POWER PLAY

Pepper waited until a quarter past five before she unlocked the drawer. This time there was no hesitation as she took out the files and walked into her secretary's office, sitting down at the electronic machine on her desk. Miranda would have been chagrined to see the speed and accuracy with which she typed. There was no hesitation; Pepper knew exactly what she was doing.

Four files.

Four men.

Four letters that would bring them here, all too anxious to see her. In some way it amused her that she retained enough of her mother's racial heritage to feel this deep, atavistic need for retribution - for justice . . . Not justice as some people would see it, perhaps, but justice none the less. The years had developed within her an ability to stand outside herself and observe and analyse.

Four men had taken from her something which she had deeply prized, and now it was only just that those four men should, each of them, lose what they prized most.

POWER PLAY

BY

PENNY JORDAN

Harlequin Books®

TORONTO • NEW YORK • LONDON
AMSTERDAM • PARIS • SYDNEY • HAMBURG
STOCKHOLM • ATHENS • TOKYO • MILAN

*First published in Hardback in 1988
by*
© Penny Jordan 1988

ISBN 0-373-15121-7

Printed in U.S.A.

CHAPTER ONE

IN LONDON perhaps more than any other city in the world there are certain streets whose names are immediately synonymous with money and power.

Beaufort Terrace is one of them; a graceful curve of stone-faced three-storey Regency buildings. Spiked black railings curve away from the flights of stone steps that lead up to each Adam door. These railings are tipped with gold, and rightly so—the rents for the suites of offices in these buildings are reputed to be the highest in the city.

Pepper Minesse was probably more familiar with this street than anyone else who rented office space on it. Her company had been one of the very first to move in when the renovators and interior designers moved out. She owned the three-storey building right at the heart of the Regency curve. As she paused briefly outside it she was conscious of the fact that a man walking down the opposite side of the street had stopped to look at her. She was wearing a black suit from Saint Laurent. It had a deep 'V' neck and looked as though she wasn't wearing anything underneath it. In actual fact she *was* wearing a black silk camisole, but Pepper had learned long ago the value of distracting people she was negotiating with, whether those negotiations were for business or personal reasons; she was one of those few women who exude both sexuality and power, and men felt challenged by her. When it suited her she let them think she was a challenge they could master.

Expensive cars were parked either side of the road, testifying to its exclusivity. Merchant bankers and money men fought like rabid dogs for premises here. Minesse Management did not pay any rent: it earned it. In addition to the building she owned in the centre of the terrace Pepper owned two others.

It had been a long hard fight for her to get where she was today. She knew she didn't look like a woman who headed a multi-million-pound empire; for a start, she looked too young. She was fast approaching her twenty-eighth birthday and there was nothing she didn't know about the complexities of human nature.

Minesse wasn't really her surname; she had adopted it by deed poll. It was an anagram of the word nemesis, and so, she thought, a fitting title for her business. She liked Greek mythology; its almost wholesale indictment of the emotions that ruled mankind appealed to the cynical side of her nature.

It struck her as ironic and very revealing that a society that could bury under the carpet child moles-tation and abuse could throw up its hands in righteous horror at the very sound of the word revenge. She liked it, but then she came from an old culture; from a race that knew the rightness of exacting a just penalty for a man's crimes.

As she walked into the building the sun caught the coiled chignon of her hair, throwing out prisms of dark red light. When she stood in the shadows it looked black, but it wasn't. It was a deep dense burgundy. An unusual colour; a rare colour even, nearly as rare as the dense violet blue of her eyes.

As she walked into the building the man across the road studied the slim length of her legs acquisitively. She was wearing sheer black stockings. They were pure silk and she ordered them by the gross.

As she caught sight of Pepper the receptionist smiled

nervously. All her staff held Pepper faintly in awe. She set very exacting standards, and she was known to be a tireless worker herself. She had had to be. She had built up the agency from nothing, and now it handled some of the world's top media and sports stars, negotiating for them advertising revenues that bolstered their incomes well into the millionaire bracket.

The girl behind the reception desk was twenty-one years old. She was a pretty blonde with the longest legs Pepper had ever seen. That was why she employed her. Looking at them kept the clients' minds occupied while they waited to see her.

Beyond the cool grey and black décor of the reception area, with its discreet touches of white and its Bauhaus chairs, was a luxurious interview room. Concealed behind its banks of pared-down designer wall units was the most up-to-date video and sound equipment on sale anywhere. Anyone who wanted to use one of her clients in any sort of televised promotion had to prove to her first that they knew what they were doing.

Pepper skirted the waiting room, knowing that she didn't have any appointments. Had anyone asked her she could probably have run through her diary for a whole month without missing out a thing; she had a brain that was needle-sharp and far more flexible than the most advanced computer.

Her secretary looked up at her as she walked into her office. Miranda Hayes had been with Minesse Management for five years, and she still knew very little more about her boss than she had done on the first day she started work there.

She caught the scent of the perfume that Pepper had specially blended for her in Paris, and envied the cut of the black suit. The body inside it was almost voluptuously curved, but Miranda suspected that her boss didn't carry an ounce of surplus flesh.

She wondered if she exercised and if so where. Somehow Pepper Minesse didn't look the type; Miranda couldn't in a thousand lifetimes imagine her cool, controlled boss hot and sweaty after a physically demanding workout.

"Any calls?" asked Pepper.

Miranda nodded.

"Jeff Stowell called to remind you about the cocktail reception for Carl Viner at the Grosvenor tonight."

A briefly upraised eyebrow suggested a certain degree of impatience that the young tennis star's agent should find it necessary to remind her.

"He said there's going to be someone there who wants to meet you," Miranda added.

"Did he say who?"

Miranda shook her head. "Do you want me to get him back?"

"No," Pepper told her decisively. "If Jeff wants to play cloak-and-dagger games he must play them alone. I'm too busy to join in."

She opened her office door and walked inside, closing it behind her, leaving only the lingering trace of her perfume.

There was nothing feminine about the room. When she had commissioned the interior designer, she had told him she wanted it to exude a subtle aura of power.

"Power?" He had stared at her, and she had smiled back sweetly. "Yes—you know, the kind of thing that goes with being the person who sits behind that desk."

"Men don't respond well to powerful women," he had told her nervously. Pepper reminded him of a large lazy cat just waiting to pounce, but then he was gay, and sexual women always made him feel nervously defensive.

Pepper hadn't argued with him. After all, he was right, but there wasn't a man born with whom she didn't know how to deal. It was her experience that the more powerful the man, the more vulnerable his ego; learning how to turn that fact to her own advantage had been the very first lesson she had mastered.

Through the closed door she could hear the muffled, staccato sound of her secretary's typewriter. The sun streaming through the window caught the delicate gold chain on her left wrist. She always wore it, and she looked at it for a moment with a strange smile on her lips before taking it off and using the gold key hanging on it to unlock one of the drawers of her desk.

This drawer contained her most private files. There were only four of them. Four very special files indeed, and they didn't belong to any of her clients. Those people who thought they knew her would have said it was typical of Pepper that she should carry the key to that drawer with her at all times, wearing it as other women might wear a lover's gift.

She paused for a moment before taking out the files. She had waited a long time for this moment; waited for it and worked for it, and now at last the final piece of information was in her hands, and from it she would forge the tool with which she would orchestrate her revenge.

Revenge—not a word for the squeamish.

In the writings of every religion known to man were warnings against the usurpation by man of that power belonging to the gods alone. And Pepper knew why. The pursuit of revenge unleashed into the human spirit a dangerous power. For the sake of revenge a human being would endure what would be inconceivable for any other emotion.

There were no names on the front of the files; she

didn't need them. Each one had been built up painstakingly over the years; information garnered in minute amounts until she found what she wanted.

She paused again before she opened the first one, tapping a dark red fingernail on the folder.

She wasn't a woman who hesitated very often, and people who had heard about her were often surprised to discover how small she was, barely five foot two, with a delicate almost fragile bone structure. They soon learned that her fragility was like that of steel wire, but Pepper hadn't always been like that. Once she had been vulnerable, and like any vulnerable creature . . . She moved her head and stared out of the window. Her profile was pure as an Egyptian carving, her skin moulded firmly to the perfection of her bones. Her eyes slanted slightly, giving her face a mysterious allure.

She looked at the files for a long time before putting them back and locking the drawer. A smile curved her mouth. It had been so long, but now the game was about to begin.

Her phone rang and she picked it up.

"It's Lesley Evans," Miranda told her.

The young skating star had only recently become one of Pepper's clients. She was being tipped to win a gold medal at the next Olympics. Pepper had spotted her over twelve months ago, and had instructed her management team to keep her under observation.

It was said in the business that Pepper Minesse had a gift for putting her money on the right horse, and what was more she always backed outsiders, on good odds.

Pepper said nothing. It made good business sense to let the Press build her up into some sort of prophetess even if it wasn't true. It added to the mystique that surrounded her, and in actual fact her decisions were based on carefully accumulated facts, leavened by a flash or two of the intuition she had learned to trust.

The skater had been approached with a contract to advertise a range of clothes intended for the teenage sports market. The company involved was well known to Pepper. They liked cutting corners and they tied their young stars up with punitive contracts. The mere fact that they hadn't approached Lesley Evans through her told its own story.

The afternoon brought a rash of further telephone calls. Pepper's clients were big stars in the sports and média world with even larger egos, and she was prepared to massage them—up to a point.

At five o'clock Miranda knocked on the door and asked if it was all right for her to go.

"Yes, do . . . I shan't be here much longer myself. The reception at the Grosvenor starts at seven."

Pepper waited until a quarter past five before she unlocked the drawer again. This time there was no hesitation as she took out the files and walked into her secretary's office, sitting down at the electronic machine on her desk. Miranda would have been chagrined to see the speed and accuracy with which she typed. There was no hesitation; Pepper knew exactly what she was doing.

Four files.

Four men.

Four letters that would bring them here, all too anxious to see her.

In some ways it amused her that she retained enough of her mother's racial heritage to feel this deep, atavistic need for retribution—for justice . . . Not justice as some people would see it, perhaps, but justice none the less.

The years had developed within her an ability to

stand outside herself and observe and analyse.

Four men had taken from her something which she had deeply prized, and now it was only just that those four men should, each of them, lose what they prized most.

Each of the letters was perfectly typed on the thick headed notepaper of the company. Pepper folded them efficiently and put them in the envelopes, using the stamps she had bought especially for this purpose: part of the ritual.

The security guard smiled at her as she walked out into the early summer sunshine. She was his boss and he respected her, but he was still man enough to cast an admiring glance over her indolently curved figure and slim legs as he watched her stepping out into the street.

There was a post box on the corner where she deposited the letters. Her car was parked outside the building, a very dark red Aston Martin Volante with the number plate PSM 1. Pepper unlocked it and swung her body gracefully into the driver's seat. The upholstery was cream leather, the seat piped in the same dark red as the coachwork. The cream leather hood was electrically operated, and as she started the engine she pressed the button that would lower it.

She drove as she did everything else; with economy and skill. It took her less than half an hour to drive through the traffic to her home in Porchester Mews. A special card was needed to operate the wrought iron gates that guarded the enclosed development. Like her offices, the buildings were Regency. It was one of the most exclusive housing developments in London, a collection of mews houses and apartments constructed round a shared enclosed garden. All the owners and tenants had access to the special sports facilities within the complex. The Olympic-sized swimming pool was one of the most luxurious in London. The gym had all the latest Nautilus equipment, and the squash courts had been designed by the world champion. In addition to her own home Pepper owned an apartment, which she kept for the exclusive use of her clients.

Her house was three storeys high. Downstairs was the drawing room, a dining room and the kitchen. On the first floor were two guest bedrooms with their own bathrooms, and on the top floor were her own private quarters—a huge bedroom, her bathroom, a sitting room, and a dressing room lined on both sides from floor to ceiling with mirrored wardrobes.

Her daily maid had already left. In the fridge was a blender full of the fresh ingredients of her favourite health food drink. Pepper took it out and switched it on. Her figure was the sort that could all too easily take on weight, so she was scrupulous about what she ate and drank. And she did exercise—discreetly.

She thought about the letters while she sipped her drink. Four men about whom she knew more than they knew about themselves. Years of painstaking detail built up layer upon layer until she could almost crawl inside their skulls.

She glanced at her watch. It had a plain gold wafer-thin bracelet and came from the Royal jewellers. She always avoided the obvious. Let others wear their Cartier Santos or their Rolex Oysters; Pepper didn't need that sort of security. This watch had been specially designed for her and owed nothing to fashion's whims. She would still be wearing it in twenty years' time and it would still look good.

Her clothes for the evening were already laid out for her; she had left a note for her maid this morning, telling her what she would wear. She gave the same careful attention and thought to her clothes as she did to everything else, but once she had put them on she put them out of her mind.

Tonight she was wearing a Valentino outfit. Unlike many of the other top designers, Valentino acknowledged that not all women were six foot tall. The suit Pepper was wearing tonight was black—a black velvet skirt cut short and tight, and a black velvet long-sleeved top with a long knitted welt that reached from just under the full curve of her breasts to the top of her hips. The knitted welt was designed to hug her body like a second skin. On anyone with a less than perfect figure it would have been a disaster.

She showered first, luxuriating in the warm spray of the water, stretching under it like a jungle cat. This was the other side of her nature; the one that no one else saw—the sensual, sensitive side. The heat of the water brought out the evocative smell of her perfume. It was the only one she ever wore and it clung to her skin with subtle emphasis.

Pepper stepped out of the shower and patted her skin dry before carefully smoothing in body lotion. At twenty-eight her body must already be ageing, according to the laws of science, but she knew without having to look in the mirror that her flesh was luminously firm and that her body held an allure that few men could resist.

Her mouth tightened over the thought and she tensed abruptly. The male sex and its desire for her was not something about which she cared to think. She had been careful over the years to build up an image of herself as a highly sexual woman. It was an image that was so carefully constructed that as yet no one even thought to challenge it. And no one ever would.

A tiny silvery mark low down on her body caught her eye and she frowned, touching it uneasily with one fingertip. The Valentino clung far too tightly to her to allow for any underwear other than a pair of special stockings that hugged the tops of her legs. She had discovered them in New York long before they had been available in British shops.

While she waited for the body lotion to sink into her skin Pepper padded comfortably about her room. Here, alone in her own home with the doors locked and the windows closed, she felt secure enough to do so, but that security had been a long time in coming, and she was intelligent enough to know that no woman who professed to be as sexually experienced as she chose to appear could afford to seem ill at ease with her own body.

Men were like predators, and they had a predator's instinct for female weakness. Pepper controlled the shiver that threatened her, tensing until only the tiny hairs on her skin showed any reaction, standing up sharply as though subjected to an ice-cold blast of air. Ignoring her betraying reaction, she put on her make-up with the ease of long habit, re-coiling her hair into a fresh chignon. Round her neck she wore a fine gold chain suspending a single flawless diamond. It nestled in the hollow of her throat, flashing fire against her smooth golden skin. Pepper rarely exposed her body to the sun; holidays were not something that held any appeal for her and a sunbed was far less hazardous to her skin. Her face she never allowed to tan.

At a quarter to seven she let herself out of the house and stepped into her car. The hood was back up. She inserted a tape into the machine in the dashboard and switched it on. As she drove to her destination she listened to the sound of her own voice relating every piece of information they had on file about Carl Viner. It was part of her credo to know everything there was to know about her clients. By the time she handed over her car to the doorman at the Grosvenor, she had virtually memorised the tennis star's biography.

Over her suit she was wearing a short evening cape of black velvet lined with white mink, spotted in black like ermine. It was pure theatre—a necessary part of the façade she presented to the world, and although Pepper didn't show it she was humorously aware of the looks people gave her as she walked indolently through the foyer.

One of the staff behind the reception desk recognised her, and within seconds she was being escorted to the suite where the private party was being held.

The party was being hosted and paid for by the manufacturers of the tennis shoes that the young star Carl Viner had agreed to endorse. Pepper had negotiated a six-figure advance payment plus royalties for the deal. She took ten per cent.

Jeff Stowell, the star's agent, was hovering just inside the door. He grabbed hold of her arm.

"Where the hell have you been?" he demanded.

"Why? It's exactly seven o'clock, Jeff," she told him coolly, detaching herself from him and allowing the waiter standing behind her to take her cape. She could see that Jeff was sweating slightly, and she wondered why he was so nervous. He was an ebullient man with a tendency to bully those beneath him. He treated his clients like children, exhorting and coaxing the very best out of them.

"Look, there's someone here tonight who wants to meet you—Ted Steiner, the yachtsman. He's with Mark McCormack, but he's looking for a change." Jeff saw her frown. "What's the matter? I thought you'd be pleased . . ."

"I could well be," Pepper agreed coolly. 'Once I know why he's thinking of leaving McCormack. It's only six months since he won the Whitbread Challenge Trophy and signed with him. If he's into drugs and he's looking to me to supply them he can forget it."

She saw the dull flush of colour crawl up under the agent's skin and knew that her information had been correct.

"Moral scruples," he bluffed.

Pepper shook her head. "No. Financial ones—apart from the obvious potential hassle with the police and the Press, a sports star who's hooked on drugs doesn't stay the best in the world for very long, and when he loses that status he loses his earning power, and without that he's no use to me."

She stepped past him while Jeff was still pondering on her words and looked round for Carl Viner.

He was fairly easy to find. He liked women and they liked him. Half a dozen or more of them were crowded round him now, tanned long-legged beauties, all blonde, but the moment he saw Pepper walking towards him they lost his attention. He had a well-deserved playboy image and for that reason some of the other agencies were wary of him, but he was shrewd enough to know what would happen if he played too hard, and it was Pepper's private conviction that he was a definite contender for next year's Wimbledon title.

Unlike all the other men present, who were wearing formal lounge or dinner suits, he was dressed in tennis whites. His shorts were brief enough to be potentially indecent. His hair was blond and sun-streaked, and fell over his forehead in unruly curls. He was twenty-one and had been playing tennis since he was twelve. He looked like a mischievous six-foot child, all appealing blue eyes and smooth muscles. But in reality he had a mind like a steel trap.

"Pepper!"

He rolled her name round his mouth, caressing it as though he was caressing her skin. As a lover he would be the type of man who liked to kiss and suck. Pepper knew even before his eyes moved in that direction that his tastes ran to women whose breasts were high and full.

One of the blondes clinging to his side pouted, teetering between sulky acceptance of Pepper's presence and aggressive resentment. Pepper ignored her and looked down at his feet. He was tall and muscular and took a size eleven tennis shoe. The grin he gave her when she lifted her eyes to his face contained pure lust.

"If you want to see if the adage is true, I'm more than happy to oblige."

The gaggle of blondes erupted into sycophantic giggles. Pepper eyed him coolly.

"You already have," she told him drily, "but as it happens I was just checking to make sure you're wearing the sponsor's shoes."

Carl Viner's face reddened like a spoilt child's. She leaned forward and patted him on the cheek, digging her nails gently into his smooth flesh. "Real women always prefer the subtle to the obvious. Until you've learned that you'd better stick to playing with your pretty dolls."

The sponsors were a relatively new company in the sports footwear field and they had wanted a racy, sophisticated image for their product. Pepper had read about them in the financial press, and it had been she who had approached them. Their financial director had thought that that gave him an edge over her, but she had soon disabused him of that. She already had several tennis shoe manufacturers clamouring with offers of sponsorship. She had never had any intention of allowing her client to accept an offer from anyone but the company she had chosen—they had the soundest financial backing; and they had also designed a shoe whose efficiency and style would soon outstrip the others, but they had allowed Pepper's self-confidence and coolness to undermine their own faith in themselves, and Alan Hart, their Financial Director, had been forced to back down and accept her terms.

He was here tonight.

There had been a time when he had thought he could get Pepper into bed, and his ego still smarted from her rejection of him.

For a woman who wasn't very tall, she moved extremely well. Someone had once described the way she walked as a sensual combination of a leopardess's feline, muscled prowl and a snake's hypnotic sway. It wasn't a walk she deliberately cultivated; it was the result of generations of proudly independent women.

Alan Hart watched her as she moved gracefully from group to group, and he also watched the effect she had on people around her. Men were dazzled by her, and she used her sexuality like a surgeon with a sharp knife.

"I wonder what she's like in bed."

He turned his head and said without smiling to the man standing beside him,

"She's a tease."

The other man laughed.

"Are you speaking from personal experience?"

He ignored the question, his eyes following Pepper's indolent walk.

How had she done it? How had she built up her multi-million-pound empire from less than nothing? For a man to have achieved so much by the time he was thirty would be awe-inspiring enough. For a woman . . . and one who by her own admission had barely received the most basic sort of formal education, never mind gone to university . . .

Alan freely acknowledged his own sense of almost savage resentment. Women like Pepper Minesse challenged men too much. His own wife was quite content with her role as his mental and financial inferior. He had given her two children and all the material benefits any woman could possibly want. He was regularly unfaithful to her and thought no more about it than he did about changing his shirt. If he gave it any thought at all he assumed that even if his wife was aware of his infidelities she would never leave him. She would lose too much; she couldn't support herself, and he had been careful to make sure that she never had more than pin-money to spend. He didn't know it, but for the last three years his wife had been having an affair with one of his closest friends. *He* didn't know it, but Pepper did.

She left after she had got what she had come for—a tentative offer of sponsorship for one of her other clients; a boy from the back streets of Liverpool who was one day going to win a gold medal for his speed on the running track.

The preliminary skirmishes were over; now the hard bargaining would begin. It was a game in which Pepper was a skilled player.

In a London sorting office, electronic machinery relentlessly checked and despatched the unending sacks of mail, and four letters slid into their appropriate slots.

It had begun. On the chessboard of life the pieces were being moved into position.

CHAPTER TWO

THE FIRST member of the quartet received his letter at nine-fifteen exactly on Saturday.

Although Howell's bank did not open for business on Saturdays, it was Richard Howell's practice as its chairman and managing director, to spend a couple of hours there checking through the mail and attending to any small matters of business that might have been overlooked during the week.

It was only a half hour's drive from the Chelsea mews flat he shared with his second wife to the small private car park that belonged to the bank. A uniformed commissionaire was there to let him in. Harry Rogers had been with the bank since the end of the Second World War, in which he had lost his right arm. He was due for retirement at the end of the year—something he wasn't looking forward to, despite the generous pension he knew he would receive. He liked working at Howell's. For one thing, it gave him something to boast about when he joined his pals at the Dog and Duck on Friday nights. There were very few people who didn't recognise the Howell name; the merchant bank was famous for its meteoric expansion and profitability under the chairmanship of Richard Howell. It was regularly quoted in the financial press as an example to others of its kind; and those financial correspondents who in the early days had dubbed him as "reckless" and "lucky" now described him as "a man with diabolically keen financial insight; an innovator and a challenger." Howell's had been behind

several of the more dazzling takeovers in the City in
recent years, and the clients who came to them tended
to stay.

At just turned thirty, Richard Howell still had the
same relentless energy and drive he had when he first
entered the bank, but now it was tempered by caution
and a discreet amount of guile.

He was a man whose photograph regularly appeared
both in the financial pages, and more latterly in those
gossip columns that focused on media personalities,
but very few people looking at those photographs
would have recognised him in the street. No photograph could convey that restless, highly strung energy
that became so evident when one met him face to face.
He was not a particularly tall man; just a little over
five foot ten, with a smooth cap of straight dark hair
and the olive-tinged skin that was his Jewish heritage.

Several generations ago the Howells had anglicised
their name and given up their Jewish faith; judiciously
they had married into the lower and even sometimes
upper echelons of the British aristocracy, but every
now and again a Howell was born who looked
remarkably like the Jacob Howell who had first
founded their empire.

Richard Howell had the sculptured, pared-down
face of an ascetic. His eyes were a very intense shade
of blue, and they burned like the incessant fires of
ambition that burned inside him. He knew quite well
where it came from; this desire to build and go on
building. His father and his grandfather had both
been ambitious men in their different ways. It was
unfortunate that in his father's case that ambition had
not led on to success but to death! But that was
behind him now.

His first wife had accused him of being a worka-
holic, and he had denied it. Workaholics were driven

purely by the pedestrian need to work; Richard wanted more; he was and always had been driven by a particular purpose, and yet now that that purpose had been achieved he couldn't stop.

Inside his traditional striped shirt and Savile Row suit was a man who was basically a gambler. But unlike those men who must win and lose fortunes across the baize-covered tables of the world's casinos, he had had the good fortune to be granted an entrée into the most exclusive of all the world's gambling circles—the world of high finance.

Richard picked up the letter and studied the heading thoughtfully. Minesse Management. He knew of them, of course; there was talk in the City that it wouldn't be long before they went public, but privately he doubted it. Pepper Minesse would never give up her empire to others, no matter how many millions going public might earn her.

Richard had seen her once, briefly, at a cocktail party he had attended with his second wife. There had been something elusively familiar about her, but though he searched his memory all night, he hadn't been able to recognise what. It had annoyed him, because he prided himself on having a good memory for faces, and hers was so strikingly beautiful that he couldn't imagine how, having seen it before, he could possibly have forgotten where. In fact, he could have sworn that he hadn't, and yet . . . and yet that elusive, faint tug on his memory told him that somewhere he had. Linda, his second wife, worked for one of the independent television companies. Like him, she was career-orientated. Pepper Minesse had been at the party with one of her clients.

Richard Howell wasn't a man who had a bias against successful women, and Pepper Minesse had intrigued him. She had built up her business from nothing and no one seemed to know anything about where she had come from or what she had been doing before she signed on her first client, other than that she had once worked for the American entrepreneur Victor Orlando. She was a woman who was skilled at appearing to be completely open and yet at the same time remaining conversely secretive about her past and her private life.

Richard tapped the envelope thoughtfully on his desk. It wasn't all that unusual for him to receive correspondence from people he did not know; it happened all the time. Howell's bank was known to be extremely discreet about dealing with its clients' affairs.

He opened the letter and read it, then got out his diary. There was nothing booked in for Monday afternoon. He made a pencil note in it. The letter intrigued him. Pepper Minesse: he was looking forward to meeting her. It could be very . . . interesting.

He went through the rest of his mail and then his phone rang. He picked it up and heard the voice of his wife. They had arranged to spend the weekend with friends and she was just telephoning to remind him.

"I'll be home in half an hour." That would just give them time to make love before they set out. The adrenalin bounced round his veins, released by the intrigue and anticipation of Pepper's letter. It was always like this—the merest hint of a new deal, a new game, always gave him a sexual boost.

Linda was the perfect wife for him; when he wanted sex she was both receptive and inventive; when he didn't, she didn't pester him. As far as he was concerned they had an ideal relationship. His first wife . . . He frowned, not wanting to think about Jessica. Linda had accused him once of wanting to pretend that his first marriage had never happened. She put it down to his Jewish blood and its inherited need to preserve old-fashioned values, and he hadn't argued with her. How could he? His marriage to Jessica was something he couldn't discuss with anyone, even now. He felt the beginnings of anger build up inside him, draining his physical desire, and checked them automatically. Jessica was in the past, and she was better left there.

Alex Barnett received his letter when the postman dropped it off halfway through Saturday morning. His wife Julia picked it up from the hall carpet and carried it through to the sunny sitting room at the back of the house where they breakfasted in leisurely relaxation on weekend mornings.

Alex looked quickly at her as she came in, dreading seeing the now familiar signs of the depression which so often seized her. This morning there was no sign of it. She was still buoyed up by the visit from the adoption authorities. He and Julia had everything that an ambitious couple could want. Everything, but for one thing . . .

At thirty, Alex Barnett was known as one of the most forward-thinking and successful men in his field. The computer age had still been at the toddler stage when he took over his father's sewing machine factory. From sewing machines to computers had been quite a leap, but he had made it safely, and although the big boys tended to look askance at some of his innovations, he held a very generous share of the market.

In less than six weeks' time he would hear from the Government whether they intended to accept his tender and install his terminals in British embassies throughout the world. The contract was far more important to him than he had allowed anyone else to know. Their sales had slipped slightly recently—not enough to cause concern, yet enough for him to realise that they badly needed the profits from this Government contract to finance new development.

That was the key to success in the computer world, and it was a young man's business; at thirty, Alex already felt years older than most of his design staff.

"Anything interesting in the post?" he asked as Julia walked into the room.

They had bought the house four years ago when he first became successful. They had been spending a weekend in the Cotswolds, celebrating both their wedding anniversary and the success of his new computer. They had seen the house and the "For Sale" board, and both of them had known immediately that it was just what they were looking for.

They had always planned to have a family. Alex was an only one himself and so was Julia. Children were important to them both, and this was a house specifically designed for a family. It had large private gardens, surrounded by shrubbery, and a paddock large enough for a couple of ponies. The village was only ten minutes away by car, and there were enough good private schools locally for their children to attend as day pupils.

They had managed to buy the house at a good price, and Julia had given up her job to settle down to the business of renovating and furnishing it, and of course, getting pregnant.

Only she hadn't; and since the news last month that the second in-vitro fertilisation attempt had failed, Julia had developed a brittle gaiety that scraped on Alex's raw nerves like wire.

What made it worse, according to her, was that he could have children, but she could not be their mother. He had tried to reassure her that she was more important to him than any potential child they might or might not have, but she wasn't willing to be reassured, so they had come back to the possibility of adoption; something they had discussed and eventually discounted in the early days after they had first discovered Julia couldn't conceive.

But now they had tried every alternative avenue, and none of them had worked.

The strain of the last few years with their hopes and bitter disappointments had scarred them both, but Julia more so than Alex. She had pinned everything on the in-vitro fertilisation working, and when it had failed, nothing had been able to rouse her from her depression.

But now at last she seemed to be recovering slightly. She was smiling at him as she handed him the mail.

"There's a letter from the adoption people. A social worker will be coming to interview us soon to find out if we're suitable candidates to adopt."

She paused beside his chair to read through the letter again. The sunlight caught her blonde hair and Alex reached up to push it back off her face. He had fallen in love with her the moment he saw her, and he still loved her. Her unhappiness was his, and there was nothing he wouldn't do to give her the child she so desperately wanted.

"Mm . . . what's this?" she asked him, holding out a cream envelope. He took it from her, his eyebrows lifting slightly as he studied the insignia.

"Minesse Management—those are the people who sign up sports stars to endorse sports equipment and the like. It's very big business."

"Why are they writing to you?"

"I don't know . . . perhaps they're arranging some sort of pro-am tournament and they want us to participate." Alex opened the letter, read it and then handed it to her.

"Well, it doesn't tell you much at all, does it?" she commented.

"No, not really."

"Will you go and see them?"

"I don't see why not. Advertising is always useful, although of course it depends how much it's going to cost. I'll give them a ring on Monday morning and see what it's all about . . ." Alex stretched back in his chair, his muscles tautening, then laughed as he saw the expression in Julia's eyes. They had always had a good sex life, although neither of them had really enjoyed those years when they had had to make love to a timetable in the hope that Julia might conceive.

"I thought you were due to play a round of golf."

"Perhaps I'd rather just play around?" he teased her, ducking out of the way as she flapped the newspaper threateningly in his direction and then grabbing her in his arms. Even without children they had so much, but Alex sensed that Julia would never give up; they had come too far down the road to go back.

But if they weren't accepted by the adoption people? He shivered suddenly and looked into his wife's face. She was thinner and there were tiny lines drawn on her skin by tension. She had invested so much hope in this test-tube thing; they both had, and he had feared that she might have a complete breakdown when their last attempt failed.

She was so fragile, so vulnerable; he could feel her bones through her skin. A wave of love and compassion washed through him. He buried his face in the smooth warmth of her throat and said gruffly, "Come on, let's go to bed."

They went upstairs hand in hand, Julia praying that

he wouldn't sense her reluctance. Since it had been confirmed that their final attempt to conceive via the in-vitro fertilisation method had failed she had completely lost interest in sex. Sex, like marriage, was ordained for the procreation of children; knowing that there would be no children robbed the act of its pleasure; of that glowing excitement she had felt in those early days when every act of love had been enough to make her climax wildly, elated by the knowledge that this joyous climatic act was the start of human life.

That joy had faded over the years, but she had still enjoyed sex; still welcomed Alex's body within hers, but now suddenly there seemed no point any more. No matter how many times he made love to her she would not conceive his child.

Upstairs in their room as Alex took her in his arms she closed her eyes so that he couldn't look into them and see her rejection.

Simon Herries, Member of Parliament for the Conservative constituency of Selwick, on the northern borders between England and Scotland, received his letter just before eleven o'clock on Saturday morning.

A long meeting with a select and powerful group of Conservative lobbyists the previous evening had kept him out of bed until three a.m. and in consequence, it was well into Saturday morning before he walked into the breakfast room of his Belgravia home in Chester Square. As was his habit, the first thing he did when he sat down was to glance through his mail.

The butler had brought the mail in earlier on a silver tray, and the thick cream envelope with the Minesse Management crest caught his attention straight away.

As a politician it was his business to know those

companies and institutions who discreetly funded the
Conservative Party machine, and he remembered at
once that there had been an extremely respectable
donation from Minesse at the end of the last financial
year.

Conservative Members of Parliament, in the main
a product of the English public school system, are
trained almost from birth to adopt the "under" in
preference to the "over" statement. It is a British
tradition that some say started with Drake playing
bowls while he watched the Spanish Armada
advancing. The "respectable" donation had in fact
been close to a million pounds.

Even so, Simon didn't open the letter straight away,
but eyed it cautiously. Caution was a prime requisite
of politicians, and in politics, as in every other power-
based structure, favours have to be paid for.

The unanticipated cream envelope disturbed him. It
was unexpected, and he wasn't a man who adjusted
well to anything that did not fall within the strict
controls he set around his life.

At thirty-two he was privately being tipped, in all
the secret and powerful circles that really matter, as a
future leader of the Tory party. He deliberately played
down his chances, smiling ruefully, adopting the role
of impressed but humble student, to the political
barons who had taken him up.

He had known since coming down from Oxford
that nothing but the ultimate seat of power would
satisfy him, but he had learned while he was there to
harness and control his ambitions. Overt ambition is
still considered both suspicious and ungentlemanly by
the British ruling classes. Simon Herries had everything in his favour; he came from a North Country
family with aristocratic connections. It was well known
in the corridors of Westminster that no one could be

an MP without an additional source of income—left wing politicians were financed by their trade union; establishment right-wingers got theirs from private sources. It was from trusts set up by his wife's family that Simon Herries received the income that enabled him to live in a style which very few of his colleagues could match. As well as the Belgravia house he also owned over a thousand acres of rich farmland and an Elizabethan manor house near Berwick. The Belgrave Square house had been bought on his marriage by his new in-laws. It was conservatively valued at half a million.

He picked up *The Times* and turned to the first leader, but his eye was drawn back to that cream envelope.

At eleven o'clock exactly, the butler pushed open the baize-covered door that separated the kitchen from the rest of the house and brought in his breakfast. Fresh orange juice, squeezed from the Californian oranges that he preferred; two slices of wholemeal bread and a small pot of honey that came from one of his own farms; a pot of coffee made from the beans that were bought fresh every day, apart from Sunday, from Harrods Food Hall and which Simon drank black. He liked his life to be orderly, almost ritualistically so. When people commented on it, Simon said it was the result of his public school upbringing.

He was as careful about watching his weight as he was about everything else. Image was important; one didn't wish to project the glossy, too well packaged look of one's American colleagues, of course—the voters would find that insincere, but Simon would have been a fool not to take advantage of the fact that at six foot, with a well muscled athletic build which came from public school sports fields, and rowing for his college, he possessed an enviably commanding presence.

His hair was thick and dark blond. In the summer the sun added distinct highlights, and his skin tanned a healthy brown. He looked arrogantly aristocratic. Women liked him and voted for him and for his policies, men envied and admired his success. He was known in the popular press as the only MP with sex appeal. He pretended to find the description distasteful.

His wife was probably one of the few people who actually knew how much he relished it, and why!

She was away at the moment, visiting her family in Boston. She was a Calvert and could trace her family back to those first arrivals on the Mayflower. She had spent a post-graduate year at Oxford, after graduating from Radcliffe. Her cool Bostonian arrogance had amused Simon; just as it had amused him to take her back to his family's ancient stronghold in the Border hills, and show her the documents that traced his lineage back to Duke William's Normans.

Elizabeth in turn had invited him to Boston. Her parents had been impressed with him. Her father was a partner in the family bank, and it hadn't taken Henry Calvert very long to discover that Simon Herries came from a family that was almost as clever and conservative with money as his own.

The wedding had made headlines in all the Society papers—discreet ones, of course; after all, there was Royalty present. Simon's godmother was a Royal, and she had graciously consented to attend.

Of course the ceremony had had to take place at St Margaret's, Westminster. Mrs Calvert had been torn between elation and disappointment. It would have been very pleasant indeed to have hosted a dinner in Boston for her future son-in-law's godmother, but Simon had been adamant: the ceremony was to take place at St Margaret's.

There was a piece in *The Times* lauding the new legislation he was pressing for to tighten up the laws regarding child abuse. He was building up a reputation for being a fierce campaigner for law and order and a return to a more strict moral climate. He was known among his peers, sometimes acidly, as the "Housewives' Choice." He smiled as he re-read the piece. There were an awful lot of housewives, and all of them had the right to vote.

His assistant would no doubt cut the piece out for him and clip it to his PR file. She was a twenty-three-year-old Cambridge Honours graduate, and Simon had been sleeping with her for the past three months. She was intelligent, but a little too intense. His mind shifted gear. It was probably just as well that the long vacation was coming up; it would help cool things down a little. He had no intention of getting too heavily involved.

Simon opened the envelope, slitting it carefully with a silver-handled knife, which had been given to his grandfather by the monarch.

The letter was brief and uninformative. It simply invited him to present himself at the offices of Minesse at three on Monday afternoon, to discuss something of mutual benefit.

It wasn't such an unusual letter; and he checked in his diary to see if he had the afternoon free. He had, and he pencilled in the appointment and a note to ask his secretary to produce everything she could on Minesse and its founder Pepper Minesse. He had never met her, but she had the reputation of being a beautiful and very clever woman.

Miles French, barrister at law, and quite possibly soon to be Judge French, didn't receive his letter until

Monday morning.

He had spent his weekend with his latest lover. He was a man who liked to concentrate on one thing at a time, and when he was with a woman whose company he enjoyed, he didn't like anything else to distract him. He and Rosemary Bennett had been lovers for almost six months, which was quite a long time as far as he was concerned. He liked beautiful women, but he also liked intelligent conversation, and his mind frequently grew bored before his body.

Rosemary was an editor on *Vogue*, and occasionally if she felt he was stepping out of line, she liked to punish him by exhibiting him in front of her fashion trade cronies.

A barrister was a rara avis indeed in their enclosed world; the men derided his Savile Row suits and white-collared starched shirts, while the women eyed him sideways, stripped off the suit and shirt, and wondered how much of a chance they would have of stealing him away from Rosemary Bennett.

He was six foot two with a body that was solid with muscle. He had black hair that curled slightly. His eyes were the colour of iced water, and Rosemary claimed that it gave her the most delicious frisson of dread when he looked at her in his "courtroom" manner. They suited one another. Both of them knew the rules; both of them knew exactly what they could and could not have from their relationship. Miles didn't sleep with other women, but she knew that the moment she began to pall he would drop her and that there would be no court of appeal.

He picked up the letter along with several others as he opened the door of the flat he owned, conveniently close to his chambers. Along with the rest of his mail he dropped it on his desk before going upstairs to shower and change. He had no appointments for the day. He was a man who didn't like to rush anything he did; a man who was patient and thorough, and to those who didn't know him, surprisingly passionate. He had a dangerous temper, although it was slow to be aroused.

His phone rang as he stepped into the shower. He cursed and went into his bedroom to answer it, dripping water on to the carpet. His body was strongly made and taut with muscle from his bi-weekly games of squash at his club. His torso was shadowed with dark hair, silky fine and alluringly sensual to the female sex.

The phone call was from his clerk, and Miles answered the query, then rang off.

Once dressed, he went into the kitchen and made himself a cup of coffee. He had a daily woman who kept the apartment clean and sometimes shopped for him, but he preferred to be independent. He had never known either of his parents. As a very small baby he had been abandoned on the steps of a Glasgow children's hospital, and had eventually ended up in a children's home, where he had learned to value his privacy and independence.

He took his coffee with him into his study. It was a spacious room, the walls lined with bookshelves, and it was one of the reasons he had bought this particular apartment. He sat down at his desk and glanced through his mail, frowning slightly as he came to the Minesse envelope, his bottom lip jutting out slightly, a habitual gesture he wasn't particularly aware of but which women found sexy. The name of the company was familiar to him, but as far as he knew he had no legal dealings with them, and in any case most of his dealings with clients were via the medium of a solicitor.

Miles opened the envelope and read the letter with

a smile. Intriguing, and he would have known that it was a letter from a woman even without his knowledge of who headed Minesse Management. He couldn't recall if he and Pepper Minesse had ever met, although he had heard about her. He wondered what on earth she could want, tossing several possibilities around in his mind. There was only one way to find out, and he had a free afternoon. Miles picked up the phone.

Pepper spent the weekend with friends who lived just outside Oxford. Philip and Mary Simms were the closest thing she had known to a family since the death of her grandmother when she was fifteen. She arrived just after eleven o'clock on Saturday morning, having timed her journey to avoid the traffic.

The bright early summer sunshine had tempted her to put the hood down on the Aston Martin, and her hair, left loose from its chignon, had been tousled by the wind. She was wearing a linen suit in a soft shade of olive green, the skirt cut short and straight, and the jacket fitting the contours of her breasts and waist. Underneath it she was wearing a cream silk blouse. As she stopped the car engine and swung her legs out on to the gravel drive she saw Oliver Simms disappearing round the side of the shabby Victorian semi.

She called to him, and he turned and waited for her, a grave-eyed boy of ten. He blushed slightly as she approached him, but the good manners instilled by his parents made him wait until she reached him.

"Hi, Oliver."

Of all his parents' friends, Pepper was his favourite. She didn't try to ruffle his hair, or worse still, to kiss him, and she always remembered his birthdays and Christmas with presents that were exactly what he wanted, plus a small sum of money for his post office savings account. At the moment he was saving up for a new bike. His birthday fell in June and he was hoping that as a present his parents would make up the shortfall on his savings.

"Mum and dad are in the garden," he told Pepper.

He had arrived in his parents' lives when his mother was just over forty and his father was eight years older, and in all the ten years of his short existence he had never for one moment doubted how much they had wanted him. He wasn't spoiled in the sense of being indulged with material possessions—his father taught at the local comprehensive and the family were comfortably rather than well off, but there had never been a second in Oliver's life when he had not known the security of being deeply loved.

He was a good-natured boy who had learned quite young to analyse and judge logically, and already he knew that although there might be times when he envied those of his school friends who possessed the latest computer, or the latest BMX, in reality many of them came from families where their parents led such busy lives that their fathers and sometimes their mothers were almost strangers to them.

Oliver knew that it was a struggle for his parents to send him to the exclusive prep school he attended, but no matter what sacrifices had to be made there always seemed to be just enough money for things like new school uniform, and extras, like the skiing holiday he had had just after the New Year.

Once he had seen Pepper safely round into the back garden, he excused himself, telling her gravely, "I'm just off to cricket practice . . . I might make it on to the first junior team this year."

Pepper watched him until he had disappeared then headed into the garden.

"Pepper, my dear! You're early . . ."

"The traffic was in my favour for once." Pepper

kissed Mary's cheek and allowed the older woman to hold her close. Mary Simms was the only person she ever allowed to embrace her in that way. Instinctively Pepper always held herself aloof and remote from others, but Mary was different. Without Mary . . .

"You're looking very well, Mary—both of you are, in fact."

There was no emotion in Pepper's voice as she studied their faces. No one looking at her could guess how close were the bonds between them.

Mary Simms, who had grown up in a rambling old vicarage near Cambridge, populated by not only her parents but a collection of ancient aunts and uncles as well, had almost from birth been used to showing her affection freely and physically. It hurt her more than she could ever put into any words that Pepper had been denied the love she herself had known as a child, and with which she surrounded her husband and son.

Philip Simms greeted Pepper with his usual absent-minded bonhomie. Philip was a born teacher; he had the gift of communicating to his pupils the desire for knowledge. He had taught her so much . . . given her so much. Here in this shabby house she had . . .

"Did you see Oliver?" Mary's voice cut through her thoughts.

Pepper smiled at her.

"Yes. He was just leaving. He said something about cricket practice."

"Yes, he's hoping to be chosen for the school's junior team." Love for her son and pride for his achievements shone out of her eyes as Mary talked.

Philip was carefully transplanting some young plants, and Pepper watched him. He was always so gentle and careful about everything he did, so endlessly patient and understanding.

"Come on inside, I'll make us all a cup of coffee."

The kitchen had changed very little since the first time Pepper had seen it; true, there was a new washing machine and fridge freezer and a new cooker, but the large cupboards on either side of the fireplace and the heavy pine dresser were just as Pepper remembered them from long ago. The china on the dresser had belonged to one of Mary's aunts, as had much of their furniture. Money had never been of prime importance in the Simms' lives, and for Pepper coming back was like crawling back into the security of the womb.

As Mary made the coffee they talked. Neither of them ever ceased to marvel at Pepper's success; they were as proud of her as they were of Oliver, in some ways perhaps more so, but they didn't totally understand her—how could they?

As she sat on one of the battered formica-covered stools Pepper wondered what Mary would say if she knew what she had done. For a moment her eyes clouded, but it was pointless trying to apply Mary's code of ethics to her own actions. Her life, her emotions and reactions were so complex that neither Mary nor Philip could ever really understand what drove her.

They had been so upset when she first decided to leave Oxford, but neither of them had ever tried to dissuade her. She had spent nearly a year living in this house, cared for, cosseted and protected by its owners. They had sheltered her and given her something that she had never experienced before in her entire life. They were the only true good and Christian people that Pepper knew; and yet she knew many who would disparage and deride them for their simple lives and their lack of interest in wealth and success.

Coming here was something she needed almost as much as she needed revenge. She had to force herself to limit her visits. Once a month, Christmas, and birthdays . . .

She and Mary drank their coffee in the sort of silence that only exists between people who know one another well and are completely at ease with themselves and each other. Afterwards Pepper helped Mary to wash up and then prepare the lunch, simple domestic tasks that none of her executives or her staff would ever have imagined her doing, but no one else was ever allowed to see her like this, vulnerable and dependent.

After lunch they all went out into the garden, not to sit down and drowse in the early afternoon sun, but to attack the weeds that relentlessly threatened Philip's flower beds. As they worked, he talked. He was concerned about one of his pupils. Listening to him, Pepper was flooded with love and humility. But for this man she would still be exactly what she had been at sixteen, an uncivilised, uneducated, little savage, who knew only the laws of her gypsy tribe, governed by emotion rather than logic.

She left shortly after five o'clock on Sunday, after afternoon tea on the lawn, eating Mary's homemade scones and some of the jam she had made the previous summer. Oliver was there with a couple of friends, who studied her car with amused nonchalance. While she watched them Oliver had grinned at her, a conspiratorial, engaging grin that showed quite plainly the man he was going to be. Already in Oliver Pepper could see seeds of great personal charm; of intelligence and drive, and more.

All his life, wherever he went, whatever happened to him, he would have these years to look back on; the love of his parents, the security they had given him, and all his life he would benefit from those gifts, just as a seedling plant growing in good, enriched earth would grow stronger and hardier than one that had to struggle in poor soil.

Handicaps of any kind could be overcome, but they left scars like any other injury. Oliver would grow into adulthood without those scars.

Pepper got up and bent to hug and kiss Mary and then Philip. All of them walked over to her car.

"It's Oliver's school's Open Day in three weeks' time," Philip told her. "Will you be able to come down for it?"

Pepper looked at Oliver who grinned bashfully at her.

"Well, since he's my godson, I suppose I shall have to make the effort."

She and Oliver exchanged smiles. She knew that she had struck exactly the right sort of note in front of his friends. They had all reached the stage where any display of adult emotion was deeply frowned upon.

She got into the car and turned the key in the ignition. Ahead lay London, and Monday morning.

Would they respond to her letters? Somehow she felt they would. She had dangled a bait none of them would be able to refuse. All of them, for their varying reasons, would expect to benefit from a connection with Minesse Management. Pepper smiled grimly to herself as she headed for the motorway—a brief twist of her lips that held more bitterness than amusement.

CHAPTER THREE

ON MONDAY morning Pepper overslept and was late. She could feel the tension building inside her as a traffic jam in Knightsbridge delayed her still further.

Up ahead of her she could see people milling in and out of Harrods, Knightsbridge, the Brompton Road, Sloane Square; all of them had become a shopping paradise for those with money to spend.

Elegant women in Sloaneish Caroline Charles outfits, wearing Jourdan shoes, paused outside shop windows. It was here in Harvey Nichols that the Princess of Wales had shopped prior to her marriage to the heir to the throne, and in nearly every department in the exclusive store were girls whose sharply cut British upper-class accents mirrored hers. American and Japanese tourists gathered outside Harrods' main entrance. Pepper noticed absently that Arab women were much less in evidence now than they once had been.

She glanced impatiently at the clock on the car's dashboard. She had no morning appointments, but she hated being late for anything because it implied that she was not in full control of her life. Even so, she fought down her impatience; impatience made people careless and led to mistakes. Mistakes—unless they were other people's—had no place in her life.

It was so unusual for her to be late that the receptionist had already commented on it when Miranda went down to collect the post.

"Perhaps she's had a heavy weekend?" Helena

murmured suggestively as she handed over the envelopes.

Miranda was as curious as the other girl about Pepper's sex life, but she was too well trained to show it. Gossiping about one's boss had been the downfall of many a good personal secretary, and there wasn't much that slipped Pepper's attention.

"I wonder if she'll ever marry?" Helena mused, obviously reluctant to let the subject go.

"A lot of successful business women do combine careers and marriage," Miranda pointed out.

"Um . . . I saw a photograph of her in one of the papers with Carl Viner. He's terrifically sexy, isn't he?"

Miranda raised her eyebrows and said drily, "So's she."

Out of the corner of her eye she saw Pepper come into the building. There was no mistaking that distinctive, deceptively languid walk, a lazy flowing movement of hips and legs.

"Morning, Miranda—Helena."

Pepper acknowledged both young women and walked past them towards her office, leaving her secretary to follow her.

"Miranda, I'm expecting four gentlemen at three o'clock this afternoon. I'll see all of them together. Here are their names. She passed a piece of typed paper to her secretary.

"Right . . . Would you like coffee now?"

"Yes, please. Oh, and Miranda, you might alert the security guard to make sure he's on the premises while they're here, please."

Although she was far too well trained to betray any surprise, Miranda tried and failed to remember a single other occasion when Pepper had made such a request. Curiously she glanced at the names, recognising only two of them. An MP and an entrepreneur. Mmm. She shrugged her curiosity aside, knowing it would be satisfied when Pepper dictated to her her notes from the meeting. Pepper was meticulous about keeping records of all her conversations, both with her clients and with potential sponsors.

Putting the piece of paper down on her desk, Miranda walked into the small kitchen hidden away behind her office. A staff room opened off it—an airy, attractively decorated room with bookshelves and comfortable seating. Minesse Management did not provide their staff with canteen facilities; the small number of employees did not merit it, although there was a formal dining room adjacent to Pepper's office, where she sometimes lunched clients and sponsors. The food for these lunches was provided by a small firm that specialised in doing lunches and dinners for executive functions. It was often Miranda's task on these occasions to check out their guests' religions and preferences, and once Pepper had these facts to hand she would call in the caterers to discuss with them the type of meal she wanted them to serve.

In this as in everything else Pepper always displayed an insight and authority that was almost intuitive. If Miranda had ever expressed this view to Pepper, Pepper would have told her that she had long ago learned that attention to even the smallest detail was important when you were gambling for high stakes.

In the small kitchen Miranda made fresh coffee and poured it into a coffee pot. She set an elegant silver tray with the pot, a matching cup and saucer, and a tiny jug of cream. The china was part of the dinner service used in the clients' dining room, white with a dense blue band and edged in gold. It was both very rich and severely restrained—rather like Pepper herself in many ways.

When Miranda took in the coffee Pepper put down the papers she was working on to say,

"If any of the men on that list telephone, Miranda, I don't want to speak to them. If any of them cancel their appointments please let me know."

She didn't say anything more and Miranda didn't ask her any questions. Pepper didn't delegate. The success or failure of Minesse Management lay in her hands and hers alone.

She drank her coffee while she studied the newspaper clippings from the weekend's newspapers. It was part of Miranda's job to go through the papers and clip out any mention of their clients or sponsors.

At quarter to twelve she cleared her desk and rang through to her secretary.

"I have an appointment with John Fletcher at twelve, Miranda. I should be back around two, if anyone wants me."

John Fletcher was an up-and-coming designer. Pepper had seen some of his clothes in a *Vogue* feature on new designers, and she had commissioned him to make two outfits for her. As yet he was not very well known, but Pepper planned to change all that. She had on her books a young model who was being tipped to go far, and it was in her mind to link model and designer in a way that could promote and draw attention to them both.

Louise Faber had introduced herself to Pepper at a cocktail party. She was eighteen years old, and knew exactly what she wanted to do with her life. Her mother had been a model, and so through her Louise already had the looks and the contacts to get into the business. Several of her mother's contemporaries had grown from modelling into other more powerful areas of fashion, and Rena Faber had been able to call on old loyalties to give her daughter a good start. But

Louise was no ordinary dewy-eyed eighteen-year-old whose ambition was to get her face on the front cover of American *Vogue*.

Louise had her own ambitions. She wanted to own and run a Michelin-star restaurant, but for that she needed money, and training. Without money and influence she would have very little chance of being taken on at the kind of restaurant where she could get the training to fulfil her ambitions. Women were not chefs, they were cooks, but Louise aimed to prove that that was wrong.

Her parents had divorced while she was quite young, and from what she had told Pepper there was not enough money in the family anyway to finance either the training or the sort of restaurant she would eventually want to own. A chance remark by one of her mother's friends, that she would make a good model, had led to her deciding that modelling would be an excellent way of earning the money she needed. Once having made that decision she was determined that if she was to model, then she wanted to be the best.

She needed an image, she had confided to Pepper, something that made her stand out from the other pretty, ambitious girls, and remembering John Fletcher, it had occurred to Pepper that designer and model could well have something to offer one another. If in her off-duty hours Louise wore only John Fletcher models, both of them would benefit from the publicity. Pepper had the contacts to make sure the press picked up on the story. She had already discussed it with John, and today he was going to give her his decision.

Initially she would make very little from the deal; but this was her forte, to spot original and new talent, whether in sport or any other field, and to nurture it towards success, and then to reap financial benefit.

No sponsor would ever risk his money on an

unproven outsider, but only let one of her outsiders start winning and Pepper was then in a position to make her own terms. That was how she had started off—spotting a potential winner before anyone else.

John Fletcher had premises just off Beauchamp Place, an enclave of designer and upmarket shops off the Brompton Road. Because of the lunch-time traffic, Pepper hadn't used the Aston Martin, and her taxi dropped her off several doors away from her destination. Two model-thin girls emerging from Bruce Oldfield's premises turned to look at her. Neither of them was a day over nineteen.

"Wow!" one exclaimed to the other. "Now that was real class!"

There was no one in the foyer as Pepper walked up the stairs to John Fletcher's showrooms. She knocked briefly before walking in.

Two men were standing by the window, studying a bolt of scarlet fabric.

"Pepper!" John Fletcher handed the silk to his assistant and came to greet her. "I see you're wearing the black."

Pepper smiled at him. She had chosen to wear the black suit he had designed for her quite deliberately. Wasn't it a black skull cap that judges used to wear when pronouncing the death sentence? Miles French should appreciate the finesse of her gesture, even if the others didn't, but somehow she was sure that they would.

The skirt of her suit had been cut in the new short, curvy shape that clung to her hips and waist. She allowed John's assistant to help her off with the jacket. He was one of the most beautiful young men she had ever seen, sleekly-muscled, golden-skinned and golden-haired. A covert look passed between the boy and John which the latter acknowledged with a brief shake of his head.

Pepper intercepted it, but waited until she and the designer were alone before saying lightly,

"Very wise, John. I'd be extremely mortified if you were to offer me the services of your tame stud."

"He hasn't been with me very long, and I'm afraid he's still a bit gauche," John apologised.

"Do you get many clients asking for that sort of service?" Her voice was slightly muffled as she stepped into a cubicle and stripped down to her underwear.

"Enough. But how did you know? Most people walking in here take one look at him and assume . . ."

"That you're gay?" Pepper stepped out of the cubicle and flashed him a mocking smile. "I know when a man likes women and when he doesn't, John, but I should have thought you were making enough profit from your clients without that sort of sideline."

"Oh, I don't provide it. Any arrangement my clients come to with Lloyd is their affair entirely."

Pepper's mouth twitched. "But word gets round, doesn't it, and there are plenty of bored rich women who'll patronise a designer who can do more for their bodies than simply clothe them."

John shrugged. "I have to make a living."

"Mmm. Speaking of which . . ."

As he worked, Pepper discussed with him her plans that Louise Faber should exclusively model his clothes.

"I like it." He stood up and studied the dress he was pinning on her.

"Do you think you'll be able to get the tie-in with *Vogue*?" she asked.

"I should think so. I've got several contacts there. There should be a number of their fashion editors at the charity do you and I are going to tonight. We could talk with them and if it looks good, then Louise and I can get together to thrash out the details.

Pepper left half an hour afterwards, picking up a cruising taxi that deposited her outside her favourite restaurant. The head waiter recognised her instantly, and escorted her to a table that made her the focal point of all other diners.

The restaurant had originally been a decaying three-storey building in a row just off Sloane Square. Pepper had bought it when she first suspected that the rich were transferring their loyalty along with their cheque books and credit cards, from Bond Street to Knights-bridge. All three floors were let out at extremely good but not extortionate rents. She had provided the finance for the restaurant, and she had also been the one who had tipped off the chef manager that Nouvelle Cuisine was on the way out and something a little more substantial on the way in.

There wasn't a day of the week when every table in the place wasn't taken. A subtle PR campaign had made it the "in" place to go. Coveys of elegant well bred women sat round the tables, nibbling at food they had no intention of eating—their size ten figures were far too important. Anyway, they hadn't come here to eat; they'd come to see and be seen.

An artist who was another of Pepper's clients had transformed the drab interior of the building with outrageously erotic trompe l'oeil, and if one was sufficiently in the know it was possible to discern in the features of the frolicking nymphs and satyrs the facial characteristics of many prominent personalities. When a person faded from the limelight, their faces were painted out and someone else's, someone who was new and newsworthy, painted in. It wasn't entirely unknown for actresses and even politicians to discreetly suggest to Antoine that their faces would look good on his walls.

Pepper's involvement in the restaurant was a well

kept secret; her face did not appear on any of the gambolling nymphs, but as she followed the head waiter across the smooth dark grey carpet, every pair of eyes in the place marked her indolent walk.

She sat down and gave her order, without reference to the menu, her forehead creased in a slight frown. Most of the women lunching together were in their early twenties or late forties, young wives or bored divorcees. The other women, those with careers, those with money, spent their lunch hour dining clients or extending their range of contacts; the sort of business that their male equivalents carried out in their clubs.

Soon these women would need the cachet of the same exclusivity. As yet there were very few clubs catering for the new breed of career women; somewhere they could entertain their clients, have lunch and even stay overnight if necessary.

If Pepper's clients had provided the bulk of her cash flow, then it was her own careful investment of those funds that had given her the very secure capital base underpinning her business. Pepper was always in the market for a good investment. She smiled to herself, her mind sliding easily into overdrive, exhilarated by the challenge of her thoughts.

Although she knew people were watching her, she ignored their covert looks, mentally weaving the threads which could form the pattern of a new business venture, at the same time thoroughly enjoying her fresh salmon and its accompanying vegetables. Pepper had gone short of food too often as a child not to appreciate it now. She was fully aware of how many of the women toying with their plates of salad were secretly gnashing their teeth over both her appetite and her apparent disregard for the effects of what she was eating on her figure.

What they didn't know was that tonight she would

eat a very meagre meal indeed, and then before she got ready to go out she would also have half an hour of tennis coaching on the indoor courts belonging to the private sports complex attached to her home. Dieting in public drew attention to a possible weakness, and Pepper had learned long ago never to let anyone see that she could be vulnerable.

She arrived back at the office at five minutes past two. Miranda followed her in to tell her that she had received phone calls from all four of the gentlemen on the list. Three of the four had asked to speak to Pepper personally, but on being told that she wasn't available had settled for confirming their appointments.

"And the fourth?"

Miranda consulted her list.

"Miles French? Oh, he simply confirmed that he would be here."

She thought as she left Pepper standing beside her desk that her boss was looking rather abstracted, but she knew better than to ask questions.

At two-thirty, Miranda prepared a trolley ready for the tea she would be asked to serve later in the afternoon. The fine china was Royal Doulton and like the coffee cups had been specially designed to Pepper's specification.

All four of the men arrived within ten minutes of one another. The receptionist showed them into the waiting room, then rang through to Miranda to tell her that they had arrived. She glanced at her watch. Five to three.

Inside her office Pepper refused to give in to the temptation to glance through her files one final time. She had already checked her make-up and clothes, and she fought against a nervous impulse to check once more. At five to three her internal telephone rang, and her stomach lurched. She picked up the receiver and acknowledged Miranda's advice that the four men had arrived.

Taking a deep breath, she said calmly, "Please show them in Miranda, then bring us some tea."

Across the hallway in the comfortably furnished waiting room the four men waited. They had recognised one another, of course, each a little surprised to see the others, but acknowledging the acquaintanceship. Their lives touched only rarely these days. Only Miles French seemed totally relaxed. What was *he* doing here? Simon Herries wondered, frowning slightly as he studied him. Was he somehow connected with Minesse? Retained by them to handle their legal affairs, perhaps?

The door opened and an attractive brunette stepped inside. "Ms Minesse will see you now, if you would just come this way, please."

When they were shown in Pepper was standing with her back to the door, pretending to study the view outside her window. She waited until Miranda had brought in the tea things and closed the door behind her before turning round.

All four men reacted to her, but she could only see recognition in the eyes of one of them.

Miles French. Pepper deliberately let her expression go blank, hiding from him her fury and loathing.

Across the desk Miles studied her with curiosity and amusement. He had recognised her face immediately, but it had taken him a few seconds to place her. He looked at his companions and realised that none of them had; his senses, honed by his legal training, picked up on her tension. She had come a long way since Oxford, a long, long way.

Simon Herries was the first to speak. Pepper let him shake her hand and give her his practised smile, a judicious blend of male appreciation, sincerity and seriousness. He had filled out since she had last seen him, and it suited him. He looked what he was—a prosperous and successful man. The others followed suit. Miles French was the only one to look directly into her eyes, trying to put her at a disadvantage, she acknowledged, her heart thumping unpleasantly fast as she met the recognition in his smile.

That was something she hadn't anticipated. None of the others had recognised her, and that he should have done so threw her slightly off guard.

"I'm sure you're all wondering why I asked you to come here." Her smile was professional and tempting, promising that none of them would be disappointed in their anticipation. She had already unlocked the drawer that held their files, and now she reached down with one smooth practised movement and removed them.

"I suggest that it might facilitate things if you were all to read these." The files held only copies, of course. Duplicates of them were safely deposited with her bank. Pepper had no intention of seeing almost ten years of work torn up in front of her eyes.

While she poured the tea she waited to see how long it took for the secure, self-satisfied smiles to disappear.

Richard Howell's went first. She saw his eyes narrow and then leave the papers he was studying to stare at her.

"Milk, Mr Howell?" she asked him sweetly.

Each of those files held a secret that if made public could destroy their professional lives for ever. Each of them had thought that secret so deeply buried that it would never be uncovered. Each of them had been wrong!

Richard Howell was now a highly respected and respectable merchant banker; but once he had simply been a younger and much poorer relative in the banking empire run by his uncle David.

It had taken a lot of digging to discover how he had got the money that enabled him to secretly buy up enough shares to challenge and eventually overthrow his uncle's control of the family business. It had taken Pepper months of painstaking work to discover that he had first started buying up shares while he was working in the safe deposit department of the bank.

For many people their safety deposit boxes are simply a place where they leave their valuables to prevent them from being stolen. There are, however, those who find that safety deposit boxes are excellent places to conceal funds—or other items—gained by other and often illegal means: tax evasion, fraud and sometimes outright theft.

It had been Richard Howell's good fortune during the time he was in charge of the safe deposit department to come across a man who fell into this last category. In addition, since it was a rule of the bank that they should hold duplicate keys for their safety deposit boxes, he was able, by carefully choosing his moment, to unlock it and discover for himself exactly what was inside—but that had only come later, following the death from a heart attack of the man who called himself William Law.

"William Law" had had his heart attack in the street, half a mile away from the bank's premises. The evening papers had carried his photograph and a small paragraph on his death, only his name hadn't been William Law but Frank Prentiss, and he had at one time been a member of a gang who had been suspected of carrying out several wages snatches involving hundreds of thousands of pounds. The police had never been able to get enough evidence to convict Frank Prentiss and the other members of the gang, and when three months went by without either the police or the bank connecting Frank Prentiss with William Law, Richard Howell went painstakingly through the records, and then when he was sure that no one would ever know, he removed from William Law's safety deposit box everything but a couple of hundred pounds.

He had no fears about the money being traced back to him—a man as clever as Frank Prentiss must surely have had the stolen notes laundered, and if the police did make the connection between William Law and Frank Prentiss, and find the safety deposit box, then they would just assume that Frank had spent the money.

There was now two hundred and forty-five thousand pounds in Richard Howell's private account with Lloyds Bank, and by the time his uncle decided to query where on earth the money had come from it was already too late—Richard was the new majority shareholder of Howell's bank, having used that original £245,000 as the basis of a fund which through clever and informed dealing on the Stock Exchange he very quickly managed to turn into a very large sum indeed.

Pepper smiled gently at him as she handed him the cup of tea. It amused and exhilarated her to see the panic in his eyes. No doubt he had thought himself safe and invincible—now he knew better.

And what of Simon Herries, the up-and-coming politician; the upholder of decency and family life; the closet homosexual who got his real sex thrills with young boys—the younger the better! When he was at Oxford he had been the ringleader of a select group, all bound to secrecy, who had dabbled in black magic among other things.

Pepper smiled dulcetly into the furious blue eyes that glittered dangerously across the width of her desk.

Alex Barnett had also been a member of that select group—if only briefly. Still, it was long enough to prevent any adoption agency from ever allowing him on their books. Pepper knew all about Julia Barnett's desperate need to have a child, and she also knew how much Alex loved his wife.

And so, on to Miles French. He had disappointed her. It was true that he had a highly active sex life, but he was very selective when it came to choosing his partners and faithful to them while the relationship lasted. Pepper had waited a long time to get something sufficiently damning on Miles, but at last her patience had been satisfied.

Three months ago, the eighteen-year-old daughter of a friend had been smuggling cocaine into the country. She should have been caught. Pepper's information was that she had got on a plane in Rio de Janeiro, carrying the illicit drug disguised some way in her back pack. But somehow when she arrived at Heathrow the cocaine had gone.

Her flight had put down briefly in Paris. Miles French had also been in Paris at the time, and the pair of them had returned to London together. Somehow Miles had managed to persuade the girl to give him the cocaine, Pepper was convinced of it, even though as yet she had no conclusive proof. Even without proof, though, there was enough on her file to irrevocably destroy both his career and his reputation. A potential High Court judge involved in a drugs scandal—he would be de-barred at the very least.

She waited until they had all finished reading. Only Miles French was still smiling. He had far more control than the others, she acknowledged, but she wasn't deceived.

Simon Herries spoke first, flinging down the file and demanding savagely, "Just what the hell is all this about?"

Pepper didn't allow herself to be affected by his rage.

"All of you will now have read your files, so all of you will, I'm sure, realise the precarious position you're in. In those files is information which if it became public could adversely affect your reputation and careers."

"So that's it!" Simon Herries sneered. "Blackmail!"

Pepper froze him with an icy look.

"No, not blackmail," she told him softly, "retribution."

She had their attention now. All of them were staring at her, watching her without comprehension— all of them apart from Miles French, whose mouth was twisted in a very knowing smile indeed.

"Retribution—what the hell for?" demanded Alex Barnett acidly.

Pepper smiled and got up.

"For rape, gentlemen. Eleven years ago all of you, in one way or another, contributed to the fact that I was raped." She paused as she saw their faces change, and offered mockingly, "Ah, I see you do remember after all!"

"Why have you sent for us . . . what are you going to do?"

It was Alex Barnett who spoke, struggling against his growing feeling of disbelief. He remembered the incident, of course. He had never forgotten it, but he had thought he had successfully buried it along with his guilt, and all the other unpleasant aspects of his past that he preferred to forget.

He looked at Pepper and saw the expensive groomed

elegance of her, wondering at the transformation. The girl he remembered had been bone-thin, wearing shabby clothes, her accent thick and hard to understand. She had fought them like a wild animal, lashing out at their faces with her nails . . . He shuddered deeply, closing his eyes.

"What are you going to do?" he muttered.

Amazingly she was still smiling at them. "Nothing. Unless of course you force me to."

Behind her calm smile she was alert, with adrenalin-based energy, watching and assessing.

Rape. To her it was the most vile four-letter word in existence, especially when it applied to the sort of rape that had been inflicted on her. The terror of that night was something she would never forget. She wouldn't let herself; it had been her single motivating force for too long. It had brought her from poverty and deprivation to where she was today.

"You took from me something that was irreplaceable, and I've decided that it's only just that each of you in turn should lose something of similar value.

"You, Mr Herries," she told him, watching him with her mouth curved into a smile and her eyes as hard as metal, "will resign from the Conservative Party. I hear you're tipped as being a possible candidate for their future leader. However, I'm sure they wouldn't think you such a drastic loss if they knew the contents of that file, do you?"

Her smile assessed his rage and then dismissed him as she turned to Richard Howell.

"The bank means an awful lot to you, doesn't it, Mr Howell? But I'm afraid you're going to have to give it up."

"Resign?" He stared at her in disbelief.

Her smile was gentle but implacable. "I'm afraid so. I'm sure your uncle will be only too delighted to step into your shoes."

Alex Barnett waited, anticipating the blow falling, knowing what she was going to tell him. He had fought ever since leaving Oxford to establish his business; he had put everything he owned into it, all his energy, nearly all his time, and he felt a sudden savage desire to take that smooth white throat between his hands and squeeze until those full lips were silenced for ever.

One look at his face told Pepper he had already anticipated her ultimatum, so she passed on to Miles French.

"I know," he told her drily, "but you've forgotten something, Pepper . . ." She frowned at him, disliking his use of her christian name. Unlike the others, he seemed more amused than appalled.

"Vengeance is mine, saith the Lord," he mocked softly. "You're treading a very dangerous path, you know."

Pepper turned away from him.

"You all have one month to consider my . . . suggestions. If at the end of that time I have not heard from you, the contents of these files will be revealed to the press. Of course, I need hardly tell you that they're only copies."

"And that you've left a letter with your bank and your solicitor to be opened in the event of your disappearance or death," Miles mocked.

It irritated Pepper that he should continue to pretend that he was merely amused by her. He had as much to lose as the others. She met his eyes and shuddered, remembering. It had been his room she had woken up in that morning, his shirt had been wrapped around her bruised body; he had been standing looking down at her.

"You can't get away with this, you know . . ."

Richard Howell blustered.

Miles touched him on the arm and shook his head.

"A month, you say?" He looked thoughtfully at Pepper and then said to his companions, "A month isn't a long time, gentlemen, so I suggest we don't waste a moment of it."

Pepper didn't watch them go. She rang through to Miranda and asked her to come in and show them out.

"You may keep your files," she told them mockingly, then she turned her back on them and walked over to the window.

It was over, and somehow she felt curiously empty . . . drained, and yet unsatisfied in a way she hadn't expected.

She heard her office door open and knew they were leaving. Miranda came back five minutes later to remove the undrunk tea, but although her secretary waited for the rest of the afternoon Pepper did not call her in to dictate to her any notes on the meeting.

Outside in the street four men eyed one another.

"Something will have to be done."

"Yes," Miles agreed. "We need somewhere private where we can talk."

"Where that bitch can't overhear us," Simon Herries swore savagely. "She must have had us followed . . ."

"I suggest we go back to my place and talk the whole thing over." Miles flicked back a white cuff and glanced at his watch. "It's half past four now. I have an engagement this evening. Is there anyone who can't make it?"

They all shook their heads. They were each in their own individual ways very powerful and authoritative men, but now they were reacting almost like bewildered and dependent children. As he looked at them Miles suspected that none of them had really yet accepted what had happened to them. For him it was different; he had recognised her when they had not, and in recognising the tremendous leap she had made from what she had been to what she was, he had already been half way to acknowledging her power.

"I just can't believe it!" Alex Barnett shook his head like a man coming up for air, confirming Miles's private thoughts. "All these years she's been waiting . . ." His face changed, shock giving way to reality.

God, what on earth was he going to say to Julia? To withdraw their application for adoption now would destroy her.

"She's got to be stopped."

Numbly he heard Simon Herries speaking, without monitoring the words, until he heard Miles saying coolly,

"What do you have in mind, Herries? Not murder, I hope."

"Murder?"

"No way." That was Richard Howell.

"She *has* to be stopped." Simon Herries glared at the others. Inwardly his heart was thumping furiously. That bitch of a woman—she had enjoyed bringing them down, having them within her power. He could kill her for that alone, never mind the rest of it.

"If you are in agreement I suggest that we talk the whole thing over in private. Since I live alone my place would seem to be the best venue."

God, how could French remain so calm! He seemed almost amused by the whole thing. Staring at him, Simon remembered how little he had trusted him in the old days, and how much pleasure it had given him to . . .

He realised abruptly that Miles was watching him, and quickly veiled the hostility and resentment in his eyes. For now it suited him to play along with everyone else.

It was Miles who found a cruising taxi and flagged it down, giving his address in a crisp, contained voice. As a barrister he had trained himself long ago to step outside his own emotions and reactions and study things logically, and he did so now. Viewed from Pepper Minesse's—where on earth had she got that name from?—standpoint it was perhaps quite natural that she should want to punish them all for what they had done to her, but it took a remarkable strength of will to wait so patiently, and build so carefully.

He could feel the tension from his companions; Simon Herries was the worst, tense to the point of violence; he had always been a dangerous, volatile man. At Oxford he had been very much the gilded youth and very sought after, but beneath that gilding had lain something malevolent, cancerous even.

And the other two? Alex Barnett still looked blank and shocked. Richard Howell was sitting on the edge of his seat, hyped up with nervous tension.

None of them wasted any energy speaking until they were inside Miles's study. "Drink, anyone?" he invited. All of them nodded.

Although they had seen each other casually over the years, they had not kept up the relationship they had had at Oxford, and each of them registered the changes in the others, as they waited for someone to speak first.

"She isn't going to get away with this!" Simon Herries downed his whisky in one gulp and slammed down the glass. "I'm damned if I'm going to be told what to do by some upstart bitch of a gypsy brat!"

"I'm sure your female admirers would be very interested to hear that speech, Simon," Miles remarked coolly, "but you seem to be forgetting that we aren't dealing with an uneducated seventeen-year-old this time. Ms Minesse is an extremely successful and powerful woman."

"She wants to destroy us!" Alex Barnett's hand shook as he put his glass down. "We've got to stop her . . ."

"For God's sake, we all know that. How the devil are we going to do it?" Richard asked impatiently.

Miles pursed his lips and offered mildly, "I have a suggestion." They all looked at him. "As I see it, we need to be able to put Ms Minesse in a position where she will not only be willing to hand over those files to us, but where she will also refrain from attempting to gain . . . er . . . retribution again."

"Threaten her in some way, you mean?" Alex Barnett looked uncomfortable. Miles ignored him.

"It seems to me that the success of Minesse Management rests entirely in the hands of its founder. If Ms Minesse were to disappear for a while, it follows that without her Minesse Management would slowly start to collapse."

"If you're talking about kidnapping her, it won't work," Richard interrupted flatly. "You heard what she said about that."

"Yes, I did, and I agree. She can't disappear. However, she could go away with her lover—and then stay away long enough for her clients to start losing faith in the company. Superstars have super-egos which need constant attention. Without Ms Minesse to provide that attention . . ." Miles lifted one eyebrow and waited for their reaction.

"Great idea!" Simon Herries sneered. "How the hell do you propose to make sure that her lover keeps her out of sight, or that she'd even agree to go with him?"

"Why, by making sure that her lover is one of us," Miles told them silkily.

Stunned silence followed his words.

Richard Howell spoke first, turning restlessly in his seat. "For God's sake, Miles, this isn't the time to start making jokes! You know she'd never accept one of us as her lover . . ."

"She doesn't need to accept it."

They all stared at him.

"Of course she wouldn't agree to going away with one of us—or with anyone else, if it meant leaving her business unattended, I suspect. But if we can convince her staff, and everyone else close to her, that she has gone away willingly with her lover, then her absence would not be considered a disappearance and consequently the instructions she has left with her solicitor and her bank would not be activated. And of course, once having abducted her, we would both have ample time and opportunity to persuade her to withdraw today's ultimatums."

"There's only one problem," Richard Howell interrupted sardonically. "Which one of us is going to play the part of the supposed 'lover'?"

Miles raised his eyebrows.

"I thought I'd take on the role myself." He smiled at them. "I'm single; I can take as much leave from my chambers as I wish without causing anyone to question my absence." He smiled again and raised his eyebrows. "Of course, if one of you would prefer . . ." They were silent as he looked at each of them in turn, and then Simon Herries spoke,

"Very noble, but why should you do that for the rest of us?" he demanded suspiciously.

"I'm not," Miles told him calmly. "I'm doing it for myself, and to be honest, I'd prefer to rely on myself rather than anyone else. However, if one of you has a better idea . . ."

"Short of murder I can't think of a single thing,"

Richard admitted bitterly. "God, she's got us all by the short and curlies, and she knows it."

No one disputed his comment.

"So, then it's agreed." Miles stood up. "I would suggest that from now on until her disappearance has been accomplished we don't get in touch with one another. She's obviously had all of us watched, at one time or another, and could still be doing so, if she thinks we plan to move against her."

"Surely she can't expect that we'd just accept her ultimatums?" Alex Barnett still looked bewildered, but now he was getting angry. The reality of what was happening had brought a thin sheen of sweat to his skin. He thought he had put all that business with Herries behind him long ago—God, what a fool he had been, but he had been flattered by Herries' friendship—way, way out of his depth.

Richard Howell was engrossed in his own thoughts. How on earth had Pepper found out about that safe deposit box? He couldn't give up control of the bank. He had fought too hard for it, but would French's plans work? At the end of the day what they were talking about was abduction and kidnap, and if French couldn't keep the girl hidden, if his plan didn't work . . . He swallowed nervously. But what the hell alternative was there?

Simon Herries watched Miles. He didn't trust him— he never had; he didn't like him very much either. At Oxford French hadn't been one of his court. That cunning bitch! Could French pull it off? He hoped so, he had fought too long and hard to give everything up now. There had to be another way, but until he found it he had to play along with French.

"Well, gentlemen, what do you say—do we go ahead with my plan, or not?" He looked at them all in turn, waiting for their responses.

"I don't see that we have any alternative." Alex Barnett looked almost ill, haunted in fact.

"I hope to God it will work." Richard paced tensely. "Yes . . . Yes . . . All right, I agree."

"And you, Herries?" Miles looked across at him.

"I agree." But I don't trust you, French, I don't trust you one little bit, he thought silently, and I'm going to be watching you.

"Right. We have one month's grace, and I intend to use that time to our advantage." Miles shot back a white shirt cuff and glanced at his watch. "I'm sorry to be inhospitable, gentlemen, but I have an engagement for this evening."

His engagement was with Rosemary. He would have to tell her that their affair was over. He wondered a little wryly how she would react. It was a pity that Pepper had managed to learn about Sophie, he had thought he had covered both their tracks rather neatly.

Pepper Minesse . . . Where on earth had she got that name? he wondered ironically again after the others had left. In their Oxford days he had known her simply as "Gypsy." Everyone had called her that.

When and how had "Gypsy" become the founder of Minesse Management? Miles reached for the phone and then put it down. Tomorrow would be time enough to start uncovering the mystery of Pepper Minesse; tonight he would have to concentrate on disengaging himself from his affair with Rosemary. It saddened him that he was able to contemplate doing so with so very little regret. Hadn't he always chosen the women in his life with a view to his ability for distancing himself from them?

Pepper Minesse . . . He remembered how she had looked that morning, huddled in a corner of his locked room. She had been a virgin; he remembered having to destroy his sheets. He closed his eyes and swore suddenly.

Pepper lay supine in her bath, letting the warm water soothe away her tension. She didn't want to go to tonight's party, but she had promised Louise.

Half of her couldn't believe that it was over; that she had actually done it. Behind her closed eyelids images writhed and danced. She saw Alex Barnett's shocked face; Miles French's impassive one. Simon had been furious, and Richard disbelieving. What were they doing now? Probably trying to think of a way to stop her, but that was something they wouldn't be able to do. She had had ten years to plan; they only had a month, and she had protected herself. If anything happened to her . . . But nothing was going to happen. She had the upper hand now. She wasn't a semi-literate nobody now, of so little importance that she could be kicked about like a stray dog. Did they really think that she had forgotten; that they could get away with it?

She moved restlessly in the cooling water, wondering why she wasn't feeling more euphoric. Beside the bath was the bottle of champagne she had taken out of the fridge. She had put it there this morning to chill so that she could celebrate, but now she didn't want it. It irked her that she was able to take so little pleasure in her achievement. What was the matter with her? She had wanted to enjoy her triumph. Perhaps she would have enjoyed it had she had someone to share it with . . . The thought startled her and she examined it suspiciously, pushing it away from her as she got out of the bath.

The charity do was being held at the Grosvenor, in the ballroom. As her partner Pepper was taking one of her oldest friends. Geoffrey Pitt had been her financial adviser for several years.

She had met him just when Minesse Management was starting to grow from a small concern to a very much larger one, and it had been Geoffrey Pitt who had guided her first tentative steps when she started to expand. It had also been Geoffrey who had advised her to buy her premises rather than rent, who had helped her to invest her profits so that they too could make money for her.

These days she knew almost as much about the world of high finance as he did himself, but officially she still retained him as her financial adviser.

When Pepper first met him he had just been getting over a traumatic divorce. It had been inevitable that they should become very close, although Geoffrey, like those men who had come both before and after him in her life, had found that she had a trick of withholding from him the most essential part of herself. Most people thought she was frigid. But how could she give herself to any man after what had happened to her? It had left her with an acute and deeply rooted distrust of the entire male sex. Her fear of them she had managed to conquer, just—and only she knew what an effort of will it had been, but to allow one to be intimate with her; to even think about permitting for a second time the humiliation and degradation she had already suffered, made her flesh turn to ice.

She was not a fool; she knew that perhaps with counselling, with care, she could possibly overcome her fear, but Pepper didn't want to overcome it. As an observer she had seen what their relationships with the men in their lives did for other women, and she didn't want that kind of bondage for herself. All her life in so many ways she had been alone, and she had come to relish that aloneness—to see it in fact as the only way for her to live. And so cleverly, discreetly she had learned how to keep the whole sex at bay.

With Geoffrey it had been almost too easy, and now they had the sort of comfortable friendship that exists only between two people who both know and like each other and have no curiosity about one another sexually. There were still times when Geoffrey looked at her and ached to take her to bed, but he knew that Pepper did not feel a corresponding desire for him. And besides, since Nick Howarth had come into her life . . . He grimaced slightly to himself. If Howarth hadn't been abroad on business Geoffrey doubted that he would have been invited to accompany Pepper tonight.

He picked her up promptly at eight o'clock.

Geoffrey was the type of upper-class Englishman who looked his best in evening clothes, Pepper reflected as he helped her into his Rolls. He was tall, with mid-brown hair and kind hazel eyes, the sort of man mothers thought would make their daughters a good husband.

As they drove down Park Lane they joined the tail end of a convoy of cars, all disgorging their passengers outside the entrance to the Grosvenor's Ballroom. The charity ball was for mentally handicapped children. Its patroness was the Princess of Wales, and she and the Prince were expected to be present.

As Geoffrey followed Pepper into the ballroom he couldn't help speculating about her relationship with Nick Howarth. He knew that Howarth was one of her major clients. There was a discreet rumour among those in the know that they were also lovers, and it was certainly true that they partnered one another at a variety of social functions—functions often associated with the sport that Howarth sponsored.

Were they lovers? Geoffrey felt the old familiar jealousy at the thought of someone sharing Pepper's bed, and then valiantly dismissed it. At heart he was a kind, rather gentle man; the kind of man who, he told himself wryly, could never hope to hold the attention of a woman like Pepper—a woman who was so intensely and vibrantly female that no man, surely, could remain immune to her.

Pepper would not have been surprised if she could have read his thoughts. Geoffrey wasn't the only person who speculated about her relationship with Nick Howarth. They had known one another for several years now, and although both of them were regularly seen with other partners, it was generally accepted among their circle of friends that they were lovers.

Nick wasn't like Geoffrey. Not so very long ago he had given her an ultimatum. He wasn't the first man to do so; and he wouldn't be the last.

He was away at the moment, but soon he would be coming back, and when he did . . . When he did she would find some way of dealing with him, Pepper promised herself. At the moment she had more important things on her mind.

A tense spiral of excitement began to wind inside her. In four weeks, but no, she mustn't think about that now. There would be time enough when . . . She had long ago learned to control her thoughts and impulses, and so, dismissing everything else from her mind, she started to concentrate on her surroundings.

As she stepped inside the ballroom she saw that it was awash with Emanuel creations in tulle and chiffon. Her own ballgown had been designed by Bellville Sassoon. The rich blue raw silk skirt floated round her as she moved, the tightly fitting bodice just revealing the upper curves of her breasts. The off-the-shoulder sleeves and the hem of her skirt were trimmed with antique lace that had cost almost as much as the dress itself. She was wearing her hair drawn softly back off her face and caught back with a matching silk flower. Among the soft pinks and peaches of the other women her gown stood out dramatically.

The Duchess of York had made red hair fashionable, but that was not why so many of the other guests stopped to look discreetly at her as she walked into the room.

John Fletcher and Louise Faber were already seated at the table when Pepper reached it. She introduced Geoffrey to them and accepted the glass of champagne offered to her.

They all made small talk for several minutes while the tables around them filled up. A tiny frisson of excitement ran through the room when the Prince and Princess of Wales were announced. Chairs scraped back over the floor as everyone stood up.

"She's lovely, isn't she?" Louise whispered to Pepper as they listened to the chairwoman's welcoming speech.

John, who had been studying the Princess's dress, announced, "She's wearing a Bruce Oldfield. It must be a new one, I recognise his latest line."

Over supper they discussed business. John had had time to consider Pepper's suggestion and he liked it. He already had in mind the sort of wardrobe he would design for Louise.

"I spoke to *Vogue* after I left you today," Pepper told him. "One of their assistant editors is here tonight, apparently—Rosemary Bennett—do you know her?"

"Yes, I do. In fact I've seen her somewhere." John turned round and searched among the tables. "Over there—look, Pepper. The woman in the Giorgio Armani—the white satin. Do you want me to introduce you?"

"No . . . not here, I'll go and see her at *Vogue* later in the week." Pepper looked away from the table, and her body froze as she saw the man making his way through the tables. For one moment she thought he was heading for her, and her face lost all its colour, her body tense with shock.

"Pepper, what's wrong?"

Somehow she managed to drag her attention away.

"Are you feeling all right?"

John's forehead was creased in an anxious frown, his eyes dark with concern. God, what was the matter with her? She had everything under control, but just one unexpected glimpse of Miles French had thrown her so completely off guard that she was still fighting the shock.

This afternoon must have been more of a strain than she had realised. Miles French hadn't reacted like the others. He had been far more cool, far more in control of himself, and he had also recognised her. That was something she hadn't expected him to do. She had changed so much from the girl she had been that she had thought there was nothing of that girl left.

Miles French had shown her otherwise, and she had found the experience disquieting.

On the other side of the room Rosemary Bennett reached out and scored her long nails delicately over Miles's wrist.

"You're looking very pensive, darling, is something wrong?"

Miles gave her a perfunctory smile.

"Not specifically."

There was something different about him tonight, Rosemary recognised; something distancing. She was far too experienced and knowledgeable about men not to recognise the signs. Miles was bored.

It was time to end their affair. She didn't really want to lose him. As a lover, physically she doubted that she had ever met his equal, but emotionally there was always a part of him that he withheld, that remained aloof and unobtainable. Rosemary veiled her eyes and studied him. Miles was not the sort of man who could live without a woman for very long, which probably meant that he had already chosen her successor.

She wondered without rancour who the woman was. Whoever she was, she hoped she had the good sense not to fall in love with him. Miles turned his head and looked at her.

"I thought tonight we might leave early."

Trust Miles to deliver the coup de grace with style! she thought wryly, and wondered if he intended to tell her before or after he had taken her to bed. Knowing Miles, it would probably be beforehand, then he would make love to her as a way of saying goodbye.

Once she had seen Miles, Pepper couldn't relax. Sensing her tension but at a loss to understand the reason for it, Geoffrey asked her if she would like to leave once they had finished their supper.

She got up gratefully, making her excuses to John and Louise. "I'm afraid I have a rather bad headache," she lied, letting Geoffrey take her arm and lead her away.

"You stay here. I'll get your coat for you," he instructed once they were in the foyer.

Pepper sat down on one of the small gilt chairs and stared abstractedly into space. Another couple walked into the room, the woman's voice cool and faintly metallic, the man's deeper, almost laconic and somehow familiar.

She tensed and looked at them.

"Pepper, what an unexpected pleasure!"

She saw Miles coming towards her and was conscious of a tight aching tension constricting her throat. She struggled to stand up, catching the heel of her shoe in the hem of her skirt, overbalancing slightly. Miles reached out to steady her, and she flinched beneath the unexpected warm pressure of his hands on her bare arms.

Five feet away Rosemary saw the way Miles was looking at the other woman and knew that she had seen the lady who was going to take her place in his bed. She smiled bitterly to herself. At least he had taste. Pepper Minesse was no pretty fluffy doll.

They had gone by the time Geoffrey returned with her coat, but as he helped her into it Pepper was still struggling to obliterate the small scene from her senses.

CHAPTER FOUR

PEPPER didn't sleep well that night. The old nightmare haunted and pursued her. It always came at times like this when she was under stress. Long-suppressed memories surfaced and twisted through her mind, and she lay back against the tangle of satin sheets, her hand over her heart feeling it steady, as she forced herself to block out the too-intrusive memory of smothering darkness, of hands and voices, whispers pitched just too low for her to hear. In her nightmare she struggled to catch what they were saying, but in reality she had heard; had known what was happening to her.

Rape. The taste of the word on her tongue was sour and foetid. Her mouth twisted bitterly. It was a full mouth, wicked and sensual; men always looked at it, imagining its red moistness against their skin.

She was too hyped up to even try to go back to sleep. If she did she knew what would happen. She would be back in that shadowy room in Oxford with the door guarded by the men who had taken her there, while . . .

Her body shook, sweat glistening on her soft silken skin. Once more she felt the smothering sensation of fear engulfing her and fought against it, pushing away the terrifying memories of unseen hands touching her body, voices whispering softly just outside the stretch of her ears.

She reached out abruptly and switched on the lamp beside her bed, deliberately controlling her breathing as she willed herself to regain control. She was both hot and shivering, pursued by demons that owed nothing to any human life form. The May night was warm, but inside she felt deathly cold.

"You can have whatever you want from life," Philip had once told her, "but there's always a price to be paid for it."

Pepper had paid her price, and now it was time that others paid theirs.

She got up and padded downstairs, ferreting about in the kitchen cupboard until she found the tin of drinking chocolate. It had been there since Mary's last visit two years ago, for Christmas shopping. Mary and Philip had never felt totally at home in her London house. Its cool designer exclusivity overwhelmed them.

Happiness and contentment had always been the meter by which they had measured their own lives, and she knew that both of them in their different ways worried about her. Although they didn't know it, they had good reason to be worried. Pepper grimaced faintly to herself, as she made a milky drink and carried it back to her bedroom, curling up against her cream satin sheets and pillows, her dark red hair spilling out over the antique trimmings. Without make-up, with her hair curling extravagantly round her face, she looked about seventeen, like a little girl who had strayed into her elder sister's room. But she wasn't seventeen . . .

At seventeen . . .

She sighed and compressed her body against the intrusive memories, but it was too late, already they were flooding back, drowning her in pain and fear. She let herself relax and admit them.

Perhaps after all it was only right that tonight she *should* remember, she thought tiredly, with the acceptance of her mother's race, for the vagaries and implacability of fate.

Very well then, if she must remember, let her at least remember it all. She would go back to the beginning . . . to the very beginning.

In January of 1960 the gypsy tribe to which Pepper's mother belonged was camped in Scotland on a tract of land belonging to the laird of the clan MacGregor. It had been a bad winter, with thick snow and howling east winds straight off the Russian seas. Sir Ian MacGregor was a kindly man brought up in a tradition that made him, as chief of his clan, as responsible for their welfare as he was for that of his own immediate family.

The MacGregors had never been a particularly wealthy clan; they owned lands, yes, but the land was fit for nothing but running sheep and renting out as grouse moors to rich Americans. When his factor told him that the gypsies had arrived and were camping in their usual valley his first thought was relief that they had arrived safely. The gypsies had been camping in that valley for more than two hundred years, but this year the heavy snowfalls had delayed them. His second thought was concern for their survival in the bitter cold, so he sent his factor into the valley with bales of straw for the ponies and some meat from the deer that he and his ghillie had shot just before Christmas.

Duncan Randall was not just the MacGregor's factor, he was also his nephew and heir, a tall, rather withdrawn eighteen-year-old, with black hair and a narrow bony face. Duncan was a dreamer and an idealist. He loved his uncle and the land, and in his soul he carried the poetry of his Celtic heritage.

An overnight fall of snow had blocked the pass through the valley so that the gypsies were completely enclosed. Dark faces and wary eyes monitored his progress in the Land Rover as he drove towards their encampment. Smudges of smoke from their fires hung on the horizon, small groups of wiry, silent children huddled round their warmth.

It had been a bad year for the tribe. Their leader had died in the autumn, leaving the tribe like a rudderless ship. He had been sixty-eight years old and it was to Naomi, his widow, that the rest of the tribe now turned.

There had been only one child of the marriage—a girl. Layla was fifteen and according to the custom of their tribe she must now be married to the man they had chosen as their new leader.

Rafe, her husband-to-be, was thirty years old, the younger son of a leader of another Lee tribe. To Layla at fifteen he seemed both old and faintly alarming. Her father had spoiled her, because she was the child of his old age, even though her mother had warned him against it, and she was a wild, almost fey creature, as changeable as April skies. Naomi worried for her, knowing that hers would never be an easy way through life.

Naomi had pleaded with Rafe to wait until Layla was sixteen before marrying her. Her birthday fell in the spring, and Rafe had reluctantly agreed, but all the tribe could see how he watched the girl with jealous, brooding eyes.

Layla had always been contrary and awkward; Naomi despaired of her. Rafe was a man any other girl would have been proud to call husband, but when he looked at her, Layla tossed her hair and averted her eyes, giving her smiles instead to the boys she had grown up with.

Since this was his first year with the tribe, Rafe had

not visited the valley before, and he watched suspiciously as the Land Rover made its slow way in towards their camp.

"Who comes here?" he demanded of Naomi in their Romany dialect.

"It is the nephew of the MacGregor," Naomi told him, putting her hand on his arm to stop him as he moved forward. "He is a good friend to us, Rafe."

"He is a *gorgio*," Rafe protested bitterly.

"Yes, but we have been made welcome here for many generations. See, he has brought fodder for our animals," Naomi told him, watching as Duncan stopped the Land Rover and climbed into the back to unload the bales of hay.

The children ran to help him. Layla was with them, Naomi noticed, frowning as she watched the way her daughter's skirts lifted as she ran.

To a Romany it is a wanton act for a woman to reveal her legs to any man other than her husband, and although she knew this very well there were times when Layla almost seemed to deliberately flout their conventions.

Layla didn't want to marry Rafe, Naomi already knew that, but she had no choice, like must marry like, and Layla, like Rafe, was descended from one of their greatest leaders. Both of them carried his blood in their veins and it would be breaking an unwritten Romany law for Layla to marry outside her own blood. Even so, her heart was troubled for her wayward child.

The bales of hay were heavy and shifting them was hard work, but a year of outdoor activity had tautened and developed Duncan's body so that he was able to take the weight quite easily. He was aware of the gypsies' silent scrutiny, but he strove to ignore it even while it unnerved him.

Across the small clearing containing their fires he could see the old woman and the man watching them. He could feel the man's resentment and dislike and it made him uncomfortable. Poor devils, it was no wonder that they resented him. He would hate to live the way they did, almost on the verge of starvation, constantly moving from place to place. He shifted his glance away from the brooding intensity of the man's stare and saw the cluster of children staring up at him. Several of them had running sores on their faces, all of them looked thin and hungry. His uncle had sent down a sack of porridge as well as the meat, and as he reached into the Land Rover to get it out he saw the girl for the first time. She was standing slightly apart from the others, watching them as he did, but there was pride in her eyes and she had a way of holding her body that defied him to feel pity for her. Where the children were thin, she was slender and supple, reminding him of the reeds that bent beneath the wind at the edges of the lochs. Her hair was long and black, shining in the harsh sunlight, her skin smoothly golden. Her eyes flashed anger and arrogance at him as she met his stare; golden eyes like her skin. She was the most beautiful thing he had ever seen. The sack he was holding slipped in his slackened fingers and he caught it up, feeling the red tide creeping up under his skin and with it a fierce upsurge of desire.

Layla knew enough about men to recognise his desire. Although she hid it from him it excited her. There were very few young men of her own age in the tribe, and certainly none as handsome as this dark-haired, fair-skinned *gorgio* boy, who was so much taller and broader than the men of her tribe, and whose eyes betrayed his wanting for her.

She tossed her hair as she walked past him, filled

with a sudden surge of exhilaration. She didn't want to marry Rafe; he frightened her, although nothing would ever make her admit it. She sensed a cruelty within him that instinctively she feared.

Her mother called sharply to her and she scowled. She was not a child who needed to heed its parents' every sharp word. She was a woman; and she would choose her own way through life. Avoiding Rafe, she darted through the snow and into the caravan.

Duncan saw Naomi walking towards him and knew from his uncle's description that she was the wife of the leader of the tribe. Her English was thickly accented, but Duncan understood enough of what she said to realise that her husband was dead, and that Rafe was now their new leader.

Later, while he and Sir Ian ate the hot potato cakes smothered in melting butter and drank strong dark tea in front of the peat fire in his uncle's study, Duncan told his uncle how surly and uncommunicative he had found the gypsies.

"It is just their way. They are very slow to trust us, Duncan, and you can understand why. They are in many ways a persecuted and little understood race, whose habits and customs are not ours. They adhere to a much harsher code than our modern laws allow for, but then their life is much harsher than ours. Their women are still cruelly punished for adultery, and they consider their marriage to be a sacred rite that can be set aside by death alone. They are a fascinating people, though, and a very proud one."

It was on the tip of Duncan's tongue to tell his uncle about the gypsy girl, but before he could, the housekeeper came in with a plate of fresh scones.

Sir Ian lived well but simply, and already Duncan was ceasing to miss his more sophisticated life in Edinburgh at the University. His mother was Sir Ian's sister. She had married outside the clan, and her husband, Duncan's father, was a solicitor.

Ian MacGregor was much older than his sister. His only son had been killed at the end of the war. His wife had died shortly afterwards, of a broken heart, so some said, and Ian had refused to marry again, so that now Duncan was his only heir. Duncan had willingly given up his law studies to take over the job as his uncle's factor—a training for the inheritance which would one day be his.

Layla was bored and restless. She hated the confinement the snow enforced on them. She wanted to get away from Rafe's brooding presence. She wanted to escape . . . She wanted to see Duncan Randall again.

No one else was stirring when she slipped out of the camp in the early morning light. She moved quietly and silently across the snow, climbing as agilely and surefootedly as one of Sir Ian MacGregor's sheep as she headed up the narrow track that led out of the valley.

It took her half an hour to climb to the top. From there the moors stretched all round her in every direction, bordered by even higher hills. Here and there a dark crevasse in the snow indicated where other narrow valleys might lie, and against the skyline she could see a smudge of smoke. Layla was drawn to it even while caution urged her to retreat.

Duncan was also up early. He wanted to drop feed off with the shepherds before they had a fresh fall of snow.

Layla heard the sound of the Land Rover engine long before she saw it, the noise carrying well on the crisp cold air. She watched as the blue grey smudge came towards her, her body outlined against the sky, her hair flowing back like a dark banner.

At first when he saw her Duncan thought there must be something wrong with the tribe, but when he stopped alongside her and looked at her, there was no mistaking the look in her eyes. He felt the heat run through his body, and silently opened the Land Rover door for her.

She had dreamed about the *gorgio* last night, and now this morning she had found him. He was her fate, suddenly Layla was sure of it. Marriage to Rafe was not for her, she wanted more from life than that.

Uneducated, inarticulate, knowing only the feelings that flowed through her blood, she knew nevertheless that the feelings inside her were the same ones that flowed through the body of the *gorgio* boy beside her.

Layla was a virgin, but she was not ignorant of the ways of a man and a woman together. Her mother had told her when she protested that she did not want to marry Rafe that she would know when she was ready to be his wife. She knew now that her body was ready for a man's possession; she felt it in her responses to the way Duncan looked at her. She reached out and touched his arm and felt the muscles contract beneath his skin.

When he stopped the Land Rover they kissed as urgently and hungrily as though they had known and wanted each other for years. Despite their inexperience there was nothing fumbled or clumsy about the way they came together, both of them overwhelmed by a force stronger than their separate or combined wills.

Layla's sharp cries of delight, her firm thighs gripping his body, the soft feminine scent of her; these were the things Duncan remembered late at night, lying awake in his bed, aching for her, wanting yet again to expend his life force inside her.

Curled up in her narrow bunk, Layla too was thinking of him. She had enjoyed the pleasure they had shared, but more than that she was exhilarated by what they had done. Now Rafe could no longer claim her in the ancient gypsy rite; now she would not have to bow her head to him or acknowledge him as her lord and master.

She knew that many of the others thought her proud and stubborn and said that her father had spoiled her. Maybe it was true, but she was not a horse to be sold into a man's keeping. All the resentment she had experienced since Naomi had first told her that she was to marry Rafe surfaced and coalesced into fierce rebellion. She had taken the *gorgio* boy as her lover and in doing so she had broken the most sacred of all gypsy laws, but she didn't care. No laws could bind or chain her. She was Layla . . . she was free.

For over a week the young couple continued to meet and make love. Duncan became so obsessed with Layla that nothing else had any importance. He lived for the brief time they could snatch together, when she managed to escape from the tribe. The fact that she knew that Rafe was watching her only served to increase her exhilaration whenever she managed to sneak away to be with Duncan.

It was only when the snow started to thaw, and Rafe started saying that it was time they were on their way, that Layla began to fear the consequence of her actions. She confided her fears to Duncan one afternoon as they lay together in the hay loft of one of his uncle's barns.

"Then don't go with them," he begged fiercely. "Stay here with me . . . we'll get married."

Layla moved restlessly in his arms. Marriage to Duncan? Was that really what she wanted? She loved him; she loved the smooth young feel of his body; she loved the desire he could make her feel; but she also loved the excitement of stealing away to be with him, the dangerous elixir of doing the forbidden.

If she stayed with him the tribe would reject her . . . her name would never be spoken by them again. Her mother . . .

Her mother had problems of her own. This Scottish valley had always been one of her favourite stopping places. Normally they spent two months or so here, but Rafe was now their leader, and Rafe did not like the valley. Rafe was also growing impatient and bitter about Layla's foolishness, Naomi knew that, but Layla was so headstrong, such a child still, as wild and fey as the most spirited filly.

She was getting old, Naomi thought tiredly. Her bones ached in the cold wind, and life had lost its savour for her since she had lost her Leon.

Rafe's surliness seemed to have infected the rest of the tribe as well. Some of the men were saying that the valley was not a good place any more. What was needed was a celebration of some sort to lift the tribe's spirits . . . a wedding feast. But Layla was the only girl of marriageable age with the tribe, and she . . .

Sighing faintly, Naomi picked up the worn pack of Tarot cards she alway carried with her, absently setting them out. One card stared up at her and her body froze colder than the snow outside her caravan. Death. She put the cards down with trembling fingers.

The Tarot cards never lied, she knew that. She shuddered deeply, sensing danger, aware of it waiting, lurking, not visible to the human eye, but there all the same, an indefinable presence that cast its shadow over the whole tribe.

One morning Rafe announced that they were leaving. No one queried his decision, not even Layla— no one could query the decisions of the leader of the tribe, but just as soon as she could she slipped away from the valley, heading for her meeting place with Duncan.

Only this time she was followed.

Rafe tracked her with the cunning skill of their race, keeping her easily in sight without letting her know that he was there. Panic had made her grow careless. Once they had left the valley behind Layla knew that Rafe would insist on marrying her. Now that she and Duncan had been lovers the idea of marriage to Rafe was even more abhorrent to her.

Duncan would marry her, she knew that, but to cast herself off from her mother, from their way of life . . . Her thoughts tumbled through her mind like a mill race in full spate. She was deaf to the tiny, betraying sounds Rafe made as he followed her.

Outside the barn, Layla hesitated briefly, glancing over her shoulder. There was no one in sight. She ran inside, and Duncan, who had heard her come in, hurried to meet her, taking her in his arms and kissing her passionately.

When he released her Layla told him of Rafe's decree.

"Don't go," he urged. "Stay here with me."

"I want to."

Neither of them knew that their whispered confidences were being overheard. Rafe had crept into the barn while they were kissing, and was now standing in a shadowy corner, watching and listening.

A fierce rage possessed him. Layla was his . . . but she had shamed him by giving herself to this *gorgio*. She had broken the most important of the Romany rules. She was a wanton who would be cast out by the tribe if they knew what she had done. She wasn't fit to be his woman, but even so he would take her and show her just what she had scorned by giving herself instead to her pretty *gorgio* lover. But first . . .

Neither of them saw him move until he was close enough to reach out and push Layla away from Duncan. His knife, so sharp and so deadly, slid between Duncan's ribs with ease, and up towards the heart.

Duncan made a small sound, a choked protest, that brought a rush of blood to his lips as he dropped to the floor. Rafe had stabbed him through the heart, and as Layla watched with horrified, disbelieving eyes she saw him die in front of her, still reaching out towards her, his eyes so terrified and frightened that she knew she would carry their expression with her to the grave.

As Rafe bent to retrieve his knife, Layla whirled away from him, running as fleetly as a hare over the snow-packed ground, not daring to pause to look behind her.

Rafe let her go. After all, where could she run to? He wiped the blade of his knife clean of Duncan's blood and stared emotionlessly down at the inert body of his rival. The *gorgio* had stolen his woman from him and it was only right that he should forfeit his life as punishment. Layla he would punish in a different way. His mouth curved in a cruel smile as he contemplated just how he would punish her. He would not take her as his wife now, of course; she was unclean, tainted by her physical contact with the *gorgio*, but she would lie in his bed nonetheless.

Rafe had a rare taint in a Romany; he liked to inflict pain. As a small child he had enjoyed setting traps for rabbits and other small animals, not because he needed the food, but because he liked seeing the tormented look of agony in the small creatures eyes.

His father had tried to beat the trait out of him, but all that had done had been to suppress it. Normally Rafe was only able to indulge his taste for inflicting pain on the women he bought whenever he had enough money to do so, but now Layla had provided him with a convenient opportunity to indulge himself to the full without restraint. By her own actions she had set herself apart from the rest of the tribe; by Romany law now, no one would lift a hand to stop him punishing her.

He was in no hurry to pursue her. Where could she go? Her *gorgio* lover was dead, the tribe would not allow her mother to shelter her from his wrath.

One look at her daughter's face was enough to tell Naomi that something was wrong. She had a clear mental vision of the Tarot cards, and saw death grinning up at her.

Layla was too distraught to conceal the truth. Naomi recoiled from her in pain and shock when the girl revealed that she and Duncan Randall had been lovers.

"And now Rafe has killed him," she told her mother.

Naomi's mind worked furiously. Her first and most important loyalty was to the tribe. Through Layla's folly, and Rafe's reaction to it, they would all suffer. The tribe needed a leader . . . they needed Rafe. They would have to leave the valley, and quickly, and once they were gone from here some story could be concocted that would prevent the truth from coming out. Once the *gorgio*'s death was discovered the police would question them, of course, but somehow . . . there must be a way out.

"Go into the van and stay there until I come to you," Naomi told Layla abruptly.

There was so much to do . . . and Rafe was not here. She went from van to van, urging everyone to pack up ready to leave. The camp fires were stamped out, the children and animals suddenly restless as they scented the imminent departure.

When Rafe returned to the camp half an hour later he saw from her face that Naomi knew.

"She has told you, then?" was all he said.

Naomi nodded, unable to meet his eyes, so great was her sense of shame. Layla . . . her daughter had shamed her. How grieved Leon would have been had he lived to see this day!

"We must leave here. The police will come. They will ask questions . . ."

"To which our people will not know any answers," Rafe warned her. He looked at her. "Tonight you will send your daughter to me."

One look at his face was enough to silence Naomi's protests, and she returned to her own van with a heavy heart. Layla had offended against one of the strongest of their tribal taboos, and it was only right that she should be punished, but the look in Rafe's eyes had chilled her through to her bones, and Layla was after all her child.

She found Layla curled up on her bunk staring blankly into space. When Naomi told her of Rafe's edict, she shook her head vehemently.

"I will not go to him!"

Pain and grief shadowed Naomi's eyes as she looked at her daughter, so beautiful and so wild. Even now she held her head proudly . . . too proudly, perhaps. She was completely untouched by her own shame.

"I will not go to him!"

"My child, you will have no choice."

"No choice." The words hammered at Layla's brain. She hated Rafe . . . if she could she would have killed him herself for what he had done, but she had no skill with a knife, and her strength was puny when compared with his.

Even now she could not comprehend what she had

lost. It was impossible to believe that Duncan was dead, shock protected her from reality, and she had not yet accepted that she had lost him.

When the police came to the camp to question the gypsies, all of them responded stoically to their questions, each providing an alibi for the other. Rafe stood apart, silent, watching.

Sir Ian, who had come with the police, looked shrunken and old. Naomi pitied him sincerely. He had lost one who had been as a son to him, and she saw defeat written across the kindly face.

The police had already questioned Rafe. He had been hunting for game, he had told them, producing two other men as his witnesses.

No matter how many questions the police asked they could not break through the wall of silent suspicion emanating from the gypsies. They knew that one of them had killed Duncan; it had to be, and a knife, used so expertly and efficiently, had to have been wielded by a Romany hand.

"Clannish as the devil, if you'll excuse me from saying so, Sir Ian," the police sergeant said, as they walked back to the Land Rovers. "We'll get nothing out of them."

"But why . . .why? I don't understand it. Duncan was such a kind boy . . ."

"That's something we'll probably never know."

"One of them's done it, for sure," the sergeant told his superior later at the police station, "but I doubt if we'll ever find out which one. They've given each other alibis that we'll never break."

At dusk, the tribe ate in silence, a pall of mistrust and fear falling over the entire camp. Not a word had been spoken to Layla since her return. She had eaten alone in her mother's van, and now the time was fast approaching when Rafe would demand his vengeance.

She shivered as she contemplated what he might do to her. Duncan's lovemaking had opened her eyes to her own sensuality. She had responded to him as joyfully as a flower unfolding to the sun, but she felt no desire for Rafe, only fear and hatred. He had killed the man she loved, and she hated him for that and always would, but she feared him as a woman always fears a man who she senses wants to inflict pain upon her.

"You must go to him," Naomi told her quietly. "If you do not, you will be taken to him by the other men, and that will be worse. Better to endure what must be with your pride intact."

"Even though my body might be destroyed!" Layla cried hysterically. She was still young enough to want to cling to her mother and weep tears of fear, but Naomi was right. And her mother would not be able to protect her, no matter how much the tribe might revere her.

It was a night that would haunt Layla for the rest of her short life. She went to Rafe's van sick with fear. When she managed to crawl out of it hours later when he had finally fallen asleep her body was a mass of bruises and raised weals.

Naomi bathed them for her, her own eyes stinging with tears, but there was nothing she could say. Layla looked at her with the eyes of a wildcat caught in a snare. Her daughter's spirit was as broken as her body.

Layla did not have the stoicism to endure such physical abuse; hatred for Rafe was the only emotion she could feel now. Not even to her mother could she describe the things he had done to her; the manner in which he had abused her, taking her not as a man but as a perverted animal. Her body shook as she tried to blot out what had happened. Naomi gave her a soothing potion to drink, thinking to help her sleep, but while her mother's back was turned, Layla poured it away.

She could not endure another night like this one; she would *not* endure it.

While the rest of the camp slept she crept silently away. The constable on duty at the police station listened to her story in stunned shock, wondering whether or not to believe it. The sergeant, woken from his bed and brought grumbling to the station, took one look at Layla's white, bitter face, and knew that he had found the motive for Duncan's death.

They arrested Rafe at dawn; and he was sentenced to death two months later. He never reached the hangman's noose. Somehow, from somewhere, he obtained a secret poison. He was found dead in his cell one morning, his body already stiffening, his eyes glaring bitterly into emptiness.

The rest of the tribe shunned Layla. They elected a new leader, who decreed that Naomi must be allowed to stay among them, but that Layla must leave.

When Naomi discovered that her daughter was pregnant, she pleaded with the tribe for clemency, and it was granted; Layla would remain as an outcast from the tribe, but she would be allowed to travel with them.

Her daughter's frail, wraithlike condition appalled Naomi. The thought of the coming child was the only thing that kept her alive. Duncan's child. Layla said the words over and over again to herself like a mantra.

"It could be Rafe's child," Naomi told her.

Layla shook her head, and looked at her mother with eyes far too old for such a childish face.

"No, it could not. He did not take me as a man takes a woman; he did not spill his seed inside me."

Rachel Lee was born to her mother during her

eighth month of pregnancy. To see Layla's thin, almost sticklike body bloated almost obscenely with her pregnancy caused Naomi almost constant pain. Some fierce spirit seemed to burn in Layla, giving her a pride and a determination she had never thought to see in her fey, spoiled child.

The birth was a difficult one, and although they paused to listen to the cries coming from the caravan, none of the other women came to help. Naomi did not mind. She was an experienced midwife, and the child was well positioned, although perhaps a trifle large for Layla's emaciated frame.

It was only when she placed the child in her daughter's arms that she saw Layla smile properly for the first time since Duncan's death.

"She is beautiful," she told her mother. "You will call her Rachel, and you will love her for me, won't you, Mother?"

Already a swift-flowing river of red blood was carrying Layla away from them, and Naomi knew it could not be staunched; that her daughter was dying. She had known it from the moment Layla gave birth. In some ways she felt her daughter had willed herself to stay alive only as long as she carried her child. She had in any case been as one dead to the rest of the tribe from the moment she betrayed Rafe.

There was no burial pyre for Layla, no grieving or lamenting for the brief life so quickly extinguished, and although the tribe accepted Naomi, little Rachel grew up knowing that she was not truly part of it; that there was something mysterious about her own birth and the death of her mother, that set her apart from the others.

She soon learned that her mother's name was one that must never be spoken and that she and Naomi were allowed to stay with the tribe as a favour rather than as a right.

Her pain at the way she was excluded was something she learned to cloak with pride and indifference, and she was soon being described as far too much her mother's daughter. She was not popular with the other children, and she knew it. It made her only more aloof and withdrawn. Only Naomi loved her, only Naomi stood between her and the hostility of the others.

CHAPTER FIVE

YES, SHE HAD learned young what it meant to be an outcast, Pepper reflected wryly.

Almost from the moment she could toddle she had been shunned by the other Romany children, but through their cruelty she had learned two valuable lessons.

The first had been to conceal her hurts. As a child she had been sensitive to a degree that had meant the other children's contempt and dislike of her had constantly lacerated her. She had known as children always know that they neither accepted nor liked her, but she had not known why, and so she had learned to cover her feelings with a protective stoical acceptance. That had been the second lesson she had learned—not to let others see that they had the power to hurt her.

Not that the others had deliberately wanted to hurt her; it had simply been that she was not one of them; that her mother had offended so far and so deeply against their code that her child would never be one of their number.

Pepper's childhood had been spent moving with the tribe through the country in their nomadic annual journeyings; formal schooling for gypsy children in those years had been spasmodic at best—not even the most ardent of school inspectors could spare the time to check up on the constantly caravanning tribes and their children—but Naomi had been taught to read and write by her husband and she was immensely

95

proud of her skills.

She too had seen what was happening to her grand-child, and while she grieved over it, she knew that according to the rules of her people they were not being deliberately unkind.

Occasionally it crossed her mind that she should approach Sir Ian MacGregor, but she doubted that he would welcome Rachel any more than her own people did, and then the winter that Rachel was seven Ian MacGregor died and the land passed to a very distant member of the family.

Since Duncan's death, the gypsies had not revisited the Glen, knowing that they would not be welcome, and the loss of the privileged campsite was chalked up as another black mark against Rachel.

It was Naomi who insisted that she learn to read and write; who sent her to school whenever the tribe stopped long enough for her to do so.

Knowing how proud her grandmother was of her own ability to read and write, Rachel never told her of the purgatory her own schooldays were. Just as she was unacceptable to the tribe, so she was also an outcast to the non-Romany children. They laughed at her clothes, calling them rags, and they sneered at her heavily-accented voice and the gold rings she wore in her ears. The older boys tugged on them until her lobes bled, and called her a "dirty gypsy", while the girls huddled together in giggling gaggles to gaze at her darned jumpers and patched skirts.

With no man to protect them or hunt for them, Naomi and Rachel were forced to depend on whatever Naomi could make from telling fortunes and selling pegs. Occasionally in the depths of the night, one of the women of the tribe would knock on her door and ask Naomi for the special potions she made in the summer months from wild flowers and herbs.

Rachel watched these transactions wide-eyed and curious about what it could be that brought the women of the tribe to her grandmother's door late at night, but all Naomi would say when she asked her was that she was too young to understand. The herbal lore which she had learned from her own mother and which she had tried to teach her own feckless daughter was something Naomi was not going to pass on to her granddaughter. None of the women of the tribe would come to Rachel for advice and potions the way they did to her. She was, after all, one of them, and still respected, although now their respect was tainted with pity, but Rachel never would be; she was the daughter of a *gorgio*, and it had been for the love of this man that Layla had betrayed one of her own, breaking the sacred gypsy code. Now when she grew older Rachel's life would lie apart from that of the tribe, and this troubled Naomi.

She was getting old, and her bones ached in the cold and the damp. She hoped that by sending Rachel to school she could in some way prepare her grandchild to enter into the *gorgio* way of life, and because Rachel loved her grandmother she didn't tell her that she was derided and disliked as much by her father's people as she was by her mother's.

School, which had been a place of fascination and delight at first, when she had absorbed everything the teachers could tell her, had now become a hated prison from which she escaped as often as she could, often spending her days in complete isolation in the hills and the fields.

When she was eleven her body started to change, and with it the reactions of her peers. Boys at school who had pulled her hair and jeered at her now tormented her in different ways, trying to pinch the small swellings that tightened the fabric of her shabby clothes.

Her hair, always thick and lustrous, seemed to darken and curl with a vivid life of its own, her body alluringly changing shape. Rachel knew what the changes portended; her tribe lived close to nature, and its girls were taught to be proud of their womanhood.

Even one or two of the young men glanced at her sideways as she helped her grandmother to gather kindling or worked with her on her pegs and baskets, but they didn't forget who her mother was, or what she had done.

While the other girls of her age in the tribe tested their new-found femininity, laughing and flirting with their male peers, Rachel instinctively suppressed hers. She was a child of the shadows, her grandmother often thought sadly, watching her pensive face and too knowing eyes. As though she had been gifted with second sight Rachel knew instinctively that the rest of the tribe were looking for signs of her mother in her; as long as she was quiet and unobtrusive no one bothered about her.

But some things are impossible to hide, and the way her body was blossoming and developing was one of them.

The pinches and lewd remarks of her schoolmates was something she quickly learned to ignore, just as she had learned to ignore their jibes about her clothes and her speech. She wasn't the only girl who had to endure this rough male teasing, but the others all had friends, families, supporters and protectors whom they could call upon if the boys' tormenting became too familiar. Rachel had no one; she knew it and her tormentors knew it.

The gypsies' progress through the country was an annual one. At the time of the Whitsun fairs they were

always in the north of England; among the mill towns
of the north-west; grimy, enclosed ribbons of towns
set in stark valleys, whose inhabitants were the inher-
itors of the Industrial Revolution; a grim and starkly
realistic people who had often known the harsh bite
of poverty.

The lives of the people were as enclosed as the hills
surrounding their valleys; their minds as narrow as
their habitat.

The mills were closing, being driven out of existence
by imports from Pakistan, cheap cloth produced by
cheap labour. The secondary school in the valley was
overflowing with teenagers who would have no jobs
to go to; the mills that had employed their parents
and grandparents were closing, and the atmosphere
within the valleys was one of resentment and bitterness.

This particular stopping place on their annual
pilgrimage was one that Rachel had always detested.
The poverty of the people in the valley was almost on
a level with that of her own tribe, and because of it
the valley people jealously guarded their rights and
privileges. Outsiders weren't welcome whoever they
were; and the gypsies were disliked and detested here
much more than they were in the richer south of the
country.

There were few pleasures to be had for the people
inhabiting these valleys full of "dark Satanic mills".
Whitsuntide was one of them.

The religious persuasion of many of the inhabitants
sprang from Methodism, the cornerstone on which
the Industrial Revolution had been built, but this did
not prevent the people from throwing themselves into
their Whitsuntide celebrations with enthusiastic vigour.
The highlight of these celebrations was the Whit
Walks. For weeks beforehand the females of the

family would gather round to gaze consideringly at the "catalogues" to choose the all-important outfit for the Walk. The Whit Walks were an unashamed opportunity to show off. A new outfit was an absolute essential, if family pride were to be upheld. Everyone would line up to walk through the streets in their new clothes; afterwards families would gather for high tea, and then later still the teenagers would be let loose to attend the fairs that had set up in the market squares.

It was these fairs which brought the gypsies to the north-west. There were rich pickings to be had from them, what with fortune-telling, working on the fairs themselves and selling their wares.

Rachel hated the whole thing. She hated the taunting looks the other girls in her class gave her while they giggled behind their hands about their new outfits. She hated knowing that she was an outcast, that she was being made fun of, but now this particular spring, with her body burgeoning into that of a woman, she hated it even more. The girls resented her glowing prettiness, and the boys lusted after the growing development of her body. The fact that she wasn't one of them, that she was an outcast, made her an easy target for their malice and male vulgarity.

She had long ago perfected the art of ignoring all that was said about her, of pretending that she simply hadn't heard the insults. But this particular morning, knowing that the whole school would be seething with excitement over the coming Whitsuntide break, she knew she could not face them. Always sensitive to the opinions of others, she had found that with the onset of puberty her sensitivity had increased. Sometimes the effort of forcing herself not to cry in the face of the jeering taunts of her schoolfellows made her drive her nails deep enough into the palms of her hands to draw her own blood.

The northern valleys possessed three modes of transport; the road, the railway and the canal. Rachel was walking alongside the latter, pausing now and again to watch a moorhen with her chicks or to study the fleeting shadow of tiddlers as they changed direction at the sight of her shadow. The canal had been abandoned as a transport route long ago, and the rotting lockgates and weed-filled waters gave silent testimony to its decay. Mills long abandoned by owners who could no longer afford to compete with foreign imports reared up darkly alongside the towpath, casting dark shadows, their windows gaping emptily, the glass broken, their interiors long silent.

Occasionally a golden bar of sunlight slatted through the bleakness of the building. Rachel liked walking. It soothed her, gave free rein to her thoughts. She shivered as she walked beneath one of the narrow bridges, feeling the cold and damp seeping down through the stone. She passed few people as she walked. The occasional old man walking his dog; courting couples, giggling. Across on the other side of the valley she could see men working in their allotments alongside the railway lines, the narrow black lines of terraced houses blotting out the sunlight.

This particular valley was very long and narrow, the hillsides treeless. It was a grim and depressing place and Rachel hated it. Whenever they came here she suffered a sense of being shut in; she loathed the oppressive atmosphere that infiltrated the place.

Outside a row of terraced houses overlooking the canal she could see one woman donkeystoning her steps. She was wearing the all-enveloping pinafore that was the uniform of the married woman here. She looked up and saw Rachel and scowled at her.

"Be off with you!" she called out harshly. "We don't want no dirty gypos round here!"

Rachel was impervious to her insults, and walked on to where the river Calder ran alongside the canal. The towpath had crumbled away at the edges here. On one side it was level with the canal and on the other it dropped away to where the river ran sluggishly below, its progress choked with the detritus of human living—old rusty prams and bicycles, tin cans, and a variety of other rubbish that had been slung out of back yards and into the river.

She paused by a gap in the dismal line of terraced houses to enjoy a warm bar of sunlight. In front of her was the back door to a small pub. A man came out and staggered across to the gents', and then changing his mind, instead relieved himself into the river.

Rachel moved on, ignoring him. One day she would escape from all this, from people who disliked and taunted her. One day . . .

Daydreams were the only things that made her life bearable, and she escaped into them whenever she could. She enjoyed reading and from the books she read she knew that there was another way of life, very many other ways of life, and one day . . .

Her daydream was brutally crushed when she heard someone call out her name in a jeering voice. Her whole body tensed as she recognised the harsh male voices and came to an abrupt halt in front of a gang of boys she recognised from school. They were all older than her, due to leave school at the end of the summer term. They were all dressed in grubby jeans and cheap leather jackets. The rank smell of young male bodies closed offensively round her as they came closer. Resolutely Rachel stood her ground, deliberately avoiding any form of eye contact. Her heart was pumping like a terrified rabbit's, but her body was completely still.

"Lost yer tongue, gypo?" one of them taunted. His eyes shifted from her face to her breasts. "Got a fine pair of tits growing there, ain't yer? They say gypos make good lays . . ."

The coarseness of his comments and the laughter of his friends increased her terror, but Rachel knew it would be madness to even try to run. That was what they wanted her to do. They could hardly rape her here in broad daylight, she reassured herself stoically, as the lad reached out and pressed a filthy hand against the front of her dress. She had to fight against her instinctive desire to tear at him with her hands and nails, to rid her body of his unwanted presence, but long after they had jeeringly let her go past, calling out obscenities after her, she felt tainted by the encounter, her body still shaking with a mixture of outraged pride and feminine fear.

During the Whit week festivities her grandmother was busy telling fortunes, and Rachel escaped to the hills, ranging over the moorlands where thin half-wild sheep foraged and the land was barren and bare. Here and there the remnants of some long-ago drystone wall boundary darkened the landscape, but in the main it was untouched by man's hand apart from the odd reservoir mirroring the swift movement of the clouds across the hills.

At Whitsuntide the people of the valleys went on holiday, the more affluent of them sometimes for as much as three or four days, the poorer just on a day trip, but all of them to the same venue—the Lancashire coast and Blackpool. Rachel watched the coaches depart filled with them, and heard them come back at night. The gypsies were camping on a spare piece of land, close to the market square where the buses terminated, and late at night the coaches would disgorge their passengers, replete on beer, candy floss and fish and chips.

Here in the small town centre a viaduct spanned the canal and road, carrying the railway overhead, and at night these arches were the haunt of eager lovers. The tribe looked down on the *gorgio* teenagers and their lack of modesty, but Rachel knew that many of the young men, especially those who worked on the fairs, slipped away late at night to enjoy the favours of the girls who gathered in giggling masses beneath the viaduct.

One night as she walked beneath them on her way back to the camp, she recognised one of the intertwined couples. Ann Watts was in her class at school, although she was two years older than Rachel. Ann Watts was described as "slow", but there was nothing slow about the way she responded to and attracted the opposite sex. Jealous of her position as acknowledged sex queen of the school, Ann Watts was one of Rachel's most vindictive enemies.

It would be many years before Rachel would be able to recognise the other girl for what she was and to pity her for it, that night as she saw Ann voluptuously pressing her body against that Tyler Lee.

Tyler Lee was the oldest of the three brothers; tall for a gypsy, with a shock of wildly curling black hair. At seventeen his body was hardened and well muscled by the work he did on the fairs and labouring in the fields during the summer. His skin was brown, his eyes black as jet. He was proud of his Romany blood and destined to marry his second cousin. Rachel knew this, but Ann Watts did not. To her Tyler Lee epitomised the glamour she saw every week when she visited the local flea pit. He was the best-looking boy she had ever seen, far better-looking than the lumpy dull boys she was at school with; and better still, Tyler was dangerous. He rode a motorbike that he had put

together from parts garnered here and there during
his travels, and he knew exactly the effect he had on
a girl when he looked at her from out of those night-
dark eyes.

Although Ann Watts didn't know it Tyler despised
her, just as he despised all the *gorgio* women who
desired him, and Ann Watts was very far from being
the first. Tyler had first realised the potential of his
sexuality when he was fourteen years old. He had lost
his virginity to a bored, thirty-odd-year-old housewife
in Norfolk, exchanging it for his motorbike and enough
money to buy himself the coveted teenage uniform of
black leather jacket. Since then there had been more
bored housewives and Ann Watts than he had cared
to count.

Ann Watts was not destined to remain in his memory
for very long. She wriggled against him provocatively,
enjoying the rhythmic thrust of his hips. Tyler would
be the third boy with whom Ann had "gone all the
way", and already she was enjoying savouring what
she was going to tell her friends afterwards. She liked
the shocked, wide-eyed way they listened to her confidences. They were all younger than she was, and still
virgins.

Out of the corner of her eye she watched Rachel go
past, and glared at her. She disliked the proud way
the younger girl moved, almost as though she thought
that somehow she was better than anyone else. How
could she be? Everyone knew that gypos were nothing
better than thieves, and that they never washed.

Ann had a bath once a week, in the new bathroom
that had just been installed in the terraced house.
Theirs was the only house in the street to have an
indoor lavvy as well. Ann's father was a foreman in
one of the few mills still working and her mother
served school dinners at the local Tech. And Ann was

their only child. Already Mrs Watts was boasting proudly that her Ann would marry young, she was that pretty. All the boys were after her.

Sensing that he had lost her complete attention, Tyler pushed her firmly against the hard stone of the viaduct wall, thrusting himself against her open thighs, demanding, "Who you looking at?"

"That Rachel Lee."

Ann saw the expression on Tyler's face and realised that he liked Rachel no more than she did herself.

"What's up?" she asked him curiously. "What you got against her?"

"Her mother was a murderer," Tyler told her.

No one in the tribe had talked about Rachel's mother, but they all knew the story, and Ann's eyes widened in malicious glee. She had always known there was something odd about Rachel Lee. Just wait until she told the others at school about her! At that moment Tyler moved more determinedly against her, pushing up her skirt and pulling down her pants with one experienced movement, and Rachel was forgotten . . . but not for long.

Rachel knew the moment she walked into the schoolyard that something was wrong. Her senses, always attuned to danger, alerted her to the menacing quality of the silence engulfing her the moment she walked into the tarmacadam yard, but she looked neither to the right nor to the left as she walked past the silent huddles of watchers.

Ann Watts waited until Rachel drew level with her before launching her first salvo.

"Whose mother's a murderer, then?" she sang out, swiftly followed by her friends, as they picked up the taunting chorus and rang it across the schoolyard.

By now Rachel knew the story of her conception, but she still felt sensitive about it, and about the cloud hanging over her birth. She lashed out instinctively and her open palm caught the side of Ann Watts' nose, and almost instantly blood spurted from it.

Almost as though the scent of blood drew them like hounds to a fox, the schoolyard was in an uproar. It took four teachers to separate the seething mass of bodies, and when they dragged Rachel out from beneath her attackers, she had a broken collarbone and three cracked ribs.

Despite questioning from her teachers and from the police Rachel refused to say what had caused the fight. The police constable was only young—he had recently been moved into the area from Cumbria and he was finding the brooding violence of the valley difficult to take. There was poverty where he came from too, but it was a different sort of poverty from this, just as his people were a different sort of people. Privately he felt sorry for the little gypsy girl, but his expression betrayed nothing of this when he questioned her. She looked very forlorn and alone in the starched hospital bed, and he suspected that the nurses weren't any kinder to her than her peers had been.

It was after her stay in hospital that things began to change for Rachel. She saw the change in her grandmother almost from the moment she came out. Naomi had aged, but more than that, there were new lines on her face that could have only been put there by pain. For the first time in her life Rachel knew the terrible fear of being all alone. What would happen to her if her grandmother should die? The tribe didn't want her.

Would she have to go into a home? Rachel knew very little about these institutions other than the fact that they were held over the heads of hapless gypsy children as a threat of what could happen to them if they misbehaved. Somehow in Rachel's mind, children's homes had become confused with prison, and she thought of being sent away to one of them as a form of punishment.

Every day she saw her grandmother fade away a little more. Sometimes when she thought no one was watching her Naomi massaged the outside of her breast. She was in deep pain, Rachel knew that. She also knew that her grandmother had to drink some of the special poppy drug she made to help her sleep at night.

Rachel was frightened, but as with everything else she learned to lock the fear up inside her.

Naomi knew that her time was short. There was pain inside her that ate into her, a gnawing, bitter pain that was destroying her from within. The pain came from the lump she had discovered in her breast, she knew that. She was going to die, and when she did what would become of Rachel?

Winter came and the tribe was once again in the far north, not camping in the tranquil valley on the MacGregor lands this time, but on a barren piece of waste ground outside a small town.

Where once they had commanded a certain amount of respect and fear, gypsies were now almost consistently reviled. The townspeople called them "dirty thieves", and Rachel was more conscious than ever of the way others looked at them. She had never felt more alien and alone. There was no one she could turn to. Naomi was dying, but Rachel still doggedly hoped that somehow her beloved grandmother would grow well and strong again.

She spent hours searching for special herbs that were supposed to have magic properties to heal her. She saved the choicest pieces of meat for her, but none of it did any good; Naomi was dying.

The spring that Rachel was fifteen they stopped off

in the north for the Whitsuntide fairs again. Ann Watts was still at school, but now she was in her last year. Last year's plumpness had given way to unsightly fat, and she eyed Rachel with spite and bitchiness when she arrived at school.

"I see the gypos are back," she sneered, giving Rachel a wide berth. "I thought I could smell something bad!"

Blotting out the laughs and jeers, Rachel held her head high and walked into the classroom. She loved the deep tranquillity of its silence almost as much as she hated her fellow pupils. Inside her something was yearning desperately for knowledge, but her lessons were so fragmented that in all her years of schooling she had learned almost nothing.

To the teachers she was just another gypsy brat, who would be gone before she could learn anything worth knowing. She could read and write and add up simple columns of figures, which in a school like the one she was in now was as much as many of their pupils would achieve by the time they were ready to leave.

They had been back in the valley for almost a week when one afternoon Rachel was struck by the knowledge that Naomi needed her. When the class stood up and the teacher left, Rachel darted out after him, taking the short cut to the gypsy camp, along the canal tow path. She ran all the way, and arrived out of breath and scared out of her wits. This was the first time she had felt for herself the power that ran so strongly in the women of her family.

As she had known she would, she found her grandmother close to death. Naomi recognised her, and forced away her pain for long enough to take her hand. She had spent many hours worrying about this child, this changeling who was neither Romany nor *gorgio*.

Pulling Rachel close to her so that she could whisper in her ear, she told her where she had hidden the small amount of money she had managed to scrape together since she had realised she was ill. She had saved the money with one purpose only in mind, and now she told Rachel what she was to do.

"You must leave here now, before . . . before I die. You must pretend that you are older than your years. You must get yourself a job and live as a *gorgio* would, Rachel. The Romany way of life is not for you, and I do not want you to become any man's whore. Remember always that my spirit goes with you."

Hot tears fell on her cold hands as she pushed Rachel away from her. Rachel was losing the only person on earth who cared about her, but if she stayed the tribe would reject her, and the school authorities would come and she would be put in a home. Naomi was right . . . she had to leave.

Alternately shivering and crying, Rachel found the small store of money. She bent down to kiss Naomi's cheek and murmured the secret Romany words of farewell. She would not be here to see her grandmother's funeral pyre; she would not be here to wish her spirit well.

Naomi opened her eyes and saw the indecision on her grandchild's face. Summoning the last of her strength, she took Rachel's hand in hers. "Go now . . . go with my blessing, my child . . . Go now."

From the moment she had learned to read Rachel had realised that it was education that was the only escape route from poverty, and now she was drawn as countless thousands of others had been drawn before her to the gilded spires of Oxford.

She had passed through the town many times with the tribe. She knew from her reading what it was . . . but in her ignorance she knew nothing of the taboos and rituals it represented; just as strong and damning as those of her own people.

Rachel reached Oxford in the late summer of 1977, when she was just short of her seventeenth birthday. She travelled mainly on foot, using the ancient Romany paths, carefully eking out the money her grandmother had given her by taking casual work along the way— mostly on farms, but always taking care to choose a farm where she could be sure of being taken under the wing of the farmer's wife. Rachel had learned enough about the male sex in her short life to make her wary of putting herself into any man's powers. She still remembered the hated sensation of being touched by male hands, and it was a man who had led to her mother's rejection by her people. Men of any age were to be avoided.

By the time she reached Oxford she had added to her small hoard of money and had two hundred pounds tucked away in the leather bag she had tied to the inside of her skirt. Her clothes were in rags, too short, too skimpy, augmented here and there by the odd cast-off given to her by kind-hearted farmers' wives who had taken pity on her.

Where once their pity would have offended her, now she accepted it with a brief smile, because Rachel was realising for the first time in her life the power of freedom. Oh, she missed her grandmother, but she didn't miss the oppressive disapproval of the tribe, which she was only just beginning to recognise for what it was; nor did she miss the contempt and dislike of the people in whose towns they stayed. Here in the

country it was different—she was different, because
she no longer wore the hated tag of "gypsy".

Only now was she coming to realise that she was
free; that she had the power to choose what she would
be. The farms where she stopped off to work thought
she was just another of the itinerant band of teenagers
who spent their summers working in the fields; gypsies
didn't travel alone, and her skin was pale enough, her
hair dark red enough for her not to be picked out
immediately as a member of the Romany people.

She was willing to work hard and she was consequently awarded respect by the farmers' wives who
employed her. Rachel didn't mind what kind of work
she was asked to do, just so long as it didn't bring her
into too much contact with any male members of the
households where she stopped, and that too was a
point in her favour. Several times she was asked to
stay on, but she was slowly coming to realise that
there might be more for her in life than the drudgery
of such menial tasks.

At one farm where she stayed in prosperous Cheshire
she was allowed to sleep in a room which had once
belonged to the now adult daughter of the family, and
this room came complete with its own television.
Several members of the gypsy tribe had had television,
of course, but her grandmother had not been among
them, and Rachel spent her free time absorbing information via this new source like a desert soaking up
rain. She watched all manner of programmes—educa-
tional, political, cartoons, American cops-and-robbers
series, and everything she saw only confirmed to her
that there was another form of life out there.

She remembered how her grandmother had always
told her that education was the key that unlocked
many doors, and how she had believed her. But how
could she get the sort of education she needed? Because

now Rachel had a goal. She wanted to be like the women she saw on television, polished, glamorous . . . loved. How did they get like that? They were like no women she had ever seen before, with their long blonde hair and their pretty faces—and their clothes.

Up until now as far as Rachel was concerned clothes had simply been something she had worn to protect her body from the weather, but now she was seeing girls wearing pretty clothes, and she ached to wear them herself.

When she wasn't working she spent more time than she had ever done before exploring the various towns she passed through on her way south. She stared in through shop windows and watched . . . and soon she had plucked up the courage to walk in through the plate glass doors of one of the stores. If the girl who served her was shocked by the state of the clothes she was wearing, or surprised that Rachel didn't even know her own size, she kept it to herself.

Rachel spent her money carefully. She knew exactly how she wanted to look. When she came out of the store she caught sight of herself by accident in a plate glass window, and froze, shocked by this new image of herself. She no longer looked different—poor. She looked just like everyone else.

She turned her head to make sure. All around her young girls dressed in the timeless uniform of the young strolled, flirted and laughed, and she was now one of them. She stared down at her jean-clad legs— her grandmother hadn't approved of girls wearing any form of trousers—then touched the soft fabric of her new T-shirt. The feel of clean new fabric beneath her fingertips was sensuously pleasing. It felt good to know that no one had ever worn these clothes before her, that they were hers and hers alone.

By the time she reached Oxford Rachel had lost all

but the faintest tinge of her Romany accent, and she had also removed her gypsy earrings. She was dressed just like any other teenager, and wore her new-found confidence like a patina of pleasure.

Oxford drew her like a magnet. She had seen a programme on television about it, and that had increased her yearning to be there.

She arrived just before the start of the Michaelmas term, and the town was almost empty of students; the bicycles that later would fill the narrow streets were few and far between, and the pubs and discos that later would be the haunt of the young were almost empty. During the long summer recess Oxford belonged to its inhabitants and its tourists—American in the main, come to stroll among the colleges, and examine the quaintness of this ancient seat of learning.

Rachel found a job easily enough in one of the hotels, but the pay wasn't as good as it had been on the farm, and the work was hard. The majority of the other chambermaids were foreign; an Irish girl with an accent so thick that Rachel could barely understand it made friendly overtures towards her, and by the end of the first week she was beginning to feel she was settling in.

When she complained to Bernadette about the poorness of her wage the Irish girl grinned at her.

"Well, why don't you do what I do? Get yourself a job in one of the pubs in the evening? They're looking for someone at the place where I work. I could take you along and introduce you if you like?"

Rachel agreed. Although the hotel provided its chambermaids with board and food, the meals they were served were very meagre indeed, and she was almost constantly hungry.

She got the job in Bernadette's pub. The manager was a plump cheerful man in his late forties, with two girls of his own who were away at university, and his wife kept a stern eye on the more flirtatious of the barmaids.

Rachel felt happier than she had ever been in her life, but when she shyly asked Bernadette if she knew how she might go about joining a library, the Irish girl filled the dormitory they shared with the other chambermaids with her rollicking laugh.

"Joining a library, is it, you're wanting? Well, sure there's a fine thing! Oi'm thinking that a pretty girl like you can get all the learning she wants from the men . . ."

Bernadette was a flirt, Rachel had quickly realised that, but she hadn't realised until now how great a gap yawned between them. For the first time since she had left them she felt homesick for the tribe. They were, after all, her people.

When Bernadette asked her if she wanted to go to a disco she refused.

"Ah well, suit yourself, then . . . I'm sure I don't mind having all the boys to meself." Bernadette tossed her dark hair as she walked out, and Rachel knew she had offended her.

Fortunately Bernadette had a mercurial temper and a kind heart, and by morning she was her normal friendly self, chatting animatedly to Rachel about the boy she had met the previous evening, as they worked.

"Keep away from Number Ten," she warned Rachel. "Helga . . . you know, the German girl, she was telling me that when she went in this morning he came out of his bathroom stark naked and asked her if she'd mind giving him a rub down! Dirty old man, he's fifty if he's a day . . . and married. I mind he's stayed here before with his wife . . ."

All the chambermaids gossiped, although Rachel tended to keep herself aloof. She wasn't used to such friendliness, and she treated it with caution, half expecting them to change and turn on her, unable to forget what she had suffered during her schooldays, but now she was different, now she wasn't a despised gypo but simply another young woman like themselves.

The seventies were a good time to be young; the world was full of optimism, and youth was petted and fêted by all. To be young was to hold the world in the palm of your hand. Rachel was constantly meeting other young people who, like herself, cherished their freedom, but who, unlike her, had travelled the world. They came into the pub in their faded jeans, carrying their backpacks, the men thin and bearded, their girlfriends long-haired and kohl-eyed, drinking beer while they told their tales of Kathmandu, and worshipping at the feet of the great ashrams. Everyone who was anyone was into meditation; Rachel read the magazines left behind by the guests and learned that she was living in an almost magical era.

As the summer heat faded into autumn, and mists began to hang over the river in the early morning sunlight, Oxford gradually began to stir back to life. Students arrived in dribs and drabs, trickling back into the town; life began to stir beneath the somnolence of the summer, as the tourists left to make way for the undergraduates.

By the beginning of Michaelmas term life in the town had changed, its pulse hard and heady. Bernadette was delighted.

"Now we'll see some foine young men," she promised Rachel one morning as they finished their work. "You wait and see!"

It was impossible not to respond to the surge of excitement beating through the air. Rachel felt it in her own thudding pulse. The crisp tang of late summer with its nostalgic undertones of autumn hung on the air. Almost every night the pub was full of young men in shabby jeans or corduroy trousers, University scarves wrapped round their necks, their long hair brushing their shoulders. They talked with a multitude of accents, but almost always in the same studiedly throwaway fashion; they were the cream, the *jeunesse doré*, and they knew it.

In some of the staider colleges it was still necessary to have permission to run a motorcar, and so the traditional bicycles were very much in use. Rachel had to run across the road to avoid being knocked down by one of them one evening as she hurried to work. Behind her she heard a great shout and then a crash, and turning round she saw a tangle of jean-clad legs and bicycle wheels.

Instinctively she started to walk away, until a plaintive voice halted her.

"I say, don't go and leave me here! I might have broken my leg . . ."

His voice was cultivated and teasing; the voice of a male used to being courted and flattered. As she turned her head to look back at him Rachel caught the blond flash of his hair. She hesitated.

"Come on . . . it was your fault I fell off, you know. I haven't ridden one of these damn things for years, and when I saw you . . . pretty girls oughtn't to be allowed to cross the roads in front of learner bicycle riders!"

He had called her pretty, and immediately Rachel stiffened, but there had been none of the hated near-violence and dislike in his voice that she had heard from the other men.

Caution urged her to walk away, but something deeper, stronger, and much more potent, urged her to stay. Slowly she walked towards him and watched him disentangle himself from his bicycle. He was tall, over six foot, with shoulder-length fair hair, and the bluest eyes Rachel had ever seen. They were the sort of eyes that always seemed to be full of light and laughter. He was laughing now, grinning ruefully as he brushed himself down.

"Damn! I think I've twisted my front wheel. That'll teach me to look at pretty girls!" He moved and then winced, taking his weight off his left foot. "I seem to have twisted my ankle as well. My rooms aren't far from here . . . If you give me a hand I should be able to make it to them without too much difficulty."

At any other time Rachel would have found his assumption that she would automatically agree to help him off putting, but for some reason she found herself responding to his smile and walking towards him.

"If I could just put my arm round your shoulders . . ."

His arm was muscular but thin, and she could smell the scent of his body mingling with the oily odour of wool from his sweater. He smiled at her, his teeth white in the tanned darkness of his face. For some reason she almost wanted to reach out and touch him. Shocked by her own reaction, Rachel dragged her gaze away.

He was like no other boy or man she had ever known. There was an aura about him that she could feel herself responding to. She looked at his hand, cupped round the ball of her shoulder. His fingers were long, the nails well cared for.

"Cat got your tongue?" he demanded with another grin.

Rachel shook her head. He was going to make her late for work, but recklessly she didn't care.

He said it was only a little way to his rooms, but in actual fact it was half a mile. Rachel gazed up in reverence at the ancient buildings of his college. She had explored them all during the summer recess, combining her walks through their hallowed grounds with knowledge she had gained from the books she had borrowed from the library. It had been the publican's wife who had come to the rescue and shown her how to join the library, and now she touched the weathered stone as they rounded the corner of the building and entered the enclosed quadrangle.

"Tom Quad," her companion told her cheerfully, glancing sideways at her.

Rachel only smiled. She knew all about the history of Christ Church College; that it had first been commissioned by Cardinal Wolsey, four years before he fell from Henry VIII's grace. Christopher Wren had added the Tower over Wolsey's gate, in 1682, and Rachel glanced up towards it automatically, just as Great Tom, the bell, tolled its curfew.

"Bang on time as usual! Come on, my rooms are up here."

His weight was beginning to make her shoulder ache, but it never occurred to Rachel to refuse to go with him. During the summer recess she had learned to parry the flirtatious remarks of the pub's patrons, but both Bernadette and the landlord's wife had warned her that Oxford's students could be remarkably persistent.

"You'd think they'd have better things to do with their time than spending it trying to get you into bed with them," Bernadette sniffed disdainfully.

It was from Bernadette and the other girls at the hotel that Rachel had gradually learned to be a little more worldly. Now when she worked she often hummed the latest pop tune. She wore make-up—something her grandmother had always disapproved of, and she was gradually adopting the manners and fashions of her peers.

For the first time in her life she felt that she was actually accepted on equal terms with her peers, and she liked that feeling, but Rachel was by nature cautious. When the other girls disappeared for the evening with flurried giggles, and didn't appear until the following morning, Rachel listened to their whispered confidences about the boys they had been out with, but when anyone tried to date her she kept them firmly at bay. She wasn't interested in boyfriends and romance; there wasn't time in her life for them. She had so much to do; coming to Oxford had opened her eyes to all that was missing from her life.

These students who flocked through Oxford's streets would one day go out into the world and become people of eminence, secure and respected. The bitterness of her childhood haunted her and Rachel was determined to make herself inviolate. The only way she could do that was by achieving financial security.

She had a quick intelligence and had soon realised that she could never be content with the goals Bernadette and the other girls set themselves. They were happy to drift from day to day, spending their wages on new clothes, dating a different boy every night. They were like the poppies that bloomed in the cornfields in the summer, Rachel thought wryly— pretty and giddy, blowing this way and then that at the will of the wind, but once summer was gone they wilted and died; they could not survive without the sun, without warmth.

"Think you can get me up the stairs?"

Rachel frowned and looked consideringly at him. He wasn't the first student who had shown an interest in her, and caution warned her to tread carefully.

"I have to get back," she told him. "I should be at work."

"You work?"

He said it with such amused condescension that Rachel could feel her skin flushing with resentment.

"Yes," she told him curtly, "at the King's Arms."

"Ah . . . Yes. I see."

He was looking at her differently now, consideringly; and Rachel knew what was going through his mind. In her almost teenage uniform jeans and cotton peasant blouse, her long hair down on her shoulders, he had mistaken her for a fellow student. Now that he knew she was not, he was looking at her in much the same way the village children had regarded her and her contemporaries when they camped near their homes. Only the suspicion was absent from his eyes, and in its place was an intense glitter of sexual speculation.

"So you're not a student."

Her head lifted, her eyes coolly meeting his and dismissing the look of desire he gave her.

"No."

"What's your name? Mine's Tim . . . Tim Wilding."

His abrupt change of tack caught her off guard, and unwillingly Rachel found herself telling him,

"Rachel."

The blue eyes laughed down into hers. "I don't like it . . . it's far too biblical for you! I shall call you Gypsy . . . it suits you far more."

Her heart almost turned over with shock and fear, but he seemed not to see it.

"Are you a gypsy at heart? I am."

Up above them a window opened and he stepped back to look up. Rachel followed his glance and saw a man leaning out to look at them. He was about the same age as her companion, but physically very different. He had a shock of dark hair, worn slightly shorter than the prevailing fashion, and wildly curly.

His face was all planes and angles, his skin brown and his eyes a clear sharp grey.

"Miles, I've ricked my ankle, and this fair charmer came to my rescue. Come down and give me a hand, will you?"

The dark head was withdrawn, after the cool grey eyes had cast a sardonic look at them both, and the window closed.

"Miles French, my room-mate." Tim Wilding pulled a wry face. "He's a mite too Celtic for my taste, but I suppose that comes of studying law. Very phlegmatic, is our Miles, unshockable and unshakeable, although it's always fun to try."

Rachel pondered his comment as his fingers wrapped round her wrist, preventing her from leaving. She got the feeling that Tim didn't entirely like his room-mate, and she shivered a little as she remembered the cool amusement in the other's almost analytic scrutiny of her. Something about him had frightened her, in a way that someone with Tim's overt sexuality never could.

"Bit of an enigma, is our Miles," Tim continued in his light drawl. He reached into his jacket pocket and produced a packet of cigarettes. "Want one?"

Rachel shook her head, and watched him extract and light one, the smile curling round his mouth making her feel curious. He looked like a naughty cherub. As he drew on the cigarette and expelled the smoke, she knew why. The unmistakable scent of pot surrounded her. It had been one of the other chambermaids who had enlightened her about the curious sweetish, sickly smell coming from one of their guests' bedrooms. It was a scent that sometimes seemed to pervade certain parts of Oxford, and Rachel drew back from it instinctively. Her grandmother had imparted to her some of her knowledge of herbs and plants and their uses, and she had learned from her of the dangers of abusing their powers.

The outer door opened before she could say anything to Tim, her attention drawn by the young man coming towards them.

Like Tim, he was wearing jeans and a cotton shirt. Rachel saw his mouth compress slightly as he too caught the scent of the doctored cigarette.

"Judgemental Miles!" Tim taunted him, catching his expression. "My dear, what sort of lawyer will you make if you haven't tasted for yourself all life's delights and dangers?"

"I don't need to smoke those to know that they addle your wits." He had a much deeper voice than Tim's, now it was crisped with mockery and a finite edge of anger. "Come on, Tim, stop showing off for the girlfriend, and let me get back to work."

He ignored Rachel and hoisted Tim towards the steps.

Rachel paused, angered by his indifference. Tim turned to look at her, and called over his shoulder, "See you soon, Gypsy!"

Turning on her heel, Rachel walked through the lengthening shadows back out of the quadrangle. She wouldn't see him again, of course; because if she did she would make it plain to him that she wasn't going to bed with him. This was the seventies, and sex was free and easy, a new toy to be explored and played with, but Rachel's heritage was an older, darker one. She had suffered too much from her own parents' careless rapture to ever treat sex lightly. It had held her mother in thrall, making her dismiss the dangers of what she was doing, and Rachel intended to make sure that nothing ever had such dominion over her. Nothing.

She was late for work that evening. Bernadette

frowned at her when she arrived behind the bar.

"You're late!" she declared. "Old man Wells has been looking for you."

Jobs weren't difficult to come by in the seventies, and Rachel was a good worker, besides being attractive to the customers, so George Wells, the bar manager, soon forgave her for her small transgression, although he kept her behind after the others had gone, making her do the final check of the tables for empty glasses.

It was dark when she finally stepped outside, and the street was empty. She turned to leave—then gasped as a hand closed over her arm, fear storming through her.

"Hello, Gypsy. I thought you were never going to come!"

She recognised his voice instantly, her head turning to look into the smiling blue eyes.

"Let's go and find somewhere where we can talk and get to know one another," he suggested winningly. "I want to know all there is to know about you, Gypsy."

The scent of drugs still clung to his skin, and his fingers when they laced with hers felt hot. Rachel wanted to pull away, and yet part of her wanted to stay with him. He was so different from her . . . she thirsted for the insight that he could give into another way of life.

Without even having to ask herself how she knew Rachel knew that he came from a wealthy background and that he had been shielded and protected by that wealth all his life. He lived a life she could only learn about second-hand, through books, and she ached to know what it was that gave him his patina of self-assurance and made him so uncaring of all the hazards that daily tormented her.

She *wanted* to talk to him, and she remembered that

there was a small café which she passed on her way home at night that always seemed to be open. They could go there.

CHAPTER SIX

TIM WILDING had never known what it was to want
something and have that want go unsatisfied.

From the day of his birth he had been surrounded
by adoring females, and as he grew older he had
learned to take their adulation for granted, to manipulate and exploit them, and in so charming a manner
that they continued to love and praise him.

He was the grandson of the Earl of Marchington;
an earldom that went back to the time of Elizabeth
the First. His family owned rich acres in Pembroke-
shire and the North. His grandfather's main seat was
in Dorset—a huge rambling mish-mash of buildings
extended and improved upon by a succession of
wealthy men rich enough to amuse themselves by
enhancing their home to suit whatever fashion had
held sway.

It was from Dorset that the first Earl had come—a
seaman turned pirate, turned one of Queen Elizabeth's
favourite courtiers, who had been repaid for his loyalty
and, some said, for his prowess in bed, with the hand
of one of the Virgin Queen's richest wards. Kate
Sothey had brought to her husband a fortune amassed
by her parents and grandparents, plus land in the
north of England.

Will Wilding had been forty-eight at the time of his
marriage, and rumour had it that his bride had been
more than unwilling. She was in love with someone
else, but the Queen's will had prevailed, and in due
time Mistress Kate provided her spouse with one son

and three daughters.

Not even the title of Countess had been enough to compensate for all that she had lost, though, and in family portraits she was shown as an unsmiling, frail-looking woman, very much in the shadow of her big jovial husband.

Will Wilding had set a standard that his ancestors carefully upheld, and the Wilding men had always married well, conserving and adding to what was theirs, with the result that the current Earl was a millionaire several times over. He and his son and his family lived at Marchington Place, and although his son's marriage had produced several children, only one of them was male—the only male heir, in the absence of any other near male relative. Tim had grown up perfectly aware of his own importance; of the fact that one day he would be the Earl. The fact that physically he was very attractive was something he had also learned young and played ruthlessly upon.

At Eton he had fagged for one of the school's most notorious bullies—until he caught the eye of one of the other seniors, who had bought him away from his peer. Paul Somerton had been wildly in love with his newly acquired fag, and Tim had deliberately encouraged and fostered his feelings, liking the power it gave him. For Paul he had no feelings whatsoever, but he had already learned how to manipulate people with his charm and his looks, and it was a skill he would use throughout his life as clinically and determinedly as any prostitute.

Sex to Tim was simply a means of subjugating his victims, and he was equally adept at making love to a male or a female. Age, looks, personality—none of these entered into his calculations, or influenced his choice of lover, until he met Simon Herries. Simon was one year his senior and thus ahead of him at

Eton. Being in different Houses they only came into contact with one another by accident, but Tim knew the moment he met him that Simon was different. He had a power, a fascination that held Tim in thrall, and under Simon's expert tuition he had learned to choose his lovers with more care.

At Oxford, among others, he had his eye on one of the tutors, a man whose influence extended widely throughout the college. They weren't lovers yet, but Tim knew that they would be.

He and Simon laughed at the ease with which their victims succumbed. They were still lovers, as they always had been, but sex was only a small part of their relationship, and Simon knew Tim well enough to accept that his sexuality demanded a very free rein. Sometimes Tim simply enjoyed the pleasure of the subtle chase and the ultimate downfall of his victim, at others he chose his lovers because they had something he wanted or needed.

His and Simon's room-mate fell into the former category, but as yet he had refused to succumb. Tim wasn't worried. He could afford to wait; it would make his ultimate victory all the sweeter. He and Simon had already been sharing rooms with someone else when Miles arrived at Oxford, and Miles had been moved against his will to fill the gap when the third member of the original trio had been sent down. Miles suspected that Simon Herries was as displeased with the arrangement as he was himself, and they both tended to give one another a wide berth.

Tim operated in a different way, delighting in tormenting Miles with deliberately provocative remarks. How he would enjoy seeing that enigmatic exterior crumble beneath the drive of desire! Tim thought, smiling to himself and watching Miles—and it *would* crumble. He had never failed yet. Perhaps he ought to invite Miles home for the Christmas vacation.

He frowned slightly, anticipating Simon's reaction to such an invitation, a petulant, almost adolescent rebellion darkening his eyes, and then his attention switched back to Rachel. She was still a virgin—he was ready to stake his life on it. He could always tell. So much the better for what he had in mind. A pulse of excitement thudded through him, a mellow sensation of pleasure yet to come as he anticipated the delights the future held in store.

Through this girl he would surely succeed in raising the Devil. Simon . . . Simon didn't really believe it could be done, he suspected, frowning again. Simon had been the one to instigate the formation of the revived Hell Fire Club, but the power and fascination it held for him was lost on his friend, Tim suspected. Simon had not as yet felt that strong pull of darkness with which he was so familiar.

But he would do; somehow he would convince him . . . Somehow? He knew how. Excitement kicked through him again. Virgins were scarce on the ground these days, and this one was perfect . . . perfect. He sensed the pride in her and the battened-down wildness. She would fight. He would like that. He could feel his body hardening, and immediately he switched off his thoughts.

The girl might only be a barmaid working in a pub, but Tim had sensed that she was intelligent, and wary too. He didn't want to alarm her . . . not at this stage. Later she could be as terrified as she wished.

The café that Rachel had mentioned was busy, but there was one table for two empty. Rachel sat down while Tim went to get them something to drink. She had noticed when they walked in how all eyes turned in his direction. He was one of the most perfectly beautiful human beings she had ever seen, and yet something in her was chilled by his perfection even while she was drawn to it. Age-old instincts warned her to be careful, but she told herself that no harm could come of simply sitting down to talk with him. They were among the last to leave the café. Tim insisted on walking her back to the hotel, but once they got there, Rachel turned firmly and repulsed him when he tried to kiss her. He accepted her refusal with a lazy smile and an amused look in his eyes that told her that he would not find it hard to find someone who was willing.

She was glad Bernadette was already asleep. She didn't want to talk to anyone about Tim. Not yet.

It was gone two o'clock when Tim eventually returned to his rooms. After leaving Rachel, he had felt so excited and pleased with himself that he had gone on to one of the discos. He had found a girl there, cheap and tarty, and more than willing to take him back to her bedsit with her. He left her in a tangle of grubby bedding, fast asleep, revelling in the way her cheap scent mingled with the odour of sex and clung to his body.

Miles looked up but didn't betray any reaction when he walked in. "Still up? I thought you'd have been tucked up in your chaste little bed hours ago, or were you too frightened to go to bed in case I joined you there?" jeered Tim.

It was part of his technique to goad his victims, normally it drew some sort of response, but Miles merely smiled impassively and said nothing.

His lack of reaction brought Tim down from his earlier high. He reached for a cigarette, inhaling deeply, watching the controlled way Miles moved as he started to clear up his books. Damn the man, he was far too controlled and clever about the barriers he put up. Tim wanted to see that control shatter, to break through that reserve and trample his pride into the dust.

"Herries is looking for you."

Miles didn't look at him as he spoke, but Tim felt the slight tension in his body. So he wasn't completely impervious after all! He grinned to himself and stubbed out the cigarette.

"Jealous?" he purred softly, taking a step towards him. "My dear one . . ."

"Cut it out, Tim." The cool command was laconic enough to betray a certain degree of amusement. "You know, you really ought to try for OUDS. Who you choose to make friends with is your own concern, but I don't like Herries."

"Because he's homosexual?" One blond eyebrow lifted teasingly. "My dear, at least half of Academe . . ."

"Enjoys having sex with and then beating up ten-year-old boys? I don't think so."

So French knew about that. Simon must be slipping—he was normally more careful about keeping his vices hidden. Tim would have to warn him to be more cautious.

"Did he say what he wants?" he asked carelessly.

"Something about a meeting. Apparently the date's been changed to tomorrow night."

There were any number of secret and not so secret clubs and coteries at Oxford, so there was no real need for the exceedingly sharp glance that Miles gave him, but as always the scent of danger fired his own excitement. This was how he liked to live, always on the edge of that danger, always flirting with violence . . .

Miles watched him as he roamed round the room, still half high on drugs, and unless he was wrong about the smell clinging to him—sex. Odd, he hadn't thought that dark-haired girl he had seen him with earlier had been Tim's type. He normally preferred them far more overtly sexual.

Miles wanted to throw open the windows and let in some fresh air, but he knew from long experience that if he did so, he would be subjected to all manner of taunts and digs, designed to undermine his self-control. Sexually he had no interest in Tim, or indeed in any member of his own sex, but he did have a deeply buried vein of hot temper that he was always careful to keep well under control, and there were many times when Tim pushed him close to the edge of it. He suspected that like Simon Herries Tim enjoyed the frisson of sex with violence. Although unlike Herries Tim enjoyed receiving the violence rather than inflicting it.

His room-mate's sex life was no concern of his, he reminded himself. He was damn lucky to be up at Oxford, and he was here to work, not to get involved in precious cliques.

The undergrad who had shared with Tim before him had been sent down in disgrace, supposedly for supplying drugs. Smoking pot was endemic among the students, and it seemed an overly harsh punishment. Oddly, Tim never mentioned his former room-mate, although he had shared with him for twelve months.

Tim was one of a number of gilded youths up at Oxford because it was what the male members of their families had done for generations. Miles doubted very much that Tim would get a degree, or that he would care. For all his gilded beauty, Miles sensed something disquieting about him, and not just because of his sexual ambiguity. There was something essentially cold and dangerous about Tim; something that ran deeply contrary to his open face and lighthearted pose.

Had he been able to choose, Miles would have preferred to share with someone else; someone closer to his own background and ambitions.

His degree was important to him because it was the first step towards his ultimate goal. He had wanted to go into law for almost as long as he could remember, and to achieve even as much as he already had had been hard work for a boy brought up in a Doctor Barnado's Home.

He had been left on the steps of a hospital as a day-old baby in the classic fashion. His mother had never been traced, and because of medical complications following on from his exposure, he had been almost two years old before he had been given a completely clean bill of health—too old then to appeal to prospective parents who wanted to adopt only small babies.

He was philosophical rather than resentful of his fate. The orphanage had been well run, the staff kind, and he had developed early on in life a matter-of-fact resilience to protect himself from thinking too deeply about his mother's rejection.

If he had been lucky at all in his life, and he liked to think that he had, it had been having been placed in an orphanage situated on the outskirts of a small Cotswold village. One of the most generous patrons of the orphanage was a local JP and retired Army officer, Colonel Whitegate. The Colonel, a strict disciplinarian and a widower, was one of those men who although having no children of his own, had a genuine rapport with them. Small groups of children from the orphanage were regularly invited to the Manor House to help the Colonel with the small stud farm he ran, and afterwards to have tea with him in the informality of his comfortable study. The Colonel bred and trained polo ponies, having become an aficionado of the sport during his days in the Army. Although reasonably

well off he did not have the means to support a full
polo string, and to travel round the world attending
matches, so instead he had turned his skill to the
breeding rather than the riding of the ponies. He was
also a well-read man, simple in his tastes and in many
ways oddly innocent about life, one of the few people
who genuinely deserved the title 'gentleman'.

He was kind to all the children he came into contact
with—the orphanage was a relatively small one and
he made it his business to know most of them by
name, but it wasn't until Miles won a scholarship to
Rugby that he began to take any particular notice of
him.

It just so happened that Rugby was the Colonel's
own public school, and when the director of the
orphanage confided to him that he was concerned that
Miles might have to forgo the scholarship because of
the expense of equipping him to attend, he had
immediately said that he would pay all the incidental
expenses. These extended to far more than merely the
cost of the uniform and spending money and covered
the whole range of extra-curricular activities, all of
which the Colonel insisted that Miles participate in.

When Miles had tried, at the end of his first term,
to protest diffidently, the Colonel had told him that
part of the benefit to be reaped from a public school
education was to take full advantage of everything
that it had to offer.

"Do you think I'd ever have taken up polo if I
hadn't gone into the Army? Got any plans for the
future?" he added brusquely.

"The law, sir . . ." Miles told him hesitantly. He
couldn't explain where this fascination with the legal
profession had come from, it was just something that
was there deep inside him. The ramifications and
diversity of the law enthralled him and challenged

him; he also liked debating, and he had already discussed with his housemaster his desire to enter the legal profession.

If Colonel Whitegate was disappointed he hid it well. Miles already knew how expensive in both money and time acquiring legal qualifications could be. The law was also a very enclosed world, nepotistic and tightly gathered in upon itself. His ambition to become a barrister could only be fulfilled if other barristers opened their chambers to him and invited him to join them. There was no automatic right of entry, but the simpler, more workaday world of the solicitor was not the one he wanted to enter.

All this had been discussed with his housemaster, and he already knew how long and arduous the road ahead would be. He would need a degree, and if he could win a place at Oxford the worth of that degree would be increased tenfold. After that there would be more periods of study, more exams, a period of apprenticeship in counsels' chambers.

All this he already knew, and explained to the Colonel as he told him of his ambitions.

"He's a bright lad and intent on reaching high," the Colonel commented to the orphanage director later.

"Too high, perhaps."

"No . . . no man can ever do that."

The Colonel financed Miles through his last two years at school, and was enormously proud of what he had achieved. Miles had an open invitation to spend his holidays with him, but during the summer he had spent all but two weeks working as a roustabout off one of the North Sea oil rigs. The roustabouts were the lowest form of life on the rigs, the work was hard and dirty, but it paid well, and Miles now had enough in the bank to see him through to his finals if he was careful.

He had learned a lot in Aberdeen. Going ashore with his workmates, he had discovered that to say one worked on an oil rig was a magic incantation as far as a certain section of the female population was concerned. He hadn't been a virgin when he went up to Oxford; there had been a couple of fumbled, hasty episodes beforehand, but in an Aberdeen pub he had been picked up by the bored wife of one of the oil company executives, who had taken him back with her to her neo-Georgian home and taught him the difference between more immediate sexual gratification and intense sexual pleasure, and all the delicate nuances in between. Miles had been surprised to discover within himself a deep well of sexuality, and he had put the lessons the woman had taught him to good use since.

He didn't have a current girlfriend; he preferred to keep his relationships casual. The last thing he wanted was to be tied down into the sort of steady relationship some of the other students were burdened with.

His workload was heavy and he studied hard. His degree was important to him, but he still left himself with enough time to enjoy some of the peripheral pleasures. He was a member of several debating societies; he rowed and he played tennis. He enjoyed both folk and classical music, although he didn't play an instrument, and occasionally he submitted a witty piece to *Isis*, the university magazine.

What he didn't do was get involved in the heavy drinking and drugs scene favoured by the *jeunesse doré* he was too intelligent to get caught in that particular trap. He knew exactly why Tim Wilding was goading him. With another man he would have told him quite simply that he was wasting his time.

He had come across homosexuality quite early on

at Rugby. It wasn't his thing; he liked women, although he numbered several homosexuals among his group of friends and enjoyed both their wit and their intelligence, but in Tim Wilding he sensed something different; something destructive and dangerous.

Although they shared a set of rooms they didn't have the same friends. Tim wasn't the slightest bit interested in gaining his degree. He and his set tended to look down on the students who had made it to Oxford through the grammar school and direct grant system. Their petty snobbishness bored Miles; he suspected it sprang from unadmitted inferiority, rather than from the much vaunted superiority that they seemed to cherish and demonstrate at every opportunity.

The fact that Tim was the grandson of one of the country's premier earls had no effect on Miles whatsoever. If anything he felt rather more sorry for him. His grandfather had a formidable reputation; his father was an immensely successful businessman and Tim had a lot to live up to. Far better to be in his own shoes, Miles reflected, where he was not constantly being overshadowed by those who had gone before. No, he didn't envy Tim, and in fact he didn't particularly like either of his room-mates, although of the two of them, he recognised that Simon Herries was the more dangerous.

There was an aura about him, a power, that Miles instinctively mistrusted. He was a very charismatic man, there was no doubt about that, but sometimes . . . just sometimes when things were not going his way Miles had witnessed a darker, far more dangerous side to his personality, and he instinctively avoided both Simon and Tim, having no desire at all to be drawn into their circle.

Their sexual proclivities were no secret, but they

were far from being the only two bi-sexual men at Oxford. Miles watched the two of them together, and it sometimes seemed to him that Tim deliberately on occasions tried to incite Simon to sexual violence— incited it and enjoyed it, Miles suspected distastefully, but they were both grown men and their private relationship was no affair of his.

There was far more between them than just a homosexual relationship, and even the reality of that was suspect, given the fact that Tim made no secret of the fact that he had many other lovers of both sexes. And yet for all his sexual conquests there was an air of almost asexuality about him, a bogus air of innocence, like that of a child before the onset of puberty. But where Tim could be both charming and witty, Simon Herries had a brooding air about him that repulsed all but his chosen band of friends.

Miles wasn't a member of that small clique, nor did he want to be. He suspected that Tim and others had formed some sort of secret club, although what its purpose was he had no idea, nor did he really care. Secret clubs abounded within the colleges; some lasted, some died, some became hallowed institutions and admission to them was highly prized. Miles doubted that anyone would remember what Herries' club had stood for once he had left Christ Church.

Tim had once told him that it was Herries' ambition to enter the Church. It seemed very unlikely to Miles, who thought he had never come across a more worldly and less Christian human being, but he kept his thoughts to himself, knowing Tim's propensity for jokes.

He had overheard one of the tutors commenting that Simon Herries would make a good politician.

"He's devious and dishonest enough for it," had been the cynical comment.

Tim waited until he was sure that Miles was asleep before leaving their rooms. Curfews were no longer maintained at Oxford and there was no penalty to pay for being out of doors after a certain time, but to Tim secrecy was the very breath of life, and he enjoyed the challenge of slipping out silently, and hugging the shadows of the stairs as he made his way to their prearranged rendezvous outside the college.

Simon was waiting for him as he had known he would be. Unlike Miles, he didn't make any attempt to conceal his recognition of the scent that Tim brought with him, pushing him away abruptly when Tim reached out to embrace him.

Tim laughed softly, knowing he held the power to make Simon cry out with desire for him, should he want to do so.

"I got your message. Why has the meeting to be changed?"

"We've got to change the venue—apparently the vicar's getting suspicious. We'll have to find somewhere else."

"Oh dear, the original Francis Dashwood didn't have these problems, did he—but don't worry, my dear, I've found something that will cheer you up. A deliciously untouched virgin."

It was while he was at Eton that Simon Herries had first become attracted to Satanism. A history lesson mentioning the notorious Sir Francis Dashwood and his cronies had sparked off his interest in the occult, and over the years that interest had grown.

There were plenty of young men like Tim Wilding who were attracted to the idea of violence and sex, and when that was combined with secrecy and power, its lure was irresistible. The aim of their 'Society' was not so much to raise the Devil as to investigate whether or not such a thing was possible; thus by stating this as the society's aim, Simon was able to cloak it in an aura of respectability and spurious study.

Of course, in order to validate the claims of Dashwood and his coven, that they had been able to raise the Devil, Simon and his friends had to mirror their methods.

Up until now they had used a remote church in a small local village for their rites, but the vicar had obviously become suspicious. Now they would have to find somewhere else.

Simon himself had little belief in Dashwood's claim—he suspected that like himself he had enjoyed the sexual licence his role gave him, and the power. Because there always had been and always would be those who were chained in superstitious fear to the old pre-Christian beliefs. Simon had learned at Eton quite by accident that it was possible to control others through the threat of hidden power. Now he used this power in a different way.

Those he chose as his disciples were only people who were useful to him in some way. First he tantalised them with subtle promises of the pleasures in store, and then once they had partaken of those pleasures, he used them as a threat against them. Unlike Simon, however, Tim believed that Francis Dashwood had raised the Devil; the pull of Satanism for him meant far more than the means by which he could control others—after all, he could do that already.

The next important date in the Satanist calendar was All Hallows' Eve; the new Hell Fire Club would celebrate it with a Black Mass. And for a virgin to be sacrificed at that Black Mass would invoke the most powerful of all of black magic forces.

Tonight, quite casually, Rachel had revealed to him

that she was an orphan. He had felt the excitement beat up through his veins then, dancing like fire behind his eyelids, making his whole body come alive. Already he could picture the scene, feel the power that would be his, first at the moment when he penetrated her body and then later when he made the ritual sacrifice and offered her up to the power of the Dark Master.

No one, not even Simon, who had shaped and indeed initiated his exploration of black magic, knew how deeply Tim had been affected by his research into Satanism. He had followed its development through the centuries, traced it back over many lifetimes, and had felt the thrilled pulse of his blood. To raise the Devil would be the ultimate thrill, the pleasure to end all pleasures, a greater high than any drug, more sexually stimulating than any mere contact with alien flesh. He could feel himself grow hot and float away from his body at the thought of what was to come.

Simon watched him, and frowned. Tim had been smoking pot again; his eyes were glazed and vacant, a thin drool of spittle escaping from the corner of his mouth. Simon had warned him before about becoming too reliant on the drug. He used it himself, but only carefully.

A virgin sacrifice. He liked the idea, although personally he would have preferred the pale, sexless body of a young boy. He felt himself grow hard at the thought. There had been a boy last week . . . He shuddered and felt the sweat break out on his skin.

As a fag at Eton he had once walked into a senior's study when he was forcing Tim to perform the act of fellatio on him, and the thrill it had given him to see someone else being forced to another's sexual demands had remained with him for a long time. In fact that had been the first time he had realised that there could be pleasure in sex as well as pain.

He had been less than five years old the first time his father abused him sexually.

His mother died shortly after he was born, and he had been handed over into the care of his father's aunt. His father had been a remote, distant figure, spending most of his time in London on business and returning to the borders only at rare intervals.

Then when Simon was four his great-aunt had died, and his father had returned home for good. A sombre, brooding man, he frightened Simon, who kept out of his way, although he had had no reason then for his fear.

The first time his father had slid into his bed and started to touch him with rough urgent hands, he had cried out in terror. He had soon learned never to make that mistake again. The next day his father had birched him, leaving thin red weals across his buttocks that oozed blood. The memory of his parent going down on his knees to lap the bright beads of blood from his lacerated flesh was something that would stay with him always.

By the time he got to Eton he was stoically accustomed to his father's abuse of him, and he had learned to endure what he inflicted on him in silence. At the least possible excuse his father would beat him until his flesh bled and he was driven to an orgy of lust.

When Paul Somerton sold Tim to his friend, Simon took his place. The cruelty of his senior made little impression on a boy who had already endured all there was to endure at the hands of his parent.

For the rest of his life there would be no pleasure for Simon without his inflicting pain on the pleasure-giver, and just as he had learned as a child to blot out the anomalies in his relationship with his father, so he learned to blot out the sadistic impulses that governed his own life.

By the time he reached Oxford he was a past master at the art of throwing a cloak of camouflage over his true personality. People might not like him; they might sense deep, uncharted chasms within his personality, but none of them knew why. Not even Tim knew about Simon's childhood; it was something he had locked away inside himself and would never ever set free.

Already he loathed Rachel even without knowing her. He could feel the waves of sexual excitement emanating from Tim, and all because of some female bitch. Simon hated women; it was a woman who had died and left him at the mercy of his father; two women, in fact, first his mother and then his aunt. Sexually they left him cold, but he already knew that one day he would marry. His father was dead, and had left him his house and lands but very little else. Simon was ambitious, but ambitions had to be fuelled with wealth, and for that he would need to marry. He had already drawn up a short list of candidates.

Abruptly he turned his mind to more pressing matters. Since one member of the coven had been stupid enough to leave behind a small portion of their black candles at their last mass, they would have to find a new site for their next one.

"I have an idea!" Simon could hear the excitement in Tim's voice. He looked across at him. He was silhouetted against the window, his head thrown back challengingly, his eyes glittering. It was a pose Simon recognised. This was Tim at his most lethally charming and determined. "There's a chapel at Marchington. We could celebrate our next Mass there."

"Don't be a fool! It would be far too dangerous."

Simon forgot for a moment how much Tim loved danger, recklessly so. He had said completely the wrong thing, as he realised almost instantly, but it was already too late.

"The harder the achievement the more worthwhile," Tim told him softly. "Think about it, Simon. No one can interrupt or stop us at Marchington. We'll be able to do it there. We can raise the Devil. Think of the power that will be ours!"

Simon shifted uncomfortably from one foot to the other. Did Tim really believe..? He grimaced to himself. He already knew the answer to that one. Tim was almost obsessed by his belief that these ancient black magic rites held the secret of total power.

"We shall hold the Black Mass at Marchington, and we shall sacrifice our virgin there and I shall raise the Devil."

Simon checked abruptly. He started to speak warningly, then fell silent as he looked into Tim's face. He looked like someone in the thrall of some blinding revelation . . . or some blinding obsession. Tim meant every word he was saying. Simon could stop him . . . perhaps . . . but the girl by all accounts would never be missed, and he couldn't help thinking of the power that would be his if he let Tim go ahead with his plans. Not the power Tim dreamed of, but a far more earthly power. He would let Tim stage-manage the Mass. He would stay on the sidelines, in the background, making sure that everything was properly recorded for posterity. They would pick the acolytes for that night carefully . . .

His mind ran ahead, busily cataloguing those among their members who could potentially be most useful to him in the future. Those who would be weak enough to succumb to blackmail. Rachel was forgotten . . . whether she lived or died meant nothing to Simon. She was as dispensable as an empty cardboard carrier, as unimportant in his scheme of things as an insignificant ant. She was no more than a means to an end; if Tim wanted this Mass then let him have it. The knowledge of his own duplicity made Simon's eyes glitter with satisfaction. It always gave him a thrill to know how completely Tim was under his control.

"Very well," he said slowly. "But it must be carefully planned, and no one, no one at all must know what's happening until the very last moment. We don't want anyone getting cold feet and running out on us to tell tales, do we?"

"It will be perfect," Tim told him. He was breathing steadily, his lean body suddenly taut with desire. Simon, who had seen that look in his eyes many many times before, recognised it instantly and laughed softly.

"Here," he suggested knowingly. "You want me here . . ."

It was cold and dark, but neither of them cared. The sudden upsurge of lust carried them both far beyond any mundane awareness of their surroundings or the lack of heat.

Afterwards, as he lay surfeited on the ground, Tim opened his eyes and said softly, "What a shame dear Miles isn't here to share this with us."

"Be careful," Simon warned him, not sharing his amusement. "He isn't like the others, Tim. He won't succumb."

Tim felt he was wrong, but he was too relaxed to argue. He closed his eyes and started mentally planning his Black Mass. The thought of it excited him so much that he reached towards Simon again, but Simon pushed him back. In their relationship, he was the one who made the rules—a fact which just occasionally Tim was inclined to forget.

CHAPTER SEVEN

SIMON and Tim had instigated their own version of the Hell Fire Club during Tim's first term at Oxford. Tim's original room-mate had been one of the founder members, but he had started to talk too much and so they had had to get rid of him. Simon had been the one to suggest they plant the drugs on him, and he had also arranged for him to be caught with them— Simon was very good at "arranging" things. Since then they had been very careful about who they recruited to their ranks.

For the coven to be fully operational and effective they needed thirteen members; in addition they also had several novice members; and among these were Richard Howell and Alex Barnett.

Both of them had been drawn into the Club almost by accident. Alex Barnett had come across Tim in the College library and had fallen into conversation with him. As a boy he had always been fascinated with the alchemists' search for the magic incantation to transform base metal into gold, and when he had seen that the book Tim was reading was on this subject he had found himself agreeing to join Tim and some of his friends at one of their meetings, not realising exactly what was involved.

Secretly he had been flattered by the invitation. He had arrived at Oxford via a State-run grammar school, and in his first term was very much in awe of Tim and his friends, and the air of aristocratic superiority that clung to them.

Richard Howell had joined the coven by a different route. His sex drive had always been phenomenal, and when he heard on the grapevine that a club existed to promote the sexual orgies indulged in by the eighteenth-century Hell Fire Club he had lost no time in making known that if such a club *did* exist he would very much like to join.

Both of them were now novices, and neither of them took at all seriously the Satanistic side of the club. To them it was simply a rather daring and exciting secret circle to which they were privileged to belong. Both of them would have laughed aloud if Tim had confided to them that he genuinely believed in Satanism; they thought that he, like they, considered it to be nothing more than a game. By the time they realised that they were wrong it was almost too late.

As novice members so far they had only been allowed to take part in the opening stages of one Black Mass. Simon was very careful about whom they recruited into the coven. By the time a new member was finally initiated Simon had secured enough material against him to ensure that if he ever did leave the coven, he would keep his mouth shut.

As far as Simon was concerned the club was simply another stepping stone on the path he had marked out for himself. He hadn't decided yet what form his career would take, but he had already determined that the more people within his control the better.

The new recruits to the club would have been surprised if they had known the mental files that Simon kept on all of them.

Richard Howell had connections in the banking world—small ones, maybe, but who knew where they would lead, who could tell how valuable such a connection might be in the future?

Alex Barnett belonged to a stratum of society that

frankly bored Simon. His background was middle class, and there was little money, but there was still something about him that Simon's well developed sixth sense told him was worthwhile cultivating.

As novices both Richard and Alex were to be initiated as full members at the next formal meeting of the club. They discussed it one afternoon in the library, where they had met by chance.

Of the two Alex was the more nervous, the less self-assured. He was perfectly well aware what his parents would say if they knew what he was contemplating doing, and he envied Richard Howell his amused sangfroid as the latter unashamedly discussed the sexual revels he was already anticipating.

If it wasn't for Richard's careless insouciance, Alex suspected that he himself might have backed out. He had felt acutely uncomfortable at his first Black Mass, conscious of an atavistic prickling of his scalp during the unhallowed service, coupled with a sensation of treading on very dangerous ground, but Oxford was a new environment for him, and he didn't have the self-confidence to say what he thought. Having come to the University via the grammar school system, he was consequently somewhat in awe of its traditions; of its students with their careless air of self-confidence; of their contemptuous mockery of those they considered beneath them, and so he trod very warily indeed.

He knew that both Simon Herries and Tim came from landed, wealthy families, and he couldn't help but be impressed by them, even while the still developing analytical side of his mind told him that the only worthy measure of any man came from within himself and not from his birth.

His parents had been thrilled and proud when he had won a place at Oxford. His father, remembering the rumours of the University and the life of its undergraduates during the thirties, had warned him to stay clear of politically biased groups, but the real life of the place was centred on its cliques and societies, and almost without being aware of what was happening to him Alex had found himself gravitating towards the group that surrounded Tim and Simon.

Both of them awed him; he longed to emulate their confidently arrogant manner, to be able to be as careless of wealth and position as they were, and without being aware of it he found himself adopting Tim's lazy drawl.

"I wonder what they've got in store for us with the initiation ceremony," Richard commented to him with a grin.

Immediately Alex felt his stomach muscles tighten. Oxford abounded with horror stories of the violent and sadistic "hazing" ceremonies popular in some of the country's top schools, and he couldn't stop himself from shivering slightly.

"Perhaps they'll give us a virgin apiece?" Richard suggested with another grin.

Unlike Alex, he had no dread of the coming ceremony. He had never suffered an excess of too much imagination. He had been brought up by a father whose bitterness at being ousted from the board of the family bank had hung over his entire life, permeating every corner of it. Almost before he could understand what his father was talking about Richard was aware of his bitterness. He had been brought up to feel that he had been deprived of something that was his right, and for a long time he had not been able to understand why his father was so bitter.

It was a simple enough story. Jacob Howell had been the younger son. His father had left a controlling interest in the bank to his elder son, and Jacob had never been able to forgive him for it, just as he had never been able to forgive his brother for being the elder.

On the morning of Richard's thirteenth birthday, Jacob Howell removed the gun he kept in the right-hand drawer of his desk and shot himself through the head.

His wife found him. Richard came home from school at the end of term to discover that his father was dead and his mother had gone to a "place where they would make her well again". From henceforth he was to consider his uncle David's house as his home.

But he never could. Unlike his father, though, he quickly learned to control and hide his feelings, screening them with a mask of cheerful insouciance, adopting a clowning pose which deceived everyone but his great-uncle Reuben.

"Mark my words, that one will be trouble," he told his nephew, but David Howell only laughed.

"The boy's a fool," he told his uncle. "He's more interested in making laughter than making money."

"No, nephew, *you* are the fool, if you can't see the way he looks at you when he thinks no one else is looking," Reuben Weiss told him, but David would only shake his head and tell his wife that her uncle was getting old and losing his once sharp wits.

Howell's bank, or at least the English branch of it, had first been opened in London in 1789, just in time to assist the fleeing French aristocrats as they came flooding to London, clutching their family jewels; delighted to discover that in London there was a bank presided over by someone who not only spoke French fluently but who also treated them with the deference they had once commanded by right. It was immensely soothing to sit in Monsieur Howell's office that was furnished so comfortably like one of their own *salons* at home, and to have their trials and just anger listened to with sympathy and understanding.

Monsieur Howell was understanding also about the need to convert their jewels into cash, and quickly—there were family members still in France and in the greatest danger. Monsieur Howell knew just how to help. He was in touch with a group of brave men dedicated to rescuing the French nobility from the rapacious jaws of the mob. It was a costly process, of course, and success could not always be guaranteed . . .

Jacob Howell was a cautious and a sensible man—too cautious for dangerous greed. It was enough if simply one in ten of those who came to him seeking succour for other members of their families should not succeed. And if that one was also very wealthy and prepared to pay very, very well, then how much more gratifying financially it was to Howell's bank when the rescue attempt failed.

Of course Monsieur Howell was always désolé to report a failure on the part of his friends—all the more so because some of his friends too had disappeared along with the person they had tried to rescue. Monsieur Howell could only wish that he could repay the sum that Monsieur or Madame had advanced, but unfortunately . . . Here the very gallicness of his shrug was sufficient to convey that when such a venture failed money was the very last consideration to be taken into account, and Monsieur or Madame found themselves leaving the bank with their views that Monsieur Howell was one of the kindest and bravest of men alive stalwartly reinforced.

Monsieur Howell's caution paid off. He had enough successful attempts to smuggle émigrés out of Paris to guarantee that he had a steady source of income for quite some time. When he was not successful—well, sometimes the fates were not kind, and because his failures were so few and so well planned, no one seemed to realise that it was always those who were prepared to pay most for the rescue of their relatives who had the least success.

Once Jacob had got a taste for this novel method of earning income, it was but a short step, given the complexity of the Howells' family connections throughout Europe—Jacob Howell was the fifth son of an Austrian pawnbroker, with brothers spread out throughout most of Europe—from rescuing émigrés to supplying both the French and the English secret services with information for which both sides paid well.

In France, Fouché knew Jacob Howell's brother as one of his most rewarding sources of information, and who would ever connect Raoul Lebrun, a staunch supporter of the Revolution, with either Felix Lewotiz in Austria, or Jacob Howell in London? The brothers had not grown up in the ghetto for nothing and knew well how to cover their tracks.

In London William Pitt treated Jacob Howell with respect and courtesy. Wars are expensive, and bankers who show their willingness to support their adoptive countries are always welcome, especially such wealthy bankers as Jacob Howell.

No one suspected that along with the letters he had smuggled into the country there also came smuggled goods of a more financially beneficial type—French silks and brandies, carried across the Channel by the route Jacob had established for his émigrés.

Thanks to his communication lines with his brothers, like the Rothschilds, Jacob Howell knew of the English victory at Waterloo before the Government and people of the country—and in plenty of time to buy heavily into "the funds", so recklessly and foolishly sold by those people who had dreaded and expected a French victory. Overnight his fortune more than quadrupled, and Howell's bank was now firmly established.

In 1818 Jacob Howell bought himself a peerage and married the only child of a wealthy London merchant. He had one son and three daughters. On his death his son inherited the bank, and his daughters nothing. The Howell tradition of primogeniture was thus established.

Richard's grandfather was not quite as hard-headed as his ancestor; but then *his* sons were twins, born only ten minutes apart, and of the two the one he loved was always Jacob, the most emotional, least rational.

Even so he could not entirely break with family tradition. On his death he split his shares in the bank between his two sons, but gave David the controlling interest, and the chairmanship, as was his right by birth.

All might have gone well, but young Jacob, always relentlessly jealous of his brother, was foolish in other ways as well. David followed family tradition and married the daughter of a wealthy, respected family— the only daughter, while Jacob fell recklessly in love with a girl whose family owned nothing more than a small suburban semi-detached and who moreover was not even pretty. Always stubborn in the face of opposition, he married his Phyllis against family counsel, and privately Richard suspected that he had lived to regret it. The heavy gambling and drinking that became part of the pattern of his father's life surely didn't come only from jealously of his older brother?

The crunch came when it was discovered that Jacob had given an IOU that he couldn't meet. David called him into the bank and told him that the IOU would not be paid unless he made over to him the major part of his shares, and agreed to resign from the board of the bank. Jacob had little choice other than to agree.

A month later he was dead, leaving his son with a legacy of bitterness and resentment that Richard was careful to hide from everyone else around him. He had been brought up in the knowledge that but for a minor circumstance of birth, a matter of ten minutes in time, *he* would have been the one to inherit the bank and not his cousin Morris.

Morris was three years younger than Richard, three years behind him. His uncle had already promised him that if he did well at Oxford there would be a position for him with the bank. Richard *wanted* that position, and he wanted more—much more.

His uncle had been impressed when he had casually mentioned Tim's name; he would be even more impressed when he heard that Richard had actually been invited to visit Marchington. Of course he would never know why.

It added an extra fillip of excitement to the situation that they were actually to be initiated in Marchington's chapel.

All of them were to go down for the weekend. Richard had read up on the place in the library. Unlike the original Francis Dashwood's estate, Marchington had no caves in which they could perform their secret rites, but Tim had informed them that his family would be away, and quite frankly Richard felt that he would prefer the comfort of one of Marchington's luxurious bedrooms to Medmenham's Gothic caves.

Every night for over a week Tim had met Rachel after she finished work in the evening. At first she had treated him warily, waiting for him to invite her into his bed. When he didn't she started to relax.

He was the first male of her own age she had talked to at any real length. When he wanted to be Tim could be an amusing raconteur; he had a string of stories about his family and their friends and a careless throwaway manner of telling them that had enchanted far more worldly and sophisticated people than Rachel.

Another girl of her age and looks in the seventies would have immediately questioned Tim's apparent lack of sexual interest in her, but Rachel wasn't like other girls. She had learned to fear sex, and Tim, like the skilled hunter he was, could sense that fear. It amused him to see how far he could go without frightening her. When he touched her apparently by accident she stiffened immediately and looked at him with wary, cautious eyes. What a rare find she was! She was as virginal mentally as she was physically, so perfect for his purpose that he thought he saw the Devil's hand in her almost magical appearance in his life now, at this point, when he needed her the most.

After that first evening he was careful only to take her to places where they could not be seen—long walks along the river; drives in the car kept outside the college.

When he told Simon that he intended to invite Rachel down to Marchington, the latter was furious.

"You can't do that, you fool!" he exclaimed.

"Why not? Marchington is my home, after all, my dear."

"She'll never fit in. Your sisters . . ."

"My sisters will tolerate her as they tolerate all my friends, including you. Besides, they won't be there."

Tim had a malicious streak when he cared to use it, and it amused him to see the dull red colour run up under Simon's fair skin.

"You were awfully obvious, you know," he taunted him. "Father would never have let you marry Deborah, even if you'd got as far as proposing to her. He's got other plans for her."

Simon glared at him. Sometimes, despite his physical desire for him, he almost wanted to kill Tim. Always sensitive where his pride was concerned, he had to grit his teeth against commenting that if Deborah hadn't been who she was he wouldn't have looked twice at her. She wasn't a beauty, none of Tim's sisters were—it was as though having poured out a cornucopia of gifts over him, the fates had turned their backs on the children that followed.

An invitation to visit his family home was the last thing Rachel had expected from Tim. She knew from his accent and his manner that he came from a wealthy family, but she had no idea of his true social position.

"Well?" he prompted, watching her with enjoyment, knowing he had completely bowled her over. Such a naïve little innocent! What did she think he had in mind—a proposal . . . marriage? He almost laughed out loud.

"You want me to come to your home for . . . for the weekend?"

"Isn't that what I just said?"

Watching him, Rachel was suddenly shaken by a frisson of sensation that wasn't pleasant, a shiver of something that chilled her to the bone but which she shook off, ignoring the warning of her mother's blood.

"I'll have to see if I can get the time off work."

Tim fought to control his impatience. He wanted to tell her to forget her stupid little job, but caution urged him to tread carefully. There was something pleasurably exciting about stalking this particular prey. He had a sudden mental image of her naked body laid out on the altar of the chapel at Marchington, of her bright blood dripping on to its pure white floor. A heat mist of wild excitement swirled through his brain. His head pounded with the force of it; he felt himself swell with power . . . the excitement of it all but choked him. It was going to be so good. He could almost feel the power growing in him at the very thought of what was to come. But he forced himself to the discipline of patience, skilfully coaxing away her doubts.

When she left Tim Rachel could scarcely believe what he had said. She was to go home with him. They would drive down in his car. She would meet his family. Judiciously he hadn't told her that they would be away—his grandfather in Scotland, his parents and sisters in the Algarve taking a late holiday, after the crowds had gone.

Bernadette noticed Rachel's silence as they prepared for bed. Always inquisitive, she asked archly.

"Seen the boyfriend again, have you? Where'd he take you tonight?"

"Oh, just for a walk," Rachel told her.

Bernadette sniffed.

"You want to be careful of that. Tell him to take you somewhere nice. You don't want to let him hide you away like he wasn't proud to be with you."

"He wants me to go home with him this weekend."

Until she said the words out loud Rachel hadn't really believed it herself, but as though Bernadette's shock was in some way an antidote to her own, she found herself facing the open-mouthed stare with a smile, amid a sudden lightness of spirit.

"You don't mean it!" gasped Bernadette.

"Of course I do. Why should I lie? Do you think they'll let me have time off?"

"Oh, sure, and if they don't we'll all cover for you

somehow," Bernadette told her, her generous nature overcoming her surprised envy. "Don't you be going saying anything to anyone. I'll speak to the others— you've done favours enough for us before. You'll have to tell them down at the pub, though, but they'll understand. It'll be the first weekend you've had off since you started. What will you be taking with you to wear? You'll want something besides your jeans."

Bernadette might have joined the rootless community of youth, but she hadn't left her Irish upbringing behind her entirely. Where she came from a girl always took special trouble when she was meeting her man's family, and in her eyes, an invitation to his home meant that that was exactly what Rachel would be doing.

What would she wear? Rachel hadn't even thought about it.

"Sure and you'll find something," Bernadette comforted her. "We could go shopping tomorrow if you like."

Rachel smiled and said nothing. Her keen eye had already noticed that there was a vast difference between the cheap clothes Bernadette and the other girls bought and wore like throwaway paper handkerchiefs and those worn by the female undergraduates.

Jeans were the anonymous uniform worn by them all, but the female students had other clothes as well, clothes the like of which Rachel had never seen before in her life, but which she instinctively recognised as a subtly different but equally give-away uniform—a uniform worn only by the privileged.

Bernadette pulled a face when she saw the groups of girls walk by in their skirts and sweaters worn over neat collared blouses. Tim had mentioned his sisters. Those were the kind of clothes they would wear, Rachel knew that by instinct. But even if she knew where to buy them she didn't have the money.

"You'll need something to wear in the evening if he's really posh," Bernadette warned her. "You know, something dressy."

Something dressy . . . Rachel worried about it nearly all night. Clothes were important to her. The taunts and slights she had suffered as a child had never been forgotten.

She was still worrying about it when she got up the next morning. At eleven o'clock, just as she was about to go for her break, the housekeeper told her she had to go and clean Room 112. Rachel knew better than to object.

Outside the door she knocked, then used her pass key, expecting the room to be empty. But a girl of her own age and build was standing in the middle of the room, surveying the tumble of clothes and carrier bags strewn across the bed and spilling out of an open suitcase.

"Hi," she greeted Rachel. "Look, could you give me a hand with this lot? I'm off to India with some friends. Running away, in fact!" She made a droll face and laughed. She spoke like Tim; her fair hair was artfully streaked and she had long beautifully manicured nails. "We're leaving this afternoon—five of us in an old bus, it should be terrific fun, but Gil says I can only take one case . . ."

Rachel was already automatically folding the clothes into neat piles.

"No, not that stuff," the blonde girl told her. "I'm leaving all that behind. I'm starting a whole new life." She made an expansive gesture with her arms and grinned at Rachel. "The parents will go mad when they find out! They sent me to Oxford to find a suitable husband." She made another face. "I'm going to send them a letter—once we're out of the country.

Gil and I will probably get married in Delhi . . ."

She kept on chattering while Rachel packed her clothes, breaking off from her confidences occasionally to say, "No, not that . . ." or "Yes, I'm taking those."

When the case was full there was still a large pile of clothes on the bed. Rachel looked at her.

"Is it full? Well, I'll just have to manage with what's in there. Help me close it, will you?"

When the case was locked she swung it down to the floor and picked up her handbag. She had reached the door before Rachel realised that she was actually leaving.

"But what about all these things?" Rachel protested.

The girl turned her head and looked at the clothes folded on the bed, then shrugged.

"Oh, get rid of them for me, would you? I'm already running late, and Gil said he wouldn't wait." And then she was gone, leaving Rachel staring at the closed door.

She must have sat there for a full five minutes, Rachel realised afterwards, and then she started to clean the room, all the time expecting the girl to come back to claim her clothes, but nothing happened.

She couldn't leave them there. She touched her tongue to her lips and walked over to the bed, carefully unfolding each item and holding it up. There were sweaters of the finest wool she had ever seen, cashmere in fact—although it would be some years before she had enough knowledge to realise that detail—neatly round-necked and long-sleeved, and blouses in fine sheer cotton and soft wool. There were skirts, pleated like kilts, such as she had seen some of the female students wearing, and two fine wool dresses with small lace collars and neat waists.

It would be years before she realised that what she

had inherited was the wardrobe of a girl who in the eighties would be described as a Sloane Ranger. All Rachel did know was that the clothes were different from anything she herself had ever seen or touched.

They weren't fashionable, Bernadette would have turned her pert retroussée nose up at them and so would the other maids, but they had something that Rachel instinctively recognised. Her mouth dry, she slipped off her uniform and tried them on.

She was a little taller and slimmer than the girl who had originally owned them, but they were still a good fit. She looked at herself in the mirror and her heart swelled with delight and relief. These were the sort of clothes she wanted to wear for the rest of her life, she thought, touching the soft wool of the skirt. In them no one would laugh at her, or taunt her. These were the sort of clothes that the girl Tim eventually married would wear.

Tim married! He would never marry a girl like her—Rachel knew that instinctively. Despite the way he treated her she had sensed within him his contempt for those whom he considered his social inferiors. She couldn't delude herself. She was just someone who had caught his interest, like a new toy that he would eventually grow bored with.

As she looked at herself in the mirror she was gripped with a burning ambition to be the sort of girl who would wear these clothes by right . . . to speak with the same careless insouciance as the girl who had just left here . . . to be one of the elite, privileged band who floated through life without responsibilities or cares. But how could *she* be like that?

She took off her clothes and put on her uniform. What was the point of going home with Tim? Their relationship could not lead anywhere. She looked at the clothes and remembered how she had looked in

them, and her chin tilted proudly, her eyes flashing
storm signals at her reflection. Was she not descended
from one of the proudest races on earth? Had her
father not been the nephew of the Laird of the
MacGregor clan himself?

For the first time in her life Rachel felt pride surge
through her body. She *would* go with Tim. Perhaps
their relationship was only to be fleeting and transi-
tory, but while it lasted she would learn from it.

She opened her mouth and made an attempt to
mimic the speech of the girl who had just left. Somehow
it didn't sound right, but one day it would. One day
she would have that patina of wealth and security . . .
one day she would be the one to offhandedly throw
away half her wardrobe, without so much as a
backward glance. For now, she decided, she might as
well look on her good fortune as a sign that she was
meant to join Tim this weekend.

She didn't say anything to the others about her new
wardrobe. Bernadette wouldn't have understood.
Instead she took everything to the cleaners, and then
went out and bought herself a new suitcase. She spent
a long time choosing it. Nothing she saw in the chain
stores she visited appealed to her. Nothing they had
on sale looked quite like the suitcase she had seen on
the hotel bed, and that was the kind of case she
wanted.

When she did find one it wasn't on sale in any of
the stores, but pushed to one side of the window of a
second-hand clothes shop down one of Oxford's
narrow side-streets.

Rachel went inside rather uncertainly. The air
smelled fusty and was faintly oppressive, and she had
a panicky urge to turn tail and flee. Before she could
move a woman emerged from the back of the shop,
rattling the cane curtain. She was one of the weirdest

sights Rachel had ever seen. Her hair was hennaed bright red, and despite the fact that she must have been well over fifty, she was dressed in an assortment of layered skirts and shawls more suitable to a girl of eighteen. In her ears she had large hoop earrings, larger than any Rachel had ever seen the women of her tribe wearing. Thick dark kohl surrounded her eyes, and the rest of her face was chalk-white.

"Can I help you?"

For a moment Rachel was too startled by the woman's appearance to speak. The shop was full of rails of clothes, hats, shoes, and an assortment of general clutter that made it impossible for anyone to move more than half a dozen steps in any direction from the small counter.

"I . . . I . . . wanted to look at the suitcase in the window," she managed to get out at last.

The eyes within their kohl surround were shrewd and dark.

"The Vuitton? You have excellent taste. Wait a moment and I'll get it out."

It took considerably more than a moment for the woman to remove the case from the window and drag it to the rear of the shop. It was covered in dust which she swished away with one corner of her shawl, before inspecting the locks.

"You're lucky, this one isn't initialled—most of them are. I had a whole set of them—they were specially designed to fit in the boot of a Rolls; this is the last one left. Do you want to see inside it? It's lined in silk. Look . . ."

Rachel couldn't resist touching the silk. It felt soft . . . and more than that, sensuous almost beneath her fingertips. Her fingers, rough from her work behind the bar, snagged on the fine fabric.

"How . . . how much is it?" Her mouth had gone

dry. She wanted this case more than anything in her life. Somehow it had become a symbol of all that she wanted from life . . . a goal that she could aim for.

The woman pursed her lips and said shrewdly, "To you, ten quid."

Ten pounds. It was more than twice the price of the cases in the other shops. Ten pounds . . . It would take a considerable sum out of her savings.

"When it was new it would have cost more than ten times that much . . . if I held on to it I could probably get twenty quid for it . . ."

It was only sales talk, Rachel knew that. She knew all about the different ways of tempting a buyer's appetite; she had spent her formative years among the greatest exponents in the world of that particular art.

"I'll . . . I'll take it," she said breathlessly.

The woman smiled, and it seemed to Rachel that there was a gleam of understanding in her eyes.

"You won't regret it," she promised. "This case will still be going strong in fifty years' time. You've got good taste." She looked at Rachel rather thoughtfully. "I've got something else here you might like. Hang on a tick."

She disappeared into the back of the shop before Rachel could tell her that she neither wanted or needed anything else. She was gone about ten minutes, and when she came back she was carrying something wrapped in what looked like a white cotton shroud.

"I got these in the other day—a house clearance. Just feel this fabric!"

She was unwrapping the shroud and revealing to Rachel's astonished eyes two dresses. The first was in a soft shade somewhere between amber and peach, the fabric so finely pleated that Rachel couldn't imagine how it had been done. When she held the dress up in front of her, it was nothing more than a long narrow tube.

"Fortuny," the shopkeeper told her admiringly. "Now there was a designer! Feel it." Rachel touched the rich fabric. No one wore dresses like this one, and yet . . . and yet there was something about it that appealed to her.

"And this one."

It was a twenties-style flapper dress in rich satin, heavily beaded and cut on the bias in pale cream. Never in a thousand lifetimes would she have any occasion to wear dresses like these, but even Rachel recognised their quality, and knew instinctively that they represented a way of life that was way, way out of her reach. For that reason if no other she yearned for them. She touched them lovingly, her eyes full of dreams.

"You can have them both for ten quid," the woman told her. "There's no market for stuff like this round here. I ought to keep them . . . one day . . . but when that day comes, I'll probably be dead and gone. Buy them!" she urged, and as she dug into her purse for the money, Rachel knew she was buying far more than two old-fashioned gowns—she was buying a way of life, a dream . . . her dream . . .

She walked out of the shop in a daze, quickly followed by a sick feeling of dismay. She had just spent twenty pounds—money it had taken her months to save. She turned round. She would take the things back, explain that she couldn't afford them—but even as she turned, she saw the woman putting up a closed sign. It was too late. She had bought them. She couldn't let the other girls see them; they would laugh their heads off at her stupidity.

Miserably she dragged the case back to the dormitory and hid it under her bed, the two dresses still wrapped inside.

Tonight Tim would ask her for her answer to his invitation. She might as well go, she decided recklessly. After all, what had she to lose?

The day Tim's father came home from honeymoon with his new bride, the church bells rang out to greet the newly married couple. Since then the church bells of Marchington village church had been rung on four separate occasions—each time to celebrate the birth of another child to the Viscount and his wife, but never so proudly or so joyously as the day they were rung to celebrate the birth of the heir.

The road to Marchington led through the village and swept past the church in a triumphant arc before curling languorously and then revealing Marchington Place itself through a veil of trees, like a magician performing an especially favourite trick.

Rachel saw it first in autumn, rising breathtakingly through the late afternoon mists, cloaked in the full splendour of its trees, glowing rose red like a jewel set in a crown of green and gold.

Tim had picked her up outside the hotel just after lunch. His car was long and low, its hood up against the fine autumn drizzle. Inside, the smell of the cream leather seats engulfed her. She was aware of his faint start of surprise when he saw her. She was wearing the pleated skirt, and a demure blouse, with its collar neatly out over the round neck of the jumper she had on. She had bought some toning fine wool tights, and a pair of plain brogue type shoes. Her hair fell in a shining curtain to her shoulders, her face free of all make-up apart from a gloss of lipstick. She knew that outwardly she looked no different from those female students she had envied so deeply, and her smile as Tim handed her into his car had a new confidence.

Once or twice during the drive to Dorset, Tim glanced at her. She looked different today. She was dressed more like his sister than was appropriate to her true status in life. For the first time he wondered if she had lied to him; had pretended to be an orphan. Doubts trickled coldly through his mind, upsetting his carefully laid plans. The closer they got to Marchington, the greater his doubts became. The others weren't due down until tomorrow: he had planned it that way deliberately. His body twitched suddenly, and he ached for a joint. He had kept off drugs all week, knowing that he would need a clear mind to plan. Now, suddenly, he felt depressed and edgy. He wanted Simon—Simon, who never seemed to experience doubts or to deviate from a chosen course.

Rachel sensed that something was wrong, but Tim's silence did not encourage her to ask what.

And then miraculously they were there, with the full splendour of Marchington spread out before them. Awe gripped her by the throat, tears suddenly filming her eyes. At her side she heard Tim saying conversationally,

"We have a ghost, you know, so don't be alarmed if you hear footsteps during the night!"

She looked at him with apprehension, suddenly longing for the familiar security of the hotel dormitory.

The gates stood open and he drove through them with a flourish, beneath the eagles with outstretched wings, whose beaks supported the ribbon of stone carrying the family motto, "Through our own endeavours shall we survive." A very apt motto indeed, and one that successive generations of Wildings had followed to the letter.

The deserted, empty air given off by the house

disconcerted Rachel. Where was the family Tim had brought her here to meet? The three sisters he had spoken of with brotherly contempt, the parents and the grandfather who also lived here.

She looked at Tim questioningly.

"Mmm, doesn't look as though there's anyone about—odd!" He stopped the car and got out. "Never mind, they'll all turn up sooner or later. Let's go inside."

Uncertainly Rachel followed him. The double doors opened into a cavernous and rather dark hallway. Rachel paused on the threshold, glancing back towards the car.

"My luggage . . ." she began.

"Don't worry about it, one of the maids will bring it in later."

One of the maids! A girl like her . . . Rachel quelled her feeling of panic.

"Come on, I'll give you a tour of the place while we're waiting for the family to turn up."

Tim caught hold of her hand, dragging her through a succession of rooms, all huge and sparsely furnished, all giving off a cold musty scent of age and decay. Rachel sensed the excitement in him, and the tension, and put it down to the fact that he was as apprehensive about introducing her to his family as she was about meeting them.

They were in a narrow corridor, icily cold, with a stone-flagged floor. There was a door at the end of it, and as they approached it Rachel had an intense reluctance to go any further. She stopped dead, and Tim, who was still holding her hand, turned to frown at her.

"What's the matter? I'm only going to show you the family chapel. It's famous, you know." He opened the door, ignoring her shudder of apprehension. "The family priest was murdered right here in front of the altar," he told her carelessly, dragging her inside. "There's a stain on the floor that's supposed to be his blood, and it won't come out . . ."

Rachel couldn't move. Her whole body was held fast in the grip of an intensely primitive fear. She couldn't have explained what she was feeling to anyone; she only knew that to walk into that small, essentially simple room with its altar and cross, and its stained glass window depicting Christ's suffering on the Cross, was to come in contact with something so evil and dangerous that her whole life would be contaminated by it.

Many, many times she had heard her grandmother talk about the "sight", and only once had she come anywhere near experiencing it, but now as she looked towards the altar it seemed to alter subtly, a grey mist darkening the room and obliterating the sunlight outside. Round the altar she could see dark formless shapes . . . men in robes. On the altar lay a body . . . a woman's body . . .

A deep shudder of panic and horror engulfed her, her body convulsing on a bitingly sharp pain. She felt the coldness of death, as she had felt it once before when her grandmother died. Instinctively she started to back away, not daring to take her eyes away from the altar, not daring to turn her back and run as she longed to do, in case to do so was to make that macabre and frightening mental vision she had had become real.

Tim, who had released her hand to walk further towards the altar, turned to look at her.

"What is it?" He was frowning . . . angrily almost, Rachel could see, but nothing, no power on earth, could make her go into that room. It was evil, the very air was rank and sour with it. She made the gypsy gesture to ward off evil spirits and stepped back into the narrow passageway.

"Rachel . . ."

"No . . . no! I can't go in there!"

Tim was fascinated, his original annoyance with her fading as he looked into her eyes. She had sensed something . . . seen something, maybe. God, she was going to be so perfect for his purpose . . . so very, very perfect. He could feel the power growing in him already. Almost dizzy with the strength of it, he laughed softly.

"Silly girl, there's nothing to be afraid of!"

There was a gloating, almost triumphant note in his voice, as though he found something intensely pleasurable in her fear.

She shouldn't have come here, Rachel acknowledged. She wanted to leave. There was something dangerous and alien here . . . something she didn't understand but knew instinctively threatened her. There was a smell of corruption and evil about this place . . . and about Tim, she realised. She looked at him, and it was as though she was seeing him properly for the first time.

He was weak, and dangerous, and he had brought her here for some purpose that she didn't understand but that she instinctively knew to be threatening. She had to leave . . . she had to get away. A fear like nothing else she had ever known in her life engulfed her; an awareness of evil and danger that obliterated everything else.

All the way back down the narrow passage she felt as though she would choke from lack of air, and when they finally emerged into an inner hallway with several doorways off it, she found that despite the intense feeling of cold inside her, her skin was bathed in perspiration.

From outside she heard the sound of a car. Tim frowned and went over to a window. The others were early. They weren't due until tomorrow. What were they doing here now?

As he looked out into the courtyard and realised that the car was his grandfather's Daimler, a feeling of helpless rage overcame him. What was the old man doing here? He was supposed to be in Scotland. Tim's hands clenched, his nails digging into the palms of his hands.

Lord Marchington had never been deceived by his grandson's good looks and facile charm. Long ago, as a little boy, he had once happened to come across an old woman wandering round the Elizabethan knot garden. She had been talking to herself as little Adam approached her to find out who she was and what she was doing in his mother's private garden. He had been aware of such a feeling of power and evil emanating from her that he had instinctively shrunk back. She had come towards him, so very fast and agile for such an old woman that she had taken him off guard, and even though he had been tall and strong for a boy of six it had taken the combined strength of her nurse and his governess to get the old woman's death-grip from round his neck.

Later his father had explained gently to him that the old lady was *his* elder sister and that until his birth she had expected that one day her son would inherit the title and lands. She was her father's only child and there were no other male relatives who would inherit the title. She had been twenty and a young wife and mother when, against all odds, her parents had at last produced a son and heir. When her husband realised that their son would not after all inherit the title, he had left her. The shock had turned her brain, so Adam's father told him, and it was several years before he realised that it was not so much the shock of losing her husband that had brought on her madness but her vicious hatred of the brother who had supplanted her.

Sometimes when he looked into his grandson's eyes Lord Marchington saw within them the same look of hatred and envy he had seen in the old woman's. A little insanity was not an uncommon thing among titled families where cousin had married cousin for generation after generation, but madness and the desire to kill . . . these were not charming eccentricities of the very rich, these were dangerous, inexcusable traits.

And not for the first time Lord Marchington worried about his grandson; his eventual heir.

This latest telephone call from an old friend at Oxford, warning him that Tim was known to be involved in drugs, was what had brought him back from Scotland. Until his chauffeur drove past Tim's stationary car he had no idea that his grandson would be home for the weekend, and he frowned a little, his concern increasing.

"What is it?" asked Rachel, watching the shadows close in on Tim's face.

"My grandfather's arrived."

He said it flatly, quietly, and yet Rachel was still intensely aware of the hatred running through him.

"Come on," he told her abruptly. "We're going back to Oxford."

And in that moment she knew that whatever it was he had brought her to Marchington for it was not to meet his family. Once again she felt that same chill that had invaded her in the chapel, saw in her mind's eye that white body on the altar, felt the presence of death.

Lord Marchington was surprised to see the girl with Tim. He never brought his lovers, of either sex, to

Marchington with him. The Earl was no fool . . . **He was well aware of his grandson's sexual proclivities** . . . but as long as one day he married and produced a son and heir, they did not concern him; but that Tim might bring the Marchington name into disrepute through his excesses did.

He listened grimly as Tim announced that they were just about to leave. He could not take him to task in front of this shy, almost fey little girl. He had not even expected to find his grandson at Marchington, but instead had anticipated having to go to Oxford to talk to him there.

What he had to say to his grandson could wait— another few hours at least. He bade Rachel a courteous goodbye and smiled at her, but Tim was not deceived.

Running side by side with his hatred of his grandfather, interwoven with it, was an even deeper vein of fear and resentment. A superb athlete in his time, a war hero, a man of great wit and charm, his grandfather was everything that Tim knew he could never be. But one day he would die . . . and one day he would be the Earl, and there was nothing his grandfather could do about it, and therein lay his own power, his own strength, and if it had not been for his grandfather appearing, interfering, this weekend, that power would have been intensified tenfold. They could not hold the Black Mass at Marchington now, and it was too late to make alternative arrangements.

All the way back to Oxford, Tim fed his growing sense of bitter hatred. Sitting silently at his side, Rachel knew that their relationship was over. Today she had sensed something in him that frightened her too much to allow her to see him again.

Tim dropped her off outside the hotel, unceremoniously. His greatest need now was to find Simon to tell him what had happened and to cancel their arrangements, to be buoyed up again by Simon's strength.

Rachel was forgotten, obliterated by the greater need. How he hated his grandfather! But he would not always be the one in a position of servitude. One day . . . one day . . . Inside him his hatred raged like a caged beast, demanding release.

CHAPTER EIGHT

TIM FOUND Simon just about to leave their rooms, and explained what had happened in a burst of angry, staccato speech. Simon had an appointment outside the town, so he suggested that Tim came along with him.

Simon knew all about Tim's hatred of his grandfather. He made it his business to be a sympathetic listener . . . for despite all that Tim had said Simon was determined that one day he and Tim would be brothers-in-law.

Tim could be very indiscreet when he was angry, the way he was now . . . very indiscreet. Tim's sister adored him and would do anything for him. If pressure could be brought to bear on Tim—and he would see that it was—all these thoughts and many more were in Simon's mind as he listened to Tim's rantings. Rachel's name spewed out alongside that of his grandfather, her ridiculous refusal to enter the chapel somehow becoming part of Tim's general vicious torrent of verbal hatred.

Simon was glad in a way; he had never liked Tim's suggestion that they held their Mass at Marchington, but he agreed with him that Rachel must be punished.

"She has to be sacrificed," Tim told him wildly, turning round and grabbing hold of his jacket lapels. By this time they were crossing a narrow bridge spanning the river, the current eddying forcefully round its stone supports. "It has to be, Simon . . . that's the only way I can get the power!" Rage was making

Tim's speech lunatic. Simon listened in growing shock and unease . . . he didn't like all this talk of sacrifice and spilling blood, but the moment he tried to remonstrate with Tim, Tim's speech became even more violent, his fingers white and rigid where they clutched hold of him.

"Come on, Tim . . ." Simon tried to release his grip on his jacket, dreading someone walking past and overhearing what was going on. He was physically stronger than Tim, and the only way he could release himself was to push Tim backwards against the low parapet of the bridge.

He heard the coping stone fall, and then as though it was happening in slow motion he saw Tim fall, striking his head against the stone support of the bridge as he hit the water.

He knew before he dived in that Tim was dead, the sickening sound of his head crushing against the stone had told him that, but still he dragged him out, torn between guilt and shock. He heard someone call out as he knelt over Tim's body.

Another student, someone he didn't recognise, came running up.

"He fell . . . he fell off the bridge," Simon told him.

They were the words he repeated until they were burned into his brain . . . to the police, to Tim's distraught family, to the Dean of the College . . . so many times that he actually believed them himself, and as his belief in his own innocence grew, so did his hatred against the person he thought of as the cause of Tim's death and the destroyer of all his plans for his own future. Rachel—she was the one to blame. It was as though at the moment of death Tim's madness had passed on to him and become his own.

Tim's death was recorded as "accidental", but Simon knew that it wasn't. Rachel had killed him, and she must be punished. But he couldn't punish her alone. He would need help. He remembered how Tim had raved about her being the perfect sacrifice . . . a virgin . . . and a plan grew in his mind.

But first he would need to choose his accomplices. His mind raced. The two new acolytes . . . Yes. Yes . . .

They both refused, and went on refusing until Simon pointed out to them how easy it would be for him to arrange for them to be sent down. And after all, what was he really asking for? Nothing really . . . only that they kidnap the girl and bring her to his room, that was all.

They had no other options . . . they had to agree. Richard Howell thought about the position his uncle had promised him and knew he had no choice. Alex Barnett remembered the sacrifices his parents had made for him, the hopes they had for him, and gave his reluctant agreement.

Simon arranged it for the evening of Tim's funeral— his own private farewell to him.

Rachel had heard about Tim's death, and following her initial shock had come a certain inescapable knowledge that it had been inevitable. She didn't know why she should feel like that . . . it was the same sort of inner knowledge she had had in the chapel at Marchington, something beyond logic and reason.

The shock of the evil she had sensed in the chapel, and which she had known instinctively emanated from Tim himself, had killed her burgeoning feelings for him, but it hadn't killed the desire, born at the same time as her knowledge that she could never be the sort of girl Tim would take home to his parents as his future wife, that somehow she would have to find a way to have all the things that life had so far denied her. Respect, wealth, status, education; she would have all of them . . . all of them and more.

Tim's death, not surprisingly, made the headlines in some of the national newspapers; there was talk around the colleges of a severe clamp-down on the smoking of pot and what the authorities considered to be the general licentiousness of the undergraduate body.

The funeral was well attended. Simon stood at the back of Marchington's village church, a sombre figure clad in black. Once or twice Deborah Wilding turned her head to look at him. She knew that he had been Tim's best friend, but there was something about him that frightened her. She had the inescapable feeling that somehow he was responsible for her brother's death. It was an instinctive, alarming feeling, and one that she had not dared to communicate to anyone else.

She knew that her mother liked him and that her younger sisters, still at the giggly, adolescent stage, thought him sexy, but she always felt uncomfortable in his presence. He was like the light to which heedless moths were drawn to die in its fierce heat. Tim had followed him blindly in all that he said and did. He had almost worshipped him, and sometimes Deborah had worried that their relationship held such blatantly sexual undertones. She had longed to be able to discuss her fears with someone, but she had no close friends of her own age; her father was too remote, and her mother too naïve. She looked back over her shoulder again and was chilled by more than the cold of the chapel. Was she really the only person to see the evil in that bland good-looking face?

She had loved her brother, but she had not been blind to his faults. Tim had been heedless and hedonistic. He had been spoiled by them all, and now his golden precious youth was gone and he was dead, and she was sure . . . so sure, that the man standing at the back of the church, claiming to be his best friend and wearing his grief like a sombre cloak, was somehow responsible for his death.

Rachel didn't go to the funeral. How could she have done? She remembered the stern and proud face of the old man getting out of his car, though, and mourned for Lord Marchington even though she could not mourn for Tim himself.

That sudden awareness of evil that had struck her in the chapel had brought home to her the reality of her roots. She felt as though she had walked unknowingly deep into the shadows of intense danger, and she knew that it was her gypsy heritage that had recognised that evil.

Tim, so beautiful and perfect externally, had been rotten and corrupt inside. Rachel didn't know how she knew this; it was just a knowledge that was as much a part of her as her knowledge of her own name and background.

For a while he had bewitched her in a way that evil does bewitch, but now she was free of his spell.

She was not free of danger, though. She sensed it all around her, pressing in on her almost suffocatingly. And that worried her. It shouldn't be there. Tim was gone. But her own sense of danger hadn't. For some reason it was still there, hovering, waiting for her, all the more frightening because she did not know from where it came.

Simon had laid his plans carefully. The desire for revenge burned deeply in him, supplanting his guilt in a crazy inversion of reality, transmuting what had really happened into what he wanted to believe had happened.

This facility to deceive himself so completely had begun long ago in his childhood, its roots so darkly enmeshed with his own deep-rooted fears that they were lost to him. He couldn't see that what he was doing was a frantic attempt to escape from the truth, from his own guilt, from a need to make someone other than himself responsible for Tim's death.

He had lost his closest friend, his most prized acolyte, the one person he could rely on to do his bidding no matter what. He had enjoyed his power over Tim. It had sustained and nourished him, and now it had gone. And that gypsy whore was to blame.

Simon had never shared Tim's belief that it was possible to raise the Devil, but now somehow it was as though, in dying, Tim had communicated part of that belief to him. Simon couldn't know that these bouts of megalomania were a psychological illness brought on by the horrors of his childhood, and if anyone had tried to tell him so he would have laughed at them. His belief in his own power, in his destiny of greatness, was all-consuming.

Rachel had got in his way. She had destroyed one of the tools he had intended to use to achieve his destiny, and for that she must be punished. It wasn't he who was responsible for Tim's fall and subsequent death, it was her . . . the gypsy whore . . . and she must be punished for it.

He hadn't eaten since Tim's death, having discovered during puberty that fasting in some magical way clarified and intensified the workings of his mind. Sometimes he didn't eat for days at a time, occasionally hallucinating and enduring horrible nightmares when his father manifested himself and came to him. He started to shake, and then controlled himself, concentrating instead on a mental image of Tim. Almost he believed that he could hear Tim crying out to him for vengeance. In his own mind his plans had taken on the cloak of a holy war of righteousness; it was as though some higher power had appointed him as Tim's avenger. Muddled images swirled in and out of his mind. If he closed his eyes he could see Tim crying out to him for vengeance, his dead eyes suddenly magically alive; he could hear him reminding him of the power that would one day be theirs; a power they would have shared in secret. And now Tim was gone, and Simon feared that his death might in some way diminish that power.

It was as though in exercising his ability to punish Rachel he was re-establishing that power, laying claim to it in the same way that King Arthur had laid claim to Excalibur. Reality blurred and became indistinct, and as always when he entered and elevated the state brought on by fasting, Simon tasted and succumbed to the heady wine of his own ego.

He had planned it all carefully. It hadn't been difficult to find out what time the girl finished work in the evenings. Simon had learned how to collate and use information during his days at Eton, and the simpering receptionist behind the hotel desk had been only too easy to persuade. He had made the excuse that he wanted the information for a friend.

As luck would have it, the evening of Tim's funeral was the night that Miles French went to a monthly meeting of one of his societies so that he would be safely out of the way; another sign that fate blessed his plans. Simon hadn't any real fears that Rachel would do anything like report him. Girls of her class didn't.

As always when he thought about Rachel hatred spewed up hotly inside him. If he had ever felt any

emotion for another human being that human being
had been Tim. And now Tim was gone, destroyed by
that milk-faced bitch. The anger that had always been
there within Simon against her sex boiled up fero-
ciously, pushing at his self-control. He had always
hated the female sex . . . it was weak and destructive
and deserved to be punished. His fingertips tingled
and he felt an enormous surge of power and euphoria.
It blanked out reality completely; a sickness that
would manifest itself over and over again throughout
his life, turning him from a logical, charismatic man
into something approaching a dangerous psychopath.

"I don't think we should be doing this," Alex confided
unhappily to Richard, as they waited for Rachel to
emerge from the pub.

"We don't have any choice," Richard reminded him
harshly, and Alex fell silent, acknowledging the truth
of his words. He was uncomfortable with what they
had been told to do; it went against everything he had
been brought up to believe in. Man cherished and
protected woman; that was the way his own parents
behaved, and it was the way he firmly believed to be
right, and now here he was waiting to abduct a young
woman and turn her over to . . .

"Stop worrying," Richard told him abruptly. "It'll
be easy. We'll just walk up behind her. I'll gag her,
and you tie her hands. We'll take her to the car and
then drive her over to Herries' rooms and leave her
there."

"What do you suppose he means to do with her?"

Alex couldn't help asking the naïve question. It was
beginning to haunt him. Simon had told them that
the girl in question had been leading both himself and
Tim on for weeks. He said he wanted to teach her a
lesson, not just for himself but for Tim as well, but

whichever way he looked at it Alex came up with the same unacceptable word—rape.

He said as much to Simon only last night and had then shivered, watching the other man's face harden dangerously. "It isn't rape when she's been asking for it the way she has . . ."

Alex hadn't wanted to be dragged into the affair, but he hadn't been able to back out.

The Hell Fire Club had disbanded amidst panic and fear following upon Tim's death; its members might think they could destroy his memory along with their robes, but they would find out that they were wrong, Simon reflected. Both Alex and Richard knew how much they were in his power.

Richard, less squeamish than Alex, hadn't liked what he was being told to do either, but he was worldly enough to know that Simon was quite capable of carrying out his threats, so he had given in. He had too much to lose now, and especially over a girl he didn't even know. One sighting of that damning photograph of himself, naked, dancing round a grave-yard illuminated by black wax candles, would be enough to destroy any chance he had of getting into the bank; he wasn't going to risk everything he had planned for the sake of some stupid little bitch who had the idiocy to get on Simon's wrong side.

Rachel was slightly late leaving the pub. She had refused to allow the landlady to send the nephew who was staying with them with her as an escort back to the hotel and stepped out confidently into the dark alley behind the back door.

She had no awareness of anyone behind her, no sixth sense to warn her before she felt the hand clamp across her mouth, and then the rough arms grabbing her like a vice. She tried to scream, but her throat muscles were paralysed, as a strip of sticking plaster was stuck across her mouth, her flaying hands held and tied behind her back.

Instinctively she knew that what was happening to her had something to do with Tim, but Tim was dead . . . She shuddered deeply, the superstitions of her Celtic and gypsy forebears stirring strongly within her. She tried to kick out, but she was lifted and imprisoned between two hard bodies. The car that Richard had hired was parked at the end of the alleyway and they bundled her into it, Alex sitting in the back with her, to prevent her from trying to escape.

Richard drove back to Simon's rooms, taking a long and circuitous route as Simon had instructed.

Beneath the terror that had engulfed her from the moment of her attack Rachel's natural strength reasserted itself. She was being taken somewhere and for some purpose; and she knew that purpose had something to do with Tim. Tim was dead . . . but the dead could reach out from beyond the grave. She thought of her own grandmother and clung hard to the memory of her goodness and power, trying to remember the incantations she had taught her as a child to ward off evil.

There was no evil in this car, rather a sense of fear that did not come from her alone, but evil waited for her.

The car stopped and she was bundled out, carried up some stairs, strong hands resisting her attempts to break free.

Simon had seen them arrive. He opened the door to his rooms in silence, indicating the bed which had been stripped down to its white undersheet. It was Miles's bed, not his own. He watched as Richard and Alex put Rachel down on the bed, then motioned for them to go, quickly locking the door behind them.

Beneath his robe he was naked, his body throbbing with a savage need to punish and denigrate this woman who had been responsible for the destruction of the one human being he loved. Tim dead was no use to him. No, he had wanted—had needed Tim to stay alive. He stared down at her, the coldness of his eyes boring into the fear of hers, his lips curled back from his teeth in a feral snarl.

Rachel knew immediately that he did not mean to kill her, even though she couldn't have said how she had come by the knowledge. She also knew that what he intended to do to her would be far, far worse. After all, execution could be carried out only once. She thought of her mother and wondered despairingly what it was about the women of her family that attracted all that was most vile in mankind.

"You're frightened, aren't you, you little bitch? So you should be, you . . . Do you know why you're here?"

Instinctively Rachel shook her head, sensing his need to talk, praying that a miracle would occur and she would be rescued.

"You're here to atone for a man's death, that's why. It was you, you little bitch, who killed him. You . . . casting your spell on him . . ."

Tim! He was talking about Tim! He had to be.

"He planned to sacrifice you to the Devil, did you know that?"

Shock turned Rachel's blood to ice. She heard Simon laugh.

"He thought he could raise Lucifer. All he needed was a virgin sacrifice. He had it all planned."

The chapel at Marchington . . . the sense of evil . . . Tim's fury when his grandfather arrived. Yes, she could understand it all now, and more. This man had been Tim's lover. She didn't know how she knew, she just did. She also knew that he had killed him. A vision flashed in front of her—two men struggling on a bridge, one of them falling . . .

"You did it . . . you killed Tim!"

"No!" Simon hit her hard, on the side of her head, almost stunning her. He reached out and she saw the knife blade flash in his hand. He grabbed hold of the top of the plain dress top she was wearing and slashed through it. The knife point touched her skin, raising a bright red weal.

A red mist danced in front of Simon's eyes. He was doing this for Tim, not for himself, but there was something about this pale, white girl . . . something about her fear, that was a thousand times more satisfactory than any other sexual encounter he had had with her sex.

He slashed through the waistband of her jeans in a frenzy of excitement, tearing her clothes from her body like a hyena stripping the flesh from one of its victims. Reality faded, the words of his own father thundering in his ears until he was repeating them in a thick hoarse chant.

"You've got to be punished . . . I have to do it . . . I've got to punish you."

He entered her awkwardly and roughly, and Rachel thought she would never survive the pain. Her body was tense with fear and rejection, the mere sight of his erection alone enough to fill her with fear. He thrust into her, breaking the delicate membrane of her virginity, his body powered by a lust to inflict pain that had its roots deep in the traumas of his own childhood. She felt his semen spurt hotly inside her, and the pain of his rough withdrawal from her was almost as great as the entry had been.

He was still erect, his body still charged with the pulsing force of his hatred. Her arms, still tied behind her, ached appallingly, her head was swimming, her body bruised and defiled in a way she would remember for the rest of her life, but deep inside her anger grew alongside her fear. She would remember this man, this night, and one day he would pay a thousandfold for what he had done to her . . . They would all pay, she thought hazily, remembering the two who had brought her here.

Simon got up and for a moment she thought it was over, and then with a cold rush of fear she realised it wasn't. He rolled her over, panting slightly.

"That was for Tim . . . for what you did to him, and just so that you'll never forget him . . ."

The scream flooded deep inside her as she felt the knife against the flesh of her right buttock, a vertical slash into her tender skin and then a horizontal one. T . . . T . . . for Tim. T . . . for terror.

"And that was for me . . . in memory of the man you destroyed!"

Rachel felt the sickness and pain rush from her stomach to her throat, and while she endured his degradation of her body and knew that it would live within her for the rest of her life, she promised herself that there would be retribution, and a retribution so terrible that he would long, as she now longed, to die rather than face another sunrise.

Before he left Simon ripped the plaster from across her mouth, making her eyes sting with tears, and proffered her a glass of some colourless unscented liquid. When she refused it he slapped her and said savagely, "Drink it, you little fool. It's only a couple of sleeping tablets."

Rachel didn't want to drink, but he held her nose and poured the vile mixture down her throat so that she was forced to swallow.

He watched her until she started to fall asleep, then

quickly went to work, picking up his clothes. They would have to be burned. He looked at his watch. At least half an hour before Miles was due back. Good, he would be long gone by then. Simon tried to picture his room-mate's face when he discovered what was lying in his bed.

French might even be stupid enough to think the bitch was lying there waiting for him . . . Well, he would soon find out his mistake if he tried to make love to her! Simon looked down at the pale colourless face with its halo of dark red hair. He had done it— he had avenged Tim's death. The madness of his lust was gone, leaving him feeling calm and refreshed.

He would need an alibi for tonight, just in case the girl was foolish enough to talk, but he doubted she would. Girls of that class . . . little nobodies, with no money or family behind them . . . if she told anyone her tale, who would believe her?

He was smiling the calm peaceful smile of an angel when he let himself out of the room and locked the door behind him. The last thing he had done was to cut through the rope binding Rachel's hands. It had rubbed her skin raw.

Miles was later leaving the meeting than he had planned. He had got involved in a heated debate, which he had won, but underlying his satisfaction at having made his point was an irritating sense of unease.

Simon Herries was up to something. He sensed it, smelled it in the air almost, if that wasn't too fanciful a thought.

Tim's death hadn't surprised him; somehow he had always been half expecting it, although in a rather more spectacular manner than a simple fall from a bridge—if Tim had fallen. He had seen the way Tim

had taunted and manipulated people, and had often
wondered how long it would be before one of his
victims retaliated. What did surprise him was that
Simon Herries had been the one to be with Tim when
he died. As far as he could see, and his perception
was very good indeed, Tim was far more valuable to
Simon Herries alive than dead. Tim was Simon's
tool . . . without him Herries would be dangerously
vulnerable. And Herries would not like being vulnerable.

As any budding lawyer must be, Miles was
something of a student of human nature. In observing
the interplay between Simon and Tim he saw much
that neither of them would have wanted him to see.
He knew, of course, that in part their relationship was
sexual, but he also knew that it was far more complex
than that. He recognised and acknowledged the aura
of power and danger that both of them gave off,
Simon more strongly than Tim. Simon was a man
who was driven by a relentless ambition to dominate
everyone around him, while Tim preferred to toy with
others like a cat with a mouse. Now Tim was dead,
not killed by one of his enraged lovers as Miles might
have expected, but dead from a drug-induced fall, his
death witnessed by the one person Miles was convinced
would have sold his soul to keep him alive. And yet
something told him that there was far more to Tim's
death than a simple accident, far, far more. There was
something . . . something dark and dangerous,
something almost evil . . . but he couldn't put his
finger on it, and the logic that had been his training
for so many years dismissed his thoughts as fanciful.

Taking the stairs to his rooms two at a time, he dug
into his pocket for his key.

The study the three of them had shared was in
darkness and he was tired enough to make his way

straight to his own bedroom. An odd, unfamiliar scent hung on the air. It wasn't drugs. It wasn't even sex, but it was something that made the skin on his scalp tighten with tension.

It was fear, he recognised in surprise, fear and . . . and blood? He reached for the light and flicked it on, staying in the doorway, his eyes searching the room, noting its heavy stillness, and then fastening on the untidy disorder of his bed, and the naked girl sprawled across the white sheet.

Miles walked over to her, light-footed as a cat, recognising her instantly. Tim's girl . . . the little redhead. Little fool, what was she doing here? Surely she hadn't been stupid enough to get herself involved with Simon; to go from Tim's bed to his?

Nothing that happened at Oxford could shock Miles any more. It was a time of complete sexual freedom and uninhibitedness, when the only thing that caused any raised eyebrows was a refusal to throw oneself into the hectic sexual climate of the times.

He reached down and shook the inert body gently. Whatever her reason for being in his bed, he wanted her out of it. He noted in detached amusement that her body was particularly good . . . good enough in fact to make him suddenly achingly aware of how long it had been since he had had a woman—but he wasn't going to get involved with this particular woman.

"Very delectable," he said out loud in a bored voice. "But I'm afraid I'd like my bed to myself tonight, if you don't mind." He had no idea what she was doing in his bed rather than Simon's but presumed it was one of the latter's malicious jokes.

When she didn't wake he took hold of the edge of the sheet and yanked it tight, ready to tip her unceremoniously on to the floor, only as she started to roll to the end of the bed he saw the blood on the sheet and the initial carved deep into the flesh of her small bottom, and he knew that whatever had happened in this room in his absence, it hadn't been anything as innocent as a practical joke—at least not as far as this small delicate-looking girl was concerned.

With fresh eyes he studied her naked body, and saw the rope burns on her wrists. He saw the glass, picked it up, and dipped his finger into the residue of fluid in the bottom. Had she been drugged before or after Herries had abused her? he wondered. Knowing his room-mate as he did, he was pretty sure it had been after. Now he understood the reason for the smell of fear infesting the room, and he also thought he understood why Simon had left her for him to find.

By the looks of it she had been a virgin. He touched the cuts on her buttock that were still seeping blood and gave a faint sigh.

Even if he knew where she lived he could hardly wake her up and turf her out in this state, but he was tired and wanted to go to bed. There was a bolt on the inside of the door. He looked at it steadily for a moment and then made up his mind.

Somehow he doubted that Herries would come back to their rooms tonight. In the meantime . . .

Miles had done enough work on farms not to feel offended by bruised and broken flesh, but a woman wasn't an animal, even if she had been abused like one. His mouth tightened perceptibly as he realised just how much Simon had abused the girl, and he wondered detachedly if she would ever recover enough to have a normal sex life after what she had endured . . . All the time he was cleaning her up she didn't move. He put her into one of his own shirts, fastening all the buttons and rolling back the cuffs, then he lifted her out of his bed and stripped off the soiled linen.

Despite his tiredness he didn't sleep much. He knew exactly the moment she woke up just before dawn, and got out of the chair he had slept in immediately to go over to her.

For Rachel to open her eyes and find another man standing over her staring at her was almost as terrifying as what had gone before.

She screamed as she scrambled off the bed and made for the door. It was bolted, and she heard Miles coming after her as she tugged the bolt free. Sheer panic lent her speed; panic and fear and the certain knowledge that she would die rather than endure another pair of male hands on her body.

Miles let her go. To go after her would only add to her fear. He recollected the terror he had seen in her eyes and involuntarily his hands curled into fists. He was not a violent man, but no one could have cleansed that fragile, delicate body without being sickened and disgusted by what had been done to it. He wasn't a naïve man, he knew that there were both men and women who found violence and pain sexually stimulating—and that was their affair, unless and until they began to inflict that pain and degradation on others who did not share their tastes. When *he* made love with a woman he liked her to share his pleasure, he liked to make her cry out with joy and fulfilment.

Only Bernadette knew that Rachel had been missing for most of the night, and like the good friend she was she had covered for her.

Rachel spent two full days in bed, shivering under the bedclothes, suffering from what the housekeeper thought was a bad attack of the "monthly curse". Because Rachel was such a good and willing worker she didn't reprimand her.

For two days Rachel thought of nothing other than how she might exact revenge for the crime committed against her. There was no point in going to the authorities, her gypsy upbringing had taught her that. How could a girl without connections or family, poor and ill educated, ever inflict vengeance for what had been done to her? She would find a way . . . She would *make* a way.

Simon returned to Oxford three days later. The shock of Tim's death had been too much for him and he had to get away, he told those who enquired. He had also taken the precaution of putting all his files in a bank safety box . . . In them were his records on all the other members of the coven. But safety deposit boxes have keys, and keys can be lost and found, stolen and forged.

Miles was waiting for him. He had known that eventually Simon must come back, if only to get his degree. He had never been a man of violence, had never thought he had it in him; but he beat Simon up so hard that afterwards he couldn't even crawl to his bed, but simply lay whimpering on the floor with tears pouring down his face.

"Now you know what it feels like to be hurt and vulnerable," Miles told him emotionlessly.

He had already made arrangements to move into other rooms. Perhaps he should have made an effort to seek out the girl and make sure she was all right, but he had been so sickened by the whole incident that all he wanted to do was forget it.

Rachel wanted to forget it as well, but she couldn't . . . The memory burned in her, causing her to be constantly sick and nauseous. It was over a month before she realised the truth. She was pregnant . . . she was carrying her attacker's child.

If she could have torn it from her body with her own hands she would have done so.

It was Bernadette who guessed first, approaching her quietly and worriedly to put her suspicions to the test.

"There's a woman that the girls go to who can get rid of it for you if that's what you want," she told her, "but you'll have to pay her."

An abortion! Rachel's grandmother had performed them occasionally. They could be dangerous, even with the most skilled of herbalists. Ergot, the fungus on the rye used to bring on the child early, could cause madness and death. But she didn't want the child. How could she?

She went to see the woman Bernadette had told her about. She was taken upstairs to a cold clinical-looking bedroom with a narrow bed, a sink and not much else.

"Umm . . . well, I'd say you were about six weeks on," the woman told her when she had finished her examination. Rachel had been tense throughout it, hating the intrusion into her body and its reminders of how this unwanted child had been conceived. "Twelve weeks exactly you'll have to be before I can do anything . . . That's the best time. A hundred pounds it'll cost . . . you'll have to bring your own soap—and a bucket. That way it means there's no chance of any infection, and no suspicion on me."

She saw Rachel's face and grimaced irritably.

"Gawd, you don't even begin to know what it's about, do you, lovey? What happened? Some young spark sweep you off your feet? And in these days! Why wasn't you on the pill? Well, it's done now, and if I was you I'd ask your young man for the money. A pretty girl like you . . . he'll be able to afford it. If he proves bothersome, tell him you'll go to the authorities. I'll bet he's a student, isn't he? Think they can get away with it, they do . . ."

"The soap," Rachel said, intervening huskily.

"A pound bar—good strong household stuff. We boil it up with plenty of hot water and then— well . . ." The woman looked at Rachel's pale set face and said wryly, "There's nothing to worry about. I don't go around ruining my ladies' insides, not like some I could name. After you've been here, you go home . . . twelve hours later it'll all be over. Just like having an especially heavy period, that's all it'll be."

Rachel stumbled from the room sick with cramping fear. Where was she to get a hundred pounds? Get it from your young man, the woman had told her. If only she knew!

No, she would never get a hundred pounds. That left only one way . . . Rachel felt her skin grow clammy with fright and nerves as she tried to remember what her grandmother had told her about the diseased seeds of the rye grasses which used properly could cause a woman's womb to contract and expel its foetus and which used incorrectly could cause the most agonising stomach cramps, and then gangrene, followed by death.

She knew what was needed, but how much . . . how often and when?

She walked far beyond the town and into the countryside, and kept on walking until the road shimmered dully in front of her and walking was simply a reflex action that kept her from thinking.

The woman saw her first, as her husband drew round the corner. She called out to him, and he braked immediately, but too late to stop the car bumper from catching Rachel. She fell awkwardly, tumbling on to the grass verge. The man cut the car's engine and they both got out, racing over to the unconscious figure.

"She's alive! We'd better get her to a hospital, though."

CHAPTER NINE

RACHEL woke up in a small sunny bedroom that was totally unfamiliar to her, and with no memory of how she had got there.

The door opened, and she stared at the woman standing there. She was small, plain and pin-neat, and her eyes were warm and very compassionate, Rachel noticed.

"Hello. How are you feeling?"

"I . . . What am I doing here . . .?" Rachel frowned as she tried to remember the woman's face, and then began to panic when she couldn't.

"It's all right." A gentle hand covered the restless movement of her own. "I'm Mary Simms. There was an accident—our car knocked you over. We took you to hospital and you've been heavily sedated ever since. Your friend at the hotel told us that you had no family of your own, so we brought you back here." For a moment the woman looked uncertain. "If you don't want to stay . . ."

Not want to stay! Rachel looked at her surroundings, felt the warmth and caring that came not just from the room but from the woman herself, and for the first time since her grandmother's death experienced an emotion she could only describe to herself as a feeling of no longer being totally alone.

And then she remembered why she had been walking down that empty lane and her hand went instinctively to her flat stomach. She saw pain flash in the older woman's eyes and wondered at it.

"No, you haven't lost your baby."

Rachel turned her head away.

"I wish I had!" She said it fiercely, bitterly, consumed with hatred for the life still growing inside her.

"Bernadette told us that your . . . your boyfriend had died in an accident. Have you . . . have you told his family you're carrying his child?"

It took Rachel several seconds to understand what she was being told, and when she did she looked at the woman and said bitterly,

"It isn't Tim's child. I was . . ." She swallowed back the venom threatening to choke her and spat out viciously, "It isn't anyone's child. I hate it!"

She felt Mary Simms flinch and looked curiously at her.

"You'll feel differently once he or she is born."

Rachel shook her head.

She wouldn't. She couldn't ever love the life that had been left within her in such violence and degradation. To her horror she felt tears gathering in her eyes and rolling down her face.

Mrs Simms made a sound of distress and remorse.

"There now, I've upset you! Let me go and get you something to eat and then you can rest. The doctor says you mustn't get up for another couple of days."

"Why . . . because I might lose the baby?"

Already, instinctively Rachel knew that in some way her child was important to this woman, more important than her, and she was jealous of that fact.

"No—because of the concussion you suffered when you fell."

Mary Simms went out, leaving Rachel alone, coming back almost immediately with a bowl full of homemade broth and some freshly made rolls. Rachel ate hungrily, appreciating the wholesomeness of the food.

"Rachel, you aren't fit enough to go back to work

yet. My husband and I would like you to stay here with us until you are. Would you like that?"

Would she? The sensation of pleasure and relief that rushed over her as she heard the suggestion was its own answer, but even so she was suspicious, unused to such kindness and concern.

"Why would you want me?" she asked baldly. "Is it because of the baby?"

She wasn't sure what made her ask that, but she saw from the shadow crossing the woman's face that she had hit on a vulnerable nerve.

"Not entirely. Philip and I are concerned for you . . . we feel responsible in a sense, because we were the cause of your accident. You're all alone in the world . . . a girl of only seventeen. Philip and I have been married for fifteen years, and we have no family of our own. Oh, several times we hoped, but . . . We'd like you to stay with us, Rachel, for as long as you care to do so."

"And the baby?"

"And your child too, when he or she arrives." The woman got up and picked up the tray. "You try and rest now. The doctor will be coming to see you later on this afternoon."

The doctor when he arrived proved to be a jovial man in his late fifties, and rather more forthcoming about her rescuers than Mary herself had been.

Yes, he had known the Simms a long time, he told Rachel in answer to her questions, looking shrewdly at her as he surveyed her pale face and set mouth. She didn't want this child she was carrying, and his guess was that left to her own devices she would try to abort it. He felt sorry for her; she reminded him of a small wild creature caught in a trap and desperate for escape.

Mary had told him of the child's vehement denial

of the suggestion that Tim Wilding was the father of her child, and yet according to her friend, he had been her one and only boyfriend, a fact which had been confirmed by the couple who ran the pub where the girl worked.

Something more than merely an unwanted pregnancy lay behind her almost savage resentment of her child, and the recently inflicted cuts on her bottom must have had something to do with her distraught state of mind, but whatever it was she wasn't ready to talk to them about it yet, so he talked to her instead, telling her about the couple who had taken her in.

"Philip is a schoolteacher . . . you'll like him, everyone does. Basically he's a very kind man."

And Philip himself would appreciate the agility and potential of her untrained young mind, the doctor reflected, as he got up to leave.

Rachel discovered that the doctor was right. Hard though she tried to hold the Simms at a distance, she found herself responding to their caring warmth. Days slipped by into weeks and weeks into months. The child inside her grew as she herself flourished in the tranquil backwater of the Simms home.

The old house they lived in was several miles outside Oxford and surrounded by a huge garden which Mary tended by herself. When she discovered Rachel's knowledge of herbs she was overjoyed, and gradually Rachel found herself disclosing more and more about herself to her unofficial guardians.

"What will you do, after the baby . . .?" Philip asked her one night over supper. He saw the suppressed look of need and intensity that crossed her face and wondered at its cause.

"I want to be rich," she told him simply. "So rich that . . ." Suddenly aware of the silence she had caused, Rachel broke off. Money wasn't important in this household. There wasn't a lot of it, anyone could see that, but it wasn't missed.

Had she grown up here, cherished by this secure background, how different her life could have been. How unfair it was that this couple who had so much to give a child, that Mary, who yearned so desperately for a family of her own, should be denied it, while others . . .

"I . . . I want you to have my baby," she said abruptly.

Colour fluctuated wildly in Mary's face as she stared at Rachel unbelievingly. Both she and Philip had learned to avoid the subject of the coming baby. Rachel hated any mention of it, bitterly resenting their attempts to get her to take an interest in her child. She had said nothing to them other than that she didn't want it, and Mary assumed that when the time came she would opt to have the child adopted. Never once had she allowed her thoughts to dwell on the possibility of Philip and herself adopting the baby.

Once, yes . . . but now they were both considered too old by the adoption societies. They had not married until Mary was in her mid-twenties, and then there had been the years of those hopeful pregnancies, all of which had ended in tragedy, and then the years when she couldn't even bear to hear the word "baby" whispered, and now when she and Philip would have gladly considered adoption she was forty and Philip almost fifty, and it was too late.

Too late, or so she had thought—and now here was this child abruptly offering them her unwanted baby. It seemed like a dream, a mirage, and she desperately wanted to reach out and grasp it before the offer was withdrawn, but sanity prevailed, and she remembered that Rachel was little more than a child herself, and that her emotions were in such a turmoil that she couldn't be allowed to make such a decision.

She reached out and covered Rachel's clenched fingers with her hand. "Oh, my dear, you can't know how much I want to say 'Yes', but when your baby comes you'll feel very differently, you'll see."

"And if I don't?" Rachel protested stubbornly.

"If you don't," Philip told her calmly, "then both you and your child will always have a home here with us, Rachel. You've become a part of our lives . . . an important part, and Mary and I love you for yourself and not for the child you're carrying. When I asked you what you planned to do with your life after the baby's birth, it wasn't because we want to get rid of you, but I can't bear to see you wasting the brain and the intelligence God gave you. You say you want to be rich. Be very careful, my dear, not to wish for the wrong thing from life, because you may very well get it."

Rachel felt as though he had twisted a knife deep inside her, and she wanted to cry out to him that he couldn't know what it was like to be her . . . that his soft words were all very well for others, for people with families and homes behind them, that until he had known as she had known what it was like to have nothing, he had no right to preach to her about not wanting to be rich.

Her labour pains started one Saturday evening in June. Mary stayed with her, soothing and reassuring her, but when her son was finally born, Rachel refused to look at him, saying tiredly,

"I don't want to see him. You take him, Mary."

She maintained her determination not to see her son all the time she was in hospital, and it was Mary who hung over his perspex cot and watched his every tiny movement, anxiously following his progress.

It was Mary who went out and bought the frilly Moses basket and the tiny sets of clothes, and it was Mary who held him when Philip came to take them home.

"Rachel, please . . . just hold him!"

Resolutely Rachel looked away. She had been back with the Simms for three weeks, and not once during that time had she touched or looked at her son. Inside her where her hatred and loathing of him had once been, there was now a tight knot of pain, and she knew instinctively that if she touched him, if she held him, there would be a bond between them that nothing would ever break.

Mary had been right, it was impossible for her to hate her own child, but Rachel had had plenty of time to think during the dragging months of her pregnancy, and with a clear-sighted determination she had deliberately plotted out a life for herself that excluded her child.

Here with Mary and Philip he would have the sort of love and security she could never give him. It was right that he should be here with them, and from the first moment she had thought of it, she had taught herself to think of him as their child. Here he would grow up free of the taint of his conception; here he would absorb from these kind, gentle people the sort of virtues and caring she could never teach him alone; here he would be safe, because when she took revenge for what Simon Herries had done to her, Simon would surely seek to hurt her in turn, even if that meant destroying his own child.

With her baby's birth, her determination to seek revenge had grown and intensified, and so too had her maturity, so she looked directly at Mary and said honestly and quietly,

"I can't. If I hold him now I may never be able to let him go. He isn't *my* baby, Mary, he's yours." She took a deep breath and told Mary what she had never told her before. "I was . . . raped by his father. I can't forget that. I don't want him to grow up in the shadow of that. *You* can give him so much . . . all the things I can't . . . love, security. I want him to have those things. I want him to have you and for you to have him. Don't you understand, Mary? I *want* him to be your child, because then he'll be safe, secure, loved."

It was all arranged very quietly and privately. The Simms had no close family, no one who knew their circumstances. Philip was a man who kept himself very much to himself. A change of house, a change of job, the quiet information dropped in one or two ears that they had had a child and that they had kept the pregnancy quiet because of Mary's age and previous medical history, and it was accepted that Oliver was their baby.

"And you, Rachel?" Philip asked her, as she helped him to pack away his books prior to the move. "What will you do?"

She had it all planned out.

"Go to college. I want to study languages, and secretarial skills."

She saw the disappointment in his face and knew why. He was convinced she could make it through university, but that took time—more time than she had.

"Then one of those cookery-cum-grooming courses . . . a short one. I'll work in the evenings to pay for it."

Rachel had learned a lot during recent months both from Philip and Mary's conversations and from what she had read. She knew that for what she wanted from life it wasn't enough just to have the ability; she would need connections as well . . . the sort of connections that were made at the very exclusive, very expensive girls' courses that abounded in select private colleges around Oxford.

"You must let us help you. At least stay with us," urged Philip.

Rachel shook her head.

"No, I can't, Philip. For one thing, there's . . . Oliver."

He didn't argue with her, but when she left to start her first month's tuition at the private secretarial course she had chosen, he gave her a cheque for a hundred pounds, which he told her she was not to give him back.

Because she worked hard, Rachel was soon well ahead of anyone else in the class. At night she worked behind the bar in a pub—a new one where she was not known—and she already had plans to get herself a full-time typing job the moment she finished the course. That would leave her evenings free for her to take in night school language classes.

Philip found her her first job. He knew of a colleague who was looking for someone to help him work on a treatise he was preparing during the summer recess. In addition to the straightforward typing there was also a certain amount of research work to be done. Although she was nervous, when she went for her interview with Professor Crompton, Rachel hid it well. She was still wearing the clothes she had been given by the unknown hotel guest. They never went out of fashion, and Professor Crompton's first impression of her was of a neatly dressed, demure child.

He rapidly revised it when he discovered how well she could work, and when he discovered by accident that in addition to working full-time for him during the days she was also taking evening classes in French and German he was astounded.

"Why?" he asked her curiously. It was so patently obvious that she would be married by the time she was twenty-one that he couldn't for the life of him see why she was bothering.

Rachel simply shrugged her shoulders and evaded the question. Already she knew the sort of job she would go after when she had the qualifications she felt she needed, the gloss to go with them. Something in the media . . . something where she would be in contact with rich and influential people . . . something that would put her on the road to achieving her ambition.

At the end of the summer vacation, his treatise typed on time and to perfection, his files in immaculate order, and his books immaculately catalogued, the Professor gave Rachel a bonus and the offer of a full-time job as his secretary-cum-assistant. She turned it down. She wasn't going to make her fortune in Oxford.

Philip and Mary were disappointed. Oliver was a plump, contented baby now, who laughed and waved podgy limbs at everyone who came near him. Sometimes when she saw him Rachel's compulsion to touch him was almost uncontrollable, but she resisted it. She couldn't allow herself regrets, she couldn't allow herself to love him as her own child. He wasn't hers. He belonged with Mary and Philip. They loved him in a way that she could never have done. They loved him selflessly, and they would bring him up cocooned in care, protected from all the harsher realities of life.

She had almost saved enough now to pay for what she privately called "the gloss". Another couple of months' work and she would be ready to start it at the beginning of the Christmas term.

She bought herself a second-hand typewriter, and in addition to her night school courses, and her daytime job working for an agency that provided temporary secretarial staff—because that way she could get plenty of variety—she also took on the task of typing students' theses. These were hard work and didn't pay all that well, but it was work she could do in her own time, and extra income that she badly needed.

When she started her final course, she wanted to leave her present digs and move into something more upmarket. She knew the sort of place it would be . . . full of girls with languid accents and county backgrounds. These last months Rachel had started to erase the country burr from her own voice, mimicking the accents of those she sought to emulate. By Christmas she would have it just right.

Sometimes Philip and Mary were bewildered by her determination, her singlemindedness, her fanatical determination to achieve what seemed to them to be impossible dreams, but they loved her nonetheless, not for the gift of the child they loved so much, but for herself, and Rachel, sensing this, absorbing it, slowly let down her defences with them, allowing herself to love them in turn.

She found the new digs she wanted almost by accident, one windy Thursday afternoon in October. She was hurrying down the street, wanting to catch her bus, when she collided with a girl coming in the opposite direction. The package of papers the other girl was carrying burst open, depositing untidy typewritten sheets all over the muddy street.

"Oh gawd!" the girl exclaimed ruefully. "Neil's going to kill me!" As Rachel bent to help her pick up her papers, she went on, "He's my brother, and I promised I'd type his thesis for him. It's already almost a week late!"

She was a small brunette with a cap of shiny curls and dancing hazel eyes, and instinctively Rachel felt drawn to her. She was wearing a raincoat, woolly tights and brogues, and she exuded happy confidence in much the same way as a cossetted little puppy.

"Let me help you with them," Rachel suggested.

"Oh, would you? Look, my place is just round the corner. Do come back with me and have a cup of coffee. It will fortify me to face Neil!" The girl made a face which told Rachel how little she actually feared facing her brother's potential wrath.

Her "place" turned out to be an immaculate terrace house, with pretty shutters and a heavy front door.

"Ghastly, isn't it?" she said as she ushered Rachel inside. "But the parents insisted on buying it!" She rolled her eyes and grimaced. "Neil has the flat upstairs, and I live down here. Actually until recently I was sharing with someone, but she's left to go to Switzerland. The parents are now agitating for me to find a new flatmate. Heaven knows what they think I can get up to with Big Brother upstairs!"

The furnishings, the area, everything about the house told Rachel exactly what sort of background the other girl came from . . . discreetly moneyed and protected.

"By the way, I'm Isabelle Kent," the girl told her.

"I'm Pepper—Pepper Minesse."

Rachel had had the name there ready at the back of her mind for some time, but this was the first time she had actually used it, and she waited a little breathlessly to see what Isabelle's response was. There was none, apart from a total calm acceptance that let her release her pent-up breath in a faintly leaky sigh.

For her new life, Pepper had constructed a

completely new background. Her parents were dead, she had no guardian, and she had been living with family friends (the Simms) but was now branching out on her own. There was no money. (She had even perfected the face she would pull when she made the admission.) She had learned a lot during these last few months, and she had learned that money didn't necessarily matter if one had the right background and the right accent. Well, she had no background, but the accent . . .

"What are you doing here in Oxford? You're not at one of the colleges, are you?" Isabelle asked her nervously.

Pepper laughed.

"No. I'm . . . I'm not doing anything much at the moment, but I'm starting at Benton's, the Cordon Bleu place after Christmas."

"Oh, heavens, what a coincidence! I've just started there." Isabelle pulled a face. "It's awful! Well, not as bad as St Godric's—I was there for a while doing secretarial work, but I was hopeless. Mummy was furious with me when she found out I was still typing with two fingers! Daddy's a partner in a merchant bank and she wanted me to go and work there . . . well, you know the sort of thing, not so much work as find myself a suitable young man." She made another face and they both laughed. "Where are you living?" Isabelle added.

"Nowhere at the moment, actually. I'm between digs, and staying with friends of my parents."

"Oh, that's marvellous! Look, would you consider moving in here?"

Rachel's heart started thumping. It had never even occurred to her that Isabelle would make such an offer, she had simply seen her as an excellent person on whom to practise her new person, but now that the offer had been made . . .

"I don't know," she began cautiously. "I'm afraid I'm not frightfully well off. I . . ."

"Oh, that! Heavens, don't worry about it. Daddy pays for all this. All you'll have to pay for is your share of the food. Look, do consider it, because if you don't, I'll probably have one of Mummy's chums' awful daughters inflicted on me. You know what it's like . . ."

Rachel smiled. Her conscience pricked her for deceiving Isabelle like this, but if she told her the truth . . . that she was an illegitimate half gypsy . . . if she spoke to her in the Lancashire accent of her youth, if she told her she had worked as a chambermaid, had been raped and left with an unwanted child . . . if she told her all those things would Isabelle accept her so readily and welcomingly? No, she would not.

Her new life started here . . . today, she told herself firmly. The past had to be forgotten. From now on she had two aims, two goals . . . financial success, and revenge against the four men who had contributed to her rape.

From now on, Rachel Lee no longer existed. She was Pepper Minesse.

She changed her name by deed poll and moved in with Isabelle. Neil, Isabelle's brother, at first inclined to be a little suspicious of his slightly feather-headed sister's new "friend", soon relaxed his initial stiff distance.

At Christmas, just before she started her first term on the cookery course, Isabelle invited Pepper to go home with her.

Pepper refused. She wasn't ready yet to risk her new persona in front of too many others, it still needed practice and gloss. She thanked Isabelle for the invitation, wrote her parents a charming letter, and explained that she was spending the holiday with friends of her parents in Oxford.

Mary and Philip were delighted to have her back. The baby was now six months old, a happy, sunny-natured child whom both Mary and Philip adored.

Pepper resolutely refused to think of him as anything other than the Simms' child. She played with him, bought him a Christmas present, but was careful to remain in the background of his life.

Mary didn't know whether to be appalled by or envious of the strength of her willpower. Neither was she quite sure how to take the self-contained young woman with her neat bell of dark red hair and her laid-back upper-class drawl. Impossible to believe, if she hadn't seen and heard it for herself, that less than eighteen months ago this selfsame self-possessed girl had been little more than a terrified child.

And it wasn't just outwardly that she had changed but inwardly as well. Philip had never doubted Pepper's intelligence, but now when he listened to the cool positiveness of her conversation he marvelled at the way she had developed it.

When she had first asked him how she might best extend her general knowledge, he had suggested she start reading the *Financial Times*, he had always found it one of the only true unbiased reporters of world news, but she seemed to have an ability to soak up information like a sponge, and to retain what she learned.

Privately Philip was beginning to suspect that she had first-class honours degree material, but the academic life wasn't for Rachel—or Pepper, as he must now get used to calling her. She wanted material success.

He sighed a little, then reminded himself that every

human being has different wants and needs. He looked at the downbent head of her small son as he played with his first set of building bricks and felt a familiar twinge of conscience. Perhaps they should have been firmer . . . Perhaps they should have tried harder to persuade Pepper to keep her child. Much as both he and Mary loved him, they were not Oliver's real parents. They . . .

"I'll never change my mind."

He looked up, stunned by Pepper's accurate reading of his thoughts.

"Look at him," she said softly. "Look at his eyes. He's loved and content. He's secure here with you, and I never want anyone to be able to take that away from him. Promise me you'll never, ever tell him the truth."

Did she know how much that had been exercising Philip's thoughts? All his life he had believed in total honesty, and yet at what stage did one tell a dearly loved and wanted child that he was not truly yours, that he was a gift? There would be bound to come a time when Oliver would want to know more, when he would need to discover himself the people who had given him life.

"It's for his sake that I'm asking you this," Pepper told him seriously. "Knowing the truth will do him no good, and could harm him. The man who fathered him . . ." She shuddered, then blanked her mind off from the tormenting images that still terrorised some of her nights. "I want for him what I never had . . . a safe, secure home. That will be something he'll carry with him all his life, my gift to him—the only thing I can give him. Promise me you'll never tell him."

And so Philip promised.

It was all for the best, Mary assured him when Pepper had gone, and he only wished he could accept that that was so as easily as his wife and Pepper.

Pepper's first few weeks at Oxford's premier cookery school might have been difficult if she hadn't had Isabelle to ease the way for her.

Isabelle, or rather Isabelle's parents, it seemed, knew everyone, as well they might. Isabelle's mother had been the most popular debutante of her year, and no one had been surprised when she carried off the cream of that year's eligible crop of young men, the heir to one of London's most exclusive private banking houses, Kent's. In fact, although no one but Pepper knew it, she had actually been accepted on the course in the first place following an introductory letter purporting to have been written by a close friend of her late mother's.

She had taken a chance on the fact that Tim's mother's handwriting would not be known to the principal of the college, since she remembered Tim saying that his sisters would all follow their mother to finishing schools in Switzerland, and that notepaper she had picked up on impulse from the desk in the hallway at Marchington had proved to be far more useful than she had ever imagined. She had taken it for no other reason than the fact that she had loved the thick expensive feel of it, so different from the notepaper provided in the hotel's bedrooms. Later she had burned with guilt over what she had done and had hidden the paper away, remembering it only when she had overheard two girls talking about a third, who would not be joining them at their exclusive secretarial school because her family was "not the right sort."

What she had done was wrong, of course, but justified, surely, since it would harm no one apart from those who deserved to be harmed . . . those who had harmed her. If she was ever to have the revenge she craved soul-deep she would need every advantage she could command, every advantage that her circumstances had so far denied her.

But even a letter of introduction from Tim Wilding's mother meant little when every other girl there knew or had heard of every other, through the social connections of their parents. She would have been very much the odd girl out, without Isabelle, Pepper recognised.

During their lunch breaks—the school had its own dining room and all the girls were expected to eat there—the talk was all of various parties and events that had taken place during the winter holidays. Some of the girls had been skiing with their parents, others had stayed at home in the country, but it seemed to Pepper, silently sitting at Isabelle's side and taking it all in, that all of them knew immediately to what the others referred.

Gstaad had gone dreadfully, frightfully vulgar, she learned, and the most awful types had started riding to hounds, and yet in almost the same breath the same girl would talk breathlessly about the absolutely super job one of Mummy's friends was giving her working in a shop. But Pepper learned that the "little shops" were always in Knightsbridge, and the holiday villas always in the South of France or the more exclusive parts of the Caribbean.

If anyone's parents owned a yacht, it was always a "tiny little thing really . . ." Large was vulgar, Pepper learned, and vulgarity in any shape or form was the biggest give-away in the world as to one's lack of social standing.

"What about you, Pepper, what will you do when you leave here?" one of the other girls asked her one lunchtime.

Pepper had no idea, but something Isabelle had once said to her popped into her mind and without even having to think about it she said airily,

"Oh, I'm not really sure, but I'm thinking of doing business lunches."

Business lunches, as a means of getting to know new young men and additionally proving that one had more between the ears than empty space, was a relatively new thing in the seventies. The rest of the class looked amazed.

"One of my cousins went in for that," a rather bored young woman remarked spitefully, "but she found it was horribly boring, and it meant she couldn't go skiing, so she gave it up in the end."

"Well, I think it's a marvellous idea," Isabelle leapt in defensively. "And what's more, Pepper and I are going to be partners."

Now it was Pepper's turn to be surprised. That was not what she had had in mind at all. She knew quite well from all that Isabelle had said to her that her friend had no thoughts of independence or making her own way in the world. For all her airy insouciance, she would marry young and well and settle down to much the same sort of life as her mother. And yet . . . and yet she owed Isabelle a lot, and she liked her. And then there were the connections she could make through Isabelle, Pepper reminded herself, telling herself that she was behaving logically and not emotionally, even while she knew the latter to be the case.

It was a very true adage that "he travels fastest who travels alone."

Perhaps Isabelle would forget all about the idea, she comforted herself as the bell rang and they all hurried back to their classes. But Isabelle didn't, and her excitement and enthusiasm for the idea was such that Pepper didn't have the heart to put her off.

"I was telling Mummy about our plans," Isabelle announced one weekend, after she had been home. "She thinks it's marvellous. She's dying to meet you, Pepper. I do wish you'd come home with me."

"Next time," Pepper promised, correctly interpreting Isabelle's mother's words. Dorothea Kent wished to inspect her, and in her shoes she would feel exactly the same. "Daddy thinks it's a good idea too. He said he'd give us a start by letting us do some for them . . . just for the Board at first," she added on a giggle. "He says he isn't prepared to let us loose on his clients until he knows we won't poison them!"

"And your brother?"

Incredibly, although they had passed occasionally on the stairs, Pepper didn't see much of Isabelle's brother. She sensed that there was a certain amount of disharmony between the two siblings.

"Oh, Neil! He's such a bore, and so dull. He doesn't think we'll be able to do it. He said we'd get bored within a fortnight. We've *got* to do it, Pepper, just to prove to him that we can! Oh, and I forgot . . . Daddy's told him to make sure he gets us tickets for the Commem. Ball at Magdalen—it's always one of the best bashes there is. Mummy's promised me a new frock for it. What will you wear?"

Pepper hadn't the faintest idea. Now that she was living with Isabelle it was impossible for her to work as well, and as it was she was having problems eking out her small savings. The only thing she had that remotely resembled a ballgown was that dress she had bought from the second-hand shop, she acknowledged grimly. She would just have to find some excuse not to go.

Only it didn't prove to be as easy as that.

Isabelle's great-aunt in Scotland fell ill, and her

mother had to go up and stay with her, and so
Pepper's proposed visit to London to stay with the
Kents had to be delayed. She had received a letter
from Isabelle's mother apologising for this, and stating
that she hoped they would meet at the time of the
Ball, when they would be staying close to Oxford with
some friends.

In other words, Pepper would have to attend the
Magdalen Ball.

In the privacy of her room she took the fluted
Fortuny dress from its protective wrapper and studied
it. Beautiful though it was, it just wouldn't do.

Isabelle's mother subscribed to the *Tatler*, and
Isabelle always brought the magazine back with her
from her weekends home. By studying the photographs of Society's do's in its pages, Pepper had
developed a fair idea of what she would be expected
to wear.

She took the problem with her when she went to
visit Mary and Philip. Oliver was walking now and
trying to talk. He gave Pepper the impartial beam he
gave everyone and hurled himself into her arms. She
picked him up automatically, wondering a little at her
own lack of mother love for him. Deep down inside
she knew she had denied herself the right to such
feelings from the moment of his birth when she had
refused to hold him. Although she studied his features
carefully she could see nothing of herself in him, nor
anything either of the man who had fathered him.

He was just another chubby, smiling toddler.

The moment Mary walked into the room his head
swivelled round and he wriggled in Pepper's arms. She
put him down and watched the eager way he ran
across the room. Yes, she had made the right
decision . . . the right decision for herself and the
right decision for him.

"Something wrong?" Philip asked her over supper. She had been quiet all day, and there was obviously something on her mind.

Pepper told them, pulling a wry face.

She had become more and more the girl she had created by her own hard endeavours and less and less the gypsy child she had been, Mary reflected, watching the naturalness of her gestures and speech. No one meeting her now would ever doubt that she had come from anything other than a comfortably wealthy upper-class home, the sort where the virtues and traditions of generations of established and orderly forms of life came as easily as breathing.

"Oh yes, you'll need something special for that," Mary agreed, when Pepper had finished telling them.

"I hadn't intended to go, but Mrs Kent is more or less insisting. She wants to inspect me and approve of me as a suitable friend and business partner for Isabelle."

"Probably more than that," Mary told her with an unusual touch of shrewdness. "You *are* sharing the same house as their only son!"

"Oh, heavens, we barely see Neil . . . he and Isabelle don't get on. I don't think he even realises I exist."

Privately Mary doubted that. Pepper was a startlingly beautiful young woman, and the new gloss of self-confidence she sported only made one all the more aware of that fact.

"I think I might be able to help out with a dress," Mary told her unexpectedly, "if you don't mind something second-hand."

"Anything," Pepper told her cheerfully.

"Well, I've been helping the Vicar's wife to sort out clothes for our 'good as new' sale for the annual fair, and I came across a bag of the most marvellous things.

Apparently they belonged to the niece of a friend of the Vicar's wife who had run off with an Arab prince . . ."

"Good heavens, what on earth possessed her to do that?" interrupted her husband.

"She's a woman, my dear," she told him wryly. "I believe the young man in question was extraordinarily handsome, and as rich as Croesus with it."

A short discussion followed on the folly of romantic indulgence and the reality of life that followed such folly, often with unpleasant consequences, which kept them all occupied for another half an hour, then Mary got up and said firmly,

"Yes, well, that's all very well. Left to it, I'm sure the pair of you could debate the issue for the rest of the afternoon, but if Pepper wants to see these things . . ."

Pepper did, she and Mary, with Oliver clinging to his mother's hand and refusing to get into his push-chair, set off for the Vicarage, which wasn't very far away. The Vicar's wife proved to be a sensible if somewhat harassed woman in her mid-thirties, who was quite agreeable to Pepper going through the bundle of things.

"They're far too good for our stall really, and because of that they probably wouldn't be bought . . . they're not the sort of thing the ladies round here would wear. Come and have a look."

There were three or four high-fashion outfits, that Pepper dismissed immediately despite their obvious quality—no one else at the college wore clothes like these, and standing out from the rest of the crowd was the last thing she wanted to do at the moment. As she looked at them she prayed that the dress wouldn't prove to be too outré.

It wasn't. It was white broderie anglaise, with an

off-the-shoulder top threaded through with blue ribbon to match the sash round the waist. The skirt was cut on the bias, and full, and there were several petticoats to go with it. It looked like an upmarket version of everyone's favourite Laura Ashley, and Pepper knew immediately that it would be ideal—demure enough to earn Dorothea Kent's approval and similar enough to the dresses other girls would be wearing not to merit any particular notice.

"It's ideal," she announced firmly.

The Vicar's wife was more than happy to accept ten pounds for it, and the three of them left with the dress bundled into a Marks & Spencer carrier bag.

"I'll wash and starch it for you," Mary promised, "and I think we ought to get some new ribbon. What do you think about a soft peach?"

For all that she herself was not particularly interested in clothes, Mary had an excellent eye for colour and style, and Pepper was happy to agree with her.

It was the fashion to have one's hair put up for formal balls, and Isabelle and Pepper spent a giggly afternoon the Saturday before the Commem. Ball, arranging and rearranging one another's hair.

"It's not fair! Yours is fantastic . . . thick and obedient, while mine curls all over the place," Isabelle wailed.

She had just spent half an hour meticulously ironing the curls flat, beneath a thick wad of tissue paper, and now she complained that her neck ached from the effort and her hair was still insisting on curling.

Everything went according to plan.

Dorothea Kent took one look at the girl with whom her only daughter was sharing and knew immediately which of the pair was the stronger. Beneath the neat blouse and pleated skirt, and later, the very pretty and appropriate white dress, she sensed a determination and power that Isabelle would never have. But five minutes' conversation with Pepper was sufficient to assure her that she was the last person likely to suggest that the pair of them take off for a trek across Australia, or indulge in any of the other equally inappropriate ventures that so many of Isabelle's previous friends had suggested.

It was a pity, of course, that she had no family to speak of, but apart from that Mrs Kent could see nothing to disapprove of.

Before they left to spend the night with their friends, she graciously suggested that Pepper might like to spend part of her summer holiday with them, and Pepper equally graciously accepted.

Dorothea was also able to reassure herself that her son, who was reading P.P.E., ready to follow in his father's footsteps, was apparently in no danger of succumbing to the girl's quite startling looks. That was as well, as she and his father had other plans for Neil . . . plans which in due time would include marriage to a distant cousin whose father owned a huge amount of Scotland, and a title.

Yes, it was all quite satisfactory really. Pepper was rather an odd little thing, so earnest and determined to make their little business venture work, but she would be a good influence on Isabelle, and after all, it wouldn't be for long . . . If Isabelle wasn't engaged before her twenty-first birthday, Dorothea would be very astonished indeed.

The Ball itself was an anticlimax as far as Pepper was concerned. The all-important event of the day for her had been meeting the Kents, especially Isabelle's mother, who she sensed was the more determined of the two adults. Isabelle's father had acknowledged her and said he was looking forward to tasting the results of the girls' time at college, but had said very little more.

While Isabelle's mother had not previously been loquacious, what she had said—or rather asked—had been very much to the point. Pepper knew she had created the correct impression, and that now she could relax, but strangely, all she really wanted to do was to go and spend the evening quietly with Mary and Philip, talking over her plans for her future. In an odd way they had become not only Oliver's family, but her own as well. She loved them as much as she was ever likely to be capable of loving anyone, she acknowledged, as she listened to Isabelle's excited prattle with half her attention.

Neil was escorting them to the Ball . . . Neil, who tended to look down on his excitable, rather dim sister. Neil was currently dating a fellow student. He went for brains rather than beauty, Isabelle had laughingly confided to Pepper.

"I wonder what they do when they're alone together? Make love, or add up columns of figures!"

Isabelle was at the moment extremely preoccupied about the extent of other people's sexual experience . . . probably because she herself had none, she had drolly confided to Pepper.

"I bet we're the only two virgins in the whole of Oxford!" she had exclaimed ruefully one evening after she had ditched her date and walked home, having gone out with the express purpose in mind of ridding herself of that unwanted stigma. "It was his hands," she told Pepper. "They were all clammy . . . I mean, can you imagine . . .?" she appealed, giving a theatrical shudder. "No, I shall just have to find someone else."

Pepper was now an accepted member of the small circle of girls who attended the cookery college. Via them she had made several contacts of her own and knew several young men, some of whom were present at the Ball. She wasn't left partnerless for very long, and while Isabelle was dancing with her latest conquest, Pepper was being swung round the floor by a succession of eager young men. None of them impressed her. A man . . . a lover . . . a husband. A man in any context was the very last thing she wanted, so she barely glanced at them.

Someone was looking at her, though.

Miles French had been persuaded to get tickets for the Ball by his latest girlfriend, an American on an exchange from Vassar. Tall and energetic with a waterfall of straight dark hair that she claimed came from some long-ago Red Indian blood, to Miles she seemed exotic and different from the other women he had dated. She wasn't a virgin and had no intention of settling down for a long, long time yet, she had told him frankly after their second date, when she had suggested they go back to his rooms to make love. They had been lovers ever since. Miles liked and admired her, but he was glad that he wasn't her chosen mate. She would be hard work to live up to, he thought in amusement, watching her as she danced with someone else.

It was then that he caught sight of Pepper. It was her hair that did it. That so unusual and vivid dark red banner of hair—that and the haunting beauty of her face. His eyes narrowed as he searched the milling crowds, seeking another look at her.

He had never forgotten the events of that night . . . nor quite forgiven himself for the violence he had felt afterwards. He had often wondered what had happened to the girl, and now, as he suddenly caught a glimpse of her cool shuttered face, he thought grimly that he knew.

She had changed, almost drastically so, but he still recognised her. That expression in her eyes, that cool wariness that warned against anyone trespassing too closely. Herries had put that there—Miles was ready to swear to it.

She was beautiful, almost flawlessly so, most men would say, but they would be wrong. She was flawed, inside, emotionally, he knew it as instinctively as though she had told him so himself, sensing the icy coldness within her even across the distance that separated them.

He thought about his energetic, ebullient American girl with her huge appetite for life in all it forms, her enthusiasm for sex and for living, and he looked for corresponding signs of such an enjoyment for life in Pepper's cool face, and knew he wouldn't find them.

Rape was an ugly word . . . a word he didn't even want to think about. He heard Beth call his name and turned towards her in relief, the decision whether or not to go across to the redhead and talk to her taken from him. She probably wouldn't have wanted to talk to him anyway . . . wouldn't have wanted to be reminded of what had happened to her. No, it was for the best—and yet Miles was left with a curious sensation of somehow having just made a very wrong and important decision.

CHAPTER TEN

ALEX BARNETT stood in Tom Quad waiting for his father. It seemed strange to think he would not be returning here in the autumn. He would miss Oxford, even though he had had divided feelings about coming here.

When he looked back from the vantage point of the sophistication he had gained over the last three years he felt rather amused by his younger self. He had been so anxious to do the "right thing" . . . to be seen to be au fait with the moods and manners of his new surroundings. With the benefit of what he knew now he realised that he should have chosen Cambridge and not Oxford. There he would have been right at the heart of the new computer industry.

Strange to remember that when he first came up to Oxford computers had meant nothing to him. Now . . .

He remembered quite clearly the first lecture he had attended on the subject, and those that had followed. He had known all along that when he finished university he would be going into his father's business, and that his degree and his years here at the famous college were simply icing on the cake . . . achievements that his proud parents could boast about to their friends, and to be fair, he had never imagined he might want anything else. And yet . . . and yet he envied those among his fellow graduates who would be making careers for themselves in what he privately considered to be the most exciting new development in British industry that there had ever been. Alex wanted desperately to be part of that industry. He knew that beyond any shadow of a doubt, but he also knew what his father was expecting. The company had been owned and run by their family from his great-grandfather's time, making sewing machines that were a household name. His father was proud of the business, proud of the reliability and sturdiness of the machines they produced—machines that were still exported to all four corners of what had once been the British Empire. Lonely homesteaders in New Zealand and Australia bought them; missionaries' wives in Africa and China, the wives of captains who sailed to South America and the Caribbean.

Nowadays their export sales were only minimal compared with what they had been at the time of the late Victorian and the Edwardian era, but the company was still very soundly based. In the Nottinghamshire town where the factory was situated they were known as responsible and caring employers. His father was the leader of the local Chamber of Commerce and his mother was involved in all manner of local charity work.

Had anyone asked Alex at the end of his first year at Oxford how he saw his future he would have replied confidently that he saw it falling into a similar pattern to his father's. Now he was not so sure. He felt disloyal in even admitting his restlessness. Others he knew from Cambridge were travelling to Japan and California to study the very latest technical developments; they were already talking about the future and the changes their bright new technology would make, like prophets granted a special vision.

He wanted desperately to be a part of that select and small band, but he knew he didn't have it in him to turn his back on his father and disappoint him.

And he would be disappointed. Alex had tried to talk to him about how he felt, but his father had frowned and dismissed computers as "a new-fangled idea that'll be dead within a couple of years."

But he knew his father was wrong.

He frowned, brought out of his reverie by sounds behind him, his frown deepening as he recognised the man strolling towards him.

Richard Howell. It seemed a long time ago since their first term together, and all that nonsense with Herries' Hell Fire Club. God, how idiotic they had been . . . dangerously so, he thought, remembering how close both he and Howell had been to being sucked into something that could have ruined their lives if it had ever come out into the open.

With hindsight it was easy to perceive his own folly. At the the time he had been too impressed by Simon Herries and his crowd to realise what he was getting himself into.

It had taken that incident with the girl Herries had ordered them to kidnap to do that. Alex wondered what had actually happened to her, then shivered, even though not a breath of wind stirred in the quad. It was pointless regretting that youthful weakness; he couldn't go back and undo what had been done. He had the future to think about now.

He saw his father's car approach and picked up his bags, calling out a brief goodbye to Richard.

He and his father didn't talk on the drive home. In addition to being a rather withdrawn and undemonstrative man, Gilbert Barnett preferred silence to speech, especially when he was driving.

It was early evening when they drove through the small Nottinghamshire village and up to the large Victorian house his great-grandfather had built. Still as solid and plain today as it had been then, it surveyed its surroundings from a slight hilltop, and Alex registered the familiar change in the car's engine note as they turned in through the gates and drove up to the front door.

His father was not a mean man, but he didn't believe in ostentation either. His Rover was four years old and was still as immaculate now as it had been on the day it had left the showroom. Alex already knew that when his father got his new car he, Alex, would inherit the Rover. Privately he would have preferred a nippy MGB in traditional racing green. Several of his Cambridge friends drove them—or if they could afford them, bright red Morgans. However, he knew that his father would not approve of his desire for a sports car. The Rover was solid and reliable . . . to match the company image.

Alex's mother was waiting for them in the drawing room. She reached up and kissed him a little shyly. His father did not approve of sons being too close to their mothers, and consequently she tended to remain rather in the background of his life.

"We're having dinner early tonight, because your father has a business meeting tonight. It's your favourite . . . roast duckling."

His room hadn't changed in ten years, and as he looked round it, he felt almost uncomfortably alien in it. It was only as he looked out of his window at the surrounding countryside that he acknowledged how little he had wanted to come home.

He knew it would be years before his father allowed him any real say in the business, but how could he simply turn his back on him and tell him that he found it boring? That he wanted wider, more exciting horizons? He knew he couldn't, so he showered and changed, then went down to dinner, where he listened to his mother's chatter about her social activities, broken every now and again by a comment from his father. It was a scene that was as familiar to him as his own face, and yet now for the first time it felt alien. *He* felt alien.

He offered to join his father in his business meeting, but was told that he would only be bored.

"Which reminds me—better get you into the local golf club now, I think. You'll meet a good crowd there."

Golf! Alex grimaced to himself. He preferred something more active such as squash or tennis. A dull lethargic feeling settled round him like a grey cloud. Was this what he had gone to Oxford for? This . . . this stifling boredom?

At his father's suggestion he was taking a couple of months off before he started work officially, but he had expected to be going into the factory most days of the week, so that he could learn the business informally from the shop floor upwards.

However, his father surprised him by being rather evasive on the subject of when he should start work, and suggested instead that he take the Rover and give himself a well deserved holiday. Alex was too grateful for the opportunity to escape to question his father any more closely.

Although there hadn't seemed to be much point in keeping in touch with his fellow computer buffs, a letter from one of them had advised him of an informal group meeting to be held once a month, in Cambridge, just so that they could all keep abreast of new developments. Since he had been given a month or so's freedom, there was nothing to stop him from packing a suitcase and spending a leisurely fortnight driving through the Cotswolds and stopping wherever the fancy took him in a gentle peregrination which brought him to Cambridge just two days before the meeting was due to take place.

The acquaintance who had written to him lived on the outskirts of Cambridge itself, and on impulse, having found himself a hotel, Alex decided to drive out and visit him. He found the village easily enough and learned that his acquaintance was the local Vicar's son. The Vicarage was pointed out to him, a long rambling building set in a tangled, untidy garden.

Alex parked the Rover on the weed-infested drive and made his way to the front door. It was opened by a small, slim girl, with a cloud of soft blonde hair and large sherry-gold eyes. She was dressed in the shortest skirt Alex had ever seen, and her toe nails in her pretty sandals were painted a vivid fuchsia. She looked nothing like a Vicar's daughter, and his expression must have said so, because she gave him a rather aloof look before asking him to come in.

"I'm a friend of William's," he told her hesitantly. "He isn't expecting me, but . . ."

"We're in the garden. You'd better come on through."

She started walking away from him before he could object, and so, rather reluctantly, he had to follow her.

The back garden of the Vicarage proved to be almost as overgrown as the front, although someone had made an effort at mowing the lawn. William was sitting in a deck chair, immersed in some technical data, but his look of surprise quickly turned to one of pleasure when he recognised his visitor.

"I'm here for Wednesday's meeting," Alex explained a little awkwardly. "I just thought I'd call round on spec. Your sister . . ."

He looked round for the girl and discovered that she was sitting down in a deck chair applying another coat of varnish to her toe nails.

William frowned and then grinned at him.

"Julia isn't my sister."

To his chagrin Alex found himself flushing slightly. Trust him to put his foot in it!

"The folks are away at the moment," William explained, making him feel even worse. The very last thing he wanted to do was to play an unwanted third to a pair of lovers. "So Julia, being the kind little cousin she is, has come over to look after me."

So they weren't lovers but cousins . . . but that didn't mean . . . Alex looked from Julia to William and then back again, and still couldn't make up his mind as to whether or not there was a sexual relationship between them. In other circumstances he would simply have asked bluntly if he was in the way, but since leaving Oxford, some of his parents' genteel morality seemed to have rubbed off on him, and he found the words impossible to frame. He felt awkward and uncomfortable, and also very conscious of the fact that the girl Julia was watching him.

"Look, it was only a brief call. I'd . . ."

"Why don't you stay and have supper with us?"

Her invitation was the last thing he had expected. He turned round to look at her, but the golden eyes were veiled.

"Yes, do," William agreed easily.

It was gone midnight before Alex reluctantly stood up and said he must go. "Otherwise I'll be locked out of my hotel," he explained.

"Why bother going back at all?" Julia asked him, watching him with her quiet, unreadable eyes. "We've got plenty of empty rooms here."

"My things . . . I . . ."

What was it about this tiny slip of a girl that made him so tongue-tied and self-conscious? For a start, she was probably at least two years his junior.

She gave a delighted peal of laughter.

"Oh, William can lend you what you need. Have you got a spare pair of pyjamas, William?"

"Never wear 'em," William told her cheerfully, giving her a mock leer. "Look, forget about your hotel, Alex. We'll go over in the morning and collect your stuff. Like Julia says, there's tons of room here, and I'll be glad of your company."

And so Alex found himself agreeing to spend what was left of the holidays at the Vicarage. William, it seemed, was in touch with several other computer buffs who lived locally, and could introduce Alex to them.

"You see?" teased Julia. "What more could you ask for?"

Alex wasn't sure if he was imagining it or not, but he could have sworn at times that Julia was deliberately flirting with him. He had now established the fact that the only relationship between her and William was a strictly cousinly one, and he had also discovered that she was an excellent conversationalist, intelligent and witty. Her parents had brought her up to do "nothing more than become a wife and mother", she told him wryly, and it seemed that she divided her time between her home in Gloucester and the flat she shared with a couple of other girls in London. She had a job in an art gallery, and when she chose she could be quite amusing about the various personalities she met there.

They were late getting back from the meeting which had been the whole purpose of his visit to Cambridge in the first place, and Alex was buoyed up on a high from the conversation and stimulating company. He and William had gone there in the Rover and now they were driving back.

"What do you intend to do with your life, Alex?"

William asked him.

"I don't have much choice. I'm expected to go into the family business. And you . . .?"

"I'm working on my own personal design for a small computer . . . so small that it could become a household item, and so easy that a child could programme it. I've run into a few problems, though." William sighed. "A friend of mine's working on a similar thing, however, and I plan to fix up a meeting with him tomorrow. Would you like to come? How much longer can you stay?"

"Well, I've got another ten days of my holiday left, but . . ."

Alex had been going to say that he could hardly stay that long, but to his delight William said immediately,

"Great! How about staying on here? We could work on my project together."

"Your parents . . ." Alex began.

"Won't be back until the end of the month, and besides, they won't mind. We've got the room, so it's no problem. Unless of course you want to spend what's left of your free time roaming the fleshpots?"

William lifted a querying eyebrow, but Alex shook his head. He had had girlfriends through his time at Oxford—never anything serious, just the usual sort of experimentation. He enjoyed sex, but had never felt obsessive about it . . . and he had certainly never desired a girl to the point where his need for her obliterated everything else.

Until now.

It was the first time he had acknowledged how he felt about Julia. Every time she so much as looked at him, he could feel the surge of need dominate his body. He had hardly stopped thinking about her from the moment he met her. When he went to bed at night he had the most erotic fantasies about her. Sometimes he suspected that she knew exactly what effect she had on him. She had a certain way of looking at him, a certain knowing gleam in her eyes.

It was gone one when they got in, and Alex went straight to bed, showering in the bathroom adjacent to his room. Like William, he too no longer slept in pyjamas, and as he walked into his bedroom he simply wrapped a towel round his hips. His room was in darkness, a slight breeze moving the curtains. He reached for the light which he was sure he had left on—then froze as he heard Julia saying softly,

"No, don't switch it on."

He shut the bedroom door automatically, staring into the gloom.

She was lying on his bed; he could see the pale blur of her body. He walked uncertainly towards her, his breath catching in his throat as he realised that she was naked. Her skin gleamed like mother-of-pearl, tipped with rose over the fullness of her breasts. As he hesitated Julia lifted herself up off the bed.

"You do want me, don't you?"

Her voice was liquid with laughter, he could see it shaking the slender arc of her delicate frame.

A fierce mixture of anger and desire burst into life inside him. Beneath his towel he felt the fierce throb of his erection. She knew what she was doing to him, damn her! He wanted to punish her for that taunting laughter, to show that he was a man, and not to be made fun of. He reached the bed, and leaned over her, pinioning her there, his mouth smothering the taunting sound. He found her breast and caressed it urgently. She was making soft animal sounds in the back of her throat, her nails digging into the muscles of his shoulders, tracing the line of his spine.

He felt the heat explode inside him and reached

down between their bodies to find the moist feminine warmth of her. She trembled as he stroked the soft delicate petals of flesh, arching up against his hands.

"Now . . . I want you now . . ."

There was no laughter in her now, only a demanding urgency that found an answer in his own need. Alex parted her thighs and moved between them. There had been women before, but none like this, and his body seemed to echo the sentiments of his mind, swelling tautly as he filled her. She felt tight and hot, encasing him firmly, making him want to plunge himself into her until she was completely and entirely his.

He heard her cry out and smothered the sound with his mouth, caught up in the fierce tide of his own need. His flesh pulsed with it, driving him mindlessly on until he was spilling himself endlessly inside her. Only then did he realise that she had not reached her own climax. As he withdrew from her he was conscious of the tightness of her body, and of her small wince of pain.

Alex was not a particularly egotistical man; he knew that nature had endowed him neither more nor less than the majority of his fellows, and certainly not to the extent to cause that brief spasm of pain, unless . . .

"Was this your first time?"

He knew the moment he blurted out the question that it was the wrong thing to say, conjuring up all sorts of emotional taboos that no modern, free-thinking woman would ever acknowledge, and he cursed himself inwardly for his stupidity. Far better to have left it and discovered the truth discreetly for himself later. He felt Julia's body stiffen in rejection and tried to salvage what he could.

"I'm sorry you didn't . . . that I . . ." He swore under his breath as he felt her coldness grow and added helplessly, "I've wanted you so damn much. You've been driving me mad, and now see what you've made me do! I promise you it will be better next time."

He waited for some smart rejoinder that there wouldn't be a next time, and when all he got in response was a small sniffle, he jettisoned all his own carefully fabricated barricades and took her in his arms, comforting her with tender kisses, telling her how much he loved her. ·

They made arrangements to marry as soon as they could.

When Alex discovered that not only had Julia been a virgin, but that she was also not on the pill, and that nor did she intend to take it, he had hardly dared to allow himself to make love to her again. He wanted her as his wife, desperately so . . . but he didn't want to make her pregnant before their marriage.

Julia could be reckless, abandoned even in her attempts to get him to break his vow not to make love to her again until they were married

She had refused to take the pill. She wanted a family and she had heard that it could make some women sterile. She refused to allow Alex to use any form of protection, so what were they left with?

There were weekends, when he went up to London to stay with her in her flat, when she brought him so close to the edge of breaking his vow that he thought he would go mad from it. She seemed to enjoy driving him to that edge, touching him, caressing him with her hands and her mouth until he couldn't hold back any longer. There were no barriers between them now, she knew his body as intimately as she knew hers, but no matter how often he brought her to her climax she claimed that it wasn't enough until she felt the pulsating heat of him deep inside her.

Later Alex marvelled that he had held out as long as he had. The week before they were to marry, Julia greeted him at the door of the flat wearing nothing other than what looked little more than a brief silk G-string and a floating see-through robe. She had darkened her nipples with rouge and she was wearing a sensual, heavy perfume. As she drew him inside her hand went to his zip. She teased him until he was aching for satisfaction, withdrawing from him with a secret smile.

"You know what I want . . ." she whispered.

His child. Julia told him so over and over again, and with only a week to go to the wedding, her pleas were impossible to resist.

That weekend he seemed to have been granted the stamina of a stallion. They made love over and over again, as frantically as though they felt that life itself was about to tear them apart.

When he looked back Alex often wondered if for that brief space of time they had both shared a deep unacknowledged premonition.

Two days before the wedding his father had a fatal heart attack.

Alex had never even known that his father had a heart condition. He was stunned, but he had his mother to think of. She had gone completely to pieces.

The wedding had to be cancelled, of course, and instead Alex attended his father's funeral.

Julia stood at his side, a delicate, fragile figure in black. Her parents had agreed with Alex that the wedding would have to be delayed—"for at least six months, darling", her mother had told Julia in Alex's presence. Alex will be in mourning."

"Mourning? God, Mother, that's so old-fashioned!" protested Julia.

"Nevertheless," her mother continued with quiet calm, "the wedding will have to be delayed."

Alex had been tempted to suggest to Julia that they get married quickly and quietly in a register office, but he knew her parents would be horrified. She was their only child, this wedding was something they had planned for and anticipated for years.

"Six months will soon pass," Alex had promised her. He had a meeting the Monday after the funeral with his father's solicitor. By a rather outdated arrangement, the house would come direct to him, as it had done to his father on his father's death. He would buy his mother a cottage somewhere close by, he knew that it was what she would want. Julia pulled a face when he told her. She didn't care for his parents' house, and he couldn't blame her. It was gloomy and old-fashioned.

There was the business to sort out as well. So far he had done little more than mooch around the shop floor, his father showing a rather odd reluctance to involve him more deeply in what was going on. Alex had put it down to the old lion fearing the roar of the new, but on Monday morning he discovered just how naïve he had been.

Charles Willshaw had been his father's solicitor for as long as Alex could remember. He and his father were contemporaries, and Charles had attended the funeral. He looked gravely at Alex over the wide expanse of his desk.

"How much did your father take you into his confidence, Alex?"

"Not an awful lot—he wasn't that kind of man. It was understood that I would follow him into the business, but . . ."

"Yes Alex, I'm afraid I have some rather bad news for you."

It was worse . . . far worse than anything he could have imagined, and yet coupled with the shock was a tiny thread of relief that now . . . now he was free. Sales had dropped drastically over recent years; his father had borrowed heavily and at high set interest rates. He hadn't been able to pay back the loan, and now the threat of bankruptcy hung over the business.

"Just the assets are there?" Alex asked when he had digested his initial shock.

"Nothing in the business. Your father hated getting rid of anyone. He's been carrying far too much dead wood for years. There's the house, of course, that should fetch a reasonable sum, although it could take a while to sell. There isn't the call these days for such a large and expensive home."

A week of almost constant meetings followed—with the bank, with their creditors, with the foreman, with the accountants, and at the end of it all, Alex realised that he would be lucky to come out of the whole thing with anything more than ten thousand pounds. Perhaps not a small sum, but certainly not enough to provide his mother, Julia and himself with a home.

He thought back to his initial interview with Julia's father when he had asked his permission to marry her. Mr Henderson was the old-fashioned type, who sincerely believed that women were too fragile to worry themselves about financial matters, much less to work outside the home. Julia had been cherished and protected all her life, and Alex was honest enough to admit that her vulnerability was part of her attraction for him. He wouldn't change her in any way, but he was also very much aware of the fact that Julia was not the wife for a potentially poor man with his own way to make in the world. Always supposing that her parents would agree to such a marriage. Julia was still very young, and Alex very much suspected that once he knew the true situation her father would insist on them waiting until he was more financially secure.

The only decent, honourable thing to do was to go to Julia's parents and explain the position, and to temporarily cancel the wedding.

Julia took the news badly. In her parents' presence she clung to Alex and wept, begging him to change his mind. They could live with her parents, she pleaded, and in the end it had been her mother who had led her out of the room, leaving Alex alone to face his future father-in-law. It was just as he had expected. Politely but quite definitely he had told Alex that there was no way he would allow Julia to marry him until he was sure Alex could support her properly.

Later, as Alex tried to comfort Julia, he couldn't help reflecting a little bitterly that if his father had not died for another month he and Julia would be safely married. He was trying to see things from her parents' point of view, but it was hard, very hard.

Refusing to give in to Julia's pleading that they went ahead and married anyway was the hardest thing he had ever had to do. He pointed out to her that if they wanted to please her parents they had no choice. He hated leaving her with the tear-stains still damp on her face, but he would hate himself even more if he agreed to her suggestion that they marry secretly and then live with her parents. That was something his pride would not allow him to do. He wanted to marry Julia, desperately so; he would marry her tomorrow if he could, but not behind her family's back; not when he knew that such a marriage would virtually mean him being financially dependent on his father-in-law.

He was touched by Julia's earnest plea that they marry immediately, wondering what had happened to the girl who had so lately insisted that it was impossible for her to marry without all the trimmings of the large wedding her mother had organised. It strengthened his confidence in their love and made him all the more determined to find some way of re-establishing himself financially, even though he knew it would take time. He and Julia were young, they could afford to wait . . . at least for a little while, even though Julia herself at the moment didn't seem to think so.

Her parents had fully understood and supported Alex's decision; they had been the first people he had told of his father's unexpected death, and now he had to explain to them that his financial situation was such that the wedding might have to be put off indefinitely. He knew he might lose Julia, but he couldn't tie her down to the type of poverty he might have to endure if he couldn't find himself a job.

He had gone overnight from being a comfortably off young man with his future securely laid out ahead of him to someone with nothing . . . less than nothing if he couldn't sell the house.

Julia's father heard him out in silence. He was a remote, old-fashioned kind of man, rather like his own father had been, and while he applauded his decision to make finding a job his priority, Alex sensed a new air of reserve about him, and guessed that Tom Henderson was considering whether he was still worthy of being considered a prospective husband for his daughter.

Alex said as much to William when he met him less than a week later in Cambridge. He had made the journey at William's specific request.

"Have you found anything yet?" William asked him.

Alex shook his head.

"No . . . and I'm not likely to be able to until I sort out the unholy mess of the company's finances.

I've got the house up for sale."

He couldn't tell William about his mother's reaction to the news that she was to lose the home that had been hers all her married life. At the moment she was staying with a cousin in Norfolk. A sort of nervous breakdown, was how their doctor had described her condition. Alex grimaced faintly.

"How's Julia taking it?" William asked him.

"She's not too happy, and I can hardly blame her . . . having to postpone the wedding almost at the last minute." Alex shrugged. "And until I get myself some sort of decent financial status, no way do I see us getting married . . . do you?"

"I might," William surprised him by saying.

"What do you mean?"

"That small home-size computer we were talking about . . . I think I've found someone who's got the answer to one or two of our problems. He's got some money he can invest—not much, but I've been working out some figures, and . . ."

"Just a minute! Are you suggesting . . .?"

"That the three of us take a chance, set up our own company."

"But we're years away from producing anything!" protested Alex. "We don't have the facilities, the . . ."

"I don't think we're as far from a breakthrough as you think. Those last ideas you came up with could be made to work. We could have the equipment manufactured under licence. It would be less profitable, but it would give us a start . . . I reckon with, say, six to twelve months' real graft, we could have ourselves a product that no one else is anywhere near producing. "It's worth a chance," William finished.

Alex wasn't sure if it was fear or excitement that was coursing through his veins, he only knew that suddenly he felt more alive than he had felt in months.

Here was the opportunity to involve himself in the sort of project he had yearned to be part of. It would be hard work—the financial problems would be almost insurmountable, but . . .

He looked at William.

"When can I meet this other guy?"

Alex left Cambridge three days later buoyed up with plans and new confidence. When he got home and discovered the estate agents thought they had a buyer for the house, it seemed like a good omen.

He decided to go to London to see Julia. He didn't normally go during the week, but this was something special. She had been so disappointed about the wedding, so down . . . they might not be any nearer to getting married quickly, but at least now Alex had some prospects ahead of him.

Julia shared a flat with two ex-school friends, and one of them opened the door to him. Alex had never really taken to Frances Napier. There was something about her that he didn't like. A year older than Julia, she was far more worldly; her men friends were invariably a good twenty years her senior and rich.

She raised her eyebrows when she saw him, contempt darkening her cold blue eyes.

"Julia's in bed. She isn't feeling too good."

For a moment Alex thought she was going to refuse to let him come in, but then she stepped back, and he walked past her, heading for Julia's bedroom. She was sitting propped up by half a dozen pillows, her face almost waxen-pale. She looked at him when he walked in, her eyes lifeless and dull, and when he bent to kiss her, she turned her head away.

"Oh God, Julia darling, please don't be like this with me! I want us to be married just as much as you do . . ." he pleaded.

He tried to cheer her up by telling her about William's plans, but she seemed lethargic and uninterested. Her pupils seemed twice their normal size, almost as though she had been drugged, he thought worriedly. When he asked her what was wrong, tears filled her eyes, and then she said abruptly, "It's just the time of the month, that's all."

He stayed for a couple of hours, but she remained distant, wrapped up in her own thoughts, not the Julia he knew and loved at all really.

"He's gone, then?" asked Frances as she heard the front door of the flat close. "Did you tell him?"

Julia shook her head.

"No. What was there to say? I was having your baby, but I've had it aborted?"

"Come on, kid! Things aren't that bad. There'll be other babies . . . lots of them. Anyone can see that the guy's crazy about you!"

Julia didn't respond. She couldn't. Tears blurred her eyes. From the moment Alex had dropped his bombshell about their wedding being postponed, she had been living in a nightmare. She had known the evening they made love that she would conceive. She had deliberately planned it that way, knowing that Alex wouldn't be able to resist her . . . sensing that once they were married he might insist on them being sensible and waiting for a year or so, but she hadn't wanted to wait.

She hadn't been able to believe it when he told her that his father was dead, and when only days later her own belief that she was already pregnant was confirmed, she simply hadn't known what to do. Her parents were old-fashioned; an illegitimate grandchild was the very last thing they would want. Oh, if she had told Alex, he would have married her, she knew that, but how could she tell him . . . how could she burden him with not just her but a baby as well, when he had no money and no prospects? Julia had never had to budget in her life, and wouldn't have had the first idea how to do so. Her father was indulgent financially . . . but once she was married he would expect Alex to support her.

She had been panic-stricken then when she realised her position, and she had turned instinctively to Frances.

"So you're pregnant," Frances had shrugged. "So what, it's no big deal."

And Frances had proved right. A discreet visit to a small and very expensive private clinic where Julia had been treated with antiseptic indifference by the doctor and staff. An overnight stay, then back to the flat. She hadn't suffered any physical pain or discomfort, there had been none of the horrors one reads about.

No, the horror was locked away deep inside her, she acknowledged. She had destroyed her child . . . and it made no difference how many times she told herself there would be other babies, she knew that she would always grieve for this one. That would be her punishment, and she welcomed it. She ought to be punished . . . she needed to be punished, and Frances, who had had cause to visit the discreet private clinic on a couple of occasions herself, looked at her with cynical contempt.

If only she could tell Alex, but how could she? Had he known of her pregnancy he would have married her, no matter what, she knew that. But she hadn't been able to endure the thought of telling her parents, of people knowing, of . . . If only Alex's father hadn't died everything would have been all right. They would have been safely married.

Julia burst into tears and buried her head under her
pillow, her hand automatically going to the empty
flatness of her smooth young stomach.

Alex was lucky. A buyer was soon found for the
factory, and when all the creditors were paid off he
was left with almost twenty thousand pounds—double
the amount he had hoped for. His mother had decided
to stay with her cousin, and Alex divided the money
between them, suggesting that his mother invest hers
to bring her in a small income. It wasn't much, but it
was better than nothing, and once their new venture
took off he would be able to do more for her.

Within a year the new company was being praised
for its innovative ideas, orders were pouring in, and
Alex was able at last to tell Julia that they could set a
fresh date for their wedding. They bought a small
cottage not far from Cambridge, so that Alex could
travel everyday. At night they made love, and Julia
responded to him with a satisfying intensity, and then
when they had been married for two years and she
had still not conceived the child she so desperately
wanted, he had bought her the house in Cotswolds,
an old rectory, a graceful, mellow home—a family
home.

The business had gone from strength to strength,
but the home computer market was overloaded, and
so three years ago they had started spending money
on developing a new system. Because it hadn't been
tried and tested, and because it was so revolutionary,
orders were slow in coming in, but once they got the
Government contract . . .

Alex arched his head back and stared out of his
study window, not seeing the verdant spread of the
lawn. Everything was going wrong. They should have

heard by now . . . and this damned Pepper Minesse business hanging over them . . . If the Department ever got wind of the contents of that file of hers . . .

He broke out into a sweat at the thought, and found himself wishing to God he had never heard of Simon Herries, or the Hell Fire Club . . . never gone to Oxford. But no, that was stupid.

He saw Julia coming towards him. The tiny stress lines round her eyes seemed to have deepened recently. He knew how she felt about her inability to conceive their child. He wished there was something he could do to help her, but there wasn't. They were going ahead with the adoption process, but their social worker couldn't make any promises. There had been so many questions . . . endless enquiries into their private lives . . . Alex thought bitterly of what it might do to Julia if they were rejected. She looked so frail, her bouts of depression were surely more frequent . . . nights when she would lie beside him, silently weeping when she thought he was asleep.

Julia saw Alex turn away from her as he saw her and her stomach clenched in a familiar sense of panic. He seemed to be doing that so often at the moment, turning away from her . . . and why not? What man wouldn't turn away from a woman who couldn't give him a child, a woman who had destroyed the child he had given her. The black pit of despair that never seemed to leave her these days started to whirl round her, sucking her down into its dark depths.

Maybe Alex had found someone else, someone who could give him children. After all, he was an attractive man . . . a very attractive man, well off, kind. What would she do if she lost him?

Please God, haven't I suffered enough? she cried silently. Haven't I paid enough?

It was that abortion, of course, that antiseptic,

clean, painless operation that had taken away not only her child, but all her chances of ever conceiving again, because despite his air of calm assurance and competence, that doctor had made a mistake . . . a mistake that meant she would never be able to conceive. But only she and her specialist knew that. In the face of her near-hysteria when he had broken the news to her he had agreed that there was no need for him to tell Alex exactly why she could not conceive, and Alex, being the man that he was, simply accepted Julia's explanation without question.

He had been so patient with her. But what if he was running out of patience? What if . . .

Her footsteps slowed. She felt reluctant to confront him in case all her fears were justified.

Alex heard her come in and waited. He heard her go upstairs and sighed. He would have to go up and comfort her, but not now. He was too on edge, too tense. If only he could get word on that contract. If only Miles French would ring and say that everything was going according to plan . . .

CHAPTER ELEVEN

RICHARD HOWELL left Oxford the same summer as
Alex. He too had a ready-made job waiting for him,
but not as heir apparent. That role was reserved for
his cousin Morris.

He spent his summer vacation working in the bank
as holiday relief for members of the permanent staff,
getting what his uncle David called a good grounding
in banking principles. Richard hated it. At that level
the pace of life within the bank was slow and pedantic.
The daily routine of dealing with the bank's customers
bored him. He wanted more . . . he deserved more,
he told himself bitterly, especially when he learned
that he had got a first-class honours degree.

David Howell was surprised, but not so his uncle-
in-law Reuben Weiss.

"I told you to watch him! If you're not careful he'll
snatch the bank from under young Morris's nose."

Morris was a plodder, a nice enough boy, but he
lacked his elder cousin's cutting edge and both men
knew it.

"What nonsense," David said uneasily. "Why,
they're practically brothers . . . they've been brought
up together."

"So were Cain and Abel," Reuben Weiss reminded
him sardonically, and David remembered his own twin
brother's bitter resentment of him and he looked
rather thoughtfully at his nephew.

Morris wasn't going to Oxford—or to any other
university. Only to himself was David prepared to

admit his son lacked the brains of his cousin. There were times when Richard reminded him very much of his own father, that sharp-brained entrepreneur, whose shrewdness was responsible for the bank's present-day standing.

Perhaps a spell away, a reward to Richard for getting his degree . . . Morris was to start work in the bank within the next fortnight or so. He would be grooming him himself to take over his role as chairman. Morris was already a little inclined to take a lead from his older, far more sophisticated cousin, and it wouldn't do for the next chairman of the board to be seen to be in awe of someone who while they held the sacred Howell name was still destined to be little more than acting manager of the bank at the very most.

David Howell frowned thoughtfully. Yes, it would be a good idea to send Richard away for a while, but where?

In the event he had to push the problem of his nephew to one side. The morning brought a phone call from a fellow banker in New York who informed him that he and his wife and family were coming over to London for a brief holiday. David knew Dan Lieberman quite well. They had had business dealings over the years and David had stayed with the Liebermans on some of his visits to New York.

He and Dan had even tentatively talked about the possibility of Morris marrying Dan's daughter Jessica. It would be a good marriage . . . Lieberman's bank, while not of the status of Howell's, was well known, and its control rested solely in the Lieberman family's hands. Dan's son would follow him into the business, and Dan's father before his death had established trust funds for both his grandchildren, which would mean that Jessica Lieberman would one day be a very wealthy young woman.

David rang his wife and told her that he had invited the Liebermans to spend the weekend with them at Windsor.

The Windsor house with its surrounding acreage was a recent acquisition. David had been rather dubious at first when his wife suggested the move, but in the two years they had owned it, several prestigious new customers had found their way into Howell's books via the contacts David had made at Windsor. There was also the not inconsiderable cachet of owning a property in the Royal Borough, and he had sensed that Dan Lieberman had been impressed when he had casually mentioned the town.

Anna Howell was the ideal wife for a prominent banker. She was a superb hostess, and managed to combine the gift of making their home seem both elegant and welcoming. She had a placid nature and seldom allowed anything to ruffle her. She was also discreet and tactful and never made the mistake of interrupting her husband or any of his business colleagues, even when their conversation threatened to ruin her carefully planned meal.

As soon as she put the phone down she was busy planning.

Morris walked into her sitting room as she sat making lists. He had been playing tennis with the son of one of their neighbours, and Anna wrinkled her nose slightly at the smell of fresh sweat.

"What are you doing?" asked Morris.

"Your father has invited the Liebermans back for the weekend. They're coming to London later this week. You remember them, don't you? Their daughter . . ."

"The Jewish American princess," Morris interrupted with a grin. "Oh yes, I remember her."

His mother smiled indulgently. Morris might not have the intelligence and determination of his cousin, but he had something else . . . something that to her mind was far more important. Morris had a sweetness, a gentleness of manner and mind. Like his father, she regretted his subservience to his elder cousin, but for different reasons. She didn't like Richard. He reminded her too much of his grandfather, her father-in-law.

Anna knew quite well why David's father had been so anxious for them to marry . . . not because he liked or approved of her, but because she was Jewish and rich. And she didn't delude herself either. David would have married her no matter what she looked like, no matter what his private feelings had been, because it was what his father had wanted.

No matter how illogical it was, she feared that her son, her precious lovely Morris, might be held in thrall to his cousin in much the same way that her husband had been to his father. It didn't matter that David had never been the favourite son, the favoured and loved child, that he had time and time again been passed over for his brother . . . even when that brother had proved beyond any doubt that he wasn't worthy of his father's love or respect. Anna had known, just as they had all known, that her father-in-law, had he been able to change the order of things, would have preferred Jacob with all his faults to be his eldest son and heir.

"Don't call her that!" she chided Morris lovingly now. "She's a very nice girl."

Morris made a face. "She's spoilt to death and you know it."

"Well, never mind about that . . . you just make sure you're at home for the weekend."

"If I have to, but you won't be able to bring Richard to heel as easily."

It was another thorn in Anna's flesh that Richard continued to live with them, long after, in her opinion, he ought to have found a home for himself. It was the Jewish tradition for families to stay together, David reminded her, but they both knew that Richard stayed because there was no other way he could afford the life-style he had with them. And while he stayed he continued to overshadow Morris in everything they both did, whether it was swimming, playing tennis, or even dancing.

Unlike Morris, he received the news of the Liebermans' visit without comment when his uncle informed him of it. He and his uncle normally travelled down to Windsor together at weekends—the small salary Richard was receiving at the bank did not allow him to run a car . . . at least, not the sort of car he would have wished to be seen driving. He preferred to travel in the comfort of his uncle's Rolls to driving the sort of run-of-the-mill second-hand vehicle that would be all he could afford.

He also accepted without comment his uncle's statement that he should go to Heathrow and pick up the Lieberman family. As he inclined his dark head in agreement, David told himself that he had been imagining that flash of fury in those intense blue eyes that could only have come from his mother's blood. There were times when Richard made him feel acutely uncomfortable, times when he sensed within him that calculating, waiting intensity that Anna's uncle had warned him about.

Richard picked up the Liebermans as instructed. He had met them all before, and he greeted the older couple with the polite deference that he knew went down well.

Daniel Lieberman Junior wasn't with them. He was in his last year at Harvard and had elected to spend

his vacation with friends at Bar Harbor, Mitzi
Lieberman announced in response to Richard's polite
enquiry.

Mitzi Lieberman liked Richard. She gave him a
coquettish smile, something that Jessica observed with
a sense of revulsion. Would her mother never realise
that she was a middle-aged woman and that she was
making herself ridiculous?

One only had to look at Richard Howell to know
that he was the sort of man who would never go short
of a woman. He must be laughing at her mother
inside. Jessica writhed inwardly at the thought.

Jessica Lieberman was what is called a "Jewish
American princess". She had known ever since she
could remember of the trust fund set up by her
grandfather and the millions she would inherit on her
thirtieth birthday. It had given her an arrogance that
had made her unpopular at her exclusive girls' school,
with its antiquated WASP ideals and worship of
lineage rather than wealth. She was not the sort of
girl who could ever have been popular, no matter
what her background, and her wealth emphasised her
disdain for her fellow human beings, which was as
much a part of her as the colour of her eyes.

One day of course she would marry. *That* was
understood, but that was a distant event somewhere
far off in the future. At the moment her mother was
busy making plans for her fall debut into New York
society, and Jessica went along with them.

Privately she couldn't think of anything more boring,
but Jessica Lieberman was adept at hiding her real
feelings and thoughts. The only thing that could move
her to real emotion was art. Already she knew that
the moment she could elude her mother her time in
London would be spent in its famous galleries. There
had been a time when she had dreamed of painting

herself, but the pedantry of her work, its sheer medio-
crity, had infuriated her to the point where she simply
refused to pick up a paintbrush. All through her life
she would never be able to bring herself to accept
anything less than excellence, in herself as well as in
others. If she couldn't be the best, then she wasn't
going to compete.

She sat in the back of the Rolls with her mother.
The boot was full of case after case of matched and
initialled Gucci luggage. Her mother firmly believed
that nowhere in the world could produce anything as
well as New York, and consequently when she
travelled, she did not travel light.

Although they had stayed with the Howells before,
they had never visited the Windsor house, and Richard
answered Dan Lieberman's questions about it, as he
drove them skilfully away from the airport.

Every now and again he looked at Jessica Lieberman
through his driving mirror. She had that gloss that all
rich American girls seem to develop. Her clothes were
expensive but unobtrusive—Mitzi Lieberman did not
approve of "fashion". Jessica's teeth, the product of
eighteen years of the most expensive dental care that
New York provided, gleamed white in the olive round
of her face as she talked. Her hair, dark and thick,
was naturally curly, her figure although petite was
curvy; she was almost the antithesis of the prevalent
fashion for tall, bone-thin girls with yards of water-
straight hair, and anyway he preferred blondes,
Richard thought, looking away from her.

The Liebermans were obligingly impressed with the
Windsor house. Anna Howell had taken a careful note
of the way her husband's non-Jewish acquaintances
furnished their homes and had firmly borne what she
had seen in mind when it came to re-vamping the
house. The result was a carefully subdued blend of

Colefax and Fowler, with just a modest dash of modernity in the Persian rugs and the plain walls.

David approved of what his wife had achieved, and the discreet diamond necklace he had bought her for their wedding anniversary proved it.

Mitzi Lieberman liked the house, but felt smugly pleased that for style it came nowhere near their New York apartment with its acres of off-white carpet and pastel leather couches. She had had the room copied from an article she had seen in *Lifestyle*—with one or two little touches of her own, like the pair of gold horses' head statues that supported the glass coffee table and the gold velvet floor-to-ceiling curtains.

She had had the entire apartment done out while Jessica was in her last year at Vassar. Jessica was such an odd girl, she thought fretfully. She had no interest in young men, or marriage. She hadn't even remarked on all the work that had been done to the apartment, Mitzi reflected indignantly. Sometimes she wondered how on earth Jessica came to be her child . . .

Jessica, who had been admiring a carefully grouped selection of small English watercolours that Anna had found in a local antique shop, looked at her mother and had a fair idea what she was thinking. Nothing on this earth would ever change her conviction that the New York apartment shrieked bad taste. She personally found it offensive even to look at it. This was much better . . . much more subtle, and somehow "right" for the house with its mellowness and large rambling garden.

Morris came in just as his mother was serving tea. Richard had been pressed into handing round the teacups, and the two cousins exchanged glances as David walked in.

Jessica had met Morris before; she found him dull and uninteresting, but she knew that her father was considering him as a prospective husband for her.

It was after dinner that David decided it was time to give Morris a delicate hint of what was in his mind.

"Jessica doesn't know any young people in England, Morris," he told his son when Anna was showing the Lieberman family round her garden. "I want you to make yourself available to show her round while she's here."

Richard knew instantly what was in his uncle's mind, and the jealousy he always kept meticulously under control raged inside him. Here was Morris, heir apparent to the wealth of Howell's bank, being handed the opportunity to marry a girl even wealthier than he would be himself!

Richard had no false conceptions about life. He felt sure that had his father married as had been planned his life would have taken a far different course. He resented his Englishness, the non-Jewish blood that came to him from his mother. Morris married to Jessica Lieberman, with that huge trust fund to come to her when she was thirty.

He saw the Liebermans walking towards the house and went forward to open the French windows.

Later, when his uncle accused him of deliberately setting out to seduce Jessica, he denied it.

He was telling the truth. He hadn't thought he would need to take things that far. But Jessica didn't want to get married . . . and that was really all he wanted from her.

Despite her years at Vassar Jessica had remained a virgin. She was too aloof, too self-contained to have much appeal on the casual dates she had had. Her remote manner put men off, and when there were so many other girls far more willing to give them what they wanted why should they bother with the Jessica Liebermans of this world?

And those young men who would have paid court
to her she avoided like the plague, knowing that what
they had in mind was the one thing she didn't
want . . . marriage. She wanted her independence,
the right to control her own life, and her own trust
fund. Jessica was no fool. She knew exactly why she
was being courted.

Even sensible young women can fall victims to their
hormones, though. To her horror Jessica found herself
responding to the physical presence of Richard Howell
in a way she had often dreamed of but never imagined
could ever happen to her.

He wanted to take her to bed, to make love to her
all night long, to kiss and explore every inch of her
body, he told her in the dark shadows of the garden,
and Jessica wanted it too. She wanted the brief indulgence of a passionate and intense summer-long affair
more than she wanted anything in her life. But Richard
wasn't after an affair, and when he realised that that
was exactly what Jessica did have in mind he knew he
would have to change his tactics.

He did it by keeping her in such a state of frustrated
anticipation that she made no demur at all when he
suggested coming to her hotel room. Her parents were
going to be out that evening . . . they were dining
with the Howells as a "thank you" for their hospi-
tality.

Richard knew that the evening would be over long
before Jessica or the Liebermans anticipated, because
he had purposely arranged, by bribing one of the
juniors, that the bank's alarm system would ring
halfway through the evening, necessitating his uncle
being called out by the police. The Liebermans returned
just in time to hear Jessica's guttural cries of fulfilment
pulsating round her bedroom as Richard made good
the promises he had been making her.

They had to get married, of course. Richard played his role to the hilt. He was contrite and guilty, but steadfast in his determined stance that he loved Jessica and wanted to marry her.

Jessica fought against her parents' edict like a caged fury, but it was no good. She would have to be married . . . *couldn't* she see that? her mother demanded.

The wedding took place in London, a lavish, full-scale affair, with the bride's face as white as her gown, and her mouth set in a bitter uncompromising line. She had no illusions. She knew now exactly why Richard had made love to her, and she could only marvel that she had been ever idiotic enough to want him to the point where she had been so blind to reality.

Dan Lieberman was irritated by his daughter's attitude, and by her stupidity. By rights she should have been marrying the Howell heir, not this cousin. David was furious with Richard, but said nothing, apart from pointing out to Morris that his cousin had snatched his prospective bride away from under his nose.

"But if Richard loves her, Dad," Morris protested, "I don't mind. I hardly knew the girl . . ."

Impossible to explain to Morris that he suspected that Richard didn't give two hoots about his bride and that his only interest in her was her trust fund.

Things wouldn't have been so bad if Dan Lieberman had suggested taking his new son-in-law back to New York with him, but he didn't. Richard's place was with Howell's, he announced firmly.

If Richard felt anything for Jessica it was mild contempt. She was far from being the first girl he had been to bed with, and it amused him that she should have wanted him so desperately. As yet she was too inexperienced to satisfy him, but he wasn't looking for sexual gratification in his marriage . . . he could find that elsewhere. His present girlfriend was a tall, leggy blonde, with a repertoire of sexual know-how that had even given him a few surprises.

In due course Jessica would produce a family—a son, he hoped. And if that boy should be Dan Lieberman's only grandson . . . but now, it didn't do to tempt fate too much.

The bridal pair honeymooned in the Caribbean—a wedding gift from the groom's uncle David.

Richard hadn't given any particular thought to how Jessica would react to their marriage. She was Jewish, therefore she must have been brought up to expect that she would one day be a wife and a mother. That she should be so furious about the way he had trapped her that she refused point blank to have sex with him was the last thing he expected. He tried cajoling, and when that didn't work he told her coldly that she was his wife and that he intended that their marriage would be consummated. It wasn't rape . . . but it wasn't anything like any of his previous sexual experiences. The cold rejection of her flesh irritated him, and by the time they returned to London they were barely speaking to one another, never mind making love.

Jessica's father provided them with a luxurious flat in one of London's exclusive Georgian squares. When Jessica taunted Richard with the fact that her father had had to pay for their home, he simply shrugged her taunt off. She could say what she liked to him. He didn't care. He had what he wanted, a wife who was going to make him rich.

Before they had been married six months they were sleeping apart in separate rooms. Richard wasn't dating the blonde any more . . . she had been supplanted by a redhead. He neither knew nor cared what his wife did in his absence. He spent as little time as possible at the flat, and made only duty visits to Windsor.

Morris was now working at the bank, and the bitterness and resentment which had subsided on his marriage to Jessica surfaced again. It wasn't just money he wanted, Richard acknowledged. He wanted the bank.

His first intimation that it was in financial trouble came when he walked into his uncle's office and overheard part of a telephone conversation. He gave no sign of what he had overheard, but started to delve discreetly into his uncle's financial dealings.

A speculative investment in the commodities market had wiped out a large part of his uncle's personal fortune; the bank had lost several important clients, and there were rumblings in the city that all was not well at Howell's.

And then, as though fate had finally decided to favour him, Richard was sent to work in the safety deposit section to cover for a member of staff who was off on extended sick leave.

By the time he and Jessica had been married four years Richard was well on the way to making his first million pounds, and Howell's bank was in grave danger of collapsing. There were rumbles from the board, open speculation in the financial press. Morris confided to him that he was worried about his father. Richard knew he had to act and act fast.

On the same day that he leaked the news of his uncle's financial misjudgements to the press, he also announced that he, as the son of David Howell's twin brother, had been approached by certain members of the board to take over as chairman.

The share price tumbled in the general panic, and Richard bought secretly and rapidly. When his uncle taxed him with the press announcements he said innocently that neither of them had anything to do with him. David Howell thought he knew better, but he had no proof . . . nothing. He was a man without power now, a man who had failed the great tradition of his family. The pains he had been having in his chest recently grew. He thought of his brother and his face . . .

Reuben Weiss found him, face down, at his study desk. He had died instantly, the coroner reported.

There was pandemonium at the bank. Someone had to take charge.

Richard had the authority. Richard had the shares . . . and now Richard also had the board's support. He had finally found his rightful place.

It struck him that he hadn't been home for almost seventy-two hours. He showered in what had once been his uncle's private bathroom, and which was now his, and got himself a taxi. He would sell the Rolls and get something else . . . He was pondering on what as he unlocked the door and walked into the hall.

He found Jessica in the drawing room reading a magazine. Despite his absence she evinced no surprise at his arrival.

"Guess what?" he told her flippantly. "I'm now chairman of Howell's bank!"

"Guess what?" she told him back acidly. "You're also about to be divorced."

She had all the evidence. She had been gathering it for months . . . or rather her private detective had been gathering it. It didn't matter how much Richard raged and argued; Jessica refused to back down. She wanted her freedom and she was going to have it.

Richard stormed out of the house an hour later, swearing under his breath. If she divorced him . . .

He thought of the settlement that would be hers on her thirtieth birthday and cursed again. Other men had affairs without their wives divorcing them. But other men weren't married to Jessica, he admitted bitterly. He hesitated for a moment on the pavement outside the house, then shrugged his shoulders. Since Jessica already knew that he was having an affair and that it wasn't his first, he might as well keep the date he had made with Rose.

He had been involved with Rose Marshall for just over three months. She was a model working for one of the new London fashion designers; a blonde English rose as different in temperament and looks from Jessica as it was possible to be.

She was waiting for him when he reached her flat. Richard was still so furious with Jessica that he forgot his own most important rule of never discussing either his wife or his marriage with his other women.

"Why not let her divorce you?" Rose asked him with a careless shrug.

At twenty-five she was beginning to be conscious of the fact that her looks and youth were not going to last for ever. And Richard Howell was a wealthy man.

Richard saw his mistake too late and cursed under his breath. Much as he enjoyed his sexual relationship with Rose there was no way he wanted to turn it into something more permanent.

"I can't," he told her baldly, adding, "Anyway she doesn't really mean it. She's found out about us and she's as jealous as hell."

"Oh, come on—I know all about your wife, Richard, I've heard about her from a friend of mine. How could she be jealous, darling?—unless of course you're trying to say that she fancies me?"

She saw from his face that he hadn't known, and she laughed shrilly, caught between triumph and a faint frisson of fear. Richard wasn't looking at her at all as though he was pleased by her disclosure.

"Don't tell me you don't know?" she asked him uncomfortably. "It seems to be pretty common knowledge."

Richard knew that Rose had a lot of friends and colleagues—people she had met through her work— who were members of the gay community, and suddenly he realised that she was speaking the truth. Little things that had meant nothing to him at the time . . . phone calls for Jessica from women he had assumed must be social contacts and friends, an oddly smug and defiant look in her eyes when she refused him sex . . . so many small pointers that he had either not noticed or had ignored. His wife . . . his wife would not allow him into her bed because she preferred to share it with a member of her own sex!

Rage and chagrin swelled up inside him. Rose saw it in his eyes and knew an increasing surge of fear. Even so, she had not expected him to head back to the door and leave.

"When . . . when will I see you again?" she asked him as he turned to leave.

Richard ignored the question. His wife . . . Jessica . . . God, how she must be laughing at him! No wonder she wanted to divorce him! Well, she could, but only at a price . . .

Jessica lay in bed staring numbly at the ceiling. She had been too confident, too careless somehow. She had never dreamed that Richard would find out, but he had, and now he was blackmailing her . . . threatening that if she didn't agree to stay with him until after her thirtieth birthday, until after she inherited under the trust fund, then he would tell her parents what she had become. And she knew he wasn't bluffing.

She wouldn't be thirty for another two years. It was unendurable. She couldn't stand it.

She got up and walked downstairs, pausing outside the door to Richard's study. If money was what it took to buy her freedom, then money he should have.

They were divorced two months later, but only after Jessica had signed a legal agreement to hand over to Richard two million dollars on the day of her thirtieth birthday.

As a woman she meant nothing to him at all . . . as a wife she had been important. He cared nothing for her feelings, and even less for her sexual preferences, Richard told himself, congratulating himself on having pulled off a good deal.

Under his guidance Howell's bank had gone from strength to strength. It seemed that the gods always smiled on him, and even more so, he had thought since he met Linda. She was his kind of woman. They had been married four years now, and life was good— at least it had been until that confrontation with Pepper Minesse.

He had to admire her. After all, she was doing no more than he himself had done, but she was a woman, and she wouldn't succeed. Miles French would see to that. Richard frowned, thinking back over the years. They had all of them changed. Nowadays he wouldn't do any man's bidding . . . And Simon Herries . . . There was something odd about him, something dangerous . . . something almost obsessive, but hadn't that always been there? That furious determination of his that Pepper was responsible for Tim Wilding's death and that she should be punished.

It was too late to go back and change things now. He only hoped that Miles French knew what he was doing. He hadn't struck him as a man who would make false claims about his abilities. What he had suggested had been so simple, and yet if he could pull it off it would be completely effective.

If he could pull it off.

Could he?

Richard mulled over what he knew about Miles, and then remembered that an eminent High Court judge had recently transferred his personal accounts to them, and made a mental note to get his secretary to make an appointment for him to have lunch. A little discreet foraging for information might be as well.

CHAPTER TWELVE

SIMON HERRIES left Oxford two years ahead of the other two. He had no money to speak of; the estate was bankrupt and he had to sell almost all of the remaining land to clear the debts. He knew that he needed money, and he also thought he knew how to get it.

He went first to Marchington, and Tim's mother, a gentle unworldly woman who thought she sensed loneliness behind the cold blue eyes and remembering that Simon had been her only son's best friend, invited him to stay.

He stayed for two months, and was quietly relentless in his pursuit of Deborah Wilding. The title would go to a distant cousin—the grandson of the Earl's mad aunt—eventually, but the Earl was an extremely wealthy man and so was his son, and all the Wilding girls had their own trust funds. If he could persuade Deborah to marry him . . .

Deborah guessed what was in Simon's mind and did everything she could to avoid him. She hadn't liked him when Tim had first brought him home, and she liked him even less now. In addition she blamed him for Tim's death. He was his friend, he had been with him . . . But she had kept her views to herself, knowing how much they would hurt her mother, who still grieved terribly for her only son. Deborah's two younger sisters couldn't understand her. They considered that Simon was both good-looking and sexy. Deborah couldn't explain her own feelings of revulsion to them; couldn't explain that she considered him to be evil and threatening; that she shuddered with fear every time Simon even touched her, and that the thought of marriage to him made her skin crawl. There was something about it . . . him . . . an aura which emanated from him that carried the smell of corruption so strong that she was amazed that only she was aware of it.

Her grandfather and her father had been away in Australia where they had joint business interests when Simon arrived, but when they returned the Earl was quick to notice the air of constraint about his favourite grandchild. She reminded him so much of his own wife, this quiet, withdrawn girl, who seemed to prefer to keep in the shadows rather than to live in the sunlight. Sometimes he thought there was almost something a little fey about her. She had an innocence, a modesty that was totally out of line with modern-day life, and often he worried about her future.

He had observed her Australian second cousins while he was away and had dismissed from his mind a half-formed idea that one of them might make her a good husband. She needed cherishing and spoiling, this granddaughter of his; and she would surely waste away and pine in the arid heat of the Australian outback.

He hadn't been pleased to discover Simon Herries in residence at Marchington. He had never liked nor trusted him, and when he saw how openly Simon was pursuing his granddaughter it added to his disquiet. When he tried to talk to Deborah, though, she refused to discuss what was troubling her. How could she, when she could see how much her mother enjoyed having Simon staying with them? It was as though having him there brought Tim back to her. After Tim's death, for a while they had thought that they might lose her too, she had grieved so intensely. The Earl wasn't deceived. Something was bothering Deborah and he intended to find out what it was.

He watched the way Simon followed Deborah and drew his own conclusions. Like her, he didn't like him, but with his much broader experience of life he knew why. Simon was a wrong 'un. The Earl could sense it . . . smell it almost. He had lived a long time and had come across other men who carried that same taint of inner corruption.

He didn't leave for Scotland at the beginning of August as was his normal habit but elected to remain at Marchington.

Deborah was glad. It didn't matter how often she told herself that there was no way Simon could make her change her mind, she still felt threatened and vulnerable. Having her grandfather there made her feel stronger, protected.

Simon was growing impatient. He needed a rich wife, and his own pride demanded that she be well connected, that she came from the same class as he did himself.

He knew Deborah didn't want him, and it infuriated him. What was she, after all? Nothing, if you took away her family and her wealth. She wasn't even particularly attractive, he thought sneeringly, watching her one afternoon as she and her sisters played croquet.

Simon's taste in women ran to narrow, athletic, boyish-looking girls with flat chests and long legs. He didn't question his preference, merely dismissing it in the same way that he had dismissed and turned his back on his homosexuality after Tim's death. He had the foresight to see then that what had been acceptable at school, that what was accepted in the cloistered confines of Oxford, would not be equally acceptable in the outside world. He had also recognised his own

need to marry well. Once he was married . . .
Deborah was annoying him with her stubborn resistance. He knew that physically he was attractive . . .
far more attractive than a girl with Deborah's plain
plumpness could ever realistically merit. She ought to
have been falling into his arms in gratitude and adora-
tion, but she wasn't.

He was determined to have her . . . all the more
so because she insisted on resisting him. Somehow he
would find a way. He had already decided that they
would be married before Christmas, in the
Marchington chapel. His stomach gave a kick of
mingled remembered fury as he recalled the use to
which Tim had wanted to put the chapel . . . and the
tragic train of events that the decision had put into
action.

He had made her pay for it, though . . . that
common little tramp who had been the cause of his
friend's death. Simon remembered the sensation of
her body beneath his hands. She hadn't cried out a
great deal, but he had sensed her fear . . . felt it
almost, and that knowledge had charged his own
excitement. He had enjoyed possessing her, dominating
her. As he remembered, it came to him how he should
deal with Deborah . . . Nothing as crude as rape,
although he would have enjoyed punishing her defiance
with the dominance of his body . . . No, that would
have to wait.

Deborah was not a modern girl; quite the contrary.
No pill for her to give her the freedom to take as
many lovers as she chose. The Marchingtons were a
devoutly Catholic family. As Simon turned these facts
over and over in his mind, his excitement grew. Fate,
it seemed, was disposed to aid him.

The whole family were due to spend the weekend
with Deborah's uncle, but at the last minute Deborah

developed all the symptoms of a heavy summer cold, and it was decided that she shouldn't go. Simon tactfully announced that he would return home for the weekend, and Deborah heaved a small sigh of relief.

He left two hours before the family, but he didn't go very far . . . only far enough along the road to pull off it and wait until he had seen that they had actually left. He waited a further hour after that, and then when he felt comfortably sure that they would not be coming back, he turned round and drove back to Marchington.

It was still only early evening, but the sky was overcast; thunder had been threatening all day. The butler let him in, and accepted his plausible excuse that he had forgotten his house keys.

Instead of going straight to his room, though, Simon went into the library and poured out two glasses of the heavy, rich port that the Earl favoured. Into one he tipped the contents of a small sachet of paper which he had bought from a fellow student. It contained a powder nicknamed "stardust"—a powerful amphetamine-based drug that removed inhibitions and gave the user an intense sensation of power and freedom. It also had the benefit of being extremely fast acting.

Simon already knew which bedroom was Deborah's. He walked in without knocking. She had been half asleep, but the moment she saw him she sat upright, trembling with shock and dread.

"I forgot my keys," he told her, smiling at her, but neither of them was deceived. "Look, I've brought you a glass of port."

He sat down on the side of her bed and put her glass beside her, drinking slowly from his own.

There was no one in the house apart from the staff.

Deborah trembled, her brain numbed by his audacity. She had never imagined he would do anything like this. She felt sick as she reached blindly for the glass. Perhaps this would make it better . . . make her feel better. She knew what Simon meant to do . . . she could read it in his eyes, and there was nothing she could do to stop him. Even if she were to call out, no one would hear her. He had chosen his time well. She had just had her supper and the staff would be in their own sitting room watching television.

She wanted to plead with him, but the words stuck in her throat. He had no mercy for her . . . no feelings for her at all, she recognised as she looked into his eyes and saw her fate written there. He wanted only what she could give him.

He had finished his port and she drained hers quickly, wishing there was more . . . wishing she could drink enough to pass out.

"You know what's going to happen now, don't you?"

His voice lowered to a silken, whispering sound that shivered across her skin. It seemed to mesmerise her. She felt dizzy as she listened to it. Simon reached out and pulled the bedclothes away from her body, and she heard herself sigh in mingled resignation and dread.

As he looked at the lush curves of her breasts Simon quelled his own inner revulsion. He closed his eyes and pictured Tim's face. The remembered familiar heat surged through his body.

Beneath the crushing weight of him Deborah felt her mind and body spin out of control. Amazingly her sense of panic and revulsion was fading and in its place was a growing, dizzying excitement. She moved restlessly beneath him, catching her breath on a gasp as she felt the aroused hardness of his body against her own. Her mind disintegrated beneath the assault of the drug; she became a creature of pure physical need. She felt the fierce surge of him within her and went eagerly to meet it. How could this ever have been something she feared?

She wasn't Tim, but she held the key to so many things he wanted. Before he finally allowed her to fall asleep Simon had made use of the state of euphoria induced by the drug to introduce her to every sexual deviation he had ever learned—and had taught her to find sexual pleasure in them. It amused him intensely that this haughty, cold young woman could be reduced to such a demeaning, grovelling state, and he hoped that when the effects of the drug had finally worn off, she wouldn't have forgotten the events of the night.

Even if she had it didn't really matter. He had taken her and, he hoped, possibly he had impregnated her too. In the morning when the maid came to wake her she would find them both in bed. He would plead the folly of youth and love . . . he would say that he was the one to blame for agreeing with Deborah's plan that they take advantage of their elders' absence. There would be no arguments, no avoidance. They would be married.

He fell asleep on the thought.

Deborah woke up first. Her body ached unfamiliarly. She moved uncertainly, and stiffened as she encountered Simon's sleeping form. And then she knew . . . instantly and irrevocably she knew. She recoiled from the sleeping male body beside her, her mind playing back to her over and over again the events of the night. What had happened to her? Why had she allowed him to do such things to her? Why had her body craved his, like an alcoholic craving drink? She had broken every moral tenet that had formed her life. And she had destroyed for ever her own inner image of herself, creating instead a creature of such base grossness that she could not endure to live with what she had done. Her mind, never strong, and tormented by these horrifying images, disintegrated beneath the force of what had happened to her. She got up and stumbled into her bathroom, heaving sickly. She couldn't bear to look at herself, but scrubbed despairingly at her skin. The foul images still would not go away.

It was almost as though Simon had put some sort of evil spell on her. She remembered her own sharp cries of pleasure, her feverish, demanding response to even the worst of the atrocities he had inflicted on her, and she knew quite simply that the burden of her sin would be with her all her life. It could never be washed away. She let the sponge drop and got out of the old-fashioned shower. She didn't bother drying herself or wrapping herself in a towel.

No one saw her as she made her way down to the chapel. It was too early for the staff to be up. Deborah took down the ceremonial sword that had been her grandfather's, holding it carefully because it was heavy, and moving like someone in a trance.

She went towards the altar, images crowding one another for prominence in her mind. Her nausea had gone, but in its place was an implacable, cold determination to escape from what she perceived to be lying in wait for her. Her mind was suddenly crystal-clear, showing her the degradation that would be her future. She had sinned grievously, and in a way that had shown her how vulnerable she was to sin. She who had always held herself aloof, who had looked down upon those whom she considered to be weaker vessels. Now she was being punished. If her grandfather knew . . .

Tears shimmered in her eyes. Her last mental image

as she flung her body forward on to the sharp point of the sword was of the Earl. She felt the pain searing her flesh, cleansing her with fire, and her last conscious thought was that she had finally and completely escaped. Never again could she be dragged down into the pit of degradation she had known last night.

She sighed, not knowing that her breath bubbled from her throat on a wave of bright scarlet blood.

Simon found her. He woke up and found her gone, and some instinct, some sense of awareness he hadn't known he possessed, took him down to the chapel. Fear and revulsion held him by the throat, his flesh crawling with loathing as he stared at Deborah's blood-spattered body.

He backed out of the chapel and looked round like someone in a deep trance. He had to get away, to escape, he thought feverishly . . . No one knew he was still here. It was still early, only just gone six o'clock. His car was outside, but the staff slept at the back of the house. They wouldn't have known that he hadn't left last night. He went upstairs, picked up both the glasses and washed them, then he hurriedly washed and dressed himself. He was just about to straighten the bed when he remembered the stains on the sheet.

He thought quickly, then stripped it off, going to the cupboard just outside the bedroom to remove a fresh sheet and make up the bed, deliberately untidying it so that it looked as though it had been slept in. The soiled sheet he bundled under his arm to dispose of later.

He used the main staircase and let himself out through one of the french windows. He drove twenty miles before he stopped shaking.

It was Deborah's father who rang him to give him the news. The shock of his granddaughter's suicide

had killed the old Earl, who had suffered a massive
heart attack. There had always been a rumour in the
family that they carried a streak of insanity, and now
that he thought about his aunt he wondered uncomfortably if it had held any truth.

Simon went to the funeral, haggard and pale in
dense black. He refused the invitation to go back to
the house afterwards. One of the local papers had got
hold of the story and there was some talk in the press
about a family curse.

Simon escaped to America. He felt no guilt for what
had happened, only a furious bitter anger. He was
quite prepared to believe that Deborah had carried
the taint of insanity—otherwise why on earth would
she have chosen death in preference to marriage to
him?

He pushed the entire incident to the back of his
mind, locking it away with all those other things he
preferred not to remember. His life had entered a new
chapter.

The Americans loved him. They loved his accent,
the way he looked, and most of all his air of breeding.
He had armed himself with several introductions and
talked nonchalantly about the family estate, shrugging
dismissive shoulders when he added the fact that death
duties had all but wiped out his inheritance. He
fulfilled their image of what a member of the British
aristocracy should be, and he in turn felt charged and
challenged by their ambition, their drive.

He was introduced to Elizabeth Calvert by a mutual
acquaintance. She was tall and slender enough to
appeal to him physically, and when he discovered who
she was he knew that he had found what he was
looking for.

They were married just after Christmas. Simon's
new father-in-law pressed him to remain in the States—

a place could be found for him somewhere within the family empire, which embraced both politics and the law—but he shook his head. He wanted to go home and restore his own family estate, he told him. In reality he had no intention of remaining under the watchful eye of Henry Calvert the Sixth, but he kept that bit of information to himself. His new wife's inheritance would make it more than possible for him to reclaim all that his father had lost, and besides, he had other reasons for wanting to return. Money, he was now discovering, wasn't enough. He wanted the power to go with it.

He thought of all that he had learned at Oxford; power came in many different guises. He would have to find the one that was right for him.

It was his new brother-in-law who first broached the subject of his entering the political arena, casually mentioning that he was due to go to Washington to address a small group of Senators.

Peter Calvert was a lawyer, and what he had to say made Simon think hard about his own future.

In their time both his grandfather and one of his uncles had represented their local constituency in Parliament. His father had had no taste for politics, and certainly it was not a career for a man without any financial backing behind him. But with his wife's family's wealth . . .

Before the newly married couple returned to England, Simon knew exactly what he intended to do.

Elizabeth Calvert wasn't sure exactly what she had expected from marriage. She had been at first astonished and then later triumphant when Simon Herries started paying court to her. At twenty-one, she had already and painfully realised that her narrow, almost curveless body did not appeal readily to the male sex. The brothers of her school friends, the young men who went to Harvard with her brothers, none of them actively ignored her, but they weren't attracted to her either. She had had only one love affair—born more out of sexual curiosity than anything else—with a totally unsuitable boy she had got to know while she was at Bryn Mawr. Neither of them had wanted anything permanent from the relationship, and when the time had come they had said their goodbyes without any regret.

Now at twenty-one Elizabeth was aware that she was becoming a social embarrassment to her family. Calvert women married young and produced families; they then went on to emulate their mothers and grandmothers by doing what generations of Calvert women had done. They worked for charity. If they didn't marry they either lived at home, or if they were very daring went abroad, and were henceforth known by other members of the family as "slightly eccentric."

Elizabeth fell into neither of those categories—yet! And the very last thing she wanted to do was to become the family spinster, aunt to her brothers' children, pitied by her female cousins and despised by her brothers' wives.

But one had to be seen to make the right kind of marriage. She knew that, just as she knew that her inheritance would find her a husband any time she wanted one, just as long as she set her sights on someone lower down the social scale than a Cabot or an Adams or a member of any of the other leading Bostonian families. And she had too much pride for that.

She had too much pride, full stop, she admitted. Far too much. Thus she had been at first wary and then reluctantly thrilled when Simon started paying subtle court to her. She wasn't a fool. She knew that financially she had a lot to attract him . . . several million dollars, in fact . . . but here was a man who could trace his family history back through countless generations more than any of Boston's first families. A man, moreover, who spoke with that upper-class English accent that no one could properly imitate . . . a man intelligent enough to hold his own with her father and brothers . . . a man who in short she could respect.

That she didn't love him didn't seem to matter. A Calvert woman did not have a career. It was a straight choice between marriage or remaining at home.

The thought of marriage had never particularly attracted Elizabeth; she knew that there was an odd coldness about her nature, a lack of responsiveness to men that she simply accepted as being part of her personality. Calvert women were not encouraged to discuss their sexuality. One married, one produced children—sons, for preference—and one worked for charity, and that was it.

Because she had never made any close women friends she had no one with whom to discuss her lack of feelings for Simon. He offered her an escape route from the label of "spinster sister" and she took it, telling herself that marriage at least offered a degree of freedom.

At first she thought she had made the right decision. After the first couple of nights of their honeymoon Simon seemed to be disinclined to make love to her— which suited her fine. He would want a son, of course . . . Elizabeth had heard all about his ancestral acres, and had quickly grasped that quite a considerable part of her inheritance would be used to buy back these lands and to pay off the mortgages on the Elizabethan house in the north. This did not worry her, her father had looked deeply into Simon's financial background, and since he had not been responsible for the debts that had overwhelmed his inheritance, Henry Calvert was quite content for his son-in-law to take charge of his daughter's financial affairs. He considered Simon to be an astute young man.

Simon had already confided to him his intention of securing the Conservative candidacy of his home town, and Henry Calvert approved of his plans.

He had never got on well with his only daughter. She was not like the other Calvert women, content to acknowledge the superiority of the male. There were even times when she made him feel uncomfortable. Privately he doubted that had he been Simon that he would have married her. There were plenty more wealthy young women in Boston far more compliant than Elizabeth. But Simon had his own reasons for choosing Elizabeth, and Henry Calvert would have been surprised to learn that her sexual coldness was one of them.

Simon did not want a highly sexed wife. He had no intention of being sexually faithful, and a wife who had little or no interest in sex herself was more likely to turn a blind eye to his own affairs—and less likely to exact retribution in the form of taking a lover of her own. As a potential MP, he would not be able to afford the scandal.

Already, though, he wanted more than merely to be a Member of Parliament. Already he was running through the contacts he had made at Oxford. Already his sights were set on a far higher goal . . . ultimately the very highest goal. He would make a good Prime Minister, he decided.

The newly married couple returned to England in the spring. Simon took Elizabeth first to the Borders, where he left her in the draughty, unheated, damp manor house while he went subtly into action. By the time he was ready to take his wife to London he had fulfilled his own goals. The local Conservative party would be adopting him as their new candidate at the next election.

Left alone in the house, Elizabeth had discovered she had more of the Calvert woman in her than she had supposed. Workmen were called in, central heating installed, damage repaired, decorators hired and antiques bought to replace those sold. By the time they left for London the house was already beginning to glow with the burnish of money. One day it would be featured in glossy upmarket magazines as an example of all that was best about traditional English country house taste, already it was beginning to show all the hallmarks of what Simon privately considered to be a "gentleman's residence".

He left a manager in charge of the home farm, and told him that whenever land became available he wished to be informed about it. So gradually he would buy back all that his father had sold.

In London Elizabeth repeated the pattern she had started in the Borders. The London house bought for them by her parents as a wedding gift was an elegant Regency building. Her parents came over on a visit for the second Christmas of their marriage, and Simon was delighted to be able to tell his father-in-law that not only was he likely to secure the Conservative seat for his own town at the spring by-election but also that he had fathered his first child.

Elizabeth smiled wanly and accepted her family's congratulations. She hadn't wanted a child quite so soon. She seemed to spend the major part of her day alone at home being sick.

Simon was out most of the time. She didn't ask where . . . she didn't really care. Marriage, she was discovering, was just as much a trap as spinsterhood. She couldn't say that she disliked Simon, but there were times when she almost ached to have her freedom. Now she could never be free. The birth of their first child would tie her to him even more firmly. And almost the entire Calvert family stood firm against divorce—not from any moralistic view point, rather from a financial one. Calvert marriages were always carefully arranged. When they broke up, so too did family fortunes . . . monies carefully garnered and cherished over many generations. Divorces were wickedly wasteful and totally unproductive. A Calvert man instead indulged his sexual proclivities with discreet and carefully picked mistresses who were content to remain in the background.

And as for the Calvert women . . . Elizabeth wondered idly if her mother had ever imagined making love with anyone apart from her father. She dismissed the question as irreverent, and tried to convince herself that she was fortunate to have so attractive and well liked a husband, and then wondered why it was that they had so few friends. Her husband dined out a lot with business and political acquaintances, but he seldom brought them home. They had very little social life.

That was something Simon too had been giving thought to. He had been using the connections he had made at Oxford to make sure of his future as an MP, but he needed spheres of influence . . . more power. He needed to please and flatter people into giving him their support, he recognised.

He looked at his wife. The right kind of wife was an undeniable asset to a politician, and Elizabeth was the right kind of wife.

She was surprised at the extravagance of his Christmas gift to her—a single strand of beautiful pearls. He added earrings when she gave birth to their first child—a son. And a delicate little pin with her initials on it when he secured the candidacy.

Only Elizabeth knew of the strain of months and months of dinner parties, of being pleasant to more local dignitaries than she could name . . . of constantly playing the part of the devoted wife of the ever charming and pleasant Simon Herries. Other women looked sideways at her, wondering what on earth Simon saw in her, she knew that. She also wondered how many of them discreetly found their way into his bed. She told herself that she didn't really care just as long as it kept him out of hers.

Once just after little Giles's birth he had lost his temper with her over some trifling incident. He had come to her room that night and made love to her, abused her, with such violence and menace that she could never forget it. She hadn't spoken of the incident to anyone, knowing instinctively that it sprang from far more than a mere male frustration at the long weeks of abstinence over her pregnancy and Giles's birth. There had been deliberate intent to hurt and humiliate her in the way Simon touched her, the things that he demanded that she do.

Elizabeth was no Deborah . . . no ignorant, shy teenager. She had immediately refused . . . and had carried the bruises on her body for weeks afterwards as a result of her defiance.

They never spoke of it, and it never happened again, but as she looked into the envious and sometimes amused faces of other women, she wondered if they would envy her if they really knew what her husband was like.

Simon was pleased with the way his life was going. At last he was getting somewhere. People treated him with respect and deference. He enjoyed all the small perks that went along with being an MP, just as he enjoyed the status which his wife's millions afforded him. For the first time he began to know the meaning of the word contentment. He no longer even thought about his relationship with Tim; that part of his life was over. An up-and-coming young politician could not afford to have any scandal attached to him.

When he wanted release from his sexual frustration he found it in a series of discreet alliances with sophisticated married women who shared his tastes. They weren't difficult to find, and although it wasn't anywhere near as satisfying as what he had once known, it was an adequate substitute.

When Giles was two and a half Elizabeth became pregnant again—much to her disgust. She hadn't wanted another child, and in fact had assumed that she and Simon would never sleep together again, but she was wrong. Simon wanted to have the perfect politician's family, and to that end he was even prepared to spend time in his wife's bed.

Luckily she became pregnant almost straight away. He sent her home to her family for a month's holiday as a reward, and thus established the future pattern of their lives.

Emma Catherine Herries was born just in time to celebrate her father's first appointment as a very junior junior minister.

Simon had changed outwardly over the years. No one looking at him now would ever imagine the young man he had been; the passions that had burned in him, his connection with the Hell Fire Club, and those who remembered it were too much in thrall to their own fear of their connection with its being revealed to betray him.

Simon sought every opportunity to prove his worth as a member of parliament. He was still too young to be considered for Cabinet membership, but he was making his presence felt. He was bound for success and nothing and no one would stop him. Elizabeth had broached the subject of a divorce and been told that she couldn't have one. Her family supported him in this decision and she had her children to consider, so she resigned herself to her life, and tried to tell herself it was no worse than many another woman's.

The friction between her son and his father worried her. Giles was a quiet, gentle boy, who had avoided coming into too much contact with Simon almost from the first day of his life. Elizabeth had objected when Simon wanted to send him away to school, and for once she got her own way.

Giles contracted glandular fever just before he was due to go, and Simon was forced to heed their doctor's advice that he remain at home and attend a local private school. Elizabeth knew that her son was aware of the tensions in their marriage, just as she knew that Emma was very much her father's daughter. She had his arrogance, and sometimes Elizabeth suspected, some of his cruelty.

They never shared a bed now, and she was glad. She knew he had his affairs, but he was always discreet. She longed to divorce him but knew that if she did her family would disown her. They were proud of Simon.

Her father thought, like Simon, that she was raising Giles to be a weakling. Calvert men weren't allowed to experience emotion. Like Simon, her family preferred Emma.

It saddened Elizabeth to watch her daughter growing up spoiled and arrogant. She wasn't popular with her school friends, and although Simon made light of it, Elizabeth had already had to deal with a couple of complaints from Emma's exclusive girls' school about her tendency to bully the young girls. Sometimes Elizabeth felt herself shrink back from her and knew that her own inner dislike sprang from Emma's resemblance to Simon. She wondered how much she was to blame for the way her daughter was growing up, but she couldn't bring herself to reach out to her.

As she did every summer, she dreaded her return to London. Simon had reached the point in his career where he was being seriously considered as a future candidate for the Party leadership. He had been tense and on edge before they left. He had embarked on a new affair—Elizabeth could always tell. She didn't want to go back . . . but she had no choice.

She arrived in London three days after Simon had received Pepper's ultimatum, to discover that her husband had gone up to the North, and that he wanted her and the children to join him. She had learned years before the folly of ignoring his commands, so she packed the clothes they would need for a week or so and told the chauffeur that they would leave immediately after supper.

The manor house, which had everything to make it a home full of warmth and serenity, was a place Elizabeth dreaded visiting. It had been here that Simon had launched his savage and never forgotten attack on her . . . and even before that there had been times when she had an awareness of an oppression of the spirit so strong and fearsome that it had almost made her cry out loud.

The house had been Simon's childhood home, and yet at times he seemed as reluctant to visit it as she was herself. Even the children seemed subdued when they were here, and yet it was the most beautiful place, built in cream stone, with views over one of the most unspoilt pieces of countryside Elizabeth had ever seen. The gardens had been designed at a later date, the grounds set out with rare specimen trees and an artificial lake. On an island in the lake stood a Greek-style temple built by one of Simon's ancestors on his return from Italy. The house and its grounds were regularly described as architectural gems, and yet there were times when Elizabeth felt she hated them.

The house was in darkness when they drove up, and this made her frown. Where was Simon? It wasn't that late . . . he would be expecting them. They only kept a skeleton staff at the house normally, and their estate manager normally took on extra help when he knew they were coming up.

They spent a month here each summer, normally in August, and then a week just after the New Year, when Simon insisted on holding a lavish ball for the local residents. He was a popular figure in the locality, for all the short lengths of time he spent here . . . but that was Simon all over, intent on maintaining and polishing his image.

Elizabeth got the chauffeur to open the heavy door and help them in with their luggage. She followed him, snapping on lights, and shivering as she realised the central heating wasn't even on! Where were the staff?

She saw a thin light burning under the study door and pushed it open. Simon was lying sprawled out in a chair, and the smell of brandy hit her as soon as she walked up to him. She saw the empty bottle and hid her shock. Simon drunk! But he never drank . . . She dismissed the chauffeur and quickly urged the children upstairs, ignoring Emma's strident questions.

There was no one other than her to help them get ready for bed. She saw to it that they had baths and then went down to the kitchen to get them some supper.

The cupboards and fridge seemed well stocked. Her thoughts buzzed desperately inside her head as she worked. What was going on? Had Simon gone mad and dismissed all the staff? But no, he would never do anything like that.

Elizabeth took their supper upstairs and settled the children, and then went back into the study. Simon was snoring. She decided against waking him, and went down to the flat above the garage which the chauffeur occupied whenever he was with them.

She told him that the housekeeper must have gone out for the evening and suggested that it might be as well if he got his own supper. That would stop him from coming back to the house. Simon would never forgive her if someone other than her saw him in his present state.

She went back to the house and started brewing black coffee. She had just finished making it when she heard a car outside.

The housekeeper looked flustered when she saw Elizabeth. She and her husband took care of the house and its gardens on a full-time basis, and Elizabeth had always found her very reliable, even though she had had trouble in understanding her North Country accent at first.

It seemed that Simon had given them the evening off . . . because he had intended drinking himself to a stupor? The woman avoided looking directly at her, and Elizabeth's heart sank. What had been going on? Surely Simon hadn't been stupid enough to bring one of his women back here with him?

She took the coffee into the study and left it there on a hotplate she plugged in. She wasn't going to wake Simon and risk his temper. Giving him a bitter look, she closed the door on him.

Simon woke up abruptly, not sure where he was, only knowing that he was in danger . . . he couldn't breathe properly. He seemed to be tied up . . . a figure loomed over him . . .

His father . . . He screamed out wildly, his body
already anticipating the pain, and then his mind cleared
and he realised that the figure standing watching him
belonged to his son. A surge of rage and hatred raced
through him as he saw the rejection in the boy's eyes.
All the frustrations and fears brought on by Pepper's
disclosures coalesced into one fierce burning need. He
reached for Giles, swinging him off his feet, holding
him under his arm as he unlocked the French window.
It had been a long time since he had been there, but
he knew exactly what to do. He found the punt and
dropped Giles on to its floor. When the boy started
to cry he hit him, revelling in the sensation of the soft
flesh beneath his fist.

There was no clear thought pattern in his mind, he
was simply following an ancient inbuilt urge; exacting
from his son the same payment that his father had
exacted from him. He didn't question his motives or
his feelings, ignoring Giles's strained, hoarse cries as
he dropped him into the rocking punt and prepared
to cast off.

The very act of getting into the punt had triggered
off a wild excitement inside Simon. He felt his body
stir with pleasure and a dangerous maniacal sense of
power. It was only right that his son should suffer
this . . . as he had had to suffer it.

He was unaware of Giles looking up at him, beyond
words, beyond tears, beyond anything except a
primaeval fear of his father. He shivered in the cold
night air, and Elizabeth, who hadn't been able to sleep
and who had come down to check on her sleeping
husband, stood transfixed at the open doorway, staring
at the small tableau in disbelief.

Where was Simon taking Giles? What was he doing
with him? It was a cold damp night. Giles could get a
chill . . . and then sickeningly she knew exactly what

was happening, and she started to run, her heart pounding with fear and shock. She reached the punt just as Simon pushed it free of the bank. Desperately she reached forward, grabbing for the pole, and managed to wrench it away from him.

She had caught Simon off guard, appearing almost from nowhere, to shock him into a moment's carelessness, but now he was turning towards her, his lips drawn back against his teeth in a rictus snarl of rage as he tried to take hold of the pole.

At some time she must have waded out into the water, Elizabeth realised as she felt her feet becoming stuck in the mud. Her terror for her son lent her a fierce strength that enabled her to resist Simon's attempts to wrench the pole from her, and she prayed desperately that somehow someone would see them and come to her aid.

Giles sat huddled up in the bottom of the punt, his eyes dazed with shock and fear, his body shaking convulsively. He seemed to be looking past them at some unimaginable horror, Elizabeth realised, and her determination to protect him sent a strong surge of adrenalin racing through her blood. By some miracle she managed to grab the pole from Simon, and then without thinking about what she was doing she raised it and hit out wildly at him, smashing the slightly flattened end of it into his body. He stumbled and the punt rocked wildly. Elizabeth saw him fall and catch his head on the side of the punt as he collapsed into it. Throwing the pole, she waded out to the boat and grabbed her child, and then with him held tightly in her arms she stumbled back to the house.

It seemed to take a lifetime to wake Emma. She protested bitterly that she did not want to leave, but for once Elizabeth ignored her strong-willed daughter, the horror of what she had glimpsed in her husband's eyes too strong to allow her to hesitate.

There was a small Ford in the garage, used mainly by the staff. The keys were kept in the kitchen. Elizabeth was shaking as she inserted them into the ignition, dreading with every heartbeat seeing Simon suddenly appear around the corner of the garage block.

It was only when they were on the southbound motorway that she could finally accept that they were safe. But for how long? Simon would hunt them down—he could not afford to let her go free to tell the world what he had tried to do to his own child . . . what he might actually already have done, Elizabeth realised on a shudder of sickness.

Knowing her own family's unshakable support of Simon, she realised she couldn't turn to them for help—at least not until she could prove her husband's depravity. She mentally reviewed her London friends. None of them were close enough for her to turn to in a crisis like this. She had always held herself rather aloof from the women she knew. And then she remembered reading about shelters that had been set up for women like her . . . women whose husbands physically violated and abused both them and their children. She had enough money with her to book into a hotel. She wouldn't use her own name. And tomorrow she would find out how she could approach one of these refuges. There wouldn't be much time; Simon was bound to come after them. Elizabeth dared not risk going back to the London house. In the back seat Emma whined and complained, while Giles slept. She would have to take him to a doctor . . . not her own doctor. Feverishly her thoughts ran round and round in tormented circles, while she castigated herself for not realising what her husband was doing to their son, and while she did so, she prayed that it was not too late and that Giles might be safe from his father's corruption.

CHAPTER THIRTEEN

THROUGH the good offices of Colonel Whitegate, Miles was able to leave Oxford, complete his law studies, and go straight into chambers. At first the others were a little wary of him. He had no legal connections, no background, and it was well over twelve months before he was really accepted.

It was gruelling, demanding work, made more so by the additional studying he did at night. Unlike most of his contemporaries, Miles had no family to finance him, so in his free time he worked. He held a variety of jobs, but it was while he was working behind the bar in a sophisticated West End club that he heard about an escort agency that was looking for presentable young men to escort some of their female clients.

"It's all straight and above board," he was told. "The agency's quite genuine . . . of course, if you want to come to a private arrangement with the client then that's something else."

"What's the pay like?"

"Good—and you get a dinner suit thrown in."

"So why are you working here?" Miles asked laconically.

"I blotted my copybook—got too involved with one of the clients. It turned out that her husband found out what was going on and made a complaint, so I got the push."

Working as an escort—paid to accompany rich old women; it sounded the very last thing he wanted, but the money was good. He needed a new set of textbooks, and his flatmate was getting married and wanted the flat to himself.

Halfheartedly Miles gave the agency a ring and made an appointment.

Marilyn Vernon had started up her agency when she discovered that the permissive age was leaving many of her contemporaries marooned on the shores of divorce; these were women in their late thirties with sufficient energy and income to enjoy themselves, but still tied by conditioning and upbringing to the need for a male escort when they went out.

She was scrupulously determined that her *escort* agency would be exactly that. The young men she employed could make whatever private arrangements they wished with her clients, but private they must be.

Miles French immediately struck her as being out of the ordinary run of well-born but impecunious young men she normally employed. Despite his relative youth he already carried about him an air of masculine authority that piqued her interest. She asked him the questions she asked all her potential employees. Miles answered them honestly and openly. Marilyn's eyebrows lifted a little when he told her that he was studying for the bar, and her mouth twisted wryly when he countered her surprise by commenting smoothly that since her agency was exactly what it was supposed to be he need feel no scruples about taking a job with her.

"The pay's better than the money I earn working in a pub . . . and to be quite frank, I need the money."

To test him she hired him to accompany one of her clients to the opera. Lady Pamela Dulwich was one of her richest and most difficult clients. She was forty-five and had the brittle brilliance of a bitchy, brittle socialite, with a penchant for attractive young men.

Marilyn knew in advance the sort of offer Lady Pamela would make Miles. If he accepted it he wasn't for her. A discreet private arrangement was one thing . . . out-and-out prostitution was quite another. She wasn't sure whether to be pleased or disappointed when he rang her at her office the following morning and explained calmly that there seemed to have been a misunderstanding and that he was not prepared to provide the kind of service Lady Pamela wanted.

Marilyn hired him. She would have been a fool not to do so, and Miles, who had initially taken on the job purely through financial need, found as the months passed, that it was impossible not to feel sympathy and compassion for the loneliness of many of the women he was hired to partner.

Very few of them made sexual advances towards him. He had that type of maleness that made it next to impossible for all but the most determined of women to treat him as nothing more than an available body.

One of his favourites was Lady Ridley. She had in her prime been a well-known opera singer, but she had married and retired to become a wife and mother. Now in her seventies, she announced that she was far too old for anyone to look askance at her if she chose to be escorted by a handsome young man. Miles liked her. She had a salty, keen wit, and a deep appreciation of the human condition that he found endlessly entertaining. Their relationship was almost one of grandmother and grandson—her only daughter lived in Australia, and she was very much alone, apart from one goddaughter, who regularly visited her but whom Miles had never met.

He had heard a lot about her, though. Amanda Courant had married young—almost straight from school. She was the only child of an extremely rich and very eccentric Scottish peer, and she had been married at her father's insistence to her second cousin.

"Hamish believed that because they both had Stuart blood they could between them produce a second Bonnie Prince Charlie."

Miles already knew that Amanda's father was obsessed by the Stuart cause, but that because of his wealth his mild eccentricities were generally accepted. He also knew that the marriage hadn't been a happy one. The second cousin had been too poor to refuse the offer of such a rich wife, but he apparently loved someone else.

"They never produced a child—I suspect the marriage wasn't even consummated, and of course, Hamish blames poor Amanda. She's living in London now . . . her mother left her a small inheritance, luckily. She won't go out, though. Her father's instilled into her the fact that she's a failure to such an extent that she actually believes it. She should marry again . . . but how can she if she won't go out and meet people? I want you to take her out, Miles. I'll pay you."

"If you mean you don't want her to know . . ." he began.

Lady Ridley shook her head. "Oh no, nothing like that! My dear boy, I've just told you—Amanda suffers from a massive lack of self-worth, there's no way she'd ever believe that a handsome young man like yourself would actually want to take her out . . . but her inheritance isn't very large and I've only managed to persuade her to go out by insisting that it's my duty as godmother to make her do so. She needs to meet people, Miles, to put the past behind her."

Miles agreed to escort Amanda to a fashionable society cocktail party.

He didn't really know quite what he expected, but

it certainly wasn't the almost flamboyantly beautiful brunette who opened the door of the small Chelsea mews house to him, and then he saw the apprehension in the huge golden eyes and he realised that Lady Ridley had been right and that he was looking at a woman with absolutely no confidence in herself at all. Her voice was husky with nervous tension, and he sensed that it would only take the slightest thing to have her backing out of the evening.

His taxi was waiting, but as he turned to take her arm he felt her flinch away from him. She was so patently nervous that he was at a loss to know how to reassure her, and even close to in the taxi, she looked closer to twenty-five than thirty-five.

The evening wasn't a success. Amanda shook visibly every time anyone male came anywhere near them, and Miles saw in her eyes that she was painfully conscious of the fact that he had been paid to accompany her. Every attempt he made to talk to her was blocked by a deflective "Yes" or "No", and he sensed that she couldn't wait for the end of the evening to arrive.

In the taxi on the way back she kept rigidly to her own small corner of the seat, looking straight ahead, her whole body taut, and Miles knew that when he was called up to report to Lady Ridley on the success of the evening, he would have to concede that it had been a failure.

As Amanda stepped out of the taxi, her heel caught and she stumbled. His protective movement towards her was completely instinctive, something he would have done for anyone, but the way she shrank from even that casual contact was so palpably obvious that he released her immediately.

He felt a slow wave of anger burn through him as he got back in the taxi to go home. This was the second time in his life that he had been made aware of the irreparable damage the male sex could inflict on its female counterpart. First that girl at Oxford . . . and now this woman.

He wasn't surprised at not being asked to escort her again. Lady Ridley suffered periodically from bouts of arthritis which kept her housebound, and Miles visited her when he could, tactfully saying nothing when she continued to fret over her goddaughter's single state.

"I've found the ideal man for her too. He's a Cabinet Minister . . . a widower with two children. Like Amanda he was brought up in Scotland. He's just perfect for her, Miles, but how can I get her to meet him?"

After that the very last thing Miles expected was to see Amanda at a celebrity publicity party he was attending as the escort of a well-known soap opera star.

When he first caught a glimpse of her he stared in astonishment, and as though the concentration of his attention caught her awareness Amanda raised her head and looked at him. Her face burned, but whether with anger or embarrassment he couldn't say. She had the clear pure skin colouring of a Celt, and the way the colour ran up under its paleness gave him a sudden urge to feel its heat beneath his fingers. He was familiar with sexual desire, certainly sufficiently so not to be caught off guard by it, but on this occasion he was, and it was several seconds before he could drag his attention away from her averted profile. Already he could feel the familiar ache and pulse of his body, the sensation of wanting to reach out and touch . . . He shook his head, amazed at his own reaction. He had only seen the woman once before, damn it, and here he was aching for her with an intensity he hadn't even experienced with his first girl.

For the rest of the evening he avoided coming into any sort of contact with her whatsoever, physical or visual. Commitment . . . marriage . . . they were not included in his plans at the moment. His career was all-important. It had to be if he was ever to make a success of it, and everything he already knew about her underlined the fact that Amanda Courant was not the sort of woman to participate in the physically pleasurable but emotionally unconstraining relationship he favoured. He made it a rule never to get involved with a woman who wanted more from him than he was prepared to give. So far that rule hadn't caused him any problems; there were plenty of young women about who wanted the same sort of casual no-strings-attached relationships.

Since leaving Oxford Miles had been involved in relationships with half a dozen or so different women, all of whom he remembered with affection. He never slept with a woman he didn't like and admire . . . he didn't need to; and sex was only part of what he wanted from his relationships.

He was an ideal lover, although he didn't know it, physically attractive and male enough to treat women with that very special brand of male tenderness. In bed he was a thoughtful and instinctively skilful lover, and out of it he was an intelligent and entertaining conversationalist, who never made the mistake of underestimating a woman's intelligence.

It almost made him hurt inside to see the way Amanda shied away from his sex; it was like looking at a delicate work of art that had been carelessly damaged by rough handling. He would have liked to have been able to show her all that a man-to-woman relationship could be, but he knew he would never get the chance.

He saw her once more before he left the party. The woman he was escorting had subtly indicated to him that she no longer required his company. She was flirting with a producer whom Miles knew only by sight, and he was discreetly about to slip away when he caught sight of Amanda Courant. She was hemmed into a corner by a large ex-rugby player type who appeared to be talking at her rather than to her, and Miles could sense her fear from all the way across the room. He told himself that the last thing she would want would be for him to interfere, and yet still he found himself going over to her.

He thought he saw the faintest flicker of relief lighten her eyes as he approached. The rugby player glared possessively at him, but he ignored him and to his own surprise he heard himself saying quietly,

"You did say you wanted to leave early!"

Was that relief in her eyes, or was it shock? Either way she was stepping past the hovering hulk and coming towards him. Neither of them spoke as they walked outside. Miles felt Amanda shiver beside him and he realised that she wasn't wearing a coat. He saw a taxi and flagged it down, ushering her into it.

To his astonishment when they reached her house, she invited him to come in. She was terribly tense, her body rigid with the intensity of it. She offered him a drink which he refused, wondering why she had invited him in when she so plainly wanted to get rid of him. She poured herself something and then put it down untouched, her movements jerky and uncertain.

The house was rented, Lady Ridley had told him, and its modern fashionable décor did not really suit Amanda. She belonged to another age, he told himself, then wondered at his own idiotic romanticism. He could see her dressed in rich velvets and satins . . . a tragic Stuart heiress . . . or was that simply because he knew her history?

She picked up her glass again, and Miles shifted uncomfortably in his chair. Her tension was obvious to him, and he suddenly wanted desperately to leave. She had her back to him and abruptly she turned round, hectic patches of colour burning in her face.

"Well, I suppose we might as well get it over with, mightn't we?" she said bitterly. "And then you can report back to my godmother that you've done what she's paid you for. How does it feel to be paid to go to bed with women no one else wants?" Her eyes glittered and he saw that they were filling with tears.

Beneath his own anger compassion rose up inside him. He got up quickly and went towards her.

"Is that what you think? That your godmother has paid me to take you to bed?"

"Why? Isn't that what you do?" Her head lifted arrogantly, but he could see behind the proud mask to the pain hidden inside her. "I hope she's paying you well, because . . ."

As Miles reached out to restrain her, she pushed his hand away, and suddenly he saw beyond the pain and the rage to what lay beneath those feelings.

His breath caught in his throat as he recognised her desire. She wanted him. He had seen desire too often not to recognise it now, and as he reached for her, despite the fact that she pushed him away, he refused to let her.

"Let's get one thing straight," he told her. "No one pays me to take anyone to bed."

"But you were paid to take me to that party . . ."

"As your escort, nothing else. Is that really how you see me? As a man who makes love for money?"

He felt the shudder run through her as he forced her to look into his eyes. He was already aroused and he knew that Amanda must be aware of it. He saw

the knowledge flare in her eyes along with a frantic
panicky disbelief.

"I want you." He mouthed the words against her
lips and felt her muscles quiver.

"You can't . . ." He caught the shaky, breathless
whisper of hope hidden beneath the flat statement.

"Why not? Because your husband didn't?"

Amanda shuddered again, and the feel of her, so
light and fragile in his arms, intensified the pulsing
ache of his flesh. He wanted her, and he wanted her
now. He bent his head and silenced her protest with
his hands. For a long time she didn't respond, then
her body jerked spasmodically as the tension eased
out of it and her mouth moved beneath his, uncertain,
tentative, untutored little movements that made his
heart ache with tenderness.

She had less experience than girls of seventeen. He
felt emotion burn his throat at the waste of it. He
wanted to give her all that she had never had . . .
show her what she could be, what she deserved to be.

He eased her slightly away and looked down into
the blind, white face, "I want to take you to bed . . .
now."

For a moment he thought she would reject him; in
fact he was more than half expecting it, and then with
an effort he could almost see, she seemed to gather all
her strength together. He saw her swallow nervously,
the movement ridging her throat. She looked at him,
wary and uncertain as an animal more used to kicks
than caresses.

"I . . ." Her voice cracked and she swallowed
again. Miles couldn't help her, much as he ached to
do so. "I . . . I haven't had a lover before. My
husband . . ."

She refused to look at him, but he knew what she
must be thinking . . . waiting for.

She looked defiantly at him.

"Well, don't you think it's pathetic? A woman of my age still . . ." her mouth twisted bitterly, "untouched and virginal, still so undesired by the male sex that . . ."

Miles put his fingers to her lips to silence her and said savagely, "I don't give a damn whether you've had no men or a hundred. Right now I want you so much that I'm likely to take you here where we're standing. Can't you see what you're doing to me?" he demanded thickly, and he saw the hot colour run up under her skin as he deliberately took her hand and placed it against the pulsing heat of his body.

She swayed close to him on a small moan of acquiescence, and Miles picked her up, feeling the urgent hammer of her pulses.

Her bedroom was furnished with the same stark modernity as the rest of the house. By rights he should be making love to her in the depths of a huge fourposter, he thought absently as he stripped off her clothes and then his own.

He felt the tension invade her at the sight of his nudity, and he knew without her having to say so that she was terrified—not so much of him, he suspected, but of herself. It was cool in the bedroom, and he wrapped them both in the quilt, stroking Amanda's shivering flesh until it grew warm and pliant and began to quiver slightly.

He was possessed by a need to make up to her for all that she had missed . . . to give her such pleasure that the past would be completely wiped out. His own desire was pushed to one side as he used his skill to arouse her. He felt her tension as he fondled her breasts, small and dark-nippled. He kissed the narrow curve of her shoulder and the thudding pulse point in her throat, opening his mouth so that he could suck

gently on it. Against his palms he felt her nipples peak
and harden and he heard the tiny gasp of shock rattle
in her throat. By the time he had kissed his way down
to the swollen urgency of her breasts she was moaning
softly deep in her throat, her nails digging into the
muscles of his arms.

He sucked gently on the turgid peaks, taking care
not to frighten or hurt her. He made love to her as
though they had all the time in the world, gradually
arousing her by such delicate degrees that she was
barely aware of the transition from dread to aching
wanting.

His hand opened her legs, gently stroking her. He
felt the shock course through her and silenced her
protest with his mouth, mimicking the delicate
movement of his fingers with the soft stroke of his
tongue as it rimmed and teased the outline of her
mouth.

Even though Amanda was aroused she was tense;
Miles could feel it in the underlying rigidity of her
flesh, and he knew if he entered her now he would
hurt her. His own flesh ached for release. Later he
would show her how to caress and arouse him, but
for now all his attention was concentrated on giving
her pleasure. Her body was beginning to respond to
the subtle rhythm of his stroking fingers. He kissed
her deeply, thrust his tongue between her parted lips,
not releasing her until he felt her response. He could
feel her body starting to relax, to welcome him. Her
nipples pressed eagerly against his hands as he caressed
her. He took one gently into his mouth, sucking on it
until he heard her moaning softly, and then he sucked
harder.

Her skin was beginning to burn, her hips lifting as
she pressed herself against the caressing intrusion of
his hand. He released her breast and let his mouth

drift lingeringly down her body until he reached the top of her thighs. As he had known it would, her body went rigid with shock when his mouth first touched her intimately. He felt her urgent movements to escape from him, her shock at the intimacy of what he was doing, but he had judged his moment well and the desire he had coaxed slowly into life flared hotly beneath the persuasive caress of his tongue.

The control which Miles had striven to maintain for so long splintered and shattered as he tasted the soft femininity of her body and felt its unmistakable response. His erection already pulsing and aching with need grew as he heard the soft, tormented cries of pleasure stifled in her throat and felt the tiny convulsive contractions of her flesh. He entered her quickly and determinedly, minimising the shock of pain and quickly reaching his own climax.

Later he made love to her again, this time bringing her to a brief but unmistakable climax with the controlled thrust of his body. She cried in his arms like a little girl, and he knew that nothing in his life had given him as much pleasure as restoring to this child-woman the power of her own sexuality.

They remained lovers for six months, and then one day Amanda told him that she was in love with someone else. She introduced them several weeks later at a party, and Miles was not surprised to discover that he was the Cabinet Minister Lady Ridley had mentioned to him.

He had always known that their relationship wouldn't last, but it hurt to lose Amanda, even though he had known she didn't love him.

His days with the escort agency were over as his bar examinations loomed, and then just after they had finished he got a telephone call from Colonel White-gate's butler-batman to tell him that the Colonel had

had a bad fall. He went down to see him immediately, shocked to see how much his benefactor had aged in a matter of months.

"Not the leg," the Colonel told him gruffly from his hospital bed. "Nothing to do with that . . . Got some damned thing inside me eating away at me. Only a matter of time now. Never thought I'd go like this, stuck in some damned hospital."

Miles knew what he was trying to say. The Colonel's only living relative was the second cousin who would inherit from him, and so Miles made the arrangements for the Colonel to come home; he hired and paid for the round-the-clock nurses who were needed in the latter stages of the Colonel's illness, and he also arranged to take leave from his chambers so that he could be there with him.

Colonel Whitegate died peacefully in his sleep four weeks after Miles's twenty-sixth birthday. As it happened, he had had a bad night the evening before and Miles had elected to stay with him, so that he was there when the old man opened his eyes for the last time. He saw them cloud and darken and heard the creaky bluff voice soften as he called out a woman's name. Miles heard the death rattle in his throat and wasn't ashamed to realise that he was crying.

He had lost the first real friend he had ever had. Men like Colonel Whitegate were the unsung heroes of the world, and Miles knew that without him he might well have made nothing of his life.

Despite their closeness, he was astounded to discover that the Colonel had left everything but the house and its lands, which were entailed, to him, with the proviso that he fulfil the Colonel's wish that provision was made for his batman.

Miles bought him a small cottage in the same village where his sister lived, and provided him with a pension.

There was sufficient money left for him to invest in the purchase of his own house and his first car. The case of vintage port the Colonel had left him he kept, to be drunk on suitable occasions. All apart from one bottle, which he and the batman shared on the evening of the Colonel's funeral.

Miles felt it was a gesture that the old man would have appreciated.

It is a long slow climb up an archaic and slippery ladder for any young man aspiring to become a leading barrister, and Miles was hampered by his lack of connections, but he got there. The year he was first tipped to become one of the country's youngest Q.C.s—that select band of lawyers entitled to call themselves Queen's Counsel and thereby to take precedence over other barristers—he had an unexpected visitor at his Inner Temple chambers.

He recognised her immediately she was shown in by his clerk, even though she had given him a false name. The years hadn't really changed her and she was still a very beautiful woman.

"Amanda! What a lovely surprise!" Miles rose to greet her, kissing her affectionately.

She looked tense and he could see there were lines of strain around her mouth. He asked her gently, "What is it?"

"Miles, I need your help." Her hands twisted the platinum wedding ring and its matching diamond ring loose on the long fingers. "It's my stepdaughter—I've just found out she's heavily involved in drug smuggling. Gordon, my husband, has just been tipped off by a friend at Scotland Yard that Sophie is being used as a carrier. She's in Brazil at the moment and due to fly back to England, stopping over in Paris on the way. She's already booked on to the flight, but we can't get in touch with her to warn her. Once she gets on that plane . . ."

"Why have you come to me?" Miles asked her gently.

Amanda smiled nervously at him.

"I was reading in a magazine about the work you do with young drug addicts, and . . ."

There had been an article about Miles recently in one of the Sunday supplements following press interest in his elevation to the ranks of Queen's Counsel. He remembered that the young interviewer had accused him of being very establishment and out of touch with reality until she learned that he worked free of charge for several organisations which helped the under-privileged, one of which was an organisation that provided help for young drug offenders. Not pushers, though. Miles had seen too much of the destruction that drugs could wreak on innocent lives to have much sympathy with those who made their living from such misery.

Amanda must have seen the distaste in his face, because she said unhappily, "Yes. Yes, I know, she deserves to be punished, but Miles, she's only eighteen, and very much under the influence of a boy she's been going out with. She's always been rebellious. She's doing this to punish us . . . her father and me. I don't think she really realises exactly what risks she's running."

"Why come to me?"

Miles was frowning now, remembering the last drugs case he had handled. He had got the girl off, but uselessly, because she had died of an overdose several months later. He never handled cases unless he was absolutely convinced that the person he was defending was innocent. He held no brief for those who deliberately inflicted pain and degradation on their fellow human beings, no matter who they were.

"There wasn't anyone else." Amanda's hands twisted again. "Gordon can't do anything. His position in the Cabinet . . ."

Miles could see that. He looked down into her face and was half irritated by his own burgeoning feeling of responsibility . . . a need to protect and shield the weaker sex. That had always been one of his own weaknesses, and it hadn't lessened over the years. He wanted to help her, he acknowledged. He wanted to wipe away the pain and fear, just as he had wanted to all those years before. As he looked at Amanda, his mind was running over all the possibilities. If the girl was flying back from South America on a known flight the police were bound to be watching the airport. The only way he could stop her would either be to fly to South America, or to intercept her when the flight touched down in Paris.

"We can't even get in touch with her by telephone," Amanda told him, cutting off the former avenue. "We don't know where in Brazil she's staying, only that she's booked on to this particular flight home."

The timing would be difficult, almost impossible, and when Miles thought of the risk he was running, he knew what he was contemplating was pure idiocy, and yet when Amanda smiled her tremulous thanks he felt as though he was St George and had just been handed his sword. The irrationality of the male ego, he derided himself wryly as he rang the TV newsreader he was currently dating and cancelled their evening date.

Half an hour later he had made arrangements ostensibly to travel to Paris to consult with a legal colleague on a matter of international law.

He took the precaution of ringing the French lawyer he knew and arranging to have lunch with him. There was a case he was involved in concerning a French wine label . . . if questioned. His mind ran on, seeking out problems and trying to find answers for them, while all the time he acknowledged the sheer implausibility of what he was setting out to do.

The girl's flight was due to leave Rio two days later, by which time Miles had made all his arrangements. He flew out to Paris as arranged, and if Jacques Premier thought it odd to be asked out to lunch at eleven-thirty in the morning he did not say so. They discussed the problems of international law at some length, and then Miles called for the bill. If the French lawyer was somewhat confused about the purpose of their luncheon engagement he did not show it.

Miles arrived back at the airport just in time to meet Sophie's flight. Luckily his French was fairly good, and the girl at the check-in desk had been all sympathy when he explained that his niece was travelling on the Rio jet bound for Heathrow and that he had intercepted her flight while on business in Paris to give her some very grave news about her father's health.

The stewardess who brought Sophie from the plane was more interested in Miles than in the sulky, unkempt girl at her side. What wouldn't she give to have an uncle like that! she thought enviously as she handed Sophie over into his charge.

"You're not my uncle!" Sophie complained sulkily the moment they were alone.

Miles had taken the precaution of drawing her out of earshot of anyone else. She was dressed like one of a hundred thousand teenagers in jeans and a thin T-shirt, a backpack on the floor beside her. She looked both defiant and wary, and beneath both emotions Miles could sense her fear. If she was frightened so much the better, it made his task all the easier.

"We can't talk here," he told her calmly. "Come on."

He could feel her muscles bunching beneath his fingers as he led her towards the door. If he had to detain her physically she would be no match for him, but he hoped it wouldn't come to that.

"Here, I'll take that . . .".

As he made to take the backpack off her Sophie snatched it back, her face white. So it was true, Miles reflected tiredly. He had hoped . . .

"Who are you, and what do you want?" she demanded.

"I'm a friend of your parents," he told her quietly. "And what I want, or more properly, what I'm here for, is to stop you from being arrested."

Her mouth fell open, but she had herself under control again quickly.

"What for?" she sneered. "Being young?"

"No—smuggling drugs."

Miles watched the way her eyes slid away from his. "You don't know that . . ."

"Oh yes, I do, and so do the police. Why else do you think I'm here?"

Sophie digested what he had to say in a sullen silence, and then objected bitterly,

"I don't believe you! If the police really do think I'm smuggling drugs, why did they let me board the plane in the first place?"

"Because they want to pick up your London contact as well," Miles told her curtly, forcing himself not to give in to his growing desire to give her a good shaking. Didn't she have any conception of what she was doing? No, she didn't. She was a spoilt, petted child, who was defying her family in the most satisfactory way she could imagine, with one blow destroying both her father's career and her stepmother's peace of mind.

"They've already got your boyfriend," he added brutally, watching her pale and flinch.

"Joachim? No—he's too clever . . ."

"You really think so? He doesn't love you, Sophie— he was using you, just as he in turn is being used. Smuggling drugs might be exciting and dangerous to you, but there are others in it purely and simply for money. Do you use the stuff yourself?"

She shook her head and grimaced.

"Do you think I'm a complete fool?"

"So, and yet knowing what they can do you still agreed to bring the stuff back with you?"

Sophie wasn't totally hardened, Miles acknowledged, watching her wince and seeing pain flare briefly in her eyes.

"Have you ever seen anyone *die* from drug abuse?" he asked her harshly. "It isn't an easy death, contrary to what you might imagine. And in my opinion anyone who contributes to that sort of death deserves whatever punishment they get. Don't think I'm doing this for your sake. I'm not."

The fight had gone out of the girl. She looked frightened and sick. Pity for her touched Miles briefly. She was young and vulnerable and had been dragged into the whole sordid situation by men old enough and cynical enough to know how to make best use of teenage rebellion.

"You can't stop me getting back on the plane," she told him.

"No, and I can't stop the French and English police taking you into custody either," he agreed. "No one likes drug pushers . . . you won't have an easy time in prison."

Prison . . . he saw that Sophie hadn't even thought

of that possibility and gave an inward sigh of relief. It was going to be easier than he had thought. She wasn't as hard as he had imagined.

In the end he managed to persuade her to leave the airport with him. He took her into Paris and booked them both into a quiet back-street hotel. When she gave him the incriminating package, he destroyed its contents, his face concentrated in grim disdain.

Afterwards he took her out and bought her an outfit more suitable for the teenage daughter of the Member of Parliament for Rochford West than the scruffy jeans and shirt she was wearing. Once she was reluctantly clad in the neat and unexceptional uniform of a Sloane Ranger teenager, Miles took charge of her passport and ordered a taxi to take them back to the airport.

Luckily they were able to get two empty seats on the next B.A. flight out. Sophie fidgeted impatiently beside him, and he could sense that she was still angry with him. He was aware of the quick silent scrutiny the airport officials gave them before they were allowed through to the departure lounge. Sophie looked like any other demure young schoolgirl in her cotton shirt and pleated skirt.

He could tell that she was stunned by the thoroughness with which their luggage was checked at Heathrow. The passport official stared and then frowned as he checked both their passports, and then they were asked to wait while their luggage was examined.

Sophie went white with shock when she saw the way the Customs officials took her backpack apart, and Miles hoped grimly that she was now aware of the risk she had run. There was no way she would have got through Customs, and he could tell from the grimly bitter expression on the faces of the men who had stopped them that they knew quite well what had happened. However, there was nothing they could do about it. Sophie was not carrying drugs. That did not help Miles to feel any better about the derisory look he was given by the senior Customs official as they were finally let through.

He found a taxi and escorted Sophie home. She sulked all the way, and Miles had seldom been more relieved to rid himself of a woman.

He found himself very uncomfortable with the thanks he received from the girl's father, mainly because had it been anyone else but Amanda who had asked for his help, Miles's own code of morals would have obliged him to have refused.

The whole incident had left an unpleasant taste in his mouth . . . a feeling of having done something Colonel Whitegate would not have considered honourable, but how could he have refused her? He pushed the incident to the back of his mind as one does with things that one feels do not reflect to one's credit.

CHAPTER FOURTEEN

To ISABELLE'S constant and ruefully expressed astonishment, the business she and Pepper started together after leaving college was an almost overnight success.

That this was due as much to Pepper's overwhelming appetite for hard work as to her father's influence and the patronage of his friends was something Isabelle was equally loquacious in mentioning.

Within four weeks of their starting up the business, it became obvious that Pepper was the one with the business brain; it was she who got up at four every morning to be at the markets to get the freshest and cheapest deliveries of foods; it was she who meticulously worked out budgets and profit margins; it was she who was scrupulous about keeping their books in order. Isabelle announced cheerfully that she found that side of their small business a boring chore.

Their first commission had been from Isabelle's father—a luncheon party for the bank's board of directors. Since every one of these gentlemen was related to Isabelle in one form or another, and since all of them had known her since she was a child, the description "sinecure" had slid almost instantly into Pepper's mind. But she was realistic enough to know that the old adage "It's not what you know but who you know that counts in life" was very true, and so she set to work, tactfully coercing Isabelle into the preparation of a menu that would make the board of Kent's bank sit up and take notice.

Alastair Kent was impressed enough to say privately

to his wife that it was one of the best, and most efficiently served lunches he had had in a long time. What he did not say was that the two extremely attractive girls who had served their meal had done nothing to detract from its appeal.

Pepper had learned during her chambermaiding days that male guests were always more ready to overlook a mistake in a pretty face than in a plain one, and she used this information ruthlessly when it came to hiring girls to serve their meals.

Isabelle had said breezily that there was no need for them to hire anyone for this task and that they could do it themselves, but Pepper had demurred, and Pepper had had her way. The sort of amateur, happy-go-lucky type of catering Isabelle was contemplating was not the image that Pepper wanted to project at all.

Within six months they had built up a reputation in City dining rooms that made Alastair Kent tell his wife that he was amazed by what the two girls had achieved.

Dorothea grimaced slightly. She had no illusions. Without Pepper, Isabelle would not have stuck it out for much more than six days, never mind six weeks! Even so, it was rather pleasant to hear that one's daughter was getting a reputation for having just a little more than feathers between her ears. Several of her contemporaries' daughters were doing similar things, and when she and Isabelle went to watch her husband playing polo at Smith's Lawn, it was rather nice to be able to take a maternal pride in her offspring's achievements.

Alastair Kent had been a polo fanatic ever since he was in the Guards. Lucky enough to have the wealth to indulge in such an expensive hobby, he was a member of a team headed by the Duke of Raincourt.

On several occasions during their first year of

business, Pepper was also invited to accompany the family down to the exclusive polo grounds at Hurlingham or Smith's Lawn at Windsor. She observed with a detached and often cynical appreciation the wealthy upper classes at play. This was a world that was as yet closed to the entrepreneurial and the mega-rich of the commercial world, but Pepper could see a day when this might no longer be the case. The polo-playing world was still small and enclosed, but wealth, the kind of wealth that was needed to be able to play this exclusive sport, no longer lay solely in the hands of the old-established families of rank and privilege.

Isabelle made no secret of the fact that she heartily resented these duty attendances. She even tried to persuade Pepper to fib to her mother that they were too busy at work to be able to go, but Pepper refused. Slowly, oh, so slowly, she was beginning to build up a network of contacts and acquaintances. Slowly, oh, so slowly, she was gradually being accepted and absorbed into Isabelle's social circle.

And then almost overnight things changed. Two events were responsible for this change.

The first was that Isabelle met and fell in love with a young ex-Guards officer.

The Honourable Jeremy Forster was everything that Dorothea wanted for her daughter as a husband. He was well connected, and wealthy; he was charming and not too intelligent, with a comfortable London home and a position with his father's stockbroking firm. In short, marriage to Jeremy would fit Isabelle as snugly and comfortably as a handmade glove.

Both families were pleased with the match. There was no need for a long engagement—Isabelle would be married at Christmas. And of course it went without saying that immediately upon the announcement of her engagement, she would cease working. For one thing, she simply wouldn't have enough time.

She explained all this gaily to Pepper the week before her engagement was due to be made public. Pepper accepted the information stoically. She had expected as much, and besides, she thought she had built up sufficient reputation to employ someone else to take her place. Someone from the same social set as Isabelle would be an ideal candidate, and she cast around, mentally wondering who, out of those young women she knew, would best fit into the gap left by Isabelle's departure.

Two days after Isabelle's announcement Pepper received a visit from Neil Kent. Mainly because she had shared so many of Isabelle's social activities she had come to know Neil a good deal better, and discovered that behind his reserved and rather formidable exterior there was a very sensitive and shy young man.

He did occasionally call round to see her when he was in the vicinity of the small Chelsea house she was renting, although normally it was by prearrangement.

It was gone eleven o'clock. She had spent the evening working on the business's accounts, and making out a list of possible substitutes for Isabelle. The previous weekend she had been to Oxford, and even while she knew that as far as both Oliver and herself were concerned, her decision to allow Mary and Philip to adopt him had been the right one, every time she saw him it left her faintly unsettled.

To counteract the feeling of tension that gripped her she had had a long hot soak in a bath full of scented hot water, and now she was wearing the tatty towelling robe she had put on afterwards.

To her Neil was simply Isabelle's brother. Pepper liked him as a person, but sexually she was completely indifferent to him—as indeed she was to all men, but with Neil she felt she did not need to hide behind her carefully cultivated role of a sexually experienced and available woman. She invited him in, conquering her surprise at seeing him.

For once he looked slightly dishevelled, and as he walked past her she smelled the sweetness of spirits on his breath.

Although the Chelsea cottage was rented, Pepper had added some decorating touches of her own. The mint green satinised cotton sofa was a perfect foil for her colouring, but when he sat down on it. it only served to emphasise Neil's sickly pallor.

"Neil, are you all right?"

She heard him groan and watched in dismay as he buried his head in his hands. She had seen too many men in the throes of drunkenness to mistake his condition, but what did shock her was that Neil of all men should arrive on her front door in such a state. He was normally very abstemious. Indeed, Isabelle often made fun of him because of his staid and slightly worthy image.

"I had to see you." The words were muffled by his hands. And as she looked at the vulnerability of his downbent head, for the first time in her life Pepper knew compassion for a man. She reached out to touch him comfortingly, an automatic reaction to his distress, shocked by the way his whole body went rigid under her touch.

Instantly a nebulous but thoroughly frightening alarm began to invade her.

"Neil, what is it? Is something wrong? Isabelle? Your parents?"

"No . . . no, nothing like that," he groaned, still refusing to look at her. "It's me . . . me, Pepper. Oh God, I'm so desperately in love with you! I don't

know what to do, where to turn . . . You fill my
heart and mind to the exclusion of everything else. I
never knew it was possible to feel this way about a
woman. I know you don't love me."

In an appalled silence Pepper watched his shoulders
heave as he struggled to master his feelings.

"I know I'll never be anything more to you than
Isabelle's brother, but wanting you is driving me
insane." He gave a high cracked laugh. "Me, of all
people! I've always thought sex was something I could
control rather than the other way round, but just the
thought of you is enough to send me crazy with
wanting you."

As she listened Pepper felt the chill inside her deepen
and spread, accompanied by a growing sense of panic.
She didn't want to hear any of this. She didn't want
to listen. She wanted Neil to go away. She wanted to
pretend he had never said any of this.

He raised his head and looked at her with tear-
blurred eyes, and she shuddered, knowing what he
was silently begging from her. He wanted her to invite
him into her bed. He wanted to stay here for the night
and make love with her.

She could feel the perspiration breaking out all over
her body, even though the room wasn't over-warm.
She wanted to scream and run, she wanted to blot out
the sight of him. She wanted . . . She shuddered
tensely, her voice hoarse and raw as she whispered
thickly,

"No . . . No! You mustn't want me like that.
I . . . I'm Isabelle's friend, I . . ."

She had no real idea of what she was saying, her
body and mind held in the fierce grip of the panic
clawing through her. It wasn't enough to tell herself
that this was Neil; gentle, kind Neil who wouldn't so
much as crush a spider, because somewhere deep down

inside her all she could think was that he was a man. All she could remember was what another man had done to her. All she wanted was to run away and hide herself from him.

"Pepper, please . . . I want you so much. Please let me!"

He was reaching for her. Her whole body froze in shock and rejection as his fingers touched her wrist. She wanted to turn and run, and she just couldn't move. A scream bubbled up in her throat. She opened her mouth and found that her throat muscles had paralysed with fear.

"Pepper, what is it?"

The doorbell rang, the sharp sound cutting through the thick tense silence. Instantly Neil released her, and her fear evaporated, and she was once more her usual self, in control, self-assured.

She went to the door and opened it.

"Hi, I've just dropped Jeremy off at his club and I thought I'd drop round and see you on my way home. Were you just on your way to bed?"

There was no way Pepper could stop Isabelle from walking into the sitting room, and no way either she could prevent her from leaping to the conclusions she saw in her eyes as they went first to her brother and then back to Pepper.

"Oh dear, I'm rather de trop, aren't I? I had no idea . . ."

"Neil was just calling in for a chat," Pepper told her firmly, knowing as she did so that there was no way Isabelle would believe her.

As she had known she would, her friend grinned.

"Ok—it's ok. I'm broadminded," she assured them both with a teasing smile. "How long has this been going on? I never guessed a thing . . . Pepper, you cheat! You might have told me. Is it serious?"

"Isabelle, it's nothing. Neil just called round by chance, just like you."

But it was no good. Isabelle wasn't going to believe her, Pepper recognised, not even when Neil elected to leave with her.

As all three of them stood in the small hallway, Isabelle turned her head and whispered in Pepper's ear,

"Sorry I spoiled your fun. Poor Neil, he's so staid and stuffy, the poor old dear. I suppose he thinks it might be setting me a bad example if he stays the night now." She gave a deep chuckle. "Much he knows!"

Of course it was too much to hope that Isabelle would keep her conclusions to herself. She was far too delighted at the thought of gaining her friend for a sister-in-law for that. Even so, Pepper was surprised when she received a telephone call at home one evening from Isabelle's father, asking if he could some round.

She had rather less contact with Alastair Kent than she had with the rest of the family, but she had always found him to be a fair, although somewhat aloof man, who still considered that women had a specific role in the scheme of things and that this role did not include the cut-and-thrust of business activities. Even so, he was an intelligent man and one who did not believe in wasting time in getting to the point.

He arrived punctually, on the dot of nine. Pepper led him to her small sitting room and offered him a drink. He refused.

"Isabelle tells me that you and Neil are rather involved," he began without preamble. "Is it true?"

Pepper, shrewder and more worldly by far than Isabelle, knew exactly why and what he was asking.

"Not as far as I'm concerned," she responded honestly, meeting his questioning look head on. She paused, choosing her words carefully. "Neil believes that he has feelings for me which he thinks are much stronger than they actually are." She paused delicately, and Alastair Kent relaxed a little.

Good, the girl was being sensible and open about the whole thing. He had half expected that she might be. It wasn't that he didn't like her. Pleasant enough girl and sharp as a needle, but not the wife they had in mind for Neil . . .

"And you . . . you don't share Neil's feelings?" he probed, watching her.

Pepper lifted her head.

"No, I don't. I want to make a career for myself, Mr Kent." She hesitated and then took a deep breath. "Marriage does not play any part in the way I visualise my life at the moment."

Subtly she had let him know both the depth of Neil's feelings for her, and her own reaction to them. She wanted it made perfectly plain that there was no question of there being any furtive sexual relationship between Neil and herself, or indeed of her ever even considering contemplating one.

Alastair Kent frowned. The affair was obviously more serious than he and Dorothea had realised. Although they had never spoken openly of their plans to Neil, they had been gently steering him in the direction of Alastair's cousin's girl; making sure that he accompanied them to Scotland in August, and then again in the New Year.

Fiona Campbell had the kind of lineage and background that made her eminently suitable to become Neil's wife, and in addition to that she was her father's sole heir. The crumbling castle and its grouse moors might not have a great deal of monetary value, but it had a heritage, a history that Alastair Kent valued far more. And now for this to happen!

Neil was a sensible enough lad—most of the time, but he was inclined sometimes to venture into a certain degree of sentimentality that his father suspected he must have inherited from his mother's family. It was no good appealing to his common sense, but Pepper was a different proposition.

He had not been quite sure how he would tackle the problem when he arrived. He had half expected tears and tantrums, pleas even. This cool, self-possessed rejection of his son's feelings had come as both a relief and a slight shock. It was the first time in his life he had ever heard of a woman decrying marriage in favour of a career, and he wasn't quite sure how to respond to it.

He and Dorothea had both discussed the matter. There had even been a mutual but soon dismissed suggestion that perhaps the offer of money . . .

"She won't take it," Dorothea had opined, slightly regretfully, conscience forcing her to add, "and she is one of Isabelle's friends . . ."

Left unsaid, but there nonetheless was the tacit understanding that friend of Isabelle's Pepper might be, but she was not really "one of us", not really totally socially acceptable. Even without the fact that they wanted Neil to marry Fiona, they would not have wanted him to marry Pepper.

Alastair Kent shifted uncomfortably.

"Well, you will understand, Pepper," he began with false heartiness, "that Dorothea and I have certain . . . plans for Neil." He avoided looking at her. There was something about that clear-eyed unwavering stare that increased his discomfort. Which was ridiculous when one took into account the fact that he was a partner in a reputable and highly professional merchant bank, while she was nothing more than one of his daughter's friends.

"You want me to tell him he's wasting his time. I've already done that," Pepper told him crisply.

"Well, yes . . . I'm sorry to say that I don't think that would be enough. Both his mother and I feel that it would be better if . . . well, if the pair of you didn't come into contact with one another for a time."

Pepper said nothing. She had already learned not to make it easy for any would-be adversary, and as though her silence somehow unsettled him, Alastair shifted awkwardly, his frown deepening.

Originally he and Dorothea had thought of sending Neil away for a time. They had cousins in America, although God knew what on earth Neil would find to do on a cattle ranch. It was already decided that he would follow his father into the bank, and really Alastair wanted him there now so that he could begin teaching him all that he himself knew.

He had come tonight to see Pepper chiefly to find out the lie of the land. Now that he knew she had no intention of encouraging Neil's infatuation with her, he needed to discuss the whole affair again with Dorothea. She was always much better than he at making this sort of decision.

Pepper's control and self-possession had thrown him. It wasn't what he had expected, and as he made his excuses and stood up he was visited by the uncomfortable realisation that had she actually wanted Neil, there would have been precious little he could have done to stop her from having him.

That realisation left him both disturbed and discomfited. It was not a good state of affairs for a senior partner of a merchant bank to feel that he was in a position where he could be bested by a little chit the same age as his daughter.

He said as much to Dorothea when he got home. She pursed her lips and shook her head. She was as alarmed as her husband. She contemplated making an appeal to Pepper to absent herself completely from their lives, but regretfully renounced it. It held too many pitfalls and problems.

"It's a pity that Pepper doesn't want to make her career in cattle raising," she said eventually with a rare touch of humour. "Then we could have sent *her* out of the way to your cousin's."

As though their conversation was an omen, the very next day, when Alastair was interviewing a potential client from America over a very formal lunch at his club, the latter told him that he was looking for a young woman to work for him as his P.A.

"You know the style of thing . . . one of your classy English girls, with a laid-back accent and the right connections. They're all the rage in New York at the moment."

Concealing his distaste, Alastair listened politely. His client was one of a new breed of amazingly wealthy entrepreneurs who almost made a virtue of bragging how they had amassed their new-found wealth. In the case of this particular man he had made his initial fortune by representing American sports stars and acting as their go-between-cum-agent in sponsorship deals.

He spent almost the entire luncheon describing to Alastair in detail how he had pulled off a succession of deals, but Alastair wasn't really listening. This could be the answer to his problem. Clever, ambitious Pepper could just be what this brash American was looking for.

He cleared his throat and interrupted his guest in mid-monologue.

"I think I know a girl who might suit you. A friend of my daughter's . . ."

"Classy, is she?" Victor Orlando asked, narrowing

his eyes. "The type of broad that's got plenty of SA?"

Hiding his distaste, Alastair said carefully,

"I think you'll find that Pepper will more than suit your requirements."

"Ok, give me her number. I'll call her."

Alastair frowned. Not even his desire to remove his son from the dangers of his infatuation for her would allow him to agree to place Pepper in such a potentially embarrassing situation.

"I think it would be better if I arranged a meeting," he said carefully. "Perhaps dinner one night . . . I won't say anything to Pepper beforehand."

"Sounds good to me. Gives me a chance to get a look at her without her putting on any special airs and graces, eh? Good thinking!"

Inwardly wondering which of their friends were least likely to be offended by the American's unfortunate manner, Alastair discreetly signalled for his bill.

The biggest hurdle would be Pepper herself. She had said herself that she was ambitious, and he suspected that working for Victor Orlando would be far more stimulating and demanding than running her own small catering business.

Alastair discussed the whole thing with Dorothea that evening.

"Well, she may agree to it," she said uncertainly, "but he sounds a dreadful man, Alastair."

"Pepper will cope with him."

Pepper did.

Dorothea Kent, who was not as sure as her husband that they should say nothing to Pepper about the purpose of the dinner party, called round at the Chelsea house when she knew Pepper would be there. Frankly and determinedly she told Pepper what the purpose of the dinner party really was.

"It could be an excellent opportunity for you," she explained.

And for you, Pepper thought cynically, saying nothing, instead reserving her judgement.

She disliked Victor Orlando on sight, recognising him as the very worst kind of male chauvinist bully, but the job as his P.A. was too tempting to pass up.

It took Victor less than six days to proposition her, and it took Pepper less than six minutes to convince him that not only was he wasting his time, but also that she could be of more value to him out of his bed than in it.

Thereafter an uneasy truce developed. Victor flew back to New York, leaving Pepper to follow him.

She arrived in the city in the first few days of the fall. It was quite a culture shock to discover women dressed in heavy tweeds in weather that would be considered hot at home, but New York was like that. On the first day of fall women wore fall clothes no matter what the weather, and Pepper quickly realised that she was going to have to follow suit.

As a gesture of goodwill, Isabelle's mother had arranged living accommodation for her, through her network of friends, and Pepper was sharing an apartment with the daughter of one of her friends, in a walk-up block in Greenwich Village.

Lucy Sanders was very like Isabelle, but she had a better defined sense of humour and a shrewdness that the other girl had lacked. She made Pepper welcome in a careless sort of fashion, once she had assured herself that Pepper hadn't been chosen by her mother to spy on her.

"Ma wants me to go home and get married, but that isn't what I want from life. New York is a crazy city and I love it—far more than I like the idea of marriage. A woman can be whatever she wants to be here." Lucy pulled a face and grimaced. "Provided she's prepared to be it without a man. They're a commodity that's in very short supply!"

Victor's offices were in an extremely expensive building on Madison Avenue, and Pepper soon accustomed herself to the advertising hype she heard all around her in the bars and restaurants.

Lucy introduced her to some of her friends, a gregarious crowd mainly involved in the theatre and design world, and Pepper soon became accustomed to listening to conversations that dealt almost exclusively with the latest off-Broadway shows. It was in New York that she put the final unmistakable gloss to her new persona.

Victor was a demanding employer and she had a lot to learn, but there was still time for dates with Lucy's friends, and business acquaintances she met through Victor. When she did date she employed the same tactics she had used at home, taking care only to date men whose own opinion of their sexuality would not allow them to admit to anyone that they had not taken her to bed. It was a wise ploy, establishing for her a very safe barrier behind which she could conceal the truth.

In the six months she was in New York she learned to call pavements "sidewalks", honed the perfection of the classy English accent; shopped at Bergdorf's and a variety of small food shops in SoHo; learned where to buy the cheapest designer clothes and where to get her hair cut, and beautiful though Central Park was in early spring, she was not sorry when the time came to leave.

Victor Orlando was astounded with her business flair—so astounded in fact that he very quickly sent her back to London to do the groundwork which would allow him to set up a similar sort of operation in London to the one he had in the States.

By the time Pepper got back Neil was safely married and living in Scotland. Isabelle welcomed her back affectionately, and she was very quickly drawn into the small élite upper-class circle she had inhabited before she left. She had an extra gloss now, a patina which once applied to her cool British upper-class accent and manner made her instantly stand out in a crowd. A good many men propositioned her, some even fell in love with her, but she had become skilled at holding them all at bay without causing offence. To one she would claim that she was involved with another, and to another that she was still heavily emotionally involved with a third. Only she knew the reason she kept them all well away from her bed. Only she knew the way she tensed up and froze when an unknown male so much as reached out and touched her.

Pepper was not stupid. She knew why she felt the way she did. She even knew how she might be able to overcome those feelings. An expensive and fashionable analyst would only add to the prestige she already had, but something told her that no amount of analysis, expensive and fashionable or otherwise, could undo the damage that Simon Herries had done. It would be with her all her life, and something atavistic and primitive deep down inside her hinted that perhaps she even deserved it, although she couldn't have said why.

Just as she couldn't have said why she still kept in touch with Mary and Philip. After all, she needed nothing from them now. She had her life and they had theirs, and they had nothing in common. Except Oliver.

Regular reports on Oliver still arrived from Mary, photographs, long newsy letters. Mary was not going to allow Pepper to simply vanish out of their lives, and even while part of her resented it, part of her rejoiced in it.

She had been back in London, working hard to establish the kind of network Victor would need, for six weeks when she had her first intimation of where the future of her life might lie.

Tennis and baseball were Victor's major sports, and Pepper had an appointment with a new up-and-coming tennis sportswear manufacturer in Berkshire who was keen to launch a new and expensive range of tennis wear, and who wanted an equally expensive and fashionable tennis star to sponsor it.

Pepper had heard about the company through one of her many contacts, and as she drove down to her late morning appointment with the sales director, she mentally reviewed all that she knew about them. The company was headed by a new and very dynamic boss who had acquired the sportswear company as part and parcel of a bigger deal. He was now completely revamping its image, and Pepper was hoping to persuade him that the as yet rather young but potentially very successful tennis player she had her eye on as one of Victor's first British sports stars would be an ideal candidate to become associated with the new label.

As she drove, Pepper mentally reviewed everything she knew about the company and its head. Nick Howarth was thirty years old. He had inherited a small scrap metal business from his father when he was eighteen, and in twelve short years he had built it up into a multi-million-pound business empire. She had heard about him through contacts in the business world. She still kept in contact with Alastair Kent, and Alastair was grateful enough to her for her co-operation over Neil's infatuation to give her the odd bit of information he thought might be useful to her.

A little to his own surprise he had found that he had come to like as well as admire Pepper. He sensed that she had lost nothing of that integrity which he had been so aware of being an intrinsic part of her, while she was in New York, and that he admired. It was so easy to be seduced by the lure of money and power, and Pepper had plainly not succumbed to it. She was still the same cool, self-assured young woman who had so disconcerted him.

In Nick Howarth, Pepper recognised a kindred spirit straight away. He was wickedly attractive, with almost wheat-blond hair and cool green eyes, tall and very lithe, sexually powerful in a way that very few men are. Even Pepper was aware of his sexuality, which was both heightened and muted at the same time by the rigidness of his immaculately pin-striped suit and white shirt.

Here was a man who liked using disguises, she recognised, a man who was well versed in the art of melting into his surroundings. What did he want from life that he didn't already have? she wondered thoughtfully. Pepper had learned in New York that it was the desire for new and more possessions that kept the commercial world turning, and where no such need existed—well then, it had to be manufactured.

What did *this* man want? she wondered, smiling dulcetly at him across the width of his desk.

The report she had prepared on her proposals lay on the blotter. Nick Howarth smiled at her, his smile as vulpine and controlled as her own.

"Well now, I must say your report packs a pretty powerful punch—very powerful indeed." He looked at her. "Are you sure that using such a very junior tennis player is a good idea, though? Wouldn't a more well known name be better?"

He was trying to throw her, to disconcert her and take the advantage, Pepper recognised.

"An *establishment* image?" she questioned thoughtfully, lifting an eyebrow.

He had made it plain enough that the image he wanted for the company was one of verve and style, and she hid her smile as she saw him check and frown. Round one to her, but round one wasn't the entire game.

He shrugged gracefully, as though humouring her.

"Perhaps you're right. But this young man . . ." he looked down at her file, "Tony Richmond, he looks promising now, but he's only, what? Sixteen. How do we know that he's not going to burn out in three months' time and never make it?"

Pepper showed him her teeth and said coolly,

"How did you know that you would make it, Mr Howarth? It's part of my job to be able to recognise and channel the kind of ambition that makes successes, not failures. That's why Victor Orlando chose me to set up the British side of his business."

"Umm . . . I was wondering about that. You do the work and Victor collects the prizes."

She smiled again, refusing to be drawn.

"I do have another appointment." She glanced at her watch. "I appreciate that what I'm suggesting is rather . . . radical, rather more . . . adventurous perhaps than you might want."

She was watching him and could see that he didn't like that. And well he might not. She had heard on the grapevine that he prided himself on his innovative style and flair.

"Perhaps you'd like a few more days to think it over?" she finished. She stood up, then tensed as he said abruptly,

"What are you doing this weekend?"

Normally they waited a little longer before propositioning her, but she had heard that Nick Howarth was a man in a hurry.

"I'm watching polo at Windsor," she told him truthfully. "A friend of mine's husband plays and she's invited me to spend the weekend."

It was true. Isabelle, newly pregnant and bored, had demanded her company, and Pepper hadn't been able to think of an excuse quickly enough to refuse.

"Polo?" queried Nick.

"You know, the game of kings," she told him flippantly, then realised that he was watching her closely. Her scalp prickled, all her senses alive and alert. Had she, albeit unknowingly, discovered his Achilles heel? Carelessly she added, "If you wished you could join us. I'm sure my friend wouldn't mind."

Childishly she crossed her fingers behind her back. She was taking a gamble based on instinct alone, something she very, very rarely did.

"You move in very exclusive circles for a PA. Polo is a very establishment sport. You might almost call it a closed shop." Nick Howarth laughed, but there was no amusement in his eyes. She had been right, Pepper thought, tiny goosebumps of excitement rising on her skin. Here was a very rich and a very successful man who wanted something he couldn't have. Adrenalin charged through her like electricity. Perhaps after all there might be a way she could persuade him to accept her plans. If so . . .

"Isabelle and I were at college together in Oxford. You may know her father—he's Alastair Kent.

"He plays in the Duke of Raincourt's team, doesn't he?" Nick Howarth responded, inadvertently telling her exactly what she wanted to know. No one who was not almost obsessed by the sport would have used that description of Isabelle's father, and especially not

someone who might more reasonably be expected to
say something along the lines of "Oh yes . . . the
banker, I know him."

"I really must go now . . . but if you want to join
us, please give me a ring. You have my number."

He was too careful and too experienced to commit
himself there and then, Pepper recognised, and she
would have thought less of him if he had. All the way
back to London she wondered if he would take the
bait. If she had judged him correctly. If . . . So many
ifs . . . but then life was composed of them, wasn't
it?

Nick rang her on Friday evening, quite late on
Friday evening, just as she was about to leave the
office, his voice carefully free of any hint of any
enthusiasm.

"If the offer's still on for Saturday, it might be a
good opportunity for us to discuss your plans in more
detail. I'm off to Paris on Sunday morning and I
shan't be back for some time."

Accepting his face-saving explanation, Pepper
demurely agreed to his suggestion. Isabelle and Jeremy
had recently bought a house several miles from
Windsor. She gave him directions as to how to find it,
and then phoned her friend.

Isabelle, scatterbrained as always, offered no objec-
tions when Pepper told her what she had arranged.

The afternoon went just as Pepper had hoped. Nick
Howarth was totally involved and enthralled with the
game. She had the lever she needed to make him agree
to her sponsorship plans, and she had got that lever
quite by chance.

Only days ago, Isabelle had happened to mention
that one of Jeremy's friends, an ex-Guards player, was
hoping to set up a new team, but that he couldn't find
enough potential players wealthy enough to make up

a full team.

Nick didn't join them for dinner, and when she got the opportunity to do so, Pepper discreetly sounded out her friend's husband on the subject of how his friend might feel about a new player who could well be in a position to underwrite the major proportion of their expenses.

"Well, it's the coming thing, isn't it?" Jeremy admitted. "The old guard don't care for it, but even HRH has said that if the game is to succeed, it needs new money to support it. Let's face it, there just isn't enough of the old stuff left to support it."

Pepper let that one pass and pressed on.

"So the team wouldn't be averse to—well, let's say at this stage, just talking to someone who might be interested in underwriting it?"

"Well, that depends on who it is." Jeremy could be shrewd enough when he wanted to be, and he looked at her consideringly. "Are we talking vaguely here or are we talking specifics?"

Pepper took a deep breath. "I was thinking of Nick Howarth."

There was a long pause and then Jeremy said thoughtfully,

"Well, he seems a decent enough sort of chappie . . . Not one of us, of course. It would have to go before the rest of the team. I could sound them out . . ."

A week later Pepper rang Nick Howarth and asked if she could see him. Over lunch she put to him her proposals that in addition to sponsoring an up-and-coming tennis star, he might also fancy getting his design team to come up discreetly with something new but subtle for a brand new polo team that was being formed.

"Several ex-members of the Guards team will be in

it. They're very keen to recruit, and . . ." she paused,
delicately sensing his tension and deliberately drawing
it out, "there could be a chance that they're also
looking for some sponsorship money, discreetly given
of course . . ."

Nick Howarth knew when he had met his match.

"How much, and what's in it for you?" he asked.

Pepper named a sum that he seemed to accept
without so much as blinking an eyelid, then added
coolly,

"And of course sponsorship of my up-and-coming
tennis player."

He frowned and for one appalled moment she
thought he meant to refuse. When he did speak he
said in surprise,

"That's all? Nothing for you . . . no . . . special
payment, no little sweetener?"

Pepper looked coldly at him.

"That isn't the way I do business."

"Well then, you're out of line with your boss," he
told her frankly. "And Pepper, let me give you some
advice. Orlando will drain you dry and then toss you
on one side when he's finished with you. Don't look
to him for concern or loyalty, because you won't get
it." He frowned and then added, "Have you ever
thought of going it alone?" He saw her expression
and smiled.

"Ah, so now I've found something that *you* want,"
he said softly.

And so it began. Pepper owed Victor nothing. She
gave him her notice and set up her own company.

Her very first deals were the ones she organised
between her tennis player and Nick Howarth, and
between Nick and Jeremy's new polo team. The
commission she earned on those deals alone was more

than she would have made in ten years of work for Victor.

Victor was furious with her. He gave interviews in the sports press verbally assaulting her, but they did her no harm. Rather they simply enhanced her reputation. A woman who could get the better of Victor Orlando was one tough cookie indeed, and within a surprisingly short period of time Pepper discovered that the sports stars were the ones coming to her, rather than the other way round.

Her foot was on the first rung of the ladder of success, and for the first time she was able to give her time and attention to something else. To Simon Herries, for instance, and to retribution.

She made discreet enquiries and found out the name and address of the best private investigator London could boast.

A man like Simon Herries, who enjoyed violence and degradation for its own sake, was not going to stop at one little rape. Oh no . . . sooner or later he would step out of line again, and when he did . . . She could afford to wait, Pepper reasoned. And she *would* wait . . . for however long it took.

CHAPTER FIFTEEN

MILES frowned as he surveyed the flimsy sheets of A4 paper on his desk. They might not be as detailed as Pepper's files, but each of them contained enough information to make him realise how very real and appropriate her threats of retribution were.

It was remarkable how much she had achieved in the years since Oxford, and along with the pity and anger he had felt all those years before was a growing admiration. And more, he admitted. There was a sense of comradeship . . . of pride almost, that he knew sprang from the fact that like himself Pepper had come through much adversity to achieve her present-day success.

This intense awareness he had of her as a person had a logical basis; both of them were after a fashion orphans; both of them had endured hardship and a sense of separateness as children; both of them had been lucky in having someone in their lives whose kindness and caring enabled them to rise above these setbacks and to go on and achieve their ambitions.

Miles, however, had not been savagely raped at the age of seventeen.

He had occasionally dealt with rape cases and he thought he had taught himself to adopt the correct distancing logic; to evaluate the facts without allowing his emotions to hold sway.

He remembered his first rape case as a junior barrister. The woman had been in her thirties, and nothing like Pepper, and yet all through the case it had been Pepper's body he had seen, Pepper's terrified condemning eyes.

She was, he acknowledged grimly, woven into the very fabric of his life in a way that he had not even previously recognised. He had never forgotten her, and perhaps even, who could tell, she had indirectly been responsible for his own attitude to the women in his life. He abhorred inflicting pain, either emotional or physical, and perhaps that was why he never allowed himself to get too involved with any of his lovers. There was always something of himself that he held back.

In the same way that Pepper held much of herself back.

Miles moved restlessly in his chair. He was here to evaluate the situation with a cold and critical eye, dammit, not to wallow in sentimentality. But he couldn't stop thinking about her; about the vulnerability so apparent to him and yet, it seemed, hidden from everyone else.

From the moment he had seen Pepper sitting behind that damned desk delivering her ultimatums he had ached to protect her; to cherish her and let her see that with him she need never be afraid.

He had wanted women before, but never like this. He admired women who made their own way in life, independent, slightly acid women who could match him intellectually as well as physically, and he had never, apart from Amanda, wanted to protect them. Pepper touched something inside him that was an elemental part of his life; a deep well-spring of emotion. It was almost as though some part of him had always known they would meet again and that she would be part of his life.

He wanted to go to her and plead with her to retract her demands, to make her see the risk she was running; to show her how dangerous Simon Herries really was, but he knew she wouldn't even listen to him, never mind believe him.

The frustration of not being able to talk to her, to show her . . . To show her what? he asked himself wryly. To show her how much he wanted her? He could just imagine her reaction to that!

At the time she had delivered her ultimatums he had acted impulsively, doing the first thing that came into his head to protect her. Would it work? It could do, if he could manage to convince the world at large that the pair of them were lovers.

Which brought him back to the problem of Simon Herries. Simon hadn't liked him taking charge—Simon didn't trust him, he had seen that much in his eyes. Miles was going to be walking a tightrope between the two of them. Herries would check every move he made, he knew that. No, for Pepper's own sake it was better that she continue to believe he had been a party to her rape.

He suspected she didn't realise how very dangerous Simon Herries actually was . . . Miles frowned again as he picked up the sheet of paper relating to Simon Herries. Pepper knew about his violent streak, of course. Against his will his mind replayed back for him in faultless detail the scene in his room at Oxford the night that Simon had raped her. Yes, he could understand how a woman would want to exact retribution for an act such as that.

Richard and Alex he dismissed as being merely pawns caught up in the real game; they posed no true threat to Pepper; not in the way that Simon Herries did.

His researcher had penned a handwritten note at the bottom of Simon Herries' sheet, and he read it thoughtfully. It seemed that Simon Herries had returned from Cumbria after what was an annual family holiday without his wife and children and that moreover the staff at the London house had not seen Elizabeth Herries or her two children since the day she left to join Simon in the country. She had left him, obviously, but why? And why had he not made any attempt to gain custody of his children? A man like Simon Herries, ambitious, driven by a powerful need to succeed, could scarcely be blind to the fact that it could only improve his public image if he was seen to be a caring father, especially since Elizabeth seemed to have been the one to have left him. She had not gone to her family in Boston, so the researcher had established.

Miles leaned back in his chair thoughtfully, putting Elizabeth Herries out of his mind and concentrating instead on Pepper. He had been a lawyer for long enough to know that there were men, perfectly respectable, upright and honest men, who genuinely believed that no good decent woman was ever raped. He had seen some of his colleagues waste years of their lives trying to show them otherwise, and he himself had come face to face with the reality of mindless and appalling violence in too many of its various forms to be naïve about it any more. Even so, what he read in the brief report worried him.

He had always known about Simon's homosexual tendencies, but he had hitherto dismissed them as youthful experimentation—Herries hadn't been the only student to indulge in that particular form of gratification and then later produce both a wife and a family—but this statement about young boys being picked up off the street and then left half beaten to death. There was no evidence to corroborate it; it was merely a comment, but Miles was a lawyer and he knew that the most respectable and reputable of men could have the most secret lives.

He had seen the shock and hatred in Simon's eyes when Pepper handed them her ultimatum and he had no illusions about how Simon felt about her. He would have killed her on the spot if he could.

As he had once before, he felt again that in Simon Herries' case the thin line dividing sanity and madness was very fragile indeed in places. His hatred of Pepper was almost obsessional—a sure sign of a deranged mind.

If he could prove it, get the man committed even if only temporarily . . . but Miles knew already that that wasn't the answer. He told himself that there was no reason for him to be involved. Even if Pepper did reveal the truth he doubted that it would have much effect on his career. He was not in as vulnerable a position as the others; he could afford to turn his back on her and walk away, but he knew he wasn't going to.

He was attracted to her—he might as well admit it. Attracted to her and challenged by her. And he was also increasingly afraid for her. She was a very brave and courageous woman, and in some ways he admired the stand she had taken, but she didn't know the danger she was putting herself in.

If he hadn't stepped in and taken matters into his own hands by assuming command he suspected that Herries would have gone to almost any lengths to silence her, even murder.

And maybe not for the first time.

All kinds of gossip had gone the rounds at Oxford after Tim Wilding's death; the kind of macabre black-humoured jokes that undergraduates delight in. Then he had dismissed the whole thing as merely another speculative item of gossip. Now . . . Miles frowned again . . . there was no doubt in his mind that

Herries had some sort of hold over the other two. He had watched them carefully and observed the way they allowed him to take control. Alex Barnett he could understand—he had never been a particularly forceful type, but Richard Howell . . .

It made no difference to the outcome of Pepper's attempt to blackmail them, of course, but still it might be interesting to see just how and why Herries held them in his power.

It was his lawyer's mind that hated loose ends, Miles told himself as he checked in his diary and then rang through to his office.

His clerk wasn't used to him cancelling appointments at such short notice, and Miles grinned to himself as he heard the disapproval in the older man's voice. Barristers' clerks were the real power in chambers; they ran and ruled the small élite world, and woe betide anyone who didn't acknowledge it.

Now that he had the week free, he needed to decide what he intended to do with it. He couldn't afford to waste too much time. Herries would soon grow impatient, he suspected, and even if he were of a mind to warn Pepper Minesse of the danger he suspected she was courting he doubted if she would listen to him.

He packed a small case and booked himself into a hotel on the outskirts of Oxford. He had friends in the area whom he could visit, and thus kill two birds with one stone. He had a godson in Oxford whom he hadn't seen since he was christened, and if he was lucky and everything went according to plan he might just have sufficient time to be able to call at the Manor on the way back.

Colonel Whitegate's heir had not been able to maintain the house for very long, and when it eventually came on the market Miles had helped to raise the money to buy it and convert it into a home for mentally handicapped children. Whenever he was in the area, he tried to make time to call in, and to visit the orphanage where he had been brought up. Things had changed since his day, but he still recognised the intense loneliness and apartness of the children there, and he knew it was something that no amount of community care and charity could ever wipe out. It was a burden they would have to carry all their lives. Something they would have to come to terms with as he had done.

Like him, there would be times when they would yearn desperately for a family of their own; when they would question what it was they had done that had put them in such a place, but he also hoped that like him, as time went by, they would be able to develop enough self-confidence to realise that the blame was not theirs. He had had to do so. There were times when he had been tempted to try to trace his parents, but he had seen too often the outcome of such heart-breaking searches to believe that it would really solve the problems that being deserted as a child had fostered.

He was one of the lucky ones, he acknowledged. He had found the strength to put the past behind him and go on into the future. Many others did not.

He knew quite well what had brought on this introspective mood. He looked down at the two sheets of closely typed paper again. This was the dossier his informant had prepared on Pepper. One fact leapt glaringly off the paper again and again. During the time she had been staying with the Simms, Mary Simms had produced a son. Was Miles being unduly suspicious? Was it not, after all, possible that a woman of forty might well conceive after fifteen years of marriage despite the fact that she had previously had a history of miscarriages?

And yet by his reckoning the child had been born just about nine months after the night Simon Herries had raped Pepper. Coincidence, or . . .

Miles could feel the beginning of a migraine building up behind his skull. Too much tension, too many late nights. For the first time in his life, the variety of a constant parade of women through his life was beginning to pall. Marriage had always been something he had scrupulously avoided. He didn't have what it took to make a permanent commitment, he had often told himself. He had tried to put himself in Pepper's mind . . . to imagine what it would have been like to be that seventeen-year-old, alone in the world. The Simms had taken her in. Might she not out of gratitude to them have . . . have given them her child?

He thought of the controlled, triumphant woman behind that imposing desk and grimaced wryly. It seemed too out of character. He was after all simply leaping to conclusions. But what if these conclusions were the right ones? What if Pepper had actually borne Herries a child?

He tried to think of the sort of heritage a child of that conception might carry, and acknowledged, not for the first time, that sometimes it was in a child's interests for it not to know its antecedents.

It was a disturbing, challenging thought and he pushed it to one side. Every instinct he possessed—and he was that rare kind of man who did not take his instincts lightly—told him that Pepper Minesse was in danger. But how to remove her from it, and at the same time not alert Simon's suspicions? Because he was suspicious, Miles had seen it in his eyes. He had not liked having control of the situation taken from him.

Simon Herries was a man poised on the edge of a

chasm which if successfully crossed could lead on to the peak, the ultimate seat of power, or so he believed. Pepper was a burden coiled round his ankles, and he would kick her down into the chasm without a qualm to free himself if he had to, without even realising that she could, by clinging to him, drag him down there with her.

Herries, Miles suspected, had no awareness of the real harshness of life. He seemed to believe himself inviolate, and Miles believed he was dangerous enough to kill if he had to. He wouldn't get away with it, of course. He would be caught and there would be a cause célèbre in the papers for a few weeks, but none of that would breathe life back into Pepper's corpse.

No . . . somehow he had to get Pepper away.

His phone rang and he picked it up. It was his secretary, reminding him that he was due to meet a client later in the day. He had been asked to represent a women's refuge in North London who were having problems with their landlord. The popular press were beginning to refer to him as a knight in shining armour, always ready to champion the underdog. It wasn't quite true, but Miles's own upbringing left him with a strong sense of gratitude, a need in some small way to pay back the kindness and generosity he himself had received, and so from time to time he took on these cases virtually free of charge.

He made a note of the appointment and went back to his mental résumé of his progress with Pepper. His campaign to establish himself as her would-be lover was well in hand. He had bombarded her office with flowers and telephone calls, and had even on one occasion parked his car virtually on her doorstep.

Pepper had seen him as she emerged from her office and had determinedly turned her back on him. In other circumstances Miles would have found the challenge of breaking through barriers an intoxicating one, but because he knew the reason behind her hatred of him he felt no amusement at her behaviour.

The security guards at both her office and home now recognised him. Pepper had told them both that she wanted nothing to do with him. He had countered by telling them that he and Pepper were lovers who had quarrelled. Two newspaper gossip columns had run items on them, both carefully and deliberately leaked by himself. As far as the world was concerned, it would no longer be surprised to hear their names linked together. All very well as far as it went, but Miles was still a long, long way from keeping her safe from Simon.

He was due to play squash this evening and then he was having dinner at his club. He needed the expertise of a doctor, and he thought he knew where he could get it.

This weekend in Oxford he would find out as much as he could about Herries' activities while he was there, and then next week—Miles checked a list he had on his desk. It covered all Pepper's social engagements for the coming fortnight. His eyebrows lifted slightly as he saw that she was due to attend the polo match at Smith's Lawn on Saturday. Windsor wasn't that far from Oxford. The father of his godson was a polo aficionado who used to play for the Guards.

The gods, it seemed, were smiling on him.

The women's refuge was in a run-down, shabby building, down a narrow side street. It was a Victorian villa with a narrow strip of front garden. As Miles rang the bell he could hear a child crying, a thin wailing, despairing sound.

The woman who opened the door to him looked at

him cautiously. She was in her thirties, blonde and too thin.

Miles introduced himself and saw her expression lighten. Had she thought he was an angry husband come in pursuit of a runaway wife?

It wasn't really so amusing. He knew that it happened.

The woman who ran the refuge was an ex-nurse. She took Miles into the room she used as her office and outlined the problems she was having with the landlord, explaining that he was trying to increase their rent.

"Most of the women who come here have no money; they can't afford to pay their way, and so we're funded in the main by whatever we can raise. Quite frankly, it isn't enough to line the pockets of a greedy landlord."

They talked for a while, while Miles decided how best he could help, then Sarah James offered him a cup of tea. He accepted, and Sarah disappeared for several minutes, returning to announce that tea would not be long. As she opened the door Miles heard the sound of children's voices.

"Just back from school," Sarah explained. "We send two mothers with them to take and collect them just to make sure they aren't snatched by their fathers. It does happen," she assured him. "Violent men don't like losing control of their wives, and they're quite ready to use any means they can to blackmail them into going back; even if that means hurting their own children."

"And do they?" Miles asked her.

She looked at him and frowned.

"We don't handle cases of child abuse here, if that's what you mean. We aren't qualified to; that's a matter for the proper authorities, although getting a woman to tell them exactly what's going on isn't always easy. We've a case in point now . . . a woman with two children. She came to us some time ago. Her husband had been violent to her throughout her marriage, but she's only recently discovered that he's also been sexually abusing their son. She knows she ought to report him, but she's too terrified to do so. She's worried that she won't be believed, and that somehow she'll be forced to go back to her husband. And this is an educated woman, Mr. French—a woman, moreover, who's married to an extremely prominent man!"

Her indignation showed in her voice, her eyes sparkling with the force of her emotion. The door opened, silencing her for a moment, and Miles turned to smile at the woman bringing in their tea.

He recognised her straight away. Elizabeth Herries! Only his legal training allowed him to control his shock. He waited until she had gone and then relied on his instincts, asking quietly,

"I presume that's the woman you've just been telling me about?"

"Remarkably quick of you, Mr. French," Mrs James frowned. "You realise of course that what I've just told you was in the strictest confidence." She was plainly rather put out that he had recognised Elizabeth as the woman she had just described, and Miles could understand why.

He thought fast, not sure yet how he could use the information to his advantage without endangering Elizabeth Herries herself. He would have liked to have talked to her, but he suspected she would simply clam up on him. If he was going to get her to talk to him he was going to have to enlist the help of the woman sitting in front of him.

"I should like to talk to her," he said quietly,

holding up his hand when Sarah James would have interrupted to add, "No, I promise you I mean no harm. Quite the opposite. I know who she is and I know her husband—a very dangerous man."

After a brief pause she told him reluctantly, "She wants to divorce him, but she's terrified he'll try to take the children from her."

"I think I can help her," said Miles, and he meant it.

Mrs James looked at him consideringly and then said abruptly, "I'll go and have a word with her, if you'd like to wait . . ."

He wasn't going to make it for his squash game, Miles acknowledged as he drove away. Elizabeth Herries had been nervous to the point of dread, but eventually she had told him everything. He had assured her that he believed her and he had managed to convince her that she needed to divorce Simon, for her own sake and that of her two children, but he had not disputed the very real danger she was in. She badly needed her family's support, but she was too afraid to approach them, convinced that they would not believe her. She had confided to Miles that her husband was determined to be a future Conservative Prime Minister. It was no secret that the existing PM was planning on retiring, and Simon was one of several men being groomed for eventual leadership.

The PM was known as a man who had very strong moral views. Elizabeth Herries' family could hardly refuse to support her if Elizabeth had the Prime Minister's condemnation of Simon to substantiate her claims.

But Elizabeth was totally against any form of publicity. She was terrified about the effect it might have on her children.

There had to be a way round the problem, and Miles was determined that he would find it.

Pepper frowned as Miranda tapped on her door and walked in carrying a vase full of flowers. They weren't the usual hothouse type of blooms, but soft pastel-coloured cottage garden flowers nestled in a mist of silver-white foliage.

Pepper looked and pretended to be studying her diary, but inwardly she was seething. She knew without taking the card from Miranda who they would be from. What did Miles French think he was trying to do? Did he honestly think that in pretending to be physically attracted to her he could swerve her from her chosen course? The man must have an ego the size of a mountain if he really believed his sexual appeal was such that she would simply give up all she had worked for, because he chose to smile at her!

"Aren't they gorgeous?" Miranda enthused, putting the flowers down on her desk. She looked surreptitiously at the downbent red head. The whole of the office was agog with the very obvious and lavish attentions of their boss's new man. There had been other men before him, of course, droves of them, but never one like this.

"Take them away and put them in the boardroom, please," Pepper commanded her curtly. "They give me hay fever."

It was a lie, and had she had her way she would have picked up the flowers, vase and all, and thrown them into the street, but she couldn't afford to behave so emotionally. It would be totally out of character.

"Mr French rang four times this morning," Miranda told her. "Er . . . I told him you'd said you didn't want to speak to him . . ."

Pepper felt her skin prickle with irritation and

something else she didn't want to name. She refused to look up, but she knew that Miranda was still standing beside her desk.

"He . . . he—er—told me to tell you that he'd be round tonight as usual and that if you really want your key back he'll bring it with him."

Pepper gripped hold of her pen and stared disbelievingly at her secretary. She opened her mouth to deliver a blistering retort, then realised that nothing she could say would do any good. One look at Miranda's face had convinced her that her secretary could never be convinced that she and Miles French were not engaged in a very passionate affair.

Damn him! If he was here now . . .

She let Miranda escape and then paced her office angrily. Miles French thought he was so clever, putting her in this position, making it impossible for her to refute his claims that they were lovers. Pepper stopped pacing and discovered that she was actually grinding her teeth. She stared out of her office window and into the busy street.

She needed to get away. She was tense and on edge. To get away . . . She laughed to herself. She never needed to get away; she loved her work and devoted herself to it wholeheartedly. Nick had given up trying to persuade her to take time off. He had asked her to go away with him often enough, but she always refused. She knew she was safer on her own home ground, and she always knew that Nick was still determined that they were going to be lovers.

Miranda came back in with some letters for signing just as Pepper was massaging her aching neck.

"Tired?" Miranda asked her sympathetically. "You need a holiday."

"Yes . . . Yes, I think I do," Pepper agreed tiredly. She certainly needed something, if only the opportu-

nity to get away from Miles French's constant
bombardment of tokens of his totally fictitious affection.

She was due to spend the weekend with Isabelle
and Jeremy, but that would hardly be relaxing. She
thought of Oxford and Mary and Philip, but visiting
them this weekend was out unless she left the office
early on Friday.

She nibbled on the edge of her pen. The polo match
she was attending with Isabelle and her husband was
an important one. Nick Howarth's team would be
playing. He was captain of it now and no longer quite
the rarity he had once been. Smith's Lawn abounded
with millionaire pop stars turned country squirearchy,
and wealthy businessmen ready to put their hands
into their pockets and sponsor such a socially potentially rewarding sport.

Pepper mentally reviewed her wardrobe, deciding
what she would wear. Isabelle was giving a dinner in
the evening and it would be a formal affair. She would
wear the new creation she had just bought from
Parker's. It wasn't in her usual style, being slightly
less sexy and rather more softly feminine. She frowned,
checking slightly, wondering why she had chosen to
deviate from her habitual style.

She had lost two pounds this week—a sign that she
was worrying about something. And yet hadn't she
every reason not to worry? Hadn't she just reached a
goal she had been striving for for ten years? Surely
that was just cause for self-congratulation? So why
then was she suffering this faint feeling of malaise;
this sombreness that shadowed her thoughts and her
dreams? Why was she allowing Miles French's pseudo
attentions to unsettle her so much? She had far more
important things to worry about. She had delivered
her ultimatums and there was no way her victims

would dare not to meet them. For now she had work to do if she was taking the weekend off. She had heard reports of a new potential tennis star, in Cheshire of all places, and she wanted to go and check out the report for herself. Tennis sponsorship was very big business. So far Pepper only had a small slice of it, but in five years' time it would be much larger. She waited for the thrill that planning the expansion of her business always brought her, but strangely it didn't come. A tiny frisson of anxiety rippled across her skin, but she dismissed it, concentrating instead on the report on her desk.

It was one of her major gifts that she could be single-minded enough to concentrate on the here and now, rather than drift into time-wasting thoughts of the past and the future, but despite her concentration she still remained vaguely unsettled. And she knew deep inside herself that somehow this was due to Miles French.

She looked up and realised that Miranda had forgotten to remove the flowers. They reminded her very much of Philip's garden, or going even further back, of the wild flowers that she had seen growing during the years of her childhood.

Miles's choice of bouquet surprised her. She would have expected expensive hothouse blooms, not these delicate, pastel-hued, velvet-petalled flowers, and it disturbed her that he was capable of doing something she had not associated with him. It made her wonder how accurate her total assessment of him had been— or more worryingly, how *in*accurate.

Julia Barnett stared unseeingly out of her bedroom window. She had started sleeping in here alone on odd nights six months ago, consumed by a guilt she could no longer fight. Alex was at work—at least that was where he told her he had gone. Her once pretty mouth twisted bitterly. She had rung him half an hour ago, and his secretary had sounded surprised that Julia didn't know he wasn't due in.

She picked up the piece of paper she found on the floor of their bedroom, only now Alex sometimes slept alone in it. She had smoothed it out and now it lay on the bed beside her.

Alex's strong handwriting was instantly recognisable, even if she hadn't kept every love letter he had written her. There were only two words on this piece; a name, written over and over again, with a compulsiveness that spoke volumes.

Julia stared at it, and blinked.

Pepper Minesse . . . another woman . . . the other woman . . . Julia knew who she was. She had seen her on television not long ago, in a BBC 2 series featuring successful women.

Alex, her Alex, was having an affair with Pepper Minesse. She felt the tightness inside her chest grow and clamped her teeth together, to prevent the scream of hysterical fear engulfing her. She had known this would happen. She had known all along she would be punished for what she had done to their child. She started to tremble, and the faintness she often experienced these days started to overwhelm her.

She wasn't conscious of passing out, only of coming to, to find herself lying on the bedroom floor. She got up awkwardly, still dizzy, pressing her hand to her flat stomach. She hadn't eaten for two days, but she didn't connect that with her dizziness. It was all part of her punishment—punishment she justly deserved. But Pepper Minesse should be punished too. She was stealing her husband. She would give him the children that she, Julia, could not.

She remembered how remote the adoption people

had been . . . kind but remote. She knew they would not get their child, but would find out about what she had done, and then . . . And then Alex would leave her and she would be completely on her own. But wasn't that what she deserved? She had killed their child . . .

She wasn't aware of walking to the station or of getting on the London train. She arrived at Pepper's office just after lunch. Pepper had not eaten out, and she was sitting at her desk, studying a report, when her secretary came in.

"There's a woman outside asking for you." Miranda frowned uncomfortably. "I'm afraid . . . she's rather odd . . ."

"Odd? In what sense?"

"Well, she seems to think you've . . . you've stolen her husband."

Pepper's eyebrows rose. There had been many times over the years when her name had been linked with that of men both married and unmarried, but this was the first time an angry wife had turned up outside her door.

"What does she expect me to do?" Pepper asked coolly. "Unlock a safe and hand him back? Who is she, by the way?"

"Well, we had some difficulty getting her name. She's . . . well, she looks very distraught. She said her name was Julia . . . Julia Barnett."

Julia Barnett. Alex Barnett's wife. Did she really think that Pepper was having an affair with her husband? On the point of telling Miranda to get rid of her, Pepper changed her mind.

"Show her in here. I'll have a word with her."

"Do you think you should?" murmured Miranda. "She's in a pretty bad state . . ." The girl flushed under Pepper's querying stare. "Well, maybe not dangerous exactly, but . . . well, verging on the hysterical, almost certainly." She bit her lip and added uncertainly, "She isn't even dressed properly."

"Show her in," Pepper repeated firmly.

She saw what Miranda meant the moment the door opened. The woman standing on its threshold must have once been very pretty and could still have been very attractive. Instead her blonde hair was unstyled and faded, her face free of make up and drawn into harsh lines of pain. She was wearing clothes that made Pepper's fastidious mouth curl; a pair of what looked like old slippers on her feet and a loose smock-like dress that did nothing to hide her appalling thinness.

"You've stolen my husband and I want him back."

The bald trembling statement broke the silence. Pepper said nothing, just sat watching. The woman stirred a feeling of pity deep inside her that she would much rather not have felt.

"I know why he wants you." The words came out in a rush. "It's because you can give him a child . . . Well, I'm not going to let you!" She moved so quickly that Pepper was caught off guard. One moment the woman was standing by the door, the next she was up against the edge of the desk brandishing what looked like a carving knife.

Pepper didn't have time to be frightened; there was only an overwhelming sensation of unreality; the incongruity of the whole situation struck her as ridiculously funny. Here was this woman accusing her of stealing her husband, threatening to end her life, when in reality . . .

"I'm not trying to take your husband away from you." Pepper spoke calmly and quietly. "I promise you that. Look, why don't you sit down and we'll have a cup of coffee and talk about it?" She saw the woman's face change, soften and then crumple into almost childish lines.

"I lost my baby," she said helplessly.

"I know. I know all about it."

"God keeps punishing me. That's why he let you take Alex from me."

"God doesn't want to punish you, really. He understands what you did."

She saw the uncertainty flicker in the blue eyes as they focused on her for the first time. She saw the tiny gleam of hope lighten them and wondered disbelievingly what on earth she was doing. Counselling distraught women was not her line of work; she couldn't care less about Alex Barnett's wife. So why did she have this appalling sense of compassion for her? Why did she have this need to reach out and help her? She could not understand it.

"Let's sit down and talk," she suggested quietly. "I know all about your baby, Julia. I know all about you."

"You do?"

"Yes . . . and I promise you I'm not going to take Alex away."

"He doesn't know what I did. I lied to him . . . I can't have any more babies, but he can . . . He . . ."

"Alex only wants *you*."

She had the woman's attention now. The hand holding the knife relaxed, but Pepper made no attempt to reach for it. Oddly, she had not felt a second's fear that she was in any real danger, but she waited until Julia had placed the knife on the desk before reaching for it and taking it from her.

She rang for Miranda and when the girl came in she said evenly, "Miranda, two cups of coffee, please, and then I'm going to take the rest of the day off. Mrs Barnett and I will be going out shopping."

"Shopping?" The blue eyes stared at her, the faded lips forming the word as though it was totally unfamiliar.

"Alex likes you to look pretty, doesn't he?" Pepper said firmly.

"Yes. Yes, he does." Frail fingers plucked nervously at the worn dress.

Here was a woman suffering under an immense burden of guilt; a woman in desperate need of proper psychiatric help, Pepper recognised. A woman she would have expected a man like Alex Barnett to have discarded years ago, and yet he still loved her. All the reports had confirmed the fact. Could a man who loved a woman so faithfully and intensely really . . .?

Really what? She hadn't imagined being kidnapped by him and then raped. She owed it to herself to exact her just measure of retribution, and yet here when she was faced with the ultimate weapon when she could have so easily have called the police and had his wife forcibly and publicly removed and held up to ridicule, she hadn't done so. Why?

Perhaps it was because of the woman sitting in front of her. She had photographs in her file of the old Julia and the difference was almost painful, and yet what had this woman done? Nothing that Pepper had not contemplated doing herself. Her guilt, her punishment, was all self-inflicted. It was one thing to read in a report that to destroy Alex Barnett's chances of adopting a child would send his wife over the edge into complete despair. It was another to be confronted with the reality of that woman and her pain.

Even without being ready to admit it to herself, Pepper knew that she just could not do it . . . That she would have to find another way of punishing him.

The decision was made almost without her being

aware of it, and with its making came an odd lightness of heart.

She got Miranda to track down Alex Barnett, who was eventually found in Whitehall, trying to discover the outcome of his tender. Pepper had asked Miranda to leave a message that he was to call at her office. In the meantime, as she had promised, she took Julia shopping. It was almost like being in charge of a helpless child, and she was in turn angry and appalled at what could happen to a member of her own sex, simply through guilt.

When she felt her charge had had enough she shepherded her back to her office. Once inside she sat her down and said firmly,

"Julia, you must tell Alex the truth."

She felt the woman tremble beneath her light touch on her shoulder.

"I can't . . . I can't!"

"You must," Pepper insisted. "You must be strong. That's what Alex would want. You must share your . . . your pain with him."

She had no idea why she was doing all this. She should simply have rung the police, she told herself angrily. She hated what this woman was doing to her own emotions. They were see-sawing up and down like mercury in a thermometer . . . She hated herself for being so ridiculously emotional.

"God won't let me," Julia protested.

Pepper took a deep breath.

"Yes, yes, he will. That's why he sent you here to me, Julia, because he wanted me to tell you that he *has* forgiven you. He wants you to tell Alex everything . . . because he wants Alex to take care of a very special child for him."

She could tell that she had Julia's attention.

"God has a child for us?"

The whole thing was like a farce, Pepper thought
fiercely, but she had to see it through. She was being
pulled apart by her own conflicting feelings, and yet
she couldn't sacrifice this woman to the hell of her
own depression. She was still governed in so much by
her gypsy genes, and they told her that there was a
higher purpose; a higher awareness, a higher ordering
of much that occurred in life, and that this was a test
for her. Almost she could feel her own grandmother
at her side, and the skin on her scalp prickled with
prehensile awareness. She never thought about that
other life now, those other mores . . . but they were
still there, and she carried her awareness that there
was much in life that is inexplicable and not subject
to reason without her being aware of it. This woman
had been sent to her for a purpose . . . she could
sense it. In her mind's eye she visualised Julia as a
desperate creature trapped in a pit of sticky clinging
mud, which would eventually drag her down and
destroy her. She was reaching out her hands to Pepper,
and if she ignored her, if she turned her back on
her . . .

She took a deep breath and with only her instinct
to go on, said firmly, "Yes. Yes, he does, Julia. Soon
Alex will be here. He'll take you home and you'll tell
him all about your baby."

"And then . . . then God will send us another
child?"

She was trembling visibly, and Pepper fought to
control her own inner panic. What was she doing,
interfering like this? She wasn't God, she couldn't
make such promises, and yet . . . and yet . . . As
though the words came from someone else, she heard
herself saying an old Romany blessing, a favourite of
her grandmother's, and almost instantly the tension
in the room disappeared, and it was filled with a

warmth like the sun coming out on a cloudy day.

Julia felt it too. Suddenly her trembling ceased and her eyes cleared. Pepper held her breath. Her internal phone rang, cutting through the golden stillness.

"Alex Barnett has just arrived," Miranda told her.

"Right. Give me two minutes and then show him in.

"Alex is here," she told Julia as she replaced the receiver. "When he comes in just tell him that you want to go home. And then when you get home, tell him all about your baby. You must do that, do you understand, Julia?"

"If I do will God forgive me?"

"God wants you to tell Alex," Pepper told her firmly. "And when you have done you're going to feel a lot better. God will forgive you."

She only hoped that the woman would forgive herself, Pepper thought as she let herself out of her office via another door that led into the private meeting room.

The last person Alex had expected to discover in Pepper's office had been his wife. He rushed over to her in concern.

"Julia . . ."

"Take me home, Alex. I want to go home."

He saw the way she was dressed, but the wild and unfocused look in her eyes that went with these increasingly common depressed moods wasn't there.

"I want to go home . . . I have to talk to you . . ." she muttered.

"What are you doing here?" Alex demanded.

"I had to come," Julia told him quietly. "I had to come."

"While they were talking Pepper walked into the foyer.

"I'm leaving now, Miranda. Would you go into my

office and give Mr Barnett a message for me? Please tell him that his wife arrived here in a rather distressed state, and I think that it would be best if he took her home."

Alex received the message in a state of semi-shock. He had no idea what was going on, or what had brought Julia here, and even more important, exactly what Pepper Minesse had been saying to her. And yet Julia seemed calmer and more rational than she had been in a long time.

He smiled rather distantly at Miranda, unaware of the length of her legs, or the lush promise of her smile, but when he looked at his wife his entire expression changed, softening and warming, and as Miranda commented wryly to one of the girls after they had gone,

"There aren't many of that kind around, worse luck!"

Pepper was late leaving the office on Friday afternoon after all. Alex Barnett had rung her several times during the week, but she had refused to take his calls. She couldn't understand what on earth had motivated her to behave in such a stupid and emotional fashion. And as for thinking that her grandmother . . . Well, that was total idiocy. Firmly dismissing both the Barnetts from her mind, Pepper got into her car.

Her clothes were already packed. A quick bath and something light to eat and she could be on her way.

With any luck she could reach Oxford before Oliver went to bed. She checked the thought as it formed. Oliver meant nothing to her. She had no right to want to see him. Oliver was Philip and Mary's child.

If she carried on like this for much longer she was likely to become as mentally unstable as Julia Barnett, she derided herself—first imagining that she could sense her grandmother's spirit and now mooning over a child she never wanted in the first place.

And yet . . . and yet when she reached Oxford just after nine and she was greeted by Oliver's welcoming smile, she couldn't disguise the curious fluttery, pleasurable sensation that rose up inside her.

Her visit was only a brief one. She left in the morning straight after breakfast. Mary kissed her gently as she drove off.

"She loves him," she said quietly to Philip later when they were alone. "I knew one day she would." He squeezed her hand and wondered why it was that fate so often decreed that those who were most meek and innocent among human kind should suffer so dreadfully.

"Does it hurt badly?" he asked her.

She shook her head.

"No, not really." She got up and smiled at him. "Oliver will be in soon. I'd better make a start on lunch."

Isabelle had organised a picnic lunch to be eaten at Smith's Lawn.

Jeremy had already gone on ahead, and watching as Isabelle manoeuvred the huge picnic basket and what seemed like half a dozen children and was in fact only three, into the back of a large Range Rover, Pepper was both amused and saddened by how much her scatty friend had changed. Now she was the complete Sloane Ranger wife and mother; those days in Oxford might never have been, and Pepper knew with certainty that the Isabelle of these days would never have stopped to talk to a stranger in the street, nor certainly to have so quickly and impetuously offered her friendship. Without their mutual connection with polo to tie them together Pepper suspected the friendship would have faded long ago.

"I'm thrilled that you're presenting the Cup. It's quite an honour, you know. Last year the Princess of Wales did it".

"Jeremy thinks Nick's team will win," said Isabelle. "He's quite miffed about it really. He says it isn't fair that they should be able to buy in so much South American talent. We don't know who half of them are, you know . . ."

There was a good deal more in the same vein, and Pepper wished she could drive to the game in her own car. However, Isabelle had made all the arrangements, and Isabelle hated her arrangements being changed.

"In fact Jeremy's not himself at all these days. I expect it's something to do with all this 'big Bang' fuss in the City." She pulled a wry face, and Pepper, who suspected that Jeremy was far more likely to be involved in an extra-marital affair than concerned about an event that could only lead to a huge increase in his income, said nothing. She knew Isabelle of old, and if she wanted to she would eventually find a way to get round to the subject that was really bothering her. Isabelle was no fool; she was also an extremely attractive woman—plumper now after the birth of three children, but Pepper suspected that she wasn't entirely true to her marriage vows herself. Of course, everything was done discreetly, one didn't flaunt one's small peccadilloes, but Pepper hadn't missed the glances Isabelle had been exchanging with the husband of one of her cronies, the last time she had been down.

She settled herself in the front of the Range Rover, while Isabelle cautioned the children to be quiet. Jeremy's black Labrador was in the back, his tail thumping against the grille separating him from the children.

"All ready?"

The match they were attending was one of the most important in the polo sporting year. Sponsored by Cartier, it was of international importance, and when they arrived at the Guards' Polo Club at Smith's Lawn, it was to find the ground sprinkled with an assortment of elegant marquees.

This was the fourth year that Pepper had attended this particular event, but it was the first occasion on which she had been asked to present the winner's trophy. She had no delusions about what Isabelle had told her in an awed whisper was a great honour; if the Princess of Wales and the Duchess of York had not been away on holiday with their respective husbands, she would not have even been considered. However, her company had become so closely involved with the game and her face so well known that as she and Isabelle made their way to Cartier's reception marquee, they drew curious and envious glances from the huge crowd of onlookers.

Luckily the day was fine and the flower-decorated marquee not too crowded. Pepper acknowledged smiles from several members of the Hurlingham Polo Association as she made her way to the top table. Once not so long ago this old-guard governing body of the sport would have looked askance at sponsorship for their game, but now it had become so much the norm as to draw very little attention at all.

Lunch was the noisy, gossipy occasion Pepper had expected it to be; she smiled and talked, and all the time she kept her ears open and managed to pick up two rather interesting bits of gossip which she suspected she would be able to turn to her own advantage later. Isabelle had drifted away to talk to some of her county cronies. Nick was deep in conversation with a fellow player.

Pepper glanced across the crowded marquee—and

suddenly froze. That man with his back to her . . . that dark head . . .

Miles had already seen her—how could he not? She was the cynosure of all eyes, both male and female. She played her part well, he acknowledged, amused and admiring of her skill and dexterity. She was dressed elegantly, in a white spotted cornflower blue silk suit with a matching hat that set off her extraordinary hair. Pearls gleamed lustrously at her throat. She was wearing decorous white gloves. He knew all about her relationship with Nick Howarth. They were supposed to be lovers. He knew a lot about Pepper now, and about how she kept her men at a distance. Inside that beautiful packaging she was a woman who was unable to come to terms with her sexuality. Miles was ready almost to bet his reputation on his belief that none of the men who so assiduously danced attendance on her had ever shared her bed. He didn't know why he was so convinced of this; all the evidence dictated otherwise. She had been very clever with her camouflage. One man would be put off by the intimation that she was in love with another; someone else the promise that one day perhaps . . . and yet another with a further piece of adroit manipulation. Pepper Minesse was one very clever lady, he admitted, still watching her; clever enough not to antagonise the male sex with an outright refusal, clever enough to manufacture for herself a reputation that made it next to impossible for anyone to believe that her sexual experience was limited to one frenzied act of lust.

He looked at Nick Howarth. He was a supremely fit male specimen; physically attractive, wealthy . . . and obviously very attracted to Pepper.

The announcement that the formalities of the day were about to begin intruded into his thoughts. There was a general exodus outside during which he was careful to ensure that he kept out of sight. Pepper looked in vain for the dark head as the bands of the Artillery Company and the Irish Guards played the national anthems of the two competing countries.

The first chukka started, the game fiercely contested and played dangerously fast. The week had left Pepper curiously drained and weak in a way that she found disconcerting. She must have imagined that brief sighting of Miles French, she comforted herself. She was beginning to feel as though the wretched man was almost haunting her. Dismissing him from her mind, she tried to concentrate on the game in progress.

Halfway through the afternoon there was a break for tea. Jeremy and Nick joined them, and the talk at the table was all of the merits and demerits of the rival teams. Pepper was not a particular devotee of polo, but it disconcerted her to realise how much that intrusion of Miles French into her mind had unsettled her. She felt restless, almost bored even by Nick's conversation, relieved, and yet at the same time in some odd way disappointed that Miles French wasn't really there. Disappointed? She caught herself up on the thought, frowning so deeply that Nick broke off his conversation to ask if she was all right. He touched her wrist as he did so, and she had to stop herself from flinching away from him.

Nick had introduced a new pony to his string, and soon he was deep in discussion with Jeremy about the animal's potential.

"It's a little on the nervy side as yet, but it's early days . . ."

Pepper shut her mind to the conversation, glancing away. Why on earth was Miles French occupying so much of her attention? It was ridiculous, it was dangerous.

The men got up, and Pepper and Isabelle followed

them. Pepper and Isabelle resumed their seats; the second half started. Nick's team had been knocked out before the afternoon tea interval, and he came over to talk to them.

"Come and have a look at my latest acquisition," he invited Pepper. She didn't want to go, but guilt and a certain irritation with herself for allowing Miles French to intrude so much into her thoughts made her do so.

Nick placed his arm proprietorially around her shoulders as they walked over to where the ponies were tethered. She wanted to move away, but restrained herself. There had been many women in Nick's life since they had first met, but she knew that he still had hopes of their becoming lovers. It would never be; she knew that, but he did not . . . not yet.

Nick stopped to talk to someone and she broke away from him. She heard someone cry out a sharp warning, and wheeled round. One of the polo ponies had broken loose from its string and was heading straight towards her. Paralysed with shock, she could only stare at it . . . someone was screaming in the distance, a high pitched terror-stricken sound, and then the breath was forced out of her lungs as someone grabbed hold of her and pushed her to the ground. She felt the weight and warmth of an unmistakably masculine body covering her own, pinning her down.

Time spun crazily out of focus and she gave into the surge of blind panic engulfing her. She tried to fight, to push the weight off her. She couldn't breathe, her lungs laboured to take in air, panic and fear obliterating the concerned sounds of the onlookers. Only one reality reached her, and that was that for the second time in her life a man was inflicting himself on her, touching her, terrifying her.

She opened her mouth to scream, but no sound

came out. Blackness engulfed her, dizzily speckled with a thousand bursting coloured stars.

"She's fainted!"

Miles got up, carefully examining Pepper's inert body for broken bones. The crowd of admiring onlookers praised him for his quickwittedness. Isabelle, who was standing at his side with her children, said shakily,

"Oh my God! Pepper could have been killed! She just stood there . . ."

"Shock and fright," Miles told her, giving her his lazy, warm smile.

"She hasn't broken anything. I'll carry her over to my car, out of the way of this crowd . . ."

Flashbulbs exploded, but no one took any notice apart from Miles. If he had arranged the whole thing deliberately, it could not have been better. Tomorrow morning their pictures would be plastered all over the press. He had seen what was happening from yards away, but no one else had made any move to snatch Pepper out of the way. Like her, they had all been stricken by shock.

"Do—do you know her?" Isabelle was obviously puzzled.

"Yes. Yes, I do know her." Miles gave her a smile and a look that said quite explicitly what their relationship was. Instantly Isabelle was all flustered. "Oh. Oh, I see. I thought I hadn't seen you here before . . . That is, one becomes accustomed to a certain set of faces and I . . . Oh dear!"

"You and she were at college together, weren't you?" he added, mentally blessing the handiwork of his informant. Isabelle liked him. There was something about him, something very masculine and yet at the same time very gentle.

"She hasn't said anything about you . . . Oh look,

she's coming round."

Pepper froze as awareness flooded back. She was instantly conscious of being surrounded by man smell, by man strength, by a maleness so intense that her whole being cried out in protest against it.

"Pepper, are you all right?"

"Isabelle." She recognised her friend's voice and clung to it, opening her eyes. She couldn't see Isabelle. All she could see was Miles French. Miles French! She froze, her eyes dilating in panic. What was happening?

"My God, Pepper, what happened?"

Nick . . . She twisted round in Miles French's grasp, her breasts pushing against his chest, as she tried to extricate herself. The contact burned her, scalding her flesh, throwing her into a wild panic.

"She was so lucky, Nick . . . Miles saved her. Miles, why don't you join us for dinner tonight?"

It would put out Isabelle's numbers, but luckily she knew of a girlfriend who would be only too happy to partner Nick Howarth. Why on earth hadn't Pepper told her about this new man in her life? Isabelle wondered, a little chagrined.

"Pepper darling, why doesn't Miles run you home? You can lie down and have a rest and . . ."

"No!" The sharpness of her response drew three pairs of eyes. Only Miles French's held understanding, and she flinched from it, fighting for breath and self-control. Just that moment of awareness in his arms had made her realise how impossible it would ever be for her to take any man as her lover. Her fear of him overwhelmed her reluctant liking for Miles. She felt contaminated by his touch, whirled back to that morning when she had woken up in his bed, when he had leaned down and she had been filled with a panicky vulnerable fear that it was all going to happen again. In some way she hated him more than she hated Simon Herries . . . although she couldn't have said why. Perhaps it was because of her very vulnerability to him, because of the look she had seen in his eyes so briefly that morning—an awareness of her fear and a compassion for it. Pepper shook her head. What on earth was she thinking? He hadn't felt compassion for her . . . he had actively encouraged what happened to her. He must have done, for her to have been taken to his room.

He had released her now and she stood shakily, fighting to appear calm and in control.

"I'm fine, Isabelle. There's no need for Miles to take me anywhere." She gave him a taut smile and extended her hand. "Thank you so much. I . . ."

Isabelle interrupted.

"Darling, I'm afraid it's no good playing dumb. Miles has already spilled the beans." The coquettish look she gave them both said it all. A savage bitter anger filled Pepper as she saw the look on Nick's face. What was Miles French trying to do to her? Was this his petty idea of getting back at her?

"I've invited Miles to join us for dinner . . ."

Isabelle's prattle washed over her. She felt trapped . . . trapped and afraid. She wanted to scream out that she didn't want Miles French invading her life; that she was frightened of him. She wanted to run to Nick and beg him to protect her, and yet her pride, that fierce gypsy pride, and her intrinsic deep-rooted fear of the male sex, stopped her. How did she know that she would fare any better with Nick than with Miles? At heart weren't all men predators in the end? Didn't they all enjoy inflicting pain, damaging, destroying? Wasn't it all part and parcel of the whole male persona?

Fate was indeed favouring him, Miles reflected as

he made his excuses and went back to his friends.

Pepper reminded him of a frantic wild animal, desperate for escape, unaware of her own danger or the fact that he was trying to save her from it. He had felt the furious beat of her heart when she came out of her faint; had caught her gasp of shock and fear. What would it take to tame her? To win her confidence?

He frowned, irritated with himself for even thinking the question. Pepper Minesse was simply a problem in his life that had to be overcome, nothing more, nothing less. She did not fit into the mould of his women. She would never be the calm complacent type of lover he preferred. She would . . . He caught himself up and sealed off the thought before it could be properly formed. Emotionalism was a deterrent to achievement. He would do well to remember that simple cynical but very accurate fact.

CHAPTER SIXTEEN

THE SOUND of her office door slamming as Pepper walked into it caused Miranda and the receptionist to exchange raised eyebrowed looks.

"What's got into her?" Helena asked. "I've never seen her react like that before . . . wonder what's caused it?"

"The same thing that causes all women's problems," Miranda retorted acidly. "A man." She had had a bad weekend with her fiancé. He wanted her to give up her job when they got married and play at being Mrs Cabbage, and she wasn't going to.

In her office Pepper ran irate fingers through her hair. Her head ached with tension, her shoulders were stiff with it, and she was aware of a deep and intense inner rage that nothing could dissipate.

She knew who to blame for it, of course.

Miles French.

God, when she thought of how he had ruined her weekend . . . *Ruined* it! He had assassinated it.

On Saturday evening, when he turned up at Isabelle's for dinner, it had been bad enough, but the way he had appropriated Pepper, had begun to give a star performance as her doting lover . . . She ground her teeth. No amount of persuasion had been able to convince Isabelle that Pepper loathed the sight of him. The stupid idiot was an incurable romantic. Isabelle had giggled away Pepper's insistence that the man meant nothing to her; nothing at all.

What on earth was he playing at? She knew that he

was trying to throw her off balance, but was there a deeper purpose to his behaviour? He hadn't struck her as the sort of man who would give up nearly an entire weekend, simply for the purpose of being annoying.

The problem was that she couldn't really confide in Isabelle and tell her the truth, and Miles knew that, damn him. He seemed to have developed a sixth sense about her . . . Pepper's skin grew hot, her eyes flashing bitterly as she remembered how he had whispered to her over dinner, flirting with her, drawing everyone's attention to them, including Nick's.

It was hardly surprising that Nick had gone off in a huff. And then as though that wasn't enough, just as she was starting to bring Nick round on Sunday, who should turn up at the quiet pub where they were having lunch but Miles, claiming that she had agreed to meet him there the previous evening.

Isabelle must have told him where they were going. There couldn't have been any other way he could have found out.

Of course Nick had been furious.

Pepper sighed, leaning back in her chair, trying to massage the tension out of her forehead. It was pointless getting all wrought up about the man; he was perfectly capable of causing enough havoc without her aiding him.

She opened her diary and settled down to work. Normally she didn't have the slightest difficulty in putting aside the private side of her life, but today, irrationally, it kept on intruding. Every time her attention wandered she found herself thinking about the weekend, remembering how well Miles had fitted in to Isabelle's circle, how cleverly he had manipulated them all, and yet, like her, part of him remained outside it, and like her he had to fight to get where he was. Like her . . .

Exasperated with herself, she flung down her pen. This was getting her nowhere. She looked out of her office window. The sun was out and it was a clear bright day. She had a sudden longing to feel the breeze, see the countryside; a vague, disturbing yearning that she knew belonged to that side of her nature she had ruthlessly suppressed for so long.

She rang through for Miranda and when the girl came in said coolly, "I'm taking the rest of the day off, Miranda. If anyone wants me, I shall be here tomorrow."

She ignored the way her secretary gaped at her. Pepper never took time off, never left the office without giving a number where she could be reached.

"What's going on?" the receptionist hissed, as she watched Pepper walk out of the building. "She's never done anything like this before!"

"Like I said, it's got to be a man," Miranda told her positively.

Ten minutes later the receptionist came into her office bursting with excitement, waving a newspaper at her.

"It looks like you're right—take a look at this!"

The photograph had caught them just at the psychological moment when Miles had reached out to snatch Pepper away from the runaway polo pony. They looked like two lovers caught in a passionate clinch, and the slightly purple prose captioning the photograph hinted at more than a casual relationship.

"Miles French . . .phew! He looks gorgeous, doesn't he? I wouldn't mind a man like that myself. No wonder she's taking the day off!"

Pepper's staff weren't the only ones to see and speculate on the photograph. Richard Howell saw it and mentally congratulated his co-conspirator on his success. After the way Pepper had treated them in her office he hadn't believed for a moment that French had the slightest chance of putting up a convincing display that they were lovers. He had forgotten the appetite of the public for sentiment, he thought cynically. And then he frowned. Time was running out. All right, so French had managed to convince the world at large that he and Pepper were heavily involved, but he still had to carry out the second and more dangerous half of his plan. And Simon was getting impatient. He didn't like or trust French. Only yesterday he had insisted on having lunch with Richard.

He had been very much on edge, very tense, and if Richard hadn't known him better he might almost have suspected he was sitting across the table from a man suffering from some very deep mental problems, rather than the prominent and very astute MP he knew him to be. Simon had talked wildly about them taking matters into their own hands and ignoring Miles's plans. Richard hadn't taken up the hints he was dropping. It had been one thing to allow Simon to force him into kidnapping the girl when he was just another Oxford undergraduate. If he got embroiled in a similar sort of thing now . . . in his position . . . and somehow this time he didn't think it was merely rape that Simon had in mind. It seemed impossible to believe that a man in Herries' position could actually be contemplating what was in actual fact murder, but Herries' hatred of the woman had been so apparent, so all consuming that it had left Richard himself feeling acutely uncomfortable.

He needed to talk to Miles, he decided, reaching for the phone, and then replacing it. There was no point in taking unnecessary risks, he would ring him from the car; that way he wouldn't be overheard.

Miles was working in his study when the telephone rang, ostensibly on the case he was taking to defend the women's refuge, but in reality his mind was on Pepper and the problem of how to remove her to a place of safety. He thought he had the answer, but what he was contemplating was very risky and full of potential hazards.

He had talked to his doctor friend and had managed to extract from him a cocktail of drugs, guaranteed to give an immediate loss of consciousness with no after-effects. Miles had told him that he was sleeping badly and suffering from stress. He had claimed that he didn't want to approach his own doctor because he had a bias against tranquillisers and sleeping tablets of any kind. It had been a very thin excuse, but luckily it had been accepted.

He had several other arrangements yet to make, including finding somewhere where he could keep Pepper until he had convinced her of her danger.

He picked up the receiver, not particularly surprised to hear Richard Howell on the end of the line. They had been keeping in contact, although Miles suspected that like Simon, Richard was not altogether sure that he trusted him.

Alex Barnett, unlike the other two, had seemed frankly relieved to leave everything in his hands, and Miles suspected that if he never heard another word about Pepper or her ultimatums he would be a very happy man.

"Nice work," Richard announced. "I've seen the piece in the papers. As far as the rest of the world is concerned at least, you and Ms Minesse are now something of an item!"

"Is that why you're telephoning me—To congratulate me?" Miles asked him drily.

There was a moment's silence and then Richard admitted,

"No. Look, Simon's putting pressure on me to . . . well, to be quite frank, I don't think he's too happy with the way you're handling things. Time's running out."

Miles had been expecting something like this from the moment Pepper delivered her ultimatums. Unless he acted fast he suspected that Simon Herries would take matters into his own hands, and that was the last thing he wanted. He had had another meeting with Elizabeth Herries and had managed to persuade her to agree to see the Prime Minister. A meeting had been arranged, very discreetly, in his name, and he had only been able to achieve that much by ruthlessly using all his contacts. He had said nothing about the purpose of his appointment save that it concerned the behaviour of a prominent MP. Right now he needed time. Time to get Pepper away to a place of safety, and time to persuade Elizabeth Herries to go through with her divorce.

"Look, why don't we have a meeting?" he suggested.

"Yes, I think that's advisable and we'd better contact Alex, too. But you should know that Simon's out for Pepper Minesse's blood," Richard told Miles frankly. "We met for lunch the other day, and to be honest, he worried me. He's talking about getting rid of her—permanently." He paused and then said grimly, "If he tries anything like that we'll all be dragged even further into the whole mess."

"You could always go to the police and tell them everything," Miles suggested, knowing even as he spoke that it was a very forlorn hope.

"You know I can't do that," Richard told him curtly, confirming his thoughts. "None of us can. No, the sooner you can get her to retract, the better.

Simon doesn't trust you," he added flatly, "and unless you do something soon he's going to take matters into his own hands."

Tell me something I don't know, Miles thought grimly as he replaced the receiver. There must be some way of getting Pepper to safety, somewhere he could take her. His glance fell on a brief he had put on one side to be filed away. It had involved a very intricate copyright case for a billionaire industrialist. He had been very grateful to Miles for winning him his case— so grateful in fact that he had offered him the use of one of his many overseas properties for just as long as he wished. Miles had told him at the time that barristers couldn't afford to take indefinite holidays. A thought struck him and he picked up his telephone.

"Get me Ralph Ryde, will you, please?" he asked his secretary.

Three minutes later his phone rang.

"Ralph, do you still have that property in Goa?" he asked without preamble. He had visited it once, and the house and its setting had caught his imagination.

"Yes . . . yes, I do. Don't go there much though now . . . it's too remote. But if you want the use of it—"

Offering his thanks, Miles ended the call and sat in thought. The more he looked into Simon's past, the more concerned he became about Pepper's future. He suspected she didn't know how dangerous the man was, and Miles had been relieved to discover from a fellow member of one of his clubs that despite Simon's own convictions, the Conservative Party had no intention of proposing him for a Cabinet post.

"Too unstable, don't you know, old chap," his contact had confided. "Not quite the sort we're looking for." His fellow club member had cleared his throat and added gruffly, "Heard one or two unsavoury items about the chappie from time to time . . ."

The club was one which Colonel Whitegate had sponsored him for when he was first at the bar, and Miles kept up the membership out of a certain sentimental gratitude to the older man. Its members were all very much in the same gruff Army mould, good sterling British stock.

Phoning Richard back Miles confirmed the need for a meeting. "Could you make it this evening at my place?"

It had occurred to Miles that it might be a good idea to get Alex and Richard on their own without Simon around. He might discover then exactly what hold the other man had had on them.

Alex Barnett sounded rather preoccupied when Miles rang him, but confirmed that he would be there.

There was only one small task left to complete now. He picked up the phone and dialled. A pleasantly spoken girl answered him.

"I'd like to book a flight to Goa for two, please. Yes, Goa."

Ten minutes later he replaced the receiver and smiled rather grimly to himself. What he was contemplating doing broke just about every rule in the book. He only hoped he could get away with it, because if he couldn't . . . He picked up the phone again.

Miranda was rather surprised to find Miles French on the phone asking for Pepper. She had assumed that when Pepper took the day off it was because she intended to spend it with him.

He even managed to sound sexy on the phone, she thought, relishing the smooth maleness of his voice. She explained to him that Pepper had taken the day off.

"Ah, good!" There was a suggestion of laughter in

his voice, a hint of shared intimacy which she liked. "I wonder if I could persuade you to enter a small conspiracy with me, then. I want to take Pepper away on holiday, but I'm sure you know how your boss feels about leaving her office."

Miranda made a wry sound of agreement.

"Well, I think I've found the answer. I'm going to abduct her . . . I've made all the arrangements, but it's just struck me I'm going to need her passport. Do you have access to it?"

Miranda did. It was kept locked in the small office safe which also housed important documents and day-to-day petty cash.

As she said later to her boyfriend, it was one of the most romantic things she had ever heard of. Just think . . . to be whisked off to the airport and flown away to some secluded spot!

"You wouldn't think it was romantic," said the boyfriend. "You'd be complaining about not having the right clothes."

"Not if it was Miles French I was with I wouldn't!" Miranda countered recklessly. Even so, her boyfriend had a point. She had made a note to remind Miles when he came in for Pepper's passport that he would need to organise some clothes for her. It never even crossed her mind that Pepper wouldn't want to go. What woman in her right senses would turn down a man like Miles French?

Miles could see the moment Alex Barnett arrived that evening that he had something on his mind. Hitherto he found him rather quiet and shy. His previous impression of him had been that Alex was a man who had been dragged unwillingly into a situation which had now completely overtaken him. Miles had seen enough of the seamier side of human nature over the years to consider himself a reasonable judge of character, and Alex was the very last person he would have anticipated finding involved in something like this.

He explained to them both how far along his plans were, watching them carefully. Richard Howell expressed nothing other than relief, but Alex Barnett looked uncomfortable and for a moment Miles thought he was going to interrupt.

The moment passed and Miles asked smoothly,

"I only realised the other day that the three of you were all members of Tim Wilding's would-be Hell Fire Club, weren't you?"

The effect was electric. Richard Howell's eyes narrowed and before anyone else could speak he said harshly,

"Look, if you've got any idea of taking over from Herries and trying a spot of blackmail on your own account you can forget it!"

He broke off and flushed darkly. Miles told him calmly, "I can assure you I have no intention of doing any such thing. How long has he been blackmailing you?"

"Virtually ever since I took over the bank."

"He got in touch with *me* once my company started hitting the headlines," Alex supplied miserably, "and I suspect we're not the only ones."

"Damn right we're not!" Richard interrupted with some force. "I've done a little discreet checking up of my own, and every one of our fellow members of that thrice damned club who's made anything of his life is facing the same problem. He's got files . . . photographs . . . copies of membership papers . . . God, even then he must have been planning to use them . . . and we thought *he* was the crazy one!"

"Crazy?" Miles asked sharply.

"Well, you remember what he was like . . . Tim Wilding at least really thought they could raise the Devil, I'm sure of it, and then when Tim died . . . well, Simon simply went to pieces."

"It was just after Tim's death that he raped Pepper, wasn't it?"

"Yes . . . he called it 'just punishment'. He blamed her for Tim's death, said she'd put a curse on him or some such nonsense. We *had* to do it . . . we didn't have any choice. It was either go along with him or risk being exposed as members of the Club and sent down. Of course, neither of us knew exactly what he had in mind."

Miles's eyebrows rose. "A man asks you to kidnap a girl and dump her in his rooms and you don't know what he has in mind?"

Richard flushed again. "Come on . . . you roomed with him. You know damn well what I mean. His tastes ran in other directions . . . He and Wilding . . ."

"So what did you think he *did* want to do to her?"

"I don't know. We were too damn scared to think beyond what would happen to *us* if we didn't go along with him."

There was a small silence as though each man was reliving those days, and then Alex Barnett said uncomfortably, "There's something I should tell you. My wife—my wife went to see Pepper the other day. She'd got this idea into her head that Pepper and I were having an affair. She's not well . . ." He flushed. "An—an accident a long time ago left her sterile, and she longs desperately for a child. She went to see Pepper to beg her to give me up—I don't understand the woman. Pepper took my wife out shopping and then sent her home and told her to talk to me. She could have pushed Julia to the edge of insanity, but instead she went out of her way to reassure her. She even . . ." Alex's thin face flushed, but he went on doggedly, "She even somehow managed to give Julia some hope, something to hold on to. We've been trying to adopt, but there just aren't enough children to go round . . . now Julia's talking about there being a special child somewhere waiting for us."

It was patently obvious that it was painful for him to disclose his private grief to them. Miles could see the mistrust and disbelief in Richard Howell's eyes.

"It's all a trick . . . she's trying to gain your wife's confidence so that she can do even more damage later. She . . ."

"Julia needs something to do to take her mind off the fact that we can't have our own children. I've suggested every manner of work, voluntary and otherwise, but until now she's ignored everything I've said. Now she's talking about working with handi-capped children. There's a new place opened up near us . . . Ranger's Hall."

Miles frowned. Ranger's Hall was Colonel White-gate's old home. He had had no idea that the Barnetts lived so close to it. He made a mental note to have a word with the couple who ran it. Provided they were satisfied that she was physically and mentally capable of working there, there was no reason why a part-time voluntary job couldn't be found for Julia Barnett.

All the time new and different facets of Pepper's personality were being revealed to him. He listened without interrupting while Alex talked about Julia's abortion; his own shock and sense of failure that he had not been able to help her; that he had not known, sensing that the other man needed the catharsis of pouring the whole thing out.

"I'm confused," Alex admitted when he had finished. "This woman is my enemy, and yet she's helped my wife. What will you do to her once you've abducted her?"

Miles gave him an icy look and said coldly, *"I'm not Simon Herries.* I only intend to keep her out of the country long enough for her to become worried about the future of her company and to hand over those files, that's all."

It wasn't all, though. There was his own deep inner conviction that Simon Herries was dangerous. That if he got the opportunity he would offer Pepper physical harm. A man who had killed once always found it easier a second time.

Miles veiled his eyes. He hadn't told the other two what he had discovered in his investigations, and he was pretty sure he was right. It had been hard to discover the truth surrounding the suicide of Tim Wilding's sister . . . hard, but not impossible.

Deborah Wilding's mother had told him that once long ago there had been a curse laid on the family. She had laughed when she said it, but with two children dead it must be very hard not to believe there was some substance in the old tale. Why was it that so many powerful, wealthy families were burdened with more than their fair share of tragedy? Was it because their very power incited too much jealously, too much passion in others? Or was it more simply that great power could so often go hand in hand with great evil?

Absolute power corrupts absolutely, unless one was very strong . . . Impossibly strong, perhaps.

"I'd better go. I don't like leaving Julia on her own for too long." Alex stood up awkwardly.

Richard got to his feet as well. His wife would be at the TV studio—he frowned. She had been talking rather a lot of late about a certain producer they had just taken on. It came to him that he was almost halfway through his allotted span and yet he had not found the contentment and security he had once craved. Owning the bank had not brought him the sense of achievement he had anticipated. In point of fact he had enjoyed himself more in his old entrepreneurial days. He grinned to himself, remembering some of the more spectacular deals he had pulled off. These days he sat back and watched while others made the deals.

He was still frowning as he got into his car. What on earth was the matter with him? He had everything he had ever wanted in life; everything he had ever promised himself. It was a wise man who knew when he had achieved enough. What more was there for him? Expanding the bank? But he didn't want that . . . He shifted uncomfortably in his seat, disliking this odd mood of introspection. He wasn't given to delving too deeply into his inner self. It must have been the letter from Morris that had brought it on.

It had been a long time since Richard had had any contact with his cousin. As far as he knew he was with Rothschild's now and doing quite well in a plodding sort of fashion. It occurred to him that Morris would have been ideal for his job. He would have loved the steady humdrum daily round that so bored and irritated him.

He stopped the car, ignoring the furious and noisy protests of other drivers. Bored, irritated . . . what on earth was he thinking? He had worked all his life for what he had now, how could he be bored with it?

Angrily he took his foot off the brake and slid the car forward. He was getting maudlin, that was what it was. What he needed was a good strong Martini and then an enthusiastic blonde . . . that would soon put the life back in him. He didn't want to go home, there was no point . . . Linda wouldn't be there, and so instead he found himself heading for the bank. The sight of it no longer brought the old thrill. He remembered the excitement that had coursed through him when he realised he had the wealth and the power to take it over.

Jessica's money had helped there . . . Richard had more than doubled the money he had taken from her as the price of his silence and her freedom. He could easily afford to repay her.

Repay her. He stopped the car and stared into the darkness. What the hell was getting into him? Perhaps Herries had been right and Pepper Minesse *was* a witch . . . Well, if so, he would like to see her get the better of Miles French. Now there was a man he wouldn't like to get the wrong side of! *He* wasn't like Herries. He didn't need to be . . . One look from those cold astute eyes and you felt as though every small meanness, every greediness and vice you had ever possessed was being stripped bare and revealed to him.

Tiredly he restarted the car . . . perhaps Linda would be home by now. If so, he hoped to God she would have the good sense to keep her eulogies on her new producer to herself. An open marriage was all well and good, but there were times when there was a lot to be said for the old traditions. A man knew where he was with the woman in his life then . . . she stayed at home and produced children. She cooked his meals and washed his socks . . .

Richard laughed to himself. God, he must be more Jewish than he had ever realised! Kids . . . who wanted them? Look at the mess Alex Barnett had got himself into over them. And yet . . .

In their darkened studio Linda stood watching the

man with her.

"Have you told him yet?" he asked.

She shook her head.

"No, I can't . . ."

"Well, it isn't going to go away, is it? What are you so frightened of?"

She touched her stomach protectively.

"You think he'll want you to get rid of it."

She winced at Gary's words. They had trained together at a hick TV station, now long buried under a pile of debts so high that no one could ever remember it. He had been a shoulder to lean on when Linda discovered she was pregnant. An ear to listen to her woes . . . He was gay and happy with it, he could also make her laugh.

She had been trying to work up the courage for weeks to tell Richard, but the time never seemed to be right . . . and never would be right. They had agreed when they got married that it would be an open, "no holds" affair. Children had never been intended to come into it . . . and yet here she was pregnant, all because of one miserable bout of sickness.

It should have been the easiest decision in the world. She had never wanted children, didn't know the first thing about them and always had abhorred the messiness of uncontrolled emotionalism, and yet here she was torn in half by conflicting yearnings. Wanting Richard and yet wanting their child too . . . Well, she would have to make up her mind soon. Unless of course—darkly, temptingly, the thought slid into her mind—she could simply wait until it was too late . . .

Linda resisted the temptation, pushing it away. No, she wasn't going to sink to that. If she decided to keep the child then she would do so honestly and openly. She would tell Richard and if he didn't want them both then . . . She stopped, appalled by the way the truth had sneaked up on her. She had no intention of even contemplating terminating her pregnancy and never had had. She wanted this child, and intended to keep it.

She hugged the knowledge to herself, swept by a fierce joy, an uprush of relief and release so intense that it overcame her dread of losing the man she loved.

She would have to tell him soon. She would tell him and let him make his decision. She had made hers and she intended to abide by it.

Miles collected Elizabeth Herries himself from the women's refuge. She was trembling with nerves as she got into his car.

They arrived on time for the appointment, but had to wait for almost half an hour as the previous one had overrun.

Miles half suspected that Elizabeth would get up and run out; as it was, every time the door to the waiting room opened she tensed, and Miles knew she was dreading seeing her husband walk in.

The Prime Minister received them kindly, giving them a brisk smile that warned them time was precious and short. Miles told him calmly and unemotionally what Elizabeth had discovered, and immediately he knew that he had judged the PM's reaction correctly. He could see that the man was extremely concerned. He was also relieved that he didn't for one moment appear to doubt Elizabeth's story.

"I'm afraid what you say only confirms my own doubts about your husband. Unfortunately there are those among my Cabinet colleagues who don't agree with me. I think the best thing we can do is to initiate a full investigation into your husband's life-style. I shall let it be known that certain information has come to me without revealing who from."

"It would help if Mrs Herries could have a copy of the report once it's received," Miles interrupted. "She needs to convince her family that her accusations are just before she can ask them to support her in her divorce petition. Obviously she doesn't want the truth to come out in court because of her children, especially her son. We want to make sure that Herries will give up all rights to his children before we petition for divorce.

"He's a very dangerous man," he told the Prime Minister. "A very mentally disturbed man, in my view."

"Yes, I think you're right," he agreed. "Really it's amazing how few men do have to retire from public life because of the stress it involves when one thinks about it, but it does happen."

He was telling them what would happen to Simon, Miles suspected. Obviously the Government would not be able to come out into the open and announce exactly why one of the country's most lauded MPs was giving up his seat. If indeed he could be compelled to give it up.

"Don't worry, Mrs Herries," the Prime Minister smiled reassuringly at Elizabeth. "I promise you that your husband will have no inkling that you and I have met."

"From now until the time the divorce goes through I'd like you and the children to stay at my house in the country. I'm employing a bodyguard who'll stay there with you. It's for the best, Elizabeth," Miles told her when she would have demurred. "You'll all be perfectly safe there."

He was dropping her outside the refuge when Pepper saw them. She was considering buying a property in the area, which was at present run down, but which she had heard on the grapevine was gradually being invaded by the lower end of the up-and-coming "yuppie" market.

She recognised Elizabeth immediately from photographs on her file, but what was *she* doing with Miles French? She dismissed the thought that they were involved in a sexual relationship almost before it was born. There was nothing sexual in the way Miles was both holding and talking to the other woman. But there was concern, and compassion. Concern—compassion, from a man like Miles French.

Pepper left without either of them seeing her, her interest in the potential property boom subdued beneath her curiosity about Miles and Elizabeth Herries.

It was one of his allies in the Cabinet who told Simon Herries what was going on.

"An investigation?" he echoed. Panic hit him, clawing at him, sending him wild with fear and rage.

It was that Minesse woman's doing—he knew it. He should have got rid of her. He shouldn't have let French take control . . .

Somehow Simon mastered his reaction and smiled tightly at his colleague, thanking him for the information.

An investigation . . . They couldn't discover anything, he reassured himself. They couldn't . . . And then remembered Elizabeth. Where was she? He had to find her and make her come back to him, and then he had to destroy Pepper Minesse.

He bumped into a fellow MP as he left the building and swore vitriolically at him without even seeing him properly. Yes, Pepper Minesse was to blame. Well, he would punish her for it, but first he would make sure she was sorry for what she had done. Oh yes, she would be sorry—very, very sorry!

Simon could feel the rage rising inside him, engorging his body, obliterating everything else. He thought of Tim and how Pepper had taken him from him. Tim had wanted to sacrifice her, believing that through her death he could raise the Devil. Simon had laughed at him, but perhaps Tim had been right. He could feel the madness starting to engulf him and he pushed it back, knowing he needed to be calm, to plan . . .

First he must find Elizabeth. She had no money and few friends, so it shouldn't be very difficult to track her down.

CHAPTER SEVENTEEN

As SHE came out of the hairdressers, Pepper didn't notice the car parked at the side of the road. Why should she? It was ordinary enough, and besides, she had too many other things on her mind.

Her hairdressers was only a short distance from her office and unless the weather was really bad she always walked. She would have to ring Jeff Stowell when she got back about that new tennis player she wanted to see. She frowned as she remembered that Miranda had forgotten to give her this message. She didn't know what was wrong with her secretary at the moment; she seemed unusually forgetful. There had been an air of expectant excitement not unmingled with envy about her this morning. Pepper shrugged the thought aside. The girl was probably having problems with her love life.

Miles sat in the car and watched her, admiring the feminine movement of her hips. Only seconds after Pepper had left her office Miranda had phoned him and given him their pre-arranged signal.

He supposed he would have found a way to put his plans into action without the secretary's help, but it wouldn't have been easy. He had planned everything in the most minute detail. He had gone through Pepper's schedule with Miranda a dozen or more times. Today was the day, and had he not been able to pick her up now, he would have followed Pepper to lunch and tried again then.

He got out of the car smoothly as she drew level

with him. He registered the surprise in her eyes, and then the shock as he reached for her. He was blocking her way, stopping her from moving.

Pepper opened her mouth to scream—and instantly found herself gasping for air as Miles's mouth came down on hers. The shock of being kissed so unexpectedly and so publicly deprived her of the ability to think. She tried weakly to struggle, but Miles's grip on her was too strong. He was slowly dragging her towards the car, she realised in panic. He was going to kidnap her! His mouth lifted as he pulled her into the car with him. She felt something cold and hard pressed against her ribs and her heart bounded in fright.

"All right!" Miles called out to the driver, and then before Pepper could speak, he murmured menacingly against her ear, "One word . . . just one word, Pepper, and I promise you it will be your last!"

All her normal composure and alertness deserted her. She was completely panic-stricken. Too many memories came crowding back for her to think rationally. Miles was still holding her in that macabre parody of a lovers' embrace with his gun into the softness of her body. Her mouth still tingled from his kiss. She was enveloped in the scent and heat of him. It smothered her, choking off her breath, depriving her of enough oxygen to make her brain cells work. She made a tiny moaning protest of fear under her breath, and instantly his grip tightened.

Dazed, she stared out of the window. Where was he taking her? She remembered Oxford and that bare, old-fashioned panelled room and her stomach churned sickly, her skin turning cold with fear. She wanted to cry out . . . She ought to cry out, and yet somehow she couldn't. The man driving the car wouldn't help her anyway, she admitted bitterly. They were both in it together.

The sunshine was suddenly blanked out and they were in darkness. Panic hit her again, and then she realised they had entered an underground garage. Almost as though he wanted to soothe her fear, Miles leaned towards her and said softly,

"It's all right, I'm not going to hurt you."

Not going to hurt her, when he was threatening her with a gun? The car stopped. The driver got out and opened the door. Miles got out first, then hauled Pepper out alongside him, still holding on to her. The driver averted his eyes . . . almost as though in fact they were lovers, Pepper thought bemusedly.

Miles said something to him, in a murmur too low for her to catch, but she thought she heard him mention a time, and then Miles was half dragging, half carrying her towards a lift.

She shivered with tension. What would she find when she reached her eventual destination? Would Alex Barnett be there, and Richard Howell . . . and Simon Herries?

They were inside the lift. It was dark and hot, but Pepper still felt intensely cold. Almost as though he was aware of it, Miles started to rub the frozen flesh of her arms. In another man the gesture might almost have been comforting. It made her feel protected, cherished . . . like a little girl . . . She banished the thought, frightened suddenly by the extent of her vulnerability. This was what kidnappers did to their victims, wasn't it? Lured them into a position of false dependence, teaching them to accept and then need those whom they should most fear. Well, that wasn't going to happen to her. Wasn't it a technique the Nazis had perfected on their prisoners during the war? Round and round her thoughts circled, like vultures waiting for blood.

The lift stopped. Pepper clung to the door, refusing to move. Miles looked at her, his eyes hard and dark. She tensed as he picked her up. The ignominy of being so easily defeated frightened her. Her face was pushed into his shoulder and her body prickled with fear and dislike at being so close to him. He stopped and she heard him unlocking the door. She struggled in his arms, frantic for escape, but there was none.

She door slammed behind them and she saw the narrow walls of a small hallway. It opened out into a huge room with a panoramic view of the city.

"A flat I've borrowed from a friend," Miles told her as he dropped her on one of the cream suede settees.

It was a woman's home, Pepper recognised instinctively, a sensual, physical woman who enjoyed the stroke of suede against her skin, and the richness of thick cream rugs on the floor. Had this woman and Miles been lovers? Were they lovers now?

"Now," Miles told her calmly, "we can do this the easy way, or we can take the hard path. It all depends on you."

"Where are the others?" Her throat was dry and cracked, her voice a painful whisper. "Aren't you going to let them in on my humiliation?"

"Which one of them did you want in particular?" Miles asked her drily, giving her an assessing look. "Simon Herries?"

Pepper went white, and he had a moment's compunction. Under that closed, shuttered little face, she must be terrified, but she wasn't showing it. He didn't make the mistake of believing that she had no emotions as so many others had. He knew too much about her for that. She had them all right, and right now they would be tormenting the hell out of her.

"You and I are doing this alone, Pepper. After all, it only takes one man to . . ."

"Don't!" The tormented, agonised cry cut right across what he was saying. Pepper pressed her hands to her ears. He was going to rape her . . . to attack her as she had been attacked before. He was . . .

"As I was saying, it only takes one of us to make you realise that you're in as vulnerable a position as the rest of us, and I elected to be that one."

He had her attention now. She was staring at him, caught somewhere between fear and a small glimmering hope that perhaps after all he did not mean to hurt her.

"Why do you think I've been at such pain to establish us as lovers, Pepper?"

She frowned. "We aren't lovers!"

"No, but the rest of the world thinks we are, doesn't it?"

She couldn't deny it.

"How do you think Minesse Management will fare without you to take charge?"

Pepper stared at him in disbelief.

"You can't get away with this," she told him huskily as enlightenment dawned. Why, oh, why hadn't she thought of this?

"Give me your files and your written promise that nothing in them will be publicly revealed and we won't have to," Miles told her reasonably.

He waited, praying that she would refuse. Things had gone too far now. She knew too much. He doubted that anything other than her complete destruction would satisfy Simon Herries, but he didn't want her to know that yet. Later, when he had taught her to trust him . . . If he could teach her to trust him, he thought wryly, remembering the fear and revulsion betrayed by every part of her body whenever he so much as touched her.

"You'll never be able to do it . . . They'll be looking for me . . . for us . . . When they find out you've kidnapped me . . ."

"Kidnapped?" His eyebrows rose. "Oh, they won't think that, surely? A woman goes away with her latest lover . . . especially a woman like Pepper Minesse, no one is going to think she's going unwillingly."

Pepper stared at him. Too late now she saw his purpose. And damn him, he was quite right . . . no one would question her disappearance with him.

"And if I refuse to hand over the papers?"

"A statement in our leading papers discreetly announcing that Miss Pepper Minesse is taking—er— an indefinite rest owing to overwork and nervous strain."

Pepper stared at him, appalled. If he carried through that threat her business empire would disappear overnight. No one would want to touch her . . . she would be ruined . . .

"You can't do that!" she gasped.

"Oh, I think you'll find that I can, but it needn't be necessary—just hand over those files."

"Never!" The word exploded between them, and Pepper was too angry to see the gleam of relief in Miles's eyes.

"Very well then," he said silkily, "let's see if a short time—say two weeks away from Minesse Management, won't make you change your mind. An uncaptained ship can sail into some dangerous waters, as I'm sure you know."

She wasn't going to give in, Pepper decided. There must be a way she could escape from him.

"Two weeks?" she said derisively. "You intend to keep me cooped up here fourteen days?"

"Not here." Miles smiled at her, and there was

something in that smile that awakened every one of her primitive instincts. This man wanted more from her than simple retribution . . . more even than her agreement to his plans. He wanted . . . She looked at him, her mind unable to cope with the enormity of what her emotions were relaying to her. She had been desired by men before, countless numbers of them, but never a man like this, she admitted to herself. And his desire was different from theirs, less overt, less sexual and more cerebral . . . and much, much more dangerous.

She dismissed the thought, knowing that to contemplate it was to weaken herself.

"I'm going to have a cup of coffee. Do you want one?"

Pride tempted her to refuse, but she had missed her coffee at the hairdressers because they had been very busy, and her mouth watered at the thought.

Miles got up and said casually, "By the way, just to avoid any embarrassment for you, I might as well tell you that the phone has been disconnected, and that the only door to this place is well and truly locked."

Pepper looked at him with acute dislike. He must have guessed that she had intended to try to escape the moment he turned his back, and of course, he would have thought of that contingency and made plans against it. Miles French, it seemed, was a master planner . . . but then being a lawyer no doubt he would be . . . every 'i' dotted, every 't' crossed. He would probably be just as meticulous when he made love, she thought bitterly—meticulous and wholly unspontaneous, she added nastily to herself.

She looked up and discovered that he was grinning at her. For one appalled moment she thought he had read her mind and was about to verbally discount her theories, and then she realised he was probably amused by the thought that he had stopped her escaping from him.

"No coffee for me," she told him abruptly, and then seconds later wished she had not been so obstinate, when she caught the delicious scent of newly ground beans wafting from the kitchen. Her stomach protested at its unwanted immolation on the altar of her pride, her taste buds rioting in furious disorder at what they were being denied.

When Miles came in with a jug of coffee and two mugs on the tray he said casually,

"Just in case you wanted to change your mind."

There was also a small jug of hot milk . . . Pepper wavered, and then he poured his own coffee. He drank it black, and the smell was just too much for her.

"Perhaps I will have some after all," she said grudgingly, not daring to look at him. If he gloated . . . if he laughed . . . but instead all he did was pour the fresh-made fragrant dark liquid into the other mug. She stopped him when it was three quarters full.

"I like mine white."

"Help yourself." He indicated the jug of hot milk. "I heated some up just in case."

She poured it into her coffee and picked up the mug, warming her chilled fingers. There was something comforting both about the warmth and the smell. She took a sip and then another. Five minutes later it was gone and she looked longingly at the coffee remaining in the pot. She was just reaching for it when Miles whipped it away from her.

What *was* this? she wondered irately. Some new form of torture? "I wanted another cup . . ."

"This has gone cold. I'll make some more."

Pepper opened her mouth to protest and found to

her surprise that she was yawning. That was odd, she felt quite sleepy all of a sudden . . . very sleepy, in fact, and almost relaxed. She leaned back in her seat, and felt her eyelids close. Panic was slow to hit her, but when it did and she realised what was happening, she opened her eyes, fighting against the relentless tide of sleepiness overwhelming her, her voice blurred and soft as she cried out accusingly, "You've drugged me!"

And then, impossibly, she was fast asleep.

Looking down at her, Miles grimaced. God, but that had been a near thing! As it was he had hated giving her the stuff, but his doctor friend had assured him it would do no harm. What he hadn't expected was that she would want a second drink of coffee. That had really panicked him. Lucky the stuff worked so fast. He had been at his wits' end as to how to get it into her, disliking the idea of force, until Miranda had happened to mention her boss's love of freshly made milky coffee . . . He grimaced as he looked down at his own barely touched mug. He loathed the stuff black, but hadn't wanted to alert Pepper's suspicions by bringing in two readymade mugs.

Now all that remained was for him to put the final part of his plan into operation.

Their flight was already booked. His chauffeur would drive them to the airport. The chauffeur was the son of Colonel Whitegate's ex-batman, and had been quite happy to accept Miles's story of a romantic involvement with a lady who was pretending to be slightly unwilling.

Slightly unwilling. Miles grimaced at the memory of Pepper's taut, bitterly rejecting body. He could almost kill Herries for that alone . . .

He dragged his thoughts away from the past. What was done was done, and there was no going back . . .

only going forward. At the airport when he took his comatose 'girlfriend' on board the jet, Miles would explain to the staff that she was terrified of flying. A tranquilliser too many, plus a good stiff drink . . . it wasn't the first time it had happened, and it wouldn't be the last.

He looked down at Pepper's sleeping figure. She was slumped against the cushions at an awkward angle, and with great tenderness Miles moved them, frowning over the task as he made every endeavour not to actually touch her. It was odd, this need he felt in himself not to infringe upon her privacy more than was absolutely necessary . . . Almost as though he was thinking that at some later date she might acknowledge and be grateful for his care of her. He grimaced at the thought. Grateful! He was more likely to have a spitting, clawing cat on his hands when she finally came round.

He doubted that even revealing to her the danger he suspected she was in would soften her mood of antagonism. She probably wouldn't believe him no matter what he told her, he thought moodily.

It was crazy, this habit he had fallen into of trying to anticipate her thoughts, of almost knowing how she would think and react. He had felt it before, on some of his more demanding criminal cases, but never to this extent . . . never with this degree of intimacy. One of his tutors had once told him that he was an instinctive creature, and that no amount of logic would ever make him totally forget that deep-running vein within him. Miles knew that he had been right. It was still there, and there were many occasions when he had allowed himself to be guided by it.

It was in force now, telling him that once he was on that plane he would have set his foot on the first step of his journey from which there would be no going back. He looked down at Pepper. There were a dozen or more other places he could take her . . . and yet . . . He thought of the villa in Goa, of its tropical gardens and appealing air of decay . . . of its lushness, the warm sensuality of the air . . . His watch buzzed and he flicked back his cuff, staring at it.

Time to go.

Their cases were already in the car. Miles grinned a little to himself. Miranda had been right to warn him that no woman wants to be abducted without her favourite clothes, but he wondered what Pepper would make of the ones he had chosen for her. He hoped he had gauged the sizes correctly.

He picked her up. She was a dead weight in his arms, and yet so small that his conscience pricked at him. But what alternative did he really have? Simon Herries was a dangerous, half-crazed man, who would not even think twice about harming her, if he felt the need.

Something would have to be done about him . . . he had taken the first step, and he hoped the words of warning he had dropped gently into a prominent M.P.'s ear had had the right effect.

Everything went as planned. The girls on the check-in desk were all sympathetic understanding and mild envy for Pepper as Miles explained her delicate state. Once on the plane he tucked her into the inside seat and fastened her seat belt. She hadn't even stirred . . . he looked at his watch. She shouldn't come round until they were well on their way, and he hoped to God his medical friend had not been over-enthusiastic with his cocktail of drugs.

The droning in her ears was familiar and persistent. Pepper struggled through layers of unconsciousness to reach out and recognise it. A plane, she thought sleepily . . . she was on a plane. Why did she find the thought so comforting? Such a relief . . . something unpleasant and unwanted tugged at her memory. Behind her closed eyelids a variety of images danced . . . a car, an unfamiliar room, Miles French's face . . . fear. Muzzy unclear impressions like those recalled from a nightmare.

A nightmare . . . yes, that was it! Relief warmed her. She was on a plane and she must have fallen asleep and had a bad dream. But where was she going? Her brain felt thick and woolly . . . She struggled to open her eyes.

"Pepper."

The familiar voice, so close at hand, froze her. It wasn't a dream. It was real. Somehow Miles French was here with her on the plane . . .

Weakly she closed her eyes and feigned sleep. She didn't feel able to cope with the reality of him right now. She would wait until her brain had cleared a little bit more.

At her side, Miles, who knew quite well that she was awake, grimaced to himself but said nothing. Soon their flight would be over. Transport to their destination had been arranged for them, but once they were there they would be as effectively cut off from the outside world as though they were on an uninhabited island.

The staff at the villa spoke only Portuguese; they were a small enclosed community, descendants of the servants brought out to India by the first Portuguese settlers. There was no telephone, no transport other than mule and cart, and the owner had been at great pains to preserve the villa's remoteness.

Although she had closed her eyes, Pepper was far from unaware of Miles's presence at her side. She thought of his threat and how it held the potential to destroy all that she worked so hard for. It was sheer blackmail, and stubbornly she decided that she wasn't going to give in to it.

It struck her as the thought formed that he could well be feeling exactly the same way about her threats against him, but she dismissed such anarchist mental meanderings, reminding herself virtuously that she, unlike Miles had moral right on her side.

She felt the plane start to lose height. She had never liked flying, and instinctively her fingers clutched at the armrest of her seat. The shock of having her cold hand taken within the comfortingly warm grasp of someone else's forced her eyes wide open. She glared at Miles and tried to tug her hand away.

"Don't let go," he murmured, smiling at her. "I'm scared!"

Pepper opened her mouth to deliver a blistering put-down, and at that moment the plane hit an air pocket and lurched drunkenly, dropping several hundred feet. She managed to stop herself from screaming, but there was no way she could stop herself from flinging herself almost bodily into Miles's arms, her face buried in the curve of his shoulder. Instantly his arms came round her, holding her, his voice a soothing murmur of inanities in her ear that helped her body to stop its wild trembling and her fear to subside.

The plane levelled out; the pilot announced that they would soon be landing. Pepper, her face red with embarrassment and rage, extricated herself from Miles's body, her face deliberately averted from him. One word . . . just let him say one word, make one mocking comment, and she would kill him!

But he said nothing, and eventually she was forced to conquer her own emotions and turn to look at him.

He was calmly reading his newspaper, and as he felt her attention focus on him he put it down and looked enquiringly at her.

He really was the most complicated and unfathomable man! Where she had expected him to crow over her cowardice he was acting as though it had simply never happened. No other man she knew would have been able to resist drawing a comparison between her tough businesslike behaviour and her complete and to their minds feminine panic at the first hint of any danger.

"You won't get away with this!" she told him fiercely. "The moment this plane lands I'm going to tell the authorities that you've abducted me!"

Miles surveyed her with interest.

"Really? Well, if you're thinking of appealing to the cabin crew, I should forget it . . . I've told them that we've had a fight and that you'll probably pretend I'm abducting you, just to get back at me."

Pepper glared at him, knowing he had spiked her guns.

The plane landed; the airport was hot and busy, the night air full of unfamiliar scents and voices. Pepper stood stock still, bemused by the alienness of her surroundings. India . . . she recognised that they were somewhere in India. She heard Miles call her name, but when she turned round she couldn't see him. She was surrounded by a seething throng of unfamiliar faces speaking an unknown language.

The shock of being abducted, the strangeness of her unknown surroundings sent her into an uncharacteristic panic. She started to tremble, the blood racing fearfully round her veins. She looked desperately for Miles, searching among the turbanned figures for his bare dark head. She couldn't see him, and for one fearful moment she thought he might actually leave her here among these unknown people whose language she couldn't speak, without money or papers. The effect was instantaneous; a throw back from her days with the Lee tribe; a feeling of panicky alienation swept over her, a fear of the people around her and their reaction to her "difference". She wanted to run and hide herself to escape from their curious glances.

Someone touched her and she swung round. Miles was standing behind her, frowning slightly. He saw the way she was trembling and drew her closer to his side. Almost instantly Pepper felt comforted and reassured by the proximity of him. Although she didn't want to admit it, even in the privacy of her own thoughts, she was glad of his presence.

All through the Customs and Immigration the shock of her discovery kept her silent. She wasn't used to having to depend on any other human being, never mind one like Miles French who was actually her enemy.

Her docility puzzled Miles. Concern for her coloured his relief at having carried out his plan successfully. Rage, tantrums, even personal violence, he had all been prepared for, but not this too pacific, dull acceptance. Had the drug he had given her been too strong? Had the fact that he had abducted her had some deep pyschological effect on her connected with her previous abduction by Alex and Richard?

Now for the first time he began to doubt the wisdom of his plans, but what other alternative had he had? Pepper was so much safer away from Simon Herries, and yet if he tried to tell her that she would not believe his warning to be altruistic. In her mind he was firmly linked with Herries and the others, and he doubted that anything he could do would convince her otherwise.

The feeling that touched him as he acknowledged

this shocked him. He had liked, admired, and even loved many women in his life, but for none had he felt this protective, fierce anger. For none had he felt this sharp desire spiked with the grim realisation that it was a desire that would probably never be satisfied.

From the moment he had realised that there had been no lovers in Pepper's life he had been aware of the damage Simon Herries had wreaked. To love a woman carrying such a burden was the last thing any sensible man would do.

Love? Miles caught himself up, frowning. What on earth was he thinking? He barely knew her . . . had talked to her on a handful of occasions, no more.

But you do know her, an inner, stronger voice taunted. You know everything there is to know about her.

And it was true. He did. From the reports he had gathered; from his own knowledge, from everything he had assimilated about Pepper, he knew her as intimately and thoroughly as though they had spent their whole lives in the knowledge of one another. It was a disturbing thought . . . a disturbing acknowledgement. How often during his life had Miles been aware somewhere deep within him of an inner, relentless searching for a oneness with another human being that would fill the empty space in his life?

But that woman could not be Pepper Minesse, surely? He had grown to adulthood knowing of this inner need within him; his intelligence told him it sprang from his own childhood . . . from not having any parents, from being alone. And while his intelligence had derided it, his instinct had allowed it to flourish; had been wise enough to know that it was an essential and important part of him, and that if he tried to destroy it, he would be destroying a very vital element of himself. Without that inner vulnerability he would not be the successful barrister that he was; he was sure of it. Others might deride instinct, and call it superstition, but it was so much a part of himself he rarely even questioned it any more.

Until now . . . Until it had told him that he had found what he had always wanted in the person of the woman standing at his side. He looked at her. Even after the long flight she looked beautiful. The wildness was subdued; the gloss gone, but the essential woman remained. Miles wanted to reach out and touch her skin, push the heaviness of her hair off her face, to cushion her protectively against his side.

He grimaced to himself, imagining Pepper's reaction if she were able to read his thoughts. Most of his women friends were of the new breed of dynamic career women, and he had long ago acknowledged that womankind had no need of the male sex for her protection or existence.

"Where are we going?"

The rusty sound of Pepper's voice checked him. He looked down at her, wishing there could have been an easier way of doing this.

"Wait and see." He touched her arm, directing her towards the helicopter terminal where his friend housed his private transport. The pilot was waiting for them. A porter brought their luggage. Pepper gaped at the machine, and sensing her reluctance to board it, Miles picked her up. The pilot grinned at him, and Pepper, furious and frightened, glared at them both. It was too dark for her to see where they were going, and besides, she was frightened of doing so, in case she started to feel even sicker than she did already.

Miles took one look at her white face and clenched hands and reached out to touch her comfortingly. Pepper opened her eyes and glared at him. She reminded him of an angry, frightened kitten, all ready

to spit and claw. He smiled to himself at the blatant
sexism of his comparison, and acknowledged wryly
that, equality or not, there were still some things so
deeply ingrained in the male psyche that they were
not easily rooted out.

The helicopter ride seemed to last an eternity, but
at least they were putting down. Pepper opened her
eyes and then closed them again, blinded by the
battery of light illuminating the landing area. The
helicopter bumped on to the concrete and then settled.
Miles opened his door and got out, turning to lift her
down. She wanted to refuse his help, but the drop to
the ground was too high for her to make alone. The
pilot removed their luggage, and what seemed like a
dozen pairs of eager brown hands took it away. The
pilot got back in his seat, and as Miles drew her away
into the dark shadows beyond the lights, it took off
again.

She watched it go, shivering with a mixture of
apprehension and excitement. Excitement? She shivered
harder and risked a glance at the man standing beside
her. Excitement wasn't an emotion she was used to
experiencing in any context, and certainly not in
connection with a man; unless it was caused by an
opportunity of putting one down. She looked away,
unsettled by her thoughts, acknowledging that there
was precious little chance of her putting Miles French
down. The combination of lazy good humour and
iron determination that he used to such good effect
defeated her. And that was frightening.

"This way." He touched her arm, directing her past
terracotta pots full of tumbling plants, their colours
muted by the diffused light. The night sky was full of
stars, the moon waning. Pepper had a jumbled impression of towers and trellises, of archways, and the rich
scent of heavily perfumed flowers, as Miles led her

down a flight of steps and through a doorway into
the almost icy coolness of a dimly lit square room.

Her heels rang noisily on the chequered tiled floor.
Heavy, carved furniture hugged the walls in formal
array; rich hangings blanketing the windows.

The room was almost Moorish in conception, and
that confused her. A woman came in, gliding so
smoothly it was impossible to imagine how such fluid
movements were perfected. She was plump and saried,
a caste-mark on her forehead. She smiled at them
both and greeted Miles in a language Pepper couldn't
begin to understand.

He listened and then translated.

"Maja says that food is prepared for us if we want
it, but that also your room is ready if you prefer to
rest."

Pepper was totally disorientated. She had no idea
what time of night it was. She was totally exhausted,
and suddenly the thought of the privacy and silence
of her bedroom was so blissfully tempting that she
didn't have to think of making a choice.

Maja smiled and bowed, indicating that she was to
follow her. Pepper went with her down what seemed
to be a maze of corridors until finally they stopped
outside a heavily carved door. Maja opened it and
indicated that Pepper was to go in.

Like the other room this too was furnished with
ornate, heavily carved furniture, expensive silk draped
the huge bed, beneath the protective mosquito nets.
The floor was bare and polished, its dark expanse
broken up here and there with softly silky rugs.

Maja smiled as she waited for Pepper to absorb the
magnificence of her surroundings—and magnificent
was the only way to describe them, Pepper acknowledged, reverently touching one of the silk-covered
ottomans.

When she had judged that Pepper had had sufficient time to adjust to her surroundings, Maja crossed the room and opened another door. Pepper followed her through it. She was in a long corridor-like room lined with mirrors and cupboards, obviously a dressing room. Another door off it led into her private bathroom. The size of the round marble bath astounded her. The fitments were gold inlaid with jade and the floor a rich polished malachite. Pepper had never seen anything like it in her life. Visions of Cecil B deMille extravaganzas danced before her eyes, but they had nothing on the reality and sumptuousness of this room. It was a suite designed for a pampered woman whose only role was to please the man who provided her with such luxuries, and Pepper wondered wildly if Miles French had deliberately chosen this suite for her. He knew so much about her . . . too much. If he knew that her much vaunted sexual experience was a total sham . . . She shivered, despite the moist heat in the air.

Maja, seeing the fear darkening her eyes, touched her arm in concern. Pepper smiled at her. If only she had some way of communicating with this woman, of asking her all the questions that tormented her mind. Where on earth was she? Somewhere or other in the Indian subcontinent, but where?

Maja indicated the bath and turned on the taps, miming that Pepper should undress, and Pepper realised that the woman intended to stay with her while she did so. But in what capacity? As a maid or a guard?

Pepper was too exhausted to dwell on the question; too exhausted to marvel at the incongruity of the fact that she, who had always been so determinedly independent, should be so unquestioningly accepting Maja's ministrations, almost as docilely as though she herself were indeed just another possession among many owned by a man wealthy enough to own such a house and so many riches.

CHAPTER EIGHTEEN

She slept deeply and well, opening her eyes to the morning sunlight, stretching languorously in what surely must be the most comfortable bed she had ever occupied. The mosquito netting diffused the light, giving it a faint haziness. Pepper had slept nude, too exhausted to wait until Maja had unpacked her luggage, but now she saw that a robe had been folded carefully over the ottoman at the bottom of the bed.

She picked it up, frowning over its tobacco satin extravagance. It was cut in a severe, almost masculine style, and yet as she slid the fabric over her sleep-warm body she had a shivery, tormenting mental image of Miles French.

The heat must be getting to her already, she thought grimly. Last night she might have been stupid enough to let Miles think he could get away with abducting her, but today he was going to discover that she was far from being a passive pawn in his game.

She bathed and dressed in the clothes she found hanging in the cupboard—cool, comfortable cottons, all in exactly the right size. She frowned over the labels, recognising them; even knowing the Knightsbridge shops they must have come from. Had Miles himself bought them for her? The thought made her feel restless and uncomfortable. She disliked the idea of him handling the brief items of cotton underwear she was wearing. It was almost as though he had in some intimate way reached out and touched her.

She dismissed the thought as fanciful, and combed

her hair. Now that she was up she felt restless and trapped. She didn't even know how to find her way back to last night's salon, from her room.

Almost as though her thoughts had conjured her up, there was a tap on her door and Maja appeared. She beamed when she saw Pepper up and dressed and by mime indicated that she was to follow her. They went down another maze of corridors, emerging into the sunlight of a shadowy courtyard. A central fountain tinkled musically, the whole scene one of tranquillity, and Pepper stiffened instinctively when she saw Miles seated in one of the chairs pulled up at a table laden with fresh fruit, a pot of coffee and what smelled like freshly baked cinnamon rolls.

She looked round, trying to get her bearings, as Maja glided silently away. Pale pink-washed walls, furniture that looked Spanish, or was it Portuguese, in conception—and yet Maja was obviously Indian; the airport, the rich smell of spices in the air there . . . these did not belong to Europe. So where exactly were they?

Pepper looked again at the tropical climbers smothering the walls and felt the moist heat of the air around her. Miles pulled out a chair for her, and like a sleepwalker, with no will of her own, she subsided into it.

"Where are we?" she asked.

She had meant to demand, instead she sounded more as though she were pleading.

"Goa," Miles told her promptly. "The Portuguese colonised it in the fourteenth century, I think it was. This villa belonged to a member of the Portuguese nobility, a *conde*, in fact, but the rich spice trade that made his family wealthy has gone, and so he sold this estate to a client of mine. It's virtually inaccessible other than by helicopter."

Pepper looked at him, and sensed that he was telling her the truth.

"What were once cultivated fields have long ago given way to jungle. The nearest village is twenty miles away and the nearest railway closer to fifty. This is a forgotten part of the world, although unfortunately not for much longer. The coast is unbelievable—soft pink beaches, the deepest blue ocean I've ever seen, the kind of solitude I'd forgotten existed, but we're too far away from it for you to enjoy it."

In point of fact they were only a matter of a dozen miles from the coast and one of the villa's outhouses housed the ancient Land Rover that was capable of taking them there, but Miles wasn't going to tell Pepper that.

Without her make-up and her hair loose, she looked like a young girl. Her vulnerability caught him off guard. He wanted to go up to her and comfort her, to take away that brief flash of panic he had seen seize hold of her when she saw him. He wanted to reassure her that she had nothing to fear, and yet conversely he knew that he could not.

He had arranged that the helicopter would come for them in two weeks' time. By then he hoped to have persuaded Pepper to drop her vendetta. He hoped to have convinced her how dangerous Simon Herries really was.

"Come and sit down and have some breakfast," he invited.

Pepper wanted to refuse, but what was the point in starving herself? Shrugging slightly, she sat down, resolving that no matter what he said to her she would simply pretend that Miles French did not exist. Yes, that was what she would do. For as long as he kept her captive here she would pretend she was here alone. She would ignore him completely and totally.

Only things didn't work out quite like that.

After their mutually silent breakfast Miles excused himself and said he was sure Pepper would prefer to be alone.

"I've brought some work with me that I want to do. Why don't you walk through the gardens? They're truly magnificent. Maja will accompany you."

So Maja *was* her guard! Pepper stifled a feeling of resentment as the Indian woman appeared and she and Miles started talking away together, both of them laughing at some joke that Miles had obviously made.

It was ridiculous to feel excluded, and yet she did. She turned her head away, determined to ignore his suggestion, and yet after ten minutes or so she was so wrought up with tension and tired of her own company that she was only too glad to go with Maja when the other woman indicated with gestures and smiles that she was ready to accompany Pepper on a tour.

Over the next few days Pepper become more familiar with the grounds and the villa itself. It was one of the most beautiful places she had ever seen; and yet the very air here seemed to be imbued with an atmosphere of heady sensuality; of lazy concupiscence so totally at odds with her own personality that it made her on edge.

She knew now that a small army of people worked and lived within the walls of the villa, keeping it in a state of instant readiness for its owner. She learned also that Miles had told her the truth when describing their remoteness. There was no phone, no means of communication with the outside world at all.

While she fussed and fumed about being so out of touch with the rest of the world, Miles was calmly involved in the work he had brought with him.

Her self-imposed silence hadn't lasted very long.

Pepper was discovering that it was pleasanter to have
someone to vent her wrath upon than to maintain an
icy silence, and no matter how much she argued or
demanded, Miles maintained that same façade of easy
companionability. But Pepper wasn't deceived. Here
indeed was the iron fist within the velvet glove. Here
indeed was a man who meant what he said.

"Doesn't it worry you?" she fretted one evening
when they had finished their meal. "People might be
wanting to get in touch with you. You could be losing
important cases . . ."

"No . . . cases are like buses, there's always another
one coming along," he mocked. "And besides, I don't
believe in a man allowing his work to dominate his
life. Work is simply one facet of a whole." He smiled
at her and mocked, "All things in moderation . . .
that's my creed for living."

It was a creed that Pepper found hard to comprehend, and yet it held familiar overtones. She
remembered Naomi telling her much the same thing.
She relaxed into her chair, smiling softly at the memory
of her grandmother.

"Who are you thinking of?" Miles asked her softly.

"My grandmother." The answer slipped out past
unguarded lips.

"Of course. Naomi, the queen of the Lee tribe."

Pepper sat up tensely. "How did you know that?"

Miles shrugged. "I'm a barrister, used to ferreting
out facts. I know all there is to know about you,
Rachel," he told her softly, deliberately using her old
name.

He hadn't moved, and yet instantly she felt threatened. She tensed and her tongue clove to the roof of
her mouth. Was he going to deride her, to taunt her
with her childhood? But no, he couldn't—she remembered his had been even more bereft of love than had

her own. She ached to put some physical distance between them, but she was too proud to move.

Was this it—was this the moment she had dreaded deep down inside herself ever since he had abducted her? Was this where he proved to her that he was just like any other man she had ever known, that beneath his urbanity and good humour, beneath the compassion she had glimpsed within him occasionally, he too was driven by a lust to possess her?

He desired her, she knew that. She had seen it in his eyes when he watched her. Would he try to inflict that desire on her? Would he . . .

Her eyes grew enormous in her pale face, her tension filling the room, making the atmosphere almost crackle with it.

Miles felt it, and instantly knew the reason for it. He had been waiting for this moment, knowing that they must both some time confront it. He had been scrupulous about not touching Pepper, not invading her personal space or intruding on her privacy, but time was running out and now he needed desperately to talk to her. He had deliberately banked down his own sensuality, forcing back his response to her. He wanted to make love to her, but before that could happen he had to win her trust, to convince her that he meant her no harm. To show her that there did exist a man who could understand and break through her web of fear.

"I know everything," he repeated slowly, standing up.

Pepper froze, waiting for him to come towards her, instead he walked over to the window and stood staring out into the night.

She sensed that he was weighing up something, coming to an important decision, and her muscles clenched protestingly.

"I want to talk to you about why I brought you here, Pepper."

It was such an anticlimax after the physical assault she had been dreading that it took her several seconds to respond. At first all she could do was to simply stare at him in confusion, and then she pulled herself together and said bitterly,

"I already *know* why. You *told* me, remember?"

"I lied to you . . . at least in part. Is that really what you think of me, Pepper—that I want to hurt you, to frighten you?"

It was almost as though he was pleading with her to deny it, but why should he plead with her for anything? Miles saw her face close up and sighed. It was not going to be easy, but then he had never believed it would be.

"Look, Pepper—I had nothing whatsoever to do with your rape. *Nothing at all.* I'm a man who prides himself on his honesty, both with myself and with others. I had no part in what happened that night. Do you honestly realise what you're dealing with— what kind of man Herries is?" he demanded before Pepper could refute his first statement.

"A man who raped me!" she challenged him flatly.

"And a man who beats and abuses his wife and son . . . a man who takes young boys off the street and . . ." He saw her flinch and pushed his hand through his already untidy hair in a gesture of self-disgust. "How can I get through to you, Pepper? Simon Herries is dangerous, almost insanely so. I suspect that you're in very grave danger—in danger of losing your life, if you don't abandon this crazy vendetta."

"First Simon's crazy and now I'm crazy!" Pepper taunted him. "You'll have to do better than that, Miles. I haven't forgotten that it was your bed I woke up in. You were bending over me . . ."

"Yes. But shall I tell you why you were in my bed, Pepper? You were there because Herries hates me almost as much as he hates you. He put you there because it amused him to do so . . . because he knew you'd think I was party to what had happened, and because he knew how I would feel about what he'd done.

"At first when I walked into my room that night and saw you in my bed I thought Herries had persuaded you to wait for me there—he and Tim. It was the sort of thing he and Tim would have done, and then when I tried to wake you . . ."

He broke off, and Pepper saw the unmistakable compassion and pain in his eyes. She wanted to run from it, to cry out that it wasn't real and that he was deceiving her, but she couldn't move. For the first time since it had happened, she was sharing the horror of her rape with someone else; and moreover, sharing it with a person who had been there with her, who had known exactly what Simon Herries had done to her body and her soul. An unfamiliar sense of release rose up inside her, a sensation of a very heavy burden being shared with a fellow human being. She didn't like it, and she fought against it, but Miles was still talking.

"I'll never forget how you looked," he told her quietly. "I'm not a violent man, but if Herries had been there . . ." He turned away from her for a moment, but not before Pepper had seen the quick glimmer of tears in his eyes.

Tears . . . for her?

"I cleaned you up as best I could, put you in clean sheets and left you to sleep. I was going to talk to you, to ask you what had happened—to warn you to keep away from Herries in the future, but when you woke up you were so petrified, you so obviously believed that I was involved, that I daredn't come after you in case I terrified you even more.

"I've brought you here to try and make you see sense—not for my sake. I couldn't care less what you reveal about my past. Yes, technically I broke the law, but I did it to help an old friend who was desperate. What would you have done in my shoes, Pepper? Would you have let that idiotic teenager destroy their lives—her father's career, and her stepmother's peace of mind? Perhaps I should have done, but I couldn't. I'm not God, Pepper . . ."

What was he saying . . . that she was usurping a role that no human being should ever aspire to? The Greeks called it hubris, she remembered vaguely. He looked and sounded tired, and she wavered, caught between suspicion and a very odd desire to walk up to him and tell him she believed him.

"Simon Herries is a very dangerous man—a man poised on the edge of madness, in my opinion. Don't be deceived about him. He won't give in easily. He isn't like the rest of us, Pepper. Howell and Barnett were dragged in by blackmail. I had no knowledge of what was intended, but Herries plotted and planned to rape you. I think he would have liked to have killed you then, but he didn't dare. He had too much hanging over him already. Wilding's death, for one thing—that fall may or may not have been an accident, I don't know, but the suicide of Wilding's sister . . . that was no accident." He saw Pepper go white and start to shake. "You didn't know about that? Well, it was well covered up. But you haven't been his only victim, you know."

"He hates woman," Pepper told him flatly.

"Yes, I think you're right, and I'm certain his wife would agree with you."

Pepper shot a look at him. Why was he mentioning Elizabeth Herries?

"I saw you with her," she told him emotionlessly. "Herries' wife . . ."

"You saw us? Where?" Miles seemed more perturbed than she would have thought her comment merited.

"In London. She was just getting out of your car." She mentioned the area, and saw him frown.

"Elizabeth Herries has left her husband," Miles told her, quickly making up his mind that she might as well know the full truth. "She wants to sue for divorce, but she's terrified that somehow or other Simon will force her to go back to him. She found he was abusing their son," he added flatly.

Pepper stared at him in shock.

"I've managed to persuade Elizabeth to see the Prime Minister, who's instituting an enquiry into Herries. Backed up with what comes out at that, I only hope Elizabeth's family will support her in the divorce. Elizabeth won't bring an action against him involving her son, for the child's sake."

"But . . . but that will ruin his career!"

"Far more effectively than you could have done," Miles pointed out drily. "But until that investigation takes place you're safer here. Once the news of that breaks Herries will have far more to worry about than your attempts at moral blackmail."

Pepper sat down.

"How do I know that any of this is true? Why should you want to . . . to protect me?"

"Is it so unbelievable?" Miles queried, his mouth twisting slightly as he looked at her and saw the struggle going on inside her. He ached to take her in his arms and tell her how much he wanted her . . . how much he loved her. He frowned, wondering abruptly how long he had hidden his feelings from himself; how long he had pretended to himself that what he felt was compassion and concern, not unmixed with a very natural desire, when in reality . . . when in reality he loved her.

"You want me to believe you actually want to protect me from Simon Herries?"

"Yes . . . Yes, I do," he told her huskily. "Even if I had been a party to your rape I would hardly want you dead—think of the effect it would have on my career if it ever got out!" he added self-mockingly.

Pepper wasn't listening, he realised. At the very sound of the word rape she had gone rigid, almost trancelike in her stillness.

"Pepper." Miles went up to her. "Pepper!" He reached out to touch her, and as he did so her eyes focused on him. The horror and terror in them chilled him to the heart. She opened her mouth to scream, but no sound emerged. Instead she slid into a dead faint.

He caught her as she fell, picking her up as though she weighed no more than a child. So much for his hope that he was gradually winning her trust, he reflected bitterly. He was a fool for trying to rush her, but time was running out.

They had only ten days left here . . . ten days before the helicopter would be coming to take them back. Somehow, even if he couldn't convince her in that time that she could trust him, he must find a way of convincing her to drop her vendetta. If she didn't . . . If she didn't Simon Herries would surely find a way of destroying her. He would try to kill her. Miles was convinced of it. He knew criminals; he knew insanity. Simon Herries had no conception of the restraints other men place on their behaviour. He acknowledged no laws, no rules . . . and he was all the more dangerous because of it.

Miles carried Pepper to her room and placed her carefully on her bed. When she came round Maja was sitting with her. She could almost have believed she had dreamed the whole thing, but the concern on Maja's face told her otherwise.

The Indian woman helped her to undress, and then bathe. She was becoming almost sybaritic in her enjoyment of the warm scented water and the luxury of scarcely having to lift a hand for herself, Pepper acknowledged. She had even begun to forget about her business for whole minutes at a time. What was happening to her? Was it the slower pace of life that was putting its spell on her, or was it Miles French who was infecting her with his dangerously revolutionary ideas?

Miles . . . Pepper sat up, quivering with an unfamiliar sensation. Some instinct deeply buried and long ignored told her that here was a man who would break through all her barriers, who could be more dangerous to her than half a dozen Simon Herries.

Had he been telling the truth? She no longer knew what to believe. He had been so convincing . . . But if he *was* telling the truth then she was guilty of pursuing a vendetta against a wholly innocent man.

She remembered waking up in his bed, her body clean and sweet-smelling, where she had expected it to be putrid with the atrocities Simon had inflicted upon her. How had it got like that? The thought of Miles touching her, cleansing her, made her heart lurch and then beat at twice its normal rate.

Maja got up and picked up a tall glass of sherbet. Pepper took it thirstily, drinking almost all of it in one go. Almost immediately she started to feel sleepy, and recognised that Maja had put some sort of sleeping potion in it. The gardens around the villa abounded with herbs, many of which had originally come from

Europe. Living in such a remote spot, no doubt the chatelaines of this enormous complex must once have had to make up their own remedies for sickness. The villa was a village complete in itself in many ways. Pepper closed her eyes and let sleep wash over her. She was changing, she acknowledged drowsily. Where once she would have fought wildly against the drug, now she accepted its potency. Was it the same with Miles French? When the time came would she accept him instead of fighting him?

She fell asleep on the thought.

The dream came later. Pepper had such a vivid impression of Naomi's presence that the dream seemed totally real, and yet she knew herself to be an adult, and the Naomi who stood at her side was not the old woman of her memories, but a younger, healthier Naomi, who nevertheless she knew instantly to be her grandmother.

She was saying something to her, using the ancient Romany tongue which by some miracle Pepper herself could understand. Naomi was warning her against something . . . like a mirage Pepper saw herself in Miles's bed, and then saw Miles himself leaning over her, his face grave.

In her ear Naomi's voice said clearly,

"He is a good man . . . Your man, my chavvy."

And then the vision faded, to be replaced by another. This time it was Simon Herries whom she saw. His face was drawn into a virulent mask of hatred, and like sulphur, she could smell the scent of corruption and hatred in the air. She could smell fear too, and knew dimly that it was not her own. She saw a child, white-faced and close to the point of death. Through the mists of her dream she heard Naomi saying a name, but it was too dim for her to hear, and then incredibly she saw Oliver, her own child, and heard Naomi saying quite clearly,

"You and your son are both in danger, my chavvy. Beware . . . you must beware . . ." And then the vision faded, and no matter how much she cried out Naomi's name her grandmother would not come back.

It was Pepper's scream that woke Miles. Disorientated and half asleep, at first he thought that somehow or other Simon Herries had actually broken in and attacked her, and then the mists of sleep dispersed and he was on his feet heading for her room.

He found her sitting up, her eyes wide open but unfocused as she called out a name. He recognised it instantly.

"Naomi!" Her grandmother. He went up to her, pushing back the mosquito netting as he caught hold of her.

"Pepper—wake up! It's only a dream . . ."

He shouldn't have let Maja give her that sleeping potion. It had obviously caused her to have nightmares. Pepper turned her head and focused on him, coming slowly out of her trancelike state. She started to tremble and her arms felt so cold Miles started to chafe them instinctively.

"It's all right . . . it's all right . . . it was only a bad dream . . ." He talked to her as he would have done to a frightened child, soothing her with the sound of his voice and the action of his hands. Gradually the trembling died down. He sat down on the bed beside her and took her into his arms, half alarmed by the passivity with which she accepted him.

Pepper had no energy to object. She was still caught up in that half dream-world where her grandmother had been so real. The heritage of her ancestors rose strongly within her, both gypsy and Celtic, and she was convinced that what she had seen had in fact been the spirit of her grandmother, warning her, as Miles had warned her, about Simon Herries.

Her man, Naomi had called him. She turned her head and looked at him, and to her own astonishment heard herself saying slowly,

"Make love to me, Miles . . . make love to me now."

Miles stared at her. Did she know what she was saying, or was she still affected by the drug? What on earth was it anyway? Maja had no right to doctor her with her own weird potions . . . heaven knows what damage she might have done. And yet Pepper seemed perfectly aware of what she was saying, of what she was asking.

He reached out and pushed the soft fall of her hair off her face, and miraculously she didn't flinch away.

Through the fine satin of her nightgown he could see the outline of her breasts. A need so sharp and intense that it couldn't be denied rose up inside him. He eased her back against the pillows, careful to keep his weight off her, holding her as though he thought she was so fragile that she might break.

His heart was thumping like a sledgehammer . . . what if she should suddenly change her mind? What if . . .? He bent his head and found her mouth, feathering it experimentally with his own. Her lips felt moist and full, they parted slightly and he captured the faint sigh of her breath.

A feeling of joy filled him. He didn't know how it happened, but somehow a miracle had occurred, and Pepper wanted him. Who was he to question such a gift from the gods? He looked down at her peaceful, beautiful face, and noted its abstracted air, and was jealous of it. What thoughts did those veiled eyes hide from him? What had wrought this transformation?

And then almost as though there was someone in the room with them he heard a voice, thick and unfamiliar, saying gently.

"Take her, she is yours and you have earned her. The first plunge of the knife must always cause pain and takes courage, but once done it is over and the wound can heal."

Pepper gave no sign of having heard anything at all, but when he looked at her her eyes were not focusing on him but looking instead at the darkness in the corner of the room. His skin chilled into a rash of goosebumps as he heard her breathe softly.

"Naomi . . ."

Miles didn't believe in ghosts, spirits, call them what you will, and yet . . . Impossible, he told himself, and yet the words lingered and he even thought he knew what they meant.

"Pepper." He said her name and she looked up at him and froze, tension invading every muscle of her body.

"You wanted me to make love to you," he reminded her, correctly reading her rejection.

"No. No . . . I don't want you!" she cried instinctively, and yet she lay quietly supine, knowing that something had changed. She had changed.

She remained still as Miles removed first her clothes and then his own. Her body was completely supine, neither accepting nor rejecting. It was her mind that rejected him, her mind that knew fear and horror. She waited, anticipating the slow caress of his mouth and hands, knowing that she would react to him as she had done to all the others. He was a very physically desirable man, but she did not desire him, she could not desire him.

He straddled her body, his movements so determined and purposeful that they seemed to mock her frozen stillness. A smile curled his mouth, some hidden amusement seeming to darken his eyes. It annoyed her that he should find her amusing. She waited for him to touch her, to start trying to coax her to respond, and then realised with shock that he had no intention of coaxing her to do anything.

"No," she heard him whisper. "Before there can be anything else there must first be this." And then he was entering her, not painfully, but determinedly, his body slowly, oh, so slowly enforcing itself on herself, until her flesh was forced to accommodate the hardness of his.

There was no frenzy of passion in his eyes, no tension in his body, just its slow, sure movement within her own, as though they were both engaged in some primaeval ritual that had to be accomplished. Only when he was fully immersed in her did his movements cease.

"Now," he said softly, "now you can't block me out of your mind or retreat from me, because I'm already a part of you. There isn't going to be any lovemaking that will end in rape, because I'm already inside you." He smiled at her then, darkly and brilliantly. "Your body already accepts me. Now I'm going to teach *you* to accept me, and to want me."

Impossible, her mind screamed, but something told her that this man possessed the sorcerer's magic of making the impossible possible. She stared up at him, mesmerised by him, wanting to tell him that he was wrong; that he had simply managed to possess her by a trick, that he had been able to enter her simply because she had not guessed what he was going to do. How could he have known of those other men who had tried and been defeated, who had lost both their manhood and their desire in the face of her body's rigid refusal to accept them? She had braced herself against a long, languorous assault on her senses, and what she had got had been a basic physical possession which had nothing to do with the rape she had endured, nor anything in common with the frantic caresses of the men who over the years had tried so unsuccessfully to persuade her to share their desire.

Every time Miles moved, every time he touched her, caressed her, kissed her, his body moved with hers, and it was like being lapped in warmth, like being heated and melted; and a thousand other sensations Pepper couldn't even begin to analyse. He was a part of her, accepted by her flesh to the point where it clung moistly to the heat of him. His tongue-tip stroked along her skin, finding the pulse thudding at the base of her throat. The pulse jumped and quivered as his hand closed over her breast. An aching, unfamiliar sensation spread through her, a wanton urgent need to arch her body against his hand. She just managed to suppress the moan building in her throat, but almost as though he had heard it Miles bit delicately into her flesh. It pulsed and quivered, her nipples hard and thrusting into his palms. She moved, her body pulsing to a fierce new rhythm. He stroked, teased and cajoled, using every ounce of expertise and control he possessed to give her the ultimate in pleasure. He couldn't afford to lose control now. Not when he was so close to gaining the prize he had yearned for all his life.

Thoughts flashed in and out of his mind, weaving themselves into a complex tapestry. This was his woman, his other half. He had known it the moment he saw Pepper again. Within hers his body throbbed and pulsed, her breasts filled his hands, the heated musky scent of her filling his senses. She was everything he had ever wanted, and somehow he would teach her to want him with the same intensity. He was never going to let her go. Never.

She cried out, a thin sharp sound that he knew wasn't caused by pain, and he bit lovingly into the rigid swell of her breast, recognising and answering her need.

Pepper was beyond thought, beyond logic, beyond anything other than the fierce urgent tide carrying her along on its crest. She reacted instinctively to the call of her blood and senses, revelling in the ultimate ecstasy of her climax, hedonistically and voluptuously revelling in it, while Miles watched her with loving awareness that for her this was the first time she had known this experience.

Later they made love again. This time he showed her how to give him pleasure as well as to take it for herself. She fell asleep with her head pillowed on his chest.

He had been right to fear her, he thought tiredly, watching her sleep. His life would never be the same again. He loved her and he wanted her with him for the rest of eternity.

The shock of waking up and finding Miles lying beside her was lessened slightly by Pepper's vivid memories of their lovemaking. She seemed to have slipped so easily from the role she had cast for herself back into the more primitive role of her mother's people, that it almost frightened her. Even in the clarity of the morning sunlight she could not dismiss her conviction that Naomi had come to her. She didn't tell Miles about it, though. He was her lover, and she was prepared to admit now that she loved him, but she didn't entirely trust him. How could she? These were days out of time, unreal, an escape, but reality existed and one day she would have to return to it. For the present she was content to bask in the hot sun, and absorb its sensuality into her flesh, so that she might give it out again to Miles in the coolness of their shadowy room. From loathing and abhorring the mere thought of making love Pepper had gone to an imperious sensuality that made Miles at once both bitterly regretful for all she had missed and yet malely triumphant that he had been the one to release the passionate woman imprisoned within her fear.

Neither of them spoke of love, Pepper because she was still wary of his motives, Miles because he didn't want to crowd her. Sometimes he feared that he was in danger of forgetting why he had brought her here in the first place. He repeatedly tried to warn her against Simon, but whenever he mentioned him Pepper clammed up.

Neither of them had broached the subject of Oliver. On their last night together Miles knew that he had to do so.

After they had made love he placed his hand possessively over Pepper's belly and looked at her.

"If you conceive my child, I don't want you to keep it secret from me the way you did Herries."

Pepper went still. He *knew* about Oliver! Her mouth was dry and bitter. She turned her head and looked at him. The wide light eyes betrayed nothing other than compassion and tenderness. She looked in vain for contempt or disdain.

"I wanted to abort it." She hardly knew why she was telling him this. "I wanted to destroy his child before it was born."

She could feel the pain welling up inside her, a pain remembered from long ago and ruthlessly suppressed. Without her knowing it she had started to cry, tears welling up and running down her face. Miles cradled her in his arms, appalled by her despair, wishing he had never brought up the subject.

Both of them knew what it was to lack parents, and he knew Pepper was thinking of this when she added huskily,

"Philip and Mary wanted him so desperately; they had so much love to give him. I was eighteen . . . I couldn't have kept him. I couldn't face having one day to tell him how he was conceived, who his father was."

"You did the right thing."

He knew it was true, and somehow in saying the words, he laid for ever his own ghosts of the past. How often as a child had he yearned to know his parents? How often had he cursed his mother for deserting him, and yet hadn't Colonel Whitegate been more of a father to him than many sons ever know? Hadn't he set him an example he would be proud to follow with his own children? Against his breast Pepper wept—for her child, for herself, for the whole of mankind and all that it has to suffer.

"We must go back," Miles told her gently when she had stopped. "Tomorrow we're going home. Before we leave I want your word, Pepper, that you'll drop this revenge business."

Her mouth set in stubborn lines.

"I can't give it. It's meant too much to me for too long, Miles," she protested, when he remained silent. "I can't give it up just like that! He deserves to be punished . . ."

"But not by you," Miles told her quietly. "You can't set yourself above the law, Pepper, either God's or man's—you must see that."

Stubbornly she remained silent. Miles sighed. He had known she wouldn't be easy to convince, and the fact that they were now lovers didn't make it any easier. He knew that she still mistrusted him, just as he knew that she loved him, but for him, one had to go hand in hand with the other, otherwise it wasn't worth having.

"It's late," he told her tiredly. "We both need to get some sleep."

Pepper turned away from him, leaving a cool space between their bodies, but at some point in the night she turned back again, and when Miles woke in the early hours she was entwined with his body, her hair wrapped round his arm like a silken bond. He made love to her with passionate intensity, making her cry out sharply in the fierce throes of delight, as he drove them both from one peak to another, until they were too exhausted to do anything other than lie sated in one another's arms.

Pepper knew that she had not conceived his child. It was an instinctive knowledge, something she didn't even have to think about. Later she would question *how* she knew, and why the knowledge should hurt her, for now she had to concentrate on keeping herself from falling apart at the thought of returning to her normal everyday life.

Minesse Management had faded into almost total insignificance, and she hated herself for allowing Miles to take such an important role in her life.

It would be different when she got home, she told herself. She would feel differently away from this place, with its ancient magic. She would feel more in control, more herself . . . less a part of Miles.

She heard the helicopter while she was showering. It was over. The idyll had come to an end.

CHAPTER NINETEEN

IT WAS a small, rather nondescript room, tucked away behind the formal elegance of Number Ten's lavishly decorated reception rooms. Heavy, old-fashioned dun-coloured velvet curtains hung at the windows, obscuring almost all the natural daylight. The table around which they sat was scarred and the chairs with their shiny leather seats far from comfortable, but none of the ten occupants of the room was really aware of their surroundings. They had more important business on hand.

All of them looked grave, one or two of them, those who had actively supported and championed Simon Herries in his bid to get a Cabinet post, looked uneasy as well.

The Prime Minister opened the meeting.

"You all know why we're here," he began crisply. "Certain information has come to my attention regarding Simon Herries. As was arranged at the time, a full investigation has now been carried out."

He handed each of them a photo-copy of the report. Dutifully the other members of the committee studied the report, leaving the Prime Minister free to study them. Those who had favoured Simon Herries' bid for Cabinet rank looked most uncomfortable—and who could blame them? The kindest thing one could find to say about him was that the man was the victim of his own brutal childhood and that this had resulted in a dangerous form of insanity.

It amazed the Prime Minister that he had managed

to keep that side of his life a secret for so long. It was fortunate that it had come to light now when pressure could be put on him to resign quietly and disappear from public life.

"Do you want to speak to him, Prime Minister, or . . ."

"I think it would be better coming from you, George," he responded drily to the Deputy Chairman of the Party. "Don't you?"

George MacBride sighed heavily. He was new to the post and only knew Simon Herries slightly. However, he was not looking forward to the task of telling him that he must resign. They were both members of the same Club, which didn't make it any easier. George MacBride arranged to have dinner there with Simon.

Simon knew even before he kept the appointment; someone had alerted him to what the report contained. But he needed to know more. He needed to know who had alerted the PM in the first place.

George MacBride, not having been fully briefed, saw no reason to withhold the information.

"Well, I think it was your wife who originally told the PM, old chum. She went to see him some time ago. Took a legal chappie with her . . . French, I think his name was."

Across the table from him he noticed uncomfortably how Simon's eyes glittered, and wished he had been a little more discreet. Too late now to regret those relaxing gins he had downed before dinner . . . "Miles French," Simon said softly. "I should have guessed." He got up, excusing himself. "My resignation will be in tomorrow's post."

Feeling rather relieved, George MacBride shook hands with him and congratulated himself that the whole thing had passed off rather well. Herries had done the decent thing, without any unpleasantness. Just as one might expect from a fellow old Etonian.

Feeling as though a weight had fallen from his shoulders, George poured himself another glass of port.

Rage burned in Simon with the cold pure heat of arctic ice. The urge to physically destroy those who had worked against him raged in him like a fever, but like a dam holding back the fierce tide of his mania, cold, calculating common sense warned him not to act too hastily. French would be expecting some form of retaliation. He would have to act carefully.

The first thing he did was to summon Alex and Richard to a meeting. He needed to know how much they knew of what was going on. The answer was very little, but his instincts, always sensitive where his own well-being was concerned, warned him that they were slowly slipping out of his control.

"Have either of you heard anything from French recently?" he asked nonchalantly when he judged the moment was right.

Alex and Richard exchanged puzzled looks.

"Not since he left the country with Pepper Minesse," Richard told him, and then seeing the start of shock he was too slow to control, he added frowningly, "Surely he told you what he intended to do?"

"You mean that crazy plan of his to abduct the woman and blackmail her into giving up those files?"

"Not so crazy, as it turns out," Richard intervened. "He's managed to pull it off."

"Where's he taken her?" Simon had no intention of wasting time listening to Richard's fatuous praise of Miles French.

"That I don't know. He said it was better that we

didn't, for our own safety, just in case anything went
wrong."

Alex, listening to the exchange, felt the rage
emanating from Simon. How had he managed to
remain blind to how dangerous the man was? Before
leaving the country, Miles had alerted them both to
what was likely to happen, and he had warned them
to say as little to Simon as they could. Richard hadn't
lied when he claimed that Miles hadn't told them
where he was taking Pepper; it was the truth.

In exposing Simon, Miles had additionally freed
them from the threat of blackmail. Simon sensed the
change in their attitude towards him, like a wary
animal scenting danger. These two would not help
him now. No, now he was on his own, and it was all
Pepper Minesse's fault. He would make her pay . . .
somehow he would make her pay. She might think
she was safe with Miles French . . . the pair of them
might think they had won, but they would soon
discover that he wasn't so easily bested.

Hatred filled him, a black, tearing rage so intense
that he could almost taste it in his mouth. He would
punish Pepper Minesse, and this time . . . this time
he would do it properly. But first he had to find her.
It didn't matter where French had taken her, he would
track them down, and when he did he would exact a
vengeance so complete that she would never, ever be
able to torment him again. The madness grew inside
him, blossoming and swelling, destroying his hazardous
grasp on reality.

When Simon left them Alex shivered slightly and
reflected that he was glad he wasn't in either Miles's
or Pepper's shoes.

Richard, less imaginative, simply shrugged off the
meeting and dismissed it. He had more important
things to think about. The bank was beginning to

bore him. He had known that for some time; now he was admitting it. He thought about Morris and wondered how he would feel about taking over the chairmanship of the bank, so that he himself could head a new offshoot devoted entirely to the more entrepreneurial end of the market. It was just the sort of challenge he loved. He would have to discuss it with Linda, of course. He frowned again. She was very elusive these days, withdrawn from him, almost. She seemed to be spending a lot more time at the studios. His old insecurity, the one he thought he had banished after Jessica left him, surfaced to torment him. Jessica's refusal to share his bed had affected him on a far deeper level than he ever allowed anyone to know. And now these last few weeks Linda had exhibited a growing reluctance to make love, pushing him away sometimes when he attempted to touch her. Had she found someone else?

Perhaps if he took her away for a few days . . .

He stopped outside a travel agents on his way back to his office and on impulse booked a short luxury cruise in the Mediterranean. It was only for five days, he could manage to take that much time off, and it should appease her.

He didn't want to let himself think that it might be more than annoyance at being neglected in favour of the bank that was responsible for his wife's changed attitude towards him.

He lingered deliberately at the office, not wanting to return to the house ahead of her. It felt curiously empty when he did, and he was beginning to dread walking into its unwelcoming coldness.

Linda had in fact returned from work early. She had been feeling sick all afternoon—and not just because of the baby. She was dreading telling Richard, but soon he would *have* to be told. She was still determined on keeping her baby, no matter what Richard had to say.

At first when he unlocked the door he thought she was still out, and then he saw her sitting on the cream leather sofa, staring into space. He recognised the look and anxiety clutched at his muscles. Ignoring it, he walked up to her and bent to kiss her.

"Guess what—I've organised a little surprise for you!" Almost he winced to hear the false heartiness in his voice. "I've booked us both on to a Mediterranean cruise. I . . ."

"I can't go."

Her brusque refusal was the last thing Richard had expected, and for a moment all he could do was to stare at her, while pain exploded inside him. So that was it. Until this moment he hadn't admitted to himself how much Linda meant to him.

She turned to face him, and he saw how white and tense she looked.

"I can't go on the cruise, Richard." Her hands twisted together and he saw that her wedding ring was loose. It seemed an ominous sign.

"I . . . I'm pregnant."

Pregnant? He stared at her as though the meaning of the word was completely unknown to him.

His blank reception so neatly dovetailed with her secret and terrified belief that he would not want the baby, and she rushed immediately into her prepared speech.

"Don't ask me to get rid of it—I'm not going to. This is *our* child, Richard . . . but if you don't want it, I'm quite prepared to bring it up on my own. All right, I know we didn't plan on having a family, but now that I *am* pregnant . . ." She lifted her head and looked at him. "Now that I am pregnant I intend to keep our child, even if that means that I lose you."

"A baby . . . you're having a baby?" Richard
shook his head like a man coming up through deep
water. "But I thought . . ." He shook his head again,
his mind suddenly clearing as he recognised what she
had said. She wasn't having an affair with anyone
else. She wasn't tired of him. She was having a
child . . . their child!

"You're having our child." He said it softly and
went up to her, pulling her to her feet and into his
arms. OK, so he might not have planned to become a
father, but he was Jewish enough to feel an entirely
male thrill of pride in knowing that he had impregnated her.

Later, after they had eaten their supper and drunk
the champagne, while Linda slept with her head on
his shoulder, Richard reflected on the events of the
day and for the first time in his life suffered an urge
to appease the gods just in case they chose to punish
his son for his own misdeeds. It came to him that the
easiest way to jettison any burden of retribution his
child might be called upon to bear would be to repay
to Jessica the money he had blackmailed from her. He
could afford to, after all; that original two million had
been increased several times over through his astute
business dealings. The more he thought about it, the
more the idea appealed to him. He would do it for his
son's sake, he told himself chauvinistically. Yes . . .
Yes, he liked the idea of that very much . . . very
much indeed.

After the meeting with Richard, Alex returned home
in a very worried frame of mind. Miles had warned
him what Simon was, but until this evening he had
not really seen it. It seemed incredible that such a man
was free to walk the streets, a respected member of

society. He reflected on what Miles had told him privately about Simon's life and shivered to himself.

Miles had taken him into his confidence just before he and Pepper left the country, but he had not even told him where he was taking her. When they came back both of them would be in danger. When they came back.

Julia was waiting for him when he got home. The introduction Miles had given them to the children's home had opened a new door in their lives. Julia spent as much time there as she could. She seemed to have a gift for communicating with these very special children, and already they were talking tentatively about the possibilities of adopting.

Additionally, Alex had been approached by a large conglomerate who wanted to take over his main line of business, despite the fact that they had not won the Government contract. The money he received from them would relieve him of all his financial worries, and he would be free to do what he enjoyed the most—developing and researching more and more advanced uses for the micro-chip. They would be able to keep the house, but Julia had even said she would have been quite happy to move to something smaller. They were communicating in a way Alex had almost forgotten existed. Julia was a different woman. No, not a different woman; Julia was once again the woman he had fallen in love with.

It seemed naïve to believe that a shadow had been removed from his life, but that was how he felt, and he could almost believe that that shadow had come with his involvement in Pepper's rape, and that all that happened in his life since, both good and bad, had been part and parcel of some form of atonement.

These weren't feelings he could discuss with anyone else, not even Julia; they seemed too fanciful—*too* fairytale almost for a man of science and logic such as Alex prided himself on being, but the thought remained nestled in a far corner of his mind, and while he listened to Julia and shared in her joy at their new way of life, he also wondered about Miles and Pepper and how he could warn them that Simon's dismissal from candidacy for the Cabinet seemed to have finally tipped him over into madness.

He would have been even more concerned if he could have seen into Simon's mind.

Pepper herself had no such fears. When Miles warned her that he thought she was in danger she laughed at him. Her whole life had taken on a new meaning, the past had faded to nothing, and Simon Herries with it. Throughout the flight back to Heathrow, Miles tried to persuade her to allow him to hire a bodyguard for her.

"Then at least move into my place," he urged.

Pepper shook her head.

"No—not yet."

"You still don't fully trust me, do you?"

Pepper smiled at him and placed her fingers against his lips, a delicious sensation quivering through her as she felt the warmth of his breath. She had never known there could be such physical pleasure as that that Miles had shown her. She felt almost drunk on it, giddy with the release of discovering her own sexuality. When they made love she wanted to purr like a cat. Miles only had to look at her and she could feel her bones melting. Even now while they argued as he reached out to touch her she wanted to arch against him. She wanted . . .

"For God's sake don't look at me like that!" she heard him muttering fiercely. "Not here!"

She smiled at him—a long slow, seductive smile that made him feel he was completely losing his sanity.

There was nothing he wanted more than to take her in his arms and feel her mouth and her body beneath his own. These last days had been such a special, wonderful time. He had known before that he loved her, but he had never dreamed the woman she would be once she was freed from the trauma of her rape. He had never guessed she could be so sensual, so responsive to his every touch. He wanted to make love to her and go on making love to her until there was no way she would ever let him go, and yet at the same time he wanted to shake her for her refusal to accept the danger she was in.

She seemed to think that Simon Herries had somehow ceased to exist. In Goa Miles had been able to keep her safe, but once they were home . . . He shuddered to think of Simon's reaction to his dismissal from the Party.

Miles had picked up a newspaper before their flight left. It was several days old and had carried a leader about the golden boy of politics' sudden decision to resign. There had been a good deal of speculation about the reasons, most of them coupled with the fact that Simon was no longer living with his wife, but as far as Miles could judge the media had not got hold of the real reason for Simon's resignation.

If only he could make Pepper see sense! That suggestion that she should move in with him had been a last-ditch attempt to get her to see her danger. He had never expected that she would agree. It was something they had already discussed at great length.

This was the first time he had ever wanted any woman living with him on a permanent basis . . . the kind of permanent basis that involved exchanging vows and making promises that lasted for a lifetime, he recognised wryly.

But not yet. First he had to make Pepper see how

vulnerable she was. She had refused to have a bodyguard, but Miles was determined to hire one for her, someone who would shadow her discreetly and make sure that she was in no danger.

He wasn't sure why he should be so convinced that Simon would try to harm her; after all, it was his wife who was responsible for his dismissal from the Party, but Simon wasn't a sane man; he was a man who had already tried to destroy Pepper once, and Miles had seen for himself just how violently, almost demonically he hated her.

Simon meanwhile watched and waited. If the staff at Pepper's office knew where she was they weren't telling anyone. He dared not question them in person, just in case one of them recognised him. He had developed the sixth sense that sometimes goes hand in hand with a maniacal personality—and what if his obsession to destroy Pepper meant that he had to spend hour upon hour every day watching her office and her home? He had nothing else to do with his time now.

Once the truth about the reason behind his resignation percolated through to his one-time colleagues they dropped him like a hot brick. He suspected that he could blame the Prime Minister for that. Officially no one was supposed to know why he had resigned, but when more than half a dozen of his ex-colleagues had made excuses when he suggested meeting for a drink or dinner he guessed the truth.

He returned from watching outside Pepper's office one afternoon to discover that he had a visitor.

He hadn't had much time to think about how his father-in-law was likely to react to Elizabeth's accusations; he had been too busy thinking about Pepper, so the sight of Henry Calvert sitting waiting for him in his own study brought him to an abrupt halt.

"How did you get in here?" he demanded, crossing over to the Sheraton bureau and pouring himself a drink. Some of the whisky splashed down on to the polished mahogany that Elizabeth had taken such a pride in keeping beautifully waxed, and part of his attention watched the liquid form into a large globule on the satin surface.

Henry Calvert hated flying. He also hated being proved wrong, but there was no way he could refuse to support his daughter in her divorce petition. A cynical man all his life, Henry was not going to pretend that he was shocked by what she had had to tell him. Mentally he cursed his son-in-law for being stupid enough to attempt to vent his lust on his own son. Already he had been dropping hints in Washington that his son-in-law looked like being a future Conservative Prime Minister; now unless he could think of a good excuse to cover Simon's resignation he was going to look a complete fool, and that was one thing he abhorred more than anything else.

The Governor had been talking about inviting Simon over for Thanksgiving; the President would have been attending the dinner; useful contacts could have been made. Henry Calvert had been looking forward to the added influence he would be able to wield once Simon was in the Cabinet—and now this. There was only one way he and his family could emerge from the stigma caused by Simon's resignation with their honour intact, and that was to throw Elizabeth to the wolves and to publicly admit what Simon had done. He had it all planned already. His righteously indignant speech; his explanation that his daughter had been so desperately in love with her Englishman that he, her father, had allowed himself to be persuaded against his better judgement, but that upon discovering how his grandson was being abused he had insisted on Elizabeth returning to the good old US of A where such sickness did not exist . . . at least not among good Boston families.

"I used my daughter's key," he said now in response to Simon's harsh question. "After all, this is *her* house."

"*Our* house," Simon contradicted him. "In this country the marital home belongs equally to both partners. Where is my wife, by the way?"

"Back home in Boston."

Henry hadn't wanted to do it, but as his sons had pointed out, once the scandal broke it would look decidedly odd if Elizabeth wasn't seen to be at home, recovering from her ordeal in the bosom of her family.

Luckily she had already announced that she didn't intend to stay with them. The boy, who had spent far too much time tied to his mother's apron strings as far as Henry Calvert was concerned, would be sent to a good school and Elizabeth would be persuaded to live somewhere quietly out of the public eye.

"What do you want?" Simon demanded broodingly.

"Your signed statement admitting your sexual abuse of your son and an uncontested divorce."

He hadn't told Elizabeth about that first bit. She was determined that her children would remain in ignorance of the real reasons for the divorce. The last thing she wanted was for the whole thing to be splashed all over the papers. She didn't realise how damaging it might be to the whole family if they did not come up with a concrete reason for the divorce. Already Henry had entered into several deals purely on the strength of being a future Cabinet Minister's father-in-law. But those deals weren't going to stand up once the news got out . . . not unless he had a cast-iron excuse for it. No Calvert ever liked to lose money, even money that he had not actually earned yet.

"And if I don't?" sneered Simon.

"I'll be forced to give the whole story to the British press," Henry told Simon uncompromisingly, adding bitterly, "You fool . . . why the hell did you have to involve your own son?"

His scorn cut through the wall of fantasy Simon had erected between himself and the real world as easily as a laser through concrete. Simon wasn't used to enduring the contempt of his peers, and just for a moment he ached to give in to the searing need to take his father-in-law's neck between his hands and squeeze his throat until he had stopped breathing.

He had the strength to do it. He could do it . . . and then he remembered Pepper. His father-in-law could wait. Pepper must come first . . . Pepper's punishment was far far more important than any momentary satisfaction he might get out of silencing Henry.

The statements were already prepared. Simon signed them recklessly, and as Henry Calvert put them in his briefcase and got ready to leave he didn't know that in reality what Simon had just signed was Pepper Minesse's death warrant.

Miles and Pepper's flight arrived at Heathrow late in the evening. She ought to have been suffering from jet-leg, Pepper recognised, but instead she was on such a high that she doubted she would sleep for weeks.

When they got into the taxi she felt a fleeting regret that she had not agreed to Miles's plea that she move in with him straight away. This would be the first night they had slept apart in almost two weeks, but sensibly she knew she needed some time apart from him, back in the real world, to assess the true depth of her feelings for him. She had no doubts that she loved him, nor that she could trust him with her life. It was just that the idea of any kind of permanent relationship in her life was so new that she needed time to come to terms with it.

She knew instinctively that Miles was not the man to be happy with half measures. He would want all of her, and for ever, and she wasn't sure if she had it in her to give that sort of commitment. More, she loved Miles enough not to want to cheat him by pretending a permanency she did not feel.

No, some time apart was what they both needed. In Goa it had seemed natural and right that they should spend every waking and sleeping moment together. Neither of them had ever been bored, even when they sat in silence there was a communion between them, an awareness of one another. But they couldn't live like that for ever. Miles had his career and she had hers . . .

Miles, sensing all that she was feeling and more, squeezed her hand. "You're right. We both need time apart to come to terms with what's happened to us. I just wish you'd change your mind about that bodyguard, Pepper. Simon is very dangerous . . ."

"He'll surely be too busy worrying about his divorce now to be bothered with me."

It should have been true, but somehow Miles doubted that it was. He had a niggling sense of approaching danger, a sharply acute awareness of an anxiety that wouldn't go away.

"I take it I'm still allowed to take you out to dinner tomorrow night?" he said humorously instead of trying to persuade her. She would have a bodyguard whether she agreed to it or not.

It would seem strange going out to dinner with Miles and then going home to her own bed, Pepper thought. Would he try to persuade her to go back to his home? Would she need any persuasion? she asked herself honestly, remembering how she had responded to his lovemaking. Somehow she doubted it.

They didn't kiss in the taxi. Miles simply touched her hand and then walked with her to her apartment door. Neither of them said anything, but Pepper knew that he genuinely believed she was in danger. For herself she felt that Simon Herries would have far more important things on his mind than her. And anyway, she had decided to drop her vendetta. Retribution no longer seemed important to her, and she marvelled at the ease with which she had stepped from the old to the new way of life. Miles had become the centre of her universe, but she would never be a dependent clinging woman—that was not her way.

They kissed briefly in the shadow of her doorway, and as he walked away she ached to call him back; to tell him that she couldn't spend the night without him.

Once inside she felt a little better. She started to unpack—and then stopped as she lifted out a dress she had worn that Miles had particularly admired. Her skin quivered as she remembered with what care he had stripped it from her; with what love he had caressed her body; with what tender desire he had possessed her. She went to bed and lay there without sleep, wondering if *he* was thinking about her, and then chided herself for behaving like a teenager, reminding herself that she had to get up early in the morning.

Miles was thinking about her, but not because he missed her sexually. He hadn't gone straight home, but had got the taxi to drop him off at a small private library he belonged to which opened almost twenty-four hours a day. They had copies of all the newspapers and it didn't take him long to check through the

indexes and take photo-copies of every article relating
to Simon Herries. He read them at his desk, drinking
black coffee to keep himself awake, trying to put
himself in the other man's shoes. Simon Herries wasn't
the first mentally ill person Miles had had to deal
with. His legal training should have made it easier for
him to try to get inside the man's mind, to try to
establish what motivated and moved him, but all he
could think about was Pepper. In the end he gave in
to his anxiety, and despite the fact that it was gone
one in the morning he dialled Alex Barnett's telephone
number. Alex answered the phone himself, coming
abruptly awake as he recognised Miles's voice.

"I've been checking through the newspaper reports
on Herries. Have you seen anything of him while I've
been away?"

"Not much. He got in touch with us once. He
seemed to think you'd betrayed him," Alex told him.

"And Pepper?" Miles asked. "Did he say anything
about Pepper?"

"Nothing that he hasn't said before. He hates her,
Miles, and I think you're right when you say she's in
danger. To be honest, I don't think he trusts me
either—in fact I doubt if he trusts anyone."

Which didn't take him much further forward, Miles
admitted as he replaced the receiver. First thing in the
morning he intended to hire a discreet bodyguard for
Pepper.

He found exactly what he wanted through a contact
in the legal world, an ex-policewoman who ran her
own small agency and who he was assured would
provide just the kind of discreet surveillance that was
needed. He briefed her as best he could and warned
her that Pepper was not to know that she was being
guarded.

If his colleagues in chambers found him rather

distracted and withdrawn they were too tactful to
mention it. Pepper's staff were equally discreet—at
least to her face.

"I thought you said she was going somewhere hot,"
the receptionist whispered to Miranda once Pepper
was safely installed in her office. "I didn't see much
of a tan." She giggled when Miranda tried to frown
reprovingly, and added, "Oh, come on . . . would
you have spent any time sunbathing if you'd been
whisked off to a tropical paradise by a hunk like Miles
French."

"I should be so lucky!" was Miranda's tart response.

Lucy, the receptionist, made a face behind her back
and muttered under her breath, "Someone's having
boyfriend troubles. I'll bet!"

Lucy was inclined to be a bit of a daydreamer who
spent half her life indulging in romantic flights of
fantasy that enlivened the boredom of her routine
tasks. She was fairly new at Minesse, having been
taken on to help out during the summer holiday
season. Simon, who had been watching the office for
days and now knew enough about the staff to recognise that she wasn't one of its regular members,
bumped into her in the street as she was carrying the
morning's letters to the post on her way to lunch.

She smiled at him, her eyes widening fractionally as
she studied him. She liked fair men, and this one
looked as though he knew his way around the world.
Rich, by the looks of him . . . and good-looking too,
she added mentally, giving him another appreciative
smile.

"I'm so sorry," Simon apologised. "Careless of
me . . . Have we got them all?"

He helped her to pick up the scattered letters and
then invited her to join him for lunch. The wine bar
he mentioned was only just down the road and familiar

to her. There seemed no harm in accepting his invitation.

Over lunch he encouraged her to chatter, subtly nudging her in the direction he wanted her to go. Very soon he had learned that the head of Minesse Management was just back from holiday and moreover that she was heavily involved in a new affair. The girl could be useful to him, although she wasn't his type; too full-breasted and feminine for him.

Lucy had no idea what Simon was thinking as he escorted her halfway back to the office, explaining that his office lay in the opposite direction. She only just managed to stop herself from asking if she would see him again. He was the most exciting thing that had happened to her in weeks, and she mentally cursed the fact that she was on the reception desk on her own and so wouldn't be able to spend the afternoon enthusing about him.

Pepper didn't go out for lunch. She had too many things to catch up on. Miranda had actually seen her flush slightly when she asked if she had had a good holiday. Nothing had been said about her own part in its arrangement, but there was no doubt that the Pepper Minesse sitting opposite her now was a very different woman from the one who had left this office just over two weeks before. She had that glow that women in love are supposed to have, Miranda noted enviously, and more . . . she had the sleek supple look of a woman whose sex life is abundantly joyful.

"I want to leave early tonight," Pepper told her briskly. "About four."

She wasn't meeting Miles until eight, but there were things she had to do. She must ring Mary and . . . She bit her lip as she looked down at the list of telephone calls there had been while she was away. She had to speak to Nick some time. She owed him some kind of explanation. They were not committed to one another in any emotional or physical way, but unspoken between them had always been her own feeling that if she could admit any man to her bed that man would be Nick. He had rung several times while she was away. She would ring him tonight when she got home.

Pepper had her own very strict code of honesty, and her relationship with Miles was not something she could explain to Nick over the telephone. He sounded guarded when they spoke and Pepper suspected that he already knew what she was going to say, but she felt she owed it to him and to herself to make her explanation in person. They arranged to meet the following evening at a small restaurant that had been one of their regular haunts.

Pepper decided to say nothing to Miles about her dinner date with Nick. She suspected it would only give him a further opportunity to urge her to accept the protection of a bodyguard—something which her fiercely independent spirit railed against.

After she had spoken with Nick she walked into her bedroom to look for something to wear. Was it customary for women in love to feel that everything already in their wardrobe was completely unsatisfactory? she wondered a little wryly. She had a sudden urge to wear softly sensuous silks in drifting styles and cool misty colours. The sharp lines of her strikingly coloured existing clothes didn't feel right any more. She wanted something softer, something more in tune with her present mood.

In the end she settled for a dress she had bought on impulse only weeks ago. Not strictly in her usual style, the white jersey clung seductively to her body, the discreet smattering of emerald green sparkle scattered across the skirt adding a more formal touch to what was basically a very demure dress. Oddly enough it suited her, she recognised, and she marvelled again about the ability of the human personality to grow and change.

Miles arrived early. Pepper was just completing the finishing touches to her make-up when he knocked on her door. The security guard had already announced him, and putting down her lipstick she hurried to let him in.

Her hallway was only quite small, and with Miles inside it, it seemed even smaller. He reached for her as he closed the door, kissing her lingeringly. There was just enough passion in the hard grip of his fingers to bring a frisson of sexual arousal to her skin. He felt it and thought she shivered. Immediately he apologised, releasing his grip slightly.

"Sorry. It's just that it seems a hell of a long time since yesterday. I forget sometimes how fragile you are."

"You didn't hurt me," Pepper assured him.

The look in her eyes told him what she wasn't saying. Pepper heard him groan as he took her back in his arms, his voice thick and slightly raw as he whispered in her ear,

"Do you really want to go out to dinner?"

Immediately she knew she didn't. She had known that some time during the evening this moment would come, but she had not expected that when it did come she would be as hungrily eager for the touch of his body as he was for hers.

They might have been apart for months instead of just hours. She let him strip off the dress and drop it to her bedroom floor without the slightest qualm. The sensation of his hands sliding over her skin made her shiver with pleasure. She looked down and watched him as he caressed her and felt her body quicken with need.

They made love quickly, eagerly, like teenagers, Pepper's body matching Miles's fierce thrusts.

"I love you, do you know that?" he demanded later, cupping her face and kissing her lingeringly. "Marry me, Pepper."

She had known that it would come, and Miles cursed himself as he acknowledged that he had moved too fast. He was rushing her, and that was the last thing he had intended. She loved him, he was sure of it, but love . . . passion; these were new emotions to her and she needed time to come to terms with them.

"It's all right," he told when she didn't answer. "You need time. I know that."

He left her just after midnight. Pepper felt bereft when he had gone. She turned over in bed, automatically reaching for him, her body chilling with emptiness when she realised he wasn't there. She didn't know why she had hesitated like that. She knew she loved him. She even knew she would probably marry him. But he was right. It was still too soon. She had an odd feeling hanging over her, an awareness of something unfinished and somehow threatening.

Perhaps she would feel better once she had spoken to Nick. Whatever it was that had brought on this odd mood of disquiet, until it was gone she felt that she wouldn't be free to share Miles's life with him.

Lucy was over the moon when Simon rang her mid-morning. He hadn't given her his real name, calling himself Greg Lucas. He asked her out for lunch, suggesting that she meet him at another wine bar, this time a little further away from the office.

She didn't mind at all that she was the one who did most of the talking—normally it was the men who talked while she had to listen. Greg was different; he seemed so interested in everything she did, even her quite boring job. Blithely unaware of his real purpose in asking her out, Lucy chattered on about Minesse Management and her new boss.

He wasn't learning anything from her that he didn't already know, but there was time yet. Time was a commodity Simon had in vast quantities now . . . thanks to Pepper.

He had a score to settle with Miles French as well, but the more he listened to Lucy the more he believed that in destroying Pepper he would be punishing Miles. Miles French in love . . . He sneered slightly at the thought, remembering Tim's unsuccessful attempts to get him into bed, and Lucy, seeing that look, paused uncertainly.

Immediately Simon checked his thoughts. This stupid little girl must be the world's biggest bore, but right now he needed her. He stretched out and covered her hand with his, playing with her fingers.

"I've got to get back to my office, but why don't we have lunch again tomorrow?"

"Here?" Lucy suggested, breathless with delight.

"No, not here." He didn't want to run the risk of being recognised and remembered, although it was unlikely so far away from his normal haunts.

CHAPTER TWENTY

"WHAT do you mean, you can't have dinner with me tonight?"

"Exactly what I said, Miles. I have a . . . a previous commitment."

Pepper felt the tension humming along the telephone line and she automatically gripped the receiver harder. She ought to have anticipated this and she hated lying, but Miles wasn't in a receptive enough mood for her to be able to explain about Nick.

"I see . . . Somehow I thought the relationship we had pre-empted all other commitments," he announced silkily.

Panic struck her. She felt like a wild animal with the nets closing in around her, and she struck out accordingly.

"I'm not your private property, Miles! I . . ."

At the other end of the line Miles forced himself not to react. What the hell was the matter with him? This was crazy! Of course she had other commitments. So had he. He knew quite well what was wrong—he was going crazy with worry about Simon Herries. All his discreet enquiries about Herries had met with no response. He seemed to have disappeared. The London house was closed up and for sale, and no one knew where Simon had gone. That worried Miles. He would have felt happier knowing where he was and what he was doing. It also worried him that he couldn't seem to get Pepper to see how dangerous the man was. She seemed to think just because she was no longer concerned about the past that Herries was going to forget it as well. Miles knew that he wasn't. He couldn't have told anyone how he knew . . . he just did.

"I'm sorry," he apologised now. "I don't know what got into me . . . Frustration perhaps," he added wryly. "I miss not sleeping with you and I wake up in the morning aching like hell."

"Me too," Pepper told him softly.

"Why don't we spend the weekend together?" he suggested, then cursed. "Damn it, I can't. There's a meeting of the trustees of the children's home and I've got to be there. We could have dinner together on Friday night, though."

"I'd like that," Pepper agreed.

By then she should be feeling more relaxed. The interview with Nick would be behind her. She was sure it was that that was making her feel so jumpy and on edge. They talked for a few more moments, both of them silently acknowledging their reluctance to end the phone call and both of them still surprised by the intensity of their emotion. It was still so new for both of them; this need to give and take commitment; this sharing of feelings that extended far beyond the level of mere desire.

At last Pepper hung up. As always when she had been speaking to Miles on the phone she felt the loss of his physical presence. There were whole hours at a time when she sat at home when she should be working on the reports she had brought back from the office, simply staring into space and re-living their time in Goa . . . She loved him, and slowly, oh, so slowly she was beginning to trust him, and to admit him into her future.

A plan was slowly taking shape in Simon's mind. He

knew exactly how he was going to punish Pepper now. He was living in a small anonymous flat he had rented in a false name. The landlord had been too glad to take his cash deposit to question him deeply. The flat was tucked away in a rabbit warren of similar dwellings in a large Victorian house, run down and shabby now and housing in the main victims of the eighties mania for divorce. No one concerned themselves with his comings and goings, and, as Miles was beginning to discover, to all intents and purposes Simon Herries had disappeared.

He had brought with him very little from his old life—his clothes, his filing cabinets with the secret records that he and Tim had built up.

Tim . . . His old friend seemed so close to him these days, so close that sometimes he felt as though he actually was there with him. If Tim had lived his life would have been different, but Tim had died, and she had killed him. For that alone she should be punished. But he had already punished her for that . . . Round and round swirled his thoughts, dark and tainted with the madness growing within him. At night he dreamed that he and Tim were together again at Marchington.

He stroked the gun he had brought with him. It had been his father's Service pistol; never handed in after the end of the war. For years it had lain in a desk drawer in the house in Cumbria until Elizabeth had found it and demanded that it be locked away, complaining that it was too dangerous to simply leave lying around. Simon had kept it in his desk ever since.

He liked handling it. The cool smooth sensation of the metal beneath his fingertips was oddly pleasing to him . . . soothing almost. He had the ammunition for it as well. He had found it tucked away in the same drawer that had housed the gun.

On Thursday he didn't lunch with Lucy. He had a poste restante box from which he collected the mail and there had been a letter from his solicitors in with the others, asking him to call and see them. It would be about the divorce. When he had punished Pepper Minesse he would have to punish Elizabeth as well. She had taken his children away from him; she had betrayed him to his enemies.

Simon had enemies all around him now. Tim came to him in his sleep and warned him about them. When he went out he moved furtively, with the cunning of the dangerously deranged, choosing different routes to reach his chosen destinations, watching always to make sure that he wasn't followed. Tim had warned him that Pepper Minesse was a very clever woman and that he would have to be cautious.

This time he would do the job properly. He had been too lenient with her before.

The madness came down over him as it always did when he thought about Pepper. It was like a black cloud filling his brain, obliterating everything else. It made him feel sick; his heart pounding rapidly, as though a fever ran through his blood, and yet elated at the same time, every perception heightened so that he felt something approaching a state of euphoria. He paced his small flat mouthing her name possessed by a blood lust so strong that it overwhelmed everything else.

Afterwards when the feeling had receded it left him feeling beatifically calm and trancelike, as though he was in some state of grace, and it was while he was on this almost ecstatically elevated mental plane that Tim came to him most clearly.

Pepper was slightly late leaving the office on Thursday evening and she wondered wryly if her tardiness was perhaps due to a psychological dread of seeing Nick.

She had to rush to be ready on time for him to pick her up. The bodyguard Miles had hired watched them leave and dutifully followed in her anonymous hire car. She saw them go into an exclusive London restaurant and discreetly prepared to wait.

Inside the restaurant Pepper tensed when Nick helped her off with her coat, refusing a pre-dinner drink. She was so on edge that all she wanted to do was to tell him about Miles and then go home. She could tell Nick was aware of her tension from the way he looked at her.

The maitre d'hôtel led them to their table and flourished an ornate menu. Pepper had never felt less like eating. Around them most of the other tables were occupied. This was one of London's most fashionable restaurants. Here the aristocracy of the stage and media world mingled with the genuine article. This was no flash, here today, gone tomorrow eaterie but a restaurant that had built up its reputation over several decades.

After an unsuccessful attempt to study the menu Pepper put it down.

"Nick, there's something I have to tell you . . ."

Nick Howarth had known Pepper for several years. From the moment she first walked into his office he had wanted her. He had stalked her carefully, knowing instinctively that the slightest wrong move would panic her. He knew all about her reputation with men, but he had his own opinions on that. A hard-headed businessman who had made his own way through life, he was not inclined to put much store on human emotions. His own parents had divorced when he was seven; a vulnerable age. He had stayed with his mother until she remarried. Her new husband hadn't wanted him either. When Nick looked back on his childhood he felt a mild irritation for the child he had been; for allowing himself to be hurt. It was different now. He was armoured against that kind of pain. He liked women; he enjoyed their company; he liked making love to them, but he believed that a man was a fool if he ever allowed any other human being to become too important to him. That was the way he had run his life. Until he met Pepper.

He looked across the table at her and knew immediately what had happened. Before he had thought they were two of a kind. He didn't know why she held him at bay, but he had known instinctively that to break through her reserve he must win her trust; and he wanted her enough to take the time to do that. Almost seven long years, dammit . . . seven long years of playing it cool and hoping that one day he would pique her interest enough to get her to come to him, and now she was going to tell him that there was someone else.

And he even knew who that someone was. The popular press hadn't been slow to reveal the romance blooming between the eminent barrister and London's top businesswoman.

Everything that had made Nick Howarth what he was rose up in him now, urging him to deny that Pepper had ever meant any more to him than any other woman. Only one tiny corner of his mind refused to accept what it was being told; and that one tiny corner mourned what he knew now would never be.

Oh, he would marry, he would have a family. His wife would be beautiful and accomplished, but he would always withhold the greater part of himself from her, and she in turn would learn to give her love to her children and the odd discreet lover.

"You're in love with Miles French," he told her,

not allowing her to go on. "So what's new, Pepper?"

She swallowed hard. What had she expected? That he would be angry? That he would demand to know why she had not told him before? He had every right; their relationship . . .

She looked at Nick as he picked up his menu and started to study it, knowing that the subject of their relationship was closed.

The old Pepper would have been quite satisfied with this, would not even have wanted to prolong the conversation; would certainly not have wanted to enter into a potentially emotionally dangerous dialogue, but the new Pepper ached to explain to Nick, to show him what she had found; to tell him that it could be the same for him.

"Nick." She reached tentatively across the table and touched his arm. Immediately a muscle jumped under his skin.

"I think I'll start with oysters."

She withdrew her hand, knowing that he would rebuff all her attempts to talk to him. The only thing she could do was to take her cue from him. Over dinner he told her about the latest business deal he had pulled off in the States. Never once did he ask Pepper about her future plans; and it gave her the eerie sensation that somehow the two of them were playing out false roles.

When they had finished eating Nick helped her on with her coat. Outside the restaurant she turned impulsively to him and said quietly, "Nick, perhaps it might be better if I got a taxi . . ."

She half expected him to demur, but his face was in the shadows and she couldn't quite read his expression. Coming outside into the cool night air made her shiver, and immediately he took hold of her.

His touch wasn't Miles's and her flesh shrank

beneath it. He bent his head and even though she knew he was going to kiss her she didn't move. She owed him this final courtesy at least.

His kiss was cool, emotionless . . . the kind of kiss exchanged by old friends. The bodyguard, witnessing it, saw Nick's hand tighten briefly on Pepper's shoulders before he released her. Enviously she noted that he was a very good-looking man.

"I'm due back in the States at the end of the week. I could be gone for some time. I'll be in touch when I get back," Nick told Pepper. He smiled at her and added quietly, "I think it might be as well if you did get that taxi. I'm only human, Pepper, and I've dreamed about having you in my bed for too long, I suspect."

It made her want to cry; she who never cried. She wanted to reach out and embrace him as a mother embraces a hurt child, and yet she knew she could not. She wanted to tell him that a part of her did love him, but she knew it was not the kind of love he wanted.

He summoned a taxi for her and saw her safely into it. Her bodyguard followed her home, and then waited for her relief to come and take over for the night-shift. Twenty-four-hour protection; that was what Miles had requested, and the agency specialised in providing just that.

Her weekly report would be on Miles French's desk first thing in the morning. One of the girls she was training would deliver it for her.

Miles read the report while drinking a cup of coffee. He had arranged that they would be delivered to his home rather than his chambers, and he frowned as he came to the last bit. Pepper had said nothing to him about having dinner with Nick Howarth.

Jealousy, an unfamiliar and therefore unrecognisable emotion, curled through him. Why had Pepper not told him about her date with Nick Howarth? Common sense told him that the explanation must be innocent, but what man desperately in love ever listens to common sense? Nick Howarth was a singularly attractive man; and one, moreover, who desired Pepper and had done so for many years. And now Pepper was having dinner with him secretly.

Miles managed to resist the temptation to ring her straight away, but by lunchtime he couldn't contain his feelings any longer.

Pepper was surprised to get the phone call asking her to meet him for lunch. He sounded oddly terse and her stomach muscles contracted. She had told him that she was not concerned about Simon Herries, but suddenly she felt apprehensive.

Lucy put the call through to her and sighed enviously. She was not seeing Greg, as Simon called himself to her, until the evening, and then only for a quick drink after work. It had crossed her mind that he might be married and that she might be involving herself in a clandestine affair with a man who had no intention of ever allowing her to be anything other than a pleasant diversion in his life, but she dismissed it, not wanting to listen to that small warning voice.

They were meeting at Pepper's restaurant. Miles was there first and had to wait in growing anger as she responded to several greetings from people who knew her. He realised that he was behaving unreasonably; almost childishly, but for once was powerless to control himself. He was jealous—intensely, aggravatingly jealous, and the last thing he wanted was to admit it.

"What's wrong?" Pepper asked him quietly as she sat down. She could see how tense he was, his forehead creased in an unfamiliar frown.

"Why did you have dinner with Howarth last night?"

The harsh question took her off guard. She blinked uncertainly and stared at him.

"How . . . how do you know that?"

It was the worst possible thing she could have said, as she admitted ruefully to herself later. Miles immediately took her response as an admission of guilt and demanded to know bitterly exactly what her relationship with Nick was.

Pepper's anger rose to meet Miles's. She was not used to having to account for her movements to anyone, and it hurt that Miles so obviously didn't trust her. She didn't stop to think that his jealousy was as unfamiliar to him as it was to her; both of them were as unused to the darker side of being deeply in love as they were to the lighter.

Instead she was challenging him angrily, demanding to know how he knew she had seen Nick.

"What have you been doing? Following me around to see where I am when we're not together!"

She never imagined for one moment that he had, and so it came as a shock when he told her quietly,

"I hired a bodyguard to keep watch over you. It was in their report."

Pepper was stunned—stunned and furious. How dared he set someone to . . . to spy on her without telling her! How dared he assume that he had the right to . . . to take charge of her life, to interfere in what she did . . .

Anger, righteous and forceful, welled up inside her. They were both oblivious to the interest of the other diners as they exchanged speculative and amused looks.

Pepper couldn't remember the last time she had really lost her temper. Perhaps as a child when she was tormented by those Northern village children, but not since then. But she lost it now, standing up, her eyes glittering wildly, her hair almost seeming to give off sparks.

"How dare you have me followed and watched!" she demanded furiously. "How dare you think you have the right to interfere in my life!" And to Miles's consternation she turned on her heel and walked out of the restaurant.

Nothing like it had ever happened to him before. He liked women; he rarely quarrelled with them, and certainly never as publicly or as violently as this.

And over what? Before she stormed out on him Pepper had told him bitterly,

"I had dinner with Nick to tell him about us. As it happened he already knew, but I felt I owed it to him to tell him myself. I didn't tell you about it, Miles, because I felt uncomfortable with the fact that Nick knew nothing about our relationship—or so I thought."

She had every right to be annoyed with him, Miles admitted later when he had cooled down. He had been idiotically jealous, and in her shoes wouldn't he have wanted to do the same thing? He admitted that he would. He also admitted that at the root of his jealousy lay his fear that Pepper wouldn't commit herself to him, and he wanted that commitment. He wanted the life he knew the two of them could have together . . . But before there could be any of that he had to be sure that she was safe from Simon Herries, and now, through his own almost criminal stupidity, he had effectively destroyed his chances of persuading her to accept the necessity of having a bodyguard. He winced as he remembered the bitter comments she had thrown at him . . . how she had accused him of wanting to spy on her. Nothing was further from the truth, but what chance did he have of persuading her to believe that now?

Pepper couldn't calm down quite as quickly. This was her first experience of the intensity of love. She knew quite well that had their positions been reversed she would have felt exactly the same way, but it jarred that Miles had gone behind her back; that he had hired a bodyguard for her, without telling her about it.

She knew that he was genuinely concerned about Simon Herries; she knew that spying on her had been the very last thing in his mind, but there was still that raw sore place caused by the knowledge that he didn't fully trust her. How could he, after what he had said?

There was a sour taste in her mouth, a heaviness in her heart. On impulse she picked up the phone and rang Mary. She wanted someone to talk to . . . she needed someone to confide in, and it was only now with the new-found awareness that love had brought her that she recognised how instinctively she turned to the older woman. She had chosen Mary to be Oliver's mother because she had recognised in Mary a quality that she had ached and yearned to have for herself, she had known how much Mary would love and protect her child.

She arranged to spend the weekend with them. She needed the break, she told herself, trying to placate the conscience that had told her that it was childish to simply disappear without telling Miles where she was going.

She shrugged, angry with herself for not being able to maintain her feeling of ill-usage. He would be away for the weekend himself; he did not own her . . . she had no need to tell him what she intended doing with her time, and yet the tiny feeling of guilt persisted and grew as she tried to clear the work on her desk ready for an early departure. Miles would hardly expect her to have dinner with him after this lunchtime's débâcle.

And yet . . . On her way out of the building, she hesitated beside Lucy's desk, some impulse causing her to say to the girl,

"If Mr French rings will you tell him that I've left early and that I shall be spending the weekend with friends in Oxford."

Miles held out for as long as he could, but Pepper's angry face kept coming between him and the brief he was studying. He reached for the phone, just as his secretary came in to tell him that a client was waiting to see him. He would ring Pepper after the meeting, he decided.

It was four o'clock and the meeting didn't finish until almost five. He caught Lucy just as she was on the point of leaving, and she duly delivered Pepper's message.

Miles swore under his breath as he tried Pepper's home number. He supposed it was no more than he deserved, and as he had half expected, no one answered the phone in Pepper's apartment.

Obviously she had already left for Oxford. She would be going to see Mary and Philip Simms. She mentioned them a lot—them and Oliver—but never once had she suggested that he might like to meet them. That hurt, he recognised. They were an important part of her life—and a part of her life that in some way she seemed to want to keep separate from him. Another sign that she didn't fully trust him.

He had known that her trust would be difficult to win, but until today he had not recognised how difficult.

If it wasn't for this damn meeting tomorrow he would be tempted to throw a few clothes into a case and follow her to Oxford, but he couldn't let the other members of the committee down. They wanted to talk about installing an indoor swimming pool at the home, and how best to raise the finance for such a venture. Miles had intended suggesting one or two businessmen who he felt might respond generously to a request for a donation towards the ultimate cost.

By the time Simon met Lucy at the wine bar, Pepper was already well on her way to Oxford.

Almost he had not gone, but he had nothing else to do, and now as he listened to Lucy's irritating chatter he froze, his body tensing with excitement.

"Say that again!" he demanded abruptly.

Lucy frowned, puzzled by the glitter in his eyes and the painful way he was gripping his wrist. Suddenly she felt almost uncomfortable with him . . . frightened in some way, although she could not understand why.

"Er . . . Pepper left the office early. She met Miles French for lunch and when she came back Miranda said she was in a real temper. They were supposed to be having dinner tonight, but she's gone off to Oxford on her own. She's got friends down there . . ."

Oxford . . . Simon relaxed his grip on Lucy's wrist, unaware of the bruises he had caused. His eyes closed and a feeling of pleasure swept through him. Oxford . . . how fitting that would be, how right and proper. Almost he could see some influence that was not human at work here . . . he shivered and thought of Tim. Tim had already told him how he should punish Pepper. He had read up on what he would need to do and had been careful to buy the books from different shops . . . And yet how similar they had all been. Small secretive places where no one looked at you . . . where the very silence seemed to be imbued with a thick dangerous potency.

Once long ago Tim had sworn that he would raise the Devil and Simon secretly laughed at him for it. Now . . . His mind clouded, old images supplanting reality. Voices seemed to call him . . . Images danced before his eyes. He got up, ignoring Lucy's cry of protest, almost knocking over their glasses of wine. He didn't hear Lucy call out to him as he left. He had things to do.

He thought about the fate Tim had planned for Pepper, and how he had mocked his beliefs in the ancient ritual. Now he acknowledged that he had been wrong. Pepper Minesse was dangerous. She possessed strange powers, he was sure of it . . . otherwise how could a gypsy brat have achieved what she had? She must be destroyed. Simon went first to his flat and lovingly took the gun from the cloth in which it was wrapped. A smile lit his face as he stroked it. Soon . . . soon now . . . And he said the words out loud as though there were someone in the room with him to hear them.

CHAPTER TWENTY-ONE

LONG BEFORE she reached Oxford Pepper's mood had changed. A dull kind of emptiness took the place of her earlier anger. She ached to turn round and drive back; she ached for the comfort of Miles's arms around her, and she used the back of her hand inelegantly to wipe away the tears that had come from nowhere to cloud her vision.

Only now when the heat of her own rage was gone did she actually feel the full shock of their quarrel. It hurt almost physically, making her stomach cramp and her muscles ache. The cause of their fight was unimportant—forgotten almost. All she wanted to do was have Miles here with her.

Only the fact that she knew Mary would be expecting her stopped her from going back—that and a growing, curious sensation that for some reason she had to go to Oxford. She blinked, surprised by the momentary vision that flashed in front of her eyes.

Oliver! Suddenly she shivered, remembering the dream she had had in her bedroom at Goa; remembering Naomi and the warning she had given her that she and Oliver were in danger.

She shivered again, goosebumps lacing her skin; she was imagining things . . . it was her heightened emotional state that was responsible for this sensation she had of Naomi somehow being close at hand. And yet . . . and yet . . . She was not so sophisticated, so out of touch with her roots that she could totally deny them. She remembered things Naomi herself had told her, and her own strange awareness of her grandmother's imminent death, and she shivered for a third time.

In Oxford Mary waited. It was half term and Oliver was playing in the garden. As he grew older, his heritage from Pepper became more plain. He was a physically attractive boy, with thick dark hair and smooth, faintly olive skin. His eyes were light-coloured and very serious, but when he smiled his whole face lit up. Everyone who met him loved him—he was that kind of child, quick and intelligent and yet compassionate as well, so essentially sweet-natured that one could not help but be aware of it. Mary adored him, although she and Philip both tried desperately not to spoil him; not to let him know how precious and special they thought him.

She had had him for ten joyous years, but soon . . . The pain within her body bit deeply and she tensed against it.

Her death would be slow and lingering; she had read that in her doctor's eyes and had shrunk from it. She had always feared pain, and her fear was no less now that she was intimately acquainted with it.

There was no question of an operation, her cancer was too deep-rooted for that. Later she could, if she chose, opt to go into a hospice run to care for people like herself who were close to death.

She still hadn't told Oliver. Now she was going to do so. She sensed that it was right for her to do so now, when Pepper was here. They would need one another then, those two. Philip had a weak heart; she had always been the physically strong one. Oliver could so easily be left an orphan. That weighed heavily on Mary. That wasn't what she wanted for him. She looked at her watch. Soon Pepper would be here. If

only she had more time . . . If only she could be sure
that Pepper . . . The pain struck again and everything was suborned to it, every other thought banished.

When it finally receded Mary went to the door and
called Oliver. He came at once, and she knew without
having to say anything to him that he was aware, as
sensitive children are, that there was something wrong.

She sat him down in her own small sitting room,
where he had crawled on the floor as a baby and then
later learned to pull himself to his feet and walk. So
many memories; so much happiness . . .

Slowly and carefully she explained to him that she
was ill and that she was not going to get better. He
listened gravely, his eyes filming with tears that he
didn't shed.

"I'm telling you this, Oliver, because when I'm
gone, if anything happens to Daddy, I want you to
go and live with Pepper."

She prayed as she said it that she was doing the
right thing . . . If need be she was not afraid of
resorting to emotional blackmail, she knew Pepper
would not refuse to take him, but would she make
him happy? Would she realise the wonderful gift she
had in her child, would she . . .? Mary clamped down
on the thought, making herself concentrate on Oliver
and what she had to say to him. She had so little
time . . . so little strength; she must not waste any of
it.

She saw the surprise cross his face and said quickly,

"Pepper is your godmother. She will take care of
you and love you . . ."

Her voice thickened and she suppressed her own
tears. She had to be strong now, for Oliver's sake. He
had been their gift; but always she had had the sense
of only having him on loan. She could not tell him
the truth. Pepper had bound them to their word, and

besides . . . she looked at him and knew that Pepper
had acted wisely. No, she could not tell him the truth,
but she could prepare him for what was to come.

"I'm going to talk to Pepper when she arrives,"she
went on. "She will understand."

"And will I have to go and live in London with
her?"

"Yes," Mary told him firmly. "And Oliver, you
must promise not to forget what I'm telling you, not
to say anything to Pepper until I've spoken to her."

Some inner wisdom she had only recently come by
told her that Pepper would accept her death far less
easily than would Oliver . . . that Pepper would be
the one to rail and protest against her fate. Pepper
loved her, Mary acknowledged sadly.

Simon drove straight down to Oxford and booked
into a small hotel. Tomorrow would be soon enough
to look for Pepper. He would find her—he knew it.
For now he had other things to do.

He drove down to Marchington. The house had
been closed up for some time and the once immaculate
gates were slightly rusty. He didn't use the main drive,
but instead drove round the back, down a narrow
bumpy track that went straight to the stables and
outbuildings.

Tim's father had died two years ago, the only
remaining heir, a cousin, had died too, and since there
was now no direct male heir, squabbles had broken
out in the family over who really had the right to
Marchington. The result was that until the squabbles
were legally settled no one was living there.

Simon already knew this. From the first moment
the idea had come to him he had been working
deliberately to this end. Marchington . . . Tim's home,
the place Tim himself had chosen for Pepper's death.

It was only fitting that he should destroy her there.

He broke in through the french windows of the library. It had been one of the late Earl's foibles that he had flatly refused to install any formal type of burglar alarm. Instead they had had guard dogs which patrolled the grounds, but these were now gone and there was no one to see Simon walk through the gathering darkness of the empty rooms.

What had happened to the paintings and furniture? Stored away somewhere, no doubt, pending the result of the court case. The house looked ill at ease and shabby in the half light. He daren't take the risk of switching on the lights, always assuming the electricity was still working, but he didn't need lights to find his way down to the chapel.

He was carrying a large parcel under his arm, and when he walked into the chapel he placed it on the simple altar. It was here that Deborah had died, the blood pouring from her body in a red tide.

Simon unwrapped his parcel and set the tall candles in the holders he had brought with him. He wasn't going to light them yet, but his body trembled with excitement as he touched them. It had been surprisingly easy to find them, and the proprietor of the small shop where he had bought them had evinced no interest at all in them or in his other purchases, but then given the type of merchandise he was selling it was perhaps not surprising.

Black magic, Satanism . . . these were joke words to many, but Simon had been surprised to discover how very strong some people's belief in the power of the rituals of evil actually was. Perhaps Tim was right and he was wrong. He shivered slightly. He wasn't here to raise the Devil, he was here to pass sentence on Pepper Minesse, and this time there would be no clemency.

He used the torch he had brought with him to check that everything was in order. He had been through this ritual so many times in his mind, lying in the narrow single bed in his bleak flat, that it was now automatic, soothing almost, calming the febrile excitement beating up inside him.

As he worked he talked quietly, addressing the one companion who followed him through his increasingly insane thoughts. Tim had become as real to him as though he was in fact alive. Talking to him like this elevated him to a mental plane where he felt a power so strong that it was almost like taking a drug.

It was not just himself he was avenging but Tim as well, Tim who would not be dead if it wasn't for that bitch. So his thoughts ran, increasingly out of touch with reality, and when at last he drove away from Marchington Simon Herries, urbane Member of Parliament and hopeful future Prime Minister, was gone for ever, and in his place was a man who looked perfectly normal and sane, but who was in fact dangerously unbalanced.

Mary sent Oliver to bed before Pepper arrived. She wanted to see her on her own, although Philip had protested. In the end he had given way. It frightened him to see his strong, dependable wife slowly weakening beneath the onslaught of her illness. Every day she seemed to lose a little more ground as though slowly she was slipping away from him.

They had talked about Oliver and Philip had concurred with all she had said, but how would Pepper feel? Mary was convinced that she would take the child. But would she?

Pepper knew the moment she walked in that something was wrong; not because Oliver was missing, but because she felt it, smelled it, tasted it almost,

with every instinct she had inherited from her ancestors. Naomi's presence was so real to her that she
almost turned her head to look at her.

She had come to Mary like a hurt child running to
its mother, but now she realised that Mary was the
one who was hurt.

Mary told her about her cancer quietly and calmly.
For a moment Pepper couldn't respond, her shock
and grief lay within her like a heavy stone.

"Surely there must be some form of treatment . . .
an operation?"

Mary shook her head.

"No—it's too advanced. I'm going to die, Pepper,
and probably quite soon. If you hadn't come down
this weekend, I was going to telephone you anyway."

Pepper wanted to scream her pain and denial, but
somehow her emotion could not be released. Like a
dark shadow, grief stalked her, and not even her
awareness of Naomi's presence could ease her anguish.
She had lost so much already . . . she didn't want to
lose Mary . . . Mary who had never hurt a soul in
her life, Mary who . . .

"If anything happens to Philip I want you to promise
to take Oliver, Pepper."

The quiet words cut right across her thoughts. They
were sitting in Mary's room, and now Pepper realised
how carefully Mary had planned this whole interview,
because she reached across the small table in front of
her and picked up a worn Bible.

"This Bible belonged to my grandmother. The date
she was given it, the date of her marriage and the
births of her children are all recorded in here, as are
their deaths—theirs and hers. My mother wrote in it
too, and so have I. I want you to swear to me on this
Bible that I hold sacred that you will do as I ask."

How could Pepper refuse? Did she even want to

refuse? Oliver was her son and in her pain she found she could now acknowledge how much she loved him . . . How much she had always loved him.

She took the Bible and made the promise Mary wanted.

They talked for a long time . . . or at least Mary talked and Pepper listened . . . Mary told Pepper about her childhood, about how happy she had been then and during her marriage to Philip.

"It's old-fashioned of me, I know, but I pray that you will have a Philip in your life one day, Pepper."

"I think I already have."

The words were out before Pepper could silence them, and once spoken demanded elucidation. Even talking about Miles made her ache to have him with her. Why had she been such a fool? Why had she lost her temper with him like that? Was it really because she had been frightened by the strength of her own emotion? She knew that it was. Her need to give Miles the commitment he wanted from her terrified her, and so she had fought against it in the only way she knew.

"You look sad," Mary told her. "Have you quarrelled with him?"

What could Pepper say? How could she explain Miles's fears for her? They would only frighten Mary, and she had enough to bear as it was.

"Yes."

"Go and ring him," Mary urged her.

"He might not be in," Pepper protested, but she was already reaching for the telephone.

Miles answered it on the second ring, and from the rough urgency in his voice she knew he regretted their fight as much as she did herself.

"I'm at Mary's," she told him huskily.

"I hoped you'd ring. God, Pepper, I'm sorry . . . but I was so damn jealous. I miss you like hell. I wish

I could be there with you."

"So do I!"

His quick ear caught the undertone of despair in her voice; a despair that came from much more than their quarrel, and he had an urgent desire to put down the phone and go to her, and to hell with the committee meeting.

He took a deep breath and said quietly,

"We need to talk. When do you plan to come back?"

"Sunday," Pepper told him. She owed it to Mary to at least stay the full weekend, much as she ached to be with Miles.

"I'll take the train down on Sunday, then, and we could drive back together."

She could introduce him to Philip and Mary . . . and Oliver. Suddenly she found she was gripping the receiver too tightly.

"I . . ." she began.

"Why don't you invite him for Sunday lunch?" Mary suggested quietly at her side, but not so quietly that Miles didn't hear her.

"It's a long time since I enjoyed a traditional Sunday lunch," he said. "I'd love to be there."

Pepper gave him directions and thought of all the things she ached to say that she couldn't over the telephone.

"How long have you known him?" Mary asked her when she replaced the receiver.

The words "for ever" trembled on her lips and Pepper only just caught them back, realising with a small shock of surprise how apt they were. That was how she felt about Miles, as though in fact she had known him not just all her life, but throughout eternity itself.

"I met him briefly years ago in Oxford," she said

instead. "I think you'll like him. He's a barrister."

The only paper Philip read was *The Times*, so they were hardly likely to have seen the gossip about them. Sensing Mary's interest, Pepper told her a little more, leaving out the true reason Miles had taken her to Goa and substituting instead the small white lie that they had gone there on holiday.

"He knows . . . about Oliver," Pepper added quietly. "He knew what happened to me and he . . . he guessed that I conceived a child. He's like me, an orphan. He was brought up in a children's home."

Did she realise how much she betrayed with those few words, Mary wondered, or was it simply now that she herself was so near death that she had been granted the insight to see so much more? She knew, for instance, how much Pepper loved Oliver, something she had never been totally sure of before. She knew as though Pepper had told her so herself that she had given him to them out of love for them and out of love for Oliver himself, knowing with a painful wisdom that no girl of her age should have had that he would be better off with them than her.

Philip and Mary liked to go to bed fairly early. Pepper went up at the same time, to the same room she had had when they had brought her home from hospital. Some of her clothes still hung in the wardrobe, her small personal belongings were scattered around in its cupboards. It was her room, and oddly, for all its simplicity she felt at home here.

She showered in the old-fashioned rather spartan bathroom, wrapping herself in the thick white towel that had been part of Mary's bottom drawer, then went to bed. She lay back in bed and stared up at the ceiling. Mary dying . . . Mary being eaten alive by pain and her own flesh. She shuddered and her throat closed up with pain.

Then suddenly she was aware of a presence in the room with her, and she said the name that came instinctively to her lips, sitting up and staring at the door.

Only it wasn't Naomi who stood there but Oliver.

He came over to the bed and stood there looking at her. He was so physically like her, this child of her flesh. Pepper wanted to reach out and embrace him, but could not. She looked at him, and in the depths of his serious gaze she saw his own pain and understanding, and for the first time something within him that was purely Naomi . . . a kind of acceptance she herself with her restless spirit had never had and bitterly regretted not having.

While her eyes burned with tears of grief and gratitude she realised that she had been given the gift of a child old in the understanding of mankind with all its weaknesses . . . one of those elevated spirits who chose to return to an earthbound plane for the benefit of others. As though Naomi stood at her shoulder and told her so, Pepper saw the strength and gentleness that would one day make her child a man revered and respected by all who knew him. And many would. He had nothing of Simon Herries in him, nothing at all, and none of her own weaknesses and failings either. As instinctively as though she had held him every day since the moment of his birth she opened her arms, and he walked into them. Without words they formed a bond, a communion that went deeper than the mere bond of blood.

How long they remained like that, mourning silently for the woman they both loved, Pepper didn't know, but eventually Oliver disengaged himself and went back to his own room as silently as he had arrived. How had he known how much she needed that contact with him? Again her grandmother's face seemed to form itself in her mind.

She slept and dreamed joyously of a beautiful garden where she walked with those whom she loved. Miles held one of Oliver's hands and she held the other, and Mary was on her other side with Philip, and then suddenly the golden warmth of the garden was stolen away and she was filled with a sense of fear. Something menaced that beautiful paradise, and suddenly she and Oliver were alone in a frighteningly dangerous place. She saw Naomi again, warning her . . . urging her to do something—but what?

Pepper woke up shivering and frightened and told herself that her dream was only her fear of Mary's death.

But what if it was more? What if Miles was right to fear Simon Herries? What if Naomi herself was warning he against him? No—she wasn't going to think like that . . .

She woke up early as she always did at Philip and Mary's. The soft fruit was beginning to ripen and after breakfast she joined Mary picking raspberries. Would Mary be alive to eat this year's jam?

The thought wouldn't go away, and as though she had read her mind Mary touched her arm and said quietly,

"It won't be long, Pepper."

"You're being so brave."

Why were they both whispering? There was no one here to listen to them—unless it was the shadow of death.

"No . . . I'm terrified of the pain. It's bad enough now." Mary shivered, her eyes clouding.

"They'll give you drugs," said Pepper, trying to comfort her.

"But will they be enough?"

Both of them fell silent.

"Oliver needs new clothes—he's growing so fast," said Mary. "Come with me this afternoon to Oxford and help me buy them. We'll all go and have lunch out."

It was a beautiful cloudless day with the sun shining from a perfectly blue sky. Oxford shimmered under the warm summer heat haze, and the quality of the light seemed so pure that the ancient buildings appeared to float above the ground.

It had been on a day as perfect as this that Pepper had seen Marchington.

Marchington. Why was she thinking of that now? Pepper wondered tensely as she parked her car. Philip hadn't come with them, preferring to stay at home with his books. He wasn't a man who enjoyed shopping.

Oliver stayed close to Mary's side. Not for his own sake, but for hers, Pepper recognised, overwhelmed by her love for this child she had so desperately wanted to hate. By what miracle had fate ordained that from that bestial coupling should come this boy? She wanted to reach out and touch him . . . to give thanks for the special gift she had received. How had she managed to live so long without realising that there was this very deep emotional side to her nature; this need to be at one with her own universe; this joy in the beauty that was all around her that she had never known before?

"Because you would not allow yourself to know it."

So real was the sound of Naomi's voice that Pepper stopped in the street and looked over her shoulder. From being disconcerting this awareness of her grandmother's watchful presence had become reassuring. She saw that Oliver was looking at her, and thinking she had alarmed him she summoned a reassuring

smile—then she realised he was looking beyond her.
Was he too aware of Naomi's presence? Her heart
skipped a beat. How her grandmother would have
loved him! How she would have cherished and taught
him.

Without realising it she had parked close to Miles's
old college, Christ Church. They had to walk past the
entrance to Tom Quad and she paused for a moment
outside it, remembering.

Simon had been up early as well. He ignored the hotel
dining room—food was of no interest to him. He had
other things to do. He drove out to Marchington
while the dew was still on the grass. No one was there.
He went down to the chapel. Nothing had been
disturbed. It was as he had thought, but it was as well
to check.

As he walked through the empty rooms it was as
though Tim walked with him.

"It won't be long now," he promised him.

The madness had finally taken over, the psychosis
inherited with his genes and begun as an escape from
his father's sexual debasement of him; a fantasy land
with a gate which he could open and close at will now
imprisoned him, the gate back to reality now closed
for ever.

Only Simon didn't see it that way. He felt buoyant,
his body surging with energy and delight. He felt alive
with the power of his own thoughts; elevated above
all other men; with the strength to destroy a hundred
Pepper Minesses.

He had gone beyond hatred of her now, his madness
deepening beyond that point. He saw himself as an
executioner sent by a greater force to destroy an
enemy of that force. He was a disciple following the
orders of his master. Euphoria possessed him. He had

forgotten how he had once privately mocked Tim for
his obsession with Satanism and remembered only the
pleasure Tim promised he would experience through
the sacrifice of Pepper.

Now it was time for that sacrifice to take place, and
he had been charged with the task of doing it.

He left Marchington in an intense state of euphoria
and drove back to Oxford. He didn't want to eat; he
was too restless, too keyed up. Now he had to find
the woman.

He saw her quite by accident, just as he was crossing
the road outside the entrance to Tom Quad. She was
standing there staring at it. There was a boy with her
and an older woman, but he didn't pay much attention
to them. He had found her! It had been so easy. A
further sign that what he was doing had some higher
approval. Keeping Pepper well in sight, he followed
her, an anonymous figure in his Savile Row suit and
white shirt.

Simon hadn't been following her for very long when
he realised something. Someone else was following her
as well. Slipping into the shadows of a narrow
alleyway, he watched as Pepper and her companions
paused outside a shoeshop, and sure enough when
they moved, so did the woman in jeans and a sweat-
shirt who seemed to have been marking their every
move. Everywhere the small party went their two
shadows followed them. Simon had no idea who the
woman was, but she was interfering with his plans.
She was in his way, and he would have to find some
means of getting rid of her.

Pepper, Mary and Oliver lunched at a new seafood
restaurant, but none of them really did justice to the
meal.

Oliver's new clothes were soon bought, winter things
for the coming school term. Pepper's eyes misted over

as she watched Mary choose them, both of them knowing that she might not be alive to see him put them on. A tight strained look came over Mary's face as they left the shop and without her saying anything Pepper knew she was in pain, and seeing Oliver slipping his hand into the older woman's she suspected that he knew it as well.

It was a strain pretending to a cheerfulness she could not feel. Naomi had taught her that death was more friend than foe; death might be, but this mortal agony, this suffering . . . surely there was no virtue or reward in that?

She longed for Miles's calm rational presence. Sunday lunchtime could not come soon enough.

They left Oxford after lunch. Two cars followed them back.

As Laura Bates had already discovered, there was nowhere to discreetly conceal her car down the narrow lane that led only to the Simms' house. Last night her relief had parked hers on the main road, secure in the knowledge that no one could leave or enter the lane without her seeing them.

Country manners were not London manners, she had reported to Laura when they switched over. She had apparently lost count of the number of would-be knights of the road who had stopped to ask her if she was in difficulty.

Simon, already aware that Pepper was being shadowed, took good care to keep out of sight of the small blue Fiesta following the Aston Martin. He saw it drive past the opening to the lane Pepper drove down, and park up several yards away. He drove past it without turning his head, and then several miles on he turned round and drove back to Oxford.

It wasn't difficult to find a bookshop selling maps

of the area, and from the one he bought he was able to see that there was only one house down the lane. Was Pepper staying there or was she just a visitor?

He waited until late afternoon and drove out of Oxford again, slowing down well before turning into the lane, and skilfully mimicking the uncertain driving of a person looking for an unfamiliar landmark.

Less than half a mile down the lane he saw the house, with Pepper's car parked outside and, better still, Pepper herself playing cricket with the dark-haired boy who had been with her earlier, on a piece of uncultivated lawn to the side of the house. His instincts told Simon that she was staying at the house, but for how long? He couldn't afford to delay. This was the golden opportunity.

He drove back up the lane and wondered if the person driving the blue Fiesta was marking down his number plate. Just to be on the safe side, when he got back to Oxford he handed in the car, which was only rented, and hired out another from a different company.

Soon it would be dusk. A good time to act. Simon went back to his room and lay on the bed preparing himself for his self-appointed task.

Miles's meeting was over, but the other members of the committee were pressing him to stay and join them for dinner. There was no reason why he shouldn't; Pepper wasn't expecting him until tomorrow and he could hardly inflict himself on her friends half way through the evening. And yet . . . and yet he had this nagging feeling that he should go to her. Almost it was as though someone was telling him that he must go to her.

It was silly really. He could pick up the phone and speak to her. Almost without consciously making up his mind, he refused the proffered invitation, and somehow or other found he was in his car and heading for Oxford.

Foolish, illogical . . . both those things, perhaps, and yet the moment he got into his car Miles felt an intense sense of relief in the air all around him, coupled with a strong impulse to drive to Oxford just as fast as he could.

Not unusual behaviour in a man in love, perhaps, but Miles acknowledged to himself that it went deeper than that. That there was more to his feelings than mere emotional need to be with the woman he loved.

Laura Bates yawned and glanced at her watch. Another four hours before she was relieved. It was boring sitting here like this. So far one car and two cyclists had turned down the lane and then come back again, that was all. She was beginning to think that Miles French was wasting his money.

She saw the yellow car approach and slow down as it stopped alongside her own without any feeling of alarm. A man got out, tall, fair and vaguely familiar. He came towards her and opened the door of her car, and as she looked into his eyes she recognised him—and shock jolted through her.

She tried to cry out, but his hands were already around her throat, squeezing it with manic strength. Laura Bates was trained to defend herself, but not against strength like this. Bubbles of air gurgled in the vacuum that was her lungs. She tried to breathe, to tear at the hands clutching at her throat, but it was no use.

Darkness came down over her, and her last thought was that Miles French had been right after all, but she would have no way of telling him, because Simon Herries would have killed her.

Simon let her body sag and then pushed her into the passenger seat, fastening the seat belt. She looked as though she was asleep. He moved his own car, then pulled on the gloves he had brought with him and got into hers.

A small spinney spread out to one side of the lane and it was an easy task to conceal the small blue car in its depths. The failing light helped him. It would be discovered in the morning, no doubt, but by then it would all be over anyway.

Back in his own car he stripped off the gloves and started the engine.

The garden was empty, lights streaming from the house. Simon parked behind Pepper's car, blocking her exit. A sense of elation filled him as he walked up to the front door.

Oliver answered his knock. Simon took hold of him quite gently, pulling him against his body with his left hand while in the right he held the gun.

Neither of them spoke—there was no need. Simon had the boy and soon he would have the others. He knew from the way the old woman had fussed over the child.

He was right.

Mary came first, calling out, "Who is it, Oliver?" And then she screamed, a high petrified sound that brought the others running.

"It's me he wants," Pepper said quietly. She hadn't taken her eyes off Simon since the moment she saw him. "He'll let the rest of you go."

She stepped past Mary, willing herself not to betray her fear. She had no option but to go with him. He had Oliver.

"No!" Philip objected rawly, stepping up to Simon and trying to wrench Oliver away.

It was the wrong thing to do. Mary cried out as

Simon raised the gun and clubbed Philip to the ground. Pepper wanted to say something . . . anything, but her throat was tight with shock and fear.

"Get in the car, the rest of you," Simon demanded savagely. He had enjoyed hitting the man, even though it hadn't been part of his plan. The fool should have known better than to approach him.

Didn't he have the gun?

"Simon . . ." He turned his head as Pepper touched his arm. His eyes glittered maniacally, his mouth curled into a rictus smile of triumph. "Let Mary and Oliver go," she begged him. "They have nothing to do with this. It's just between you and me."

Please . . . please let him agree, she prayed, but even as she did so, she remembered Naomi's warning and knew he would refuse.

"Do you think I'm a fool? If I let them go they'll be on the phone to the police. You," he gestured to Mary, "you and the boy . . . in the back."

"Philip . . . my husband . . . he has a weak heart. You can't leave him lying here! He could die!" Mary protested, and Pepper felt ashamed because her fear had nearly all been for Oliver. She bent down to touch Philip and felt the stickiness of the blood on the side of his head where Simon had clubbed him. She suspected that Philip was already dead, but she daredn't say so.

"Crazy fool! He shouldn't have interfered," Simon snarled, then he laughed, a maniacal sound that chilled Pepper's blood.

Now she knew why Naomi had been trying to warn her, and of what. Why, oh, why hadn't she realised just how dangerous Simon Herries was? Dangerous and mad.

She heard Mary scream and turned in shock to see that Simon had levelled the gun at Philip's prone body. Oliver struggled in his arms and the gun went off. Pepper heard the shot, smelled the stench of burning flesh and cordite. Behind her she could hear Mary being sick. Oliver was staring at them both, his eyes huge and agonised.

She couldn't bear to look at Philip's poor body. She knew if he hadn't already been dead that that shot must have killed him.

"Get in the car," Simon repeated. "Otherwise the boy goes next."

He was loving this, high on the power of the control he had over them. He had enjoyed killing the man. It was surprising how satisfying it had been, though not as satisfying as killing Pepper would be. He looked at her and frowned. She should be more afraid—cowering, begging him for mercy.

"I think we'd better do as he says," Pepper told Mary. Privately she was wondering if there was any point in prolonging their agony. Simon would kill them all in the end, she had seen it in his eyes. She was tempted to plead for Mary's and Oliver's lives, but she suspected that if he thought they were important to her he would take even greater pleasure in killing them.

How he had found her she had no idea. She could hardly think straight at all as she got into the back of the small car. Oliver was at her side. Simon made Mary get into the driver's seat and then he climbed into the passenger seat beside her, the gun pressed hard against her side.

Mary started the engine. She was trembling so much it took her several minutes to get the car started, and all the time the tension within it grew.

"Where . . . where do you want me to go?" Mary asked Simon drily. Odd how her pain had subsided now that she actually was faced with death. She contemplated driving to the nearest police station, but she knew that Oliver and Pepper would be dead before anyone could help them. She knew who Simon was . . . she had recognised him instantly . . . and his madness.

Pray God Oliver would never learn that this madman was his father! She shuddered at the thought.

Originally Simon hadn't planned on taking anyone other than Pepper, but he had seen the fiercely protective way she had stood close to the child. He would enjoy what he had to do.

He would sacrifice the boy first, he decided calmly. He would enjoy watching Pepper's face as he made the ritual incisions. It would give her an idea of what lay ahead of her. She would die in the same kind of mortal agony she had inflicted on him. He would punish her as she truly deserved to be punished, the way Tim would have wanted her to be punished.

Pepper had only been to Marchington once, but she had recognised the route instantly, even in the dark. Generations of ancestors accustomed to living close to nature and its powers had given her instinct a deep inner knowledge out of step with modern living.

She knew instantly what Simon intended to do. He might just as well have screamed the words at her. She saw the chapel, felt its evil coldness. She saw the black candles, the words of the satanic Black Mass. She closed her eyes and prayed . . . Not to God of whom she knew nothing, but to older, stronger powers, to Naomi who she knew to be watching over her.

Oliver, sensing her tension, reached out and touched her. She withdrew slightly from him, frightened that he might sense through touch and understand what lay in her mind, and silently, over and over again, she repeated the words that her race had used almost since the dawn of time itself when committing the bodies of their young children to burial.

Miles found the turning into the lane without too much difficulty, even in the dark. He could see the light blazing from the house and in his anxiety to be with Pepper thought nothing of the fact that there was no sign of Laura Bates or one of her employees.

It was only when his headlights picked out Philip Simms' prone body that he began to feel real fear.

He stopped his car and got out. Philip was dead. As Miles knelt in front of him he was possessed by such a savage surge of urgency that he was half way back to his car before he realised what he was doing. It was an effort of will to make himself go back into the house and telephone the police. Within ten minutes they were with him.

At first they were efficient and polite, and no more, but Miles was not a leading barrister for nothing, and his story sounded too improbable not to be the truth.

"So you think this . . . Simon Herries has kidnapped your fiancée and perhaps two other people as well because of some private vendetta?"

He explained as simply as he could, and all the time the urgency inside him grew until he felt he could explode with the force of it.

"I don't suppose you've any idea where he might have taken them, have you, sir?"

The Inspector's attention was distracted when a uniformed constable came up to him, looking sick and shaken. He was only young, nineteen, maybe, no more.

"We've found a car in the spinney at the top of the lane, sir. There's a body in it . . . a woman."

Not Pepper! Dear God, no! Every instinct Miles possessed was screaming that she was still alive.

"Tall, heavily built . . . dark hair."

No, not Pepper, it sounded more like . . .

"Laura—Laura Bates, a private investigator," he said numbly. "I was worried about Pepper. She wouldn't listen to me, so I hired Laura as her bodyguard."

Now he had the inspector's full attention.

"And you've no idea where this Simon Herries could have taken them?"

"Marchington . . . he's taken them to Marchington."

Miles felt as amazed as the Inspector looked. How had he known that? Where had the words come from? Not from him, although he had been the one to speak them.

"Marchington?" the Inspector repeated.

"It's the family seat of the Earls of Marchington. Simon had a very close relationship with the Earl's grandson Tim Wilding at Oxford. They were planning to revive the old Hell Fire Club when Tim was killed. That was how it all started." Miles told them what Pepper herself had told him, willing himself not to show his impatience while with every breath he took, his sense of urgency grew.

Whoever started the rumour that the British police have no imagination was wrong, Miles acknowledged an hour later when a casually dressed, laconic detective, with an unshaven jaw and a quantity of dark, untidy hair, said, "I think we'd better check it out." He looked up at the sky and said something that Miles himself hadn't noticed. "There's a full moon tonight. If your theory's right . . . Johnson, Austin, get the cars," he called over his shoulder, and added to Miles, "You realise if he does have them there we're probably going to have to talk him into surrendering. It could be a long wait . . . I'll send one of the squad cars."

He didn't want him with them, Miles recognised, but there was no way he wasn't going, and he said so. Pepper needed him. He shook off his exhaustion, and wondered what on earth the detective would say if he told him that he was almost haunted by a thin old woman with a gnarled walnut face and distinctive Romany features who told him constantly that Pepper needed him. Probably have him locked up! he decided wryly.

"What we need now is some idea of the layout of the building. They'll try to get that for us back at the station. I can't promise you we're going to get them out alive," the Inspector told Miles frankly. "It all depends on Herries. You say he's insane? If that's true . . ."

It was what he didn't say rather than what he did that lay so heavily on his heart, Miles acknowledged, and there was much he had not told the police. Like the fact that Oliver was Simon's son . . .

As they drove past the end of the lane Miles noticed two policemen removing a shrouded body from the blue car. Laura Bates . . . he shuddered deeply. Indirectly he was responsible for her death.

No one in the chapel at Marchington heard the police arrive. Mary, beyond shock and pain, was sitting with Oliver, holding on to him. For the past three hours they had had to sit and listen while Simon talked.

Little of what he said made sense to anyone other than Pepper. She saw that he blamed her for Tim's death, even though she knew that he was responsible. His hatred of her, of her whole sex, spewed up inside him like lava from a volcano. He talked of Deborah and her suicide, and Pepper's heightened awareness made it almost possible for her to see the other girl as she lay on the coldness of the chapel floor. She had to

fight to suppress her sickness as Simon told them what
he had done to her. For a girl brought up as Deborah
had been, innocent, naïve, a girl whose sexuality had
never been awakened, the torment she had experienced
must have been unendurable.

And lastly he talked of Pepper herself, of her
rape . . . of his pleasure in it, but listening to his
ranting Pepper found that she might almost have been
listening to him talking about someone else. His words
no longer had the power to hurt her. She was free . . .
Miles had freed her.

All the time Simon talked, he never took his eyes
off them nor relaxed his grip on the gun. He would
shoot them the moment they tried to move—Pepper
knew that.

She also knew why he was delaying so long. He
would not start the Black Mass ritual that would lead
to their deaths until midnight.

She prayed as she had never done in her life before
that neither Oliver nor Mary understood what was in
store for them. She would kill her child herself before
she would allow Simon Herries to touch him, and she
fully intended to do so.

Miles had been right to warn her. Miles . . . this
was the first time she had allowed herself to think of
him. She hadn't dared before, knowing that to do so
was to weaken herself. She wanted him; she loved
him, and now too late she knew that all her dreams
of revenge and retribution had been nothing more
than a throwing away of so many years of her life.
But they had brought her Miles. Good out of bad,
love out of hate—like Oliver, the child of her enforced
union with a man who was now going to kill them
both. How could she have guessed when she had been
so desperate to destroy her unborn foetus just what
her child would be . . . would have been, she corrected

herself bitterly.

They found the car straight away. The house was in darkness. The police fanned out silently around it.

"Door forced here, sir," one of the men told the Inspector.

They went inside. The Inspector had suggested that Miles remain by the security of the police cars, but he had refused. His awareness of Naomi's presence was so strong now he was surprised that no one else was aware of her.

"They're down here somewhere," he told the Inspector, heading for the passage that led to the chapel.

The Inspector and the man at his side exchanged glances. Both of them were too experienced . . . had seen too much to question how he knew.

"Carefully now, sir," was all the Inspector said.

The chapel was illuminated with candles for the Black Mass. The wax hissed and dripped, giving off a drugging odour. The ingredients that went into their making were secret; special incantations said over them. Once, long ago, the drug content in them, made from wild poppies, had been put there to soothe the fears of a coven's victims. Then the rite of sacrifice had been an accepted part of rural village life.

Like animals, human beings have instincts that pass from generation to generation, although civilisation has glossed over them. As the men approached the entrance to the chapel all of them felt an atavistic and instinctive urge to withdraw.

Pepper saw them first, her heart leaping into her throat. She sensed them there, even while they were still cloaked in the shadows, and she measured the distance to safety with fierce eyes . . . not for herself, for Oliver, for her child. He had won the school sprint race, Mary had told her with pride. A child, no matter how fast on his feet, could not run faster than a bullet . . . unless someone stood in its way. Pepper inched forward carefully—and froze as Simon saw her.

He stopped in full spate, suspicion narrowing his eyes. Like an animal he could smell fear around him . . . fear and danger. The candles guttered slightly as though somewhere someone had opened a door.

Watching the scene, Miles felt his stomach roll over. No one spoke. The police were armed, but how could they risk rushing Simon? If they tried he would kill all three of them before they could reach him.

Simon grimaced and advanced on Pepper. It was five to twelve. Soon it would begin. He could feel the pleasure building up inside him. There was a pressure inside his skull that was almost a pain, an excitement that went beyond anything he had ever known—and then abruptly it started to fade. He stopped moving, bewildered by the sudden loss of exhilaration, his eyes unfocused and wild as he stared into the dark corners of the chapel. Where was Tim? He had promised Simon he would be here to share this with him . . . he had told him so. Confusion clouded Simon's mind. He wanted the sharpness of his earlier exhilaration back. He wanted to feel again that keenness, that euphoria, that ecstasy that would be his when he saw Pepper's body spread out on the altar . . . He told Pepper as much, relishing the words, while his unseen listeners froze.

"You were right—he is mad," the detective told Miles grimly. "We need to distract him."

"Can't risk it," one of his men said tersely. "We wouldn't have enough time. We might be able to save one of them . . ."

Simon frowned. It was almost time. Where was the

exhilaration he needed to feel . . . he had to feel? Where was Tim? He had promised he would be here . . .

Pepper watched him, her heart in her throat, sensing the dull clouding of his senses. Now . . . it had to be now. There wouldn't be a better time. The gun was still pointing at them.

Outside in the darkened corridor the Inspector turned to Miles. "We've got a marksman here. We'll get him up and into position, but at the moment there's not a damn thing he can do. The others are in the way."

Pepper gripped hold of Oliver's shoulder, and he looked up at her. She looked towards the corridor and immediately he understood. This communion between them was still so new to him and yet at the same time so very old; something that had come into this life with him and that would go out of it with him as well. Pepper wanted him to run. He knew that one of them was going to die, although he didn't know which one, but Pepper wanted him to run, and run he would.

Her fingers still gripped him. She watched Simon struggling against the darkness dulling his brain. He turned his head.

The moment was upon them. She released Oliver's shoulder and he ran. Simon called out, levelling the gun. Pepper rushed in front of him to protect her child, but Mary beat her to it, pushing her to the floor with surprising strength, flinging herself at Simon's chest, arms outstretched.

The impact of the bullet killed her instantly. Her inert body was still draped against Simon's when the police marksman's bullet entered his brain.

As death embraced her, Mary saw a woman waiting for her, her hand outstretched, and a feeling of intense happiness overwhelmed her. In the shadows behind the gypsy woman stood Philip. And as she floated towards him the gypsy woman turned her so that she could look down on the scene she had just left, and she thought she heard her saying,

"It is over. The child is safe."

In a daze Pepper saw the men emerge from the passageway, policemen, and another—another whose face she felt she should know. He was carrying a little boy. He said her name—at least she thought it was her name. He said it again, his forehead creased in anxiety, and then she knew. She got up and ran to him, and his free arm opened, gathering her close to him.

"It's over, Pepper—it's over. You're both safe."

They were safe, yes, but Mary and Philip were dead.

"It is as it was ordained to be." Pepper heard the words and yet knew that no one had spoken them. She smiled shakily, her lips forming a name.

"Naomi . . ."

She would not see her grandmother again—not in this life. She knew it instinctively. From that other world, her grandmother's task was done.

She felt Oliver's hand on her arm and looked at him.

"Mary's at peace now, Oliver," she told him.

He looked back at her, his eyes grave and knowing.

"Yes . . . I saw her," he told her quietly.

Miles watched them both, knowing they were sharing something from which he was excluded and yet not resenting it.

"I should have listened to you," Pepper admitted later when the formalities were done with and she and Oliver were safely installed in Miles's flat.

"And I should have been more understanding."

"That poor girl!"

They were both silent for a moment. Oliver was upstairs in bed, and Pepper turned to Miles and said quietly,

"Oliver is my responsibility. I promised Mary I would take care of him, and even if I hadn't done so, I would want to . . ."

"He's our responsibility," Miles amended quietly. "He's a very special child, Pepper."

"Yes." Her head was bent, her hair falling against her cheek. In the firelight she could have almost been a young girl. It was four o'clock in the morning, but neither of them felt like sleep.

"I was frightened of committing myself to you . . ." she told Miles.

"And I was frightened of losing you." He took hold of her hand. "We can't alter what happened, Pepper."

"No . . . it was already ordained," she agreed quietly.

"We could always live in London, sell both our flats and buy something bigger," Miles suggested.

Pepper shook her head.

"No, Oliver is used to the country, and that's what I want for our children."

"You'll find it tiring commuting between London and the country every day," Miles warned her. "It's different for me—I can work from home."

Besides, he had been approached with a hint that he was being considered as a circuit judge. He would be one of the youngest in the country, his work load would be heavy, but he wouldn't need to be based in London.

"No," Pepper told him. They were sitting in her drawing room discussing their plans. They had been married quietly at the weekend, with Oliver and only a handful of friends to witness the ceremony.

"I'm giving up the business." She avoided looking at Miles. "It's served its purpose now."

He understood immediately.

"Minesse—Nemesis. Was it worth it, Pepper?"

She shook her head.

"No . . . nothing is worth the loss of people like Philip and Mary, and I could have lost Oliver as well."

Sensing the guilt underlying her words, Miles took hold of her hand.

"And yet look at the good that has come out of it as well," he reminded her. "Look at Alex and Julia."

"Do you think they'll get permission to adopt Randolph?" Pepper asked him, referring to the half English, half West Indian physically handicapped baby the Barnetts were hoping to make their own.

"I don't see why not. You're a very special lady," Miles added softly, "but you aren't superhuman. None of us can change what life holds in store for us, we can't alter the circumstances, only mitigate them."

"But if I hadn't tried to blackmail all of you— Simon Herries . . ."

"Would still have destroyed himself and possibly others as well, but in a different way. It's over, Pepper, and we've all got to go on with our lives. Will you ever tell Oliver?" he asked her.

"I don't know. I don't think so. I want him to grow up free of any burdens." She paused and added quietly, "If we have a daughter I'd like to call her Naomi."

"I think she'd like that," he agreed, and both of them knew that he wasn't referring to their unborn child.

She would sell Minesse Management, Pepper

decided; she had several potential buyers for the business. She and Miles would buy an old rambling house somewhere in the country and she would direct her formidable energies to bringing up their children. They would give them all that they had not had themselves; and with any luck all that they had had.

She touched her still flat stomach, smiling secretively at her own inner knowledge. She had conceived Miles's child, she was sure of it, and its conception was a sign of her own rebirth; a sign that the past was dead and its burden of bitterness with it. Pepper had tried to bargain with fate, forgetting that others might be called upon to meet the price for her. Now she knew better.

"Come on," Miles demanded prosaically. "I'm hungry! Let's go and get something to eat, and then we'd better go and relieve Alex and Julia of the burden of our son."

The other couple had offered to look after Oliver for them for a few days so that they could have some time alone. Already Pepper missed him.

She looked down at her wrist. The key was gone and in its place she wore a small charm that was the Romany symbol for peace and hope. She touched it gently and smiled before slipping her arm through that of her husband. Sunlight touched their faces, warm through the glass. Pepper lifted hers up instinctively and Miles, looking down at her, thought she had never looked more beautiful, more desirable, more womanly. Sorrow had touched her and left its mark. He had her now and he would never let her go. Never.

He saw her smile and asked softly, "What are you thinking?"

"An old saying, one that goes. 'Living well is the best revenge.' And that's exactly what I intend to do from now on."

All things have a purpose, a meaning that it is not always given to us to understand. Out of rage Pepper had found love; out of grief she had been given hope; out of danger had come peace, and she intended to be worthy of those gifts.

THE GODS AND THEIR GRAND DESIGN

Also by Erich von Däniken

THE GODS
AND THEIR
GRAND DESIGN

The Eighth Wonder
of the World

by
ERICH VON DÄNIKEN

Translated by Michael Heron

G. P. Putnam's Sons
New York

First published in Germany 1982 under the title *Die Strategie
Der Götter*

Library of Congress Cataloging in Publication Data

Däniken, Erich von, 1935–
    The Gods and their grand design.

    Translation of: Strategie der Götter.
    1. Civilization, Ancient — Extraterrestrial influences.
    2. Indians of South America — Colombia — Antiquities.
    3. Colombia — Antiquities.   I. Title.
CB156.D35713   1984   001.9′4   83–27066
ISBN 0–399–12961–8

Printed in Great Britain

Contents

1 Legendary Times!

'We should not fear those who hold different opinions, but those who hold different opinions and are too cowardly to say so.'

Napoleon 1 (1769–1821)

Reality is more fantastic than any fantasy.

Before I can follow a trail that was laid many thousands of years ago, I must tell you about an astounding but controversial event that took place in America in the first third of the last century. It leads us back to that ancient trail.

Among the immigrants who streamed into the New World from Germany, Scandinavia, Ireland and England was the Smith family from Scotland, who lived in the small town of Palmyra in New York State.

The district in which the Smiths lived was still barely civilised. Day-to-day existence demanded hard physical toil from the immigrants. The American War of Independence from 1776 to 1783 already lay fifty years behind, but the vast country was still very sparsely inhabited and the settlers had to maintain running battles with the indigenous Indians.

The new arrivals from Europe were hard-working. Not only did they bring tools and goodwill with them, but also the many and varied religions of their homelands, which they sought to propagate with missionary zeal. Sects and religious groups spread like weeds. The apostles of salvation of countless different faiths vied with each other in making extravagant promises and capturing souls with sinister threats about the hereafter. Chapels, temples and churches shot up like mushrooms, as though the devil himself had discovered how to confuse the minds of the settlers in their new homeland.

Like many immigrants, Mother Smith and her three children were Presbyterians. Her son Joseph, who was eighteen, found things more difficult. He sought desperately for the true God, because he could not accept the fact that all the saviours claimed firmly to be in the right and at the same time fought each other bitterly in the name of Jesus. Joseph Smith (1805–1844) was a nonentity, until the night of 21 September 1823, when he had a strange vision.

Joseph was praying fervently in his bedroom, when he suddenly perceived a light, which illuminated the room brilliantly. A bare-footed angel in a white robe stepped out of the light. The vision introduced himself to the terrified youth as Moroni, the messenger of God. Moroni had astounding news for the young man!

The angel told him that in a stony hiding-place near the Smith family's home town a book was preserved written on gold plates and giving a full account of the former inhabitants

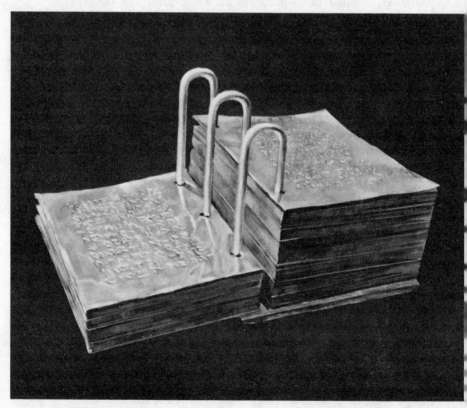

The Book of Mormon, inscribed on gold plates, revealed to Joseph Smith through a vision.

of the American continent and the source from whence they came. Near the gold tablets lay a breastplate to which two stones, Urim and Thummim,* were attached and with their help the ancient scripture could be translated. In addition the cache contained a divine compass. After telling Joseph Smith that he had been chosen to translate part of the scriptures and spread their message abroad, Moroni, the divine messenger, vanished.

Only for a while.

Then he reappeared, repeated the exciting news and added the prophecy that there would be great desolation by famine, sword and pestilence in the future.

We do not know whether Moroni was ordered to deliver his message bit by bit or whether he was forgetful. In any case he appeared for the third time on the night of 21 September to add a warning to his two previous messages. Joseph was forbidden to show the sacred objects on the Hill of Cumorah to anyone, apart from a chosen few. If he broke this commandment he would be killed.

Short of sleep after his nocturnal visit, Joseph naturally told his father about his alarming experience over their frugal breakfast. A bigoted believer like all the settlers, Father Smith had no doubt that his son had been given a divine mission — to seek out the place described by the angel Moroni.

South of Palmyra, near the village of Manchester, rises the Hill of Cumorah, which towers up steeply on its north side. Underneath the top of the hill Joseph Smith found the treasure he had been promised. This is how he himself described it:

Under a stone of considerable size lay the plates, deposited in a stone box. This stone was thicker and rounding in the middle on the upper side and thinner towards the edges, so that the middle part of it was visible above the ground, but the edge round was covered with earth. Having removed the earth, I obtained a lever, which I got fixed under the edge of the stone, and with a little exertion raised it up. I looked in, and there indeed did I behold the plates. The box in which they lay was formed by laying stones together in some kind of cement. In the bottom of the box were laid two stones

*Oracle stones used by the priests of Israel.

The Hill of Cumorah beneath whose summit Joseph Smith found the
buried treasure, the plates of the Book of Mormon.

crossways of the box, and on these stones lay the plates and the other things with them.

When the teenager, with the curiosity of any treasure-hunter, automatically reached for the objects with both hands, he immediately felt a blow. He tried again and received another crippling blow. At the third attempt he received what seemed like a powerful electric shock. He lay on the floor as if paralysed.

At the same moment Moroni, the enigmatic nocturnal messenger, appeared beside him and ordered Joseph to return there every year on the same day. When the time was ripe, he would be given the sacred objects.

That time came four years later.

On 22 September 1827 the heavenly messenger Moroni handed Joseph Smith the engraved gold plates, the breastplate and the gleaming translation aids Urim and Thummim. Moroni impressed on the 22-year-old Joseph that he would be held responsible if the ancient treasures were lost owing to his carelessness.

I do not know if this story really took place like that. However that is exactly how it is handed down in *The Book of Mormon*, the 'Bible' of 'The Church of Jesus Christ of Latter-day Saints', the Mormons. It is the firm belief of several million Mormons, those devout people who have their headquarters in Salt Lake City in the State of Utah.

I do not know whether Joseph Smith was a religious psychopath or a crafty demagogue who took advantage of the religious confusion of his day to ensnare people. I do not know if Joseph Smith was a selfless, honourable truth-seeking prophet.

Nor do I know who visited the young man on the night of 21 September 1823 and handed over the hidden treasure four years later. Was it an Indian who knew of the existence of the ancient plates? Could he, or a member of his tribe, have hidden them? Did an Indian convert to one of the many Christian communities betray a well-preserved secret? Did a white treasure-hunter, who needed a partner, initiate Joseph Smith? Or did the young man stumble on the treasure trove alone and invent the story of the heavenly vision to attract attention?

I do not know the answer, but one thing seems certain. Joseph Smith actually possessed the engraved gold plates!

With the help of the 'translation stones' Urim and Thummim, Joseph Smith had worked for 21 months translating part of the text on the plates before he showed them to three honourable and respected men in June 1829 — with the angel Moroni's permission, of course! Oliver Cowdery, David Whitmer and Martin Harris drew up a document in which they swore that they had seen the plates 'and the engravings thereon'.

This testimony carries some weight, for the three men stuck to it after they had parted from Smith and the Church of Latter-day Saints he founded, two of them even becoming violent opponents of the new religion. None of the men disavowed his oath.

Two days after revealing the engraved plates to the three men, Smith showed his treasure to eight more witnesses, who were allowed to handle the thin plates and leaf through them. These eight men also testified to the fact with their seals and signatures (2):

Be it known to all nations, kindreds, tongues and people, unto whom this work shall come: That Joseph Smith, Jun., the translator of this work, has shown unto us the plates of which hath been spoken, which have the appearance of gold; and as many of the leaves as the said Smith has translated we did handle with our hands; and we also saw the engravings thereon, all of which have the appearance of ancient work, and of curious workmanship. And this we bear record with words of soberness, that the said Smith has shown unto us, for we have seen and hefted, and know of a surety that the said Smith has got the plates of which we have spoken. And we give our names unto the world, to witness unto the world that which we have seen. And we lie not, God bearing witness of it.

CHRISTIAN WHITMER. JACOB WHITMER. PETER WHITMER JUN. JOHN WHITMER. HIRAM PAGE. JOSEPH SMITH SEN. HYRUM SMITH. SAMUEL H. SMITH.

The oaths of 11 men, not all members of the religious community founded by Joseph Smith, who defended their

Characters which Joseph Smith copied from the metal plates. Scholars classified them as 'reformed Egyptian hieroglyphs'.

ancient faith belligerently and called on their God as witness, carry considerable weight, if we remember the fantastic zeal with which the settlers clung to their congregations and sects for fear of punishment at the Last Judgement.

The two sworn testimonies are not alone in supporting the conclusion that Smith actually possessed the engraved plates for a time, the contents of the translation also support it. They exclude a *complete* forgery, although I am sure there was *partial* forgery.

Smith described the book's golden plates as somewhat thinner than the tin plate commonly used at the time. The individual pages were held together by three rings. The book was some 15 cm broad, 20 cm high and 15 cm thick. A third of the metal pages could be leafed through easily, the other two-thirds being 'sealed' to a block. Smith made copies of the characters on the plates and these were later classified by scholars as 'reformed Egyptian hieroglyphs'.

The present-day Book of Mormon of the Church of Jesus Christ of Latter-day Saints, based on the translations of the mysterious plates by the church's founder Joseph Smith, enlarged by the addition of prophecies about Jesus (which were certainly not in the original text) and a kind of continuation of biblical history, fitted in well with the Christian faith of American society around the middle of the last century.

Smith and his Church of Jesus Christ of Latter-day Saints soon became the object of mockery, but they also attracted the hostility of the American fundamentalists, who stuck rigorously to a literal interpretation of the Bible and preached zealously against critical theology and modern science. There are still fundamentalists in America today.

It was a painful business for Smith because, after their successful translation, the angel Moroni asked for the plates back to hide them again for the distant future. So apart from this translation and the sworn statements of the 11 men, poor Joseph had no proof that he had actually held the legendary plates in his hands every day for nearly two years.

The young Mormon community fought bravely and kept its spirits up. In spite of constant persecution, it increased in size and has 5 million adherents today, although internal strife in the early days led to the arrest of Joseph and his brother Hyrum. On 27 June 1844 a mob broke into the jail at Carthago, Illinois, and shot the brothers Smith. The industrious and God-fearing Mormons had their martyrs. They stuck together and during the last 140 years created a religious and secular empire without parallel.

Between past millennia and the last century there is only a rickety suspension-bridge over a perilous abyss and that is loosely anchored to the banks of time. In spite of that, many rotten planks force researchers to make reckless leaps unless they want to sink in the morass of the present. Two sections of the Book of Mormon, the plates of Ether and Nephi, are well suited to form a fairly solid bridge leading back to past millennia.

The 24 plates of Ether tell the story of the people of Jared. According to the translated plates, the Jaredites are supposed to have pleaded with their God about the time of the building of the Tower of Babel, i.e. towards the end of 3,000 BC, to save them from the warlike turmoil of the neighbouring peoples. God heard their plea and led the Jaredites in a spectacular trek, first into a wilderness and then across the ocean to the coast of America. The journey, described in great detail, lasted 344 days. The plates do not state on which coast of the American continent the emigrants landed, but extracts from the Mormon Bible, Book of Ether, 2. 4 *et seq.*, may be of interest:

And it came to pass that when they came down into the valley of Nimrod [Mesopotamia, E.v.D.] the Lord came down and talked with the brother of Jared; and he was in a cloud and the brother of Jared saw him not.

And it came to pass that the Lord did go before them and did talk with them as he stood in a cloud, and gave directions whither they should travel. And it came to pass that they did travel in the wilderness, and did build barges, in which they did cross many waters, being directed continually by the hand of the Lord.

The barges were small and light upon the water, even like unto the likeness of a fowl upon the water.

And they were built after a manner that they were exceedingly tight, even that they would hold water like unto a dish; and the ends thereof were peaked; and the top thereof was tight and like unto a dish; and the length thereof was the length of a tree; and the door thereof, when it was shut, was tight like unto a dish.

When the Jaredites had built eight windowless watertight vessels according to their 'Lord's' instructions, they thought they noticed a structural error. When the only door was closed, it was pitch black on board, but obviously it was not a mistake, for the 'Lord' gave them 16 gleaming stones, two for each vessel, and the stones gave them bright light for 344 days. Great stuff!

The craft, loaded with seeds and small animals of all kinds, must have been amazingly manoeuvrable in all weathers. Even if the translation of the Book of Ether is only partly factual, the technology the 'Lord' passed on to the Jaredites was sensational. This quotation makes amazing reading:

And it came to pass that they were many times buried in the depths of the sea, because of the mountain waves which broke upon them, and also the great and terrible tempests which were caused by the fierceness of the wind.

And it came to pass that when they were buried in the deep there was no water that could hurt them, their vessel being tight like unto a dish, and also they were tight like unto the ark of Noah; therefore when they were encompassed about by many waters they did cry unto the Lord, and he did bring them forth again upon the top of the waters.

First God created man, then he destroyed his descendants in the Flood. He made a covenant with the survivors 'for all future generations' (Genesis 9.10 *et seq.*). Rebellious mankind tried to rival God and built the mighty tower of Babel. God descended in a rage and scattered the children of men 'over the face of all the earth' (Genesis 11.1 *et seq.*). One of these exiled groups was the Jaredites, who were transported to America in vessels light as birds, with strange sources of light.

If God wanted to give a group of people a chance of survival, what was the point of the laborious construction of eight small vessels? Could not almighty God have carried them to distant parts by a miracle?

Couldn't this God have flown the Jaredites over the ocean or did he prefer not to? Their presence in America shows that he wanted to help them cross the big pond. Was he only able to give technical instructions for ship-building? If he forgot that it was pitch-dark inside the ships, was he forced to correct his error in retrospect by providing flashing stones? Even if the Lord did not want to perform a miracle, even if he made these people work hard for their salvation, why did he not give instructions for building a normal surface craft which could have crossed the Atlantic comfortably? And if the craft had to be like nutshells, almighty God, the acknowledged Lord of the clouds and winds, could at least have given his flock calm seas.

It annoys me that an everlasting omniscient God could not see any farther into the future. Did he not sense that thousands of years after the ocean crossing the traditional account might provoke doubts about his omnipotence? Did it spark the question why technology and not a miracle? He would have been wiser to make use of a miracle which would be inexplicable for all eternity. Miracles escape the bounds of critical reason.

Like all immigrants, the Jaredites sailed to America in terrible conditions. Did not their guardian 'Lord' possess adequate technology to transport his protégés over the big pond in a less dangerous way? What kind of 'God' was at work here 5,000 years ago?

The literature of dark distant ages is literally legendary. We have no precise knowledge. Mankind, stupid and incorrigible, has always managed to wipe out the traditions of previous ages. The library of the ancient city of Pergamon in Asia

Minor, with its 500,000 volumes, was destroyed. The great libraries of ancient Jerusalem and Alexandria were destroyed; the libraries of the Aztecs and Maya went up in flames. Successive generations of mankind wiped out the collected wisdom of the past, but they did not wipe it out completely. There still exist fragments of age-old traditions from which, with a little ingenuity, we can form conceptions of the 'gods' who were once active. We cannot now determine the age of the traditions from textual fragments. The chroniclers noted down indiscriminately not only what they experienced, but also what they knew only from hearsay. Primeval, old and 'new' stories were woven into a colourful tapestry. The chonological course of events was mixed as if in a cocktail-shaker. The years drew rings, but over the centuries collected around a central point.

All we have to do today is to peel off the layers of this 'onion' in order to reveal the essential core. Getting at the 'hard core' is not really miraculous or inexplicable. It is a matter for reason, i.e. analysis, and hence explicable. Working outwards from the centre of tradition — freed of chance superficial accretions — we can find trails which were once expounded for curious men in the distant future. This future has actually begun!

The *Sagen der Juden von der Urzeit* (3) (Legends of the Jews from Primitive Times) relate that, after the banishment from Paradise, the angel Raziel gave Adam a book 'at the behest of the All Highest', the text of which was clearly engraved 'on a sapphire stone'.

Raziel told Adam that he could educate himself with the help of this book. Our first ancestor realised how valuable the 'book' was and after reading it he always hid it in a cave.

Adam learnt from the engravings:

everything about his limbs and veins and all things that went on inside his body and their purpose and causes. He also learnt about the courses of the planets. With the aid of the book he could ... examine the paths of the moon and the paths of Aldebaran, Orion and Sirius. He could name the names of every separate heaven and knew wherein the activity of each one consisted ... Adam knew all about the rolling thunder, he could tell the action of lightning and could narrate what would happen from moon to moon.

A 'book' on a sapphire stone giving anthropological and astronomical instruction? The heavenly messenger Raziel's gift to Adam is as grotesque as the one Moroni gave to Joseph Smith!

For chroniclers in the remote past all this must have been rather like what journalists today call a canard, a phoney story. This 'book' on a sapphire stone was sheer nonsense.

As clever children of the computer age, we know that things that were once inconceivable are technically possible now. Everyone knows that technology uses tiny silicon chips on which to 'engrave', i.e. store, millions of bits of information. Looking at it from a modern point of view we may ask ourselves if the transmission of a text on a sapphire stone was the product of an advanced technology already far ahead of our own.

The *Sagen der Juden von der Urzeit* has it that Adam handed the book down to his son Seth and that it was inherited by his descendants Enoch, Noah, Abraham, Moses, Aaron and then by Solomon (c. 965–926 BC), the King of Judah and Israel, who acquired his enormous wisdom from the sapphire stone.

According to the *Sagen der Juden von Urzeit*, the Book of the Prophet Enoch was supposed to have formed part of Adam's sapphire book. Enoch, the seventh of the ten patriarchs, was in direct touch with God and spoke to the 'Watchers of the Heavens' and the 'fallen angels'. At the age of 365 he was carried up to heaven — without dying — in a spectacular fashion. Ancient Jewish legends go on to say that Enoch acquired his all-embracing knowledge from Adam's book and that men gathered round him so that he could spread the wisdom of the sapphire stone, teach and instruct them:

When the men sat around Enoch and Enoch spoke to them, they raised their eyes and saw the form of a steed come down from heaven, and the steed descended to earth in a storm. Then the people told Enoch and Enoch spoke unto them: This steed has descended for my sake. The time has come and the day when I go from you and from which day forth I shall never see you again. Then the steed was there and stood before Enoch and all the children of men saw it clearly.

Ancient Jewish tradition describes how the faithful did not

want to let Enoch go after his eloquent farewell before his ascent into heaven, how they ran after him and how he bade them seven times to leave him alone, how he insistently warned them to turn round, for otherwise they would die. It says that small groups of people went home after each warning, although the most persistent stayed with Enoch. Loyalty, devotion, curiosity? In the end Enoch gave up; he lost his temper!

As they insisted on going with him, he spoke to them no longer, and they followed him and did not turn back. And on the seventh day it came to pass that Enoch rode up to heaven in a storm on fiery steeds in fiery chariots.

The ancient Jewish legend shows that events at Enoch's take-off for heaven unfolded in the most 'ungodly' way. When things had quietened down, those who had heeded Enoch's warning and returned home went looking for their friends who had stuck to the prophet until the countdown. They all lay dead around the launching-pad — excuse me — the spot from which Enoch ascended with the fiery steeds.

The legendary age between Adam's appearance in the scenario of the history of mankind and the building of the tower of Babel was the first great age of the gods, of fire-breathing horses, mysterious deaths and remarkable births.

The story, then, is as old as the hills, although we have only known about it since 1947. That was when sensational finds were made in eleven mountain caves at the north-west end of the Dead Sea, near Qumran. They consisted of numerous manuscripts from the second century BC written on leather scrolls concealed in earthenware jars.

One scroll tells the story of Lamech, Noah's father and patron of nomads and musicians.

Even on the Other Side, Lamech will be glad that his intimate family history was not generally known during his lifetime, it was so painful and remarkable. Lamech's wife Bat Enosh gave birth to a child, although the head of the family had never slept with her. Later Lamech learnt from his grandfather Enoch that the 'Watchers of the Heavens' had placed the seeds in Bat Enosh's womb. Lamech showed great generosity and recognised the child as his own. The offspring produced in this remarkable way was called Noah at the request of the 'Watchers'. The same Noah became world famous as a survivor of the Flood.

To make matters worse, the arrival of an unnaturally begotten child in the family of Lamech's son Nir could not be concealed. Nir was married to Sopranima and she was barren, to the family's sorrow. Nir tried hard to implant progeny in Sopranima's womb, but without success. For a priest of the Almighty like Nir, admired by the common people for his wisdom, it was a terrible scandal to learn that Sopranima was barren. Nir was shattered and reviled his wife so grossly that she collapsed and died, although a boy the size of a three-year-old crawled out of his mother's womb. Nir summoned Noah. They buried Sopranima and called the little boy Melchizedek, thenceforth known as the legendary priest-king of Salem, later Jerusalem (5).

Tradition leaves us in no doubt that Melchizedek was a case of a 'divine birth'. Before the Lord opened the sluices to unleash the Flood, the Archangel Michael came down from heaven and informed adoptive father Nir that it was the 'Lord' who had implanted the boy in Sopranima's womb. Consequently, and we can understand this, the Lord had sent him, Archangel Michael, with orders to carry the boy Melchizedek to Paradise so that he would survive the imminent deluge safely:

> And Michael took the boy on the very night on which he had descended and took him on his wings and set him in the Paradise of Eden.

Melchizedek survived! He reappears after the Flood. Moses tells us about it:

> After his return from the defeat of Ched-or-laomer and the kings who were with him, the king of Sodom went out to meet him at the Valley of Shaveh (that is, the Kings' Valley). And Melchizedek king of Salem brought out bread and wine; he was priest of God Most High. And he blessed him and said, 'Blessed be Abram by God Most High, maker of heaven and earth, and blessed be God Most High, who has

delivered your enemies into your hands!' And Abram gave him a tenth of everything.

(Genesis 14.17–20)

Hundreds of Old Testament scholars and exegetists have been excited by this passage from the Bible. 'The strange figure of the priest — king of Salem, who appears like a *deux ex machina* and then vanishes again — has naturally interested posterity' (8).

Obviously, because something extraordinary happened here. Abraham, the first of the three Patriarchs, stands at the head of Jewish tradition. Then the almost unknown Melchizedek comes along and blesses him! And that is not all. Of his own accord, the patriarch gives the king of Salem 'a tenth of everything!' What kind of a priest of 'God Most High' was that? After all, there was only the one God, whom Abraham worshipped. Or did Abraham know anything about the most extraordinary 'divine' birth? Melchizedek appears unexpectedly; he cannot be fitted into any tailor-made accepted pattern.

Given a little less naive faith and a little more courage, the Melchizedek mystery could be solved by modern speculation in this way. An extraterrestrial crew made up of so-called gods produced Noah and Melchizedek by artificial insemination. The legal fathers, Lamech and Noah, recognise them as their own sons, but against their better judgement, for they remember the assurances that the sons of the heavenly ones would be responsible for the artificial insemination of their wives Bat Enosh and Sopranima. It was the same heavenly gods who destroyed their descendants because their genetic experiment did not develop as they liked. Saved from the Flood, both were the products of genetic manipulation. As captain of the ark Noah became founder of the new generation and the priest king Melchizedek became its teacher.

The fact that Melchizedek existed both before and after the Flood does not conflict with this theory. What Albert Einstein calculated with his special theory of relativity and what was proved in physical experiments makes it possible. If Melchizedek, thanks to Archangel Michael's friendly cooperation, boarded a spaceship that accelerated to very high speeds and came straight back to earth, decades or centuries would have passed on earth, whereas the crew of the spaceship would not have aged significantly before they landed again. Melchizedek would still be young and eager for new tasks.*

It is not a question of names or the lapse of time. 'Legendary' traditions cannot be arranged chronologically. Was the survivor of the Flood really called Noah, as the Bible claims? Or was his name Utnapishtim, as it says in the Sumerian *Epic of Gilgamesh*, which dates from c. 2,000 BC? Or was the survivor of the Flood not even called Utnapishtim, but Mulkueikai, as the Kágaba Indians of Colombia name the priest who survived the Flood in a magic craft? Names are unimportant. What matters is the substance of the traditions.

Have we lost sight of Joseph Smith's Book of Mormon? What have the angel Raziel, Enoch's ascent into heaven and the artificial procreation of Noah and Melchizedek got to do with the Book of Mormon?

In the Book of Ether translated by Smith it says that the Jaredites were sent to sea in their eight ships around the time of the building of the Tower of Babel. The Jaredites were led by one of Jared's brothers and Jared himself was Enoch's father!

Jared means something like 'He who has come down', so it is understandable that the Jaredites were a race from a 'divine line' and so enjoyed the privilege of being introduced to a new country by the gods after the Flood. The crew of the spaceship looked after their descendants. They seem to me to have invented the nepotism so widely practised today.

To recapitulate, in the Book of Ether the Jaredites come to their new home in eight windowless ships, each one as tight as a dish. A similar crossing is described in the Babylonian didactic poem about the creation, the *Enuma elis*. It, too, gives an account of the Flood, but this time the survivor is called Atrahasis (9). In the partially preserved epic the god Enki gives the man chosen for survival, Atrahasis, precise instructions for building the ship. In answer to Atrahasis' objection that he knows nothing about ship-building, Enki draws the outline of a ship on the ground and enlightens him.

The American orientalist Zecharia Sitchin, the first scholar bold enough to interpret Sumerian, Assyrian, Babylonian and biblical texts in a modern way, writes (10) that Enki demanded a well-planned ship, hermetically sealed all round and caulked

---

* See my book *According to the Evidence* (1977) for other biblical characters exposed to the effects of time dilation.

with strong pitch. There were to be no deck or openings so that sun could not shine in. It was to be like an *aspu* ship, a *sulili*, (the same word (soleleth) that is used in Hebrew today for a submarine). Enki asked for the ship to be a MA-GUr-Gur (a ship that can roll and be tossed about).

Joseph Smith held the gold plates in his hands in 1827. The poor immigrant from Scotland knew neither Aramaic nor ancient Hebrew and he had never seen Sumerian cuneiform writing. Indeed, in the days of the Mormon prophet there was no scholar in the world who could have deciphered the Babylonian tablets, because, like the Epic of Gilgamesh, they were not discovered until after Joseph Smith's death. So how can we explain the similarities between the Book of Ether and the other texts discovered later?

Our contemporaries see history through glasses polished by scholars. In so far as glasses from the workshops of the exact sciences — mathematics, physics, biology and chemistry, for example, — are concerned, they improve the sight. But since theology and psychology have been given the status of sciences, the glasses have become blurred. Those two disciplines should have been left to the blissful field of faith. When theologians and psychologists agitate old texts in the cocktail-shaker of their specialties, only turbid faith trickles out. And we are supposed to swallow that as if it were a scientific conclusion!

Although expressed more elegantly in the circumlocutions of scientific parlance, it is clearly insinuated that the old chroniclers lied. Driven into a corner, they would be more willing to agree (which archaeologists, ethnologists and pre-historians do not) that men were already capable of building seaworthy ships thousands of years ago than that they involved 'gods', alien teachers, in their logical calculations.

Did the chroniclers of the *Enuma elis* epic lie when they wrote that Atrahasis was instructed in ship-building by the god Enki? Why had Noah and Utnapishtim to be given the idea of building watertight and weatherproof ships by gods? In what magic workshop was the artificial lighting for the Jaredites' fleet cooked up? If there were no savants, how can we understand the 'miracle' of artificial fertilisation that nevertheless brought two splendid types like Noah and Melchizedek into the world?

I know that Noah is not a unique case! The oldest Sumerian

Noah was not even Utnapishtim, but the still older Ziusudra. This example clearly shows that various chroniclers obviously (a) drew on earlier sources and (b) gave former heroes the names of their own people. No matter under what names the conquerors of the Flood appear in the ancient traditions, they were all of semi-divine origin. The protagonists were certainly not purely terrestrial!

Anyone who studies the fragmentarily preserved old texts with clear undimmed glasses finds special characteristics to identify the 'gods' by.

Unlike the God dominating the universe, the divine figures of legend and myth were by no means omnipotent. They did not appear like fairies who moved groups of people from one place to another with a wave of their magic wand. To be sure, the 'gods' themselves flew across countries and even took passengers with them in certain cases, but they did not transport groups of men in their varied types of vehicle. This clearly implies that the 'gods' did not use giant spaceships, their technical capabilities being far too limited. We can assume that their craft were more probably a mixture of shuttle and helicopter. The NASA engineer Josef Blumrich has conclusively proved from the Book of Ezekiel that a mini-spaceship could have been constructed in biblical times (11).

A large mother ship in the earth's orbit that men from the Blue Planet never saw launched smaller craft in the direction of the earth. As in the American space shuttle, there was only room for a small crew. Outside the earth's atmosphere the mini-spaceship fell slowly, braked by its ram jet drive, into the thicker atmospheric layers of the earth. The ram jet drive got its energy from a nuclear reactor. (Opponents of atomic energy will complain that the crew would have been contaminated by radioactivity. Nonsense. Why are sailors not contaminated after long voyages in nuclear-powered submarines?)

The mini-spaceship stopped some 10 km above the earth. Then two or three helicopter units firmly attached to the mini-spaceship emerged. (Helicopters with rotor blades cannot emerge, scoff the sceptics. They can, because they are built to fit inside each other, like a car radio aerial. But what about energy? The main reactor supplied that.) The shuttle glided to earth by means of the helicopters and was in a position to land on plains or mountainous terrain. Fantasy? Where did the

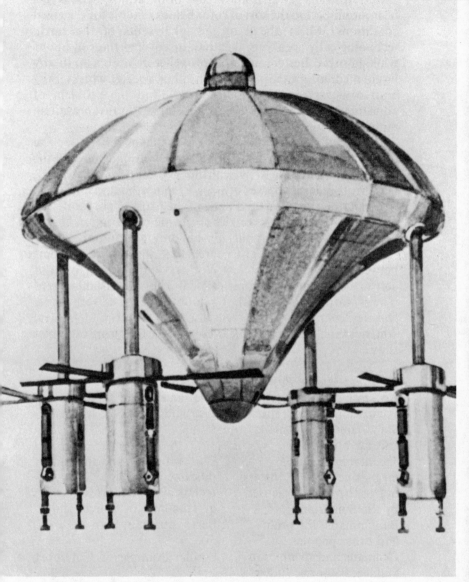

The small spaceship which the NASA engineer Josef F. Blumrich constructed from the details given in the Book of Ezekiel.

extraterrestrials get their knowledge of the atmospheric layers near the globe and the sort of rotor blades suitable for the given conditions? Miles ahead of the inhabitants of the earth, technologically speaking, they had discovered the conditions while in orbit. Besides, a ship's propeller drives a ship in any liquid medium, fresh or salt water, oil or a sea of whisky. Aircraft constructors have long since solved the problem of adjusting rotor blades to the right angle for the prevailing atmospheric pressure.

Incidentally, helicopter landings explain the noise, the thunder and uproar which all the ancient chroniclers describe as accompanying the arrival of the 'gods'.

Obviously large masses of people cannot be transported in small shuttle craft. If a 'god', one of the Most High, wanted to settle a group of peoples on the other side of the ocean, he had to impart instructions about ship-building, as tradition tells us.

Today most ethnologists agree that there were contacts between the Old and the New Worlds, via the Bering Strait or across the Atlantic on simple rafts, as Thor Heyerdahl proved by his own voyages (12). Undoubtedly there were many features common to the civilisations of South and Central America, and those of the Near East, as the following examples show:

Near and Middle East	*South and Central America*
Accurate calendar calculations among the Sumerians, Babylonians and Egyptians	The same is true of the Inca and (later) the Maya
The ability to cut megalithic stone monsters out of the rock. Practised by the Sumerians, Babylonians, Egyptians and other peoples	Pre-Inca tribes and the Inca possessed the same technical ability. Examples at Tiahuanaco, Bolivia and Sacsayhuaman, Peru
Dolmans and menhirs in Galilee, Samaria, Judea (13) also in prehistoric England and France	Similar examples in Colombia
Mummification	Also found
Prehistoric astronomically	The same finds in

Near and Middle East	*South and Central America*
aligned stone circles and rectangles	prehistoric Peru and Colombia
Enormous markings on the ground that point to the sky in the deserts of present-day Saudi Arabia	The same phenomenon in Peru (Nazca, Palpa) and on the coastal cliffs of Chile
Marriage between brothers and sisters among the Babylonians and Egyptian Pharaohs	Incest also among the Inca to preserve the 'divine blood' of the Sun God
Stories of the Flood, including details such as the dove and the raven which signalled the survivors to leave the ark, among the Sumerians, Babylonian and Egyptians	The same tradition among the Kágaba Indians of Colombia and (later) the Aztecs of Mexico The Aztec Noah was called Tapi The Aztec Flood epic is identical with the biblical one
Skull deformation of small children among the Egyptians	The same deliberate deformation among pre-Inca and Inca tribes
Depictions of cranial surgery on living patients among the Babylonians and Egyptians	The same trepannings among the Inca and Central and North American Indians
Great engineering skill in the building of extensive irrigation systems among the Babylonians	The same skill shown by the Inca and Maya. Recently vast canal systems built by the Maya have been mapped from aircraft and satellites (14)
Feather headdresses or crowns were worn to show that people had an affinity with 'that which flies'. Shown to have been used by Egyptian and Hittite popular leaders	The same custom among the Inca and all Indian tribes
Adoration of the 'flying	Inca and Maya edifices

Near and Middle East	*South and Central America*
snake' among the Babylonians, Egyptians, Hittites and other Mesopotamian peoples	teem with 'flying snakes'
Building pyramids to honour the gods and get closer to them	The steeply rising step pyramids of the Maya do not resemble the less steep unstepped pyramids near Cairo, but there were step pyramids in Egypt, too, e.g. at Sakkara. The massive pyramid of Teotihuacan, Mexico, is comparable to the Egyptian pyramids. The Mesopotamian ziggurats are stepped forerunners of the pyramids
In Genesis 11.1 it says: 'Now the whole earth had one language and few words ...'	In the Popol Vuh, (15) the Quiché Maya creation myth, in the chapter on 'Completion of Creation' we read: 'they had a single language. They prayed to neither wood nor stone ...' and in the chapter 'Wanderers through the Night': 'Lost are we. Whence the confusion? We had one language when we came to Tula.'
In Exodus 14.16 the Lord says to Moses: 'Lift up your rod and stretch out your hand over the sea and divide it, that the people of Israel may go on dry ground through the sea.'	In the traditions of the Cakchiqueles, a branch of the Maya, we read: 'Let us plunge the tips of our rods into the sand under the sea and we shall rapidly control the sea above the sand. Our red rods, which we received before the

Near and Middle East

South and Central America
gates of Tula, will aid us
... When we came to the
edge of the sea, Balam
Quitze touched it with his
rod and straightway a way
was opened.'

Exodus 14.21: 'Then Moses
stretched out his hand over
the sea; and the Lord
drove the sea back by a
strong east wind all night,
and made the sea dry land,
and the waters were
divided. And the people of
Israel went into the midst
of the sea on dry ground,
the waters being a wall to
them on their right hand
and their left.'

Popol Vuh, chapter
entitled 'Wanderers
through the Night': 'They
scarcely noticed how they
crossed the sea. They
crossed it as if there were
no sea. Round stones rose
from the sand and over the
rows of stones did they
walk into it. They called
the place drifting sand;
those who crossed the
parting sea have the name.
Thus did they manage to
cross.'

Genesis 9.12: 'This is the
sign of the covenant which
I make between me and
you and every living
creature that is with
you ...'

Popol Vuh, chapter
'Departure of the
Patriarch': 'This will
succour you when you call
on me. This is the sign of
the covenant. But, now,
heavy of heart, I have to
go.'

Daniel 3.21: 'Then these
men were bound in their
mantles, their tunics, their
hats and other garments
and they were cast into the
burning fiery furnace ...
(25) He answered, "But I
see four men loose,
walking in the midst of the
fire, and they are not hurt;
and the appearance of the

Popol Vuh, chapter 'Ball
Game and Kingdom of the
Dead': 'Then those men
went into the fire, into a
fire house. Within all was
burning heat, but they did
not burn. Smooth of body
and fair of face did they
appear in the twilight.
People wished them dead
in the places where they

Near and Middle East	*South and Central America*
fourth is like a son of the	walked, but it did not
gods." '	happen. Confusion seized
	those of Xibalba.'

It would be useful to expand the small list of the staggering concordances between ancient texts of the Old and New Worlds in a dissertation the size of a large volume, if there were any real interest in explaining unsolved mysteries of the past.

Thor Heyerdahl drew attention to still more parallels, such as identical techniques for weaving cotton, the similarity in the circumcision of boys, the same gold filigree work and so on (12). The scientific journalist Gerd von Hassler confirmed astonishingly similar names given to gods and cities on both continents (16).

The Popol Vuh removes the last doubt about the importation of civilisation into South and Central America from the Mesopotamian region. It states clearly that the Patriarchs came from the East:

> Thus did they vanish and go thither, Balám Quitzé, Balam Acab, Mahucutáh and Jqu Balám, *the first men who came over the sea from the beginning of the sun.* They came hither a long time ago. They died at a great age. And they were called 'Servants of God', Sacrificers' ... *and they brought the writings of Tula over the sea.* They called the scripture that wherein their history was written.

In 1519, when the Spanish conquerors were camped outside Tenochtitlan, Mexico, the Aztec ruler Moctezuma (1466–1520) made an impressive speech to the priests and important dignitaries. It began as follows: 'You know, as I do, *That our forefathers did not come from this country* in which we live, but that they came here *from far, far away* under the guidance of a great prince.'

Moctezuma was a highly cultured ruler of his people, well versed in the sciences of his day, and he had a thorough knowledge of the traditions of his ancestors. He knew what he was talking about. He saw the arrival of the Spaniards under Hernando Cortez as the fulfilment of his belief in the return of the god Quetzalcoatl and so he offered no resistance.

The question no longer arises *whether* civilisations were effectively influenced. What matters is to try to answer the question *when* and *why* they were influenced.

It is pointless to puzzle about the WHEN. In spite of the existence of artefacts which can be dated archaeologically, there is not even an approximate chronology. The Aztecs already referred to ancient traditions, the origins of which they knew nothing. The same was true of the Maya and the Inca. The chroniclers of the day had not experienced what they wrote about: 'It is written in the records of the fathers.' Without quoting sources, I should warn the reader. The authors did not know who these fathers were or when they immigrated.

However, archaeological datings go steadily further back into the past. In *Scientific American*, (18) the celebrated American Maya scholar Norman Hammond mentioned finds of pottery from Yucatán, the northern peninsula between the Gulf of Mexico and the Caribbean, dating to 2,600 years BC. Some of the pre-classical Maya periods may be calculated from the artistic motifs represented on the pottery. The new date confuses us considerably; for according to the previous view held by archaeologists the ancient Maya kingdom was supposed to have begun c. 600 BC and the pre-classical Maya period c. 900 BC at the earliest. So what are we to make of these troublesome potsherds, which are a good 1500 years too old to fit into their theory? Scholars would dearly love to reinter them and forget all about them, leaving a tough nut for future generations to crack. Each new dating complicates the puzzle and yet we anticipate many new finds. The latest academic conclusion is that there is nothing definite about when the legendary immigration took place from either written or archaeological evidence. Dates are still shrouded in the mists of the history of mankind.

HOW the great journey took place is equally obscure. The Bering Strait, icebound in spring and winter, which lies between Cape Prince, Alaska, and Cape Desnef, Siberia, suggests itself as a route. Even today navigation is difficult at all times of the year, owing to drift-ice and fog. This dangerous sea route sounds impracticable for peoples migrating thousands of years ago. But if we postulate rafts, canoes or primitive sailing ships as vehicles for an Atlantic crossing, we must accept that the goal of the journey was known in advance.

I do not underestimate the courage in undertaking bold ventures shown by our ancestors just out of the Stone Age, I even credit them with audacity in times of peril, but not with a penchant for suicide. As land-lubbers they were certainly afraid of the stormy seas which could crush their miserable rafts like nutshells. But if they did risk the perilous expedition, they must have been sure of a worthwhile goal. If we admit that, the question WHY becomes pretty clear. The 'gods' promised them a blessed country far, far away! This promise made it necessary for them to instruct their protégés in the arts of ship-building, navigation, etc. They showed the small groups of people — it was not a mass migration — the route to the goal. Just as it says in the traditions.

There remains the speculation about what reason the 'gods' may have had for the distribution of small groups of people in various parts of the world. Were they concerned with training their semi-divine offspring in new, safe territories? Did they foresee in outline the future evolution of humanity, the direction the further development of their intelligence would take? Lastly, did they expect that among the progeny of the artificially produced Noah and Melchizedek there might be scientists who would find and understand the 'divine' legacy? Were they sure that the trails they laid could never be lost?

Living creatures are subject to certain patterns of behaviour whether they like it or not. At night mosquitoes fly towards the light: they cannot help it. Man must eat and drink in order to live, whether it suits him or not. These are vital functions of the organism.

Intelligent reason asks questions whether it wants to or not. Intelligence wants to know what it was like in the past and how we became what we are. Who originated the idea that *homo sapiens* is different from animals? This series of intelligent questions leads unerringly back to the 'gods', whether we like it or not. Intelligent questioning can only be temporarily interrupted by fake answers; it suddenly finds itself dissatisfied with half-truths. Intelligence is an untameable beast. It keeps on asking what things were like in the past. And in the end it realises that the history of mankind without the 'gods' leads into a landscape, the map of which is blank.

Myth and legend are impregnated with the enormous impression the 'gods' made on primitive man. Chroniclers

Joseph Smith (1805–44), the founder of the Church of Jesus Christ of Latter-day Saints.

Imaginative painting of the vision of Moroni, the heavenly messenger.

The Mormon Temple in Salt Lake City.

The village square of Chavín de Huantar.

The road led upwards through a rust-coloured gorge in a series of acute hairpin bends.

picked up the red thread of tradition and spun it further. That is how the 'divine' deeds were recorded, down from their thunderous arrival to the manifold didactic instructions to the inhabitants of the earth. With their abilities our early ancestors transformed what they had learnt into architectonic master-pieces, made use of 'anachronistic' technology and created amazing objects of art.

The Popol Vuh, one of the great books from the dawn of mankind, shows how deliberately the trails were laid. It says that the servants of God 'brought the writings of Tula across the sea. They called the scripture that wherein their history was written.' The ancient traditions of the Quiché Maya refer to yet older writings and part of the Book of Mormon consisted of such writings. Joseph Smith translated the crossing of the Atlantic by the Jaredites from the 24 plates of the Book of Mormon, which form only the smallest part.

Smith translated most of the book from the plate called Nephi. Who was Nephi? He was the son of a Jewish family who lived in Jerusalem around 600 BC, i.e. thousands of years after the Jaredites. His father was called Lehi, his mother Sariah.

In chapter 1, verse 4 of the Book of Mormon, Nephi writes:

For it came to pass in the commencement of the first year of the reign of Zedekiah, king of Judah ... there came many prophets prophesying unto the people that they must repent, or the great city of Jerusalem must be destroyed.

That is right. Jerusalem was completely destroyed in 586 BC. Jeremiah and Ezekiel were prominent in this legendary age. It must have been a special period, for both prophets spoke incessantly with their 'God', who descended from heaven in fire-breathing chariots that made a frightening noise.

Nephi's father Lehi repeated the experiences of the prophets, as is described in Nephi, 1.6 *et seq.*:

And it came to pass as he prayed unto the Lord, there came a pillar of fire and dwelt upon a rock before him ... he saw one [an angel] descending out of the midst of heaven, and he beheld that his lustre was above that of the sun at noon-day.

The being from the pillar of fire ordered Lehi to assemble

Sariah, his sons and daughters (Nephi being among them), and friends of the family in order to inform them that they were destined to travel to a distant country. After initial difficulties, the migrant group built a ship under the guidance of the mysterious Lord: 'And it came to pass that the Lord spake unto me, saying: Thou shalt construct a ship, after the manner *which I shall show thee, that I may carry thy people across the water* (1 Nephi 17.8).

As if that was not enough, the mysterious alien gave the ship-builders special astronauts' food which needed neither preparation nor cooking. He knew that eating keeps body and soul together, but also that another object was even more important — a compass!

And it came to pass that as my father arose in the morning, and went forth to the tent door, to his great astonishment he beheld upon the ground a round ball of curious workmanship. And within the ball were two spindles; and the one pointed the way whither we should go into the wilderness . . . And we did follow the directions of the ball, which led us in the more fertile parts of the wilderness.

Father Lehi died during the crossing. Nephi assumed command. Nephi's brothers were jealous because of the special favour the 'Lord' showed him and they tied him to a ship's beam. In this tricky situation, they found out how indispensable the compass was. 'And it came to pass that after they had bound me insomuch that I could not move, the compass, which been prepared of the Lord, did cease to work.'

The Mutiny on the Bounty came to an end and the expedition reached the American continent, with the metal plates and the compass: 'Now I, Nephi, had also brought the records which were engraven upon the plates of brass; and also the ball or compass, which was prepared for my father by the hand of the Lord.' (II Nephi 5.12).

Following Nephi's account, Mormon scholars are convinced that the group first wandered from the Red Sea through the Arabian peninsula, then built their ship on the coast of the Indian Ocean, somewhere in the area of the Gulf of Aden and Oman, and finally reached the coast of South America across the South Pacific. James E. Talmage (19) puts this around 590 BC, a date we should take note of.

There is one amazing coincidence. The translation that Joseph Smith made from the metal plates in 1827 is duplicated in the Popol Vuh. But Smith could not possibly have known the contents of the Quiché Maya bible, for it was only translated for the first time by Wolfgang Gordan in the 1950s!

Two groups reached the American continent independently of each other. First, the Jaredites in their hermetically sealed ships in the age of the first wave of the gods. It was the legendary epoch in which flourished the chroniclers of Adam's sapphire book, Enoch's ascent into heaven, the test-tube babies Noah and Melchizedek, as well as the 'lords' of creation Utnapishtim, Ziusudra and others. Secondly, the Nephites, who set out from the east and reached South America thousands of years later, around 590 BC.

Soon after the landing Nephi had a temple built:

> And I, Nephi, did build a temple; and I did construct it after the manner of the temple of Solomon save it were not built of so many precious things. But the manner of the construction was like unto the temple of Solomon; and the workmanship thereof was exceeding fine.
>
> (II Nephi 5.16)

It is not my concern to prove which parts of the Book of Mormon are genuine, but it may please the followers of the Church of Jesus Christ of Latter-day Saints that one proof emerges as a by-product of my researches.

Nephi built a temple 'after the manner of the temple of Solomon'. In so far as this information is valid, South America must contain a temple (on a smaller scale) of the kind Solomon had built in Jerusalem — a complex with outer and inner courts, a sanctuary with a temple which had four doors aligned on the four cardinal points of the compass. This temple must have originated between the fifth and sixth centuries BC.

Moreover, Nephi's temple must have been built 'cold', so to speak, without prototypes or borrowings from typical South American architecture. The temple must have been the first of its kind, an edifice that appeared out of the blue without local traditions.

I am not only on the trail of a temple which meets these pre-requisites, I am also on the trail of the 'Lord' who led the Nephites to South America. Did this 'god' still exist after the landing or had he transformed himself into spirit? Also, where did Nephi recruit the large numbers of builders needed? After all, he arrived with only a small group. 'Immediately after their arrival, the Nephites began ... to till the earth, and we began to plant seeds: yea, we did plant all the seeds which we had brought from the land of Jerusalem' (I Nephi 18.24).

The Nephites produced progeny assiduously, for they practised polygamy (forbidden to the Mormons by govern-ment decree in 1890). Assuming that the immigrant group consisted of 100 men and 100 women, and each woman bore one child a year, the Nephites would have numbered 1,500 souls in 15 years. The firstborn, pubescent teenagers of 15 followed the example of their elders and willingly played their part in multiplying. In 30 years a good 5,000 Nephites would praise their 'Lord'. Quite enough people to build the temple, especially as there were indigenous workers to collaborate with them. The personnel was there.

The Lord was present! As soon as he arrived, he gave Nephi this task: 'And it came to pass that the Lord commanded me, wherefore I did make plates of ore that I might engraven upon them the record of my people' (I Nephi 19.1).

Thirty years later. The 'Lord' set great store by a complete log book. Once again he ordered Nephi:

And thirty years had passed away from the time we left Jerusalem. And it came to pass that the Lord God said unto me: Make other plates; and thou shalt engraven many things upon them which are good in my sight, for the profit of thy people.

Was the 'Lord' vain? Why did he want the 'Things ... which are good in my sight' noted down? The 'Lord' constantly insisted upon his golden words being engraved upon the metal plates. He considered them important for the future, otherwise he would have had them recorded on perishable materials such as papyrus, leather or wood. This 'Lord' in his wisdom took care that his communications, addressed to intelligent beings in the future, were permanent.

A difficult question. Is there a temple in South America modelled on Solomon's masterpiece? Is there some proof of the activities of the gods to be found there?

I invite you to visit that temple.

2 In the Beginning Everything Was Different

> Drawing the attention of the masses to something means putting
> healthy human reason on the right track.'
>
> Gotthold Ephraim Lessing (1729–81)

The Jerusalem of the Andes is called Chavín de Huantar.

It was raining cats and dogs on that April day in 1980 when
two young missionaries, soaked to the skin, stood outside the
door of our house in Feldbrunnen. The older one, about 30
years old, was an American called Charlie, the younger man's
name was Paul and he came from Berne. My visitors from the
Church of Jesus Christ of Latter-day Saints made me a present
of the German version of the Book of Mormon. (I already had
seven other translations in my library.) I invited the missionaries to come inside to warm up and drink a cup of coffee.

My fellow countryman Paul asked what I thought of the
Book of Mormon. I said that I found the plates Ether and
Nephi exciting and informative. Nor did I think they were
forgeries, but found it unfortunate that some rather crude
prophecies about Jesus had been added to the original text.

Naturally, the young missionaries disagreed with me. Either
the complete Book of Mormon was inspired by the Holy Ghost
and therefore 'genuine', or the whole book was worthless.
Being well up in the subject, I showed my disinclination for a
discussion that would lead nowhere, a hint that was very
quickly taken by Paul, belying the reputation the Bernese have
for being slow-witted. He asked, 'You know many ruins in
South America. Have you found any that resemble Solomon's
temple in Jerusalem?'

I told him truthfully that I had not. The missionaries said
goodbye without trying to make a hopeless conversion. It was
such a terrible April day that they would certainly have found
a willing victim if they could have promised me blue skies.

Paul, the Bernese, had put a bee in my bonnet which went on
buzzing, but another one was tormenting me even more.

Whether the temple mentioned in the Book of Nephi existed in South America or not seemed far less important to me than the question whether the temple described in detail by the prophet Ezekiel in the Old Testament existed — a temple in a distant land, standing on a high mountain, built like the temple of Solomon. If there were a temple in South America that fitted Ezekiel's description, that *would be* a thrilling story.

What has the Nephi of the Book of Mormon to do with the Ezekiel of the Bible? Well, both of them lived at the same time in the same geographical zone. Perhaps they knew each other. Both of them wrote about a flying god who came down and gave instructions. On this god's orders, Nephi had a temple built in South America and Ezekiel was flown by the same god to a distant land where he was shown a temple on the Solomonic model on a 'very high mountain'.

It is established that Ezekiel lived in Jerusalem and Babylon. If someone showed him the temple in South America — he describes it incredibly accurately — someone must have flown him there and then back to the Near East. There is no other possibility.

So my search for a Solomonic temple in South America was by no means purely inspired by the Book of Mormon, I was also looking for Ezekiel's temple and the trail of the 'flying god', who was at the back of it all. I only realised much later that both trails would meet in the most fascinating way.

My eyes were aching from looking at an endless procession of temples in books on archaeology. At the time finding *the* temple meant more to me than the sight of a blue Mauritius means to a philatelist. If I suspected similarities, the plan of Solomon's temple in Jerusalem told me that essential details were missing, that it was too early or too old, or that it did not belong to the period of Nephi or Ezekiel. I went through 39 lavishly illustrated books. In all of them Chavín de Huantar was described. I decided to visit this site, take accurate measurements and see the landscape in which it lies with my own eyes.

Nineteen eighty-one. Once again Europe was enjoying a cold wet spring. It was autumn in Peru when I rented a kind of Russian jeep, a Lada Niva, in Lima, the capital.

Long before dawn, I was driving along a smooth asphalt road, the Panamericana del Norte, one of the best roads in the world, through sandy desert bordering the coast in the direction of Trujillo, the fourth largest city in Peru. I left the Panamericana at the town of Pativilca. After that sugar-cane plantations lined the road.

When I was handing over 200 soles at a toll station, a horrible stench from the Lada Niva assailed my nostrils. The cap of the petrol tank was missing. I wrapped a piece of plastic round a stone and blocked the stinking hole with it.

After running for 30 km through a stony desert, past the menacing spurs of the mountains, the road began to climb gradually. After turning off from Pativilca — in the distance you can see the ruins of a fortress from the time of the Chimu Indians — I reached the God-forsaken village of Chas-quitambo at a height of 780 m. In ancient times this place was a handing-over point for Inca relay runners. Nowadays, too, the best thing is to keep on running.

The ascent into a rust-coloured gorge began in a series of acute hairpin bends. The lowering rain clouds now lay behind me, the fog banks cleared and opened up a panorama of light brown and black mountains.

My clattering Russian banger was becoming less willing with every curve. On the narrow road, my red star could no longer make it in second gear. Near Cajacay, at a height of 2,600 m, the old fellow was completely out of breath. Automobile asthma. The engine needed more oxygen. I unscrewed the top of the air filter. The filter which was supposed to let the air through felt like the remains of a plaster cast. I threw it away, screwed the top on to the empty filter, started and the old jalopy leapt forward. It had understood me. It *had* to get me up the mountain.

After every hairpin bend I hoped I had reached the top of the pass. For a long time these were vain hopes, for more and more mountain valleys kept appearing. The clay huts by the roadside became fewer. Indians in colourful ponchos, carrying heavy bundles on their backs, put one foot before the other in the steady rhythm of the experienced mountain climber. I was amazed that the hard-working local inhabitants could scratch a living from the sterile rocky soil up here, yet a third of Peru's 14.6 million inhabitants live in these uplands.

I reached the cloud-filled pass at a height of 4,100 m. In European latitudes it would have been a zone of permanent ice and snow, but Peru is closer to the Equator. Only dry grasses and miserable stunted bushes grow up here.

A young dark-brown Indian woman, with a baby on her breast in a cloth bag and a heavy sack of potatoes on her back, looked at me suspiciously when I asked her if she would like a lift, because friendly foreigners are rare in this region. I took the sack off her back and pushed it behind the seats of the Lada Niva. She got in and laughed self-consciously after arranging the six skirts that all Indian women wear. We drove past the frozen lagoon of Conocochca with the glaciers of the 6,600 m high Cordillera de Huyauhuish ahead of us.

I managed to worm out of the taciturn Indian woman where she was going — the town of Catac at a height of 3,540 m in the valley of the Rio Santa. I shuddered at the idea of the woman having to walk the 40 km stretch with her heavy burdens — it would have taken her two days, but we did it in half an hour. In Catac the road forks off to Chavín de Huantar.

At the only petrol station I filled my jeep with a young woman and two men. She was called Ruth; Uri and Isaac had black and red beards respectively. They were Israelis who had decided to roam through the world for a year with no fixed plans, although they did not exclude visits to archaeological sites like Chavín de Huantar. They asked why I was going there. I limited myself to vague remarks about a Solomonic temple connected with the prophet Ezekiel. They might be the sort of fanatically orthodox Israelis who would have been shocked by the real object of my research.

'Are you Swiss?' asked Uri. 'Then you must know Erich von Däniken's books. I am not sure whether the ideas he puts forward are crazy or rational.'

Instead of answering I bit my lip.

Beyond Catac the road was not asphalted and led in tortuous curves to the picturesque icy lake of Quericocha at a height of 3,980 m. The snowclad summit of Yanamarey (5,260 m) caught the eye.

Next came the tunnel through the Kahuish pass (4,510 m). The word 'tunnel' might call up false associations with the tunnels in Western industrial countries but I should point out that this 500 m long specimen is only hacked roughly out of the rock with an unmade road, full of potholes, running through it. Icy water drips from roof and walls and there are no lights or signals in the one track nightmare road. If the head-lights of an oncoming car appear, the driver nearest the exit or entrance has to back out. Naturally, everyone drives in the hope of not meeting an oncoming car in the dark hole. This tunnel does not deserve a star in the guide books.

If the uphill drive had been taxing, the steep descent on the other side of the tunnel into the Mosna valley proved really frightening, even for a veteran driver like me. The narrow un-made road winds like an endless snake clinging to the mountain in curve after curve. Your eyes cling to the left because a sheer abyss threatens on the right. We reached the bottom of the valley at the little village of Machac (3,180 m). The ruins of Chavín de Huantar are clearly visible, close to the road.

The Hotel Turistas was full to the last bed, not of tourists but archaeologists. We met the crème de la crème of German and Peruvian archaeologists. In the distinguished German group, Professors Udo Oberem and Henning Bischof greeted me politely, and their Peruvian colleagues were polite and friendly. To the Germans I am an unpredictable outsider, always planning some new trick. The Peruvians have a different opinion of me. When I was honoured by the aldermen of the town of Nazca some years ago, the mayor said in his address that there were many theories about the lines on the plain of Nazca. He could not say whether they were a calendar or a take-off point for hot-air balloons, the remains of Inca roads, magical signs, the marking lines of a sportsground or landmarks for extraterrestrials. 'As for those of who live and work here,' said the mayor, 'we are not primarily interested which of the experts is right. But one thing is certain: Herr von Däniken has brought the most tourists to our region!'

Over the evening meal the Israelis asked if they could help me in any way, for they had found out who had given them a lift. I accepted their offer gratefully, for a continuity girl was just what I needed when taking my measurements.

In the morning the Israelis were waiting for me on a sunny hill outside the site of the ruins. They were suitably draped in cameras and measuring apparatus. We passed through the massive wooden gate into the ruins of Chavín de Huantar.

The section of the complex that is still preserved is called El Castillo, the castle, although it never was a castle. It is a rectangular building 72.90 m long and 70 m wide. Large granite blocks, fitting together to the millimetre, form the rectangular façades. The lower monoliths nearest to the ground are the best preserved. The higher the building, which slopes slightly inwards, rises, the more clearly visible are the ravages of time — just like the Solomonic temple in Jerusalem which suffered 36 wars and was destroyed 17 times. At Chavín as in Jerusalem new walls were built each time on the lower blocks of stone.

The main portal of the Castillo faces east, the direction of the sunrise (and Jerusalem). Two columns, topped by a monolith nine metres long, are flanked by square and rectangular granite slabs. The squat columns are decorated with incomprehensible patterns in relief, as are the crowning monolith and the adjacent slabs. Weathering through the ages has worn down the reliefs and unfortunately man, too, has damaged the delicate work. When El Castillo first stood there in all its glory, the massive structure must have looked like a single, almost seamless block, even from a short distance. El Castillo was the termination and crown of the temple complex, the Holy of Holies, to which only the high priests had access.

Today a rubbish heap overgrown with clumps of grass is concealed behind the main portal. A few steps lower down lies a square which occupies the whole width of the Castillo — the forecourt of the sanctuary. Some 36 m from the Castillo, more steps lead down to a second gigantic courtyard (70 by 42 m), from which yet more steps lead to the so-called 'sunken square' (the length of the sides are 49.70 m).

To the north and south of the sunken square rise platforms, which have not yet been excavated, but you can recognise the artificial hill by the scattered monoliths protruding from it. The whole site is reckoned to cover an area of some 13 hectares, but so far only the temple complex has been excavated. It is known that the whole layout stood on a man-made stone platform.

Four flights of steps lead from the sunken square to the four cardinal points of the compass with absolute accuracy, as I checked with my own compass. The side of the plateau descends 80 m to the bed of the River Mosna which flows past the temple in a south-easterly direction.

The complex measures 228 m from the western wall of the Castillo to the south-east corner. The section excavated to date is about 175 m wide. These measurements do not include the wall that once enclosed the area. Remains of this wall are visible on the west side.

At all events, a huge rectangular complex stood here with outer and inner courtyards and the (still extant) ten-metre-high Holy of Holies, with inner and outer courtyards for the priests and the people. The rectangle is aligned on the four cardinal points of the compass with its steps and doors and the main portal points to the east, exactly like the Solomonic temple in Jerusalem.

Today Solomon's temple in Jerusalem no longer forms an exact rectangle; it is now an irregular trapezoid, with sides of 315 m to the north, 280 m to the south, 485 m to the west and 470 m to the east (1). However, the original temple was strictly rectangular. King Herod was responsible for the distorted shape, which doubled the area, and because the space was lacking, additional supporting walls were built on which (in those days) new platforms were placed.

Ruth, Uri and Isaac were busy measuring the courtyards, walls and monoliths, while I was taking photographs from every angle and in every corner. When we stopped for a cigarette and Ruth showed me my notepad clipped to a board, I held my breath. This was professional work! With delicate lines she had drawn a site plan that was ready for the printers. All the walls and monoliths, the steps and flights of stairs and the sunken square were sketched in. The beginning and end of the lines were marked by small arrows to show which sections the measurements referred to.

We sat on boulders, which were not in short supply. I asked my new friends what their jobs were. Ruth said drily, 'I am a surveyor for road building and land measurement.'

So that accounted for the professionalism! Uri turned out to be a teacher, Isaac a pilot. The gods had put the right team into my Lada Niva! The four of us did a job which would have taken me four times as long by myself.

Together we explored the network of passages and galleries under Chavín de Huantar. One passage on the east side of the main square was only 1.10 m high and 67 cm wide and it was impossible to stand upright in it. For one very good reason.

On 17 January 1945 Chavín de Huantar was swamped by

a massive flood. It happened like this. The little river Mosna runs past the south-east side; on the north-west side, between the ruins and the Indian village of Chavin, a stream called Huacheqsa tumbles down into the depths. It rises from a mountain lake which is fed by the water melting from a glacier in the cordillera. In December 1944 and January 1945 more water flowed in than the lake could take and the rocky banks broke like a dam. The stream became a raging torrent and covered the low-lying parts of Chavín de Huantar with a dark brown layer of mud which penetrated the underground passages. When the waters subsided, scree, sand and mud were left behind.

The passage through which I crawled with the help of a flashlight was once higher, or deeper, whichever you prefer. When I had gone as far as I could in the passage beneath the ruins, I saw five lateral tunnels, 60 cm high and 48 cm wide. They may have formed part of an irrigation system, especially as the main passage ran in the direction of the river Mosna.

However, as a 1.72 cm high passage on the west side ran in a southerly direction, i.e. not in the direction of a stream, the subterranean infrastructure cannot have been intended to act solely as water mains.

Chavín de Huantar had been flooded in earlier times. In 1919 the Peruvian archaeologist Julio C. Tello carried out extensive excavations with a group of Indians. When he returned in 1934, the stream had 'destroyed part of the main wing' (2). Tello writes that a third of the complex which he had seen when it was still intact was then destroyed and that many subterranean passages and channels had been flushed out. Kilometres away Tello found stone, metal, and pottery artefacts on a sandbank in the river miles from the temple. They had been swept out of the temple ruins.

When the temple first stood there in all its glory, the raging mountain torrents could not have affected it. The closely fitting megalithic walls were watertight, the irrigation channels around and under Chavín de Huantar functioned and the streams were under control. It was only when fallen trees and monoliths hindered the flow of the water and after grave robbers cut holes in the walls of the Castillo that the water could exercise its destructive power on the buildings.

Together we set out to explore the passages which run under Chavín de Huantar in a tortuous network.

The next day my Israelis took a local bus in which the passengers were packed like sardines. I promised I would send them all a copy of my book in Hebrew, with a personal dedication. We had only spent two days together, yet I missed Ruth and the bearded men when I drove my Lada Niva back to the ruins to take a closer look at the passages in the rubbish dump.

Two tunnels on the north side of the Castillo are shut off by iron grilles to stop tourists going into the dark labyrinth on their own. And it is a labyrinth, as I found out.

Just beyond the entrance the first tunnel leads to a remarkable stele, *El Lanzon*, the lance or spear. *El Lanzon* is situated at the intersection of the two passages which are over three metres high, but only 50 cm wide. Monolithic granite slabs form the ceiling.

In spite of its strange proportions, this passage would be hardly worth mentioning if it did not contain an inexplicable puzzle. *El Lanzon* is a giant stele more than four metres high, yet the passages are little more than three metres high. How did *El Lanzon* get here? It is not a rubber giant that could have been bent. Given its great length, it could not have been manoeuvred horizontally around the countless bends in the 50 cm wide passage. There is only one solution. Right from the start, the architects of Chavín de Huantar planned an opening in the ceiling through which the stele could be lowered into the crossing between the two passages, before the rest of the vast temple complex was erected over it.

No one knows how to interpret *El Lanzon*. The Czecho-slovakian archaeologist and ethnologist Miloslav Stingl (3) describes the stele as:

A very strange creature. Large jaguar teeth stick out over the lower lip. The eyes are staring upwards as if they were looking up to heaven. The belt round the god's body is also decorated with jaguar heads. Two snake heads hang from the belt. The god holds his right hand up, the other rests on his hip.

That is a description, not an interpretation, and I find it hard even to follow the description because I cannot recognise a 'creature' in *El Lanzon* at all. True, you can make out a

The stele El Lanzon is situated deep underground at the crossing of the two passages. It is more than three metres high, but only 50 cm wide.

El Lanzon is lavishly adorned with ornaments. No one knows what they mean. There are many explanations, but none which makes sense.

big muzzle with protruding 'jaguar teeth', but not in the place where jaguars normally have their fatal fangs. Where Miloslav Stingl sees jaguar teeth, I recognise — equally imaginatively — joints of armour, since *El Lanzon* strikes me as a technical artefact rather than an animal figure.

Apart from the passage through which I came to confront *El Lanzon*, all the passages leading from the intersection come to a dead end. After a few paces I was halted by massive walls. That struck me as odd. What was the sense of the planners of Chavín de Huantar only completing the passage to *El Lanzon*, and ending all the other tunnels in a mysterious full stop? All that work for an architectural joke? I suspected secret doors behind the dead ends of the passages. No more and no less.

As I could go no farther, I retraced my steps. Outside the sun was blinding as it can only be in the clear air at a height

A menacing helmeted figure blocked my way.

of 3,000 m. I blinked hard and entered the second tunnel which runs southwards under the Castillo. It was lit by weak bulbs along the walls and they suddenly failed. I groped my way back into the daylight. A friendly attendant lent me an old-fashioned carbide lamp. (I gave him my lighter as surety and I was soon to miss it.) The smell reminded me for a moment of my first bicycle.

The harsh light shone on passages three metres high and cut out of the rock, and on the monoliths forming the ceiling. Soon the tunnel branched off to the left and right; I chose the left-hand one.

I nearly fell over a stone head which, at first glance, looked like a helmeted being, possibly humanoid. In the past the walls were covered with reliefs depicting winged figures flying upwards. Today only vestiges remain as evidence. The figures are carved with such delicacy and in such low relief that they might have been made by a modern dentist using a high-speed drill to practise his hobby of sculpting. But nowadays dentists have no time for badly paid hobbies, they prefer to invest in lucrative high-rise buildings. This passage also came to a dead-end formed by a massive wall.

With all the zeal and patience of a Boy Scout, I went back to the main passage, tried a different entrance, climbed seven steep steps and reached another corridor. It was 1.30 m wide and 1.83 m high. Two people could comfortably walk side by side in it. Across the top of the steps ran a narrower passage with three exits leading to three chambers 5.70 m long, 1.94 m wide and 2.25 m high. The harsh light of the carbide lamp revealed grotesque figures. Strange stone heads revealed their helmets and gave me haughty, rather mocking looks. They were asking, 'What do you think of us?'

Many times I tried to find a way through the walls, but could not manage it. I trotted back to the central corridor, made two 90-degree turns on my own axis and entered another room. In it stone heads were neatly arranged on a wooden plank facing reliefs showing all kinds of fabulous scenes. How many more passages and chambers await excavation? Perhaps the secret of the 'gods' awaits discovery deep below the ruins, perhaps the architects preserved the key to the misinterpreted culture of Chavín de Huantar deep underground?

While I scrutinised every square inch of the wall which closed

There are also easily accessible passages — a good 1.80 metres high and 1.30 metres wide.

Deep in the earth stone heads with strange faces stared at me in the harsh light of the carbide lamp.

off the tunnel to see if there was any trace of an opening, the carbide lamp gave up the ghost. I was in darkness. It was as quiet as the grave. For the first time I felt a draught of cold air passing through the chambers. Although I could not see, I felt my way to the source of the draught, stumbling over stone heads and bumping into monoliths. I took several flash-light photos, as I had plenty of batteries. The current of air came from under the floor of the rear wall. Was there a passage behind it leading even deeper into the earth? I fingered the masonry, pulling hard on protruding parts of the blocks, but nothing budged.

I cautiously put one foot ahead of the other, taking flash photos. I sadly missed the lighter I had left with the attendant.

I crawled upwards on all fours.

One passage wall felt much like another; none of them gave a clue where to go. I had to find the stairway whose seven steps I had climbed up and now must climb down again. But the stairway I felt led upwards. The current of air grew stronger along the walls. I crawled upwards on all fours. Another seven steps and I saw light right above me. The tunnel led beneath an iron grille which could easily be lifted up. I hauled myself out of the depths into the open air and tried to decide where I was.

I had come out of the labyrinth roughly in the centre of the Castillo, high above the east-facing main entrance. The huge rectangle of the temple complex spread out below me. I clambered down and sat down under the main gate to catch my breath. I looked up to try to find out which hole I had crawled out of ... and discovered strange flying creatures engraved on the underside of the monolith lying across the columns.

They consisted of 14 cherubs, as the Bible calls the watchers of the heavens. Seven figures resembling birds of prey were looking northwards and seven southwards. It struck me that all the stairways I had ascended or descended had seven steps. Was the 'sacred number seven' the number giving the key to Chavín de Huantar?

The number seven has traditions which are not confined to the seven-year itch. Its magic is invoked in the seven-day periods into which the month is divided. Around 1,600 BC the Babylonians did away with their five-day week and introduced the seven-day week. In the seven celestial bodies, Sun, Moon, Mercury, Venus, Mars, Jupiter and Saturn, the Babylonians saw the whole order of the cosmos. Among the Jews, the seven days of creation and the seven-branched menorah of the tabernacle testify to the importance of the sacred seven. In the Revelation of St John we find the 'book with seven seals'. Seven has significance in Buddhism and Malayan civilisation. In ancient Greece seven days of grace were common. Thebes had its famous seven gates, there were seven wise men ... and then there were the seven wonders of the world. Was the number seven revered in Chavín de Huantar, too?

No code is safe to our modern intelligence services. Surely it should be possible to crack codes that are simply begging for decipherment?

Down below one 'sunken square' a collaborator of the archaeologist Julio C. Tello found an obelisk that today stands in the Archaeological Museum of Lima. It is called the Tello obelisk and its sign language awaits interpretation. I spent hours in front of it, taking photographs and copying the engravings on it. I asked Peruvian archaeologists about the possible meaning of the patterns. I soon realised that they knew nothing definite when they struck up the cult aria: the jaguar cult, the bird of prey cult, etc. I could equally well sing the pyramid cult, as small pyramids can also be made out on the Tello obelisk. Down below the square where the obelisk was found stands the 'Altar of the Seven Goats' (also known as the 'Altar of the Constellation Orion'). My zoological imagination was not powerful enough to make out seven goats, but the arrangement of seven holes in the altar does correspond approximately to the position of the seven satellites in the constellation of Orion.

The Tello obelisk.

Today the Tello obelisk from Chavin de Huantar is housed in the Archaeological Museum at Lima. The engraved ornamentation with its bewildering interplay of images has not yet been 'deciphered'.

The Raimondi stele.

The wretched figure seven crops up everywhere. Specialist literature (4, 5) confirms that it was also a sacred number in Chavín de Huantar. Is seven a key to the messages hidden there? Where is the master spy 007? Perhaps archaeologists should rope in a code-breaker. The old 'cult' caper is pretty hackneyed.

Every visitor to the Museo Antropológico y Arqueológico in the Plaza Bolivar in Lima walks past the Raimondi stele. It comes from Chavín de Huantar. Antonio Raimondi had the stele, made of diorite and measuring 1.75 m high, 73 cm wide, and 17 cm thick, brought to the capital in the year 1873.

What do scholars make of the reliefs on this work of art? Let them say their piece.

Miloslav Stingl:

The Raimondi stele ... represents the jaguar man. More and more highly stylised jaguar heads grow from his own divine head with great fangs protruding from their jaws. (3)

Professor H. D. Disselhoff:

A jaguar man stands upright on a rectangular slab. In each hand he holds a composite sceptre, richly ornamented with curves. The lower half ends in the stylised heads of birds of prey, the upper half in a vegetable emblem. The piled-up headdress is composed of the jaws of beasts of prey and snakes' heads ... and snakes' bodies with realistically depicted heads. The main subjects are hybrids made of men and animal, feline beasts of prey, snakes and birds of prey. (6)

Rudolf Pörtner and Nigel Davies:

Represents a figure, front face, with the head of a beast of prey. Both hands hold a decorated staff which reaches far above the figure's head. The upper two-thirds of the stone is filled by an imaginative headdress consisting of suggestions of mouths with tongues hanging out arranged one above the other. From them parallel snakes' heads emerge upwards to left and right. (7)

Professor Hermann Trimborn:

A stone slab, the so-called Raimondi stele, came from here as early as 1873. In low relief it depicts a feline monster with a sceptre in its claws. It is crowned with a series of open jaws belonging to beasts of prey, from which snakes emerge.' (8)

Professor Horst Nachtigall:

This stele is one of the most interesting sculptures of the American megalithic civilisation. It represents an upright half-human half-animal figure with an animal head and a headdress consisting of monsters' heads, framed by a crown of rays. Both hands and feet have animal claws. A snake girdle encircles the body. (5)

Dr Siegfried Huber:

The details of the relief drawings are like codes. Fangs, snakes' heads, mysterious interlacings and eyes with no symbolic explanation — surreal if one can call them anything. The petrified threatening expression of an anxiety-ridden existence. (9)

Dr Friedrich Katz:

Here, too, we find hair snakes and facial features strongly resembling jaguars. The Raimondi stele consists of the stratification of several bodies and faces in an almost monstrous way. (10)

Dr H. G. Franz:

The standing figure represents the religious leader, priest, shaman, call him what you will, in a mask, which appears in a fantastic transformation as a face mask or full head mask with an animal skin. The mask-cum-helmet becomes

a mask-cum-tower ... The feet end in jaguar or eagle claws. The built-up mask rises far above the small stunted figure ... What appears above must be included in the mask's superstructure, which consists of several superimposed animal jaws — wide open dragonlike upper jaws, which at the same time seem tipped upwards. (11)

Dr Inge von Wedemeyer:

The consummate image of the highest incarnation of the god of creation Viracocha. (12)

Gentle reader, you can just as well turn the photographs of the Raimondi stele upside down so that the enigmatic and variously interpreted figure falls from above. Of course the animal claws, the eagle's claws, the feet of the jaguar man or whatever they are supposed to be, would be at the wrong end, but it takes less imagination to recognise that the figure is falling, than to puzzle out all the zoological discoveries which make no sense in the end.

If such contradictory interpretations of the relief code, the only word that seems suitable, can be given, there should also be room for my speculative questions. Surely the peculiar sceptre has a very technical look? Is it a question not of jaguars or stunted jaguar men, with highly stylised heads or towering masks, but of the diagram of a car engine with fuel injectors and many feed pipes? Is it a picture puzzle of some future technology that we shall only understand when we ourselves have developed enough?

I do not know what the stele means, either, but one thing is obvious to me, the archaeological tap dance on the spot will never get us anywhere. People are not brave enough for unorthodox thinking. Arthur Schopenhauer (1788–1860) said that to ignore stems from ignorance. I have nothing more to add.

Chavín de Huantar plays a dirty trick on academics by the mere factor of its existence. The temple complex has no model and so cannot be fitted into a chronological development. Chavín de Huantar emerges suddenly, without any advance warning, saying here I am, the Chavín de Huantar culture. This sudden appearance brings out the sweat of doubt on academic foreheads and confuses the well-trained grey cells.

Quotations from three celebrated scholars echo this confusion.

1. Professor Walter Krickeberg:

It has often been emphasised that the development of higher civilisation in ancient America did not take place as an organic growing process in slow continuous advances, but by leaps and bounds, one might almost say explosively ... the oldest American high civilisations appear on the scene suddenly, apparently without roots or preliminary stages, for example the Olmec culture in Mesoamerica and the Chavín culture in the Andes. This remarkable phenomenon can probably only be satisfactorily explained if we postulate one or more external impulses which affected ancient America. (13)

2. Miloslav Stingl:

The appearance of the Chavín culture is more like an explosion, an unexpected discharge, the effects and consequences of which were felt throughout Peru. (3)

3. Professor H. D. Disselhoff:

I am convinced that *an as yet unexplained external influence* prevailed when the Chavín culture originated. (6)

Chavín de Huantar astonishes everyone who visits it. At the site nearly 50,000 sq. m of uneven rocky terrain were levelled. The first plans for the surface buildings already included an irrigation system deep below them, connecting or emerging corridors were cut (exploded?) out of the rock and the Castillo with all its subsidiary buildings and square matches the subterranean infrastructure exactly. A work of genius, an achievement unique in the world, in so far as it has no prototype. But: the Solomonic temple in Jerusalem also had underground corridors. Recently, more intensive excavations in Jerusalem revealed the hidden passages, and there are still many similarities between the temple layout at Jerusalem and that at Chavín de Huantar awaiting discovery. Archaeological excavations are in progress.

Chavín de Huantar could not have been built without technical know-how. As all scholars agree that such know-how did not exist on the American continent, it must necessarily have been imported. First-class stonemasons were at work, not hastily trained Indians. There were tools which had been developed down the generations by practical use. There were architects experienced in building above and below ground, who planned as a team. When the bare stonework was finished, artists with special skills were waiting to decorate the hundreds of stone slabs with their abstract art. Did they create the style of Chavín de Huantar out of the blue?

In the opinion of all the academics, this style, too, has no models. Was it just there, in all its perfection? Although uninterpreted as yet, the drawings of the flat reliefs with their mysteries are disturbing. The engravings on steles, obelisks and wall slabs represent beings made up of animal and human

The section of the complex that is still standing is called El Castillo, the castle, although it never was a castle.

The main portal of the Castillo, with two columns topped by a monolith nine metres long.

The columns are decorated with mysterious patterns in relief. Weathering through the ages has worn them down and, unfortunately, man, too, has damaged the delicate work.

The base of the Castillo was formerly faced with polished chiselled slabs.

Four flights of steps lead from the 'sunken square' to the four cardinal points of the compass.

Remains of walls typify the architecture of the complex. The 'sunken square' is on the right.

The Temple at Jerusalem. It was often destroyed and rebuilt on the foundation walls — like the Temple at Chavín de Huantar.

The Temple at Jerusalem is not an exact rectangle today, but an irregular trapezoid. However, it was a perfect rectangle originally.

The passages cut out of the rock are three metres high. They frequently turn off abruptly at angles of 45 degrees. How was El Lanzon brought here?

My lamp illuminated the strange heads with their stylised faces that peered from all sides.

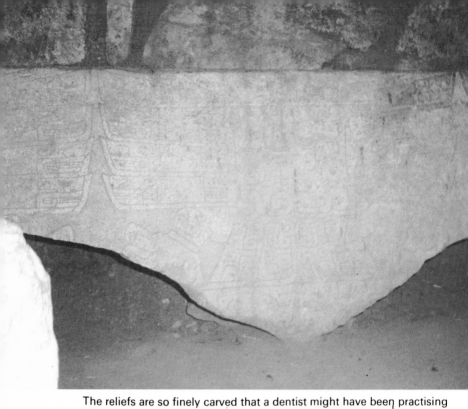

The reliefs are so finely carved that a dentist might have been practising his hobby of sculpting with a high-speed drill.

I searched every square centimetre of the wall to find a hint of an opening, a way out.

elements as identical as technical robots. We find the same style with the same codes, whether it be on the Lanzon stele or the Raimondi stele, on the Tello obelisk or the monolithic wall slabs. No one will deny that countless artists were involved and that they all came from the same school. The works at Chavín de Huantar would be a strange business if they were brewed up in their own juice. But was that so?

'Winged gods' proliferate in the Mesopotamian zone. They hovered over the portals of palaces, decorated throne-rooms and tombs; small-scale versions of them were found on the Babylonian, Assyrian and Hittite cylinder seals with which private and official documents were stamped in those days. Such 'winged gods' also fluttered and hovered in the consummate artistic abstractions at Chavín de Huantar.

The indigenous highland Indian Julio C. Tello, still the most important excavator of Chavín de Huantar, characterised the works of art as the products of an 'extraordinary race' (2). Some slab engravings struck him as a mixture of fish and dragon. He recovered images with elements of dragon, condor and man from the ruins, monsters which are reminiscent of diagrams of machines, if looked at from the present-day point of view. Stylised condors fly away with outspread wings,

A symbiosis of bird, animal and man = a monster.

although they have neither birds' faces, birds' eyes or beaks. They form a symbiosis of bird-animal-man monsters, sur-realistic works of art from another world by an extraordinary race, as if extraterrestrials had guided the sculptor's chisel.

Whole libraries about the Chavín style have been published. After reading the majority of the books, I should like to quote:

A delight in the use of curves is characteristic of Chavín. Powerful curves like these are not found in any other major Peruvian style. (14)

In its extremely complicated depictions of animals Chavín achieves a degree of perfection and refinement that is unknown in the human representations. The reliefs reveal a mastery bordering on virtuosity. Large hard stones are covered with a maze of elegant supple lines which look like pen-and-ink drawings. (15)

The intricacy and sophistication ... the strength and quality of the curving lines, in short, the entire concept, indicate that we are far from the beginnings of an art which doubtless evolved in other media than from megalithic sculpture. (17)

Why did such great religious artistic styles

originate in Mesoamerica
and Peru (Chavín) and not
elsewhere? What unleashed
this genius? I do not know.
(16)

The massive columns and heads of their sculptor colleagues
corresponded to the pen-and-ink drawings of the engravers.
The American archaeologist Wendell C. Bennett (18) found
two dozen heads, part human, part animal, all ornamented
with the engravings typical of Chavín. Originally the heads
protruded from the temple walls on tenons. Only two of them
are in their original place today.

The heads vary in character. Sometimes they have broad
noses and swollen lips, sometimes a rectangular animal muzzle
showing Dracula teeth snarls below the nose, at other times the
heads have no faces at all. Many are equipped with technical
accessories such as helmets, ear protectors, mouth filters and
what seem to be spectacles. A feature common to the faces
is a hostile, strange, alienating, cold expression.

Bennett also excavated megalithic slabs with ornaments that undoubtedly have value as evidence, but without human or animal features. Their sinuous lines are repeated side by side with the abstract-cum-figurative images. For all our intelligence we have not yet deciphered this symbolic language. However that is a commentary on us, not on those ancient sculptors who entrusted *their* messages to the stones, using *their* techniques.

We should not make too much fuss about the man–animal combinations — they occur in all ancient civilisations — were it not for the fact that the delicate style of the ornamentation at Chavín de Huantar is adhered to uniformly and so has more to tell us than we think. The visitor is forced to suspect that the artists did not know what they were depicting, in spite of their absolute mastery of shape and form. Did someone 'dictate' that they had to engrave? Were they using their own imaginative capacity when they immortalised the unknown something that came down from heaven in their drawings and adumbrations of jaguars and condors? When they drew their stone portraits, were they remembering the helmeted gods who gave them autocratic commands and hostile looks?

When the biblical Enoch and Elijah ascended into heaven, tradition has it that they departed on fire-breathing horses. Our ancestors knew that horses cannot breathe fire or fly. They were more familiar with four-legged creatures than we are. They probably symbolised or described the unintelligible by invoking the power of the horse as a symbol of the explosive energy of an alien phenomenon. The winged jaguars and condors meant the same to the artists at Chavín de Huantar as the winged fire-breathing horses did to the Mesopotamians and the intricate pictorial compositions originated because of the beings resembling humans who careered through the sky. In other words, they were not surreal in the artistic sense of the word, but attempts to reproduce what they had experienced.

In the book of the Old Testament prophet Job (40 and 41), we find the perfect example of a 'hippopotamus', except that it was not and could not have been such a creature, for:

His bones are tubes of bronze, his limbs like bars of iron ... His sneezings flash forth light, and his eyes are like the eyelids of the dawn... Out of his mouth go flaming torches; sparks of fire leap forth. Out of his nostrils comes forth smoke, as from a boiling pot and burning rushes. His breath kindles coals, and a flame comes forth from his mouth ... When he raises himself up the mighty are afraid; at the crashing they are beside themselves. Though the sword reaches him, it does not avail; nor the spear, the dart, or the javelin. He counts iron as straw, and bronze as rotten wood ... He makes the deep boil like a pot; he makes the sea like a pot of ointment. Behind him he leaves a shining wake; one would think the deep to be hoary. Upon earth there is not his like, a creature without fear.

Strong meat, panegyric of a technically equipped 'Hippopotamus'!

Old Testament scholars ascribe Job's speech and God's answer to Egyptian and Babylonian sources. Unknown creatures were lauded. The reliefs at Chavín also served as a perpetuation of actual experience.

It is just as if the Andean artists had read the Sumerian Epic of Gilgamesh (20) which contains, as part of the literary tradition, a hybrid being of the kind they symbolised in stone.

Gilgamesh and Enkidu climbed laboriously on to the top of the mountain where cedars in great profusion surrounded the dwelling of the gods. The sacred tower of the Goddess Jrnini shone forth, blindingly white.

Each of them carried an axe. Enkidu swung his and felled one of the cedars. Then a wrathful snorting was heard: 'Who was there, felling cedars?' Chimbaba himself saw them approach. He had claws like a lion, his body was covered with scales of bronze, on his feet were the talons of a vulture, on his head the horns of the wild bull; his tail and member for procreation ended in snakes' heads ... They shot their arrows at him, they hurled their throwing sticks. The weapons rebounded, he was unharmed.

Scholars claim that Chavín de Huantar was a place of pilgrimage, the religious centre of a mysterious people who suddenly appeared in the valley of the river Mosna and stamped the whole area with their culture for several centuries

— a view which the scholar Friedrich Katz (10) expresses as follows:

> Most researchers believe in a religious impulse, the emergence of a new cult which spread throughout large areas of the Andes. Many scholars believe that Chavín and perhaps the other centres of this culture were important religious towns which became the goals of pilgrimages. Afterwards the pilgrims would have broadcast the news of the new religion in the most remote villages. Even today we can still find centres of belief and pilgrims who cover hundreds or even thousands of miles to visit holy places.

In his investigation of the Chavín problem, Gordon R. Willey (21) comes to the same conclusion: 'Chavín is very obviously a great ceremonial centre,' a view shared by Julio C. Tello.

Now all religions have originators or founders. The Israelites of the Old Testament worshipped God, the Lord who created Adam and Eve, protected Noah and spoke to Abraham and Moses. The New Testament groups parables and theories about Jesus. Buddha and Mohammed also founded religions. Wherever religions originated, they have to be ascribed to semi-divine figures. Peoples were never captured by religions as the result of mass enlightenment. There were always beings, personalities, who lived among mankind or figures who set an example of what they preached.

The Chavín cult had no founder. It would be blasphemous to name jaguars, condors or snakes as the potential founders of a religion, just because we cannot root out some enlightened person.

There are scholars who connect the animal–human cult with shamanism. Shamans were the magicians who could send their souls out to the spirits or allow them to enter their own bodies. Nigel Davies (22), who has lived in Mexico for 20 years, writes:

> Anyone who escapes unharmed from a tiger in the forest is considered as one of God's chosen vessels by the Mojos (an Indian tribe in east Bolivia, EvD) and initiated into the guild of jaguar shamans. The Mojos still have a temple cult devoted to this divinity.

There is no doubt that shamanism is widespread among primitive races. We can also appreciate that the simple children of nature wanted to possess the characteristics of animals — the speed of a jaguar, the snake's cunning, the bird's ability to fly (a dream dreamt by all peoples). It is a platitude that animals were sacrificed to propitiate them. Primitive artists would never have credited wild animals with abilities they had not actually seen. Snakes crawl on the ground, but cannot fly; the jaguar runs and leaps, but cannot fly; the condor has not got legs adapted for leaping like the jaguar. It is as simple as that.

Religions and cults have laws and moral doctrines. Were they founded by jaguars, married to a shaman? Did condors spew down pious dogmas from above? And — the height of insanity — were there animal architects who built Chavín de Huantar so that they would have their own religious centre?

Assuming that the Chavín cult really was a jaguar–condor religion, would not those skilled artists have taken special care to portray their admired, feared and *revered* animals as accurately as possible? Then we should surely be able to admire perfectly realised animals on the stone monuments of Chavin, sculpted as magnificently as the sacred Apis bulls and lions of the Egyptians and Babylonians? Could not we expect to find a mummified jaguar or condor at Chavín de Huantar, since the Egyptians mummified millions of the sacred falcons of their sun god Re? Not a single mummy of a sacred animal was found at Chavín de Huantar.

What kind of god was the temple dedicated to? He could fly like a condor and also looked like a jaguar; he killed like a snake, yet had human features. He had the intelligence of a clever ruler. What kind of a god was it that combined all these characteristics?

Earlier researchers dated the building of the temple to between 1,000 and 700 BC. The theologian and historian Siegfried Huber (9), who lived in the Andes for a long time, writes:

If we can date its origins to 850 BC, Chavín emerges as the oldest, maturest art style in form and technique ... On that assumption foreigners would have come to the country around 850 BC and induced the indigenous population to accept their ideas.

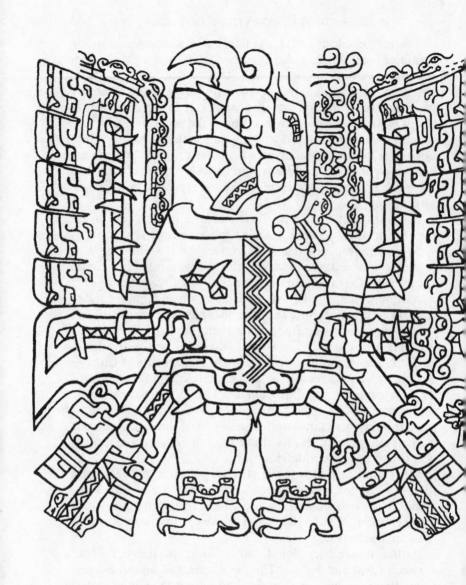

Recently scholars consider the culture to be far more recent. Peruvian archaeologists assume that it began between 800 and 500 BC. Nothing is certain, but all the dating methods in use today allow 200 years' latitude either way. Present-day physics offers modern techniques of dating ancient remains, but doubts about the dates remain.

Since an interest in archaeology is fortunately 'in', it may be of interest to say something about the techniques used for datings.

Datings are calculated by radioactive half-lives. A half-life is the period in which half the number of isotopes in a radio-active element disintegrate. A fixed value is necessary as starting-point. With the well-known carbon 14 method, the earth's atmosphere is taken as a constant with the unchanging amount of radioactive carbon isotopes. In the course of the earth's history the number of carbon isotopes reckoned to be constant was subject to fluctuations. We do not know why, but in the meantime there is no doubt that the datings are questionable.

Another point is what kind of physical artefacts are to be dated. In the same temple the shreds of a cloth and the remains of a wood fire can both be examined. What does that mean if the rags belonged to a temple dancer who practised her art in a temple that was already ancient? Nor do the carbon remains say anything about the age of the temple; the fire might have been lit in a ruined temple.

Modern physics offers eleven methods of dating, but they seldom provide clearcut dates. Each method has its snags. Analyses can often be made on specific materials and pre-suppose a knowledge of local peculiarities which are often unknown.

For example, microanalysis presupposes a knowledge of how high the concentration of nitrogen, fluoride and uranium was on the site in the past! Who can possibly say that with certainty? In the potassium–argon method the result stands and falls by the knowledge of the quantity of argon that penetrated (and was lost from) the stone during thousands of years. Amino-acid analysis has the weakness that it can only be used on objects that were preserved at constant temperatures, because chemical reactions alter at higher temperatures. Nobody can know whether the object to be examined was exposed to higher temperatures at some time. Temples burnt down and were rebuilt on the ruins. So every method has its faults.

Professor Richard Burleigh (23), a specialist in dating methods, holds out hopes for the future:

> The next major advance seems likely to depend on the successful development of the particle acceleration method ... This method of dating, using only milligram quantities of sample offers the possibility of obtaining results more rapidly than present methods, with a probable upper age limit of about 100,000 years. Cost is likely to restrict these installations to a few fortunate institutions.

But there is one snag about this procedure; the apparatus is too expensive. Given the official lack of interest in mankind's prehistory shown by governments, limited budgets would not allocate a penny to purchase it. Perhaps the technologists should combine to invent a time machine which would let them travel back into the past. Our eyes would pop out of our heads!

The correct dating of Chavín de Huantar should lie somewhere between 1,000 and 500 BC.

Archaeologists specialising in South America point out that the equally puzzling Olmec culture originated in Mexico at the same time. It is true that the Olmecs, indigenous inhabitants of the Gulf of Mexico, did produce works of art which often resemble the Chavín style. Pottery of this kind was found at Monte Alban, a Zapotec religious centre, as well as at Veracruz and Tlatlico on the edge of Mexico City. The Olmecs' stone monster heads have similarities to their unknown brothers at Chavín, save that these comrades, which today are on parade in the museum park of La Venta near Villahermosa, are very much larger. In the Museo Nacional de Antropología in Mexico City one can see stone Olmec snake heads with technical attributes which could stem from Chavín. So has the Chavín culture got a counterpart?

I do not want to get involved in the academic battle (24, 25, 26) about which culture influenced which, but I must point out that Chavín de Huantar is in the South American Andes and not in Central American Mexico. Given a latitude of 200 years for the 'copyright' dates, it is not impossible that groups

These stone Olmec works of art (above and overleaf), which might have come from Chavín de Huantar, are on show in the Anthropological Museum in Mexico City.

of Chavín people migrated northwards or sailed there by sea and influenced the Olmecs. There are no insuperable barriers between Peru and Mexico, but there were enough incentives to make the Chavín migrate, for example in order to spread their outstandingly successful religion. Religion has always favoured adventurous excursions. Just imagine all that could have happened in 200 years that were full of gaps!

On the whole specialist literature holds the view that America was settled in a southerly direction starting from the north, present-day Canada. In his book *Kasskara and the Seven Worlds* (27), Josef Blumrich used dates and facts to prove that this drive from north to south did not exclude other possibilities. There are many South and Central American datings that are older than the North American ones, just as, vice versa, archaeologists discovered artistic evidence in the north that is older than southern artefacts.

On his plates in the Book of Mormon, Nephi tells us that he brought the record of his people's past from overseas. On his arrival, he had a temple built 'after the manner of the temple of Solomon'. Chavín de Huantar suggests itself.

There is a simple answer to the question why Nephi did not build near the coast, rather than choosing a site in the high Andes. After the landing he quarrelled with his brothers:

> But behold, their anger did increase against me, insomuch that they did seek to take away my life. Yea, they did murmur against me, saying: Our younger brother thinks to rule over us; therefore, now let us slay him, that we may not be afflicted because of his words. For behold, we will not have him to be our ruler; for it belongs unto us, who are the elder brethren, to rule over this people.
>
> (II Nephi 5.2 *et seq.*)

The outcome of the conflict was preordained. 'God' advised Nephi to depart, along with his followers. Nephi obeyed:

> And we did take our tents and whatsoever things were possible for us, and did journey in the wilderness for the space of many days. After we had journeyed for many days we did pitch our tents.
>
> (II Nephi 5.7)

No matter where the immigrants landed, they must have found themselves in country bordering on the Andes, and that was desert, genuine desert, with the exception of the few fertile strips by the river. Journeying 'in the wilderness' could only mean that the Nephites turned towards the mountains, because elsewhere there was no wilderness. And what better protection for the refugees than in the mountain valleys?

In foreign countries greenhorns find their bearings from watercourses which necessarily lead to their sources. And 'God' was always there. Nephi noted this, and also that this god could fly. He ordered Nephi, his chosen one, to 'make other plates; and thou shalt engraven many things upon them that are good in my sight.'

The connection of the builders of Chavín de Huantar with the sea is undeniable. Mussels and mother-of-pearl artefacts have been found high in the mountains.

Nephi is supposed to have reached South America around 590 BC. He had the temple built 30 years later. The complex at Chavín is dated to between 80 and 500 BC, or at the most between 1,000 and 600 BC.

Nephi knew Solomon's temple from personal observation. There were some highly educated families among his followers, as he mentions in I Nephi. Perhaps among them there were architects familiar with the temple plans.

When Nephi left Jerusalem, the city was presumably occupied by the Babylonians. In 586 BC Solomon's temple was completely destroyed by Nebuchadnezzar's soldiers. A speculation that is not too far-fetched is that the plans of the sacred temple were smuggled out of the country so that it could be rebuilt in all its glory on a new site — as a memorial to the ancient homeland and symbol of the ancient faith.

The temple complex at Chavín de Huantar can certainly have been a copy of Solomon's temple:

Chavín de Huantar has outer and inner courtyards, consecrated areas, a sanctuary (El Castillo), separate sections for pilgrims, priests and high priests, a temple wall with external rooms for the 'unclean' and even the little brook mentioned in the Bible ... everything as it was in Solomon's temple.

Chavín de Huantar was orientated towards the four cardinal points of the compass ... like Solomon's temple.

In Chavín de Huantar the number seven was looked on as sacred ... as it was in Solomon's temple.

Chavín de Huantar was a sanctuary, religious centre, and place of pilgrimage ... as was Solomon's temple.

Chavín de Huantar had a ventilation system in its windowless shrine (El Castillo) and its inner rooms had artificial lighting ... as did the Holy of Holies in Solomon's temple.

Chavín de Huantar is built over underground galleries and water conduits ... like Solomon's temple.

The builders of Chavín de Huantar worshipped a flying god ... like the Israelites.

The last statement will arouse opposition. The Israelites worshipped only the one 'ineffable' God. He was the Israelite God, who descended amid fire, noise, quaking and stench, as expressively described in the Old Testament. It was this God who ordered Moses to set bounds about the sacred mountain so that the people would not perish if they broke in:

And mount Sinai was wrapped in smoke, because the LORD descended upon it in fire; and the smoke of it went up like the smoke of a kiln, and the whole mountain quaked greatly.

(Exodus 19.18)

There was also the Israelite God's ban on making images:

You shall not make for yourself a graven image, or any likeness of anything that is in heaven above, or that is in the earth beneath, or that is under the water of the earth.

(Exodus 20.4)

According to this commandment, there should have been no representations of the gods in Solomon's temple. Was the order complied with (and at the same time got round) by making abstract images of God, as at Chavín de Huantar? Even the Old Testament confirms that Solomon tolerated other gods besides his own:

Now King Solomon loved many foreign women ... concerning which the LORD had said unto the people of Israel, 'You shall not enter into marriage with them ... for surely they will turn away your heart after their gods. Solomon clung to these with love. He had seven hundred wives, princesses, and three hundred concubines; and his wives turned away his heart. For when Solomon was old his wives turned away his heart after other gods; and his heart was not wholly true to the LORD his God, as was the heart of David his father.

(I Kings 11.1 *et seq.*)

We shall never be able to prove that his temple was also decorated with abstract representations of strange gods, because the temple was totally destroyed by the Babylonians in 586 BC. When it was rebuilt, the Roman Emperor Titus Flavius had it burnt down again in AD 70. Were images of the gods in relief or stone sculptures destroyed in the conflagration? The presence of human-cum-animal depictions of the gods in this restricted geographical zone speaks in favour of their existence. The Babylonians produced many fine examples. As did Chavín de Huantar.

As a candidate for Nephi's temple, Chavín de Huantar has more similarities to the Solomonic temple in Jerusalem than can be explained as coincidences. I found them on my excursion which was intended to put me on the trail of Ezekiel's temple.

Ezekiel's report is unique. It is like a case for private detectives. A case for Heinrich Schliemann.

Let us take a look at it!

3   A Case for Heinrich Schliemann

'The fact that things happen means nothing. It is all important that they are known.'

Egon Friedell (1878–1938)

Heinrich Schliemann's great revelation came one summer evening when a drunken man came into his father's grocer's shop in Neubuknow and gave a Bacchanalian recital of Homer's poetry. The drunk had been to a secondary school, a fact he used to remember when befogged by alcohol. Fifteen-year-old Heinrich Schliemann did not understand a word of the Homeric hymns from the *Iliad* and the *Odyssey*, but the 'music' enchanted him. He wanted to learn the language.

The gods put obstacles in his path. If the young lad had not injured himself by carrying heavy loads and so made himself unfit for manual work, he would certainly have been destined for the same boring life that his father led in the little Mecklenburg town. Heinrich signed on as a cabin boy on a freighter — the dream of all adventurous young lads. The ship was wrecked and the young sailor was saved and stranded in Amsterdam without a penny. Fortunately he found work as a bookkeeper in a business house. He had a successful career. In his spare time he learned languages. He mastered Dutch, French, English, Italian, Spanish and Russian. Because of his linguistic ability he was given increasingly important positions, especially in Russia.

During the Crimean War which France, England and Turkey waged against Russia from 1853 to 1856, Schliemann first looked after the Amsterdam firm's interests in St Petersburg, but soon founded his own business and made a sizeable fortune. He travelled in Europe and the Orient until his hour came in 1868. He settled in Athens and learnt ancient Greek. In five months he could read Homer in the original; in two years he knew Homer's *Iliad* and *Odyssey* by heart.

With Homer in his head and money in the bank, Schliemann decided to take the traditions dating back to the second millennium BC at their face value, not just as the imaginings of a great poet. When he published his ideas in 1869, archaeologists burst their sides with laughter.

From 1870 to 1872 Schliemann excavated in Asia Minor at Hissarlik, which he looked on as the Troy described by Homer. He showed the archaeologists how literally tradition should be taken by his incredible finds. Schliemann uncovered nine superimposed settlements, including the old Homeric Troy, the citadel of which was destroyed by fire in 2,000 BC. Gold and silver treasure was found. Potsherds proved that the potter's wheel had existed there. With the seventh layer of settlement Schliemann came across signs of the Middle Bronze Age (c. 1800 BC). Walls and towers made of squared stone blocks stood on a diameter of 200 m; the inner rooms rested on circular terraces. Mycenean pottery proved to be imported, as Homer described it.

On the second layer Schliemann laid bare the ruins of the magnificent citadel of Priam and Hector, which was destroyed by Agamemnon, as Homer stated.

Schliemann the amateur gave the signal for a new look at archaeology. Convinced that Homer's poetry contained historical sources of tradition in full detail, he discovered the pre-Homeric world of the second millennium BC. Schliemann alone must be credited with giving the starting signal for prehistoric research in the Mediterranean countries. He gave the gold treasures of Troy and the royal tombs at Mycenae, and the gold treasure of King Priam, over 4,000 years old, to the Berlin Museum for Prehistory and Early History.

Scholars hid behind the dubious designation of the 'science of the spade' and claimed boldly that Schliemann had been lucky. Lucky? One man took the old traditions literally and became the greatest researcher of all time.

Heinrich Schliemann, who had latterly been the recipient of the highest academic honours, was buried in Athens on 4 January 1891.

If a Heinrich Schliemann existed today, I would have a good tip for him.

I suffer from stress every time I start to write a new book. When I realised my situation — even as I write this — I ask myself: what is this stress we are always talking about nowadays?

I took from my library a book by Hans Selye called *Stress beherrscht unser Leben* and learnt from the man who discovered and christened stress that this contemporary phenomenon is not really an illness, but the body's way of adapting to the conditions in which we live. 'Stress need not always be harmful; it is simultaneously the root of life, for every emotional and physical activity causes stress. The very stress that makes one man ill may be quite stimulating to another!' On that basis I am definitely one of the other men.

Hans Selye, the 'father of stress', wrote in his introduction that his book was intended for both doctors *and* laymen. Consequently he felt forced to include passages that laymen could not understand and at the same time provide explanations that were axiomatic to doctors. He got out of the dilemma by prefacing each chapter with a resumé which the specialist could skip, but which would make everything intelligible to the layman.

The problem that faced Hans Selye, born in Vienna in 1907 and since 1934 Professor of Endocrinology at Montreal, of writing *one* book for both doctors and laymen, is very like the difficulty I face of not being repetitious to readers who already know my books, and yet making them intelligible to new readers. Readers aged 20 were only five years old when my first book came out. Encouraged and instructed by Selye, I have marked a few pages with a black line in the margin. My old readers can skip them. They know the texts about the prophet Ezekiel from my books *Chariots of the Gods?* (1969) and *In Search of Ancient Gods* (1974).

Without these quotations new readers would have no idea what a time bomb is ticking away in the new enquiry into the Ezekiel mystery.

Ezekiel was an Old Testament prophet. The following report has as its subject an event that is supposed to have happened about 592 BC.

Now it came to pass in the thirtieth year, in the fourth month, on the fifth day of the month, as I was among the captives by the river of Chebar, that the heavens were opened ... And I looked, and behold, a whirlwind came out of the north, a great cloud, and a fire unfolding itself, and a brightness was about it, and out of the midst thereof as the colour of amber, out of the midst of the fire. Also out of the midst thereof came the likeness of four living creatures. And this was their appearance; they had the likeness of a man. And every one had four faces, and every one had four wings. And their feet were straight feet; and the sole of their feet was like the sole of a calf's foot: and they sparkled like the colour of burnished brass ... In the midst of the living creatures there was something that looked like burning coals of fire, like torches moving to and fro among the living creatures; and the fire was bright, and out of the fire went forth lightning ... Now as I beheld the living creatures, behold one wheel upon the earth by the living creatures, with his four faces. The appearance of the wheels and their work was like unto the colour of a beryl: and the four had one likeness and their appearance and their work were as it were a wheel in the middle of a wheel. When they went they went upon their four sides: and they turned not as they went. As for their rings, they were so high that they were dreadful; and their rings were full of eyes round about them four. And when the living creatures were lifted up from the earth, the wheels were lifted up ... And when they went, I heard the sound of their wings like the sound of many waters, like the thunder of the Almighty, a sound of tumult like the sound of a host; when they stood still, they let down their wings. And above the firmament over their heads there was the likeness of a throne, in appearance like a sapphire; and seated above the likeness of a throne was a likeness as it were of a human form ...'

(Ezekiel 1.1 *et seq.*)

Then the Spirit lifted me up, and as the glory of the LORD arose from its place, I heard behind me the sound of a great earthquake; it was the sound of the living creatures as they touched one another, and the sound of the wheels beside them, that sounded like a great earthquake ...

(Ezekiel 3.12)

And I looked, and behold, there were four wheels beside the cherubim, one beside each cherub; and the appearance of the wheels was like sparkling chrysolite. And as for their appearance, the four had the same likeness, as if a wheel were within a wheel. When they went, they went in any of their four directions without turning as they went, *but in whatever direction the front wheel faced the others followed without turning as they went.* And their rims, and their spokes, and the wheels were full of eyes round about ... *And when the cherubim went, the wheels went beside them*; and when the cherubim lifted up their wings to mount up from the earth, the wheels did not turn from beside them. When they stood still these stood still and when they mounted up, these mounted up with them ...

(Ezekiel 10.9 et seq. — my italics)

I read out the last text during an extremely heated discussion after a lecture and said that it came from the Bible. An indignant opponent shouted that I should be ashamed to say that. I took *Die Heilige Schrift des Alten und des Neuen Testaments*, Stuttgart, 1972, the so-called Zurich Bible, out of my briefcase. There is no finer German version. I handed it to the enraged heckler and he shut up like a clam. The quotations preceding it also came from the Zurich Bible. [Translator's note: English version used here.]

I was just as astonished when I first came across these passages, but was immediately convinced that they seemed too technical to be interpreted in purely theological terms.

I boldly asserted that Ezekiel, or whoever wrote the first and oldest version, had seen and described a machine that suddenly came out of the clouds and understandably made a strong impression on him. Although he was eloquent, he could only stammer. He had never seen a machine before and so could not understand the functions of the wheels and wings; to him they were the limbs of 'living creatures', because they moved. Naturally the 'four wings' (rotors) were lowered when the helicopter landed. The law of gravity saw to that. The eye-witness was astonished by wheels and rings, and amazed that he was raised from the ground together with the 'living creatures'. It is a characteristic of helicopters that they take passengers with them when they take off.

Our local reporter Ezekiel heard an incredible noise. In an attempt to describe it, he could only write of 'tumult like the sound of a host' and the 'sound of many waters'. The people could imagine something expressed in those terms. He was an accurate observer; he even saw the pilot sitting on 'the likeness of a throne'.

Now the modern technical version of the text is not lacking in convincing comparisons. It was obvious to me that Ezekiel had not had a vision, but was describing a technical reality. I was given a rare bashing by the critics for my audacity because I could not prove my claims and Bernard Shaw himself said that critics are bloodthirsty people who have not had to face the hangman. But proof came from a top technologist who originally set out to disclose my assumptions as sheer nonsense.

It was a milestone in the thousands of years of biblical exegesis when an engineer analysed the texts critically. That engineer was Josef F. Blumrich, former leader of the group for constructional research with NASA at Huntsville, Alabama, the holder of numerous patents for building large rockets and the NASA Exceptional Service Medal. In his book *The Spaceships of Ezekiel* (1), he supplied an engineer's proof of the existence of Ezekiel's spaceship in the distant past. In his foreword Blumrich writes that he really wanted to prove the untenability of my theory, but he had to admit defeat, although the effort turned out to be richly rewarded, fascinating and enjoyable. These are the result of Blumrich's investigations:

It is possible to infer the general appearance of the spaceship described by Ezekiel from his account. Then an engineer can set aside his report and reconstruct a flying machine with the same characteristics. If he then shows that the result is not only technically possible, but also practical and well thought out in every respect, and moreover finds details and processes in Ezekiel's account that tally perfectly with his own conclusions, one can no longer speak simply of indications. I discovered that Ezekiel's spaceship has very credible dimensions:

Specific impulse	I_{sp} —	2,080 sec
Weight of construction	W_o —	63,300 kg
Fuel for return journey	W_9 —	36,700 kg
Diameter of rotor	D_r —	18 m

Total power developed by rotor	N	—	70,000 HP
Diameter of spaceship proper	D	—	18 m

The conclusions reached show us a spaceship that is not only technically possible, but also very sensibly adapted for its mission. We are surprised to find a stage of technology that is in no way fantastic, but rather falls almost within the field of our present day potentialities, in other words one that is only a little way ahead of our time. In addition the conclusions show a spaceship that was used in connection with a command module in orbit round the earth. The only fantastic thing is that such a spaceship was tangible reality more than 2,500 years ago!

A splendid by-product of Blumrich's researches was a vehicle that could move in all directions constructed from Ezekiel's description. On 5 February 1974 the engineer received United States patent No. 3,789,947 for it, which was also a belated recognition of Ezekiel's accuracy as a reporter.

So I was not lying with my crazy technological interpretation, although my critics would have loved me to be wrong.

I first took an interest in Ezekiel over 15 years ago. The old gentleman would not leave me in peace. After all, his book did not consist solely of the four chapters which had stimulated my speculations about a spaceship. It has 48 chapters, crammed full of sayings, threats, commandments, prophesies and accurate reports. It is full of curiosities.

Down the centuries the Book of Ezekiel must have had countless interpretations. In a book published in 1981 (2), 270 treatises on the prophet were catalogued, quoted and commented on. Two hundred and seventy-two scholarly heads devoted years of their lives to the ancient text. Even if little new came out of the hair-splitting exegeses — all the exegetists wear blinkers — there is still keen interest in Ezekiel today. No wonder, because a time bomb is ticking away in the texts that should lead to the trail deliberately laid by the 'Lord'. Secrets have an extraordinary attraction for people.

My (brand-new) researches concern a building which could give a modern Heinrich Schliemann excavation tips just as accurate as Homer's poetry turned out to be in pointing the way to Troy.

I reveal my find in Chapter 40 of the Book of Ezekiel and close it with chapter 48.

I have taken the liberty of only including the passages relevant to my theory, and also of italicising significant points. This is not dishonesty on my part. Everyone has a Bible and can consult the unabbreviated text. I know lots of scholarly books that use quotations the sources of which are not available to the reader.

Ezekiel writes:

In the twenty-fifth year of our exile, at the beginning of the year, on the tenth day of the month, in the fourteenth year after the city was conquered ... the hand of the LORD was upon me, and brought me in the visions of God into the land of Israel, and set me down upon *a very high mountain*, on which there was *a structure like a city* opposite me. When he brought me there, behold, there was *a man, whose appearance was like bronze*, with a line of flax and a measuring reed in his hand; and he was standing in the gateway. And the man said to me, 'Son of man, look with your eyes and hear with your ears, and set your mind on all that I shall show you, for you were brought here in order that I might show it to you ...

And behold there was a wall all around the outside of the temple area, and the length of the measuring reed in the man's hand was six long cubits, each being a cubit and a handbreadth in length; so he measured the thickness of the wall, one reed; and the height, one reed. Then he went into the gateway *facing east*, going up its (*seven*) *steps* ... Then he measured the distance from the inner front of the lower gate to the outer front of the inner court, a hundred cubits. Then he went before me *to the north*, and behold, there was a gate which faced *toward the north* ... And he led me toward the south, and behold, there was a gate *on the south* ... Then he brought me to the inner court *on the east side*, and he measured the gate; it was the same size as the others ...

And he measured the court, a hundred cubits long, and a hundred cubits broad ... Then he measured the wall of the temple, six cubits thick; and the breadth of the side chambers, five cubits, round about the temple, and the side chambers were in three stories, one over another, thirty to each story ...

I saw also that the temple had a raised platform round about. Then he measured the length of the building facing the yard which was at the west and its walls on either side, a hundred cubits ...

Over against the threshold the temple was *panelled with wood* round about, from the floor up to the windows ... to the space above the door even to the inner room, and on the outside. *And on all the walls round about in the inner room and the nave were carved likenesses* of cherubim and palm trees, a palm tree between cherub and cherub. Every cherub had two faces ...

Now when he had finished measuring the interior of the temple area, he led me out by the gate which faced east, and measured the temple area round about. He measured the east side with the measuring reed, five hundred cubits by the measuring reed. Then he turned and measured the north side, five hundred cubits by the measuring reed ...

It had a wall around it, five hundred cubits long and five hundred cubits broad, to make a separation between the holy and the common ...

Afterward he brought me to the gate, the gate facing east. And behold, the glory of the LORD came *from the east*; and the sound of his coming was like *the sound of many waters* and the earth shone with his glory. And the vision I saw was like the vision which I had seen when he had come to destroy the city, and *like the vision which I had seen by the river Chebar* ... Then he brought me back to the door of the temple; and behold, water was issuing from below the threshold of the temple *towards the east* (for the temple faced east): and the water was flowing down from below the *south end* of the threshold below the temple ...

And he said to me, this water flows toward the eastern region and goes down into the Arabah; and when it enters the stagnant waters of the sea, the water will become fresh. And wherever the river goes every living creature which swarms will live, and there will be very many fish ...

And on the banks, on both sides of the river, there will grow all kinds of trees for food. Their leaves will not wither nor their fruit fail, but they will bear fresh fruit every month, because the water for them flows from the sanctuary ...

Most scholars say that the first part of the book is an epiphany. Visions of strange flashing and sparkling chariots that descended from heaven played a large part in the literature of ancient Israel. Even Eve, Adam's wife, is supposed to have seen a heavenly chariot (3):

Then Eve looked up to heaven and saw a shining chariot come, drawn by four gleaming eagles, whose glory no one born of woman could express nor look on their face, and angels went before the chariot.

(My italics)

The heavenly vehicles which flit through the traditions do not fit into any hangar! Enoch describes 'fiery heavenly cars'; Elijah went up to heaven in a similar model drawn by 'horses of fire'. When Old Testament exegetists turned their attention to Israelite tradition, they failed to note that heavenly chariots also buzz their way through Buddhist mythology (4). The great teacher Padmasambhava used such a vehicle. Ardjuna, too, hero of the Indian epic Mahabharata (5), travels gaily through the cosmos in a heavenly chariot.

Why should it not be accepted that the gods in all the myths, religions and sects all over the world actually had such heavenly chariots? Why do scholars insist on what they call a more plausible explanation of this phenomenon?

Three academic opinions are representative of the most important interpretations. The theologian Professor J. Lindblom (6) sees 'hallucinatory experiences' in the events. His Swiss colleague Othmar Keel (7) finds 'visions', while Professor W. Beyerlin (8) interprets them as part of the ritual of Israelite religious feasts. The theologian Fritz Dummermuth (9) is alone in admitting that 'the reports in question cannot readily be explained away as natural phenomena of a meteorological or volcanic kind'; and Dummermuth even remarks in a later article in the *Zeitschrift der Theologischen Fakultät Basel* (10) that 'It is about time to take a look at things from a new point of view, if biblical research is to make any progress here.'

Bravo! It would be a step in the right direction if a comparative study of heavenly chariots was made on an international scale, if Old Testament experts sat round the round table with specialists in Indian mythology and produced their respective documents.

It is senseless to confine the global phenomenon of 'heavenly chariots' to a specific local event in Israelite territory, because *it is not true.*

The figure of the 'prophet' has undergone amazing transformations during past centuries. The prophet whose word could not be questioned became the 'visionary' and, after being called 'dreamer' and 'fantast', he became a 'cataleptic'.

Man was and is inventive and will use any tricks to avoid having to tackle the inexplicable.

The Book of Ezekiel was taken apart. Semantic experts decided that style and choice of words pointed to more than one author. The prophet was abruptly relegated to the rank of 'pseudo-Ezekiel' (11), whose book was first compiled from different texts around 200 BC. A hundred years ago, the theologian Rudolf Smend (1851–1913), a distinguished Ezekiel scholar (12), wrote: 'There can be absolutely no doubt that the account is based on a visionary experience and that the vision is in no way a form of literary expression.'

The majority of theologians now think that the Book of Ezekiel was not written by the prophet, but was more probably the joint work of redactors, who mixed ancient texts (possibly including some by the prophet himself) with later additional material.

I, too, favour this explanation. 'Ezekiel' is not an original work. Practical questions make the authorship irrelevant. It makes no difference whether Ezekiel had visions or whether the book called after him originated from ancient additional traditions. My questions go to the heart of the matter:

If Ezekiel did have a vision, what purpose did his God have in mind?

If there was no vision, which parts of the text should be rated as descriptions of reality and which as the products of imagination?

If the descriptions really were phantasmagoria, we could dismiss them as science fiction.

If the accounts prove to be based on reality, where must we look for the minutely described temple?

An unanswered question is how Ezekiel, or Mister X, reached the temple and returned to Jerusalem.

The narrator of the Book of Ezekiel writes in the first person 'I saw ... I experienced ... I heard ... I was brought ...' The use of the first person has always indicated that the writer was an eyewitness. Was the man behind the 'I', whoever he was, a liar? Fabricating to make himself interesting?

The facts show that the Ezekiel narrative must be dated to the sixth century BC, whether it is attributed to the prophet (who lived at that time) or to his disciples. It was an age of strictly orthodox faith. No writer would have dared to call on almighty God as chief witness, no one would have risked putting words into God's mouth that were untrue.

'You shall not take the name of the LORD your God in vain; for the LORD will not hold him guiltless who takes his name in vain' (Exodus, 20.7).

But if lies were served up in Ezekiel's name, why does he still retain the status of a prophet in the book of books? Even if Ezekiel was not the sole author, the original was written in the first person!

Faithful to the axiom that the accused person should be given the benefit of the doubt, I believe that Ezekiel was describing real events.

In the text he says that the hand of the Lord set him down on a *very high mountain*. There are no very high mountains in Israel.

Interpretations which say that Ezekiel was describing the Solomonic temple at Jerusalem cannot be right, because that temple is not sited on a *very high mountain*. There is nothing approaching a very high mountain in or around Jerusalem, only a few hills. Moreover, Ezekiel grew up in Jerusalem and knew the hills by name. If the Lord has set him down on a hill, he would have mentioned the hill by name, given the accuracy of his bookkeeping.

From the *very high mountain* Ezekiel saw a structure like a *city*. If it had been Jerusalem, he would have recognised his home town and mentioned it by name.

There can be no doubt that Ezekiel was not describing Jerusalem and Solomon's temple.

'*And behold, there was a man, whose appearance was like bronze ...*' Since explicit sexual characteristics were not visible,

Ezekiel's instant identification of the unknown figure as a man must have come from his facial features or the fact that women, unemancipated in those days, could not give orders.

This man had the appearance *of bronze*. Excuse me, honoured exegetists, why did it not dawn on you that this man was wearing an astronaut's suit which seemed to shine like armour to the narrator?

The stranger addressed the prophet as *son of man*. Interesting, for this mode of address implies that the man with the appearance of bronze was not a man at all and that he did not know the name of the person he was speaking to. He continues to address Ezekiel as son of man. If I landed on Mars among the little green men and one of them prostrated himself in the sand before me, I couldn't say, 'Arise, John Smith.' I would have to say, 'Man of Mars, arise.' The impersonal address son of man seems to me to be a strong indication that the alien gentleman was no timeless omnipotent God. For *he* would have known Ezekiel's name.

Sceptics may ask how an extraterrestrial, for that is what I assume him to be, knew Ezekiel's language. Just as man in all ages quickly learnt the languages of newly discovered peoples, the extraterrestrials must have observed their elected groups for some time in order to master their tongue.

Now things get really exciting!

The man with the appearance of bronze tells the prophet to take a good note of what he is going to see, *for you were brought here in order that I might show it to you.*

The key to a strange story is encoded in that sentence.

If we discard the idea of extraterrestrial cooperation, almighty God had our Ezekiel transported to a *high mountain* and made a *man like bronze* measure the temple with a measuring reed before his eyes, so that Ezekiel would have the measurements firmly stamped on his memory. The detailed description shows that the prophet took his mission very seriously. What was the point of this instruction?

Theologians take the view that God gave Ezekiel a vision of the temple so that he would be able to build it in the future. But Ezekiel's temple was never built. If God showed his chosen vessel a phantom building, it means that he did not know the future and so was not omniscient.

This is the snag. In the original form of the Ezekiel text there was no grammatical future tense! Written Hebrew was made up solely of consonants; it had no vowels. In order to facilitate reading, vowels were indicated by small dots between the consonants. The original text had the imperfect and perfect tenses, but no future. But students of theology point out that the future — if need be — grows out of the consecutive perfect. Strictly speaking, the original text of Ezekiel can be transposed into the past, the present or the future, depending on which way you want it. It was a temple; it is a temple; it will be a temple.

As scholars stick to their interpretation of the text as a vision, they naturally project the building of the temple, the exact measurements of which were known to Ezekiel, into the future. The consecutive perfect makes that possible.

If we start with the assumption that Ezekiel (or Mr X) was brought to a temple which was measured before his watchful eyes, the question arises: What was the point of this accurate measurement? The text provides the answer. The prophet was to observe everything closely, because that was why he was brought there.

In my Zurich Bible, the one I usually quote from, it says: 'For thou wast brought hither for that purpose.' The same passage in the Göttingen version (14) reads: 'For I came hither to show it to thee.'

These two translations are worlds apart!

'Thou wast brought hither for that purpose,' means that Ezekiel arrived on the spot after a journey. 'I came hither to show it to you,' means that the *man in bronze* sought out the prophet. The latter translation obviously adds weight to the idea of a vision, which theologians prefer. But in context it misses its point. Ezekiel was taken to a *high mountain* and discovered *a structure like a city*. In other words, he was confronted with a new situation. He was ordered to memorise in absolute detail all the data about rooms and walls supplied by the man in bronze.

The keen observation with which Ezekiel registered the data, allow us to assume that he noted them down on the spot. In that way, the hand of the Lord achieved its goal via the bronze-clad messenger. A hitherto unknown temple entered the annals of tradition! The data for constructing a real temple — not

a visionary phantom — were to preoccupy men's brains for
millennia.

The aliens, my extraterrestrials — to let the cat out of the
bag again — had a good idea that sacred traditions were never
lost and that they would survive wars and natural catastrophes
in written or printed form. They knew that priests and
exegetists would grind their teeth over the mysterious event
introduced into the ancient text. They knew that at some point
in the future the fiery heavenly chariots would be given a
technical explanation.

Convinced that the real measurements of a real temple are
set out in the Book of Ezekiel, regardless of whether the
prophet or another author wrote it, I felt I ought to be able
to find at least the rudiments of this structure, which could
not be overlooked because of its size.

Let the paperchase begin!

The front of the temple described by Ezekiel was *facing east*.
According to the Zurich Bible the man in bronze first measured
a wall, other versions speak of a 'building' or 'structure'.

The man in bronze used a special measuring reed, which
was *six long cubits, each being a cubit and a handbreadth in
length*. Strange. Surely a normal cubit would have been used
if the whole thing was a vision. But no, a special unit was
used for the measuring. And so scholars (13) wash their hands
of such absurdities:

> Given an imaginary building, it is of minor importance to
> know whether the normal Babylonian cubit (458 mm) or
> the 'royal' Egyptian cubit (525 mm) more common among
> the Israelites is referred to ... The description is only meant
> to symbolise that the sacred place differed from all others.

Correct. If it *was* a vision, it makes no difference what kind
of measuring reed was used, but it wasn't a vision.

The text tells us about a four-cornered building aligned on
the four cardinal points of the compass. The man in bronze
measured a court that was *a hundred cubits long, and a hundred
cubits broad*. Ezekial observed that 'on all the walls round
about in the inner room and the nave were carved likenesses
of cherubim and palm trees', and that 'Every cherub had two
faces.' A cherub is defined as a semi-divine hybrid figure, half-

animal, half-human. Do the beings with two faces represent flying messengers of the gods? Or flying beings like those eagles that Eve saw when she described the heavenly chariots? Were they flying jaguars or mechanical products? The question-marks remain, but cherubs are always connected with flying.

The book contains an important fact about the complex. Water, i.e. a river, flowed from below the *south end* of the temple *towards the eastern region* to end in *a sea*.

Remarkably concrete data for a vision!

Equally precise facts are given about the structure of the temple complex:

> Adjoining the twenty cubits which belonged to the inner court, and facing the pavement which belonged to the outer court, was gallery against gallery in three stories. And before the chambers was a passage inward, ten cubits wide and a hundred cubits long, and their doors were on the north. Now the upper chambers were narrower, for the galleries took more away from them than the lower and middle chambers in the building.

The Göttingen Bible says that ledges of rock projected into the stories, that the stories were built in three steps and consequently were narrower than the lower and middle chambers. Hence the upper chambers were set back from the ground more than the lower and middle ones.

This is the Göttingen Bible's laconic commentary: 'This seems to imply that in view of the uneven site the whole building consisted of three sections each of which was slightly set back from its neighbour.'

The devoutest of all devout theologians must surely begin to doubt whether this was only a vision. Surely if almighty God desired to show a temple he wanted built in Israel in the future, one brilliant gleaming image would have been enough? Would he have given details of how the visionary building was orientated towards different points of the compass? Would a vision contain mundane details such as the measurements of the rooms and passages, and say how the building was stepped on the uneven ground? Would it mention a stream that flowed eastwards into the sea? The theologians themselves

I had climbed out of the labyrinth high above the main entrance. The temple complex was spread out below me.

The Solomonic Temple at Jerusalem also had an infrastructure of subterranean corridors.

Over the centuries the reliefs have lost some clarity of outline, but one
can still make out robot-like beings on them.

Originally the heads protruded from the walls on tenons.

The American W. C. Bennett excavated more than two dozen very strange heads.

In the Forest of the Statues I greet a person with a frightening face.

'The Bishop' in strange surroundings.

A moon-faced monolith sits on a mossy mound. It looks just like a modern work of art.

This triangular skull lies in the grass near the Bishop, guarded by a bird of prey.

A tumulus is surrounded by 30 monoliths. In the centre there is a dolmen which could equally well be standing in France! (Unfortunately the gods did not send me sun every day, or I would have used it to take photos with more contrast.)

Two figures and two menhirs support the roof; below it stands a squat figure holding a necklace from which a skull dangles.

Sarcophagi are cut out of one block of stone like bathtubs. Nearly all of them were empty when found.

(16) reject the idea that Ezekiel could have been describing the temple of Jerusalem:

> We do not know anything about such a source in the temple from the text. For we can scarcely identify it with the waters of Shiloah that flow softly; they flow in an entirely different direction.

But Ezekiel has taken special note of this stream:

> And wherever the river goes every living creature which swarms will live, and there will be very many fish ... And on the banks on both sides of the river, there will grow all kinds of trees for food. Their leaves will not wither nor their fruit fail, but they will bear fresh fruit every month ...

No stream flowing out of Jerusalem has banks teeming with life. The fuss that theological interpreters have made about the river in their religious zeal is incredible. As everything in the Dead Sea is literally dead and there can be no question of it teeming with fish, the river described by Ezekiel is dismissed as *a vision of the future!*

In order to breathe even visionary life into the river (that did not exist in Jerusalem), translators and exegetists use two tricks. There is not a single word about the 'Dead Sea' in Ezekiel, so it has been sneaked into the translation (16):

> Furthermore 'the sea' must be called the 'Dead Sea' even in the translation, since the reference is obvious to a Jewish but not to a German reader, and a translation has little value if its meaning has to be explained in a note.

Next the second trick!

After 'the river' received a name by deliberate addition to the text, it is turned into a miraculous ecological happening in the future:

First commentary (14):

> Now Ezekiel sees a second miracle. Countless trees stand in the previously barren country round the river and transform the unfertile desert into flourishing verdant land ... the river flows with the same power down into the Jordanian depression to terminate in the salt waters of the Dead Sea

... The miracle-working waters flowing from the temple leave us in no doubt about which type of narrative this chapter drew on for its images and colours; it is the river of paradise, the waters of which gladden the city of God.

Second commentary (17):

It would be a false start to waste scholarly criticism on such fantasies.
The idea of a glorification of nature is most likely ...'

Third commentary (12):

According to this, Ezekiel's expectation that in the future the temple spring will grow into a powerful river which will irrigate the barren eastern part of Judah and even make the Dead Sea pure again is perfectly intelligible. If true divine service is to take place in the temple at some time, its barren surroundings have to turn into an orchard.

Fourth commentary (18):

Describes the stream of living water which emerges from the temple and makes the land fertile and the Dead Sea pure.

Fifth commentary (16):

In the case of such visions, why look for natural connections of such doubtful value? At all events for us Christians, provided we are not merely dry as dust textual critics, this sacred river has the significance of a divine prophecy ... we recognise in it and in its workings a delightful symbol of the blessings of the holy spirit.

Vision. Prophecy. Illumination. If we follow the commentaries, Ezekiel promised an orchard and a river that would irrigate Judah, and make the Dead Sea pure. None of that has happened. Israel is still waiting for the river of paradise and the delightful blessings of the holy spirit.
In other words, criticism should not be wasted and the whole story should be accepted as a glorification of nature.

If Schliemann had treated Homer like that, Troy would probably have remained undiscovered.

In 1889 the archaeologist Georges Perrot, together with his collaborator Charles Chipiez, used the text of Ezekiel to draw a reconstruction of the temple. The two scholars took additional descriptions from the Book of Kings.

Exact reconstruction met with difficulties when it came to the unit of measurement. Which cubit had the *man in bronze* used? The Babylonian cubit of 45.8 cm or the Egyptian cubit of 52.5 cm? Or was the cubit based on some other measurement? It really does not matter, for in any case an enormous building rose from the ground.

Perrot stumbled on one fact that should not have surprised him on careful consideration:

> If we study Ezekiel more closely, we shall see that the actual temple is described in less detail than the courts and fore-courts surrounding it. Actually these outer areas should have been less important to the prophet than the sanctuary. At first sight, this disproportion is surprising, but there must be a good reason for it.

The authors came up with a paradox. They said that presumably Ezekiel did not deal with the sanctuary in detail because it was well known to the Israelites. But in fact the majority of Israelites did not go further than the outer and inner courts and so knew them better than the sanctuary, which was not accessible to everybody. Then why did Ezekiel describe the outer areas so carefully?

The theologian Rudolf Smend also attempted a graphic reconstruction (12) in the last century and was surprised that the measurements of the temple were confined to length and breadth, 'with two exceptions, which are not really exceptions (Ezekiel 40.5 and 41.8)'.

These nil returns do not surprise me. The *man in bronze* realised that not much evidence of the height would be left in thousands of years. All that mattered were the measurements of the foundation walls at ground level. But the fact that Ezekiel did not take down any measurements of heights refutes the theologians' wishful thinking that the prophet described, in his hallucinations, a building to be built in the future. Heights would have been indispensable for a future building. If the interpreters would come out of their hiding places and admit that Ezekiel recorded a real building and its measurements, the mystery would be solved.

Attempts at reconstruction constantly get confused because of the assumption by the faithful that Solomon's temple in Jerusalem must have been the model. This error produces discrepancies which Rudolf Smend freely admits:

> The remaining verses cannot possibly mean 'in the pillars of the gate' and anyway it would be absurd ... In this case the expression would also be nonsensical, because gate and hall would naturally collapse ... it seems impossible for such chambers to be by all gates, because the slaughter tables [for the religious killing of living animals — E.v.D.], from which they cannot be separated, were located at only one door, the east door ... if the burnt offerings, the sin offerings and the guilt offerings were to be slaughtered on the north side of the altar, then our passage is contradictory again.

Given an exit in the wrong position, a lot of work must have been done to fit it into the scheme of the Solomonic temple.

Like Smend, the theologian and philosopher Otto Thenius (20) was amazed by the lack of heights when he attempted a reconstruction, but also astonished by the dry exact description:

> One examines the flat description, with no adornment, of the individual measurements down to the breadth of the gates and the strength of the walls and takes into account that according to this description a ground plan, and only a ground plan, can be drawn. If we assume the description to be a figment of the imagination, we get no answer to the question why Ezekiel did not give a single measurement of height for the temple ... Of course! It was not a figment of the imagination.

The theologian Eduard Reuss (1804–91), a leading representative of historical and critical theology, had difficulties with a reconstruction:

There are insuperable difficulties regarding other elements
... the 66-cubit-high columns are suspicious to us ... in
order to find the 25 cubits of the whole breadth we must
count the thickness of the rear wall in addition to the
measurements of the passage and the watch chambers that
are not mentioned here ... What does 'doors against doors'
or 'from one door to another' mean? Are we to postulate
doors in the rear wall of the watch chambers leading to the
court?

Thenius hit two nails on the head. A ground plan can be
drawn on the basis of the Ezekiel text and there is no answer
to the question of the missing heights if we assume that it was
a vision.

Taken as a whole, the attempts at reconstruction stand on
shaky feet. Measurements and supposition — for example,
by which walls, altars and washbasins are supposed to have
stood — are taken from other biblical sources and fitted into
the Solomonic temple.

In spite of some contradictions, 'Ezekiel' supplies perfectly
practical data which give an idea of what he was shown on
the *high mountain*.

My theories:

1. The temple as described by Ezekiel did exist. Ezekiel's
descriptions — and/or those of his co-authors — are not the
product of a vision. No architectonic plan for a temple to be
erected in the future was projected in a vision.

In a vision hard facts about the terrain on which the temple
was to be constructed would have been ridiculous and indications of slopes and rocks penetrating the future temple absurd.
I think a vision which risks planting productive trees with
luxuriant fruit, trees with leaves that do not wither, by that
stream or river, borders on the grotesque. All that in the
Jerusalem area! Moreover, it is not true that the prophet
himself registered everything, the man in bronze also knew
the details. Where did he get them from?

The fact that the future is used in the biblical text for the
description, 'on the banks, on both sides of the river, there
will grow all kinds of trees for food. Their leaves *will* not
wither, nor their fruit fail,' is based on the translator's grammatical judgement.

The special cubit used by the man in bronze militates against the assumption of a vision. Ezekiel was a preacher and prophet, not an architect. He could not 'create' accurate measurements out of his conscious or subconscious mind; even the actual technique of taking measurements would have been alien to him. The temple measurements would not have existed without the man in bronze.

The use of the first person in Ezekiel's description speaks in favour of an eyewitness account. Anyone who rejects his testimony as unreal stamps the whole book as a fantastic lie.

How are our industrious exegetes going to fill this explosive vacuum?

In the Book of Ezekiel, the Ark of the Covenant is not mentioned in either the general description of the temple or the record of the sanctuary. If the Solomon's temple had been the subject of the report, the most important of all relics, the Ark of the Covenant, would certainly not have been forgotten.

2. Ezekiel was describing the temple complex of Chavín de Huantar in the Peruvian Andes.

More modest than the scholars who profess to know everything as if they had been there in 573 BC, when the prophet is supposed to have had his 'vision', I summarise more than a dozen coincidences and leave the critical reader to form his own judgement.

1st coincidence	Ezekiel was brought to a very high mountain which he did not know in a heavenly chariot. Chavín de Huantar lies on such a mountain and it was unknown to Ezekiel until his arrival.
2nd coincidence	Ezekiel saw *a structure like a city* opposite him. Archaeologists have proved that an extensive urban settlement was once located near Chavín de Huantar.
3rd coincidence	Ezekiel described a temple, the main façade and main gate of which faced east. As at Chavín de Huantar.
4th coincidence	Ezekiel' complex was constructed in three steps on three superimposed terraces — as at Chavín de Huantar.
5th coincidence	In Ezekiel's account the outer court could

be reached by three gates facing north, south and east. As at Chavín de Huantar. For the Castillo stood to the west.

6th coincidence	The 'inner court' measured by the man in bronze had sides of about 50 m. My Israeli friends and I measured 49.70 m at Chavín de Huantar.
7th coincidence	Four steps led from the inner court of Ezekiel's report to the four cardinal points of the compass. Exactly like Chavín de Huantar.
8th coincidence	The man in bronze measures the space between the side rooms as five cubits. That works out at 2.29 m using the Babylonian cubit and 2.62 m using the Egyptian cubit. My Israeli friends and I read off 2.30 m on our tape.
9th coincidence	Ezekiel saw the likeness of cherubim on inner and outer walls. As at Chavín de Huantar.
10th coincidence	According to Ezekiel a river flowed from below the south end of the threshold. In present-day Chavín de Huantar the stream flows down from the south, but touches the complex at the south-east corner.
11th coincidence	The water in Ezekiel's account became a river flowing to the eastern part of the country. At Chavín de Huantar the little Mosna at first flows eastwards to the town of Huycaybamba, where it joined the Rio Marañon. The Marañon originally flows in a northerly direction, but then turns exactly eastward for several thousand kilometres to the basin of the Amazon, which debouches into the Atlantic Ocean.
12th coincidence	The man in bronze describes to the prophet the area where the river flows as teeming with life, the water as full of very many fish. This description fits in perfectly with the Rio Marañon and the Amazon.
13th coincidence	The man in bronze praises the extra-

	ordinary fertility of this region with ever-green trees and fruits. There could be no better description of the rich vegetation on the banks of the Marañon and the Amazon.
14th coincidence	The sacred number '7' plays as an important at part at Chavín de Huantar as it does among the Israelites.
15th coincidence	Ezekiel described his experiences between 592 and 570 BC. Chavin de Huantar was built between 800 and 500 BC! Given the latitude in archaeological dating already mentioned, a gap of 200 years would still allow a chronological correspondence, even if the original text were 200 years older than is now assumed.
16th coincidence	The man in bronze told Ezekiel that his people had built him *a new temple here*. Chavín de Huantar originated out of the blue. It had no forerunners.

Far fewer coincidences stimulated Heinrich Schliemann to excavate at Hissarlik.

To be quite fair I shall also mention data given by Ezekiel which cannot be made to tally with those at Chavín de Huantar. In Ezekiel the whole temple complex is square. Perhaps Chavin de Huantar was also square originally, but then we would need to know where its eastern border was located, for it is unrecognisable today. Ezekiel's sanctuary formed a square with sides measuring 50 m. This size does not match that of the Castillo. It measures 70 by 72.90 m, only approximately a square. The crucial point is that we do not know if later redactors corrected the measurements in Ezekiel's account so that they could squash the Solomonic temple on to the vision. Professor Walther Eichrodt (14) refers to this possibility: 'Certain stylistic peculiarities suggest that here too [he refers to the measurements — E.v.D.], the text was altered by someone else ...'

Obviously the wooden panelling mentioned by Ezekiel can no longer be checked at Chavín de Huantar. Nothing is left of wood in a minimum period of 2,500 years, even if there is no fire. Nor could I discover any palm trees in the works of art, unless one tried to make out these tropical growths in some of the stylisations. In my opinion, animal-cum-human representations of the kind found at Chavín de Huantar could also have been mentioned in the original text, apart from the cherubs. These then fell victims to collaborators and censors to whom such pictorial elements were inopportune. The unintelligible was left out. No wonder that the Book of Ezekiel ends abruptly.

There is still something peculiar about Ezekiel. Some years ago a press report landed on my desk. Additions to the Ezekiel text had turned up in the caves of Qumran on the Dead Sea. I wrote to all the relevant addresses in the hope of seeing the finds. All in vain. Even a well-intentioned person is bound to think that there was information in the text that had to be withheld from the public. Some of the celebrated Dead Sea Scrolls are preserved in a special hall in the Israeli Museum in Jerusalem. I do not know why the architect of this Shrine

Some of the famous Dead Sea Scrolls are housed in a special hall of the Israeli Museum in Jerusalem. The architect conceived it in the shape of a UFO. Memories of the future?

of the Book conceived it in the shape of a UFO. Perhaps he shared my ideas about 'chariots of the gods'.

I realise that I have produced no *proof* of the correctness of my theories, in spite of that large accumulation of 'coincidences'. Somewhere in the world there may be other temples that fit Ezekiel's description better than the building at Chavín de Huantar. I hope that at least I have contributed to bringing the visions of chariots and temple more realistically under the critical magnifying glass.

The man in bronze had cogent reasons for flying Ezekiel to South America.

At some time between 1,000 and 500 BC the extraterrestrials reappeared. They enticed a group of Israelites — the Nephites of the Book of Mormon — to South America. They instructed the emigrants, gave them the compass and protected them.

This group was told to build a temple in South America on the model of the temple of Solomon. The Nephites and their helpers set to work, obeying 'divine' instructions. When the temple was completed one of the 'gods' flew the man in bronze to Babylon in a shuttle craft, landing near the river Chebar where Ezekiel and other Israelites were imprisoned. The man in bronze recognised Ezekiel as the spiritual leader of the group. He flew him to Chavín de Huantar and showed him the temple recently completed by the Nephites.

What was the point of it all?

To lay trails for the future! *We are the addressees*. The extraterrestrials intended Ezekiel's descendants to discover and recognise the connections — at some time in the future. They deposited in the past a time bomb for the future.

If extraterrestrials were on the earth in Babylonian times, they must have left traces of their presence in the art and literature of the region, I hear someone complain. *But they did*. We make the mistake of not taking the traditions literally and not interpreting the works of art through the spectacles of modern technology.

I shall never forget one long night spent in my home with some archaeologists who are good friends of mine.

As I am often ill at ease in the periphery of archaeology, I asked some heretical questions. I asked what we were to make of finds which do not fit into the framework, for example with technical relics which would make nonsense of all previous assumptions? Technical finds from the earliest times? They would be looked on as a dirty trick played by some envious colleague. And then? If such a find proved to be 'not of this earth' or not fitting into an already established civilisation, scholars would keep quiet about it. There was a lot of laughter about it, but it dawned on me how irresponsible this attitude was, even in jest. Sacrosanct doctrines must not be shaken.

The man in bronze sensed this when he said to Ezekiel: 'Son of man, you dwell in the midst of a rebellious house, who have eyes to see, but see not, who have ears to hear, but hear not.'

P.S. At the beginning of this chapter, Hans Selye saved me from an attack of stress. May I quote the professor again at the end of it?

Theories are indispensable. They arouse opposition, but that has its good side, because it reveals the weak points in our conceptions and shows research the direction it must take. Even a theory that does not fit all the known facts is valuable, so long as it fits better than any other hypothesis.

4 The Strategy of the Gods

(As Seen from Colombia)

'God created men because he was disappointed with monkeys. After that he gave up experimenting.'

Mark Twain (1835–1910)

'If you come here I can help you Stop Correspondence pointless Greetings Dr Miguel Forero.'

This telegram put a full stop to a series of letters I had written over a period of months to Bogotá, the capital of Colombia.

The reason for my correspondence was an article (1), 'Indio-Kultur im Dschungel,' which I had read in *Der Spiegel* on 1 February 1981. In it I learnt that mysterious cities had recently been discovered in the Colombian jungle and that the men who built them *had known more about relations with the cosmos than we do today*. That was not a reporter's opinion, but the view of Professor Soto Holguin, who was in charge of the excavations. Archaeologists are conservative in their judgements and do not willingly stick their necks out.

That was why the news excited me. Were the men of an extinct Indian civilisation supposed to have understood more about terrestrial relations with the cosmos than the brilliant children of the second millennium AD now drawing to its close? Perhaps I could find a new building stone for my theory in Colombia.

What kind of jungle cities were they and which ancient Indian tribes had built them? I read in the article that the excavation area was cordoned off by the army. Would it even be possible to visit it? At three-weekly intervals I patiently penned these questions to Professor Soto Holguin of the *Universidad de los Andes*, whom I had never met. All my letters remained unanswered. Perhaps he had something against me. Finally I turned to Dr Miguel Forero, a lawyer, with whom

Dr Miguel Forero, a Bogotá lawyer.

I have been corresponding for years. His telegram arrived promptly. If Forero cabled me to come in person, there must be a reason for it. Soon Bogotá was included in my travel plans for South America and I arranged to stop off there on my way back from Peru.

Forero was waiting for me at the airport with his extremely bright 16-year-old son Juan Carlos. During the half-hour taxi ride to the Hilton I came straight to the point: 'Do these jungle cities exist?'

'What you are looking for is called Ciudad Perdida, the lost city. It lies in the virgin forest of the Sierra Nevada, six days' journey from Santa Marta on the Caribbean Sea.'

'Why don't we hear more about it?'

'The excavation zone is cordoned off by the army. The archaeologists want it to themselves.'

'Have you any influence with Professor Soto?'

'Not yet, but I'll soon remedy that.'

'Will it take long?'

Dr Forero said I would have to wait four or five days. Apart from Professor Soto, he would have to get in touch with the army, without whose permission I would not be allowed to visit Ciudad Perdida.

Wait four or five days? That went against the grain. Time is the only asset that cannot be preserved or increased. The sulky look on my face must have spoken volumes, for Forero thought hard about how to keep me busy in the meantime.

'San Agustín! Have you ever been to San Agustín?'

I had. I was on the point of saying 'naturally', for South America had virtually become my home of the gods. But I had only spent one day there and that was too short for a thorough examination of the village and its unsolved mysteries. I grabbed at the opportunity. That very evening I booked a flight to Pitalito, a little town 500 km from Bogotá.

San Agustín was more than a way of passing the time.

At two o'clock the next day, the Aeropesca jet landed at the airport, recently built at a height of 1,730 m. If anyone asked me for my first impressions and the special characteristic of Pitalito's taxi-drivers, I wouldn't have to hesitate for a moment. They all had luxuriant moustaches! I refuse to be swamped by the torrent of verbiage from these hirsute gentlemen and Hernandez became my driver because of his trusty-looking Land-Rover.

It is one hour's drive from the airport to San Agustín, a delightful trip through the blue-green mountain scenery. The village is only a few kilometres from the 1,550 km long river Magdalena, the largest in Colombia. It was often visible, glittering in the sunlight far below in the precipitous depths.

The modest little village would have remained unknown had it not been for the term San Agustín Culture bestowed on it because of its famous megaliths.

Hernandez was disappointed when I said goodbye to him in front of the Hotel Yalconia outside the village, because throughout the journey he had praised himself eloquently as the best guide for foreigners. Tourists usually engage guides. Hernandez did not understand that I wanted to be alone.

In 1758 the Spanish monk Juan de Santa wrote the book *Wonders of Nature* (*Maravillas de la Naturaleza*). In it he gave a vivid description of the mysterious stone statues worshipped by the Indians in the valley of San Agustín.

Ninety nine years later the Italian General Codazzi, then Head of Colombia's Geographical Commission, travelled in and around San Agustín. Codazzi was a good draughtsman and sketched 34 statues and four altars. As a trained army man, he did an accurate cartographical job. He made a plan of the whole terrain, including the statues on their correct sites.

In 1857 Codazzi stood where I now stood and was puzzled, as I was. At first he thought that the statues were petrified representatives of a 'transcendental world', then he tried to fit the stone figures into the context of a religious system, but finally he was unable to explain the meaning and purpose of the layout. He had nothing to be ashamed of, for no one since Codazzi has found the answer.

In 1892 the famous German archaeologist, geologist and traveller Alphons Stübel (1835–1904) drew more statues, which were published in 1906 in his book *Vulkanberge von Kolumbien*. This attracted the attention of other German academics.

In 1911, Karl Theodor Stöpel, the Heidelberg professor, paid a visit and had the first plaster casts of the statues made. Stöpel found that the figures were mainly made of ferrous sandstone, granite and volcanic stone. He was the first man to discover the subterranean passages at San Agustín and explore them in detail (2). This is what he wrote about them:

> The same temple is laid out with massive stone flags on either side and is covered with a large stone slab, like the preceding one. Creeping through the roots of trees I managed to gain the interior and was surprised to find a lateral passage leading in a south-westerly direction, presumably leading to the other temple, the site of which has not yet been located. I would have dearly loved to explore this passage thoroughly, but had not the time. I followed it for about 30 m, but could not persuade my companions to go any farther with me. However, in the impenetrable forest region, one can realise from holes in the ground, often several metres deep, that these temples had subterranean connections with each other.

Remarkable. Today, only about 80 years later, no one wants to know about subterranean links between temples and statues. Did they lapse into oblivion? Did they hide secrets which it was inopportune to show to the public? Is it because the passages, if they really exist, do not fit into the schema which was cobbled up in the archaeological conjurer's workshops to explain the miracle of San Agustín? At any rate, the renowned Indian scholar Felicitas Barreto, who spent some time at San Agustín, told me that there were artificial subterranean passages stretching for kilometers.

Finally, the ethnologist Konrad Theodor Preuss (1869–1938), the then Director of the Museum of Ethnology in Berlin, made the first scientific survey of San Agustín (3) in 1912. He took precise measurements of everything he saw, opened a number of tombs, examined gigantic stone sarcophagi and was astounded to find them empty:

> The directions in which the chests and their openings point are too numerous for us to be able to draw any conclusions as to the meaning of the figures, and the tombs, too, are not all in the same lengthways direction, while the position of the head of the dead persons cannot be determined for the simple reason that no traces of the skeletons remain ... We may assume that the very small number of stone tombs,

namely those fitted with stone coffins, were only intended for important persons. As I did not find the slightest trace of skeletons in them, I had to conclude that they have crumbled to dust.

That is strange, too! Either the grave robbers worked so well that they did not leave the slightest trace behind them or the dead were never buried in the sarcophagi.

The empty burial sites of San Agustín reminded me of the celebrated dolmens in Brittany. Dolmens are artificial hills characterised by massive, erect unhewn stones topped by one (or more) flattish stones. The dolmens were often heaped with earth so that they look like bulges in the landscape. Prehistorians believe that the dolmens were graves. The only snag is that no skeletons have been found inside them.

Are we on the wrong track? Were these putative graves never really graves at all, either in Brittany or at San Agustín? Did the sarcophagi conceal objects that the people of those days believed to be dangerous and so covered them with earth? Could they have been gifts from the 'gods', relics of an unknown technology? Perhaps later generations assessed the danger of the objects differently and took them from their hiding place, or grave-robbers may have recognised their great value and stole what was hidden in the sarcophagi.

Professor Preuss christened certain statues at San Agustín 'moon queen' and 'sun god'. He was convinced that the stonemasons intended to represent a 'second I' in many figures. The idea is tempting, because many statues are two-storeyed. The main figure bears a second figure on its back. The I in the I? I do not think much of the idea.

The sights of San Agustín are divided into four main sectors: the Archaeological Park with the 'Forest of the Statues', the 'Spring of the Foot Washing', and the 'Hill of the Foot Washing', the 'Hill of the Idols', an artificial horseshoe-shaped plateau, El Tablon and La Chaquira, two sites high above the River Magdalena, with statues and figures carved out of the rock. In the evening, at my hotel I was struck by a strange idea which I immediately checked on the map. I found confirmation on it.

San Agustín is the only place in South America from which waters flow in the three main directions of the Atlantic, the Pacific and the Amazon basin.

The River Magdalena, which has its source up here, ends in the Atlantic Ocean. Only a few kilometres away streams descend from the 4,700 m high Purace to join the Rio Patia which in turn finally flows into the Pacific Ocean in the Bay of Tomaco. Lastly, there are the little rivers, Rio Orteguaza and Rio Caqueta, the sources of which are near San Agustín. They meet in the Rio Yaro, which becomes the Rio Japura on Brazilian territory and flows into the Amazon. This network of rivers represents an astonishing hydrographic situation! Did this fact turn San Agustín into a place of pilgrimage?

All we need to imagine is that Indians from various regions came upstream to see where the life-giving water came from. Inevitably Indians from the Pacific, the Amazon basin and the Colombian area on the edge of the Andes must have met in the mountain valley of San Agustín! Does this 'meeting of the peoples' explain the variety of the figures in the 'Forest of the Statues' at San Agustín? Did every Indian society once sacrifice to its gods in its own way at the source of *its* river, in order to conclude with the deities a covenant guaranteeing a continuous flow of water? Perhaps Amazon Indians placed a valuable gift in a sarcophagus, and their colleagues from the Pacific stole it, buried it elsewhere or destroyed it.

That was an idea that flashed into my head over my evening whisky. The next few days were to show that it was not so stupid.

I walk through the 'Valley of the Statues'. What a variety of figures! The some 200 robot-like sculptures on Easter Island in the Pacific, with their identical dour looks, are a boring lot of dummies in comparison with the wealth of artistic ideas found at San Agustín. So far 328 monuments have been found here.

In passing I greet a person only 1.15 m high. He crouches in front of a tree-trunk, with a broad flattened nose, terrifying Dracula teeth and hands raised as if in blessing above the relief of a kind of step pyramid.

On a mossy hillock made of layers of stones rests a

This almond-eyed figure is putting an embryonic something into its mouth.

moonfaced monolith — remains of a body? — with enormous eyebrows and a muzzle once again showing four Dracula teeth, a timeless creation which would not look out of place in a modern art gallery.

An almond-eyed figure introduces an embryonic something into its mouth. Broad noses and Dracula teeth seem to have been suggested by a characteristic prototype, which has set the fashion here.

In the hot humid jungle, a stunted figure under a corrugated iron roof licks an ice cream, excuse me, pushes a titbit between his frightening teeth, his grim face peering suspiciously from under the crescent moons over his eyes.

A demonic parade of idols!

The next free-standing figure makes me withdraw my boorish remark about the parade of idols, for its official title is 'The Bishop'. More than four metres high, the human face, with its large melancholy eyes, does command respect,

Under a corrugated iron roof in the hot, humid jungle, a remarkable type appears to be licking an ice cream.

This bird of prey is eating a snake that writhes round its stomach.

but after lengthy scrutiny I could not discover anything episcopal about this stone man. The Bishop is squeezing a tiny child, whose head and hands dangle downwards. It looks as if this fine fellow's next move would be to enjoy crushing the child between his fangs. Episcopal?

Ten metres beyond this dignitary, a triangular skull peeps out of the grass. Giant eyes, giant nose, giant muzzle and giant fangs show that he belongs to an alien race. But the head has its guardian — a bird like an eagle. The haughty bird of prey is consuming a snake which is helpfully curling round its bulging belly. A symbol to show that flying beings could also cope with the most poisonous animal on the planet?

Or did the eagle with the snake bring friendly greetings from Mexico? For, according to the German ethnologist Horst Nachtigall (4), the same representation is found there:

The eagle with a snake in its beak at San Agustín has an astonishing parallel in Mexican stone sculpture. On his second Mexican expedition Dupaix [researcher in the last century — E.v.D.] found in the Hermitage of La Soledad in the valley of Oaxaca a stone about one metre square, on which the same scene of an eagle with a snake held in its claws and beak is represented ... The Mexican state coat of arms shows the same scene today.

Yes, all very fine and most interesting, but it is about 3,000 km as the crow flies from Oaxaca in Mexico, the location of an eagle with a snake, to San Agustín, the site of the other! It is possible that one culture influenced the other, that Indians migrated from one place to another, but it is also possible that these companion pieces originated because the way in which an eagle strikes a snake was once observed both in Mexico and here in Colombia.

Not far from the standing eagle figure is an imposing tumulus, surrounded by more than 30 monoliths. In the centre is a dolmen of the kind to be found in France. Two figures and two menhirs support the stone slab of the roof. The two guardians of the tomb hold clubs — or are they axes? They are helmeted and over their heads hover faces apparently carrying the roof slab while in flight. Between the guardians and the menhirs behind them, a squat figure is holding a necklace from which hangs a skull.

There are many of these massive dolmens, vast monolithic works of granite, at San Agustín. One slab, for example, 4.38 m long, 3.60 m wide and 30 cm thick, rests as if weightless on menhirs rising 2.50 m from the ground. Such weights cannot be lifted without cranes and scaffolding. The builders of the 'Forest of the Statutes' were certainly not the primitive Indians we are asked to take them for. Like the builders at Stonehenge and Carnac in France, they must have set to work with tried and tested techniques in order to move such stone monsters in mountainous country. Oh yes, one incidental point. There is hardly any granite in the valley of San Agustín! Imported? How?

Often sarcophagi formed from a single block of stone lie under the dolmens, like giant chiselled bathtubs. So I ask: Were the sarcophagi originally containers for divine figures

Massive dolmens and menhirs lie in and on the ground at San Agustin. Such weights cannot be lifted without cranes or scaffolding. The Indians could not have been so primitive as we think they were.

and not for aristocratic corpses? Did people hope to win the favour of the gods by enclosing their stone reproductions in sarcophagi?

Were they so afraid of their wrath that they imprisoned their images deep in the earth?

Even the waiters in the hotels of San Agustín are great propagandists for the local sights.

One afternoon torrents of tropical rain poured down from lowering clouds. It was impossible to distinguish separate drops; it was as if a gigantic hose was deluging the country. The water clattered on the roofs of the dolmens, spurting back in fountains, washing the statues as it had done for thousands of years and rustling the leathern leaves of the tropical trees. The ground was steaming. By soaking gravel paths I reached the Yalconia dripping wet and sat by the fire, the heat of which dried me off outside, while whisky warmed my innards.

Long familiar with my programme, the waiter exhorted me at all costs to include a visit to the 'Spring of the Foot Washing', stretching his arms expressively to show the size of the complex. It was an absolute marvel, a maze of channels and water basins, decorated with reliefs of animals and human faces. It was a real puzzle and he was curious to find out what I would have to say about it.

At first I did not say anything, for I was speechless when I turned my astonished eyes from a framework of planks and steps to the stone miracle below me.

Over a surface area of some 300 sq m, the flattened brownish rocks contained a complicated network of handmade channels of various widths and narrow grooves, of depressions which curved through the rock like snakes, of systematically arranged large and small basins, of rectangles and circles. Reliefs of lizards, salamanders and ape-like animals appeared on the rock and the sides of the basins.

Within my range of sight, I counted 3 rectangular main basins, and more than 30 separate engravings. The labyrin-

A small selection of the many shapes at the 'Spring of the Foot Washing'.

thine channels, through which the water is led in a bewildering play, cannot be counted, but you can observe the direction of the water. It flows, dropping from one channel into another, and continues on its way as soon as it reaches a certain water-mark. The largest basin is 3.20 m long, 1.40 m wide and 81 cm deep.

In the tourist guidebook (5), published by the Colombian National Institute for Anthropology, it says:

Everything points to the fact that this was a sacred place, probably for religious ceremonies and ritual bathing. We find three water basins of different degrees of workmanship, corresponding to a certain social hierarchy. The most richly decorated was presumably for princes and priests, the second, with less ornamentation, for other eminent personages and the third and simplest for the people.

The German archaeologist H. D. Disselhoff (6) states quite boldly: It does not require too much imagination to postulate a water and fertility cult here. His colleague Horst Nachtigall (4) is a little more cautious about the purpose of the labyrinth:

> Perez de Barradas [Colombian archaeologist — E.v.D.] thinks of a water and fertility cult and believes that the basins and channels must have served to receive the blood of human sacrifices, which can neither be proved nor contradicted. The significance of the complex is unknown.

That is frank speaking! How quickly archaeologists are on the spot with some cult or other when they cannot grasp something. How quickly some pedant's catalogue description leads us astray — for example the 'Spring of the Foot Washing'!

In this particular case interdisciplinary collaboration would have been a good idea. Possibly some metallurgist would have realised long ago that the arrangement of channels, furrows and basins was ideally suited to the separation and purification of molten metals of various kinds. If that could be established — and why not? — it was not foot washing that took place at San Agustin, but applied metallurgy: molten metal flowed from basin to basin, heavy particles sank to the bottom, lighter ones were carried farther, impure fragments and slag were caught in the filters of the circles and snaking grooves — a refinery built out of the rock.

The 'Spring of the Foot Washing' is not unique, a one-off achievement. I have seen a similar layout about 2,800 km away as the crow flies at El Fuerte in Bolivia.

The barren mountain peak of El Fuerte lies near Samaipata,* a little Indian village in the Bolivian jungle, five hours' drive from the city of Santa Cruz.

The mountain top resembles a pyramid made by human hands. Two parallel lines run from the bottom to the top. If we play the game 'it looks like', the images of launching ramps aligned on the heavens suggest themselves. At the upper end of the ramp, on top of the mountain, El Fuerte is flat. *And that is exactly where the 'double' of the 'Spring of the Foot*

---

* *The Gold of the Gods*, 1973; *In Search of Ancient Gods*, 1974.

A large-scale double of the 'Spring of the Foot Washing' can be found on top of the mountain El Fuerte in the Bolivian jungle.

Washing' can be found. The same labyrinth of basins, grooves, connecting channels, writhing snakes and figures, on a larger scale.

There is one suspicious difference from San Agustín. There is no spring and thus no flow of water at El Fuerte, on the highest point of the mountain, so that the wild invention of a water and fertility cult up here rapidly fades away.

Why did Indians carry out such laborious work on this mountain top?

The idea that solved the problem came not from me, but from the engineer Josef Blumrich, for many years head of NASA's Division for Project Construction at Huntsville, USA. I visted El Fuerte with him some years ago. Faced with the artificial stone labyrinth, he came up with the idea of a metal processing plant.

The pictures of El Fuerte and San Agustín speak for themselves. Whether archaeologists accept this suggestion or prefer to take refuge in a dubious cult, is not ultimately very important. But it is correct that the images prove that the cultures of El Fuerte and San Agustín had points of contact, in spite of the vast distances between them, with no roads through mountainous and tropical forests. Moreover, a water link between San Agustín and El Fuerte is conceivable. The Indians of El Fuerte could descend the Rio Mamore, which flows into the Rio Madeira, which in turn discharges into the Amazon below the present-day port of Manaus. Then the bold canoeists would have paddled up the Rio Japura to land at its source in the San Agustín region.

In spite of this theoretical link by waterways, I find it hard to believe that it was really used in practice.

The Amazon has so many tributaries to lead navigators astray that the Indian watersportsmen would have needed extremely accurate maps to reach their goal. Who could have done such hydrographic mapping in those days? Today we at last know the network of rivers in the Amazon region, but only because they were photographed by satellite from a height of 300 km.

It remains an exciting and important task to discover how the companion pieces of San Agustín and El Fuerte came into being.

I spent hours in front of and above the 'Spring of the Foot

Washing', watching tourists, who gaped at the labyrinth and certainly went away convinced that they had seen a genuine Indian footbath. The little stream of Quebrada de Lavapatas will giggle and continue to ripple past the wonder work for all eternity.

I climbed the 'Hill of the Foot Washing' up literally endless steps. The oldest archaeological traces were found up here on an artificially levelled plateau; they date back to 650 BC. This dating was taken by the carbon 14 method from the remains of wood and bones which lay on the ground around fallen statues. It cannot be established by this method whether the stone sculptures date to this period or to a much earlier one, as it is only applicable to organic finds.

Up here, on the crest of the artificially levelled hill, stands 'the Double I', *El doble yo*, incarnate in a human figure with both arms bent and hands folded over its chest. The grim face shows four fearsome fangs under the broad nose; a piercing

The 'double I' stands on top of the mountain. This figure carries an animal on its back. It stimulates the imagination to speculate why.

Yet another 'double I'. Once again a skull with enormous jaws carrying another being on its back.

look stares far into the valley from deep eye sockets. A tightly fitting helmet encloses the head.

Something after the pattern of the marsupials which were universal in the Cretaceous, the stone man carries an animal on his back — 'the double I'. Archaeology talks about a jaguar, which I was quite unable to recognise, as were other people I asked about it. A squat crest, almost as big as the head, pressed down on the rectangular skull. Does a jaguar look like that, even from a distance? Even granted the stylisation of their technique, the ancient stonemasons were closer to their subject than that.

Nearby is another figure, odder and more mysterious than its prominent neighbour. The face is carved in an abstract manner, with slit eyes above a broad mouth showing the obligatory Dracula teeth. What kind of an object this figure holds in its left hand simply baffles the imagination. The gruesome face is topped by a second 'skull', although it could equally well be something quite different.

Archaeological literature describes this monster as a 'crocodile'. I could not recognize a crocodile.

From scaffolding I examined the miracle in stone spread out at my feet.

El Fuerte also has a labyrinth of basins, grooves and channels. Was the whole site a metal-processing plant?

My stone Stone Age writer colleague.

Did idols dressed in animal skins appear at San Agustin?

The stones of Leyva: a row of twenty-four columns with others lying nearby.

A tumescent phallus 5.80 metres long. A memory of a fertility cult?

The strangest park I have ever visited.

Once again, as at Sete Cidades in Brazil, I walk over this reddish-grey honeycomb pattern formed by the cooling of the molten rock.

The model of the raft of El Dorado in the Gold Museum at Bogotá.

It is easy to find one's way in Bogotá, thanks to an intelligent road system.

With Juan Carlos in the Gold Museum. The visitor is constantly amazed by the wealth of treasures.

The four-seater Hughes helicopter flew me into the green hell.

Just before landing I took this snapshot of the topmost terrace. Could it also have been inspected from a great height in the remote past?

There is another fascinating sculpture on the plateau between the two above-mentioned figures — a monster carved out of a single block which the literature describes as a 'crocodile'. It is the first winged crocodile I have ever come across.

Even in a stylised version, the crocodile would have had long narrow jaws, not the squat muzzle that spreads almost across its head. Suppose someone tried to interpret the monster in the light of modern technology. He would recognise behind a wide open breathing apparatus (nose) two look-out holes (eyes) for pilots and to left and right the stumps of wings.

Ridiculous? If the 'gods' had inspected the Indians from a high speed shuttle craft, I would have every sympathy for the terrified stonemasons who represented the heavenly ship as a badly damaged crocodile. Even today the Papuans of New Guinea would perpetuate a landing Concorde as a being with outspread legs that plunged on to its prey with curved-down beak.

What does the 'double I' mean? As Sigmund Freud and his successors did not exist in those days, we cannot dabble in psychology or introduce schizophrenia as a solution. Those ancient artists created stylised images of what they had seen and experienced.

On the other side of the Alto de Lavapatas, the setting sun flashed from whitish grey clouds hanging deep into the valleys, gilding the grass and trees around me, while the mountains lit up on the horizon in the unreal blue of the approaching night.

An unsuspected writer colleague stood in my way, as if trying to draw my attention to trade union hours of work. Of course he was made of stone. He was getting his kicks from stereo music coming from his headphones. In his right hand, my strange colleague held a goose quill, a primitive writing tool. Or a knife which he held with the blade upwards. What else could it be? A scalpel? A flute? A blowpipe? And what was in his left hand? An eraser, if I was right about his profession. Am I right, sir, in assuming that you took down instructions from the heavenly ones? The model for this figure must have spent most of his time sitting. His short legs look stunted.

Once again sharp fangs protrude from an ugly mug. The

uniform style of the sculptors up here seems to indicate models that were not of this world, for according to my knowledge of evolution, our ancestors never at any stage had teeth of the kind that adorn a lion's mouth. My strange colleague wears lenses in front of his bulging eyes. What with the earphones and the Rex Harrison hat on his thick skull, he makes a most peculiar dwarf.

The artists who carved away up here understood a lot about representational art; they were masters of their craft. You see this everywhere in San Agustín. They made fine differentiations between men and beings resembling men, most of whom are given four monstrous Dracula teeth. Man must have been terrified of them; they left an indelible impression and that is why they constantly recur with their special characteristics. My little colleague with his tusks was certainly not of this world, either. Earphones and writing materials are strange attributes for this Lilliputian among the giants, but writers are always modest, even if they claim to receive their messages 'from above'.

The inevitable nocturnal rain tore me from my exchange of ideas with my fellow author. I rushed down the endless slippery steps, past a bamboo hedge, past images and gods who followed me enviously with their dripping eyes. They had to stick it out in the downpour; I could seek refuge by the fireside in the Hotel Yalconia. They stood out there, members of a crew of misunderstood witnesses to the remote past.

Pedro, a native tourist guide, persuaded me to conclude my week in San Agustín with a visit to el Alto de los Idolos, 'The Hill of the Idols'. I really wanted to fly home, but Pedro's enthusiasm won the day.

At the crack of dawn Pedro drove me down to the river Magdalena in the Land-Rover and then on to the Hill of the Idols. Up there the visitor finds a man-made plateau, shaped like a horseshoe, with the excavated debris sloping down from it.

It seems most likely that it was a burial ground. Horizontal stone graves, their sides formed of massive slabs, support this view, as do vertical cylindrical shaft graves and huge granite dolmens. Pedro had not exaggerated. This was a sight not to be missed.

I don't know if I am hypersensitive, but mysteries like this excite me, they fill me with awe, I sense the self-imposed mission of making my tiny contribution to the solution of the puzzle. When I see dolmens and menhirs up here on the plateau, I am immediately reminded of the dolmens and menhirs of Brittany.

Surely it is exciting that we still do not know how and why such monumental complexes were built in an unknown past? All the researchers suffer from the prejudice that modern man was the first to have an advanced technological civilisation. From that point of view the stone images made by our remote ancestors are assessed as primitive forms of expression. Yet who knows what our descendants will make of the sculptures of Henry Moore? Perhaps they will also look on them as the expression of the primitive art of our present, which will one day become the distant past.

In order to protect human life, governments and private individuals all over the world are building deep atomic shelters, primarily for survival, but also in the lurking hope that legacies of this age could provide later generations with information about our life in the second millennium.

Were the Indian tribes of San Agustín also afraid of annihilation? Did fear give them the strength to make vast bunkers underground and cover them with earth so that their refuges were unrecognisable from above? Did they want to save themselves alone or the images of the gods and their knowledge as well? I lay no claim to omniscience; I ask questions because I cannot bear being held back by scholarly taboos. Why are identical structures found in Europe and South America? What drove our forefathers to action? With elitist arrogance — our often overrated modern art may be an expression of the age — the barriers of knowledge are placed in front of the highly artistic works of the stonemasons of ancient times. But we have no right to set ourselves up as the culmination of a grandiose evolution of the human spirit. I share the views of Lao Tse, the Chinese sage, who lived around 300 BC: 'The best part of knowledge is to realise your own lack of knowledge.' But it also a continual spur to wanting to know more.

A few kilometres from the 'Hill of the Idols', just beyond the village of Isnos, I find another example of the 'double I' on the Hills of the Stones (Altos de las Piedras). This version was mentioned by Professor Preuss as early as 1913. It was accepted as fact by his colleagues, although Preuss himself was much more cautious:

> In the Mexican cultural zone we know of many gods' heads looking out of animal jaws, for example the Aztec tribal god Uitzilopochtilis looking out of the humming-bird's beak. This animal was then called the Disguise of the God and by that we understand the special form in which he may appear. Moreover it was looked on as identical with him or as his second nature. In our case, too [at San Agustín E.v.D.], we must undoubtedly look on the second head above the figure, whether it be animal or human, as a corporal extension of the main representation, as its second I. One could also postulate the heavenly nature of the god, since this second face appears above.

It is well known that primitive peoples dressed themselves in animal skins for their ritual dances, animals whose strength and characteristics they would have liked to possess. Does this trait also apply to the figures at San Agustín?

I do not know any idols, either in the original or in illustrations, that are concealed in animal skins. They do not even wear animal masks, although most of them have helmets. On close examination the bewildering ornamentation of the 'double I' — to be specific, the figure on the Hill of Stones — shows at least three faces, the third being under the rucksack with the second face, the three faces together forming a unity. Just because a dubious psychological explanation has been given, are we forbidden to ask more questions? Must Professor Preuss's theory remain in the literature unchallenged? Below I list a few ideas which offer alternatives to the prevailing opinion.

The main figure represents a priest. Above and behind him crouches the divine being who dominates him and accompanies him everywhere.

A human figure with a homunculus on top symbolises that man always has to carry the burdens of others.

The third being only emerges from the union of two beings.

The warning: man, be careful. Look out for what is happening behind your back.

The symbolisation of ancient myths which described the gods as helmeted beings, who were always accompanied by a second god. The myths say that the gods could see in all directions.

Scholars should introduce more sense or nonsense into the forest of the gods at San Agustín, so that speculation about the unsolved mystery does not come to a full stop. The helmeted figures with their excessively large teeth are certainly not meant to depict human beings. In a great many cases, the figures hold little men *without* Dracula teeth. In my view, that is how the representatives of two worlds were exhibited in stone.

Pedro had booked a friend with two horses on whose backs we rode up a steep mule-path to La Chaquira, a site high above the river Magdalena. A human figure peers from the rust-coloured rock, apparently blessing the river with out-spread arms and hands raised high. *No* frightening fangs emerge from the large mouth with its swollen lips. Delicate eyebrows are in correct relation to the shape of the face, as are the eyes.

The last doubt is removed. The stone carvers of San Agustín knew perfectly well how to differentiate between human faces and the demonic masks of gods and idols.

An Aeropesca jet flew me back to Bogotá, time enough to give free rein to my imagination.

I have been a scapegoat for the academic establishment for 15 years, but I am alive and well and I don't care. What am I doing, apart from making room for imagination? It is mostly locked up in dark dungeons in our day and age. Frightened people dare not say what they secretly think.

We live in a grey age which turns people into a drab uniform product. Birds of paradise are turned into sparrows, because they are in the majority. What goes in 'King Nobel's Royal Domain' and the universities is made into intellectual currency which is internationally acceptable. Speculations about the possible and the still conceivable are eradicated. The really conceited scholars behave as if they had actually been present at prehistorical and early historical events, so brazen are their interpretations, although they cannot possibly be more than subjective impressions. In the unfertile wilderness I miss interdisciplinary collaboration between archaeologists, ethno-

High above the river Magdalena a figure stares out of the rock. It has not got Dracula teeth and the face is carved in the correct proportions.

logists and technicians of all kinds. Between the clearly demarcated areas of knowledge I am an indefatigable crosser of frontiers, I burn my fingers, I fling open the windows to let fresh air in. I know that I'm a nuisance, yet many critics should be grateful to me for the eminence they have achieved by elaborating on my successes.

We must always remember that pioneering revolutionary discoveries were made by intelligent laymen. The imaginative brain thinks something out, the scientist asserts that it is impossible and the engineer puts it into practice. People who can no longer enjoy using their imagination are condemned to a dreary monotonous path from the cradle to the grave.

My imagination works inside conceivable frameworks; I am always open to new possibilities, I enjoy refreshing associations of ideas and am grateful when I am steered off the wrong track. I am against all uniformity, especially when it comes to thinking. I look on it as sheer dictatorship if an accredited TV personality can arrange for unacceptable opinions to be banned from the small screen. The freedom to use our imaginations should be one of our acknowledged freedoms.

Apart from the exact sciences, there are literally no scientific opinions which have to be respected as facts. I take from my hand luggage the internationally respected article by Martin Knapp, 'Im finstern 20. Jahrhundert' (7) and read:

> We can safely assume that many virtually unopposed 'truths' of present-day science will sooner or later turn out to be mere assertions, half-true theories, clumsy opinions or narrow dogmas. It is unintelligible why precisely today our present knowledge must be free of error or even more free of error than in the past. As in all ages men make a habit of considering themselves and their achievements as important and correct. Yet in the process each generation looks back on more errors in the past than the preceding generation. So the latest generation should be in a better position and find it more easy to decide how many errors are concealed in the present.
>
> One textbook author writes off another with conviction. The experts quote from one another; they support their knowledge by the false achievements of others. They do

not always check with the newest methods or track down contradictions in the conclusions of other fields. Last but not least, students adopt the theories of their teachers out of tactical opportunism when taking exams and often cling to them for life.

The arrogance with which many researchers, technicians and scientists represent mere theses and assertions as ultimate truth and propagate them is ridiculous and imprudent.

Dr Forero was waiting for me at the airport with such a long face that it could only mean bad news. I prepared myself for trouble.

Forero told me that he would bring a colonel in the Colombian Air Force to see me at the Hilton in the evening. The colonel knew my books and wanted to talk to me.

'Is it really necessary?' I asked.

'You want to see Ciudad Perdida, don't you? Do you want a five-day ride on a donkey on top of having to engage local guides? It's easier to let the air force take you there — in a helicopter!'

This was tempting, so I agreed to the conversation. Dr Forero had been right when he cabled that my physical presence was necessary. Contacts like this could not be made by letters.

'What about Professor Soto?'

Forero said that he had been unable to chase him up, because the head of the excavations was on the very spot where I longed to be. His office at the university did not know when he was returning to Bogotá.

I welcomed Colonel Baer-Ruiz that evening. He was of German origin and a most winning and attractive personality. Over our whiskies we talked for hours about my theories and especially about my desire to reach the 'lost city' in the jungle. I admitted that I was hoping the air force would help. I discreetly dropped the word 'helicopter' into the conversation. Colonel Baer-Ruiz knew about the archaeological discovery, but was not sure exactly where it was located. He asked for a few days' grace and then I would hear from him.

A few days' grace! Life in South America is more easy-going than in Switzerland or England. '*Mañana*' is the watchword.

All I could do was to wait for a message from Colonel Baer-Ruiz and signs of life from Professor Soto.

The day seemed endless. In the evening I accepted an invitation to dinner at the Rotary Club, which was lucky, for I met the agriculturalist Dr Jairo Gallego, a small, lively restless man like myself. I had no idea that evening of the journey my new acquaintance would launch me on. When I told him about my enforced wait, he asked: 'Do you know the Piedras de Leyva?'

I had neither heard of them nor read about them, but his description of prehistoric buildings which baffled archaeologists made me curious, especially as I thought of the wasted days ahead. Better to get to know the world and its mysteries:

> Many people only grasp
> Life's missed targets far too late.
> So, man, be wise in time,
> No time to lose, so travel, travel!
> (J. W. Goethe)

One could argue whether 5 a.m. is late at night or early in the morning, but it is an ungodly hour in any case. As always when my travel timetable forces me out of bed at this hour, I was amazed on this 18 May 1981 in Bogota by the considerable number of late homegoers or early risers on Carrera No. 7 outside the Hilton. I froze as I was whirled out into the cold air through the swingdoors in the foyer with my metal chests full of cameras and measuring gear. Colombia's capital lies 2,645 m above sea-level and the nights are cold there at all times of the year.

Four men, Dr Forero and his son Carlos, Dr Gallego and Carlos Esqualanta, an archaeological student, were standing round a small black Fiat.

The tight fit I was afraid of in the little Fiat turned out to be an advantage. I soon warmed up and asked cheerfully how long the drive to Villa de Leyva would take.

Dr Gallego, who sat at the steering wheel, called over his shoulder to me in the back seat, 'About seven hours!'

I suddenly found the cramped space oppressive and was already getting some idea of the numbness I would feel in feet and ankles, and later in the small of the back in two hours' time.

Gallego must have seen my horrified face in the driving mirror, for he pulled two oranges out of his pocket: 'Eat your breakfast first. The trip will fly past; I often have to do it professionally.'

The Fiat buzzed onwards. Melancholy airs came from the radio, a sound of choirs, guitars, trumpets, and a howling tenor saxophone, obviously all well-known melodies, for the two young men joined the academics in singing them. They sang all the way.

I wiped a peephole in the blurred window. Girls and boys in brightly coloured pullovers stood by the roadside; they offered painted home-fired pottery for sale, drinking vessels, beakers and basins. Heaps of stone about half a metre high made me ask if they were only road signs.

Dr Gallego said that *chicha* was served in houses with the stone piles outside. *Chicha* is a drink like beer, with a chalky colour. The South American Indians brew it under various names and from various natural products. Here among the Andean Indians it is fermented from sugar-cane or maize. The South American Indians use manioc, the albumen-bearing plant of the rain forests; they call their *chicha kashiri*.

Making home-made *chicha* is a simple business. Sugar-canes are crushed with stone or wooden cylinders. The juice is caught in jugs, heated on an open fire or glowing stones, then poured into a trough containing the remains of *chicha* from the last brew. These remains cause rapid fermentation. Indian women stir the mass, add a little water and cover the trough with banana leaves. The *chicha* is ready for drinking in 24 hours. The transformation of sugar into alcohol takes place so quickly that the brew would be ready for distilling as spirit in two days. In the case of *chicha* it must be drunk as soon as the drink is 'mature'. A day too late and Moctezuma's revenge is certain!

From the provincial capital Tunja, 2,820 m above sea level, our road led into the mountains, a primeval landscape with rust-brown and red peaks, beyond which other Andean summits could just be made out, shimmering blue and violet in the distant haze. The view reminded me of a mountain valley in Kashmir.

The valleys were traversed by the dark green strips of potato fields. Dr Gallego told me that in the market of La Paz, the highest capital in the world at 4,000 m, Aymara women offered 200 varieties of potato for sale, all cultivated in the Andes. It is archaeologically proved that Indians planted potatoes as early as the Nazca period around 200 BC and raised 625 species. Pizarro, the Spanish conqueror, introduced the potato into Europe around 1550. I realised that without Indian agriculture we should all have starved to death long ago.

The sun was blinding; it stood almost at its zenith. With engine screaming a sports car passed us on a curve with only inches to spare, followed by eight more cars obviously all indulging in an impromptu private rally. Gallego reacted in the same way as I would have done. He pulled into the side of the road until the drivers had satisfied their outburst of South American temperament.

No one had said a word. Dr Gallego changed into first gear and suggested that we eat lunch in the Hospedería Duruelo.

On the first floor of a rambling snow-white convent with its colonnades, Carmelite sisters have installed a restaurant in the refectory which outsiders can use. It is a noble room with chairs carved out of ebony and leather seats drawn up to tables covered with spotless linen, on which were bowls of orchids in all colours of the rainbow. Orchids are not expensive plants up here; they flourish like daisies do back in Switzerland.

After a brief grace, the sisters, wearing black dresses and white hoods, noiselessly served *ajiaco*, the Colombian national dish; noiselessly because they 'floated' on velvet slippers, like ministering angels. *Ajiaco* is a thick vegetable soup made of diced potatoes, peas, maize, avocados, rice and pieces of chicken. Our angels offered us cold milk and *guayaba* juice to drink. The *guayaba* is a dark-brown fruit the size of a mandarin, rich in vitamins. The Colombians claim that one glass of the bitter-sweet juice contains as much nourishment as ten bananas.

Naturally after the meal we had coffee as black as a moonless night. Wherever you go or stop or sit there is coffee. Colombians must have hearts like horses. Not only do they like coffee at any time of day and on every occasion, they are also proud of it, because it is supposed to be the only coffee in the world that is produced and exported without any chemical additive. At all events it also helps tired men on their mules.

'How much farther is it to your pile of stones?' asked Juan Carlos when we piled into the tiny Fiat again.

'Only a couple of kilometres,' Papa Forero consoled him.

And soon a rough natural path actually did lead us to the stones of Leyva. They lie or stand in a rectangular excavated area. There are no tiles or remains of walls to indicate a building to which the blocks might once have belonged, although the number and dimensions of the relics could easily have been parts of a gigantic edifice. By my measurements the rectangle was 34.40 m long and 11.60 m wide.

Twenty-four columns, the longest of them rising 3.40 m from the ground, have survived on the eastern long side. The distances between the still extant colomns allow us to calculate a maximum of 42 columns on the long side when the structure was new. In the centre of the complex some partially round

Twenty-four columns have survived the centuries. The longest rises over three metres from the ground; the others grow old on the ground.

broken columns are found. With a length of 6.80 m and a circumference of 2.75 m they pressumably towered above their other colleagues in the past.

'What was all this junk in the past?' young Juan Carlos wanted to know — he was carrying a camera for me.

'Hand me the compass, quick . . .' My grey cells had clearly developed a picture I had seen!

The compass confirmed my presentiment. The rectangle is aligned on the four cardinal points of the compass, the lengthways axis running from east to west and the crossways from north to south.

The menhirs, the unhewn stones of the cromlech* at Crucuno in Brittany, are looked on as a sensation, a wonder, a mystery by archaeologists, because they are laid out rectangularly. Before this discovery, megalithic stone layouts had to be circular, as at Stonehenge, Avebury and Rollright. Stone circles can so easily be interpreted as calendars. Then came the irritating discovery of the rectangular cromlech of Crucuno, which has lain near the village of the same name in Brittany since time immemorial. The programmed interpretations began to look shaky.

There are stones there; they cannot be concealed. Twenty-two menhirs stand in an area 34.20 m long by 25.70 m wide at Crucuno; others lie prostrate on the ground and damaged; some may even have been taken away. Fernand Niel (8) showed convincingly that the Crucuno rectangle represents a calendar. The summer and winter solstices can be read off from the diagonals, the equinoxes from the lengthways axis. The rectangle formed by the Leyva stones, before which I stood, is aligned from east to west, as in Brittany.

A recognised specialist in megalithic complexes, Fernand Niel, verified that the length, breadth and diagonals of the Crucuno rectangle are in the ratio 3:4:5. This ratio is looked on as the Pythagorean or Egyptian right-angled triangle. It was a geometrical measurement in ancient Egypt.

Because the rectangular cromlech of Leyva is narrower than the one at Crucuno, other angles and diagonals result, but the number of menhirs seems to have been larger in Columbia than in Brittany.

*From the Celtic: stone circle.

Here at Leyva 24 menhirs stand on one long side. In Brittany the number is 22. In this God-forsaken place 76 menhirs must have stood guard once along the four sides — 24 on the long sides, 14 on the shorter sides. Now one cannot even guess how many columns adorned the centre.

My speculative brain was buzzing.

The more menhirs that were 'planted', the more angular calculations resulted and the more complicated the complex was for mathematical problems. A large number of menhirs also produced more lines of sight and combinations between them. Stars could be aimed at in larger numbers and more accurately. For the arrangement of the Leyva stones — as at Crucuno — clearly suggests that it was concerned with observation of the heavens. If not, why were the four rows of stones aligned directly on the four cardinal points?

I do not blame the Colombians for not trying to crack the puzzle nut of Leyva; they know nothing about its counterpart in French Brittany. We communicate all round the globe, but a distance of 10,000 km is still an unbridgeable abyss for archaeological research. Really archaeologists should be grateful for they could at least share my not inconsiderable travelling expenses when I refer them gratis to such cross-connections. They are neither grateful, nor do I see any travelling expenses. So be it. Perhaps my grandchildren will realise that their old grandpa gave quite reasonable hints in the year dot.

My young friend Juan Carlos had asked what the layout was in the past and even Forero the father and Gallego looked at me as if I was a clairvoyant for being able to give even a vague explanation on the spot. I said that I found a similarity to a famous cromlech in France and suggested that we inspect the surroundings, as we might find more information from the stones.

Only a kilometre away a tumescent penis, 5.80 m long, lay on the ground. A tree had grown through it and cracked it. Nearby was another bringer of happiness with the respectable length of 8.12 m.

Someone with a sense of humour and a bit of cheek could claim that emancipated women of the past had taken the tools out of the male workmen's hands in order to perpetuate the male sexual attribute in its most imposing state as a warning.

In many countries the phallus was a favourite subject for stone carvers, but we seldom find such fine specimens as this.

However, these symbols of sexual enjoyment did not suggest any conclusions about the geometrical rectangle.

Were they the remains of a fertility cult? Penises of this format do suggest an idea about the cult of which they formed a part. Supposing there were fixed days on which children could be conceived, or not conceived, in the immediate vicinity of the calendar stones? Did the sexologists of the Stone Age creep by and announce the happy message of female fertility limited by time? They would have had Rome's blessing posthumously. Or did giants frequent the spot to use and enjoy these enormous sex objects? Any suggestion may be viable.

I had not the slightest plausible explanation; I could only point out that the phallus was a favourite subject for stone carvers in many countries. Perhaps these phalli were only a leisure pastime for the Stone Age carvers, perhaps the same ancient psychologists — even without a couch — encouraged them to create these representations all over the world. If the archaeologists avert their prudish gaze from such finds, perhaps the sexologists could take the job on. How about a best-seller called *The Sex Life of Stone Age Man?* Ms Shere Hite, pack your bags for Leyva. You will be delighted.

The two cromlechs mentioned as aligned on points of the compass are typical examples of many similar layouts in all continents. To interpret them as calendars seems obvious, but unsatisfactory. There were simpler methods of establishing the beginning of spring and prophesying the onset of autumn.

There is something that has escaped us all so far. What are we overlooking in order to find out the secret of the Stone Age men? Crude predictions of the seasons were never needed for agriculture on our planet, because they normally occurred in a regular rhythm. A more accurate calendar would have been useful for casting horoscopes based on the stars. But seriously: did the cromlechs fix dates for the consecration of priests, for ritual festivals, for cults connected with the stars? Were such days deduced from cycles of fixed stars in the heavens? Were they monuments for visitors who came from heaven and vanished there again? In that sense, is the phallus a symbol of life that came from the cosmos? The calendar explanation may belong to the arsenal of solutions to a stone puzzle, but I do not think it is the ultimate conclusion of wisdom.

Working visits. An absurd term used for some time now by members of governments when they meet to discuss matters of mutual interest. If these gentlemen work normal hours, they are active at a 'working lunch'; if they start early, they chat away over a 'working breakfast'. Recently a European radio announcer said they had even met for a 'working drink'. In that sense, I am always busy over working breakfasts, working lunches and even working drinks while on my travels.

On the evening after my Leyva excursion, I was invited to a 'working meeting' with Swiss subjects who live in Bogotá. In this circle I met a fellow countryman, Raphy Lattion. He is Professor of Music in the Swiss College in the capital. He had read my books and so he wasted no time in asking me if I had seen the 'genetic disc'. The word 'genetic' immediately reminded me of the phalli at Leyva.

'No. What is it?' I asked.

Professor Lattion explained that a plate had been found with remarkable reliefs on both sides. On one side a series of pictures depicted the origin of life from spermatozoa to foetus, the other showed fertilisation of the cell and evolution into a frog.

'How old is the disc?'

'A few thousand years at least.'

My eyes must have betrayed my doubts; for the prehistoric inhabitants of Colombia, not being equipped with microscopes, did not know about spermatozoa. My grey-haired fellow countryman hastened to add: 'You can see the disc for yourself! It belongs to the father of a former pupil, Professor Jaime Gutierrez. Would you like to meet him?'

'Of course. Please make an appointment.'

Strictly punctual myself, I was pleased to find Professor Gutierrez waiting for me outside his bungalow on Carrera 9B, No. 126. I was impressed by his casual leisure gear, but even more so by his powerful nervous hands. They led me to think of some manual activity. I said so. A good natured twinkle appeared in the dark eyes set in the face of this tall, slim bearded man. He admitted that he was an industrial draughtsman, a subject he taught at three universities in Bogotá.

Technical-cum-artistic activity infected the whole family. In the large living room his wife, his four sons and his daughter, all over 18, as well as some friends, were all engaged in manual activity. The sons looked like replicas of Che Guevara: bearded in the manner of the Cuban doctor and guerrilla leader, and wearing the same peakless cap. When we talked, it turned out that they only shared the external attributes of the revolutionary.

All of them, girl and boys, and to some extent their mother, worked at their hobbies. They modelled or painted, made delicate mobiles. The eldest enlarged his own photos in a dark-room. Mrs Gutierrez was painting glass sheets with a fine brush, in the style of old painting behind glass. A South American family life we can hardly conceive of after the daily reports of unrest from the southernmost part of the New World. The media conceal this large part of the silent majority.

That was my first impression; the second was the showcases

Professor Gutierrez was waiting for me.

loaded with archaeological finds on all four walls, here and in other rooms. Gutierrez took Professor Lattion and me away from the family and led us into an austerely furnished study. A desk, a chair, a drawing-board and cases full of pottery and strange stones. The master of the house picked out at random an artefact like an amulet, about the size of a hand. It was covered with engraved characters.

Glozel! The word flashed through my brain.

Glozel, a hamlet like hundreds of others, is situated in the Departement of Allier between Lyons and the world-famous spa of Vichy. Glozel became famous through finds that were made there and the intrigues they fostered. Just like a detective story.

On 1 March 1924 the young farmer Emile Fradin was ploughing his fields. He was annoyed. Stones were damaging his ploughshare. So he gathered them up and piled them up at the edge of the field. While working to and fro carrying the stones, he felt that one was lighter than the others. When he removed the surface mud, he saw characters scratched on the stone that looked like T-H-O-U-X, a crazy mixture of letters. Emile Fradin put the find in his coat pocket and wiped it clean. A potsherd appeared. He could not decipher any of the engravings, but decided to sort out the potsherds from the pile of stones, because the relic could have come from the distant past. His efforts were rewarded by the discovery of hundreds of tablets and engraved stones.

The stones at Glozel were talked about as far afield as Vichy. Dr Antonin Morlet, the spa doctor, heard about them. Together with Fradin he found more stones and tablets with engravings.

Four years later, in 1928, a commission of Swedish and French authorities marched across virgin soil in Glozel, soil that Emile Fradin had not tilled. The commission found the remains of bones that were dated to 12,000 BC. The collection at Glozel was enlarged by several thousand interesting stones and some clay tablets, as well as urn-like vessels.

Quite recently the Swiss Dr Hans-Rudolf Hitz investigated the written characters and took great pains to decipher them (9). The result was as astounding as it was encouraging. The signs proved to be not only intelligible written symbols, but also rows of mathematical figures!

Drawings on the Glozel stones.

I asked Professor Gutierrez if he had ever heard of Glozel. Of course he had not; how could he? So I told him what I thought about them and asked where the stones in his collection came from.

Professor Gutierrez said that over 17 years ago he had talked to Bernardo Rincon, who was a smith by profession and had a small farm (*finca*) near Sutatausa, 40 miles northwest of Bogotá. Rincon had shown him some stones engraved with figures and characters and asked him how old they might be.

Gutierrez, who could not give an opinion, asked a geologist friend to make a rough estimate of the age of some stones and at least to decide whether they were old or young. The geologist assured him that the stones, including the engravings, were thousands of years old, because clear traces of the effects

Two examples from the Gutierrez collection; engraved stones from Sutatauso near Bogotá.

of water could be seen under the microscope. Gutierrez cheerfully told me that if I had the time and inclination, I could pick such stones out of the earth at the *finca* myself.

Was there a centre from which the stone engravings were ordered and produced? Did someone 'commission' large numbers of stones to be marked with messages and news to increase the probability that they would be found thousands of years later?

The stones at Glozel have been shown to be dated to 12,000 BC. None of the temple ruins from the Maya or Inca period, from ancient Egypt or Babylon, are considered to be as old as that. The stones must belong to a mysterious epoch much farther back than anything previously falling into the sphere of archaeology. Does archaeology not trust itself to enter this unmapped area in the history of mankind?

Finds so far reveal concentrated collections of stones in certain points in the world. As this phenomenon has not yet been systematically tackled, we can only accept the chance discoveries as a beginning, not as an end. Only after a worldwide exploration could we know if the stone plantations were holy places where the faithful deposited the precious stones, like modern *ex votos* in places of pilgrimage. Perhaps the stones had a fixed value for trading and barter, depending on the richness and contents of the engravings. Did merchants carry them in their baggage so that when they ordered goods from their suppliers they could back up the orders with valid 'currency'? Were they amulets, written communications to members of a tribe? Every interpretation has a chance — except for that of forgery. Let us admit that we have never known so little about so much as today.

Professor Gutierrez handed me a black disc, weighing about two kilos with a diameter of 22 cm and a hole in the middle like a gramophone record.

'Where did you get the disc?'

'It happened quite by chance. It is known here that I collect prehistoric and ancient objects. A few years ago a *guaquero*, a treasure-hunter, came to see me,' Gutierrez grinned: 'Perhaps he would be called a grave-robber in other parts. He offered me the disc for a small sum.'

'Do you know where the man found it?'

'*Guaqueros* have their little secrets. The man swore that it

The genetic disc.

did not come from a grave. He said he had laid a water pipe in the ground on his *finca* and found it there. He lives in the outskirts of Bogotá.'

'And the object is supposed to be old and authentic.'

Gutierrez exhaled the aromatic smoke from his black cigar through his nostrils. 'The blind feel it, those with sight see it, geologists guarantee it. This fine example of the stonemason's art is thousands of years old! Look at it. With the years the disc has been compressed by the weight of the earth it lay in. The figures were distorted, on the edges they are even pressed upwards. The symmetry of the representation of the snake is warped. In many places the reliefs have been worn down, eroded by flowing water. Two geologist friends at the Technical University confirmed what I sensed, indeed knew instinctively. The disc is thousands of years old; How many

Geologists say the disc is thousands of years old. It has been compressed by the weight of the earth so that it has been pushed upwards at the edges.

thousands I do not know. At all events they congratulated me on this magnificent piece.'

On the face, twelve ornaments divided by vertical lines run round the edge of the disc. Towards its centre is a sequence of six sectors interrupted by an arrow. Directly below the arrow are engravings of a foetus, a male and a female being, the latter clearly recognisable by penis and vagina.

'What is your interpretation, Professor?'

'At first I thought of a calendar because of the twelve divisions perhaps containing signs of the zodiac. But then what was the point of the two beings with their striking sexual characteristics? One can puzzle about the whole, but penis and vagina are unmistakable. I discussed the disc with biologists at the university ...'

'What did they say?'

'They were the men who called it the *genetic disc*. They looked at the representation from the point of view of their specialty. The biologists say that two frogs crouch directly below the arrow. A line starting to the right of the frog man runs half-way round the hole in the centre and terminates in the arrow. The line with the arrow points to the significance of the 'cartoons' on the edge. My colleagues said that they depicted the connection between vagina and penis, in other words the act of reproduction. Now follow the six fields to the left of the arrow: first field — spermatozoa; second field — male and female egg cells; third field — the fertilised egg; fourth field — the foetus; fifth field — the embryo; sixth field — the growing embryo.

'I did not understand the fields to the right of the arrow so clearly. The biologists think they might refer to an evolutionary development, perhaps on these lines: first field — cell division; second field — a water creature; third field — a batrachian, a reptile, a salamander? fourth field — possibly a bird; fifth field — an intermediate stage in the evolution towards man? sixth field — fairly obviously man. And as for the six sectors running round the centre, the three left-hand fields could represent cell multiplication, the three to the right a small woman and man — vagina and penis. Also a pregnant woman, recognisable by her breasts.'

'Fantastic,' I said and looked at Gutierrez and Lattion, who were watching me intently.

Obverse of the genetic disc.

'That's what everyone who has seen the disc says,' said Gutierrez, while Lattion asked: 'And what do you make of it?'

Careful study under a magnifying glass confirmed what the geologists had said. I spoke my thoughts aloud: 'We can forget the facile explanation that it is a forgery. I admit that the graphic, almost modern depiction of an arrow disturbed me, but arrows form part of the repertoire of all pictorial rock art. I saw arrows at Sete Cidades in Brazil, in the valleys of the Hopi Indians in the USA, in the caves of La Pileta in Spain and in Val Camonica in Italy. Arrows are stylised spears and they have existed from time immemorial.

'What can the reliefs mean? The images are too unfamiliar to be ascribed to a period so far accessible to us. The thoroughly modern conceptual ability permits us to assume that the disc has come down from a civilisation that had reached our present state of knowledge.

'The artists who created these images possessed knowledge thousands of years ahead of their time. They had the know-how which early peoples are simply not credited with. They did not possess microscopes which could have made spermatozoa or cell division visible to them, nor did they have any idea of the evolution they were representing. Did they have teachers to inform them? What do you think?'

Gutierrez pulled his beard thoughtfully. 'I could certainly imagine this disc as a teaching aid. The hole in the middle would make it very practical. The representations can be turned at will to come into one's field of vision.'

'I can only recognise the intelligible clarity of a teaching aid on the face, the obverse is pretty confusing . . .' I interrupted.

Professir Gutierrez, who has been studying the disc for years, thought that something could be read off the obverse so long as it was turned anticlockwise. As follows:

Eight o'clock: a loving couple with a symbolised vagina to the left of the man's head. Seven o'clock: spermatozoa penetrate the vagina. Six o'clock: kneeling woman with an unfertilised ovum outside the womb, with a spermatozoon floating above. Five o'clock: spermatozoa (chromosomes indicated by dots?) which lead to two ova, one ovum is empty — unfertilised — the other is fertilised. Four o'clock: the foetus. Then follow unintelligible signs, but the one o'clock

Reverse of the genetic disc.

position is obvious again: twins in the mother's womb.

'Professors must have a little left to interpret,' laughed Professor Lattion.

I thought to myself that a piece like this really belonged in a showcase in a museum, then asked, 'What do the archaeologists say?'

Gutierrez consulted several specialists about his pet piece, including Colombia's leading archaeologist, Soto Holguin. He took a long hard look at the disc, but finally admitted that he did not know what to make of it.

'Look, Erich,' said Gutierrez, 'a thing like this does not fit into any recognised plan or known culture. Where would the disc be placed in a museum? What kind of label would it be given for visitors' information? The age of the stone, and its signs, would necessitate a brand-new view of the early history of mankind. If such finds were accepted, our early ancestors could no longer be looked on as primitive hairy savages. Time is needed before a breach in the existing mental scaffolding can be made. Yes, we all need a lot of patience!'

That was true. As I was writing this, some words of Professor Hermann Oberth, the acknowledged 'father of space travel', occurred to me. 'There are scientists who behave like forcefed geese. They simply reject new ideas and concepts as nonsense.' That is also true.

Professor Oberth's statement can be quoted without need of examination. Undermining the traditional dogmas is no longer queried. Formerly churches were considered dogmatic, sciences as dynamic. The pillars of wisdom have changed their location. Today the church says that extraterrestrial, indeed extraterrestrial human life is possible . . . and it does not shock the faithful. The church has long since become dynamic; it is no longer dogmatic. Science has become dogmatic and intolerant; it will not stand for opinions deviating from the currently accepted norm, except in extreme necessity. Outsiders' views can only be discussed outside 'King Nobel's Royal Domain' (10). In the process institutes and chairs for all kinds of 'ologies' multiply like rabbits. The chemist, Professor Max Thurkauf, Basle, was right when he made fun of the 'wishy-washy-wushology' in the universities.

Men of courage gladden my heart.

Professor Fred Hoyle, knighted for his service to science,

is considered to be Britain's leading astrophysicist. He has a professorship at Manchester and a guest professorship at the Caltec Technical Institute in California; he works at the observatories of Mount Palomar and Mount Wilson. By modification of the equations of the general theory of relativity, Hoyle developed a theory for a homogeneous isotropic model of the universe with the continuous production of matter.

So much for Sir Fred's scientific qualifications.

For a long time Hoyle has held the view that life came down to earth along with comet-like matter. In 1982 he took a decisive step further. He queried Darwin's theory of evolution, as well as the theory that life could have originated by chance.

I smirk; I hug myself for joy.

When I attacked this Achilles' heel of current doctrine in my book *According to the Evidence* in 1977, I was ridiculed; I was out in the open, alone in the rain. So I shall simply quote Sir Fred's ideas from his London Lecture as reported by the German News Agency on 12 January 1982.

Professor Hoyle said that man was the re-emergence of an earlier intelligence that had been faced with a universal catastrophe of cosmic dimensions. This intelligence had resolved itself into a kind of building chest, whose existential building blocks were distributed throughout the universe. All the biological basic materials from which life as we know it is composed were in this building chest. When the building chest reached the earth as a suitable environment, it developed, accelerated by additional genetic material of the kind still coming from space.

Hoyle said that on this assumption the difficulties in Darwin's theory of evolution would be obviated; it would also explain why an intelligent plan must stand behind the structures of life. For these structures are so complex that they cannot have originated by chance, as orthodox scientists claim.

With this bold statement, Sir Fred rejected two theories. First, the theory according to which life originated from a primitive soup, which created by chance processes the precisely arranged chains of amino acids on which all life depends. Secondly, Darwin's theory of natural selection, which is based on chance mutations of genes that create more highly involved plants and animals. Hoyle held the view that harmful mutations are much commoner than beneficent ones, and that consequently the process must go downhill, provided that Darwin was right.

He explained that micro-organisms were diffused throughout space in interstellar gases and that they could reach the earth in comet fragments, in whose frozen matter the micro-organisms were enclosed. Thus the arrangement of bio-materials originated by intelligent planning, not by chance.

With the favourable help of a super-technology, the intelligence would find a new material structure in which the gigantic stock of information — the intelligence — could be transmitted.

So much for this extract from Professor Hoyle's important lecture. I venture to add some of my own personal observations.

My critics trumpet that extraterrestrials were never like humans, that molecular chains on distant planets would have arranged themselves into a completely different order from those on earth, and so would have produced quite different results from our own.

That is not necessarily so. The first intelligent form of life was formed somewhere in the universe. When and where that happened is beside the point; we do not know. This intelligent form of life sent the germs of life, molecular chains or basic biological material out of its galaxy in all directions — life bombs (building chests) as I postulated in *The Stones of Kiribati*. Some containers traverse the universe, reach no goal or crash into alien suns; others come into the gravitational field of a *virgin planet*.

What happens? If the surface of the planet is unsuitable for the basic genetic material, it will die; it cannot flourish. But if it is suitable, the 'sowing' proceeds according to a coded programme. It is much the same as if the seeds of a tree flourishing in Europe are planted in Australia. If the soil there is not right, the seeds will not grow; if it is, a tree like its European forebears will grow, owing to the genetic information encoded in the cells. Much the same thing happens with Hoyle's building chests. This demolishes the problem of identicality or similarity. Wherever the cosmic seed grows, it develops in exactly the same or a very similar way to the way it did in its place of origin.

This theory does not exclude the possibility of life in the universe whose forms and appearance would exceed our wildest flights of fancy. But no such form of life would ever thrive on our planet. Critics who are already prepared to consider this theory at the same time warn that it would be absurd to admit that humanoid beings in the universe would think and act like us.

Because what I said over 15 years ago is now a burning topic, I will give a brief summary of my ideas. Alien, intelligent forms of life visited our planet thousands of years ago. They took some cells from *the already existing hominids* and changed them by genetic manipulation, a process that is already practised today. Gene technicians can already deliberately alter hereditary characteristics (GEO, February 1982). Only two years ago, the view was that planned genetic manipulations would not be possible for at least 100 years, if at all.

The genetically manipulated cell was put into a liquid culture in which it grew to the egg stage. The egg was implanted in the potential mother. (Artificial insemination of human and animals has long been practised.) The resultant child had all the parents' qualities but, owing to the genetic manipulations, it possessed additional qualities and abilities which its parents did not — for example, the ability to speak, the faculty of storing experience in the brain and to summon it up as memory at any given time. I said that the theme was burningly topical.

At one time in the USA there were trials before the high courts with evolutionists and fundamentalists as the protagonists. The evolutionists (mainly from the scientific camp) wanted confirmation that life on earth originated by chance and then developed further on the evolutionary principle (as propounded by Darwin). The fundamentalists (mostly orthodox believers) wanted the biblical act of creation confirmed. God created man in his own image.

Apart from the fact that every court requires a procedural clarification, both sides only represented a half-truth. If the opponents had taken the extraterrestrial element into consideration the conflict would have ended or not even begun. the evolutionists are right in so far as evolution, mutation and selection exist, but they do not clear up the central problem

The whole steep mountainside seems to have been piled up like a grotesque birthday cake.

'My name is Sylvia. Welcome to Buritaca 200!' a bright-eyed beauty greeted me.

From the end of the gorge a steep flight of steps with a gradient of 50 degrees led 1,100 metres up to the big terrace.

Below the excavation finds there were stone mills for grinding corn — household objects, scoops and vases.

The steep slopes of the Buritaca valley were cut into and buttressed with stone, earth and supporting walls.

Sylvia pulled aside a curtain of lianas and opened up a view of still more surprises.

What in fact was Buritaca? A city of priests? A military outpost?

of how life originated or how intelligence began. The fundamentalists are right in so far as life arrived on earth from outside and that 'God' or 'gods' formed hominids and made them intelligent in their own image. Once the extra-terrestrials are drawn in, even anthropologists need not look for the missing link, which is artificial mutation by extra-terrestrials.

Perhaps the genetic disc which lay before me contains the information we are looking for. In any case, I wish the archaeologists one Fred Hoyle for the next ten Christmases!

Gutierrez spread out some drawings on the desk.

'What do you think they are?'

'Pages out of your son's chemistry book.'

'They are rock drawings from the *Piedras de Tunja*, the stones of Tunja.'

'Where can I see them?'

'Forty kilimetres north-west of Bogotá.'

'So near?' I already had Tunja in mind as a place to visit, seeing that I still had a few free days to fill in. While I was studying the chemical formulae, molecular chains (for that is what they looked like), Gutierrez handed me a book (11).

'Here. The drawings are reproduced in it. The archaeologist Miguel Priana wrote about the Tunja stones as early as 1926. He assumed that they were drawings by Chibcha Indians, but I don't agree. I know a great many Chibcha works of art and this is not their handiwork. I think that the drawings stem from a much more ancient culture. We may be the addressees of the mysterious messages, once we can read them.'

Dr Forero had not been able to reach Professor Soto, nor had Colonel Baer-Ruiz shown signs of life. Forero wanted to try other possibilities of getting me to my goal. Yesterday Professor Gutierrez said that one must have patience.

I decided to go to Tunja.

Forero sent my young friend Juan Carlos to guide me out of the maze of traffic and accompany me to Tunja.

Thanks to a road map carefully prepared by his father, with all turn-offs marked in red, we left the city in a rented Chevrolet by a first-class road in a north-westerly direction, past brightly painted houses with big metal footballs on the roof. Football fans obviously showing their premature joy about the World Cup Final in Colombia in 1986.

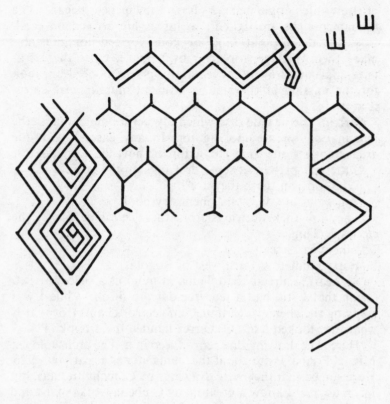

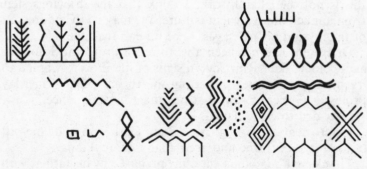

Drawings on the Tunja stones like illustrations in a chemistry textbook.

We are driving through scenery which reminds me of the Swiss Canton of Appenzell, an immaculate pre-Alpine landscape. There was activity everywhere. The land was worked intensively. Willow hedges were set up, fields ploughed, fruit and pottery were on sale; no sign of the lethargy which I observed so frequently in the highlands of Mexico and Bolivia.

In Facatativá, an eyrie with a few single-storey houses, Juan Carlos asked where the stones of Tunja were. We were told they were at the end of the village. When I parked next to the Army School, the speedometer showed 40.5 km. Gutierrez had estimated the trip very accurately.

A large sign announced that the *Piedras de Tunja* were in a government-protected zone. It said *Parque Arquelogico de Facatativá* and outlined everything that was forbidden. No fires to be lit; drive carefully and park where indicated; do not paint stones or trees with signs or scratch them with tools. All praise to the government in Bogotá!

An amazing site. Along well-kept empty roads, watched by only a few black and white cows, I strolled past colossi and square and rectangular stone blocks. They excluded any idea that nature had played eccentric games here. However prodigal she may be, nature does not make dead straight lines run round whole blocks of stone. One thinks rather of a temple frieze, a 'roof', which rested on strong columns in the past and then collapsed.

Were they relics of the legendary Masma culture, that hypothetical culture which is supposed to have existed thousands of years ago and whose traces have been suspected in all quarters of the globe?

The Peruvian geologist Daniel Ruzo introduced the concept of a Masma culture into the literature (12). He coined the concept of a putative legendary culture which left hitherto inexplicable traces. I saw them in the Peruvian Andes at a height of 3800 m, barely 50 km from the capital, Lima. They are assembled on the plateau of Marcahuasi, which has an area of about three square kilometres.

Up there Daniel Ruzo photographed statues of animals from the Mesozoic, badly eroded by weathering, among them a stegosaurus, which belonged to the dinosaur species and lived in the early Cretaceous. During his excursions, Ruzo also came across reliefs of lions and camels, which supposedly never lived in South America.

The geologist aimed his camera at various times of the day and in different seasons on the same strange rock formations of Marcahuasi and made an amazing discovery. He caught a crag with the visual outlines of an old man on the plate, but on development it showed the face of a young man.

Fascinated by Marcahuasi, Ruzo travelled the world and collected photographic proof of what he called Masma culture, for want of a better word. His stimulating book was, and is, completely ignored, although it came out in 1974.

Ruzo's photographs came into my mind during my walk through the Archaeological Park, as did the idea that keeps on nagging at me. Why do we stubbornly refuse to recognise the remains of ancient cultures in weird inexplicable rock formations? Because we all share the erroneous opinion that man never transformed rock faces into works of art?

Even people who have never been there know the monumental stone sculptures of Mount Rushmore from photographs. In the state of South Dakota, south-west of Rapid City, the gigantic faces of Presidents George Washington, Thomas Jefferson, Theodore Roosevelt and Abraham Lincoln stare out of the naked rock. Immediately next to them an eccentric artist produced his own work. Using pneumatic drills and dynamite, he sculpted the mountain face into a colossal equestrian statue of the Indian chief Sitting Bull.

The presidential heads are carefully tended, otherwise they would soon be covered with lichen and crumble away under the influence of wind and weather. Assuming that this expensive maintenance work had long since ceased, what would intelligent men read into the eroded stone sculptures thousands of years later. Would they interpret the four heads and the equestrian statue as 'geological freaks' of nature? Probably. Because no one in his right mind has overturned mountains into monuments.

Our age will not take the trouble to investigate the provenance and origin of the monoliths scattered about the stone park of Facatativá as if a giant had thrown them there. Comparative archaeology could provide a solution to what is puzzling here, to what points back to the distant past, to what lies beneath my feet in a greyish-red honeycomb pattern.

I trod the same honeycomb pattern in Brazil at Sete Cidades, the Seven Cities between the town of Piripiri and the Rio Longe. There as here the rock must have become molten hot like lava during a volcanic eruption. There as here nothing has moved. The heat must have been released like an explosion and then cooled down, so that the honeycomb pattern formed on the spot during the rapid cooling process. Iron became molten, oxidised and left the rust-red colour behind on the honeycomb pattern.

Facatativá and Sete Cidades became Indian holy places. Inexplicable rock drawings and engravings are found at both sites. Both places present the picture of a devastating catasstrophe liberating enormous heat in which stone monsters were hurled through the air.

Indians hammered and engraved the drawings which Professor Gutierrez had shown me on massive stones beneath overhanging cliffs. In the Archaeological Park they have the special rank of the 'Stones of Tunja'.

What is the message of these engravings which look like chemical formulas? Are they signs, meant as warnings? Do they tell of a catastrophe that happened here in the past? Are they notices defining a zone that it would be dangerous to enter? For possible answers, we must take a look at some very recent experiments.

The American atomic authority NRC commissioned a research group to work out how generations living thousands of years after our time could be warned not to enter a still active atomic waste depot.

Thomas Sebeok, the head of the group, was in favour of covering the storage area with gigantic warning signs on which a communications mixture of symbols, images and words were engraved, since men would not know our language and writing thousands of years later. In addition, the experts recommended taking into account the human tendency to superstition. Hidden threats should be engraved on the signs in graphic form so that future men would think that entering the zone would evoke a supernatural revenge. *Der Spiegel* (13) added: 'As experience shows that such warnings attract rather than repel inquisitive people, Sebeok also recommended sowing the surroundings of the atomic waste depot with the vile smell of long-lasting stink bombs.'

I do not know if bombs can be produced which will still stink in the distant future, but the idea of the warning signs I find very, very dubious. What material would they have to be made of to last thousands of years? If we postulate gold or platinum, lovers of the noble long-lasting metals would certainly find them. I bet that the signs would not stay put for long.

Supposing the idea was mooted of entrusting warnings to the rocks at Facatativá? As far as possible on protected rocky summits, just as the Indians transmit their information? That seems to be the most likely explanation of all. History has proved it.

Under the threat of global annihilation a great deal of money is wasted on research and on illusionary models for saving mankind. In the same way, government bakshish has been allotted to prehistoric research. Don't we realise that the fatal situation which may confront it has been survived once or even many times? I am afraid that what Montesquieu

(1689–1755) said is true: 'Man hardly ever reaches reason from reason.'

When the Spanish conquerors overcame the highlands around present-day Bogotá in April 1538, the stones of Tunja were already worshipped as a shrine. The Spaniards encountered Indian tribes whom they called Chibcha because of their communal language. They were settled between Nicaragua and Ecuador. The Muisca belonged to one linguistic group of the Chibcha. They did not erect any monumental buildings, but they produced sophisticated pottery, were skilled in working gold and knew how to weave very fine cloth.

Why were the Tunja stones worshipped as holy relics even in those days? Here, where I was walking, the Muisca held their festivals in honour of the gods, here they sacrificed boys to appease the wrath of god. Why just here? Was it not just a place like any other? We can conclude from the traditions of the Muisca that the Tunja stones were considered sacred from the very remote past.

The sungod Chiminigagua (gagua means sun) emerges from the mists of mythology. The Spanish chronicler Simon Pedro (14) followed Indian stories in relating the arrival of the god:

It was night. As yet there was nothing in the world. Light was enclosed in a great something house and came out of it. This something house is Chiminigagua and it concealed the light inside itself, so that it came out. In the gleam of the light things began to be.

Chiminigagua, the sun or light god, was the almighty ruler of the universe to the Muisca; they saw him as a beneficent god, but they did not build temples in which he was supposed to dwell. He took his something house with him. Messengers went to and fro between the Chiminigagua and the Muisca — instructing the Indians in useful activities, teaching them morals and religion and finally vanishing, but not without announcing that they would return.

This tradition has a counterpart in the myths of the Caribes Indians. The Caribes Indians lived in the hot humid Colombian region near the northern Andes. The myths of the Caribes Indians (15) relate that mankind stems from a certain

Louquo who came from heaven, like his Muisca colleague. Firstly he created intelligent men, whom he taught to catch fish, build houses and plant manioc before he returned to heaven as a god.

Chiminigagua and Louquo, the Inca god Viracocha and the Maya god Kukulkan are at the centre of traditions which have the same message. 'Gods' came down from heaven, created men, became their teachers and finally vanished into the unknown in mysterious fashion. Their 'children' were left behind, incapable of grasping the miracle they had experienced.

The strange figures were not made into constellations, nor did stars become symbols of the vanished 'gods', until after their ascents into heaven. As the concrete visions left the earth without a trace, they obviously had to be at home 'up there', from whence they had come. It was only natural that the places in which they visibly and physically lived were elevated to the status of holy places, like the Tunja stones in the Archaeological Park of Facatativá.

On the homeward journey Juan Carlos asked, 'Do you know the story of El Dorado?'

'Vaguely. I know that El Dorado means the golden; I know that concept stands for the legendary land of gold.'

'And you don't know the Muisca mythology?'

'Do you know it?'

'Si, si, señor. We learn the story at school, and now it has even come into our home.'

'Tell me about it.'

Juan Carlos sat up straight in his seat.

His vivid account was emphasised with volatile gestures of the kind only South Americans use. 'All right. When the Spaniards came to these highlands in the sixteenth century, they showed the captive Indians gold and precious stones and tortured them to find out where similar gold and precious stones could be found. In terror of their lives and as they did not know where the treasures were hidden, they told the conquerors the traditional story. Between ourselves, Erich, they did a lot of harm.

'This is the story the Indians told the Spaniards:

'Before a new Muisca ruler could be installed, the chosen one had to spend a period of solitude in a cave. On the day of the summer solstice he made his way to Lake Guatavita, 2,600 m high in the mountains. All the members of the tribe were awaiting him up there. On the shore they had built a raft of wood and reeds, decorated with flowers and garlands. In the darkness of night they placed four bowls of burning charcoal and a lot of *moque* (incense) on the raft. Because it was a feast day, the men were adorned with feathers and the women wore their finest ornaments of gold, coral and precious stones.

'In the darkness of the night the future ruler was taken out naked, rubbed with resinoid earth and then covered with a layer of gold dust. Not one bit of his body was left uncovered, not even his hair.

'After this procedure the chosen one was led to a raft, in the centre of which he had to stand motionless. A prince was posted at each corner. I do not know if it was as magnificent a picture as the one in our school books, but it must have been a fine sight. Just think about it. The dark night, a raft, five princes on it, adorned with gold chains and earrings, at their feet mountains, literally mountains of gold and precious stones. And then when the sun crept over the mountain tops, when its first rays reached the raft, at that moment the shores of Lake Guatavita sprang to life. A great chorus of flutes, drums and song sounded from the shores and could be heard deep in the valleys.

'Slowly the raft with the five men was rowed out into the middle of the lake. And then it happened!

'The young gilded ruler brought the sungod his gifts. He threw all the treasures on board into the lake and the four princes followed suit.

'Then the raft neared the shore. The gilded one entered the lake and was washed to the accompaniment of ritual hymns. Now he was the new king of the Muisca.'

'A beautiful myth ...' I had heard it before, but could not deprive the young man of the pleasure of telling it.

'No myth, señor! It did happen. When the level of Lake Guatavita fell owing to drought, a lot of gold was found. Word of honour!'

The story Juan Carlos defended so vehemently is true.

Already in 1545 Hernan Perez le Quesada tried to lower the level of the lake. Thousands of Indians scooped water out of the lake using empty gourds and wooden scoops. Because it was the dry season and the surface level was lower than usual, it was possible to lower it by three metres, enough to recover 4,000 gold pesos.

The next attempt in 1580 failed. Antonio de Sepúlveda hired 8,000 Indians whose furious prospecting changed the face of the landscape in a way that is still visible today. On the side facing the valley, Sepúlveda had a V-shaped cut made through which the water slowly drained away. By the time the artificial gorge collapsed on to the effluent water the level of the lake had sunk by 20 m. Sepúlveda was able to send to his Christian majesty, King Philip II, in Madrid a catalogued treasure of golden breast plates, snakes, eagles, rods and an emerald as big as a hen's egg. The entrepreneur kept back 12,000 gold pesos for himself, but still died in poverty. Sepúlveda was given a tomb in the church of Guatavita, near the lake whose gold had enchanted him and brought about his downfall.

The lure of the Muisca gold persisted down the centuries. Adventurers kept on trying to empty the lake to recover the rich booty. Limited companies were formed and constructed underground channels. Gold objects were constantly brought to light, but the great majority of gold artefacts is still hidden in the depths of the lake. It appears that someone once reached the bottom, but it was covered with a layer of slimy mud 20 m deep, which even the bravest diver could not face. Pumps from Bogotá came too late. The surface of the mud became rock-hard in the heat of the sun. Then the waters covered the Muisca treasure once again. Experts estimated tht it was worth about 100 million US dollars.

A myth with tangible traces.

Who inspired the poor Muiscas to sacrifice their country's treasures to the sun god? Who spurred them on to gild their tribal prince, the man they looked on as next to the gods, for a religious ritual? Had extraterrestrials worn suits that gleamed like gold? Did the naive Indians believe that gods who came down from the sun demanded sacrifices of gold and jewels?

'Do you know the *Museo del Oro*?' asked Juan Carlos, when we were saying goodbye outside the Hilton after a nerve-racking drive through the free-for-all traffic in Bogotá. Yes, I had visited the Gold Museum ten years before. Only part of its 28,000 archaeological exhibits can be on show at any given time, so that another visit could be well worth while. We made a date for the next day which I would have to keep, provided there was no news taking me into the jungle.

The harsh ringing of the telephone awoke me at an unpleasantly early hour. Dr Miguel Forero was on the line and I was wide awake at once.

'Have you contacted Professor Soto?'

'No, that won't be so easy to do, but in the meantime would you like to talk about your theories to some air force officers?'

'Of course, I'll do anything to get to Ciudad Perdida! A lecture is OK with me, so long as one of the officers has a helicopter in his pocket.'

'How are you going to spend the day?'

'I've arranged to meet Juan Carlos in the Gold Museum.'

The Gold Museum housing Colombia's outstanding gold finds was established in 1939 by the *Banco de la Republica* in the second storey of the bank's head office at Street No. 16. It is protected by massive steel doors and guarded by armed security officers.

I am delighted to say that taking photographs is still allowed,

The treasures in the Gold Museum are protected by massive steel doors.

as it was ten years ago. In most European museums the guards become hysterical when they see a camera. You have to hand them in before a visit. The idea is that the objects on exhibition suffer from being photographed. I can understand that in the case of ancient documents constantly subjected to flash photography, but now there are highly sensitive films with which you can take pictures in semi-darkness.

I claim that archaeologists — whose museums specialise in 'hard ware' — prohibit photography for two reasons. Firstly they want their own photographs to be sold. As an author who is all for sales promotion, I find that attitude scandalous. Where do the archaeologists get the money for their researches, where do museums get their subsidies? From the tax-payer's pocket. That is why I consider it a swindle when excavated objects are held to be personal possessions. Secondly, there is a desire to prevent amateur archaeologists with cameras from interpreting objects in a way which does not fit into the orthodox theories. *All* interpretations are subjective. While unaccredited intruders are kept out of 'King Nobel's Royal Domain', it is difficult for outsiders to oppose new views to the settled sacrosanct doctrines. Louis Pauwels and Jacques Bergier wrote in their book *Aufbruch ins Dritte Jahr-Tausend* (16): In addition to the freedoms which are guaranteed us by the constitution, we should demand another one: The freedom to doubt science.'

In the darkened rooms of the Museo del Oro silence reigned. Thick carpets swallowed up the sound of one's footsteps. People spoke in whispers and were frightened when they saw a strange face reflected in the glass of a showcase. One felt reverential before the piles of primitive treasures.

The guards led us into a dark room in which soft music came from invisible speakers. Theft-proof steel doors closed behind us automatically. We tried to get our bearings and then bright lights were switched on. We were in a treasure-house crammed with gold. Works of art from every tribe of Colombian Indians hung from the walls behind heavy panes of reinforced glass. Precious objects ornamented with gold, silver and platinum hung from the ceiling.

Confused by the plethora of riches, I concentrated on individual pieces, the meaning of which was inexplicable. Both then and now precious metals were and are not used for everyday objects. They were undoubtedly religious artefacts, stylised representations of important divinities, given that artists hammered figures, faces with helmets, into the precious metal.

There are rarities from the cultural heritage of the Quimbaya Indians. The museum guidebook says: 'Anthropomorphic stylisation,' i.e. human features in non-human beings. As a child of our times I could see a robot in them; legs astraddle, something like a head and on it two capsules like the casing of two alarm clocks. There are variations on these 'anthropomorphic stylisations', sometimes decorated with wings, sometimes with rods, but the alarm clocks are always there and they give the objects a technical touch.

The Calima Indians are depicted with very large skulls and wide bony noses quite alien to their racial type. Rings almost as big as the head dangle from their ears and wide gold face masks 'drop' from their noses. Moreover helmets are crammed on to their heads, terminating in wings decorated with balls,

A smart amulet with many puzzles, I was able to solve one of them.

discs, dots and rods, yet the alarm clocks are always there too. We ought to think about who or what was symbolised here. The museum guide makes it easy; he refers to these Calima works as 'diadems'. Liz Taylor is an authority on diadems. Someone ought to ask her if she would like to deck herself out in the style of this square skull.

Then there is as elegant round amulet with a figure on it. One cannot say whether it is a man or a woman. The artist was presumably symbolising a porter. The figure holds tree trunks or stone pillars leading to the lowest point of the triangular skull and a similar feature lies across its ankles. Memories of the ancestors who suffered under the burden of stones in Facatativá?

An amulet with a figure from whose skull rays shot out also interested me. In front of its chest a disc hangs over a wide belt. The fabulous creature crouches on a litter like a throne, which is carried by two embryonic monsters (animals?). Wherever there is an empty space balls appear. Balls seem to have played an important part in the repertoire of these ancient artists.

On another breast plate, an autocratic being is being carried on a litter, but here by little stylised men. The being holds two objects, the one in his left hand might be a beaker, the one in his right hand is more technical looking. Once again balls (or discs) float round the face. The ball game so favoured by the ancient Indians dictated that the only graphical accessories they could give figures were balls, varying only in size.

It is said that the balls or discs represent sun and moon. I do not believe it. Even Pre-Columbian Indians could see that there were only one sun and one moon in the sky! Why did a plurality of these emblems dominate the pictures? I find them too prominent as pure ornamentation and besides they take up too much space. Can we assume they were the Indian's conception of the world as a sphere? Were balls (or discs) a symbol of the eternal to them?

What can have gone on in the head of the Indian artist when he placed a humanoid creature with giant frog eyes, straddling spindle legs and spindle arms in another amulet? The two birds flanking the creature seem too big in proportion to the figure. This group of three appears on a frieze which is supported by long crossed legs. Stylised in the manner of

A stylised mannikin is juggling with balls. The ancient Indians were so fascinated by balls and discs that they never depicted figures with any other adjuncts. There was a reason for this.

a cornflower, eleven balls enclose two beams below the frieze. In the lower sector of the four-storeyed representation, a little chest is included with two balls resting on its lid.

Scholars say that this amulet is a nose ring because the circle is open at the top, so that it could be clipped on to the nose. They may be correct, but then the artistic depictions would hang sideways.

And of course the Gold Museum houses some model aircraft — I'm sorry, representations of insects. All the models are low-flying, with the wings brought back under the rump and vertical tail fins. Archaeologically, these golden jewels are catalogued as 'religious ornaments', attributes of a fish or insect cult. All very well, except that there is no trace of a fish

I think these 'religious ornaments' are model aircraft and I'll tell you why.
These little jewels are behind reinforced glass so thick that my colour
photographs did not come out. In gold they look good enough to steal!

or insect cult among the Colombian Indians. Besides, the model aircraft do not have fish or insect heads.

The Gold Museum was well worth my second visit. The thousands of exhibits stimulate the imagination and make one admire the ancient Indian artists. They take one far back into the world of puzzles and mysteries, the world which was so ruthlessly ended by the Spanish conquerors.

That evening my patience snapped. Dr Forero is a kind, helpful and reliable man and I did not doubt for a moment that he was making great efforts on my behalf. Over dinner he explained to me that many of the air force officers whom Colonel Baer-Ruiz wanted to invite were away on courses or commandos and that he did not want me to lecture to a tiny audience. Dreaded *mañana* was rearing its head.

Dr Forero suggested in all earnest that I should stay in the country for another three months. A big UFO congress was due to take place in Bogotá in August and the organisers would be delighted for me to lecture. And during that time I would certainly be able to achieve my aim of visiting the lost city in the jungle. *Mañana*.

I had allowed one week for this excursion in my travel plans, after that I had contracted to give lectures in Germany, Austria and Switzerland as part of my programme for the year.

'I'm going to fly to Santa Marta and try to find my own way into the jungle,' I said. Dr Foreero advised against this.

If the army had cordoned off the excavation zone, not even a Colombian, let alone a foreigner, could reach it.

I thanked Dr Forero warmly for all his help and said I was sure we should meet again.

The next day I flew back to Switzerland.

5 The Eighth Wonder of the World

'The question today is how we can persuade mankind to agree
to its own survival.'

Bertrand Russell (1872–1970)

Before my departure I had booked a room in the Hilton for
14 August. At the end of July I confirmed with Dr Forero
that I would attend the congress in Bogotá, but added that
my main reason for coming was to meet Professor Soto and
visit the lost city.

Lufthansa flight 512 landed punctually at 21.40 hours on
the rain-soaked landing strip at Bogotá. Was I dreaming? Had
nearly three months passed since I had flown away from here
in frustration? The certainty that I would now be able to see
the lost city delighted me.

My booking was confirmed at the Hilton, the youthful head
of reception told me, but there was no room available. Furious
because it was night, I was tired and no other accommodation
would be available, I tried the old joke.

Putting on my most serious face, I asked, 'Would you have
had a room for Queen Elizabeth if she had arrived unexpectedly?'

The young man looked at me with a wild surmise. 'Well,'
he said perplexedly, 'in that case we would have to make an
exception.'

'Give me the Queen's room. I promise you she won't arrive
tonight.'

The man in the black suit had no sense of humour. He
refused to offer me one of the rooms which all hotels of this
category keep in reserve. After one last question: 'So you've
no room for me?' I began to open my bags so that I could
lie down on a sofa in the hall. Why should I suffer for a
blunder by the staff? I was worn out after the flight and the
resultant jet lag; I longed for a bed. Worried about my
imminent striptease, the young man summoned the manager

and of course he had a room for me. Why couldn't I have had one straight away?

At nine o'clock the next morning I was woken from a long refreshing sleep. Dr Forero was on the line.

'So you're here. I can't believe it!'

'But we did arrange to meet today.'

I had arrived before my letter written at the end of July. We met an hour later. Apart from three lectures in the Teatro Libertador, I was to address the Rotarians on two evenings and also give the talk which Colonel Baer-Ruiz had planned during my last visit.

'What news of Professor Soto?'

Miguel Forero was prepared for my question and took a book from his briefcase entitled *Buritaca 200 (Ciudad Perdida)*, the Lost City (1). The author: Professor Soto Holguin. I flicked through it. Flights of steps overhung with lianas, moss-covered walls, terraces in the midst of luxuriant virgin forest.

'Fastastic,' I said, 'and what about Soto?'

'If it suits you, you can meet him at the University at eleven o'clock tomorrow morning.'

It is easy to find one's way about in the big city. Bogotá is covered by a network of streets intersecting at right angles. All the streets running from north to south are called *carreras*, except for occasional grandiose *avenidas*. The streets which cross the *carreras* at right angles are called *calles* and like the larger streets running from north to south they are numbered consecutively.

I arrived punctually at eleven o'clock at Professor Soto's Institute on Carrera No. 1. The tall slim archaeologist greeted me with a smile.

'So you're the man who writes those books!'

'Do you think I shouldn't?' I countered.

'Not at all. Science is open to all opinions.'

So the professor, quite young to hold a chair at the age of 38, was prepared to accept views outside the standard dogmas. I admired him as a rare example of his profession.

In an auditorium we sat in chairs with an arm rest on the right so that the students could take notes. The professor lolled on the seat and puffed at a cigarette. I asked: 'You call the lost city Buritaca 200. What does that mean?'

'The Sierra Nevada of Santa Marta extends between 32° 50′

Professor Alvaro Soto Holguin received me at his institute in the university for our first conversation.

and 74° 15′ west of Greenwich. Latitudinally the region comprises latitudes of 10° 5′ and 11° 20′ situated north of the Equator. Several small rivers have their sources in this region and some of them flow into the Caribbean in north-westerly direction. One of them is the Rio Buritaca, on the banks of which the "Lost City" is located. Hence Buritaca 200.'

'But what does the number 200 mean?'

'It is the two hundredth settlement, the two hundredth city, so to speak, that we have located so far.'

'It sound incredible. Does that mean that the whole jungle area was once dotted with settlements and urban cultures?'

'Yes, the area is enormous. You can form a rough idea of it when I tell you that we already know more than 2,000 kilometres of roads and tracks with stone surfaces. We have been excavating since 1976 and there is no end in sight. Buritaca 200 alone is ten times as big as the famous Inca fortress of Macchu Picchu in Peru.'

A girl student served us coffee. Colombian coffee tastes good all over the world, but it is never made so strong as in its home country. It would be interesting to know whether the Colombians all have heart disease or whether they hardly know where their hearts are beating because of the coffee. I asked; 'When was the city built and by whom?'

'On the basis of previous datings using the radioactive carbon isotope carbon 14, we conclude that Buritaca 200 was built around AD 800. The builders were the Tairona Indians, a sub-group of the Chibcha. Scholars also speak of a Tairona culture, but that is absurd, because the Tairona did not use that name for themselves. It was the Spaniards who gave the name to the Indians living in the Sierra Nevada. Not such a strange name when you know that the word *tairo* means something like 'casting metal' and the gold-hungry conquerors were only out after metal.'

'Did you find pottery or graves with mummies in?'

'We found ceramics and some metal objects. We discovered a few rockfaces with engravings and even some graves, but without mummies. The jungle is too humid for mummification.'

'Is it true that the excavation area is sealed off by the army?'

'Sealed off? That's not the right word. There are a few

soldiers up there to protect our personnel and keep out grave-robbers who could do a lot of damage.'

'So you have nothing to hide on the site? Theoretically, could tourists visit Buritaca 200 on organised tours?'

'We have nothing to hide, but we do not want tourists on the site. We are quite willing to allow access to experts, who could learn a lot from Buritaca 200. The social and ecological system of the complex is imposing. Although the Indian builders practised agriculture, traded with the sea ports and built cities, they did not destroy their environment.'

'Have you any objection to my visiting Buritaca 200?'

'Not the slightest!'

'How can I get there?'

'Only by helicopter. The flight from Bogotá to Santa Marta and back costs about 8,000 US dollars. But if you have the time and can wait for two months, because I have to give my university lectures, you can fly with me.'

A kind offer, but how to spend two months, a sixth of a year? I told myself that I must not be downhearted.

My first conversation with Soto Holguin was comparatively short, but later we had two lengthy talks at his flat in a high-rise building on Calle No. 7. Gradually I began to form a picture of the Lost City, as parts of the jigsaw fitted together. This is its story.

When the Spaniards Rodrigo de Bastidas and Juan de la Cosa were investigating the coasts of Venezuela in 1501, they also went in the direction of Panama. Obviously they must have traded with the Indians in the coastal regions, for they left one of their companions, Juan de Buenaventura, to learn the Indians' language. After all, merchants have to learn the language of their trading partners before they can cheat them.

The conquerors soon realised that Indians had gold objects to barter, as well as other things.

Professor Henning Bischof (2), the foremost expert on the Tairona culture, writes of the dense settlement in the region of the present-day port of Santa Marta:

In the sixteenth and early seventeenth centuries the Sierra Nevada looked quite different ... This conclusion is confirmed by the accounts of expeditions and battles, which show that the Spaniards had a much better range of vision than would have been the case in wooded mountain country. Basically, details of the density of the Indian population alone are enough to prove that the landscape must have changed considerably.

Rodrigo de Bastidas settled in Santo Domingo, the present-day capital of the Dominican Republic on the south coast of Haiti. In 1514 the Spanish king Carlos I appointed him Governor of the recently founded Province of Santa Marta. The Governor reached the small coastal town of Santa Marta with a body of two or three hundred men in June 1526.

During the next few decades the Spaniards were in almost continuous combat with the Tairona Indians, who defended themselves desperately against the white invaders who burnt their villages, plundered them and took the men prisoner or slaughtered them. The *conquistadores* knew that their barbaric methods had the blessing of the king in Madrid. He had issued a decree turning the Indians into slaves, outlawing them and allowing them to be killed or forced to perform the most degrading tasks.

The Indians met the Spaniards' modern weapons with stones, wooden clubs, spears and bows and arrows. Poisoned arrows. They got the poison from two natural sources, firstly the juice of the manzanilla tree, a highly poisonous type of spurge with fruit-like apples, which contained the poison. The arrows were dipped into the juice, dried in the air and wrapped in palm leaves so that the archers themselves would not be poisoned. Secondly, they tapped pacurine from the bark of the liana *Strychnos Toxifera*. In modern medicine it is known as curare, used as a nerve-relaxant. The Indians liked using pacurine because the game they killed remained edible in spite of the poison once the edges round the wound were cut out carefully.

Thousands of Spaniards died painfully by poisoned arrows in a hundred years' war against the Tairona, but the number of Indians who paid with their lives was far greater; it is estimated at 10,000.

Repelled by all the brutality, Juan de Castellanos (3), an eyewitness used to horrors, told how Captain Miguel Pinol gave orders that all Indians taken prisoner should have 'their noses, ears and lips cut off'. More then 70 Indian leaders were massacred, as well as women and children, and a severely wounded prince's son was executed, but not until the pagan son had been baptised into the Roman Catholic Church.

When it was all over the Spaniards had looted several hundred thousand gold pesos, as well as jewels and pearls. Indian settlements in the Sierra Nevada were destroyed. The few surviving Tairona hid in remote bays on the Caribbean coast.

The Tairona culture was wiped out and forgotten. Centuries passed. The jungle swallowed up the once flowering fields and settlements and cities. Save that in the region around Santa Marta it was rumoured that somewhere in the steaming forest-clad mountains there had once been an Indian tribe who saved a lot of gold from the Spaniards.

The kingdom of the Tairona had long since become the habitat of wild cats, apes, eagles and poisonous snakes. The humid flora of the primeval forest had conquered it. But gold has an irresistible fascination and men with gold-fever are not afraid of anything.

In autumn 1940 the treasure hunter and amateur archaeologist Florentino Sepúlveda met an old member of the Kogi Indian tribe in a quiet bay on the caribbean, only 20 km from Santa Marta. The old man told him that there were great cities and endless roads that had once been built by the Tairona in the immediate vicinity.

Sepúlveda, who was sixty years old himself, did not take the Indian's tales at their face value, but he found them interesting enough to tell his 19-year-old son Julio Cesar about them.

Julio Cesar, who did not know much more about the Spanish conquerors than that they loved gold, took the story seriously. For he was convinced of the existence of the legendary land of El Dorado and sensed that here was a chance to get rich quick — like winning the pools.

Julio Cesar followed the river Buritaca upstream from the coast. In the spring of 1975 he stumbled on one of the terraces of the Lost City. Convinced that he was on the right track, he took a spade and hacked a hole in the wall in front of him. After hours of laborious work he had to admit that the wall he was banging away at was part of a huge flight of steps.

This brought the gold-digger to his senses. He got on his horse and rode back to the port and seaside resort of Santa Marta, a difficult seven days' ride.

In a hotel bar, Julio Cesar did what a grave-robber should never do. He talked. Greedy for the gold, but not able to solve the problem of the site on his own, he showed the place in the jungle to some companions. Either out of envy or gold-fever, someone later shot Julio Cesar in the Lost City. Comrades dug his grave near the steps on which he had stumbled.

Then the grave-robbers, the *guaqueros*, swarmed in. They found their way into overgrown stone ruins. Soon Tairona cult artefacts appeared more and more frequently on the black market in antiques. The Colombian Institute for Anthropology and Archaeology got wind of this. When one grave-robber ransacked the site, the army took over the Lost City.

Archaeologists have been excavating in the jungle of the Sierra Nevada since 1976 and there is no end in sight yet, as Professor Soto told me. According to an assessment of the complexes so far excavated, 300,000 Indians must have lived there once. That is equal to the combined populations of Geneva and Berne.

Who were these wild Tairona Indians who managed to build these gigantic cities, who could not defend themselves against a handful of Spanish conquerors?

Soto told me that the present-day Kogi Indians on the coast and in the valleys of the Sierra Nevada are most probably direct descendants of the Tairona. His teacher, Professor Gerardo Reichel-Dolmatoff, spent years studying the life and history of the Kogi. In the process he established so many astonishing similarities between the present-day Kogi and the more ancient Tairona that we can assume that the Kogi descended from the Tairona.

Therefore groups of Tairona must have survived the Spanish massacres, preserved their ancient traditions and religious customs and handed them down to later generations. To find out who the Tairona were, I would have to concentrate on the Kogi, who are still living.

Once again Professor Preuss was the first man to take a scholarly interest in the Kogi and describe them in detail. After he had excavated parts of San Agustín from 1913 to

1914, he tackled the traditions of the Kágaba, as the Kogi were formerly called. Preuss discovered that the Kágaba-Kogi attributed the creation to the primordial mother Gauteóvan, who produced the sun and everything that existed from her menstrual blood. The four original priests who were the ancestors of the present-day Kogi priestly tribe also stemmed from Gauteóvan.

Tradition had it that the four original priests brought culture to the Indians, made laws and instructed them 'in all things'. The original priests had their home in space. Laws reached the Kágaba 'from outside'. It was said that these priests wore masks when they arrived and had their 'faces taken away'. If we assume that they had arrived on an interstellar flight, the faces would have been oxygen masks.

The priests bequeathed their office to their sons. They were brought up in the temple, serving a nine-year novitiate, so that the knowledge of the fathers was handed down untouched from one generation to another. The highest priests of the Kágaba-Kogi are called *Mama* (5). The *Mama* are more than what we normally understand by priests. The *Mama* is the absolute ruler of the tribe, whose orders must be followed blindly. There is no limit to the praise and punishment he can allot, because he knows that he is in direct succession to the original cosmic priests. Even today the *Mama* is convinced that he is in spiritual communication with the cosmos.

In order to reach this high-priestly rank, novices were shut up for nine years in total darkness and under close supervision in order to develop hypersensitive spirituality for cosmic contacts. The poor lads could not touch a woman during these nine years, do any work or eat salt. They were not served with food until midnight. It consisted of haricot beans, potatoes and snails; nothing with blood in it.

The primordial mother Gauteóvan and the four priests were not the only ones to emerge from the universe. There was also Uncle Nivaleue, who descended from heaven and made himself useful by laying out large fields. The demon Namsaui was another heavenly figure. The myths say that he was twice the size of normal men and killed men by the cold which flowed from him, leaving only their bones behind (4). It was said of Namsaui that his mask was red, his clothing blue and that he had protruding eyes over a very long nose. Namsaui was the lightning demon; he made the thunder and the snow that falls from heaven.

Professor Preuss described the Kágaba creation myth over 50 years ago. From the 30 pages he wrote I extract only the most important verses which show that their gods came from space and made man intelligent.

1st verse: The mother of our whole tribe bore us in the beginning. She is the mother of all kinds of men and she is the mother of all tribes ...

2nd verse: She alone is the mother of fire, the mother of the sun and the Milky Way ...

12th verse: And thus did the mother leave a memorial in every temple. Together with her sons Sintana, Seizankuan, Aluanuiko and Kultsavitabauya, she left behind songs and dances as memorials.

13th verse: That is what the priests, fathers and elder brothers reported.

Then come tales of the four priests fighting with demons and animals. 'Lightning bolts' are unleashed; there were flights all over the heavens and seeds of various plants were brought to earth. Masks of the gods were worn, one of them hidden in a mountain:

30th verse: Today it was set up to work on diseases and all kinds of evil and so that the novices who had learnt in the temple could talk to it. Afterwards the fathers, priests and elder brothers talked to it.

Did I read aright? Priests in ancient times are supposed to have talked to a mask to influence diseases? These descriptions only become intelligible when looked at from a modern point of view. The mask was a helmet with a built-in radio connection via which the priests received expert advice.

Knowledge of the Flood shows how far back the mythology of the Kágaba-Kogi reaches:

38th verse: Now centuries passed and then this world produced men with unnatural tendencies so that they used all kinds of animals to couple with. The mother desired the son, the father the daughter, the brother the sister, all being of the same blood.

39th verse: The prince Zantana saw this and opened the gates of heaven so that it rained for four years.

40th verse: When the priests observed that he would do this, the priest Seizankua built a magic ship and put all kinds of animals and other things inside it: the four-footed animals, the birds, and all kinds of plants did he place inside it. Thereupon the elder brother Mulkueikai entered the magic ship and closed the door.

41st verse: Then began red and blue rain which lasted for four years, and with the rain seas spread all over the world.

42nd verse: Meanwhile elder brother Mulkueikai lay in the magic ship which afterwards settled on the crest of the Sierra Negra. There he ventured out briefly and only very close to the ship. He stayed on the Sierra Negra for nine days.

43rd verse: After those nine days nine centuries passed before all the seas dried out, as the priests have handed down in our traditions.

44th verse: Now all evil people had perished, *and the priests, the elder brothers, all came down from heaven*. Whereupon Mulkueikai opened the door and placed all the birds and four-footed animals, all the trees and plants here on the earth. This did the divine person called father Kalgusiza bring about.

46th verse: And in all the temples they left behind a souvenir as a memorial.

How closely the texts resemble each other!

The Kágaba tradition mentioned sodomy, as did Moses in Genesis 19, before the destruction of Sodom and Gomorrah. The Sumerian *Epic of Gilgamesh* also includes a similar account of the Flood.

The Kágaba myth says that the priests all came down from heaven. The Sumerian King List says that: 'After the flood had receded, the kingdom came down from heaven again.' It sounds just like the Epic of Gilgamesh which relates that the 'gods' came down to earth after the great Flood.

Is there anyone barefaced enough to talk about coincidences when faced with such striking similarities? I mention only two myths identical with the Kágaba creation story, but they are found in ancient traditions all over the world. Everywhere real life experiences find their way into the myths.

Generations of priests continuously handed down the ancient knowledge of their cosmic teachers and preserved it. Professor Reichel-Dolmatoff (6) has shown that all the activities of the Kogi are still permeated by the cosmic laws of their Kágaba ancestors.

The Kogi are deeply religious. Their religious ideas are closely connected with their conception of order and happenings in the universe. Most villages have a chief who embodies governmental authority, but the real power of decision lies in the hands of the *Mama*, the native priests. These men have a thorough knowledge of tribal customs. They are not only shamans or medicine-men, but also in their priestly role take on tasks which they perform during ceremonial rituals after years of training.

During his years of study, Reichel-Dolmatoff discovered that all Kogi buildings could only by understood in the context of cosmic processes.

If a terrace, a house or a temple was to be built, the primary concerns were not only about the presence of water, light and shade, but the Kogi's cosmic relations to the constellations and the calendar were also 'built in'.

The Kogi looked on the cosmos as egg-shaped, demarcated by seven points: north, south, west, east, zenith, nadir (the lowest point of the heavens diametrically opposite to the zenith) and the centre. Within the space defined in this way lie nine layers, nine worlds, the middle or fifth layer representing our world. All the temples and ceremonial houses are models of the Kogi cosmos and follow this pattern.

Inside the ceremonial houses four divisions are superimposed. On the fifth division, the earth, the Kogi live, but symbolically four more divisions lead down into the earth, as symbol of the cosmos.

Apart from being religious centres, Kogi temples are also observatories. They are laid out in such a way that an accurate

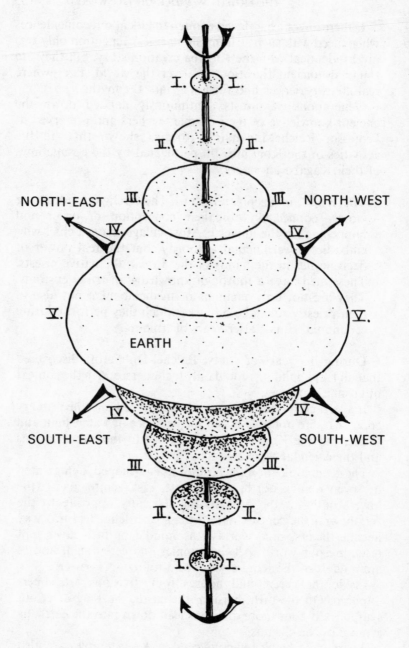

I.   I.

II.   II.

NORTH-EAST   III.   III.   NORTH-WEST

IV.   IV.

V.   V.

EARTH

IV.   IV.

SOUTH-EAST   III.   III.   SOUTH-WEST

II.   II.

I.   I.

The Kogi looked on the cosmos as egg-shaped space.

calendar reading is possible at any time. Reichel-Dolmatoff
(7) gives this example:

Men and women live apart. In every Kogi village there is
a large round men's house on the roof of which a big post
like a flagpole points up to heaven. Directly opposite — after
all, the ladies must not be too far away — is the women's
house, which is round, too. Two crossed beams emerge from
the roof-ridge. Post and beams represent a symbolical act!

Precisely on 21 March, the beginning of spring, the post
on the roof of the men's house throws a long shadow on the
ground. It falls exactly between the shadows cast by the crossed
beams on the women's house. The phallus penetrates the
vagina, a symbol of spring. Seeds must be laid in the
earth.

Inside the temple, a thick rope hangs from the ridge post
through the four divisions down to the fifth, the earth. The
high priest Mama is convinced that he is in direct contact
with his cosmic teachers through this rope.

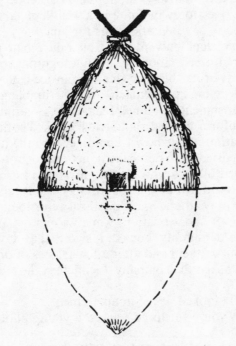

Cross-section of a Kogi house with its symbolic continuation into the
ground.

What does this tell us? Nine years' confinement in the dark might develop telepathic abilities enabling men to make contact with extraterrestrials. We know that radio connections from star to star are too slow to make interstellar communication possible. Alpha Centauri, the nearest fixed star to the earth, is four light-years away, i.e. 4 times 9.46 times 10^{12} km. Questions from earth transmitted to Alpha Centauri by radio would not get a radio answer for eight years. But telepathy is as swift as thought and it is not bound by the physical laws of time and space. Could the Kogi's knowledge make the inaccessible intelligible to us?

When I had given my lectures in the Teatro Libertador and used up the time allotted for talking to Professor Soto and visits to libraries, I was burning to see the Lost City about whose builders I now knew quite a lot.

Salvation came from an angle indicated three months before, and then by a lucky chance.

I was invited as a guest to the Officers' Club of the FAC.* The air force owns a lovely clubhouse in the centre of Bogotá, an extensive one-storey building in a well-kept garden with a swimming pool. My invitation was for lunch.

From one o'clock onwards I sat on a dark-blue plush sofa next to Dr Forero, looking at photographs of famous Colombian aviators. Neither this nor an ice-cold vermouth had any effect on my stomach. It was rumbling irritably, craving nourishment. Colonel Baer-Ruiz, wearing a smart light-blue uniform, arrived about two o'clock. The first reasonable information about how I could get into the jungle near Santa Marta dried up in polite introductions to group captains and pensioned officers who kept on arriving in droves.

When we sat down at the beautifully set-out table around three o'clock, my stomach, as loud as a ventriloquist's voice, interrupted every conversation, while we chatted about God and the world and my books. I swore that I would get something out of them and after a few glasses of dry Chilean white wine I asked the company 'Gentlemen, how do I get to Buritaca 200?'

The officers looked at me in amazement.

'Where do you want to go?' asked a young pilot.

---

* *Fuerza Aerea Colombiana*, the Colombian Air Force.

The forest flora have forced their way through the man-made paving stones.

'The whole site has a plan, a gigantic plan...'

Above:
A last snapshot: Sylvia, Margarita, Hernando and the flight engineer, shortly before takeoff.

Overleaf
Left:
Millions of cubic metres of stone were shifted at Buritaca. How? The eighth wonder of the world?

Right:
We hastened up the main flight of steps to the landing terrace. The helicopter took off and the landing place was swallowed up in the maws of the greedy rain forest.

I soon realised that Buritaca 200 was so much double-Dutch to these aviators. Admittedly they had heard of the Lost City, but no one had even a rough idea where it was. Well briefed by Professor Soto, the little Swiss gentleman was able to give the astonished Colombians the exact geographical location of their national attraction.

I asked politely if there was any chance of looking for it in a helicopter. All the officers burst into a cascade of Spanish which I could no longer follow. Finally Colonel Baer told me that only the head of the air force, General Paredes Diago, could decide about my case. However he had just returned from a ten-day visit to the USA and his timetable was so booked up that he would not be able to receive me at once. *Mañana.*

'What a pity,' I said and saw my prey escaping. How was I to get into the jungle, unless I waited for two months and relied on Professor Soto?

Over coffee and brandy, I overheard someone saying that General Paredes Diago was interested in my books and was also a passionate pipe collector.

The pipe which opened up the jungle to me.

Pipe collector? An idea flashed through my brain.

Since I got hold of a patented model which makes tiresome cleaning with dirty fingers unnecessary, I smoke a pipe for lazy smokers while working or playing chess. This pipe does not have the classical curved bowl. A container closed by a filter holds the tobacco and is in a straight line with the mouthpiece. The container can easily be emptied into an ashtray by a slight pressure. I took a brand-new example out of my jacket pocket. 'Does the general know this sort of pipe?'

Colonel Baer was interested at once. I took the pipe to bits, put it together again and asked him to present it to the general with my compliments and possibly mention that he was the only man in Colombia who could help to solve my little problem.

Colonel Baer-Ruiz phoned me early the next morning to say that General Paredes Diago would expect me in the headquarters of the FAC at 4 p.m. Dr Forero also accompanied me on this vital visit.

The air force headquarters, a modern building of glass, steel and concrete, lies on the outskirts of Bogotá. My hand luggage was checked and our bodies were searched. After showing our own identity cards, a corporal pinned numbered cards to our chests, the only military identification I have ever worn.

On the way to the general's office past glass cases full of model aircraft of all periods, we civilians were given appraising looks by officers who were waiting for their appointments on leather settees. We only sat in the waiting room for a quarter of an hour and the door to the holy of holies opened.

General Paredes Diago, with five gold stars on his shoulder straps, held my pipe in his hand when he rose from behind his desk. He asked us to sit down in a corner while an orderly served coffee. My poor heart!

I gave the general a signed copy of the Spanish version of my book *Signs of the Gods?*, *Profeta del Pasado*. Warned in advance that the general was a busy man, I came straight to the point: I wanted a helicopter flight to Buritaca 200.

For a moment the general looked at me reflectively. Then he summoned his adjutant.

'What unit is stationed in Santa Marta?'

'The No. 5 Cordova Infantry Battalion, sir,' answered the young officer.

'Find out at once whether the battalion has a helicopter and whether the machine is ready for a special mission the day after tomorrow.'

A loudspeaker somewhere interrupted our conversation. The general spoke something in reply into his microphone. I could not understand a word. The general bowed to me and disappeared. Dr Forero gave the thumbs-up sign. We had won!

In a few minutes the general returned, handed me an envelope and wished me luck and success.

In the taxi I read what the general had dictated:

Fuerza Aerea Colombiana.
Senor Teniente Coronel.
Hector Lopez Ramirez Commandante Batallón de Infanteria No. 5 Cordova Santa Marta.
El señor Erich von Däniken está autorizado por este Comando para efectuar un vuelo en Helicótero Hughes que se encuentra en esa Unidad de la ciudad de Santa Marta a la ciudad perdida.
Cordial saludo.
General Raul Alberto Paredes Diago.
Commandante Fuerza Aérea.

[Lt Colonel Hector Lopez Ramirez
Officer commanding No. 5 Cordova Infantry Battalion
Santa Marta
This order authorises Mr Erich von Däniken to fly from Santa Marta to the Lost City in the Hughes Helicopter belonging to your unit.]

The next day I landed in Santa Marta on the noon flight of Colombian Airways and lodged right by the sea in the Irotama, a hotel which had seen better days. I phoned repeatedly but I could not get in touch with Colonel Ramirez. At five o'clock in the afternoon it's packing-up time, as with soldiers all over the world. *Mañana.*

On Friday, 21 August, at 5.30 a.m., I was driven out to No. 5 Infantry Battalion. Two infantrymen with machine pistols searched me at the entrance before I could explain the reason for my visit, but the general's letter which I waved at them worked like an open sesame until a civilian in the colonel's

anteroom looked at it with wrinkled brows. Surprise depart-
ures from routine were unwelcome at such an early hour. The
civilian disappeared into the next door office without a word.

Although it was so early in the morning I was dripping
with sweat because of the high humidity. I sat on a wooden
bench, wiping the sweat from my forehead with a handkerchief
that was already wet, and waited. The civilian returned, sat at
his desk and said nothing. The waiting seemed endless. Was
there going to be some snag when I was almost there?

I determined to sit there quietly, but determined not to
budge until the general's order was carried out. *Basta*.

Basta!, repeated the young man in green uniform who was
leaning against the wall with his arms crossed. On the flap of
his right-hand breast pocket I saw the words Fuerza Aerea
Colombiana embroidered in silver. A pilot in the infantry?

He had to be my helicopter pilot! I spoke to him.

His name was Fernando, he said, and he was to fly a Mr
von Däniken to the Lost City, but he had not the faintest
idea where it was and the weather that day was not ideally
suited to the little Hughes. Besides the machine could only
stay airborne for two and a half hours. It could not spend
much time searching because if the city could not be found
in an hour and a quarter we should have to return.

Fernando did not see things through rose-coloured spectacles. He gave a gloomy account of the difficulties he had
with the marijuana cultivators in the district. They were rightly
afraid of the military pilots and opened fire on them at random.
More than one aircraft had been shot down over the forests
and the crew had never been heard of again. Santa Marta
was a centre of the trade in marijuana, a city where life was
not worth twopence since, trafficking in the drug had begun.
People could earn fantastic sums in a very short time and that
pushed up inflation. Morality went to pot and shoot-outs
were the order of the day. 'Santa Marta gold' was dealt with
on the international markets at top prices as being finest
quality marijuana.

Since the men stood to attention, the officer who looked
in and held the door open must be my Colonel Ramirez. I
leapt up, gave my name, received a brief searching look and
was invited to sit down in his office. Naturally we were served
coffee, of the kind that pours forth from morning to night.

Santa Marta — port and seaside resort on the Caribbean — is the centre
of traffic in illegal 'Santa Marta gold', valuable marijuana.

Fernando described his difficulties. Colonel Ramirez interrupted him. 'Is there anyone in the battalion who knows the
exact location of the Lost City?'

Ramirez gave an order over the loudspeaker, spread some
military maps on the table and pointed with his finger. 'It's
somewhere in that region.'

When I pointed out that it was on the River Buritaca,
Fernando asked ironically if I knew the forest. He could not
land there. I would either have to jump out or be let down
on a rope ladder. I certainly had no desire to do that and said
firmly, 'You can land in the forest on terraces that were built
more than a thousand years ago!'

Professor Soto had told me that that was how he had
reached the site.

'Do you believe that?' Colonel Ramirez looked at me
sceptically.

'I know it for a fact.'

A corporal, who was undoubtedly of Indian blood, reported.

'You've been to the Lost City before?' asked Ramirez.

'Yes, Señor Comandante,' said the Indian, thumping his chest proudly.

'Then you shall go on the flight.'

Until that moment I did not realise that even Indians can turn white. The corporal crossed himself and his face, which had been radiant, turned ashen.

Together with Hernando, the Indian and a flight engineer, I clambered into the four-seater helicopter, which crossed Santa Marta with a deafening roar, then flew along the coast to the mouth of the Buritaca valley.

The natives were called Indians (Indios) by mistake. To the end of his days Columbus believed that the country he discovered was India and so named the inhabitants Indians. The Indian shouted something I did not understand and I saw that he was showing Hernando where to fly in sign language. Low cloud cover clung to the tops of the giant forest trees. Somewhere down below there were marijuana farmers, but I was more afraid of losing our way than their flintlocks. There was nothing to orientate oneself by. From above the green hell looked like an enormous greenish-black cauliflower. Dense and impenetrable.

The helicopter banked steeply and then I saw it: one terrace with a second and a third one below it Hernando had spotted it, too, and gave me a significant look. He landed the Hughes gently on the topmost terrace. He did not stop the rotor blades. They made a whirlwind in the still air. Hernando was anxious to take off again; he did not trust the weather.

'Back here in five hours,' I shouted and put up my hand with the fingers outspread. 'OK. In five hours,' he shouted back, pointing to the terrace on which we stood.

The helicopter rose up vertically; its clatter seemed to cling to trees and lianas. When the noise had faded, there was a moment's silence in the jungle, but the animals soon recovered from their fear of the noisy visit. Monkeys roared, birds chattered and invisible animals screamed. Wherever I went I was followed by buzzing mosquitoes which proved to be very attentive. I would gladly have walked around the jungle sauna

When the helicopter banked we saw a terrace suitable for landing in the dense jungle.

like Adam, but the repulsive biters made me realise in the most unpleasant way that I was not in Paradise. I read somewhere that there were about 1.5 million species of insects. The great majority of them were represented in Buritaca.

Now I was standing lost in the Lost city, probably the first European to do so. Certainly no European had as yet photographed or written about the site.

I like adventure, but I'm no hero. I am always getting into tricky situations against my will. I asked myself what would happen if the weather made landing impossible in five hours. Or supposing the only helicopter available crashed in the meantime.

What if Hernando was given a more important military mission? Spending the night here was not a very pleasant prospect, but what could I do about it? I shouldered my cameras and clambered down to the next terrace.

Opposite, on the cliff face, clung a wooden hut among tropical undergrowth, cedars, nut trees, eucalyptus trees, advocado pear trees, rubber trees, palms and ferns, all of them smothered in lianas. It had to be the archaeologists' camp. I shouted, but there was no answer. Heaven only knew where the team were digging today to keep the greedy jungle at bay from the ruins they had excavated. They must have seen and heard the helicopter.

Suddenly two soldiers appeared from nowhere. They were wearing jungle camouflage suits flecked with brown, green and red and were armed with rifles and pistols.

'Buenos días, señores!' I cried but got no reaction from their dark-brown faces. I still had two duty-free cigars in metal tubes bought on the Lufthansa flight and I gave them to the soldiers. They said, 'Gracias!' and walked away. They were far from loquacious, but at least I knew that there were people somewhere in the green hothouse.

I slowly descended the endless steps which were a good 1.5 m wide and was surprised that the elliptical terrace on which we had landed was still within my field of vision. The lower I went, the more obvious it became that the topmost platform rested on a lower one, and that on another one and so on. A series of artificial stone plateaux carried the structure up to the summit.

Was I suffering from hallucinations? I met two delightful girls on a moss-covered path. One of them, wearing baggy trousers and a green safari blouse, smiled and shook me by the hand. 'My name is Sylvia. Welcome to Buritaca 200!'

The other Amazon, in blue jeans that showed off her appetising figure, a wide leather belt and a wide-brimmed straw hat, looked a little bit older than Sylvia. Margarita, the older girl, was an architect by profession; Sylvia, an archaeologist, had been working with the excavation team for more than half a year.

My Colombian forest angels asked me for a cigarette, the only thing they longed for at that moment. I gave them all I had left. These girls with their perfect English were just what I needed. They led me along stone paths through the tropical rain forest, commenting on the site as we went. The humidity remained steady, between 60 and 95 per cent.

Buritaca 200 lies to right and left of the little river that gave the town its name, clinging to the gorges of Cerro Corea, 3,055 m high. The structures are arranged in the form of terraces in several layers along a broad road. The main entrance to the town is 900 m high. From the end of a gorge, a steep flight of steps with a gradient of 50 degrees leads 1,100 m up to the large levelled terraces. The upper part seems to have been the centre of the city. An intricate mixture of 26 large and small terraces with areas varying between 50 and 880 sq. m occupy the heights. All these terraces have been excavated since 1976, a tremendous feat.

Complicated topographical conditions were laid down by nature. This means that the ancient architects had to level the mountain metre by metre to make room for the horizontal structures. They cut into the rock faces, filling in with stones, earth and supporting walls. The height of the wall varies from 60 cm to 10 m!

Integrated with walls and terraces, the excavators discovered a canalisation system which kept the vast complex dry in spite of the constant humidity and torrential rain.

Margarita explained to me that archaeologists divided Buritaca into four main sectors. In the first sector they found the remains of household objects such as stone mills for grinding corn, in the second pottery, such as scoops, vases and eating dishes, in the third, ceremonial artefacts including beautifully worked clay flutes, and in the fourth, cult objects such as priests' rings, figurines of the gods and funerary tributes.

In spite of these finds, archaeologists, especially Soto Holguin, the Director of Excavations, are faced with a problem. No one knows what Buritaca really was — a sanctuary on a vast scale, orientated to the firmament, the calendar? A priestly city inhabited solely by initiates in one vast monastery? A dormitory town in which 300,000 Indians slept before going to work somewhere else in the daytime? Was it a military outpost, a fortress?

However, scholars do agree that the builders of the jungle city included far-sighted architects and engineers with a variety of skills. The whole conception implies far-sightedness because the settlements in the Sierra Nevada cannot have been the work of one generation. The gigantic scale shows that there must have been an overall plan before the first great stones were moved. Astronomers must have been involved from the beginning, at least as advisers, as it has been proved that certain terraces are aligned on the constellations. The exemplary ecological system indicates the cooperation of engineers. There were only limited areas for cultivation, but maize, beans, manioc and potatoes to supply 300,000 Indians were cultivated without destroying the environment.

In order to understand the full significance of this achievement, one needs to know the state of affairs around Santa Marta before 1975, when the Sierra Nevada was placed under government protection. The population in the port, the smart seaside resort of Santa Marta, grew at an alarming rate. It overflowed the city limits and reached the slopes of the Sierra Nevada. The forest was burnt down. People planted coffee and bananas in the fertile soil for a couple of years and as yields decreased pushed further into the jungle, leaving behind the scars of civilisation. In this district, it rains virtually every day from April to November. Without the protective covering of the tropical trees and their network of roots in the ground, the soil is eroded. The land becomes arid and unfertile in a

The Tairona settled in the virgin forest, but they did not destroy it.

few years. Today the area around Santa Marta still bears tragic witness to the destructive type of agriculture practised by local settlers until 1975. A disaster.

All this happened in a relatively short time. Yet the Tairona lived in their cities for nearly a thousand years without destroying the virgin forest and still produced great quantities of agricultural products. How did the Tairona solve their ecological and agricultural problems? Professor Soto gave me this answer:

To achieve what was achieved at Buritaca there must have been a social organisation that differed from every other type. The Tairona Indians must have known and used something special. These people were anything but primitive and the modern world can only learn from them. We destroy tropical rain forests by slash and burn and keep on creating new environmental crises. The builders of these settlements proved that there are other ways of going about things.

At first I suspected that the topmost terrace had come about by a chance accumulation of stone slabs and blocks.

At first I suspected that the top terrace had been formed by a chance accumulation of stone slabs. I said as much to Sylvia and Margarita, but they pointed out that I was standing in a landscape intentionally laid out in a bizarre way, a landscape of stone circles, walls, ellipses, small towers, flights of steps and paths, in an indescribable confusion of shapes which would not have occurred to Pablo Picasso in his most daring period, when he was dissolving the objective into geometrical structures.

Sylvia pulled curtains of lianas aside and opened up a vista of new surprises which extended downhill to the River Buritaca and up to the rock faces. Wherever we went in this ill-understood monument to the past, we continuously came across artificially levelled surfaces. The Hanging Gardens of Semiramis in Babylon were looked on as the seventh wonder of the world. I make a plea for adding Buritaca as the eighth wonder of the world.

The girls watched me as I came on one surprise after another. My camera was clicking away constantly. If I could not prove

My camera never stopped clicking!

what I saw with photographs, no one would believe my description of the unique panorama. I had only to push aside the enormous leaf of a rubber tree to find myself staring at yet more massive accurately built walls and paths. With the explosive power of forest flora, thick corozo palms, bay-trees, cedars and ferns of every kind had forced their way through the neatly laid stones. It was a labyrinth as described in the dictionary: an arrangement of tortuous and deceptive paths from which it is difficult to find the way out. No matter whether I looked up, down, right or left, more platforms lay around me.

Mentally I conjured up the distant past when the priests worshipped their gods on the highest terraces, surrounded by thousands of Indians. When incense offerings rose to heaven from every platform and combined with the prayers, when the *Mama* were on intimate terms with the cosmos. If you block out in your imagination the trees which grow on the slopes today, a complete picture of this utopian landscape is present. Professor Soto's remark came into mind: 'The whole site has a plan, a gigantic plan, save that we do not know what it was for!'

One stone, more than two metres high, was covered with a plastic sack. I asked what it was. Sylvia and Margarita undid the rope and removed the protective covering from the monster, which was a monolith with many right-angled lines engraved on it. 'What is it?' I repeated.

Sylvia answered. 'The Indians say it was the plan of the complex.'

'A sort of city map, in other words?'

The girl nodded, but added at once that Professor Soto had his doubts about that. He had had the stone covered to save it from further weathering, in the hope that one day it would yield up its secret to scholars.

The literally indescribable noises of the forest were suddenly overpowered by the sound of water, although water was nowhere to be seen. Sylvia and Margarita were amused by my astonishment, then they pulled aside a curtain of lianas. A waterfall poured down the cliff until it was captured in a broad stone channel and led by another channel to a circular platform.

When you think that this area with its tropic rain was kept dry, your respect for the constructors increases enormously.

The Indians claim that this stone shows the town plan of Buritaca. It is not yet known if that is true.

I know the famous rice terraces in the mountains of the Philippines and the steep cultivated terraces of Machu Picchu in Peru. None of them is comparable with Buritaca 200.

The builders here did not set to work with monoliths of monstrous dimensions, as at Tiahuanaco and Puma Punku in Bolivia, or like Sacsayhuaman in Peru, and yet millions of cubic metres of stone were moved, for all the mountain slopes turn out to be artificially built on. After the first finds, the incredible astonishment began that always sets in in the presence of new discoveries. We shall keep on learning new things about Buritaca 200.

Suddenly monkeys and birds were silent. The noise of the helicopter's rotors echoed from the slopes. My five hours had actually passed.

Sylvia, Margarita and I hastened along narrow paths and across the main flight of steps to the landing terrace. Without the girls topographical knowledge, I would have been hopelessly lost.

Hernando was chatting to the soldiers who had been so taciturn with me. I pulled out of my pockets everything I did not need urgently and gave the conents to the helpful ladies: a light NASA windcheater, an anti-insect spray, plasters for cuts, a dynamo pocket torch, two screwdrivers and a measuring tape. Everything can be put to some use in the jungle.

The helicopter took off and flew low over the treetops in a curve back to the sea. Our landing place was left behind and was swallowed up by the mouth of the greedy rain forest.

Professor Soto had told me that the Kogi, like their ancestors the Tairona, looked on themselves as the 'elder brothers' of our planet. All foreigners are 'younger brothers' to them, for it was their ancient priests who brought life to their country from the cosmos.

The Tairona once had a blooming culture. Why do the Kogi dress so wretchedly today? Why have they stopped working in gold, spinning thread and weaving artistic materials? Why do they no longer paint mythical scenes on their ceramics?

The *Mama*, their high priests, the omniscient ones, tell the Kogi that it is no longer worth it. The gods had given the 'younger brothers' the opportunity to build dangerous playthings such as cannons, helicopters, car, submarines and rockets, but the 'younger brothers' did not know how to handle them. So the playthings would soon set the world on fire and there was no point in their former activities, although the *Mama*, and all the Kogi people are convinced that they are the ones who will preserve and continue the human race after the holocaust.

I am the opposite of a prophet of world disaster. I am an optimist, because I still rely on the intelligence of the men who recognise and try to eliminate the danger into which we have manoeuvred ourselves. Later I found that the mam-Kogi prophecies tally with the traditions of other Indian tribes from Chile to Canada.

In January 1980 there was an Indian Congress in Montreal attended by Indian priests from many territories. The representative of the Yanomano Indians from Venezuela told the Congress (8):

> In the vicinity of the country where my people live there are some mountains which are sacred to us. We call one of them the 'bear', another the 'monkey' and a third the 'bird'. Long before the white men came, our medicine men visited these mountains many times. No one else was allowed to visit this district. These mountains conceal great powers and the ancient sages of our people speak of dangerous material that lies there. Our tradition says that if these mountains were destroyed, terrible misfortune would befall. Massive rainfall would flood everything and wipe out our people.

Then the Yanomano had something incredible to say. A few years ago Japanese scientists had drilled in the sacred mountains ... and they found uranium!

How could this knowledge (confirmed two years ago) have found its way into ancient Indian tradition a thousand years and more ago; who knew that certain mountains concealed dangerous materials? Who could predict that exploitation of the sacred mountains would unleash terrible misfortune?

As the primeval Indians were certainly incapable of producing measuring instruments to locate the uranium, we must ask: where did they get their knowledge? was their unspoilt religious sensitivity enough to localise the dangerous radiation? Or did they see creatures suffering an agonising death in the vicinity of their sacred mountains? That is quite possible, for nature does not look after her uranium as carefully as modern nuclear power stations treat uranium waste. Nature makes no distinction between the living and the dead.

Yet even if we admit that the Indians had sensed the presence of dangerous matter in their mountains in some way or other, their foreknowledge of the latent danger involved in exploitation is incomprehensible. We are proud of the fact that our high technology has made the invisible measurable. But who handed on the precognition?

Who told the Yanomano about the danger hidden in the mountains? The Indians themselves supply the answer. It was their heavenly teachers!

Of course it is easy enough to dismiss the 'heavenly teachers' as figments of the imagination dreamed up by the primeval Indians, but that leads us into a complete cul-de-sac. Then we are implying that the narrators of all Indian tribes, and *mutatis mutandis* our biblical prophets, cheated and lied in their accounts of conversations with the heavenly ones.

A prophet like the biblical Enoch did not say that he had spoken to visions or travelled in the realms of fancy. Enoch makes it quite clear that he spoke to teachers who came from heaven and that they instructed him in his activities. So were Enoch, Moses, Gilgamesh, the Yanomano and Hopi Indians, the Dogon Negroes in Central Africa, the ancient Indian sages and the Kogi all lying? Are we dealing with a world-wide Mafia of imaginative storytellers?

The second 'solution' of misunderstood mythological messages and stone witnesses from the remote past by psychological interpretations founders on the hard facts which do not tolerate lengthy attempts to lay verbal smokescreens. Buritaca 200 exists. The cosmological model stems from an as yet unverifiable past. It had been in existence long before the white man occupied the terrain centuries ago and 'discovered' the Indians. They would have existed and continued to exist even if the white men had not scared them away and ill-treated them.

The way may be unpleasant and barely accessible to our scientists, but it is the only one that leads to the goal. The primordial teachers were extraterrestrials.

If we accept this (to me banal) fact, the whole history of

mankind would be brilliantly illuminated. It is high time to pull this wisdom tooth. It is high time to investigate the claims of the Kogi that their ancient priests had left in the temples 'memories' which more advanced men would understand. Perhaps the stone phalluses that rear up to heaven are symbols of the life that came 'from above'. Perhaps the 'genetic disc' is a pointer to the origin of the first life. Perhaps the engravings on the Tunja stones contain formulas giving information about the sojourn of the extraterrestrials. Perhaps the Archaeological Park at San Agustín is a gigantic memorial that was left behind – as a memory of the future.

Our blue planet affords an overpowering number of memories. What must happen before science finally takes notice of them? It will be too late after a global catastrophe. We can no longer afford to overlook warnings or ignore possible remedies.

We are not only responsible for what we do, but also for what we leave undone!   (Molière, 1622–73)

Picture Acknowledgements

The pictures on pages 2 to 7 were kindly put at my disposal by the Church of Jesus Christ of Latter-day Saints, Salt Lake City (USA)

Josef Blumrich: Page No. 19 (from *The Spaceships of Ezekiel*, Bantam Books, 1974)

Manfred Steinlechner: Indian ink drawings on pages 42, 50, 51, 61, 66, 142

Professor Jaime Gutierrez, Bogotá: Page Nos. 145–148

Patrick Utermann: Sketches page Nos. 184 and 185

Willi Dünnenberger: Page No. 187

All other illustrations are by the author

Bibliography

1 Legendary Times!

1. *The Book of Mormon*, 16th edn, 1966
2. HINCKLEY, Gordon B., *The Truth Re-established. Brief sketch of the History of the Church of Jesus Christ of Latter-day Saints*, 1978
3. BIN GORION, Micha Josef, *Die Sagen der Juden von der Urzeit*, Frankfurt, 1919
4. BURROWS, Millar, *More Light on the Dead Sea Scrolls*, London, 1958
5. WUTTKE, Gottfried, *Melchisedech, der Preisterkönig von Salem, Eine Studie zur Geschichte der Exegese*, Giessen, 1929
6. BONWETSCH, Nathanael G., *Die Bücher der Geheimnisse Henochs, Das sogenannte slawische Henochbuch*, Leipzig, 1927
7. *Die Heilige Schrift des Alten und des Neuen Testaments*, Stuttgart, 1972
8. HERTZBERG, H. W., 'The Melschisedek Traditions', *The Journal of the Palestine Oriental Society*, Vol. VIII, Jerusalem, 1928
9. LAMBERT, Wilfried G. and MILLARD, Alan Ralph, *Atrahasis, The Babylonian Story of the Flood*, Oxford, 1970
10. SITCHIN, Zecharia, *Der Zwölfte Planet*, Unterägeri bei Zug, 1979
11. BLUMRICH, Josef F., *The Spaceships of Ezekiel*, Bantam Books, 1974
12. HEYERDAHL, Thor, *Early Man and the Ocean*, Allen & Unwin, 1978
13. MADER, A. E., 'New Dolmen Finds in West Palestine', *The Journal of the Palestine Oriental Society*, Vol. VII, Jerusalem, 1927
14. BÄRWOLF, Adalbert, 'Radar entschleiert die Äcker de Maya', *Die Welt*, Hamburg, 6 September 1980

15. CORDAN, Wolfgang, *Das Buch des Rates Popol Vuh* — *Schöpfungsmythos und Wanderung der Quiché-Maya*, Düsseldorf, 1962
16. HASSLER, Gerd von, *Noahs Weg zum Amazonas*, Hamburg, 1976
17. HONORÉ, Pierre, *Ich fand den Weissen Gott*, Frankfurt, 1965
18. HAMMOND, Norman, 'The Earliest Maya', *Scientific American*, New York, March 1977
19. TALMAGE, James E., *The articles of faith. An Examination and Consideration of the Main Doctrines of the Church of Jesus Christ of Latter-day Saints*, Salt Lake City, undated
20. MAZAR, Benjamin, *Der Berg des Herrn* — *Neue Ausgrabungen in Jerusalem*, Bergisch Gladbach, 1979

2   In the Beginning Everything Was Different

1. MAZAR, Benjamin, *Der Berg des Herrn* — *Neue Ausgrabungen in Jerusalem*, Bergisch Gladbach, 1979
2. TELLO, Julio C., 'Discovery of the Chavín Culture in Peru', *American Antiquity*, Vol. IX, No. 1, Menasha, 1943
3. STINGL, Miloslav, *Die Inkas* — *Ahnen der 'Sonnensohne'*, Düsseldorf, 1978
4. KAUFFMAN DOIG, Federico, 'La cultura Chavín', *Las Grandes Civilizaciones del Antiguo Peru*, Tomo III, Lima, 1963
5. NACHTIGALL, Horst, *Die amerikanischen Megalithkulturen*, Berlin, 1958
6. DISSELHOFF, H. D., *Das Imperium der Inka*, Berlin, 1972
7. PÖRTNER, Rudolf and DAVIES, Nigel, *Alte Kulturen der Neuen Welt, Neue Erkenntnisse der Archäologie*, Düsseldorf, 1980
8. TRIMBORN, Hermann, *Das Alte Amerika*, Stuttgart, 1959
9. HUBER, Siegfried, *Im Reich der Inka*, Olten, 1976
10. KATZ, Friedrich, *The Ancient American Civilisations*, Weidenfeld & Nicolson, 1969
11. FRANZ, Heinrich G., 'Tiermaske und Mensch-Tier-

Verwandlung als Grundmotive der altamerikanischen Kunst', *Jahrbuch des Kunsthistorischen Instituts der Universität Graz*, 1975

12. WEDEMEYER, Inge von, *Sonnengott und Sonnenmenschen*, Tübingen, 1970

13. KRICKEBERG, Walter, *Altmexikanischen Kulturen*, Berlin, 1975

14. DISSELHOFF, H. D., *Alt-Amerika*, Baden-Baden, 1961

15. SÉJOURNÉ, Laurette, *Altamerikanische Kulturen*, Vol. 21, Frankfurt, 1971

16. WILLEY, Gordon R., 'The Early Great Styles and the Rise of the Pre-Columbian Civilisations', *American Anthroplogist*, Vol. 64. 1962

17. LOTHROP, Samuel K., *Essays in Pre-Columbian Art and Archaeology*, Harvard University Press, Cambridge, Mass., 1964

18. BENNETT, Wendell C., 'The North Highlands of Peru, Part 2, Excavations at Chavín de Huantar', *Anthropological Papers of the American Museum of Natural History*, Vol. 39, New York, 1944

19. EISSFELDT, Otto, *Einleitung in das Alte Testament*, Tübingen, 1964

20. BURCKHARDT, Georg, *Gilgamesh — Eine Erzählung aus dem alten Orient*, Insel Verlag, undated

21. WILLEY, Gordon R., 'The Chavín Problem', *Southwestern Journal of Anthropology*, Vol. 7, No. 2, Albuquerque, 1951

22. DAVIES, Nigel, *Voyagers to the New World — Fact or Fantasy*, Macmillan, 1979

23. BURLEIGH, Richard, 'Scientific Methods of Dating', *Cambridge Encyclopedia of Archaeology*, Cambridge University Press, 1980

24. COE, Michael D., 'Olmec and Chavín: Rejoinder to Lanning', *American Antiquity*, Vol. 29, No. 1, Salt Lake City, 1963

25. KANO, Chiaki, 'The origins of the Chavín culture', *Studies in Pre-Columbian Art and Archaeology*, No. 22, Washington, 1979

26. KUBLER, George, *The Art and Architecture of Ancient America*, Harmondsworth, 1979

27. BLUMRICH, Josef F., *Kasskara und die Sieben Welten*, Düsseldorf, 1979

General
MÖLLER, Gerd and Elfride, *Peru*, Pforzheim, 1976
MASON, Alden J., *The Ancient Cities of Peru*, Pelican, Edinburgh, 1957
MIDDENDORF, E. W., *Das Hochland von Peru*, Vol. III, Berlin, 1895
KRICKEBERG, Walter, *Pre-Columbian American Religions*, Weidenfeld & Nicolson, 1961
WAISBARD, Simone, *Die Kultur der Inkas*, Zurich, 1980
RAIMONDI, Antonio, *El Peru*, Vol. I, Lima, 1940

3   A Case for Heinrich Schliemann

1. BLUMRICH, Josef F., *The Spaceships of Ezekiel*, Bantam Books, 1974
2. LAING, Bernhard, *Ezechiel — Der Prophet und das Buch*, Darmstadt, 1981
3. KAUTZSCH, Emil, *Die Apokryphen und Pseudepigraphen des Alten Testaments*, Vol. II, Ch. 7, Das Leben Adams und Evas, Hildesheim, 1962
4. GRÜNWEDEL, Albert, *Mythologie des Buddhismus in Tibet und in der Mongolei*, Leipzig, 1900
5. BOPP, Franz, *Ardschuna's Reise zu Indra's Himmel*, Berlin, 1824
6. LINDBLOM, J., *Prophecy in Ancient Israel*, Oxford, 1962
7. KEEL, Othmar, *Zurück von den Sternen*, Fribourg, 1970
8. BEYERLEIN, W., *Herkunft und Geschichte der ältesten Sinai-Traditionen*, 1961
9. DUMMERMUTH, Fritz, Separatdruck der theologischen Fakultät der Universität Basel, *Theol. Zeitschrift*, No. 17, 1961 and No. 19, 1963
10. DUMMERMUTH, Fritz, 'Biblische Offenbarungsphänomene', *Theologische Zeitschrift*, No. 21, 1965
11. TORREY, C., *Pseudo-Ezekiel and the Original Prophecy*, New Haven, 1930
12. SMEND, Rudolf, *Der Prophet Ezechiel*, Leipzig, 1880

13. BAUMGARTNER, W., *Hebraisches Schulbuch*, 26th edn, Basle, 1971
14. EICHRODT, W., *Das Alte Testament deutsch — Der Prophet Hesekiel*, Göttingen, 1968
15. PRAGER, Mirjam and STEMBERGER, Günter, *Die Bibel*, Salzburg, 1976
16. RICHTER, G., 'Der ezechielsche Tempel — Eine exegetische Studie über Ezechiel', *Beiträge zur Förderung christlicher Theologie*, 16. Jahrgang, Heft 12, Tübingen, 1912
17. REUSS, Eduard D., *Das Alte Testament — die Propheten*, Vol. 2, Braunschweig, 1892
18. HAUCK, Albert D., *Realencyklopädie für Protestantische Theologie und Kirche*, Chap. Ezekiel, Graz, 1969
19. CHIPIEZ, Charles and PERROT, Georges, *Le temple de Jérusalem et la maison du Bois-Liban, Restitués d'après Ezéchiel et le livre des Rois*, Paris, 1889
20. THENIUS, Otto, *Die Bücher der Könige — Kurzgefasstes exegetisches Handbuch zum Alten Testament*, Leipzig, 1849

General
BRUGG, Elmar, *Tragik und schöpferischer Mensch*, Baden/Switzerland, 1965
ZIMMERLI, Walther, *Ezechiel*, Vol. XIII/2, Neukirchen-Vluyn, 1969
BAUMANN, Eberhard D., 'Die Hauptvisionen Hesekiels', *Zeitschrift für die Alttestamentliche Wissenschaft*, Vol. 67, Berlin, 1956

4   The Strategy of the Gods

1. 'Indio-Kultur im Dschungel, *Der Spiegel*, 1 February 1981
2. STÖPEL, Theodor K., *Südamerikanische prähistorische Tempel und Gottheiten*, Frankfurt, 1912
3. PREUSS, Theodor K., *Monumentale vorgeschichliche Kunst*, Göttingen, 1929
4. NACHTIGALL, Horst, *Die Amerikanischen Megalithkulturen*, Berlin, 1958

5. SOTO, Alvaro, *San Agustín*, Instituto Colombiano de Antropología, Bogotá, undated
6. DISSELHOFF, H. D., 'Die Kunst der Andenländer', *Alt-Amerika — Die Hochkulturen der Alten Welt*, Baden-Baden, 1961
7. KAPP, Martin, 'Im finstern zwanzigsten Jahrhundert', *Information der Internationalen Treuhand AG*, Heft 64, 1981
8. NIEL, Fernand, *Auf den Spuren der Grossen Steine*, Munich, 1977
9. HITZ, Hans-Rudolf, *Als man noch Protokeltisch sprach, Versuch einer Entzifferung der Inschriften von Glozel*, Ettingen, 1982
10. THÜRKAUF, Max, *König Nobels Hofstaat*, Schaffhausen, 1981
11. PRIANA, Miguel, *El jeroglifico Chibcha*, Bogotá, 1924
12. RUZO, Daniel, *La historia fantastica de un descubrimiento*, Mexico City, 1974
13. 'Stinkbomben in Atomlagern', *Der Spiegel*, 1981/51
14. SIMON, Pedro, *Noticias historiales de las conquistas de tierra en las Indias occidentales*, Bogotá, 1882–90
15. NACHTINGALL, Horst, *Alt-Kolombien*, Berlin, 1961
16. PAUWELS, Louis and BERGIER, Jacques, *Aufbruch ins dritte Jahrtausend*, Bern, 1962

General
BRAY, Warwick, *El Dorado*, New York, 1974
BUCHANAN, D., 'A Preliminary Decipherment of the Glozel Inscriptions', *The Epigraphic Society*, Vol. IX, No. 226, San Diego, Ca., 1981
CRICK, Francis, *Life Itself, Its Origin and Nature*, London, 1981
CHAVES, Eduardo B., *Mensagem dos Deuses*, Lisbon, 1977
FRADIN, Emile, *Glozel et ma vie*, Paris, 1979
HORNICKEL, Ernst, *Sonne, Strand und sowieso — Von Inseln, Küsten und lockenden Wassern*, Stuttgart, 1975
HOYLE, Fred, *Diseases from Space*, London, 1979
HOYLE, Fred and WICKRAMASINGHE, N. C., *Evolution from Space*, London, 1981
POSADA OCHOA, Mario, *Gold Museum*, Bank of the Republic, Bogotá, 1968

5   The Eighth Wonder of the World

1. SOTO, Alvaro, *Buritaca 200* (Ciudad Peridida), Bogotá, undated.
2. BISCHOF, Henning, *Die spanisch-indianische Auseinandersetzung in der nördlichen Sierra Nevada de Santa Marta (1501–1600)*, Bonn, 1971
3. CASTELLANOS, Juan de, *Elegias de varones ilustres de Indias*, Madrid, 1914
4. PREUSS, Theodor Konrad, *Forschungsreise zu den Kágaba*, Vienna, 1926
5. KRICKEBERG, Walter and TRIMBORN, Hermann (and others), *Pre-Columbian American Religions*, Weidenfeld & Nicolson, 1961
6. REICHEL-DOLMATOFF, Gerardo, 'Die Kogi in Kolombien', *Bild der Völker*, Vol. 5, Wiesbaden, undated
7. REICHEL-DOLMATOFF, Gerardo, 'Templos Kogi — Introduccion al simbolismo y a la astronomía del espacio sagrado', *Revista Colombiana de Antropología*, Vol. XIX, Bogotá, 1975
8. 'Indianer prophezeien den Untergang des Weissen Mannes', *Weser-Kurier*, 21 January 1980

General
REICHEL-DOLMATOFF, Gerardo and Alicia, *The people of Aritama*, London, 1961
REICHEL-DOLMATOFF, Gerardo, *Colombia — Ancient Peoples and Places*, London, 1965
SOTO, Alvaro and CADAVID, Gilberto, 'Buritaca 200', *Revista Lampara*, Bogotá, No. 76, Vol. XVII, December 1979

Index

Ancient Astronaut Society
World Headquarters
1921 St Johns Avenue
Highland Park
Illinois 60035
USA
Telephone: (312) 432-6230

Dear Reader,

Last but not least, may I introduce to you the Ancient Astronaut Society, abbreviated to AAS. It is a tax-exempt, non-profit membership society. It was founded in the USA in 1973. It now has members in more than 50 countries.

The Society's objective is the collection, exchange and publication of evidence tending to support and confirm the following theories:

The earth received a visit from outer space in prehistoric times ... (or)
The present technical civilisation on our planet is not the first ... (or)
A combination of both theories.

Membership of the AAS is open to everybody. A newsletter for members is published in English and German every two months. The AAS takes part in the organisation of expeditions and study journeys to archaeological and other sites of importance for the proof of the theory. A world congress takes place every year. Previous congresses were held in Chicago (1974), Zürich (1975), Crikvenica, Yugoslavia (1976), Rio de Janeiro (1977), Chicago (1978), Munich (1979), Auckland, New Zealand (1980), Vienna (1982).

Please write directly to the Society for membership information and a free copy of the Society's newsletter *Ancient Skies*.

Most sincerely,
Erich von Däniken